I0563608

BY NEVA'S WATERS

"REMAIN HERE," SAID THE DUCHESS, ADDRESSING
HER TWO ATTENDANTS.

"By Neva's Waters." (Page 146) Frontispiece.

BY
NEVA'S WATERS

Being an Episode in the Secret History of
Alexander the First, Czar of All the Russias

BY

JOHN R. CARLING

AUTHOR OF

"THE SHADOW OF THE CZAR," "THE VIKING'S SKULL"
"THE WEIRD PICTURE," ETC.

———

BOSTON
LITTLE, BROWN, AND COMPANY
1907

Copyright, 1907,
BY LITTLE, BROWN, AND COMPANY.

All rights reserved

Published October, 1907

ALFRED MUDGE & SON, INC., PRINTERS,
BOSTON, MASS., U. S. A.

TO

MY DAUGHTER, WINIFRED

CONTENTS

CONTENTS

ILLUSTRATIONS

BY NEVA'S WATERS

CHAPTER I

A MODERN FREE-LANCE

On a cold January night in the first year of the nineteenth century, a state ball, given by command of the fair young queen, Louisa, was held in the Royal Palace at Berlin.

Of those who attended this fête, many, chiefly of the masculine sex, were indifferent to polonaise or waltz, finding their entertainment in the galleries where, somewhat after the fashion of a modern restaurant, stood little tables, at which parties of two or more, while glancing at the dancers, could at the same time regale themselves with a supper and converse upon the topics of the day. This was a feature recently introduced by the Russian Count Wengersky, and though Court fossils stood aghast at the innovation, it had met with the approval of Queen Louisa and had brought immense popularity to the Count.

In one of these balconies sat round a table some officers, who, though of youthful aspect, were more interested in politics than in the charms of the ladies. Their talk, which was extremely animated, turned chiefly upon the question whether their sovereign lord, Frederick William III., would permit himself to be drawn into the confederacy formed by the four Powers, France, Russia, Sweden, and Denmark — a confederacy whose object was to resist by armed force the right claimed by Great Britain of searching on the high seas all vessels suspected of carrying contraband of war.

As these fire-eaters talked, they cast cautious glances in the direction of Viscount Courtenay, an Englishman, who sat alone at a table sipping his wine. A member of a famous historic house and patriotic to the backbone, the quick-spirited viscount was not the man to allow any disparagement of his country to pass unchallenged, and as his reputation for swordsmanship was such as not to be disputed even by "Fighting Fitzgerald," then in the height of his glory, the Prussian officers took good care that any remark uncomplimentary to his native land should be spoken in a low tone.

Wilfrid Courtenay's life should have been cast in the Middle Ages. He was a romantic freelance, whose ideas were more akin to the age of chivalry than to the nineteenth century. The spirit that finds a zest in danger, the spirit that made the vikings the terror of all coasts from the North Cape to Sicily, the spirit that sent the Crusaders forth to do battle with the Paynim beneath the blazing sun of Syria, the spirit that has caused Englishmen to plant colonies in the very teeth of hostile savages — that spirit still ran strong in the blood of the Courtenays. Accordingly, on the attainment of his majority, Wilfrid, leaving to his widowed mother the care of his patrimonial acres, had set out like a knight-errant to wander over Europe in search of adventure, in which quest he had fleshed his sword in more than one campaign, earning thereby from no less a personage than the Count d'Artois, himself a pattern of chivalry, the proud title of *Le Bayard de l'Angleterre*.

To this taste for fighting was added another, in singular contrast with it. Just as Frederick the Great, in the intervals of campaigning, found a strange pleasure in writing what his admirers called poetry, so Wilfrid was wont to devote some of his leisure to the study of painting, but whereas Frederick in his art never rose above mediocrity, Wilfrid, in his, succeeded in attaining a high degree of excellence.

For the rest he was tall, with fair hair, blue eyes, and

that indefinable air that is always the accompaniment
of aristocratic birth: shapely and muscular in limb; a
giant in strength; a stranger to fear; chivalrous in
his dealings. Among his faults was that of acting upon
impulse rather than upon the cooler dictates of reason.
But where would be the great deeds of history if their
authors had always paused to weigh consequences?

Now as Viscount Courtenay sat alone toying with his
wine glass, a familiar voice suddenly broke in upon his
reverie.

"Wilfrid, that our respective countries, or shall we
say our stupid cabinets, are at war with each other, is
surely no ground for breaking off our personal friendship?"

"Prince Ouvaroff! You in Berlin!" exclaimed Wilfrid, his face brightening; and, somewhat apprehensive lest the other should salute him, continental-fashion,
with a hearty kiss, he quickly extended his hand, and
was relieved to find Ouvaroff content with the English
mode of greeting.

"'Prince' do you say?" returned Ouvaroff in a tone
of quasi-reproach. "It was 'Serge' in the old days."

"Then let it be Serge still. I am glad to see a familiar
face."

The newcomer was of Russian nationality, with a
countenance decidedly unhandsome, a genuine Kalmuck
physiognomy, though its ugliness was redeemed by the
mild expression of the dark eyes. But however unprepossessing in face, his figure was tall and well proportioned, and arrayed in the blue uniform of the Preobrejanski Guards, who formed, in 1801 at least, the *corps
d'élite* of the Czar's army.

During his term of service as *attaché* to the Russian
Embassy in London, the Prince had become well-known
in West End salons, where he had met Wilfrid, who,
in spite of an unreasoning prejudice against Muscovites,
made an exception in favour of Prince Ouvaroff, appreciating his sterling qualities. The two had, therefore,
become fast friends.

There was a mystery attending Ouvaroff. He had
been brought up by a boyar of high rank, who would

never, even on his deathbed, reveal to his adopted son the secret of his parentage.

"Your father lives and knows of your existence. 'Tis for him to speak — not me," were almost the last words of his guardian.

The matter troubled Ouvaroff a good deal. He had often talked it over with his English friend, and now, their first greetings over, that friend reverted to the old theme.

"Any nearer to — to the discovery?"

The Prince's face assumed a somewhat sombre look.

"No nearer, and, truth to tell, I hope I may never be any nearer than I am at present."

Wilfrid lifted his eyebrows in genuine surprise.

"Do you remember," continued the Prince, "that old gipsy fortune-teller, whom you and I once met near your place in Surrey? She predicted that my father would become known to me in the very moment of my killing him."

"My dear Serge, surely you don't attach any importance to her words?"

"I do, and — fear. Her prophecies were three — first, that on my return to Russia I should be created a prince; second, that I should become *aide-de-camp* to the Czarovitch Alexander. Both these have come to pass. Why should I refuse to believe the third?"

"Why? Because the old sibyl assured me that within a year I should save the life of the fairest princess in Europe, gaining her love by that act. Eight years have passed since then, and so far I haven't saved the life of any woman, whether princess or peasant. Since she can prophesy falsely as well as truthfully, dismiss your gloomy forebodings."

Ouvaroff changed the conversation.

"What's this I hear you've been doing at Paris?" he observed. "I am told that a picture of yours exhibited there last Christmas almost created a riot."

"A riot? Nonsense!"

"I see you do not like to — what do you say in England? — blow your own trumpet. But for once lay aside your modesty, and let me have this story."

"Well, since you insist on being bored. You are referring, I suppose, to my picture, 'The Last Moments of Marie Antoinette?' Despite what French newspapers may say, I had no political motive. The work was done merely to please my own fancy. When finished my poor old drawing master saw it, and begged for the loan of it, to place it among a small exhibition of his own pictures. I consented. The result was marvellous. Thousands came to view the picture. Republicans who had once yelled for the head of 'The Austrian,' and had gleefully seen her perish on the scaffold, now melted to tears at sight of her image on the canvas. Bonaparte got wind of the affair, and, on the ground that it was creating a sentiment in favour of Royalism, ordered the picture to be destroyed. The *gendarmerie* were stoutly opposed. Shouts of *A bas Napoleon* were raised, a struggle ensued, and the gallery had to be cleared with fixed bayonets."

"And is it true that you challenged Napoleon to a duel?"

"I demanded compensation for the loss of my picture or — satisfaction at the sword's point."

Ouvaroff could not help smiling at his friend's colossal audacity.

"And General Bonaparte's answer ——?"

"Was a police order to cross the frontier within forty-eight hours."

"You went?"

"I stayed. You see, the First Consul's sister, the dark-eyed Pauline, with whom I had had some love passages — platonic, of course — had invited me to a ball a fortnight later. My dear Serge, how could I refuse? On the evening of the dance I presented myself, greatly to the dismay of my friends, who were aware that the First Consul was expected. I had purposely arranged to take my departure at the moment of his arrival."

"He saw you?"

"Certainly. Figure his rage as he saw me raising Pauline's hand to my lips as I took my leave! The music, the dancing, the conversation — all stopped. The stillness was painful. 'Did you not receive an order to quit France a fortnight ago?' he thundered. 'Why have you not gone?' 'And did you not receive a challenge to fight a fortnight ago?' I answered. 'Why have you not fought?'

"He couldn't speak for passion.

"'As to quitting France, Citoyen Bonaparte,' I continued, 'in such matters as coming and going, we Courtenays are accustomed to please ourselves. I had fixed upon to-night as the time of my departure, and, as you now perceive, I — er — depart. Adieu, citoyen.'

"With that I passed, by preconcerted arrangement, through a circle of friends, and before he had time to order my arrest I had reached a private gateway, where a carriage was awaiting me. As I had taken the precaution to have relays of horses in readiness, I succeeded in crossing the Eastern frontier a few hundred yards ahead of the pursuing carabineers."

"And so General Bonaparte declined to measure swords with you?"

"Bonaparte is a Corsican — that is to say an Italian bravo, who prefers darker methods. Listen to the sequel. A few days later, as I was sitting at the card table in the *kursaal* at Homburg, a man suddenly rose, accused me of cheating, and ended his remarks by flinging the contents of his wine glass in my face. Of course, a meeting was inevitable. It was to be a duel to the death. Later that night my second came to me in great distress, advising me to cry off. He had discovered that my adversary was a secret agent of the First Consul — none other, in fact, than the famous, or infamous, Abbé Spada."

"I have heard of him. The first swordsman of France?"

"So-called. Well, we met, and considering the many men whom Spada has killed in his day, I felt justified in giving him his passport to Gehenna."

"You killed him!"

"Within three minutes."

Ouvaroff regarded the speaker with admiration.

"That's Bonaparte's way of dealing with the objects of his displeasure," concluded Wilfrid. "But I'll be even yet with the Little Corsican for destroying my picture."

Now, as Wilfrid gazed down upon the dancers swaying rhythmically to the sound of the music, his eye was caught by a lofty figure standing, solitary and contemplative, within an arched entrance that opened upon the ballroom. It was a middle-aged man with silvering hair, whose cold, handsome face wore a somewhat sombre expression. He was clad in Court costume, carried his hat under his arm, and sparkled all over with diamonds from his powdered *queue* to his shoe buckles. It was the diamonds that attracted Wilfrid's attention; he did not like to see a man so bedizened.

"Do you know that gentleman, Serge?" asked Wilfrid, indicating the magnate in question. "His face seems familiar to me."

"Count Arcadius Baranoff, one of the Czar's ministers. You must have seen him in London, for he was formerly ambassador at the Court of St. James's. As rich as Crœsus. One of the men," the Prince went on in tones of contempt, "who in the last reign climbed to power through the bedroom of the Empress Catharine. He is a proof of the power of the personal equation in international politics."

"How so?"

"He is a rank barbarian, whose polish is but skin deep. When he was in London his *brusquerie* offended the men, his coarseness the women, and he left England burning with a desire to do her hurt, and now the time has come, he thinks."

"Thinks!"

"You are aware that, after fighting each other for a year or more, the Czar Paul and Consul Bonaparte are now fast friends. This is mainly due to the diplomacy of Count Baranoff, who was sent to Paris as the Czar's envoy: it was his hand that signed the Franco-Russian treaty. While in the French capital he tickled the Parisian fancy with a pamphlet, 'Is it possible for an Englishman to possess sense?'"

"Oh, indeed!" muttered Wilfrid, with a glance at the distant pamphleteer.

"And now, on his way back to St. Petersburg, he tarries at Berlin in the hope of persuading the Prussian King to join the league against England."

"Humph! Is he likely to succeed?"

"There's no telling. He has had two interviews with the King. Frederick William is an amiable, weak-minded man. Were it not that Queen Louisa insists upon being present at these interviews, Baranoff might have carried his point. He is to have a final interview on the fourth day from this, and — mark this significant point — the Queen knows nothing of this intended meeting."

"And Prince Ouvaroff as a Muscovite patriot," smiled Wilfrid, "hopes that Baranoff will gain his ends?"

"By no means," responded the other quickly. "Personally, I am opposed to the war, and — but let this be kept secret — so is the Czarovitch. Why should we give an opportunity to your Nelson to earn fresh laurels at Russia's expense? But a truce to politics — I shall be letting out more than I ought," he continued with a laugh, and then, by way of changing the subject, he added —

"You are not married yet?"

"No, nor likely to be. Waiting for the promised princess," said Wilfrid mockingly. "But you —? What of the lady you loved five years ago?"

"I love her still," replied the Prince moodily.

"She remains unwed?"

"So far. But she is ice to me."

"Take heart. The Neva is not always frozen. That she does not marry should encourage you to continue your suit."

"Give me your face and figure and I might succeed. Is it likely that she, confessedly the most beautiful woman in Moscow, will marry an ugly fellow like me?"

"What have looks to do with love? What says your own Russian proverb: 'I do not love thee because thou art pretty, but thou art pretty because I love thee.'"

These words failed to arouse Ouvaroff.

"I have discovered of late that I have a rival, and a successful one. There is peril in aspiring to her hand."

Before Wilfrid had time to ask the meaning of these mysterious words a liveried attendant approached, carrying a silver salver, upon which lay a sealed envelope. This with a bow he presented to the Prince, who, upon opening it, found therein a card inscribed with the words : —

" He who now speaks with you is the man.
ARCADIUS BARANOFF."

CHAPTER II

FOR a moment Ouvaroff fastened his gaze upon the card
which he so held as to be seen by none but himself; then,
raising his eyes, he looked at Wilfrid. There was a
sudden coldness in the Prince's demeanour, and Wilfrid
intuitively felt that the writing on the card had something to do with it.

"The next dance is a Hungarian waltz, I perceive,"
said Ouvaroff in a changed voice. "I am reminded
by this card that a lady is waiting for me. Excuse my
absence for a few minutes. I am so ugly, you see," he
added with an uneasy smile, "that when I *do* obtain
the favour of a dance I cannot afford to miss it."

As honest a fellow as ever lived was Ouvaroff, but
the words he had just spoken were a "white lie," as
Wilfrid quickly proved; for, upon looking down during
the whole course of the waltz, he did not see the Prince
among the dancers.

While Wilfrid was puzzling himself to account for
Ouvaroff's conduct, he saw Count Baranoff coming along
the gallery, smilingly exchanging a word here and there
with those to whom he was known.

Wilfrid watched him and took the measure of the
man. His eyes, more oval in shape than those seen in
Western Europe, had the deceitful, furtive glance of the
Asiatic.

"Were I a Czar, that is not the sort of man I should
choose for my minister," was Wilfrid's comment.

"Do I address Viscount Courtenay?" said the Count
with a bow as he drew near to Wilfrid.

Yes, he did address Viscount Courtenay. This somewhat bluntly. Wilfrid had not asked for the diploma-

10

tist's acquaintance, nor was he disposed to be over polite to an enemy of England).

But the envoy was not to be rebuffed by Wilfrid's frigid manner. He sat down in the chair lately occupied by Ouvaroff. The little group of Prussian officers stared at the pair, wondering what there could be in common between the Czar's representative and the eccentric young Englishman.

As Baranoff seated himself a diamond dropped from his coat. Wilfrid picked it up and presented it to its owner, who gracefully waved it off.

"It is beneath the dignity of a Baranoff to resume what he has once let fall."

"And beneath that of a Courtenay to accept it," replied Wilfrid, placing the gem in the exact spot where it had fallen.

This diamond-dropping was an old trick of Baranoff's whenever he wished to gain the good graces of a stranger. He had always found the method very successful — with Russians. It didn't seem to answer with an Englishman.

The Count called for a bottle of Chartreuse and helped himself to a glass, first pouring in from a phial that he produced a few drops of a liquid that Wilfrid knew to be "diavolino," one of those Italian nostrums much in vogue a century ago, as warranted to keep in tone the constitutions of those given to dissipation.

Wilfrid's dislike of the man increased.

"You have business with me, sir?"

"Ah, how delightfully English! You come to the point at once. Business? Yes, we may call it that. At any rate I have an offer — a magnificent offer to make."

He eyed Wilfrid curiously, dubious as to how his words would be received. And indeed it was on Wilfrid's tongue to tell the envoy to take himself and his offer to Samarcand, or further, but he refrained for the moment, thinking that he might as well hear what the offer was.

"I wish," continued the Count, "to give you the opportunity of earning three hundred thousand roubles.

Such is the price I am willing to pay for a service to be done by you."

Three hundred thousand roubles, or, roughly speaking, £50,000 in English money, would be a welcome gift to Wilfrid, whose family estate had a heavy mortgage upon it. But, mindful of the character of the speaker, he determined to learn first whether the proposal could be honourably entertained by an English gentleman and a patriot.

"Three hundred thousand roubles! It must be a very substantial service to be worth so much."

"You speak truth. It *is* a substantial service."

"There are thousands of suitable men in Europe. Why select me for the purpose?"

"Thousands of men — true. But only one Courtenay."

Wilfrid did not controvert a remark so obviously just.

"The work," continued the Count, "is one requiring a spirit that will dare great things."

"Then, who more qualified for the task than Count Baranoff?"

"You are very good," smiled the envoy. "But I was not at Saxony in the summer of 1792 — you were."

"So, too, were many other men in the year you mention."

"True, but you were the central figure in a certain affair, forgotten by you, perhaps, but remembered by others. I will explain anon."

The summer of 1792 was about eight and a half years back. Wilfrid hurriedly reviewing his brief sojourn in the kingdom of Saxony, could recall nothing to explain Baranoff's words.

"What I require for my three hundred thousand roubles is that you shall make love — successful love, mark you — to a certain lady."

Wilfrid gave a scornful laugh.

"I thought the enterprise was one demanding a high degree of courage!"

"And so it does. There's great danger in it."

"That makes it interesting. Where is this Lady Perilous to be found?"

"In the city of St. Petersburg."

"Is the lady young or old?"

"She is in her twenty-third year."

"Seven years my junior. Ill-favoured, perhaps, and therefore unable to obtain a suitor?"

"She has the loveliest face in St. Petersburg."

"Not ill-favoured? The daughter of a vulgar merchant, or of some wealthy serf desirous of obtaining a nobleman for his son-in-law?"

"On the contrary, her father is a prince."

Wilfrid started. He thought of the gipsy's prophecy.

"Is the lady of fallen fortunes?"

"She can command millions of roubles."

"A prisoner immured within a fortress from which you would have me rescue her?"

"Nothing of the sort."

"A cloistered nun, repentant of her vows?"

"Not at all. She moves freely in Court circles."

"Demented, or that way inclined?"

"As sane as women in general."

"Subject to some hereditary taint? Epileptic or the like?"

"As sound in physique as yourself."

"Then by all that's holy!" cried Wilfrid, in a paroxysm of perplexity, "explain why a lady of princely birth, beautiful, and rich, can lack suitors among her own nation? Why must a foreigner from distant England play the lover?"

"Because there is no one in St. Petersburg bold enough to take upon himself that *rôle,* since discovery means certain death to the lover, death perhaps to her."

"Death!" queried Wilfrid, somewhat startled at the word.

"At the hands of the State."

"Ah!" said Wilfrid, beginning to receive a glimmer of light. "She is a lady important politically?"

"Very much so," replied the diplomatist with a look that confirmed his statement.

"What prospect have I of winning this lady's affections?"

"I have discovered, no matter how, that you are the only man in Europe who can succeed."

"Really! That's very flattering to my vanity," laughed Wilfrid. "The lady did not send you on this mission, I trust?"

"She is modesty itself, and would die rather than commission any one on such an errand."

"I ask her pardon for wronging her in thought. Have you got her portrait?"

The Count hesitated for a moment, and then drew forth an ivory miniature.

"Painted three months ago. It scarcely does her justice."

As Wilfrid's eyes fell on the miniature he fairly held his breath. It was a face more beautiful than any he had ever seen. The soft violet eyes and the lovely delicate features, with their sweet grave expression that spoke of a nature, pensive and *spirituelle,* might well inspire love in the heart even of the coldest; much more then in that of a romantic character like Wilfrid.

"Well, what do you think of it?" asked Baranoff.

"It is the face of an angel," replied Wilfrid as he returned the miniature. "What is her name?" he added.

"You do not recognise her?"

"No."

"I thought perhaps you *might* have recognised the face. Her name? Pardon me, I will give it if you are prepared to undertake the *rôle* of lover — if not, 'twere best, in the lady's interests, to keep it secret."

Wilfrid reflected. A lady of political consequence, Baranoff had called her, threatened by the State with death if she listened to love-vows! Wilfrid was sufficiently versed in Russian history to know that the reigning dynasty was a younger branch of the House of Romanoff, and that a return to the rights of primogeniture would deprive the present Czar of his crown. Was the lady with the angel-face a descendant of the elder line, and thus so nearly related to the throne that, in the Court of the gloomy and suspicious Paul the First, it would be perilous for any man, even the highest among

Russia's nobility, to aspire to her hand? Imbued with this idea Wilfrid began to weave a whole political romance around the person of the beautiful unknown. Was she, though nominally at liberty, a virtual prisoner at the Czar's Court, watched by a hundred suspicious eyes — pining for affection, yet forbidden to marry?

To try to set her free from such gloomy environment was no more than his duty.

And Wilfrid, if Baranoff had spoken truly, was certain of gaining her love! To woo and carry off a fair princess from the power of a jealous Czar was just the sort of enterprise that appealed to his knightly and romantic character. He could no longer hesitate.

"Do you assent?"

"Assent!" echoed Wilfrid. "Is it possible to dissent? You say that provided I succeed in marrying this lady you will add to the pleasure by paying me the sum of three hundred thousand roubles! Really, your proposal is so extraordinary, so captivating, that I am almost inclined to think that you are trifling with me. And," he added in a graver tone, "it is not wise, sir, to trifle with a Courtenay."

"No trifling is intended. But, pardon me, I have not, it seems, made my meaning quite clear. You are labouring under a slight misapprehension. I spoke of *love:* I did not speak of *marriage.*"

Wilfrid stared hard at the speaker, upon whose lips there now appeared a sinister smile. Then, vivid as fire upon a dark night, the full meaning of the proposal flashed upon him. He was deliberately to set to work to corrupt a woman's innocence! The lady in question had given some offence to the powerful diplomatist, who chose this diabolical method of revenge. The fall from purity, the shame that is worse than death, would destroy whatever influence she possessed in Court circles, and probably at the same time remove a political obstacle from Baranoff's path.

Now whatever sins might be imputed to Wilfrid, he had not yet played the rake. In an age when gallantry was considered one of the marks of a gentleman, and even the clergy were not conspicuous for purity of morals, he had kept his name stainless, thanks to the influence of a good mother, who had bidden him see in every woman a saint.

His anger, then, can be imagined. He blamed himself for holding converse with so cold-blooded a barbarian.

"I deserve this insult," he muttered. "What else could I expect? Can one meddle with pitch and not be defiled?"

"You must not talk of marriage," resumed Baranoff. "What I require is that the lady shall be induced to compromise herself."

"So that all the world shall hear of her fall?" said Wilfrid, smiling dangerously.

"Why, truth to tell, 'twill not avail me much if the *amour* remain secret."

The candour with which Baranoff spoke showed that he was quite convinced that Wilfrid had consented to his scheme.

"But you have said," commented Wilfrid, "that the affair, if discovered, may bring upon her the penalty of death."

"So it may, if it be discovered while she is on Russian ground. But I will so arrange matters that both you and she shall have every facility for escape. Once over the frontier you are safe. As I have said, the danger is great. But so, too, is the reward. Think! Three hundred thousand roubles!"

"Your Excellency," said Wilfrid with the air of one who has formed an irrevocable decision, "I will at once depart for St. Petersburg."

"Good!"

"I will seek out the lady."

"Excellent!"

"And I will warn her of your damnable designs."

"Ha!" muttered Baranoff, looking thunderstruck.

As he caught the angry sparkle of Wilfrid's eye, it suddenly dawned upon him that he had mistaken his man. Reared in the atmosphere of Catharine's Court, in its day the most licentious in Europe, Baranoff had become dead to all sense of honour, and failed to understand how a man could resist the twin temptation of a pleasant *amour* and a rich bribe.

" Do I take it that you refuse my offer? "

" To the devil with your offer! "

Baranoff elevated his eyebrows and affected the extreme of amazement.

" I hold out to you the prospect of an *amour* with a beautiful and charming woman, to be followed by a free gift of three hundred thousand roubles, and you refuse! "

" Repeat your infamous offer, and I'll — yes, by heaven! I'll fling you over the rails of this balcony! "

Unconsciously Baranoff backed a little from the table, for Wilfrid looked quite capable of putting his threat into execution.

There was a brief silence. Then Baranoff spoke.

" So you will visit St. Petersburg and put the lady on her guard," sneered he, mightily pleased that he had withheld her name. " I fear that if you seek to enter Russia at this present juncture you will be taken for a spy of Pitt's. As minister of the Czar it would be my duty to order your arrest."

" Oh, indeed! Do you really entertain the hope of returning to Russia? "

" What is to prevent me? "

" Myself."

" You! " exclaimed Baranoff disdainfully.

Wilfrid laughed pleasantly.

" I shall certainly do my best to provide you with a grave in Brandenburg's sand. In seeking to make me the agent of an infamous deed you have offered an insult not to be passed over by an English gentleman. You will have to defend your conduct with the sword."

There was a very palpable start on the part of Baranoff, and his face paled. Though well versed in the art of fencing he durst not measure swords with the man who, inside of three minutes, had transfixed the Abbé Spada, the champion duellist of France.

He sought to shield himself behind the privileges of his high offices.

" It would be contrary to etiquette," he remarked

loftily, " for a *chargé d'affaires* to accept a challenge.
My imperial master would never forgive me for putting
my life to the hazard of a duel while engaged in conducting a diplomatic mission, otherwise —— "

" Now you are talking nonsense," interrupted Wilfrid,
bluntly. " The Czar loves a duel, for only a few weeks
ago he invited all the sovereigns of Europe to his Court
to settle their international disputes by single combat."

And Baranoff, well knowing that the eccentric Czar
had so acted, felt himself deprived of his argument.

" Fight me you must! I will force you."

" Force me? indeed! " said the Count. " In what
way? "

" By publicly branding you as a coward; by putting
affronts upon you in every assembly you frequent. For
example, if you are among men I shall walk up to you
with a pair of scissors, and after asking, ' Why do these
Muscovites wear their beards so long? ' I shall proceed
to clip yours. If you are sitting with ladies I shall relate
in their hearing and in yours the story of how you propose to deal with one of their sex. It may be that
through fear of me you will keep within your hotel, in
which case I shall have to affix a notice at the chief entrance, stating the reason of your enforced seclusion!
In short, sir, I shall make your life at Berlin so abomi-
nably unpleasant that for very shame you will have to
fight. There must be a meeting unless you wish to see
the name of Baranoff turned into a byword for a
coward."

The Count listened with secret consternation, feeling
certain that this obstinate pig of an Englishman would
keep his word. A man who had not shrunk from defying the First Consul to his face was not likely to pay
much respect to the status of a diplomatic envoy.

And to whom could he look for protection? Not to
Frederick William. So long as Queen Louisa was by
his side that monarch would avow, rightly or wrongly,
that he was powerless to control the actions of one who
was not a native-born subject. Not to the British Ambassador at Berlin. That magnate, in view of the hostile
relations between Great Britain and Russia, would be

highly amused at the mortification of the Muscovite envoy.

While he was thinking of all this Wilfrid, too, was thinking, and it suddenly occurred to him that there was another and better way of punishing Baranoff — one that would likewise strike a blow at Bonaparte.

"As your Excellency seems to have no liking for the duel, I give you the alternative of quitting Berlin within twenty-four hours."

An instant feeling of relief swept over Baranoff. Here was a way of escape. Then he began to reflect that if he should depart within the time prescribed he must sacrifice the promised interview with King Frederick, and go back to St. Petersburg without gaining the adhesion of Prussia to the Northern Confederacy — a sad blow to his hopes!

Disposed to take a favourable view of matters, he had that very day sent off a despatch to the Czar stating that King Frederick seemed slowly coming over to Russian views. He must now return to report the failure of his mission, and, if he should speak the whole truth, to confess that he had been frightened from Berlin by a single Englishman! The neutrality of Prussia meant the loss of so many war vessels to the Confederacy, and was practically equivalent to a bloodless naval victory on the part of Wilfrid.

Some such thought as this caused Wilfrid to smile. Baranoff, quick to read his thoughts, was consumed with secret rage.

No, he would not withdraw from Berlin at Wilfrid's bidding, and he said as much.

"Go you shall," retorted Wilfrid. "As General Bonaparte, your dear ally, banished me from France, so I in turn do banish you from Prussia. 'Tit for tat,' as our English children say."

Baranoff gave a scowl of baffled hatred.

"How much has Louisa paid you for this business?" he sneered.

With disdain on his face Wilfrid rose.

"When next you take to pamphleteering let the theme be, 'Is it possible for a Russian to be a gentleman?' My present address is the Hôtel du Nord. If by to-morrow evening at six of the clock you have neither left Berlin nor sent me your second, you may prepare for humiliation. I take my leave. *Adieu* or *Au revoir*, whichever you please."

And so saying Wilfrid withdrew to the quietude of his room in the hotel to think over matters.

It was a fascinating thought that during a brief stay in Saxony he had been seen by a girlish and beautiful princess, upon whose imagination he had made an impression so powerful that after the lapse of eight years she still retained him in mind. True, Baranoff was a person upon whose statements little reliance could be placed, but in the present instance Wilfrid was convinced that he had not spoken falsely.

"The lady has a real existence," he muttered. "Now how ought I to act in this affair?"

It was hard that a princess who cherished his memory with affection should meet with no return. Yet, on the other hand, it would be embarrassing for both if he should be unable to requite her love.

If he went it was doubtful whether he would find her, so slight were the clues he held.

Would his friend Ouvaroff be able to identify her? The thought had no sooner entered Wilfrid's mind than he recalled the Prince's strange saying in connection with his own love suit. "There is deadly peril in aspiring to her hand." This could scarcely be a coincidence — Ouvaroff's lady must be Baranoff's princess.

"Humph! if Serge were first in the field," thought Wilfrid, "it seems unfair to cut him out. But, if the princess *won't* have him —— "

Early on the following morning he called at Ouvaroff's quarters. To his extreme disappointment he found that the Prince had taken his departure, leaving a note to the effect that he had been hastily summoned to St. Petersburg by command of the Czarovitch. "Pardon my running off without a farewell," he wrote, "but Alexander's service brooks no delay."

Ouvaroff was not the only Muscovite to leave Berlin that day, for in the evening the political circles were surprised, and probably relieved, by the news that Count Baranoff had suddenly departed for St. Petersburg, thus relinquishing his attempt to make Prussia a member of the Armed Neutrality.

And now was Wilfrid continually haunted by the lovely face in the miniature. It filled his mind by day; by night it mingled with his dreams. Sometimes he saw the face, its lips curved into a witching smile as if inviting a kiss; sometimes the eyes would assume a sad, wistful look, as if appealing to him for aid.

To visit St. Petersburg, or not to visit it? was the question to which for a long time he could discover no answer. Still in doubt he looked one night from his hotel window, and saw the face of the sky as one dark cloud. But while he gazed, there presently came a rift, and through the rift one planet sparkling bright.

Hesperus, the star of Love!

It seemed like an answer to his thoughts. Love in the shape of a fair princess was beckoning to him. His mind was made up — he would go to her!

CHAPTER III

A WINTER night, frosty and still. The northern stars, set in a sky of steely blue, twinkled over a plain of frozen snow — a plain so vast that its visible border touched the horizon. In all the wide landscape no town, no hamlet, not even a solitary dwelling was to be seen; the view, a monotonous blank, relieved here and there by clumps of dark firs, the darker by contrast with the surrounding white.

Lofty posts, painted with alternate bands of black and white, and situated a verst distant from one another, indicated the ordinary line of route over the wintry waste, and along this route a hooded sledge was moving with all the speed that three gallant mares could supply, the bells upon the duga, or wooden arch, ringing out musically over the crisp snow.

Two persons occupied this sledge, one, the *yamchik* or driver, Izak by name, an active little Russian, who sat partly upon the shaft, in order when necessary to steady the vehicle by thrusting out a leg upon the snow; the other, Wilfrid Courtenay, who, voluminous in fur wrappings, sat, or rather reclined at the rear under cover of the hood.

It was over Russian ground that the car was speeding, its goal being St. Petersburg, distant now about one hundred miles.

Wilfrid had met with considerable difficulty in entering the Czar's dominions. Twenty days had he been detained at the frontier-town of Kowno for no reason whatever as far as he could see, save the caprice of petty officials, whose insolence and greed had so galled the spirit of the Englishman that several times he was on

22

the point of turning back. However, he thought better
of it, and when at last leave *was* granted him to go forward, forward he went. Having learned by experience
that travelling in one's own equipage is more convenient,
and, in the end more economical, than the ordinary
method of posting, Wilfrid had purchased at Kowno
a covered car, together with three steeds to draw it,
accepting at the same time the proffered services of a
yamchik, who boasted that he knew every verst of the
way from Kowno to St. Petersburg.

And here he was speeding along at the rate of twelve
miles an hour. The keen cold air, combined with the
rapid swaying of the car, caused him to fall into a semi-
slumber, from which he was roused by the voice of Izak.

"If the little father will condescend to look, he will
see the village of Gora," he cried, pointing with his whip
to a light shining far off like a star.

Welcome news to the cold and hungry Wilfrid. Gora
should be his stopping-place for the night.

Fifteen minutes more and they reached the silent,
sleeping village, which, like most of its kind in Russia,
consisted merely of a line of wooden cabins on each side
of the post-road with a row of trees in front.

At one end of the village stood its only house of entertainment, the Inn of the Silver Birch — an inn very different externally from the generality of its class. As a
matter of fact, it had originally been the seat of a rich
boyar, the lord of the village and of the surrounding
land. It was a large and handsome structure of timber,
pillared and balconied, and with much carving about its
eaves and gables. On three sides grew lofty birch trees
with silvery bark; the fourth side lay open to the gaze
of the travellers.

"This is the twentieth inn I've seen painted red,"
remarked Wilfrid.

"'Tis the will of the Czar," answered the yamchik.
"Some weeks ago he gave a ball, and to it came a lady
wearing a red dress. 'What a pretty colour!' said Paul.
And lo! at once a law that all post-houses and bridges
shall be painted red. Great is the word of the Czar! He
wills, and — pouf! 'tis done."

"A pity he doesn't will a spell of warm weather, then," growled Wilfrid, as he set his half-frozen feet upon the hard ground.

As was the village, so was the inn, still and silent as the tomb. Wilfrid's summons, however, soon brought to the door the landlord, a somewhat melancholy-looking man. He was accompanied by a tall and pretty girl of about eighteen, sufficiently like him to be recognizable as his daughter.

Though wrapped in sheepskins they shivered as the keen, icy air from without, chilling the warmer air within, produced an instant fall of sleet, a phenomenon which, familiar enough to the four, was witnessed without surprise.

Now as the girl caught sight of Wilfrid there came into her eyes a sudden light. It was not the light of recognition, for she could never previously have seen Wilfrid, but it was a look that seemed to say she had been expecting him, and was glad he had come. Such at least was the impression that Wilfrid derived from her odd manner.

Turning from her to the landlord Wilfrid requested accommodation for the night, but at this the landlord put on a lugubrious look of refusal, explaining that it was neither for lack of room nor of victuals that he was compelled to turn the little father away, but the fact was the whole inn had been hired for the night by a small party, now fast asleep, whose grandeur was such that they had insisted that no other traveller should be received, lest the noise, however light, which must necessarily accompany his presence, should disturb their slumbers.

"Did they look under their pillow for a rose-leaf?" asked Wilfrid.

But this classical allusion was lost upon the landlord. It grieved him, he continued, to refuse a traveller at so late an hour of the night, but what could he do? He had given his word. There was another inn some twenty *versts* farther on; would not his Excellency ——?

No, his Excellency wouldn't, especially when he no-

ticed on the face of the pretty girl a look of disappointment, evidently occasioned by her father's words.

"Your name?" asked Wilfrid, addressing the landlord.

"Boris, son of Peter."

"Good Boris, your guests' command applies only to
noisy and drunken roysterers, not to a gentleman so
orderly and quiet as myself. Lead on — I'll not disturb
their slumbers."

Boris hesitated, but a whisper from the girl seemed to
decide him.

"His Excellency may enter," said he.

The girl's eyes danced; she could not have looked
more glad had she herself, and not Wilfrid, been the
traveller. While Boris conducted the yamchik with the
car and horses across a courtyard to the stables, Wilfrid
followed the girl — whose name she told him was Nadia
— to a large room on the ground floor, a room not
warmed by the ugly-looking closed-up stove, the usual
accompaniment of a Russian room, but by a fire of pine-
logs blazing upon the stone hearth, the ruddy glow forming a cheerful contrast to the snowy prospect without,
which could be dimly discerned through the panes of the
double lattice.

In one corner of the apartment hung a small painting
of the Madonna, before which a taper was burning.

Wilfrid was passing this negligently by when Nadia
gave a little scream.

"Ah! you are a heretic!" she cried. "Come, you
must bow before the picture — so." She showed him
how to do it, and, to please her, Wilfrid bowed. "Now
you make the sign of the cross, with your fingers bent
thus." Wilfrid imitated her action. "That's right.
Now you are a member of the True Church."

She smiled so prettily that Wilfrid could not help
smiling too.

Throwing a huge bearskin over the back and seat of
a chair, Nadia drew it to the fire, and bidding her guest
be seated, she began to bustle about, saying that all the
servants were asleep and that it would be a pity to
awaken them, so she herself would prepare his supper.

As Wilfrid seated himself, the innkeeper entered from the kitchen, where he had left the yamchik, who, when his meal was over, would curl himself up and sleep, peasant-fashion, upon the stove.

"Your Excellency has travelled far to-day?" asked Boris. His manner was in striking contrast with Nadia's free and lively style. He stood in humble fashion, as if not liking, even in his own house, to sit down in the presence of his guest; but, invited by Wilfrid to a seat near the fire, he sat down, mentally contrasting the Englishman's affability with the hauteur of the Russian grandees sleeping above.

"You have come far to-day?" he repeated.

"From," replied Wilfrid, as he set to work with knife and fork, "from a place called — let me think — Via — Via — "

"Viaznika?" interjected Nadia.

"Ah! that's the name — Viaznika."

"You set off late in the day?" pursued the innkeeper.

"About noon."

Boris looked as if Wilfrid had made a very puzzling statement.

"Your horses seem fleet enough," he murmured.

"Have you any reason to doubt their fleetness?" smiled Wilfrid.

"Why, see here, gospodin. It is now midnight, and since you say you set off at noon, you have taken twelve hours to come thirty-six versts."

Reckon a verst at about two-thirds of the English mile, and it will thus be seen that Wilfrid had been travelling at the magnificent rate of about two miles an hour! But how could this be when the horses had been kept going at a fair trot the whole of the time? Nadia sat silent, her eyes fixed upon the ground. Odd, but Wilfrid somehow derived the impression that the talk had taken a turn distasteful to her. Why should this be?

"Have you mistaken the distance between Viaznika and here?" said Wilfrid to the innkeeper.

Now whatever faults English travellers may have to find with Russia and her ways, all will bear witness to the excellence of her posting-maps. One of these, placed before Wilfrid, quickly convinced him that Boris was right. The distance by the post-road between Viaznika and Gora was a little more than twenty-four miles. The three-horse car had occupied twelve hours over a journey that a pedestrian could have performed in half the time. It was clear that the yamchik had not followed the ordinary route; in fact, Wilfrid had known thus much at the time, for on pretext of taking a short cut, Izak had frequently deviated, now to the right and now to the left. Wilfrid's suspicions being thus aroused he began to study the map, and found that the preceding day's journey could have been accomplished in a considerably less space of time than that actually taken by the yamchik. That worthy's conduct was certainly puzzling. His motive could hardly be a pecuniary one since Wilfrid, alive to the disadvantages of paying by the day, had by mutual arrangement fixed upon a definite sum for the whole journey, so that manifestly it was to Izak's interest not to retard, but to accelerate, Wilfrid's progress.

"Where did you pick up the man?" asked Boris.

"At Kowno. He came to me of his own accord, saying that as he had heard I was about to make the journey to St. Petersburg would I accept his services? According to his own account he has performed the journey from Kowno to St. Petersburg more than a hundred times during the past ten years."

"His face is strange to me. He has never stopped at the Silver Birch."

"Nay, father," interposed Nadia. "I remember him on two or three occasions."

She caught Wilfrid's eye as she spoke, and coloured. Wilfrid wondered why.

"Let's have the fellow in here, and we'll question him," said he.

"He'll be asleep by this time," said Nadia gently. "'Twill be a pity to disturb him."

Thus advised, Wilfrid put off his cross-examination of the yamchik till the morning, and the conversation flowed into other channels.

"Are you a *vitch* or an *off?*" asked Nadia, suddenly.

"I am not quite sure that I understand."

"Why, look you, my father being the son of one Peter, is Boris Petroff. Now if he were a boyar he would be Boris Petrovitch."

"I see. Well, I suppose I must put myself down among the *vitches*, for I am a nobleman in my own country."

Nadia's face fell when she heard this. In a voice that seemed to savour of resentment, she asked : —

"How many souls have you?"

"We in England are limited to one. Is it different in Russia?"

"One!" echoed Nadia. "Some of our great boyars have ten thousand souls."

"They must take an unconscionable time in dying! And how many has Nadia?"

"None," replied the girl with a flash of her eyes as if detecting some hidden insult in the question. "We are souls ourselves, my father and I."

"It is the fashion of our boyars," explained Boris, "to call their serfs 'souls.'"

"A good name," added Nadia in a bitter tone, "for they have us, body as well as soul."

"And there are twenty million like us," said Boris.

It came upon Wilfrid as a painful shock to learn that this dignified innkeeper and his pretty daughter were serfs. That serfage existed in Russia was, of course, no news to him, but it had existed as something remote, and therefore as shadowy as the helotry of ancient Sparta. It was a very different thing to be brought vividly face to face with the system, to know that Boris, head man of the village, the lessee of a government post-house, and therefore himself a master of servants and the owner of many roubles, was of no account in the eye of the law. He and Nadia could be summoned back at any time to their lord's estate, clothed in peasant attire, put to degrading tasks, and, like domestic animals, could be whipped or sold at the pleasure of their owner.

No wonder, with such fears as these always present to their mind, that Boris should wear an habitual look of melancholy, and that Nadia's flashes of liveliness should alternate with moods of gloom!

Now if Wilfrid had been some blockhead of a Russian boyar he would have disdained all further conversation with the innkeeper and his daughter, but being an English gentleman it never occurred to him that he was losing caste by conversing with a serf, and so he continued to talk on, and under his sympathetic words Nadia seemed to brighten again.

"Do you know," she remarked, looking up with a half-smile, "that you have been talking treason? You have used the word 'free' several times. It's a prohibited word."

"Prohibited?"

"I do not jest, gospodin. The Czar Paul would regulate the language of his people, so he has issued a ukase forbidding the utterance of certain words. Among such come 'freedom' and 'liberty.'"

"The devil!" muttered Wilfrid.

"You may say that. That's not a prohibited word."

"'Twere well, Nadia, to give me a list of these forbidden vocables."

"I don't know them all. However, you mustn't use the word 'revolution.'"

Wilfrid began now to understand why the officials of Kowno had confiscated from his small travelling library a book bearing the title of "The Revolution of the Heavenly Bodies." Evidently it was regarded as a dangerous political work!

"Anything more?"

"Well, 'snub' is forbidden."

"Heavens! what treason lurks in that simple word?"

"It will be taken as a reflection on the Czar, whose nose has a skyward tendency."

"Anything more?"

"Beware of the word 'bald.'"

"Ah!"

"Because if the Czar were to swear by the hair of his head the oath would not be binding. Do you know he once had a soldier knouted to death for speaking of him as the 'baldhead?'"

To the truth of Nadia's remarks history can bear witness. The last of them was not very encouraging to

Wilfrid, for if the Czar could put a man to death for an offence so slight, he would surely do the like with one who had defeated his envoy at Berlin. And Wilfrid's coming to St. Petersburg would quickly become known to Baranoff's underlings, since it was required of every stranger that he should report himself at the Police Bureau. Was it likely, then, that Count Baranoff would neglect the opportunity of exposing him to the vengeance of the Czar? But though Wilfrid began to realize more vividly than before the dangerous character of his enterprise, he was still resolute to go on with it, trusting that as he had emerged triumphantly from previous perils, so, too, he would from this.

He sought to turn the conversation from politics by making inquiries as to the other guests in the house.

The innkeeper, with a shake of his head, gave it as his opinion that there was something mysterious about them, since one and all had declined to disclose their names, a statement that did but serve to stimulate Wilfrid's curiosity.

"To-day about noon," said Boris, proceeding to tell all he knew, "there drove up to the inn door a troika containing four persons, two equerries attired in blue and silver livery, and two women, who —— "

"Who," interposed Nadia, "from their dress might have been taken for grand-duchesses, but who proved in the end to be only ladies' maids."

"The four had been sent on to prepare for the coming of their mistress, a boyarine, so they said, of the highest rank. They wished to engage the whole inn for the night. They insisted that the time of their lady's sleep must be free from the slightest noise, to ensure which they stipulated that I must exclude all other visitors, and to this I agreed, as they promised to pay well. They then went the round of the inn, selecting such rooms as they deemed suitable."

"And the airs and graces of the maids!" said Nadia. "They strutted about with their noses held high. Nothing was good enough for them."

"They selected the Tapestried Chamber as the bedroom of their lady," continued Boris.

"Yes, and grumbled because there was no room communicating directly with it. They wished to be near their lady, and actually wanted us to connect the Tapestried Chamber with the adjoining room by there and then cutting a doorway through the wall."

"And when I refused," pursued Boris, "on the ground that I could not make any alteration in government property without the consent of the government, I thought they would never cease laughing, though for my part I could see nothing to laugh at. In the evening about seven of the clock the boyarine and her party arrived."

"And how sweet and gracious she was!" commented Nadia. "Different altogether from her retinue. Do you mind that ugly haughty man in uniform, with the long spurs and the fierce moustaches. He's a fire-eater, if you like! He spent an hour after dinner in fencing with another officer, as lordly as himself. One of the maids so far condescended to me as to say that he practised this sword-play every day in order to be able to kill a certain Englishman."

"He must take care that the Englishman doesn't kill him," smiled Wilfrid. — "They have all gone to bed, I suppose?"

"All," replied Boris. "The boyarine in the Tapestried Chamber; in the room on her right the two maids, in that on the left the — the ——"

"The Ugly One," interjected Nadia.

"And the rest here and there in different rooms."

"And they are staying for the night only?" asked Wilfrid.

"For the night only. They set off at ten in the morning for St. Petersburg."

"You didn't hear the boyarine's name?"

"We didn't hear the names of any of them. They wish to remain unknown. 'The name,' said the officer with the spurs, who seems to be the boyarine's right-hand man, 'the name by which we choose to be known is Pay-well. Ask questions and it shall be Pay-not.'"

"It is the fashion," remarked Nadia, "with some of our noble ladies to spend a week or two of religious seclusion in some convent. From a few words let fall by one of the party I believe the boyarine is returning from some such a visit."

"It may be," responded Wilfrid. "Is she young or old?"

"Not much past twenty,' replied Nadia.

"And her appearance?"

"Her appearance!" repeated Nadia with enthusiastic warmth. "Her appearance! Ah! gospodin, how can one describe what is indescribable? I am told that there lives a German duchess so beautiful that once, when passing through a certain village of Italy, the simple-minded peasants knelt, believing her to be the Madonna. I think our boyarine must be that duchess, so sweet and beautiful is she."

"Dark or fair?"

"As fair as the day, with golden hair and blue eyes."

"Then she resembles you."

Nadia gave a scornful little laugh.

"My eyes are light blue; hers are of a lovely, dark azure and shine like stars. At a distance our hair may seem alike, but look closer. Mine is straw-coloured tow; hers woven sunbeams and as soft as silk. But the way she arranges it! She must be very much afraid of the Czar."

"Why so?"

"Her *coiffure* shows it."

"What! has that old autocrat been dictating in what way ladies shall wear their hair?"

"That is so, gospodin." And here Nadia, twisting her long hair into a number of thick plaits, disposed them in ludicrous fashion around her head, saying with a smile, "This is Paul's ideal *coiffure*, and this is how ladies must appear at Court. But we, who do not go to Court, may wear it as we please." And with that she let her hair fall around her like a shower of golden threads, and pushing some aside, looked smilingly at Wilfrid.

CHAPTER IV

IN THE PRINCESS'S BEDCHAMBER

A FEW more words passed and then Wilfrid, with a glance at his watch, opined that it was high time for him to go to bed.

"Will you show the gospodin to his room, Nadia?" said the innkeeper.

"He had better pull off those heavy boots first," suggested the girl.

And Wilfrid, knowing her reason, good-humouredly complied.

"And you'll not get up till after ten?" pleaded Boris. "The boyarine must not know that I have broken my word. And I must keep your yamchik out of the way till she has taken her departure."

"Very good. To please you I'll prolong my slumbers," assented Wilfrid, "though I confess I should like to have a peep at the fair boyarine." And bidding the innkeeper "good-night," Wilfrid followed Nadia, who led the way with lighted lamp.

"Tread softly," she said with a subdued laugh. "Don't disturb the repose of the Ugly One, whatever you do. So savage-looking is he that he'll think nothing of running you through the body with his long sword if he should be waked before his time."

Mindful more of the boyarine than of the Ugly One, Wilfrid stepped with noiseless tread.

"Your room," said Nadia, as they ascended a staircase, "is exactly over the boyarine's bedchamber, so you must move about as silently as a ghost."

Conversing thus in whispers she turned down the corridor that led from the second landing.

33

" This is your room," she said, pausing before a closed
door.

Wilfrid, taking the lamp from her hand, wished her
" good night."

" The last Englishman parted from me very differently." There was no mistaking the saucy invitation of
her eye and lip. Pretty faces were made to be kissed,
and Wilfrid did what any other sensible fellow would
have done similarly situated, in which pleasing business
the lamp became accidentally extinguished.

" There now! You yourself must re-light it," she
said, thrusting a tinder-box into his hand. " I cannot
stay longer," and pushing him into the room, she closed
the door upon him and hurried away.

Wilfrid's first act on finding himself alone was to lock
the door, his practice always at a strange inn; his next,
the room being in total darkness, was to obtain a light, a
somewhat difficult feat, owing to the dampness of the rag
in the tinder-box. Not till after the lapse of ten minutes
did he succeed in producing a flame sufficient for the
rekindling of the lamp.

While kneeling on the floor at this task he more than
once fancied that he caught a sound like a sigh, and at
the moment of obtaining the light he became convinced
of the reality of the sounds.

A regular succession of light breathings gave audible
proof that he was not the only person in the room.
Rising to his feet and holding the lamp on high, Wilfrid
looked about him, and discovered that the breathings
came from a bed a little distance off. Curtains hanging
around the bed prevented him from seeing the sleeper.
It was clear that through some strange blunder Nadia
had shown him to the wrong room.

Then —

" By Jove! " muttered Wilfrid.

His eyes had fallen upon a startling sight — startling,
that is, in the sense of being unexpected.

There, orderly disposed upon a chair by the dressing-
table was a pile of fair undergarments, while beneath the
same chair there peeped forth a pair of satin shoes
formed only for the smallest of feet.

RISING TO HIS FEET AND HOLDING THE LAMP ON HIGH, WILFRED
LOOKED ABOUT HIM.

Page 34.

"*By Neva's Waters.*"

The person behind the curtains was not a man!

Fortunately Wilfrid's movements had been so noiseless as not to disturb the occupant. His obvious course, then, was immediate retirement.

He was on the point of stealing off when his eye was caught by sparkles of light coming from a jewel-case that lay upon the dressing-table. It did not require the knowledge of a lapidary to pronounce that the rich gems and the wrought gold represented a very large amount of money. The owner was obviously a lady of wealth, and — Shrine of Venus! — there could not be a doubt about it; he was standing in the very bedchamber of the fair boyarine!

Nadia, paying too much attention, perhaps, to Wilfrid's talking, had not noticed that instead of ascending to the *third* landing and taking the corridor that led from that, she had mistakenly stopped and turned when upon the *second* landing, with the result that Wilfrid, instead of being in the room immediately above that of the boyarine, was in the boyarine's room itself!

"What would the Ugly One with the spurs and moustaches think," muttered Wilfrid grimly, "if he knew of my presence here?"

The sooner he withdrew the better. He had already been in the room more than ten minutes. If Nadia should recall her error, and should come flying back with clamour, the issue might be awkward, both for the lady and himself.

Just as he was about to make for the door his ear detected a movement in the bed.

His heart almost leaped to his throat. Some instinct told him that the movement was not an unconscious stirring in slumber; the lady was wide awake, and remembering that she had gone to sleep in the dark, was doubtless puzzling herself to account for the light now shining through her bed-curtains.

His first impulse, to extinguish the light, was checked by the thought that the fear occasioned by the sudden darkness might elicit a scream from her. Better to stand still and be openly seen than to glide, a terrifying black shape, from the room.

A glance toward the bed showed him a hand coming forth from between the curtains — a hand as white as the sleeve of the nightdress that clothed the arm of the wearer.

The drapery parted, revealing a beautiful face and figure — the living original of the miniature!

Overwhelmed with surprise Wilfrid stood, as breathless and as still as if he had suddenly fallen under a spell of enchantment.

He had loved her from the first moment of setting eyes upon her portrait, but now the actual sight of the living princess increased that love tenfold. Could it be true that he, and he only, held a place in her heart, and that for a space of more than eight years? If eight years previously in Saxony he had exercised so powerful an impression upon her girlish imagination, she should surely know him again? But though he hoped and looked for it, she betrayed no sign of recognition. Indeed, the only emotion expressed in her widening eyes was wonder.

"What are you doing here?" she asked.

Her voice — and one more soft and musical had never fallen upon Wilfrid's ear — seemed to have the effect of breaking the spell that had held him.

He bowed with all the grace he was capable of.

"I am an English traveller, a midnight arrival, who has been erroneously led to believe that this was his bedroom. I cannot sufficiently express my regret at having disturbed you in this unceremonious fashion."

There was about Wilfrid that air of good breeding that marked him as a gentleman, and gave to his words the stamp of truth.

Her suspicions, if she had had any, were gone in a moment.

"Then, sir, please to withdraw," she said, in a tone of gentle dignity.

"At once," replied Wilfrid, turning to the door, "trusting I may be permitted to pay my respects to you in the morning, and to apologise more at length."

Just the faintest shade of fear passed over her face.

"No, no, you must not do that! As you love your

life keep this meeting a secret! I speak with good reason. Go! But stay — one moment. Your name?"

"Wilfrid, Lord Courtenay."

A faint cry escaped the Princess as Wilfrid so held the lamp that its light fell clearly upon his face.

She knew at least his name, if she did not recognise him; that much was certain. Equally certain was it that his name or his presence filled her with some deep emotion. She caught her breath; her colour came and went. If these symptoms were due to love it was a love mingled with dismay, and the dismay seemed to predominate.

Though prudence told Wilfrid that it was high time to go, he could not resist the temptation of lingering to ask,

"Have we met before?"

"Once," answered the Princess in a softened voice, "and once only, when you saved me from death!"

It must have been in his sleep, then, for he had no recollection of it! Adventures he had known in plenty, but to save the life of either woman or girl was a pleasure that had never yet fallen to his lot, and he said so.

The Princess gave a half-smile.

"It was an event so strange that I do not wonder at your failing to connect me with it."

A more puzzling statement, this, since the very strangeness of the affair should surely be an additional reason for stamping it upon his memory.

As Wilfrid looked intently at her in the vain attempt to discover her meaning, he saw an awful change pass over her face. Dilated eyes, lips drawn apart, and cheeks perfectly bloodless — all showed her to be seized by a sudden sense of fear.

A moment more and Wilfrid, too, felt fear, not on his own account, but on hers.

A murmuring of voices and the sound of footsteps were audible on the other side of the bedroom door. A little crowd was congregating in the corridor without. What was the cause of the gathering? His striking of the flint had been accompanied by very little noise. The voices of both the Princess and himself had been scarcely loud enough to penetrate beyond the room. Why, then, was attention becoming drawn to the Princess's bed-chamber? Had Nadia become aware of her error? Was she outside, testifying to others that she had mistakenly conducted an English traveller to this chamber? Had the Princess's retinue gone to the bedroom intended as his and found it empty? Had they then decided to search the Princess's bedchamber? The discovery of a man at the dead of night in the bedroom of a lady, who had let fifteen minutes elapse without raising an alarm, would certainly place her in a compromising situation.

The confused murmur outside ceased. Then came a gentle tapping upon the panels of the door.

Now if Wilfrid had followed his **own** impulse he would at once have opened the door, and explained the matter precisely as it had happened, being of opinion that the truthful way is always the best way, but on glancing at the Princess he saw her with her finger upon her lips, which action he took as a sign that he was not to speak.

In the silence of that trying moment he could almost hear the beating of her heart.

The knocking was renewed, being followed this time by a turning of the handle and a pressure against the door, which did not yield since, as previously stated, Wilfrid upon entering had locked it.

"What is it?" cried the Princess, striving to subdue the tremors of her voice.

"Did not your highness call us?" was the reply, delivered in a deep bass voice, which Wilfrid immediately recognised to be that of Prince Ouvaroff, or, as Nadia had impolitely called him, the Ugly One.

The voice came both as a surprise and a pleasure to Wilfrid — a pleasure, because his present position would now admit an explanation, certain to be received by the Prince, who would not be likely to impute dishonourable motives to his old friend. Indeed, Wilfrid was almost on the point of answering, but thought it more prudent to await the pleasure of the Princess.

"I did not call, Prince. I would **have** rung had I wanted anything."

Wilfrid groaned in spirit. The deed was done. If the

Princess were not compromised before she certainly was now, and by her own action. Her words were tantamount to saying that nothing unusual was occurring — in effect, a tacit denial of his presence.

"But had you rung we could not have come to you," said a feminine voice, belonging evidently to one of the Princess's maids, "since your Highness has locked the door against us."

"A wise precaution in a strange house. I did not call, nor do I want anything. Return to bed, silly ones. You — you are interrupting my rest."

There was a brief whispering, followed by the sound of receding footsteps, and though all became silent in the corridor again, Wilfrid was troubled with the horrible suspicion that the speakers had merely moved off to some distant place of observation, there to wait for his appearing. If so, how was it possible for him to escape discovery?

The only other exit from the room lay through the window, but Wilfrid was well aware that Russian windows are, at the beginning of winter, so firmly secured against the cold without as to be opened with extreme difficulty. Moreover, if he should succeed in crawling through the lattice and in dropping to the ground below — honourable doings for a Courtenay! — his footprints in the snow would betray him. And how was he to re-enter the inn without attracting notice? It was impossible for him to remain all night in the bedchamber, even if the Princess, yielding to necessity, should permit it, for in the morning discovery must ensue upon the entering of the maids. He could leave only by the door, but again came the disquieting thought that there might be watchers in the corridor without, determined to see the end of the matter, even though they should have to wait all night. If this last were the case, then each moment of his stay would but deepen — nay, confirm — suspicion.

He was still standing in the place where he had first stood after lighting the lamp, hesitating to stir lest the moving of the light or the sound of his feet should lead to his betrayal. But now the Princess beckoned him to approach. She wished to speak, and for obvious reasons to speak in a whisper. Wilfrid moved forward in silence. The Princess pointed to a chair by the bedside, and Wilfrid, sitting down, placed the lamp upon the dressing-table, and bent his head to listen.

What the Princess said was almost inaudible to Wilfrid: it was more by the motion of her lips than by the actual sound proceeding from them that he understood her to say: —

" I said what I did " — alluding to her implied denial of his presence, surely a pardonable evasion considering the circumstances — " to save you from being cut to pieces before my eyes — your fate if found here. Do not go — till — till they have had time to fall asleep again."

With that she sank back upon her pillow.

To be sitting by the bedside of a fair and youthful princess was a very charming situation, but it had its drawbacks. Should discovery ensue, then, unless the Princess had the nature of an angel, how could she ever forgive the man who had made her innocence appear as guilt? From her, whose love he was so anxious to win, what could he now look for but resentment? The endearing impression made on her mind by his saving of her life, though confessedly he had no recollection of the event, would now be completely effaced by this unfortunate blundering into the wrong room at night.

As Baranoff's face, with its sneering smile, rose vividly before him, Wilfrid turned cold at the thought that he had done the very thing the minister had wanted him to do! Should this affair come to his ears how he would triumph in the Princess's shame! How quick he would be to reveal it to the world! Wilfrid recalled his words: " Death at the hands of the State for the Princess as well as for her lover." That there was truth in this utterance seemed evidenced by the words of the Princess herself; that he would be slain before her eyes if found in her bedchamber. Such a fear spoke but too plainly of her position, for if she were powerless to prevent her retinue from butchering him, it was clear that she was not really their mistress. She was, in fact, a sort of honourable prisoner of State, free to travel if she chose, but at-

tended by an escort, told off to watch for any suspicious
act.   In forecasting his probable doom she had not
touched upon her own.   Was it possible that he was
really bringing upon her a like fate?

He ventured to steal a glance at her face.   How
beautiful it was, with its soft violet eyes shaded by long
dark lashes?   Whatever may have been the arrangement of her hair earlier in the evening, it now lay upon
the pillow like a bright aureole around her face, one
golden tress twining about her white throat like a vine
tendril clasping a marble column.

If ever woman had cause to be angry with Wilfrid
that woman was this princess, and yet her face betrayed
not the faintest sign of resentment; on the contrary,
there was something in her look assuring him that, come
what might, she would be the last person in the world
to reproach him for an act unwittingly committed, a
forgiving tenderness of spirit on her part that, while it
endeared her the more to Wilfrid, at the same time enhanced, rather than lessened, his despair.

Half an hour passed without a word spoken on either
side.   Then the Princess bent forward till her golden
hair was so close to his own that he could feel her warm
breath on his cheek.

"Lord Courtenay," she said in the faintest of whispers, "before you go, a few words.   You have heard me
called 'Highness.'   Do you know my name and rank?"

"I regret to answer no," replied Wilfrid, speaking in a
tone similarly subdued.

As she did not seek to enlighten him it was clear that
she preferred to remain unknown.

"You will keep this meeting a secret?"

Wilfrid bowed assent.

"When you have found the right room let me entreat
you to remain there till after ten in the morning."

Ten o'clock, he remembered, was the time arranged
for the resumption of her journey.

"My meaning is that if a certain one among my suite
should learn that you have passed a night at this inn,
the consequences to me may be," she hesitated as to the
choice of a word, finally selecting "hurtful."

Wilfrid had no doubt that the person she meant was Ouvaroff, and for the moment he felt that he would like to do for Ouvaroff what he had done for the Abbé Spada.

"Your Highness, say no more. I stir not from my room till after the hour named."

"What other persons besides myself know that you are here?"

"The innkeeper and his daughter, but for their own sake they will not speak of me to your suite. There is my yamchik, too, but they will take good care to keep him out of the way."

Though the Princess had hinted that it was time for him to go, she did not seek to hasten his departure.

"Why do you, an Englishman, travel in Russia at a time so perilous as the present?" An embarrassing question, but before he had time to consider what answer he should give, the Princess spoke again.

"Lord Courtenay," she said in a grave earnest tone, "I am glad in one sense to have met you, for I can give you a warning. It has become known to me that your life is not safe in Russia. Leave the country with all speed. Take another name; assume a disguise; forge a fresh passport; go anywhere rather than to St. Petersburg, where you have an enemy who will not spare you."

"You allude to Count Baranoff?"

"To one greater than Baranoff."

But when Wilfrid asked for the name of this person, the Princess shrank back with a strange and troubled look, so that Wilfrid refrained from repeating the question, for he could very well guess who was meant, though why she should hesitate at naming him was a mystery.

One greater than Baranoff? Who but the Czar could be greater than the Czar's minister? And the cause of the Czar's enmity was doubtless to be found in the defeat at Berlin of his policy, a defeat due to Wilfrid alone. And yet it seemed improbable that Baranoff would have the courage to tell the story of his own cowardice and flight. It might be, however, that he had related the matter in such a way as to exculpate himself, representing that his triumph would have been certain but for a secret emissary of Pitt's, Lord Courtenay by name, who, insinuating himself into the confidences of Frederick William, had induced that monarch to side with Great Britain.

The warning given by the Princess more than ever convinced Wilfrid that his journey to St. Petersburg was likely to end in his arrest. Yet turn back he would not, now that he had once met with the Princess, whose whole manner showed that she moved in an environment of suspicion and peril, from which, if possible, he would deliver her.

" You will not go to St. Petersburg? " she said in a soft pleading tone that vibrated to his heart.

Wilfrid felt that to say he was bent on going would but increase the look of sadness on her fair face. He therefore temporised.

" I will think over the matter."

" I have warned you. If you will not take my warning you are lost. I have no more to say," she added — words that Wilfrid interpreted as a hint to go.

" Your Highness," he said, rising, " you know my name. Will you not favour me with yours ere I go? "

She shook her bright flowing hair in tantalising fashion.

" What good will it do you? " she said with a sad smile. " Let me remain unknown. Now go, and Heaven watch over you ! "

" And over you, too, Princess ! "

Wilfrid bowed, took up the lamp, and walked to the door. Arrived there, he cast one last lingering glance at the Princess. She was sitting up in bed watching him, her hand pressed to her side as if to repress the accelerated beating of her heart. Was its quickening due to fear, or to love, or to a mingling of both?

He extinguished his lamp, conscious that even in the darkness the Princess's eyes were upon him.

He cautiously turned the key of the door, the steel tongue of the lock moved back almost silently. Wilfrid paused a few moments, fearing lest the sound, faint though it was, should have attracted attention.

Finding that all remained still, he ventured to open

the door and to look forth. By aid of a faint light shed
by a lamp hung from the ceiling, he saw that the corridor was empty. His trained hearing caught neither
the hasty movement of feet nor the sound of closing
doors; nothing whatever occurred to suggest that any of
the Princess's retinue had been on the watch.

Thus assured, he stepped out into the passage, quietly
closing the door behind him.

It was a new thing for Wilfrid to be stealing along a
corridor at night like a thief, fearful of being seen or
heard — an altogether humiliating experience, made en-
durable only by the thought that it was necessary for
the honour, the safety, perhaps even the life, of the Princess. Twenty paces — he had a reason for taking accurate measurement — brought him to a landing, whence
a short staircase led to the floor above, where was a corridor, similar in all respects to the one he had just left.

Moving forward twenty paces along this, Wilfrid
paused before a certain door.

"Directly above the Princess's room, Nadia said. Then
this should be it. Now, pray Heaven, I am not disturbing some other person's sleep."

He cautiously opened the door, and quietly exploring
his way through the darkness, reached the bed. It was
empty. Re-lighting the lamp he found himself in a room
whose appointments seemed to show that it was intended
for the use of a male visitor.

Whether or not it was the room that Nadia had meant
for him mattered little; he was not going to look for any
other; so locking the door he went to bed, and was soon
sound asleep.

CHAPTER V.

" It is past ten o'clock, gospodin."

The words came from Nadia, who, having tried for some time to arouse Wilfrid by knocking at his bedroom door, had at last succeeded.

" Past ten o'clock!" echoed Wilfrid, realising what these words meant. " Then the Prin — I mean the boyarine and her party have gone?"

" Half an hour ago."

It was with considerable mortification that Wilfrid heard this news. It had been his intention to secrete himself at some loop-hole of observation in order to watch the departure of the Princess and her train. Prolonged slumber, however, had debarred him from this pleasure.

On coming down to breakfast his mortification soon yielded to a new feeling, namely, curiosity as to whether Nadia was aware of the blunder she had made. Had she discovered her error shortly afterwards, but, overcome with confusion and fear, had left him to extricate himself from the difficulty as he best might?

If she were not aware of her mistake it would be better to let her continue in ignorance of it — so much the safer would be the Princess's secret. But in what way was he to question Nadia without revealing what he wanted to hide? A lawyer might be equal to the task, but Wilfrid wasn't a lawyer, for he was too impulsive in speech, which is a fault, and too transparent in motive, which is a virtue.

As he sat down to breakfast he eyed Nadia keenly, who coloured on observing his gaze as any maiden might, whose last parting from a man had been marked by a kiss, so that her sudden blush told him nothing of what

45

he wished to know. She was the sole attendant at table, her father at that moment being engaged in superintending the delivery of a wagon-load of fagots.

"The gospodin slept well?" she asked.

"Excellently. Five minutes after leaving you," said Wilfrid, fixing his eyes intently upon her face, "five minutes after leaving you I was fast asleep."

If she had been among the little gathering outside the Princess's bedroom she must have known that he was not keeping to the truth. If she knew it she did not betray her knowledge by any change in her manner.

"There is nothing like a long drive in the frosty air for making one sleep," was her quiet remark.

"By the way," added Wilfrid with a careless air, "just as I was dropping off I fancied I heard a disturbance on the floor beneath me — a talking, or a moving of feet — muffled sounds of some sort. Was I dreaming?"

"The floor directly beneath yours would be the boyarine's room," said Nadia, opening her eyes wide with surprise. "Do you say the noise came from there?"

"There or near it, so at least it seemed to me. Did you hear the noise?"

"I! I was down in the kitchen getting ready some nice things for the boyarine's breakfast."

"Did any of the boyarine's party complain of a noise during the night?"

"None."

"Ah! Then I *must* have been dreaming."

During this brief dialogue Wilfrid had kept his eyes on Nadia's face, and became convinced by her natural and artless manner that she was unconscious of her blunder of the previous night.

That she was looking somewhat pale was nothing to the point, seeing that she had been up all night preparing with her own hand dainty dishes for the boyarine and her party.

At this point, having finished with his timber, Boris entered to see what services he could render. Naturally enough Wilfrid was desirous of learning all he could about the Princess.

"You waited on the boyarine at breakfast, I presume?" he said, addressing the pair. "How was she looking?"

"Rather pale and anxious," replied Boris. "She scarcely spoke. In fact, her lively manner of last night was altogether gone."

"And Ouva — I mean him whom Nadia calls the Ugly One? He breakfasted too, I suppose?"

"Sitting opposite to the boyarine," replied Boris, who seemed to have kept a keen eye on his visitors. "He, too, looked rather grave. I caught him more than once watching her curiously. Her eyes would droop when she became conscious of it."

"In short," said Wilfrid with a mirthless laugh, "she might have been taken for a child that has done wrong, and he for a parent that had been scolding her."

The innkeeper with some surprise murmured that Wilfrid's words exactly hit off the situation.

For appearance's sake Wilfrid went on eating, but his appetite had gone. He was possessed by a horrible sinking of heart; he suspected, nay, he felt sure, that his long stay in the Princess's bedchamber had become known, and that Prince Ouvaroff was disposed to put the worst construction upon the event.

The picture of the fair and innocent Princess, sitting mute and wretched amid her escort, exposed to coldness and suspicion, and unable to vindicate herself, filled Wilfrid with almost intolerable anguish.

Upon the woman whose love it was the one desire of his life to gain he had brought cruel reproach. Already in imagination Wilfrid heard the mocking laugh and ribald jest directed against the Princess by the immoral circle at the Court of the Czar. "She is only like the rest of us."

Second thoughts, however, induced Wilfrid to believe that perhaps after all he was disquieting himself without reason.

The apparent lack of cheerfulness on the part both of the Princess and of Ouvaroff might be due to an entirely different cause. It came suddenly upon Wilfrid that the Princess was none other than the lady to whom Ouvaroff himself had once aspired, till a State warning had bidden him put a check upon his presumption. Perhaps, regardless of the State's inderdict, Ouvaroff had once more ventured — it might even have been on the previous night — to renew his suit with the same result as heretofore. Hence the meeting between her and him this very morning would necessarily be quiet and somewhat embarrassing.

There could be no doubt that the Englishman who had so roused the deadly ire of Ouvaroff was none other than Wilfrid himself, though it was somewhat difficult to see how the Prince could have learned that his former friend had become his rival, since if the Princess really cherished a secret affection for Wilfrid, she would be the last person in the world to divulge it.

There was one circumstance which disposed Wilfrid to think that his interview with the Princess had escaped observation, and that was the peculiar forbearance of Ouvaroff. Surely, if the Prince had suspected anything he would have sought Wilfrid out and have demanded an explanation of the nocturnal incident. But the Prince had done nothing of the kind; on the contrary, he had set off next morning apparently ignorant that his old friend was beneath the roof of the Silver Birch.

But no sooner did this favourable view present itself than it vanished. Ouvaroff, aware of Wilfrid's destination, was perhaps leaving him to the vengeance of the authorities at St. Petersburg.

The breakfast over, Boris, who took considerable pride in his hostelry, made the suggestion that perhaps his Excellency would like to be shown over the building; if so, Nadia would be pleased to take him round.

Wilfrid readily fell in with this offer, moved solely by the wish to see again the chamber in which the Princess had passed the night. He accordingly accompanied Nadia through the various rooms, listening, it must be confessed, with very little interest to her remarks, till at last they reached the Tapestried Chamber. And a daintily furnished little chamber it was; but now, void of its fair occupant, how desolate it seemed!

Wilfrid's eyes roved reminiscently and mournfully around. Here was the dressing-table upon which he had set his lamp, and there the chair over which her fair attire had been cast; here, the seat in which he had sat by her bedside, and there the pillow still retaining the hollow made by the nestling of her golden head.

The faint perfume that Wilfrid had noticed on the previous night still hovered around the pillow. Moved by a sudden impulse, he lifted it, and with surprise and delight saw beneath a folded handkerchief.

On the principle of " Findings, keepings," as children say, Wilfrid took possession of the article, which was of the finest cambric, delicately perfumed, and edged with beautiful lace.

Now, although the title of princess is sometimes borne — in Russia, at least — by persons of doubtful station, Wilfrid had felt that this was not the case with *his* princess; and on unfolding the handkerchief he received a startling proof of the correctness of his opinion, for the centre of the cambric exhibited the figure of a double-headed eagle wrought in gold thread.

" The Imperial Arms! " muttered Wilfrid.

His look of blank surprise was as nothing compared with that of Nadia's. She, indeed, seemed not only amazed, but quite frightened by the discovery.

" The Czar's Arms! " she gasped. " Is she a member of the Imperial house — A Grand Duchess? "

It seemed so, if the handkerchief were to be taken as proof, but how near to the throne there was no means of telling. She might be a very distant relative of the Czar; on the other hand, she might be a niece, or even a daughter! Wilfrid's head swam at the thought. No wonder he ran the risk of being slaughtered by her suite if found in her bedroom!

That eagle in gold thread was not only a startling sight, but an unwelcome one to Wilfrid; it seemed to put a sudden stop to his love-dream. For him to think of mating with a princess of the Imperial house of Romanoff would indeed be the height of audacity; and yet, if the lady herself were willing — and the tender glance of her dark-blue eyes had given him a lover's hope — he was quite ready to brave all risks on her behalf. If she were a Romanoff, was he not a Courtenay, with imperial blood in his veins, descended from the Byzantine emperors and permitted by the Garter king-at-arms to bear the proud title of *Æquus Cæsaribus* — equal to Cæsars?

But soon his thoughts took a lower flight.

"We have jumped to conclusions too hastily," he said to Nadia. "The possession of the handkerchief doesn't necessarily prove that she is a Grand Duchess. It may have been a gift of the Czar."

This way of looking at the matter seemed to relieve Nadia's mind somewhat, though why she should look so troubled over the discovery was a puzzle to Wilfrid.

"Besides," he continued, "if she were an Imperial Duchess, her suite would select, as her stopping-place for the night, the castle of some grand boyar, rather than a wayside hostelry."

But Nadia opined there was no force in this argument, seeing that the great Catharine herself had on one occasion stopped at the Silver Birch, and had slept in that very chamber. And Wilfrid was forced to admit to himself that it was an argument in favour of the Imperial theory that the chief of her escort was no less a personage than the Czarovitch's own aide-de-camp, namely, Prince Ouvaroff. If she were not a Grand Duchess she must at least be some one of distinguished rank.

Folding the handkerchief, now the most precious of all his belongings, he placed it carefully within his breast, and descended again to the breakfast-room.

"And now," said he, "send me my yamchik, and I'll ask the scoundrel what he means by taking twelve hours to drive twenty-four miles."

Nadia departed, and presently returned, leading in the yamchik, who stood, cap in hand, smiling and fawning.

Yes, shame to him, he *had* taken a long time in coming from Viaznika to Gora. Ah! why did he ever deviate from the post-road, thinking to take a shorter cut? He didn't like to tell the gospodin so at the time, but he knew he had lost his way, and he had wandered, and wandered — oh! how he had wandered!

"Just as you are doing now," interrupted Wilfrid.

"And yet you say you have performed this same journey a hundred times?"

Yes, that was the most wonderful part of it — that he, who had travelled this route one hundred times, should go wrong at the one hundred and first. But there, man must make a certain number of mistakes in his life-time; even the mighty Czar sometimes made mistakes, much more, then, a poor yamchik.

But when it was pointed out by means of the map that he had similarly lengthened the stages on other days, the yamchik, while venturing to deny the impeachment, became less glib of tongue; professed that, being unable to read, he could not understand the condemnatory map, and finally grew so dense that Wilfrid, despairing of getting any clear ideas into the fellow's thick skull, bade him go and harness the horses for the next stage.

Was the fellow a fool or a knave?

Wilfrid was disposed to rank him among the latter class, having a suspicion that all these manœuvrings on the part of the yamchik had been prompted by some interested motive, a motive, however, that Wilfrid was utterly unable to fathom.

It was hardly worth while now to dismiss the fellow, when only three or four days' journey from St. Petersburg; but, while retaining him, Wilfrid determined not to leave these final stages to his judgment. So, after a brief study of the map, he selected both the route and the stages; and since, from motives of prudence, he did not wish either to overtake the Princess or to appear as if following immediately upon her track, he chose a somewhat circuitous road to the capital in lieu of the direct one.

And now, from without, came a jingle of bells and neighing of steeds to tell him that his car was in waiting.

Wilfrid rose, called for his bill, and paid it with a liberal overplus. Boris and his daughter accompanied him to the inn door, where a little crowd of servants had assembled to watch the departure of the rich Englishman.

Wilfrid turned to say "Good-bye" to Nadia. Her manner plainly showed that she was sorry to part with her guest, who, moved by a generous impulse, drew the pretty serf-maiden to one side.

"Nadia," he whispered, "take heart. How long I shall be in St. Petersburg, I know not; but when I return again this way I will redeem you and your father from serfdom — yes, if it cost me fifty thousand roubles."

He had thought to see her cheek colour with delight, her eyes to sparkle, and her lips to quiver with thankfulness; it was all the reward he wanted.

But, to his surprise, her emotion took a very different shape. She shrank back, staring at him, her cheek as white as the dead; in her eyes a look of wild, haunting horror.

"Isn't that promise worth a kiss?" smiled Wilfrid,

She did not give him one; instead, she presented her cheek, and on touching it with his lips he found it as cold as marble.

Somewhat mortified by this strange reception of his offer, an offer made in all good faith, Wilfrid waved his hand to Boris, sprang into the sledge, and the next moment was speeding off along the frozen highway.

Nadia staggered, rather than walked, to her own little sitting room.

"What did the Anglisky say to you?" asked Boris, somewhat suspiciously.

"Say?" gasped Nadia, who seemed scarcely able to speak for emotion — "words that he meant to be words of hope, but to me they are words of despair. I would rather he had stabbed me. And he looked at me, oh! so pityingly. My God! if he only knew the truth!"

A shudder shook her from head to foot.

Her wondering father repeated his question.

"He promised to buy us our freedom, yours and mine."

"Glory to God!" cried Boris, clasping his hands fervently together. "Glory to God who has put this thought into the heart of the Englishman! My prayer for you, Nadia, my prayer day and night for years, is answered at last. He'll keep his word, this Englishman. An Englishman always does. And he shall not lose by his goodness. I will work, work night and day, till I have paid him our ransom twice, yea, three times over. But, Nadia, Nadia, why do you grieve? Is this a thing to grieve about?"

"The offer comes a day too late, my father."

"A day too late?"

"We are already free," she replied, with a laugh dreadful in its want of mirth. "Free by the grace of the nether fiend, who is now mocking me with a deed that need not have been done."

CHAPTER VI

HEIRESS TO THE THRONE!

On the fifth morning after leaving Gora, Wilfrid and his yamchik were speeding over a landscape that presented to the eye little more than a vast expanse of virgin white, sparkling beneath the rays of a pale, northern sun, that gave light, but not warmth.

"St. Petersburg!" cried the yamchik suddenly, pointing with his whip to the far-off northern horizon, which, presenting hitherto a smooth line, began now to have its continuity broken by a series of irregularities.

As the horses raced onwards, higher and ever higher out of the illimitable sea of white, there rose to view a curious and, to an occidental eye, fantastic mingling of palaces and minarets, of cupolas and crosses, each gradually becoming more clearly defined against the pale lilac of the Arctic sky.

Now, more than ever, did Wilfrid realise the madness of his enterprise.

He was hastening to a city that held two at least of his enemies, namely, Count Baranoff and the recently alienated Ouvaroff; to whom must probably be added a third, in the shape of the Czar Paul — which was tantamount to saying that he had a whole empire against him.

Now with the aid of friends, a man has often succeeded, despite police and spies, in eluding the vigilance of the Government; but no such hope sustained Wilfrid, seeing that in all the wide city there was not one man to whom he could look for refuge.

"I am entering St. Petersburg," he mused. "Shall I ever leave it? 'Tis doubtful. I feel, for all the world, like a prisoner riding to the guillotine. No matter! Honour forbids me to go back. That my princess is to

54

be found here is a sufficient reason for going forward. If her life is threatened, let them take mine as well."

And he consoled himself with that aphorism of the desperate, " What is to be, will be."

They were now leaving the silence and monotony of the steppe. Wooden cabins, with blue smoke rising from them, began to appear by the roadside, few at first, but by-and-by increasing in number, till they formed a continuous line. Soon the appearance of stone houses and handsome shops, of vehicles and pedestrians, told Wilfrid that he had entered upon the suburbs of the city.

" Hôtel d'Angleterre," was his reply to the yamchik's question as to whither the gospodin would be driven.

The hotel in question, a palatial structure, was kept by an Englishman, who bore the homely name of John Smith, a rosy-cheeked, rotund little personage, but having at this time a most lugubrious air, due to the bad state of business. His hotel, he remarked to Wilfrid, was mainly patronised by English visitors, all of whom had taken to flight on the declaration of war, leaving the vast building almost empty.

It was doubtless a very fine thing for patriotic Britons at home to read of their victories by sea and land, but the war fell hard on the English resident in St. Petersburg.

All this, and much more, was detailed by John Smith, whose gloomy prospects Wilfrid tried to brighten with the assurance that it was simply a game of bluff on the part of Paul, who, as soon as he should learn that the tall sails of Nelson's fleet were coming up the Gulf of Finland, would quickly make peace.

Having paid and dismissed the yamchik, Wilfrid asked for a file of daily newspapers that should cover the period of the previous three weeks. He had found it impossible to procure a newspaper at any of the post-inns on the way; and hence he was in a state of ignorance as to how the world had wagged.

Going out, the landlord soon returned with a file of Russian journals, and, looking cautiously around, said: " If your lordship cares for news fourteen days old, I have here a file of the English *Times,* and that's what you won't find in any other hotel in St. Petersburg. I get them from the English Club, who contrive to have them introduced into Russia without their being seen and 'blacked' by the censor. Say nothing about this, or I shall be having a domiciliary visit from the police."

Taking the papers, Wilfrid sat down and began with the file of the *Times,* skimming the contents with a quick eye, in the course of which operation he came across a paragraph that caused him for the space of a full minute to sit dumbfounded with surprise.

The paragraph which the Russian censor would certainly have "blacked" out, had the journal in question fallen into his hands, purported to come from the *Times* correspondent in St. Petersburg, and was worded as follows : —

" A strange story, to be received with some caution, is being whispered among political circles here, to the effect that the unfortunate Czar, Ivan VI., whose life, it will be remembered, was spent wholly in a dungeon, contracted a secret marriage with his gaoler's daughter, a girl of exquisite beauty.

" The sole descendant of this union is a grand-daughter, now in her twenty-third year, and said to be of surpassing grace and loveliness. Till lately she has been living at Moscow, carefully concealing the secret of her romantic origin; but, through no act of her own, the story, by some means or other, has transpired.

" The Czar Paul is said to be convinced by documentary evidence of her legitimacy and Imperial lineage, a matter to him of grave import, since, as there is no Salic law in Russia, if the rule of primogeniture be followed, this grand-daughter of Ivan VI., as the eldest surviving representative of the House of Romanoff, should now be wearing the diadem of the Czars.

" With a view of keeping a watch over her, Paul some months ago removed her from Moscow to his Court at St. Petersburg, conferring upon her the title of Grand Duchess, and placing her among the ladies in immediate attendance upon the Czarina. Assuming that this story is true, he would be a bold prophet who, in view of the gloomy and suspicious nature of Paul, would venture to predict length of days to a lady so dangerous pol.tically to him and his heirs."

The paper fluttered from Wilfrid's hands. He had no desire to read anything more that day. The political and military affairs of the Continent sank into insignificance beside this startling paragraph. The English readers of *The Times* might regard the story as a romantic fabrication; Wilfrid had reasons for believing otherwise.

The newspaper paragraph had closed with a sinister prediction, a prediction that had sent a thrill of fear to his mind. The only way of preventing its fulfilment was the removal of the duchess from Russia; but how could he, single-handed, effect the escape of a lady watched day and night as she undoubtedly must be?

"Matters are growing interesting," he muttered. "A grand-daughter of a Czar! Lineal heiress to the throne! So that is why the lady must have no suitors; she must be prevented from transmitting her rights. And Ouvaroff and I, and all would-be lovers are to be 'warned off.' Well, for my part, I decline to take the warning. Having more than a liking for the lady, I intend to carry on my suit; for, if her eyes said anything the other night, they said love."

A few questions to his host elicited the fact that the Czarina Mary, the Czarovna Elizavetta, the Grand Duchesses, and the ladies of the Imperial Household, were accustomed to take a drive every afternoon at two o'clock along the Nevski Prospekt.

Thinking that *his* grand duchess — the *Times* correspondent had, unfortunately, forgotten to name her — might form one of this party, Wilfrid resolved to take his stand near the entrance of the Michaelhof, in the hope of obtaining a fleeting glimpse of her.

Aware that in St. Petersburg a man in civilian attire is deemed of little account, Wilfrid resolved to don the uniform of a certain Austrian regiment in which he held the honorary rank of colonel, a reward conferred upon him by the Viennese Court for his bravery at the battle of the Devil's Bridge, where he had fought side by side with Russians, as well as with Austrians.

The picturesque uniform of dark blue, rich with gold braiding, was admirably adapted to set off his graceful figure to advantage, and when, after assuming his cloak and a jewel-hilted sabre, he took a glance in the mirror, he was satisfied that he had made the best of himself.

Thus attired, he set off on foot to view the Michael-ovsky Palace, the new residence of the Czar Paul.

The building, when seen, proved quite a revelation to Wilfrid, whose very brief acquaintance with the city had hitherto shown him but two main styles of architecture, the barbaric, semi-oriental style, seen chiefly in its churches, and the *façades* copied from the boulevards of Paris, seen chiefly in its hotels and mansions.

But the Michaelhof differed from both styles. Here, in the very heart of St. Petersburg, was a feudal castle, with donjon and towers, battlements and loopholes, portcullises and drawbridges; and, finally, a surrounding moat, which, however, just then availed little for defensive purposes, inasmuch as it was frozen over.

Wilfrid had seen numerous fantastic castles in his time, but none to compare with this bizarre-looking pile. One might have fancied that a mediæval architect, given to wine, had fallen asleep and dreamed; and that this palace was the petrifaction of his dream-fortress, although the bristling cannon and sentinels with their bayoneted rifles comported somewhat incongruously with this relic of a bygone age.

The building had for Wilfrid a fascination due not so much to its strange character as to the fact of its being the residence of his princess. Which of those gloomy towers did she inhabit? Over which drawbridge would the Czarina and her ladies come forth?

"An Englishman, I perceive," said a voice close to Wilfrid's ear. He turned and saw beside him a cloaked and sworded figure, wearing the uniform of a general in the Preobrejanski Guards; a man tall and strong, broad and burly, with somewhat vulgar-looking features, and with a rich, florid complexion, evidently due to a liking for ardent spirits; as a matter of fact, his breath exhaled an aroma at that very moment. He had eyes of a light blue, a snub nose, and a truculent tawny moustache, and he carried himself with a kind of bluff swagger, probably mistaken by him for ease.

Wilfrid might well wonder how so commonplace a man should be wearing a general's uniform; yet the man was to be a history-maker; in the time to come he was to surprise Europe, and perhaps himself, by the brilliancy of his campaigns against the invading French.

"An Englishman, I perceive," he repeated smilingly.

"What is the evidence?" asked Wilfrid.

"You go on foot. A Russian gentleman never walks when he can ride."

"By the same rule you are not a Russian — ah — gentleman."

"You are right. I am a Hanoverian — General Benningsen. At your service, sir," replied the other, raising his hand in military salute.

The name might well strike Wilfrid with surprise, for Benningsen was a man great in his family connections, if in nothing else. As a youth, he had wandered forth from Hanover to seek his fortune, and entering the Russian military service, had the good fortune to attract the notice of the great Catharine, ultimately marrying a natural daughter of that Empress.

But though a sort of brother-in-law to the Czar, Benningsen was not in favour at Court. As a matter of fact, he had been exiled for a time, and though recalled and restored to his rank as general, he was excluded from the Council of the Empire, the membership of which his Imperial family connections might naturally entitle him to expect. It was openly whispered that this exclusion, together with his banishment, had made Benningsen disposed to favour a change of Government, no matter what, so long as it was a change. Indeed, it was even asserted that he had been heard to say he would have his revenge on the "little orang-outang," his name for the Czar Paul.

"As an Englishman and a soldier, you are my brother," exclaimed the Hanoverian theatrically.

The Czar being at variance with England, it pleased Benningsen to patronise everything and everybody coming from that country.

On learning the name of his new " brother," Benningsen was loud in his admiration and delight at meeting
with one who had shown the Russian troops how to pass
the Devil's Bridge by scaling the rocks above it, leading
the way in the very fire of the enemy.

" Your gallant feat of arms," he assured Wilfrid, " is
remembered with gratitude and admiration by every
officer in St. Petersburg."

It was characteristic of Wilfrid that he thought, not
of the effect that his deed might have upon the Czar, but
upon — some one else. If his feat of arms had given
pleasure to the Princess, it mattered little to him how
Paul and others viewed it.

Benningsen, with a sweep of his arm, directed Wilfrid's attention to the Michaelhof.

" ' In my father's house are many mansions,' " he
remarked. " And that's the style of them," he continued
pointing to the palace. " Truly the angels have curious
ideas respecting architecture."

As Wilfrid's face showed that he was quite in the
dark as to the other's meaning, the General proceeded
to explain.

" Evidently you are not aware that my august brother-
in-law received a visit one night from the Archangel
Michael, who, showing him the plans and elevation of a
palace, bade him build one like it. Fact! At least," he
added with a side glance at Wilfrid, " it's a fact that
Paul says so, and it is never prudent to doubt the word
of a Czar."

" You speak freely."

" Why, one may speak freely with an Englishman.
With a Grand Duke 'twere otherwise. To return to
Paul. As soon as he had received the Archangel's com-
mission he was in a devil of a hurry to carry it out.
Five thousand men were at work daily. To dry the
walls more quickly red-hot plates were affixed to them.
All to no purpose. The place is so damp that the dear
Czar, the Empress, and the Grand Duchesses, are in a
continual state of coughing. And the price of all this?
— Eighteen million roubles ! "

Wilfrid let him rattle on without interruption, perceiv-

ing that he was one of those men who are never better
pleased than when hearing the sound of their own voice.

"You see that window facing us on the third story,"
continued Benningsen, pointing it out. "What sort of
room do you suppose lies behind it?"

"A prison, if one must judge by its numerous cross-
bars."

"Wrong. Paul's bedroom. Difficult to enter from
the outside, eh?"

"Are you contemplating the feat?" smiled Wilfrid,
for Benningsen really looked as if he had some such
idea in his head.

"The window barred," murmured the General, as if
following out some train of thought rather than addressing Wilfrid, "and the bedroom-door difficult of access,
since to reach it one must traverse a network of corridors
so like a maze that to find one's way requires the thread
of Ariadne."

"Are such precautions necessary?"

"The dear Czar thinks so."

On learning for what purpose Wilfrid had come to the
Michaelovski Square, Benningsen made the disappointing announcement that a distressing cough on the part
of the Empress — "due to the damned palace" — prevented her and the Imperial ladies from driving forth
that afternoon.

Benningsen, who was a member of the English Club
situated on the Minerva Prospekt, suggested that Wilfrid
should accompany him thither, to which proposal Wilfrid
assented, moved more by the hope of there getting rid
of the General than by any other reason. So the two
set off, on foot, because, as Benningsen remarked, it was
"so English."

The Minerva Prospekt, when reached, turned out to
be a wide and noble *boulevard,* alive with pedestrians of
the lower orders and with the sleighs of the wealthier
classes. The barbaric, yet handsome, costume of the
boyars, the gay dresses and rich furs of the ladies, with
their bright eyes and laughing voices, the furious galloping of steeds and the jingling of silver bells made a
scene of colour, movement, and sound, that offered a

striking contrast to the stillness, the emptiness, the monotony of the Michaelovski Square.

Then, in a moment, all was changed!

" Gossudar zdes! Gossudar zdes!"

Such was the cry — " The Czar is coming! " — that flew from mouth to mouth along the Prospekt.

Pedestrians stopped short in their walk; vehicles were hastily reined in, and dismay appeared on the faces of all, as with a crash of military music there suddenly debouched upon the Minerva Prospekt a regiment of footguards, in front of whom, and keeping time to the music with the waving of his cane, strutted an odd little figure, who was evidently taking a huge delight in the soldiers, in the marching, in the music.

CHAPTER VII

"THE orang-outang, confound him!" muttered Benningsen savagely, catching sight of the odd little figure. "Run, before he sees us. Quick! This way!"

"Why should I run?" demanded Wilfrid haughtily. He received no answer. Benningsen, holding his cloak over his face as if to prevent recognition, was running down a side street as fast as his legs could carry him. Wilfrid watched him in amazement.

"Afraid to face the Czar, his brother-in-law! Is the fellow an impostor, assuming the name of Benningsen for the purpose of fooling me?"

But as Wilfrid turned again he saw in a moment why Benningsen with some few others had vanished down the side streets; saw, too, why the square in front of the Michaelovski Palace had been deserted by all but the sentinels and those officials whose duty took them there.

For the truth was that even loyal Muscovites had come to regard a meeting with the Czar as little short of a calamity, since it was required by him that whenever he passed through a street all traffic must be suspended, pedestrians must cease their promenading, the occupants of vehicles must dismount, and everybody, from the serf to the boyar, must kneel bareheaded, be the wind never so cutting or the snow never so deep, till the "Little Father" — the expression is not meant to be ironic — had passed by. This practice, an old usage belonging to the barbarous days of the Empire, had been abolished by the good sense of Peter the Great; but Paul, on his accession, had revived the custom in all its rigour, so that Wilfrid, glancing along the Prospekt, saw two lines of kneeling people, some of whom even, with a

63

servility truly Oriental, were touching the slush with their foreheads.

Close to Wilfrid was a landau from which there had alighted two ladies, the one aged and feeble, the other young and delicate, both obviously of noble blood since the panels of their carriage bore an armorial device; yet there they were, side by side with their coachmen and footmen, kneeling in the roadway upon a horrible mixture of snow and mud that chilled their limbs and stained their fur cloaks.

And woe to them and to any other person who should rise too quickly after the Czar had gone by! If detected by a backward glance of the Imperial eye it was well for the offenders if they escaped the knout or Siberia.

As Wilfrid beheld the obvious discomfort of these two ladies, a fierce anger flamed in his breast against the sovereign who required such humiliating obeisance. During all this time the regiment, marching twelve abreast, was drawing nearer to the place where Wilfrid stood.

Some of the kneeling throng, conjecturing from his attitude that he was a foreigner, ventured to give him good-natured advice.

"Kneel to the Czar, little father!" they cried. "Kneel if you would escape the knout. See! his eye is upon you."

That fact made no difference in Wilfrid's attitude. Determined to assert his English manhood he stood erect as a palm.

Other Englishmen besides Wilfrid had declined to bow the knee, but they had been strong in the knowledge that they could obtain the protection of Lord Whitworth, the British Ambassador. Wilfrid had no such hope to sustain him, since the withdrawal of that minister, on the outbreak of the war, had left Paul free to do as he liked with those obstinate Englishmen who refused to acknowledge his divinity.

"Halt!" yelled the little figure, who, for his size, possessed marvellous lung power. "Halt! Stop that music!"

The regiment ceased its marching, the band its playing.

There was a terrible silence as the Czar, with a glare in his eye, marched straight up to Wilfrid. A shiver of expectancy ran through the throng. Some wriggled forward upon their knees with a view of getting into a better position for watching the sequel.

Wilfrid, who had seen not a few kings in his day, thought that the being now advancing towards him was the sorriest specimen of sovereignty he had ever met with — a very Caliban of royalty. He could scarcely bring himself to believe that the grotesque creature to whom all were kneeling as to a god could really be the crowned head of a vast empire.

He beheld a man, short of stature, bald and wrinkled, with a leaden complexion and large, glaring, dark eyes. The countenance was of the true Kalmuck type, so frightfully ugly that, if history speak truly, its owner shrank from looking into a mirror. (His wife, it is said, fainted at the first sight of him.) Certain it is that, differing from his predecessors, he forbade his likeness to be stamped on the coinage, with the result that since his time the Czar's head has not figured on the Russian currency.

As if he were some character in a comic opera, whose part it was to burlesque royalty, he wore a shabby old military surtout reaching down to his heels, jack-boots with immense spurs, and an enormous cocked hat carried beneath his arm. No matter how many degrees of frost the thermometer might register, that hat was never seen upon his head. It seemed as if he had set himself to contradict the current opinion that St. Petersburg is the coldest capital in Europe. Cold? when a man can walk about in the open air without furs and without a hat! Pooh, don't talk such stuff as that, sir!

Thus arrayed he was accustomed to play at soldiering by parading through the streets at the head of a regiment of footguards, flourishing a baton, marching on tip-toe with mincing air, and looking so like a little bantam that if he had flapped his arms and cried, "Cock-a-doodle-doo!" one would have felt little surprise.

The regiment that accompanied him was the famous Paulovski Guards, a creation of his own and worthy of him. The face of every soldier, like that of his Imperial master, carried the ornament of a snub, up-turned nose; and, as if to render the face still more grotesque, the moustaches were brushed upwards to the ears.

Not only did Wilfrid's erect attitude give displeasure, but his six feet of handsome and athletic manhood was likewise an affront to a ruler, who, on account of his diminutive and ugly appearance, had been so sneered at by his mother's tall and shapely courtiers that he had come at last to hate the sight of a well-favoured person, and was jealous even of his own son's stature and beauty.

Directing a terrible glance at Wilfrid, the Czar spoke, and by that act, Wilfrid, did he but know it, had become a very illustrious character. "There are but two great men in Russia," Paul had once said, "myself, and he to whom I happen to be speaking at the moment."

"Why," demanded the Czar — and though Wilfrid had never before seen or heard him, there seemed something oddly familiar, both in his face and voice — "why do you refuse to us the homage of the knee?"

"Because, Sire," replied Wilfrid, bringing his hand up to the salute, "I revere the memory of the great Peter, who was wont to employ his stick upon the bodies of those who knelt to him!"

This was hitting Paul full in the teeth, for if there was one thing upon which he prided himself it was the imitating of his great-grandfather.

"We follow," frowned the Czar, "a custom more ancient than the reign of Peter." And then, confident that Wilfrid's boldness could spring from but one nationality, he added, "You are an Englishman?"

"A man cannot choose his own parents, Sire."

"Your name?" cried Paul, growing more angry.

"Wilfrid, Lord Courtenay."

The Czar closed his eyes in thought. He seemed as if trying to recollect something. Wilfrid wondered whether the Emperor was connecting his name with that of the Princess. Suddenly opening his eyes again sharply, Paul said — "We have heard of you from Baranoff. You are the artist who tried by a picture to create an outbreak against established order?"

"I painted a picture portraying the murder of that royal lady, whose daughter till lately was under your protection, Sire."

Paul winced, recalling first with' what state he had welcomed the daughter of Marie Antoinette, and then, how he had sent her packing at a moment's notice, merely to please his new ally Napoleon.

"We have heard of you," he repeated. "A spy of Pitt's, with whose gold you bribed Frederick William to hold aloof from the Russian alliance."

The charge of being a spy came with a good grace, Wilfrid thought, from the very head and front of the spy system.

"No Courtenay was ever a spy. Question your own officers, Sire, and they will tell you that I have shed my blood in the service of Russia."

"The more effectually to disguise your calling. A spy of Pitt's. Silence! Do you brave the Czar to his face? On your knees, rascal, or —— "

And up went the stick that had been often applied to the bodies of his subjects.

Wilfrid, his face somewhat pale, stepped back and half unsheathed his sword, and thus the two stood looking at each other. There was in Wilfrid's eye a gleam which seemed to say that, if struck, he would strike back, and strike hard. As if realising this the miserable little man slowly lowered his stick, and just as slowly Wilfrid's blade went down into its scabbard again, finishing its descent with a little clang.

During this episode no man moved, whether among soldiers or civilians — not a hand was put forth to defend the Czar. The significance of this fact, which did not escape Paul's notice, served only to increase his fury.

"You would see your Czar murdered?" he cried, turning upon his regiment. "Lieutenant Voronetz, arrest this man."

A young officer, motioning four men to follow him, approached Wilfrid.

"You are my prisoner," he said, with a look that entreated the captive to give as little trouble as possible.

For one moment Wilfrid hesitated. The wild blood of

his viking ancestors danced in his veins, urging him to
defy his enemies. He was convinced now that in any
case death would be his lot; then why not die heroically,
with his trenchant blade whirling round his head?

"Give me his sword," cried Paul, who had taken a
fancy to the weapon. He was a collector of swords, and
kept a little store of them in his bedroom.

"This sword," said Wilfrid, drawing forth the blade,
"the gift of the Prussian Queen, shall never be handled
by a Muscovite barbarian."

And ere his guards could stop him, Wilfrid snapped
the blade in half, and flung the two fragments upon the
snow.

"An honourable way of treating a Queen's gift,"
sneered Paul; and then, addressing the officer, he added,
"To the Citadel with him. To be brought to the Red
Square at the first parade to-morrow. Your life for his,
if he escapes. Forward," he cried, addressing the regiment and waving his cane.

The band struck up a march, and the grotesque Paulovski Guards, with the Czar at their head, moved onward again; and as they passed the wearied Petersburgers rose and straightened their stiffened limbs.
They took care to keep at a respectful distance from
Wilfrid, and to maintain silence. It was dangerous to
express sympathy.

At a signal from Voronetz, the four soldiers fell into
position, two before Wilfrid and two behind, the lieutenant taking his place at the prisoner's right hand.

"Draw sabres. March."

Four swords flashed simultaneously from their scabbards; and, as the guard moved forward, Wilfrid mechanically moved forward with them, scarcely able to
realise that he was a prisoner, so quickly had the event
happened.

"Gospodin," said Voronetz, "when the monkey plays
the flute you should dance. You have acted foolishly."

"Wisely; for I have maintained the dignity of an
Englishman."

"And put yourself into prison."

"No more in prison than yourself, good Voronetz. Russia is a prison."

" 'Tis a pretty large one, then. Gospodin, if one is not prepared to obey the laws of Russia, one should keep out of Russia."

"There's something in that argument," laughed Wilfrid. "Whither are you taking me?" he asked presently.

"To the Petropaulovski Fortress."

"The Pet — ? 'Tis a melodious name."

" 'Tis called the Citadel for shortness."

"Where situated?"

"On the other side of the Neva."

"Far or near?"

"Three versts away. If the gospodin likes, he may hire a vehicle to take us thither."

"Thanks; but I'm in no particular hurry to reach your polysyllabic fortress. Who is the governor of it?"

"Count Arcadius Baranoff."

"The devil!"

"I believe he is, or a near relative. The post was given him as a sort of reward for his successful mission to France. There's a fine salary attached to it."

The thought that he was to be put into the power of his enemy, Baranoff, was a somewhat disquieting one to Wilfrid. A dark cell and irons was the least merciful punishment he could expect from the malignant governor.

Wilfrid's position seemed to weigh little with the chatty lieutenant; for, as they marched along, he took upon himself to point out to his prisoner various buildings of note, thinking, perhaps, that as Wilfrid was not long for this world, it would be a pity for him to pass out of it without taking with him some knowledge of so fine a city. "See Petersburg, and then die," was evidently his motto. And as it is better to be cheerful than gloomy, Wilfrid tried to take an interest in the proffered remarks.

"And what place is this?" he asked, as they passed by a wide, open space.

"This is known as the Red Square."

"And that hillock in the centre ——?"

"Is where the condemned criminal stands."

"And the wooden pillar ——?"

"The post to which he is tied while receiving the knout."

"The knout. What is that?" asked Wilfrid with assumed innocence.

"Now you jest, gospodin. 'Tis a whip."

"Does it — ah! — hurt?"

"You'll soon be in a position to judge."

"How so?"

"You heard the Czar say that you are to be brought to the Red Square at the first parade in the morning."

"You mean that I am to be knouted?"

"As surely as the sun will rise to-morrow. If the gospodin has any money or jewelry upon him, he had better entrust them to me."

"For what purpose?"

"To bribe the executioner, so that he may accommodate you according to your taste."

"I fail somewhat to grasp your meaning."

"Why, look you, knouted you must be in some way or other, for the Czar will be present to see his orders carried out. Now, there are three ways of swinging the lash."

"Really? You interest me."

"First, there is the merciful way. The strokes are made to descend upon the back only; in which case one has a chance of surviving the lash, even though gunpowder be rubbed into the wounds and set on fire."

"Is that one of the features of the merciful way?"

"The people sometimes demand it; it pleases them, and need not hurt you."

"How is the pain to be avoided?"

"A bribe to the knouter, and he will, before beginning business, administer to you unseen a stupefying drug."

"Good! And the second way ——?"

"Ah, that is terrible, gospodin, terrible! The executioner causes the lash to coil entirely round the body, cutting the flesh as with the edge of a razor, laying the very bones and bowels bare. No one can survive this

method, which is the one he'll adopt, unless bribed to
act otherwise."

" And the third way? "

" Is the happy despatch; he kills at the very first
stroke by breaking the spine. You have but to say which
method you prefer and Vladimir will oblige. You'll
always find the friends of the condemned at Vladimir's
door on the eve of a knouting."

Wilfrid had no fear of death, as such, provided it
should come in swift and painless guise. But death by
knouting! To stand half-naked, on a grey, wintry morning in sight of a gaping crowd, his flesh hanging in strips
from ribs and spine, was an end so dreadful that it might
well have shaken the iron nerves of Zeno himself.

Just as he was preparing to make a dash for liberty at
some side street, gateway, or any other convenient opening, and was looking keenly ahead of him with a view to
this contingency, he noticed, not far off, and on his side
of the road, a man wearing the livery of some nobleman;
a man who commanded attention by reason of his stature,
for he was fully seven feet high and proportionately
broad. He stood smoking a cigar, and lounging at the
foot of a flight of steps that led up to the door of a
stately mansion. Though attentive, apparently, to nothing but his cheroot, this man was in reality keeping a
watchful eye upon the advancing escort, whose lieutenant
was walking on the side remote from the steps.

Though struck somehow by the man's manner, Wilfrid
was not prepared for his action.

As the little party came up and was in the act of
passing, the hitherto listless giant displayed a sudden and
remarkable activity. Putting forth his mighty hands, he
grasped the two near guards, namely, the one who
marched before Wilfrid, and the one who marched behind, and hurled them, each against his neighbour, with
such force that all four went sprawling to the ground,
their sabres flying with them. At the same moment,
Wilfrid found his wrist clasped by the hand of a young
lady, clad in a handsome set of sables.

" Quick," she said, her eyes dancing with excitement.
" Up these steps, and you are safe. Quick! "

Wilfrid required no second bidding. Pulled by the lady upon one side, and by the giant upon the other, he was swung up the steps towards the door; it opened at a touch, and the three disappeared before the very eyes of the astonished escort. The rapidity of the feat was the most astonishing part of it: the affair had not taken more than six seconds.

Recovering from his surprise, Voronetz called upon his men to follow him, and flourishing his sabre he sprang up the steps, bent on forcing his way into the mansion, when he suddenly stopped short at sight of some letters upon the glass lamp above the door.

"We cannot enter here," he said, his sword-arm dropping limply to his side; and then, realising the consequences of Wilfrid's escape, he muttered, "Holy St. Nicholas! I shall lose my head for this."

While Voronetz stood there, irresolute and despairing, Wilfrid, having passed the double doors of the mansion, found himself in a stately entrance-hall with a gilt gallery supported on marble pillars. The tapestries and mirrors, the statues and pictures, rivalled the splendour of Versailles.

Four lackeys in gold-laced liveries, stationed at different points, gave an additional touch of grandeur to the scene. Two well-dressed gentlemen, conjectured by Wilfrid to be secretaries, passing through the hall at this moment, glanced curiously in his direction.

The lady who had rescued Wilfrid was about twenty-five years of age, with dark hair and dark eyes. Wilfrid, who, it must not be forgotten, was an artist, contemplated her tall and graceful person with secret pleasure. He had seen only *one* face more beautiful; and it was quite possible that if his princess and this stranger were to stand side by side, an impartial judge might have awarded the palm for beauty to the latter.

She laughed with all the gaiety of a schoolgirl at the feat she had just performed.

"I was a witness of your arrest," she said, "and hurried on before you. I knew your guards would take the Nevski Prospekt, because it is the direct route to the Citadel; and I knew, too, they would take this side of the Prospekt, as being the sunnier. So I stationed François at the foot of the steps with orders to snatch you from their hands. And we have succeeded. You are safe here. The Czar and all his armies dare not enter."

"What place is this, then?"

"Monsieur le vicomte," she said, with a graceful little curtsey, "welcome to the French Embassy."

Wilfrid's face clouded at these words.

"I thank you, mademoiselle," said he, folding his cloak around him, and taking a step towards the entrance, "but I must wish you adieu. An enemy to France, I cannot in honour accept this asylum."

"Stay a moment," she replied, raising her forefinger with a pretty air. "There is a twofold France, royalist and republican. For which are you?"

"For royalist France, undoubtedly."

"You hate Bonaparte?"

"I do not love him."

"Let me whisper a secret. I hate Bonaparte; yes, that is the word — hate. Is not this a dreadful confession to come from the daughter of the Ambassador that represents him? *Mon père* is a republican, a servant of the Consulate; but as for me — '*Vive le roi*' is my motto. Now, if I, a foe of the Republic, do not scruple to reside under the roof of the French Embassy, why should you not accept its hospitality, at least for a day or two?"

"Will you let me see Monsieur l'Ambassadeur?"

"At present he is out. He will return shortly."

"It is generous of you to offer me an asylum, but — your father may object. My presence here is certain to bring trouble upon him. The Czar will demand my surrender, and —— "

The young lady drew herself up proudly.

"You are my guest, for I invite you here. *Mon père* is a gentleman, and will not hand his daughter's guest over to death merely because he has had the manliness not to kneel to a tyrant."

Wilfrid began to waver. Why should he not accept her invitation? Not only would he be escaping a terrible fate, but there would be in this new situation a piquant charm that appealed to his love of mischief. He pictured the First Consul's rage on learning that the Englishman who had defied him to his face, slain his fencing-master, and defeated his policy at Berlin, had now put the finishing touch to his audacity by taking refuge for a few days under the very roof of the French Embassy! "It will turn his hair grey," thought Wilfrid,

"Come, you must not go from here. Will you deprive me of your society, when I have been expecting it these many days?"

"The deuce you have," thought Wilfrid.

The young lady here drew forth a letter, and directed Wilfrid's attention to the signature, "Louisa R."

"Do you know this handwriting?" she asked.

"I think I recognise the autograph signature of my friend, the Queen of Prussia."

"As children we were friends together," said the Ambassador's daughter, "and though our lives now lie far apart, we still correspond with each other. In this letter she bids me exercise surveillance over a favourite knight of hers, Lord Courtenay, now on his way to Russia; for, to quote her very words, 'If I have rightly gauged his character, he will not be twenty-four hours in St. Petersburg without coming into collision with the authorities.' See how excellently she has judged you," smiled the young lady, as she folded up the letter and put it away. "You haven't been a day in the capital, and yet you have already got, as you English say, into hot water. The good queen having charged me to watch over you, it is my intention to fulfil the trust."

Her smile was so arch and her manner altogether so charming that Wilfrid could no longer resist. He would accept her hospitality, conditional, of course, on its being sanctioned by her father, the Ambassador.

"That is well," said the young lady on hearing his decision.

She now informally introduced herself as Pauline de Vaucluse, daughter of Henrion, the Marquis de Vaucluse.

"But you mustn't give him his title," she added. "He is a *ci-devant,* that is, an ex-noble, a Republican. He has dropped the '*de*,' and must be addressed as Citoyen Henrion."

"And you are the Citoyenne Pauline," smiled Wilfrid.

"My faith, no!" replied the young lady, with a flash of energy. "I am the Baroness de Runö in my own right; and claim the title due to my rank." Then, turning to Wilfrid's rescuer, who, during this dialogue, had been standing near by, but out of ear-shot, she said, "François, conduct Viscount Courtenay to the Porphyry Suite. My lord," she added, with a graceful inclination of her head, "I hope to see you again within half an hour."

"Truly, my lines have fallen in pleasant places," thought Wilfrid, as he followed François to the apartments assigned him.

CHAPTER VIII

A CHARMING TÊTE-À-TÊTE

As Pauline was about to leave the entrance-hall, the double doors leading from the street suddenly opened, and in walked her father, the Citoyen Henrion, Ambassador of the Republic.

He was a man close upon his sixtieth year, with silver hair and a dignified presence. His countenance expressed mildness and amiability, rather than force of character or diplomatic subtlety; in truth, his appointment was due more to his polished manners than to anything else. The *parvenu* ambassadors of the Republic had often, from lack of dignity and ignorance of etiquette, excited the sneers and laughter of foreign courts. The Marquis de Vaucluse was sent to St. Petersburg to show that the race of gentlemen was not extinct in France, and that the new government could count among its sons men distinguished both by birth and manners. He conscientiously strove to do his duty to the Republic, and when reproached for relinquishing the traditions of his order, he was wont to say, " I serve France, not Napoleon: a nation, and not a government."

There was at this moment a cloud on his brow, and Pauline perceived its cause in the shape of Lieutenant Voronetz, who, with a very lugubrious face, followed hard upon the heels of the Ambassador.

" This may be fun to you, Baroness," he remarked, " but it means death to me."

" And, naturally, you don't want to die," answered Pauline. " But, then, neither does Lord Courtenay."

" So the story this lieutenant tells me is true?" said the Ambassador, looking in perplexity from one to the other.

76

" Quite true, *mon père.*"

" Where is the man? " said the Marquis, casting a look around.

" Probably at this moment admiring the Gobelins in the Porphyry Suite, where he must abide till this storm be blown over."

" You have lodged him in the suite kept only for our illustrious visitors ! "

" Well, he's an illustrious visitor. Comes of one of the oldest families in Europe. Counts the Greek emperors among his ancestors. Can Napoleon say as much ? "

" He must be surrendered to Lieutenant Voronetz."

" He shall *not* be surrendered," said Pauline firmly.

The Marquis grew uneasy. When his daughter assumed that look and that tone, he knew full well that she would have her way in spite of him. Has he been the only man to be ruled by his daughter?

" Why did you do this thing? " he asked, smiting his gloves together in a helpless fashion.

" To teach a tyrant that liberty is not yet dead in St. Petersburg."

The Marquis gave her a glance intended as a caution not to speak too freely in the presence of the Czar's lieutenant. Then, after a moment's pause, he drew her aside out of the hearing of Voronetz.

" Of course, *matiushka,*" he said, using the endearing term which the foreigner in Russia soon learns to apply indiscriminately to all women, " of course, little mother, we know, between ourselves, that this kneeling to the Czar is a degrading piece of servility, and I can quite sympathise with Lord Courtenay in his attitude. But your action, Pauline, has put us all in the wrong. If you desired him to be set free it should have been done in proper form. A joint note from the ambassadors would have procured his release. As matters now stand, Paul will be justified in demanding Lord Courtenay's surrender. The meekest ruler in the world cannot submit to have his authority flouted as you have flouted it. *Nom de Dieu!* Pauline, what were you thinking of? "

" Not of the niceties of diplomatic observance, you

may be sure. But do not look so troubled, *mon père.*
The Czarovitch shall get us out of our difficulty. Go and
lay the matter before him. Ask him to persuade his
father to pardon the Englishman. He is sure to succeed.
You know how Paul — it's his only good point — respects the judgment of Alexander. ' I must consult the
Grand Duke,' he says, when in a state of doubt. ' He
has a fine sense of justice.' Go at once, before Paul has
had time to learn that his prisoner has been rescued.
The work of persuading him will be easier then."

" Alexander certainly *could* effect this for us," said the
Marquis musingly. " The question is, will he ? "

" He will, if you say that it is the wish of Pauline."

The Ambassador gave her a sharp, penetrating look,
as if he would fain learn the reason for this belief of
hers.

" Was he not present at our ball here last week ? "
remarked Pauline, answering her father's unspoken
question. " He danced with me four times, and was
extremely gracious ; nay, did he not say if ever I should
have a grievance that he could set right, I was not to
hesitate to apply to him ? *Mon père,* we'll make him
redeem that promise. Tell him that Pauline de Vaucluse
is a prisoner in her father's Embassy, unable to stir out,
because she has made herself amenable to arrest by
thwarting the Czar's will. He'll soon set matters right,
and you'll return with a free pardon both for Lord
Courtenay and your mischievous daughter. But first
you'll see our visitor ? "

Her father assented, and bidding the lackeys supply
Voronetz with wine he requested the lieutenant to await
his return.

Then, with old-fashioned courtesy, he offered his arm
and conducted his daughter to the daintily-furnished
chamber that served as her boudoir.

" Now, remember," cautioned Pauline, " that Lord
Courtenay will require delicate handling, for he is
patriotically proud and quick to take fire. If he should
come to believe that his presence here, though personally
agreeable to us, is from a political point of view embarrassing, he'll make his *congé* at once. As soon as he

learned that this was the French Embassy, he was for walking out again, his honour forbidding him to take refuge here. He required some persuading to remain. So, *mon père,* be careful."

"Now, Heaven forbid," said the Marquis, "that I should say aught to embarrass him."

And the Ambassador was as good as his word, for upon Wilfrid's entering, he greeted him in a manner so courteous and affable that Wilfrid was at once placed at his ease. Pauline looked at her visitor with a smile that plainly said, "Did I not say my father would take your part?"

"Monsieur l'Ambassadeur," said Wilfrid, "our respective countries being at war, my position beneath the roof of the French Embassy is certainly a singular one."

"And for me a happy one," replied the Marquis, with a bow. "Still, whatever the situation, it is not of your creating, but of Pauline's. You are her guest and mine; and here you must remain till we have persuaded the Czar to see matters in another light."

After a few more words of gracious import, De Vaucluse, taking Voronetz with him, went off on his conciliatory errand, leaving his daughter to entertain the stranger.

And a charming entertainer she made, quite fascinating Wilfrid with the vivacity and intelligence of her conversational powers. Part of the time was spent in showing her guest the various objects of interest contained in her boudoir, among them being a piece of silk embroidery wrought by her own hand and set as a picture in a silver frame. It represented a castle, quaint, yet pretty.

"Castle Runö," explained Pauline. "Built upon one of the islands of the Neva by Peter the Great, to satisfy a fancy of his wife, Catharine. I hope to have the honour of entertaining you there some day, for castle and island are both mine, my very own, inherited from my Russian mother. Its possession carries with it a title that makes me a baroness in my own right."

"Then you are half a Russian?" smiled Wilfrid.

Though by her own showing this must be so, the Baroness nevertheless seemed to resent the idea.

" No, indeed, I am wholly French, as I can soon prove. Vera, come here a moment," she said, addressing her maid.

The girl came forward, and at her mistress's request knelt upon the hearth.

" Vera is a pure Muscovite," said the Baroness. " Now, look at her ear," she continued, touching it caressingly. " You see it? Look at mine, and tell me the difference."

" Her ear has no lobe," remarked Wilfrid, in some surprise.

" True. Have you not noticed the like before? " asked Pauline. " No? O, unobservant man! Well, after this take due note, and you will find that every true-born Russ is without a lobe to his ear."

Wilfrid wondered whether his grand duchess was distinguished by this peculiarity. He hoped not, for Pauline's pearly little shell of an ear was prettier than Vera's.

" I suppose," he observed, " that all the members of the Imperial Family bear this Muscovite mark? "

" Not so, for the dynasty has scarcely a drop of true Russian blood, and is rather proud of the fact. ' I am a German, not a Russian,' said the Czar Ivan; and so have all his descendants said."

Pauline hitherto had been bright and lively, but all her brightness and liveliness went in a moment when she saw Wilfrid open a small album that lay upon the table.

" You may look," she said, with a heavy sigh, for Wilfrid, on seeing the nature of its contents, had closed the book.

" Indeed, I would rather that you read it."

Wilfrid opened the album again, and found it to contain melancholy souvenirs of the Reign of Terror in the shape of private letters written by some of Pauline's friends, who had fallen victims to the guillotine; written, many of them, on the very eve of execution. Their style, direct from the heart, as was natural with persons at the point of death, gave to these letters a pathos that would have touched the heart of the least emotional.

"Those letters are dear to me," said Pauline. "They are the fuel that keeps the fire of my patriotism burning. Every day I read them, in order to prevent me from ever loving the Republic, that Republic that put my friends to death."

With somewhat melancholy feelings, Wilfrid closed the album, admiring, as he did so, the creamy white of the binding.

"Is this the famous Torjek leather," he asked, passing his forefinger over its smooth surface.

Pauline's answer took a singular shape. She bent forward, and laying hold of Wilfrid's hand lifted it and drew the finger that had touched the book slowly down her cheek, accompanying her action with a weird smile.

"Is not the touch the same?" she asked; and, without giving him time to answer, she continued, "You have heard of the Princess Lamballe?"

"Good heavens! Do you mean that —— ?"

"Did you ever see her at the Tuileries in the days of the old *régime?*"

"No, but ——"

"Well, from to-day you can say that you have had the honour of touching her skin!"

Knowing that among the eccentricities of horror produced by the French Revolution human tanneries had a place, Wilfrid had no need to ask more with that binding, white and lustrous, staring him in the face.

"There is all that is left of the Princess Lamballe," said Pauline, her eyes set with a stony grief, a grief too deep for tears. "We were brought up from girlhood together. She was my dearest friend. She was young; she was beautiful; she was good. And you know her end? Taken to the prison of La Force, her only crime being that she was a friend of the Queen's, she was flung forth from the prison-gate into the hands of a howling mob. And then . . . . My God! it will not bear thinking of. . . . Pieces of the body put on the end of pikes were paraded through the streets. . . . Some found their way to the tanyard. . . ."

Overcome by the recollection, she was silent for a few moments, and when she spoke again it was in a mood fierce and dark.

"Do you wonder now why I hate the Republic? Let my father serve it, if he will. For my part, I work for its downfall."

It was clear to Wilfrid from this, as well as from previous remarks made by her, that the one passionate aim of Pauline's life was the subversion of the Republic and the restoration of the Bourbons, an aim laudable enough in itself, were she any other than she was, but scarcely compatible with her position as the daughter of the Ambassador of the French Republic.

"To work for its downfall," she repeated. "And I shall succeed," she continued, with a smile as of coming triumph. "Mark me," she added, "smile, doubt, call it vaunting, if you will, but when the secret history of to-day comes to be written, it will be found that I, Pauline de Vaucluse, Baroness of Runö, have been the chief cause of Bonaparte's downfall."

But when Wilfrid asked in what way she intended to accomplish this, he was met by a tantalising shake of her head.

However strange her words, there was in her manner something which led him to believe that they were no mere boast. Still, great as was his desire to witness the fulfilment of them, he did not like to see a daughter working in opposition to her father, especially if — he trusted he was not wronging her by the supposition — she should be availing herself of the political secrets acquired by her residence in the Embassy.

However, being as yet not sufficiently advanced in her friendship, he refrained from taking upon himself the office of Mentor.

At a sign from the Baroness, her maid, Vera, withdrew, returning with a bright samovar or tea-urn.

"Do you take sugar?" asked Pauline, who seemed to have recovered from the gloom occasioned by her reminiscences. "Yes? I fear I can offer you none but Barth's."

"And who is Barth?"

"A man who is making his fortune out of beetroot.
We have to rely upon him ever since Paul forbade the
import of your colonial sugar."

"It seems to me," grumbled Wilfrid, "that this Paul
lays his despotic finger upon every department of life."

"Too true. And he treats his own family no more
indulgently than he treats the public. He has kept his
daughters under restraint for a week upon a diet of bread
and water merely for yawning at church. And in the
Greek Church, you must know, one has to stand, and
not sit; and the service usually lasts three hours."

"Who would be a grand duchess?" smiled Wilfrid.

"Times will be different when little Sasha comes to
the throne."

"And who is little Sasha?" asked Wilfrid absently.

"The Czarovitch, to be sure — Alexander."

"Of course — called little because he is like his father
in stature?"

This remark drew a laugh from the Baroness and a
smile from her maid.

"'Little' is a term of endearment. He stands six
feet two inches high in his boots."

"My height exactly," remarked Wilfrid.

Pauline paused with her cup half-way to her lips, and
looked doubtfully at Wilfrid.

"I don't think that you are *quite* as tall as Alexander."

"Six feet two in my boots," asseverated Wilfrid.

Pauline drank her tea thoughtfully. Presently she
said : —

"You'll think me silly, but I am quite curious to know
which is the taller, you or Alexander."

"How shall we settle this weighty matter?"

"Easily enough. Alexander's exact height is to be
seen on the panel behind that curtain. He called at the
Embassy last week, and, *mon père* being out, it fell to
me to entertain his Imperial Highness. He had tea
here, just as you and I are having it now, and, if you'll
believe it, the conversation took a similar turn to ours —
that is to say, we talked of his stature. I was actually
so daring as to doubt the word of a Czarovitch, so just
to convince me, he laughingly stood against yonder wall,

like a recruit about to be measured, while I, with a piece
of black crayon, marked his height upon a panel, and
found it to be, as I have said, six feet two inches. See!"
Walking to the place indicated, Pauline drew aside the
tapestry, revealing upon the white panel behind a short
black horizontal line, and something more as well that
she had not mentioned, for the line rested upon the life-
size silhouette of a human profile, drawn with black
crayon, presumably the profile of Alexander.

"Now, if you want to measure yourself with little
Sasha —?" said Pauline.

So, to please her, Wilfrid stood with his back against
the panel, and Pauline saw that the crown of his head
was on a level with the charcoal line, showing that his
stature differed little, if at all, from that of the Czarovitch.

"And this, I presume, is his profile," said Wilfrid,
falling back to obtain a better view. "Drawn by —?"

"Your humble servant. As Alexander stood there, he
said, 'I wonder you don't draw my profile also!'
'Why, so I will,' was my reply, and placing a lamp on
this column here, I made him stand in such a position
that his side-face was silhouetted upon the panel, and —
there you have it! Now, Lord Courtenay, you are an
artist, that is to say, one who has, or ought to have, a
keen eye for beauty. Don't you think that Alexander's
profile is perfect?"

Wilfrid ventured to dissent, though with some diffi-
dence, because it was clear that his fair hostess regarded
it as an ideal head.

"Well, Sir Critic, what are the faulty points?"

"To meet the requirements of my ideal of beauty —
and mine, of course, may be a wrong ideal — the line of
the forehead should be brought slightly nearer to the
perpendicular. The nose would be perfect but for this
slight depression near the bridge, and the chin, in my
opinion, recedes a little more than it ought."

"And your opinion of his character, so far as it can be
deduced from this silhouette?"

"An amiable and intellectual youth, disposed to do
good, but likely to fail for want of a strong will. Of

course," laughed Wilfrid, "this opinion of mine is open to correction. One should see the whole face with its expression, before passing judgment."

Pauline's pout showed that she was not altogether pleased with Wilfrid's views.

"Shall I criticise the critic?" she said, and calling upon Vera to place the lamp exactly where it had been during her sketching of Alexander, she adjusted Wilfrid's position, little by little, till at last his profile — brow, nose, lip, chin — became coincident as far as was possible, with Alexander's.

"That's it; now don't move," she said. "Let us see how much difference there is, and whom the difference favours."

Taking up a piece of black crayon, she outlined Wilfrid's profile upon that of Alexander's, with a result as surprising to Wilfrid as to herself.

The defects, or assumed defects, that he had pointed out in Alexander's profile were remedied in his own. The line of the forehead had become vertical, imparting a more intellectual character to the face; the depression of the nose had vanished, and the chin had taken a firmer touch.

Though Wilfrid tried not to be conceited, his own judgment told him that the second profile was preferable to the first, and so thought Pauline.

"H'm, an improvement, certainly," she said, holding her head upon one side and surveying her handiwork. "So I am to read your character thus," she added quizzically. "Amiable and intellectual, herein running parallel with Alexander, but differing from Alexander in having a strong will. I trust that in Alexander's case you are in error, for 'twill be a pity if weakness of will should prevent him from carrying out the good reforms he has in mind."

They returned to their chairs and to their tea.

"Since you know the Czarovitch so well," said Wilfrid, "I presume you know also his *aide-de-camp*, Prince Ouvaroff?"

"Do *you* know him?" she asked.

"Serge and I are friends of several years' standing,"

replied Wilfrid, very much doubting, however, whether the term "friends" was any longer applicable to the relationship between himself and Ouvaroff.

Pauline's face assumed a somewhat whimsical expression. "Poor Ouvaroff!"

"Why that sigh?" smiled Wilfrid.

"Lovers may come, and lovers may go, but Ouvaroff remains faithful for ever."

This to Wilfrid was a most surprising piece of news.

"When last we met the Prince spoke of a nameless lady who for some years past had been saying him nay. Can it be that —— "

"He will not take my 'No.'"

Her words showed Wilfrid that he had been holding a wrong opinion. Pauline, and not the nameless duchess, was Ouvaroff's inamorata. So far, good! There was no rivalry in love between them. But why, then, was the Prince daily practising swordsmanship? Was the object of his resentment some other Englishman, and not Wilfrid at all? And what had he meant by saying he had recently discovered that it was death to court the lady of his choice, language identical with that used by Baranoff when speaking of the "Princess"? Were there, then, at St. Petersburg two ladies whom it was death to court? Now, though it might very well be that peril would befall the unauthorised suitor who should venture to make love to the grand-daughter of Ivan VI., yet why an *aide-de-camp* of the Czarovitch should not pay his addresses to an ambassador's daughter without having the fear of death before his eyes was a question that set Wilfrid thinking.

It may seem strange that Wilfrid, being now *tête-à-tête* with one who knew Ouvaroff intimately, did not ask whether she was acquainted with the lady to whom the Prince had acted as escort, but the truth was, Pauline had so fascinating and seductive a manner that Wilfrid hesitated to touch upon this theme lest she should draw from him an account of the nocturnal incident at the inn of the Silver Birch, a disclosure which would have been a breaking of his word to the Princess. Upon that matter, therefore, he determined to keep a silent tongue.

"Another cup of tea, Lord Courtenay?" said Pauline, breaking in upon his reverie. "No? You really have finished? Well then —— "

Taking the porcelain cup used by Wilfrid, she held it for a moment above the tiled hearth, and then let it fall. It was shivered to pieces.

Wilfrid wondered in what light he was to take this action.

"It means," said Pauline, responsive to his thoughts, "that no one else shall ever drink from that cup. 'Tis a Muscovite way of honouring a guest. You see, I *am* half a Russian, after all. With our grand boyars it is often the practice after a feast to cast all the plate out at the windows upon the heads of the expectant crowd below, it being thought undignified to make use of the same dishes a second time. Paul has done his best by ukase to abolish this custom, chiefly with a view to the saving of his own plate."

Wilfrid acknowledged the high honour conferred upon him, adding —

"This must be a somewhat expensive habit on your part?"

"Not so, my lord," replied Pauline with a charming curtsey. "It is not *every* guest I treat in this way."

CHAPTER IX.

A DOCUMENT MISSING

WHILE Wilfrid was thinking that if Pauline's ways with Ouvaroff were as fascinating as her ways with him, it was no wonder that the poor Prince's head was turned, the maid Vera, who had gone off on some errand for her mistress, now re-entered, bearing a salver, upon which lay two name-cards.

"Visitors, my lady."

Just the trace of a frown appeared upon Pauline's face as she took the cards in her hand. Wilfrid's society was much more interesting than that of Count Baranoff and General Benningsen. She was on the point of feigning some excuse for not receiving them when Vera remarked,

"They say they have startling news."

"In that case I'd better see them."

And bidding Wilfrid excuse her absence for a short time she descended to that same entrance-hall in which she had held her first interview with him.

Baranoff and Benningsen had met by chance upon the steps of the Embassy, each bringing the same piece of news, the Count intending to communicate it to the Ambassador, the General to Pauline.

Though apprised of Wilfrid's arrival, Baranoff knew nothing whatever of his arrest and escape, and it was only in the interval of waiting that he heard the story from Benningsen. The news filled the Count with secret rage. Hitherto hating Pauline a little, he now began to hate her more. To think that but for her he might this night have had Wilfrid a prisoner in the Citadel, subjecting him to insult and degradation! Instead of which Wilfrid had now found powerful champions in the Ambassador and his daughter!

Mingled with Baranoff's ire was a high degree of fear. Self-interest had prompted him to withhold from Paul the reason of his failure at Berlin, and in thus hoodwinking the Czar he had committed a kind of treason. Now should Wilfrid have given Pauline the correct version of that affair, it would perhaps go the round of St. Petersburg society, bringing upon him ridicule and mortification, to say nothing of dismissal from office — or worse, should the matter reach the ears of the Czar.

Had he not sent in his card to the Ambassador's daughter, he would now have retreated. A coward at heart, he glanced apprehensively at the door by which Pauline would enter. Supposing she should appear in company with Wilfrid, and he with taunting tongue should renew the challenge! Outside the Embassy Baranoff was a great man, a man to be feared, a man who, with a few strokes of his pen, could send an opponent to Siberia; but his power stopped at the door of the Embassy; inside it he was helpless, and no match for the mocking Baroness and the devil-may-care Englishman.

It was a relief to him when Pauline entered alone.

Pauline had no great liking for the coarse burly Benningsen, but was compelled by parity of political interests to keep on friendly terms with him.

Far different was the case with Baranoff: him she loathed, as every pure woman was bound to loathe the ex-lover of the dissolute Catharine. It always cost Pauline an effort to treat him with ordinary civility.

"Aha, Baroness!" cried Benningsen. "What is this you've been doing? Rescuing in broad daylight a prisoner of the Czar, and whisking him into the Embassy. By Heaven, you're a bold one!"

"And you're not," replied Pauline, whose habit it was to speak her mind freely to the General, who was accustomed to speak freely to her. "I marked you, running from the face of Paul, putting life before honour."

"Faith, my dear!" said he with a grin, and not a whit abashed by her reproach, "honour, when lost, may be recovered; one's life, never."

"You come with news, I understand?"

"Unpleasant news," returned Baranoff, affecting a mournful air, in reality secretly delighted, as knowing that the tidings would alarm her. "Unpleasant news I regret to —— "

"Hold! the Baroness must pay toll for our tidings. Toll," added Benningsen, significantly. "You know what I want."

"I do, but unfortunately the knout is not here, but at the Citadel. The Count will be but too pleased to accommodate you."

The jest was a true one. Nothing would have pleased Baranoff more than to see Benningsen tied up to the knouting-post. Baranoff gloried in the fact that it was he, and he alone, that had persuaded Paul to make war with England. Benningsen was sneeringly confident that the Count would be the first to sign a peace as soon as ever the British fleet appeared in Finland waters.

"Toll!" repeated Benningsen. "A bottle of — what shall it be? Who was it that said, 'Port for boys, claret for men, brandy for heroes'?"

"Louis, a bottle of port for the General," said Pauline sweetly.

"Ach! but you're down on me to-night," grinned Benningsen.

However, the bottle when brought, was labelled cognac.

"A corkscrew? No," said Benningsen, staying the hand of the servitor. And drawing his sabre, with one stroke he cut clean through the neck of the bottle, sending the glass fragments flying to the other end of the salon.

"That's the way we do it in camp."

The liqueur being poured out and watered to taste, Baranoff ventured to drink to the fair Pauline.

"You are guilty of treason," said she. "You know that Little Paul claims the first toast."

"O, damn Little Paul!" cried Benningsen savagely, and speaking with a recklessness that led Pauline to wonder whether he had not been taking brandy at other places besides the Embassy. "Little! Humph, that's true, but what there is of him is quite enough! Damn the powers that be! Here's to the powers that will be, eh?" he added, raising his glass with a significant wink at Pauline, who tried by a warning frown to check the license of his tongue.

"Your tidings?" she asked.

"The English consols are going up, and the Russian are going down," answered the General.

"'Tis very like, thanks to the Count," said Pauline, "but you didn't come here merely to tell me that."

"No. What think you is Little Paul's latest craze? You'll never guess, so I'll tell you. This afternoon he put the Czarovitch under arrest!"

"Our little Sasha!" faltered Pauline, with concern in her looks.

"Ay, our little Sasha!" repeated Benningsen. "And Constantine also. Both brothers are prisoners, each in his own apartment. To-morrow they are to be sent to a fortress."

"And *mon père* has just gone to the Michaelhof to have an interview with Alexander."

"Faith, then, he'll return without it!"

Alas for Pauline's hope of obtaining pardon for Wilfrid and herself through the mediation of Alexander! Her father's errand to the palace was like to end in failure.

Matters began to wear a serious look. Having done a deed certain to incense the Czar, she durst not leave the Embassy for fear of arrest. And what would happen to her father if he should defy the Czar's command to surrender Lord Courtenay?

"What have the two youths done, or rather what does Paul say they have done?"

"No one knows his reason," said Benningsen. "But this is what he said on giving orders for their arrest, 'Before many days be past men will be astonished to see heads fall that once were very dear to me.' It's my belief he'll keep his word," continued the General. "He has a craze for imitating his great-grandfather, Peter. And Peter put *his* son to death, you know."

Pauline's look of concern deepened.

"Let the Russians reproach Paris for its Reign of

Terror," she said. "It was but a brief season. But at
St. Petersburg life has now become one long reign of
terror. One rises from bed of a morning with no certainty of returning to it at night. Our lives are made
miserable by a series of vexatious edicts. Our commerce
is destroyed; the national credit sinking; the treasury
empty. Wars on all sides; Cossacks assembling at
Astrakhan for an overland march to India; troops
massing upon the Prussian frontier to compel King
Frederick to join the Armed Neutrality. And ere long
we shall have a foe in the Baltic, for I presume," she
added, turning to Baranoff, "the report is true that
Nelson's fleet has set sail."

The Count, with a sour look, opined that it was correct.

"Then with the breaking-up of the ice will come the
bombardment of Cronstadt."

"Thousand devils!" cried Benningsen, "and I've
just bought a villa at Oranienbaum. Right in the line of
fire. Thirty thousand roubles clean thrown away!
Count, this war is of your creation. Undo your work.
Persuade Paul to make peace. This morning's text
ought to dispose him to it."

"Text?" said Pauline inquiringly.

"Text!" repeated Benningsen. "His latest craze is
to turn the Bible into a book of holy divination. Each
morning he opens the Scriptures, and the first verse his
eye lights upon is taken as a direct message from Heaven.
To-day's text was, '*Thou shalt bruise his heel.*' Not
quite seeing its application to himself straight he goes
with the verse to Archbishop Plato. 'The passage, Sire,
is to be taken in connection with the preceding clause,
"*It shall bruise thy head.*" The head is a vital part;
not so the heel. The meaning, therefore, is that your
enemies, the English, will do you more hurt than you
will do them.'"

"Trust Plato for making the Scriptures speak his own
views," said Baranoff with a sneer.

"The text," continued Benningsen, ignoring the
Count's remark, "has made our little Czar thoughtful.
All day long he has been saying at intervals, '*Thou shalt
bruise his heel,*' so that — but here comes Monsieur

l'Ambassadeur," he said, breaking off in the middle of a sentence. "Now, perhaps," he whispered in Pauline's ear, "I shall be able to have a word with you on — start not — on a matter touching our personal safety."

The Marquis de Vaucluse had entered the reception-hall wearing a perturbed look, due to the discovery that the Czarovitch was a close prisoner in his own apartments, and forbidden to hold any communication with the outside world.

For a few moments the four discussed in common this latest phase of Imperial politics, and then Baranoff, desirous of conversing privately with De Vaucluse, drew him on one side, leaving Benningsen free to talk with Pauline.

"How long, think you," said Baranoff to the Marquis, "shall we be able to keep the Czar alive?"

De Vaucluse, not understanding the other's meaning, regarded him with a startled look.

"I am alluding, dear citoyen, to the privately-expressed opinion of Paul's chief physician, Wylie."

The Ambassador's brow cleared. He had thought the other was about to announce the existence of a conspiracy for the assassination of the Czar.

"Physicians' forecasts are not always right. What has the Scotsman been saying?"

"Paul has had of late several strokes of apoplexy, each one more serious than the last. In Wylie's opinion the next is likely to prove fatal. Now, neither you nor I can afford to see Paul go, for Alexander's accession will mean the end of the Franco-Russian Alliance."

This was a fact as well-known to the Marquis as it was to Baranoff.

"Any undue excitement," continued the Count, "any undue rage will carry him off."

"The remedy is obvious," smiled De Vaucluse. "His immediate *entourage* must take every precaution to prevent him from exciting himself."

"That is very good counsel of yours," said Baranoff in a dry tone, "but, unfortunately, your charming but too generously-impulsive daughter has this day done a deed likely to raise the Czar's wrath to a dangerous point."

"And, therefore," said the Marquis, "he must be kept in ignorance of Pauline's act."

"But when he demands his prisoner in the morning — what then?"

"Why, then, it will be advisable for you, the Governor of the Citadel, to take upon yourself to affirm that the prisoner died during the night."

De Vaucluse, being a diplomat, had no more scruple in suggesting a lie to Baranoff than Baranoff, in other circumstances, would have had in adopting it.

"It seems to me, Monsieur l'Ambassadeur," said the Count loftily, "that you are neglecting the safest way out of the difficulty."

"And that is —— ?"

"To surrender the person of Lord Courtenay to be taken to the Petropaulovski Fortress in accordance with the Czar's wish."

"I should be most happy to meet your suggestion, dear Count, were it not for one little circumstance."

"Ah!"

"I have pledged my word of honour to Lord Courtenay that I would not surrender him."

The Ambassador's manner plainly showed that he meant what he said, and that further arguments directed against his decision would be so much wasted breath.

"Of course Monsieur l'Ambassadeur would not talk thus unless he were sure that his action will have the approval of the First Consul?" Baranoff's smile was not that of a friend. It was a sudden revelation to the Marquis, showing how sinister the Count could be when crossed in his purpose. "You will mention this matter in your next despatch to him, eh?"

"This man means mischief," thought De Vaucluse. "He will take care that General Bonaparte hears of this matter. And then —— ?"

The Ambassador did not like to think of the "then." Never before in his diplomatic career had he been in such a strait as the present, and all due to that wayward Pauline! He glanced somewhat darkly at his daughter, little thinking that at that moment she had far greater grounds for uneasiness than he had.

"General, you are drunk!" had been her frank utterance to Benningsen as soon as she had found opportunity to converse with him privately.

"Heigh-ho! I wish I were," replied the warrior.

"You must be, or you would never, in the presence of Baranoff, have drunk to the powers that will be."

"Pooh! what matters?"

"Much. He'll be guessing our secret. He's mean enough to report your words to Paul. Do you want to be sent into exile a second time?"

"It's a case of exile for all patriots, I'm thinking. I leave the city to-night. By the waters of Finland I'll sit down and weep when I remember thee, O Petropolis, for I shall have to leave all behind me, including my villa at Oranienbaum. I'm glad it isn't paid for."

"Speak more clearly, General," said Pauline looking startled.

"Humph, haven't I spoken clearly enough? Cannot you guess why little Sasha has been put under arrest?"

She understood clearly now, and drew a deep breath, born of fear.

"Paul has discovered ——?"

"I fear so."

There followed a significant silence, during which both sat looking at each other.

"Who has betrayed us?" she said at last.

"No one. It was an accident. You know — you have reason for knowing — that there is in existence a weighty document containing the autograph signatures of those who have pledged themselves to ——"

She interrupted him with a gesture of impatience.

"Why tell me what I know already?"

"Our dear friend, Count Pahlen," continued Benningsen, naming the Foreign Minister, next to the Czar the most powerful man in the Empire, "was the person to whom we all agreed to entrust our common document, a document so precious that he durst not keep it at his bureau, locked in an escritoire, lest it should be detected by some prying secretary. He therefore carried it about on his person."

" An unwise thing to do."

" So it has proved, for he has lost our great charter."

" Lost it! " said Pauline in dismay.

" It was on his person at one o'clock; at two it was gone. Either he dropped it, or it was stolen from him. The question for us is — Into whose hands has it fallen? It may have been picked up by some mujik, who, too ignorant to read and therefore unable to appreciate its value, may use it to light his pipe. Some one, not over friendly to Paul's rule, may have found it, in which case he may hand over the document to one of the signatories occurring therein, or, at the least, he may keep a silent tongue on the matter. But I sadly fear that the document has been found, if not by an enemy, by one at any rate who, seeing in the discovery the prospect of a reward, has hurried with it to Paul. At all events three hours after Pahlen's discovery of his loss little Sasha was put under arrest."

" That proves nothing. Is he the only one? Why are not all the others arrested? "

" Who knows what may be happening at this very moment? I have come to warn you. You will do well this night to set off with me for Finland, lest in the morning Little Paul should be found demanding your head."

" Fly! And leave Alexander to his fate! No, I'll not do that. Having drawn him into a conspiracy, I'll stand by him to the last, and, if need be, share his doom."

There was a brief interval of silence.

" If Paul would but die! " murmured Benningsen.

" Oh, if he would only die to-night, our necks would be safe! But then, men never will die when they are wanted to. Look at my rich uncle now, that —— "

" Hasn't Count Pahlen determined upon any plan of action? "

" Within an hour from now he holds a meeting at his house to consider the state of affairs. But, mark my words, nothing will be done. All their resolutions will end in smoke. Fear will fall upon them when they hear that the incriminating document is in the hands of the enemy. Every man will look to his own safety. There will be a general flight. Nay, some, thinking to save their own necks, will voluntarily come forward to betray their fellows. And then, what will Monsieur l'Ambassadeur think, when he learns that his trusted daughter is a member of a conspiracy to dethrone the Czar, and more — has made use of the Embassy as a meeting-place for the conspirators?"

CHAPTER X

OF the two visitors to the Embasssy, Count Baranoff was the first to take his departure.

" To the Citadel," he said on stepping into his carriage, and the next moment he was being whirled along the Prospekt in the direction of the Neva.

The handsome stone bridges that now span that broad river were non-existent in the early years of the nineteenth century, the present Troitzkoi Bridge being then represented by a chain of pontoons, which, overlaid with smooth planks, afforded a level road from one bank to the other.

So long as the water continued frozen, and again after the current had resumed its free flow, one could rely upon finding the bridge in position, but the case was very different in early spring (and it was now the twenty-third of March), when the breaking up of the ice and the drifting of the bergs would cause the bridge to be taken to pieces and put together again two or three times in the course of a day.

The bridge was in position when Baranoff's carriage came up, and he was driven rapidly over the shaking timbers to its northern end, where rose the Fortress of Peter and Paul, a building as familiar to the Petersburgers as the Tower to Londoners, with this difference, however, that whereas the latter is a memorial of the dead past the former is, to the Petersburgers, an object of present fear.

The edifice, a work of Peter the Great, was built originally to defend his new capital, but has become useless for such purpose, being now in the very heart of the city. In reality a brick fabric, it is faced externally

with granite, and with its five bastions rising from the
water's edge has a somewhat majestic appearance.

Entering by the Ivanskaia Gate, whose sentinels presented arms as he passed, the minister made his way to
his official study, where, somewhat to his surprise, he
found awaiting him a visitor in the person of his brother
Loris, his junior by two years.

A medium-sized man was Loris Baranoff, with a cold,
hatchet-shaped face and grey eyes that in their keenness
seemed capable of reading one's thoughts. His appearing in any assembly — and all assemblies in St. Petersburg were open to him — was sufficient to send a thrill
of uneasiness to the heart of any man or woman who in
talking had been so rash as to touch, however remotely,
upon State affairs. For Loris Baranoff was Chief of the
Secret Police. " Let a man speak but three words,"
said Richelieu, " and I will undertake to find treason in
them." Loris Baranoff would find treason if a man did
not speak at all!

He was reclining at his ease in an arm-chair by a
bright fireside, his legs stretched out before him at full
length, his hands clasped at the back of his head. Usually impassive in his bearing, he had at this time a light
in his eyes that told of some inward excitement; at least,
so the elder brother judged.

" You have news, Loris? " said he, taking a seat that
stood opposite. " Good news? "

" News! " echoed the other with a sort of fierce exultation. " News! Ay! Dame Fortune is smiling on us
at last."

" Time she did. She has dealt us some reverses of late.
What happy discovery have you made? "

" Let us dispose first of little matters before we come
to the big," said Loris, taking out a pocket-book and
referring to some notes therein, written in a shorthand
of his own. " First, my spy Izak the yamchik arrived
this morning with your Englishman, Lord Courtenay."

" I am already aware of that."

" This afternoon Lord Courtenay happening to meet
the Czar —— "

" I know the whole story; his refusal to kneel, his

arrest, and his rescue by that marplot, Pauline de Vaucluse."

"Oh, so you know! Well, what's to be done? for so
long as he keeps where he is, the Czar himself cannot lay
finger upon him."

"Let him abide. His arrest is but a question of time.
You have the place under observation?"

"Trust me for that! He can't sneeze without my
knowing it. Let him but take six steps outside the Embassy and he is a prisoner. — To return to our useful
friend Izak. He timed his journey admirably, arriving
at the Silver Birch on the very night and at the very
hour appointed by you, without creating any suspicion
apparently in the mind of Lord Courtenay."

"That, too, I know. Lord Courtenay has graciously
obliged me by doing for nothing what I was willing to
pay him three hundred thousand roubles for. So much
the better for my pocket! Everything fell out precisely
as I planned it. Thanks to Nadia the affair seems to
have moved as smoothly as a piece of clockwork. Now,
Grand Duchess Marie, proud and virtuous beauty, we
will see how you look when you hear that your reputation is gone."

As Loris caught the vindictive sparkle of his brother's
eye he said —

"You have never yet told me why you hate her so."

Arcadius hesitated, then said with a sneer —

"The wisest man commits at the least one big error
in his lifetime. I committed mine when I made love to
her."

No man was better able to control his emotion than
Loris Baranoff. On the present occasion, however, he
sat perfectly aghast.

"*You — made — love — to — her!*"

"Why not?"

"An Imperial Duchess!"

"Pouf! A condescension on my part! Hasn't an
empress welcomed me to her arms?"

"Bah! don't compare the damnable old hag Catharine
with the young and beautiful duchess. So — you made
love to her! And her answer?"

As if he would give it! — give it, that is, word for word. No, not even to his brother. He would have braved the rigours of Siberia first. His cheek, seldom touched by the colour of shame, coloured now as he recalled the Duchess's flaming words of scorn.

" She took my offer of love as a deadly affront."

Loris did not wonder at it, though regard for his brother kept him from saying so.

" That day," continued Arcadius, " I made an enemy, and a dangerous one. It is her aim to expel me from office, and to see that I do not return to it. Either I must destroy her, or she will destroy me. Now you see my reason for throwing this Englishman in her way. Why do you smile? "

" At the amount of unnecessary trouble you have been taking."

" Unnecessary? "

" Entirely so. Now we stand too high in Paul's regard for her to prejudice him against us? "

" Granted."

" It is through the medium of Alexander that she hopes to do us hurt? "

" Through none other."

" Ah, well; if her power is dependent only upon Alexander, you will see, after hearing my news, that you need no longer fear either him or her."

" Let me hear the news," said Arcadius, doubtfully, as he settled himself in his chair to listen, " and I shall be the better able to judge."

Loris put up his pocket-book and began his story with commendable directness.

" This morning as I was at the Michaelhof on business the Czar chanced to see me, called me to his side, and began a conversation, while walking, in that restless fashion of his, from room to room, I keeping pace with him. Entering a certain cabinet we came suddenly upon Pahlen standing by a window engaged in the study of some document. Before the Count was aware of our presence, Paul, with that *brusquerie* so characteristic of him, had snatched the document from his hand, demanding to know what it was. The sudden fall in Pahlen's countenance told me that it was a paper whose contents he would fain hide; as a matter of fact, though I did not know it at the time, his life was hanging upon a thread, for if Paul had once begun the reading of that paper it would have been all over with the mighty Chancellor of the Empire. However, as you know, it takes a good deal to disconcert Pahlen. He was equal to the occasion.

"'One moment, Sire,' said he, venturing to take the paper from the Czar's hand, 'the document is odorous of tobacco, whose scent I know you dislike. Permit me.' And taking out a perfume-bottle he began to besprinkle the document, and while casually directing the Czar's attention to something happening outside the palace-window he —— "

"Substituted another and more innocent document."

"Just so. 'Twas neatly done, but it didn't escape me. Convinced that the document must be one of great moment I determined to become the possessor of it. Knowing that Pahlen was about to proceed to the Mint to receive a deputation of merchants, I made some excuse for accompanying him, first, however, secretly sending a note to the Police Bureau."

"What did the note contain?"

"These words — 'Send Godovin to me at once. I am at the Mint.'"

"And who in the devil's name is Godovin?"

"Once the most expert pick-pocket in St. Petersburg, now an honest — ahem! — police officer!"

"I see your design."

"Towards the close of the meeting, just as Pahlen was ending his speech to the merchants, my man entered. 'Godovin,' I whispered, 'within Pahlen's breast-pocket is a paper that I must have. Can you take it without his knowledge?' The fellow smiled and nodded."

"And he succeeded?"

"Godovin never fails. I've employed him before. Just as Pahlen was passing out Godovin simply brushed by him, and the next moment he was pushing beneath my cloak the document I wanted."

"A useful knave! And the contents of this document?"

"Are eminently adapted to make us rejoice."

"Why so?"

"Because the document — hold your breath — relates to a plot for the deposing of the Czar; it contains the autograph signatures of the conspirators; and, as many of them happen to be obstacles in the way to our future advancement, we have but to denounce them to Paul, and Siberia or death will be their doom."

Arcadius slapped his thigh savagely.

"I knew it," he cried. "I guessed there was something of the sort afoot when Benningsen took to damning the Czar in my presence, and drinking to the powers that will be! Of course that German pig is one of the conspirators! At last I have him in my power! You have brought the document with you?"

For answer Loris drew forth a roll of vellum, which he proceeded to unfold.

"Read it."

"The devil! You don't ask me to read all this, do you?" protested Loris, exhibiting the document to his brother's gaze. "It's infernally long and prosy, but it's unimpeachable in its treason, and that's all we want. It starts with a statement drawn up by a body styling itself 'The Committee for the Public Weal.'"

"What's the gist of it?"

"The Committee begin by affirming that they are neither revolutionaries nor republicans, and proceed to enumerate the advantages of a hereditary monarchy. At the same time, they admit that occasions may arise to justify the setting aside of the legitimate occupant of the throne; as, for example, when a ruler shows signs of madness. Such a crisis is now occurring in Russian affairs, and the Committee proceed to point out the strange words, ukases, and acts of Paul, all which, it is alleged, sufficiently prove that the Czar has lost his reason."

This was what all men in St. Petersburg had been thinking for a long time, but none had durst say so openly.

"In these melancholy circumstances it becomes the duty of all good patriots to unite for the peaceful deposing of Paul, who shall be maintained in honourable captivity till such time as he shall recover his reason; failing its recovery, he shall remain a captive till the day of his demise."

"Speciously put, but the conspirators know that they are signing Paul's death-warrant."

"How so?"

"What sovereign ever lived long after his dethronement?"

"The probity of Alexander is a sure guarantee for his father's safety."

"Circumstances will prove too strong for Alexander. The conspirators will take good care that Paul shall not live long to trouble the new reign. One morning he will be found dead in bed, and people will say, 'Alas! for the Little Father! He has died of apoplexy. His physicians always said he would.' Dr. Wylie is already preparing the public mind for the event. — Well, we'll defeat their plans. In the morning this document shall be put into Paul's hands. But you spoke of autograph signatures. Of course, the Czarovitch's name figures there?"

"What makes you think that?"

"Men would not plot to put Alexander upon the throne unless they had first gained his consent; they would require his signature as a guarantee for their future safety."

"You're right. Alexander's name heads the list."

"'Tis his death-warrant; and let him die! We want no reforming Czars. And, as a man's foes are those of his own household, I warrant that the second signature is that of the Grand Duke Constantine."

"Correct. He follows his brother. Here is his name in Greek characters."

"Grandmother Catharine hoped that he would one day be King of Greece," said Arcadius. "That day will never come now. Whose is the next signature?"

"Count Pahlen's."

A savage joy mantled the face of Arcadius.

"Good! A powerful rival swept from my path. I may yet live to be Dictator of Russia. And the next?"

"Is the autograph of that venerable father of the church, Archbishop Plato. Did his conscience trouble him? 'Tis a somewhat shaky signature."

"I warrant the conspirators moved heaven and earth to obtain it. Who henceforth would stand aloof from an enterprise hallowed by the Church? He is an Anglophile; let him perish!"

"Next comes Prince Ouvaroff. After him the Czar's ministers."

"*All* of them?" said Arcadius, with an emphasis on the first word.

"You are the sole exception."

Arcadius smiled bitterly.

"Their act in keeping from me all knowledge of the plot is a clear proof that I am to have no place in the new Ministry. They hate me as the author of the Franco-Russian Alliance. Let them talk as they will of Paul's madness; their real aim in dethroning him is to conciliate England."

"Here's a name that you love — General Benningsen!"

"Bragging ass! Drunken wassailer! A Hanoverian, almost an Englishman! Paul did ill not to follow my counsel. He *would* recall him from exile. Here's his gratitude!"

"Next comes a name almost illegible, but I have a strong suspicion it's meant for James Wylie."

"Paul's own physician in the plot?"

"It seems so," said Loris, scanning the name. "It's a vile scrawl."

"His Scottish cunning. If the plot miscarry, he'll be in a position to deny his signature."

"Likely enough," assented Loris. "Would it surprise you to learn that there are women in this affair?"

"Not at all. And the leading spirit among them is Pauline de Vaucluse."

"Right. There's no hesitation about *her* signature. Here it is, large, firm, bold, and differing from the others as being written in red ink."

" Ink? " said Arcadius, examining the signature. " It's my belief it's written with her own blood. I doubt not that it was she who started the plot. She hates Paul; she hates me; she hates the war with England. Conspirators can meet safely beneath her roof, since spies are unable to get a footing there. Besides, who would ever suspect a Foreign Embassy of hatching treason against the Czar. She would act as an excellent decoy, too, seeing that half the young men in St. Petersburg are in love with her. Hence the many balls given of late at the Embassy."

" By the by, why wait till morning before showing this document to Paul? Why not take it to-night? "

" Need we be so precipitate? "

" Yes, in view of Pahlen's desperate strait. When he discovers — and he must have discovered it ere this — that his treasonable document is missing, what will he do? Aware that the plot has become known to others, he and his fellow-conspirators will see the necessity of striking the blow before Paul has time to learn of their treason. It behoves them to act, and to act at once. Delay will be fatal to them."

This conclusion, so startling, yet so palpably obvious, filled Arcadius with sudden dismay.

" A thousand devils! " he muttered. " What may not be happening now at the Michaelovski Palace? We must — ah! what the devil's that? "

Hitherto quiet had prevailed outside the Citadel, but now in a moment the air became filled with a series of sounds, eerie enough and loud enough to startle the boldest. As if subjected to a well-directed fusilade of heavy artillery the fortress trembled to its very foundations, amid a confused shouting of voices, a grinding of timber, and a crashing of ice, intermingled with the dull plunge of heavy bodies into deep water.

" By heaven! the bridge is down! " cried Loris.

The bridge! Their only way to the Michaelovski Palace! The two brothers rushed to the nearest window. Finding it difficult to open, Loris shattered the glass with his sword-hilt.

Dark and starless as was the night, they could nevertheless see that not a single pontoon remained in the place where the bridge had lately been. Nature had played havoc with man's work. Between the Citadel and the opposite bank intervened a broad expanse of black water, upon whose rapid current ghostly bergs tumbled and crashed, danced and whirled, as if in glee at the destruction wrought. Here and there, in mid-stream and clinging to fragments of timber, human forms could be heard uttering cries for help.

The brothers looked at each other with pale faces, and eyes full of baffled rage.

The catastrophe had put an end to the proposed visit to the Michaelhof. No boat could live on such a tide. For hours, and it might be days, the pair would be cut off from the Imperial quarter as effectually as if they were in far-off Siberia.

" No crossing to-night," said Loris. " Now, Pahlen, do as you list. There is none to stay your hand.''

CHAPTER XI

"THOU SHALT BRUISE HIS HEEL"

UPON the departure of General Benningsen from the Embassy, Pauline de Vaucluse was left, a victim to troubling thoughts.

Dear to her father's heart was the Franco-Russian Alliance, and yet she, his daughter and *confidante,* had been secretly working to bring it to nought; and all to no purpose, so it seemed.

To be a successful traitress is bad enough, but to be an unsuccessful one ——!

In too melancholy a mood to seek Wilfrid's society again, she left her father to entertain him; and, on the plea of a headache, retired to her own room, wondering what the morrow would bring forth. Apart from the uneasiness arising from the loss of the incriminatory document, she was troubled with a feeling of self-reproach, due to an indefinable something in Wilfrid's manner. It had not taken her long to discover that he was one to whom deception of any kind was distasteful, his character in this respect affording a striking contrast with her own. If any one had reproached her with duplicity, she would have asked with a smile how it was possible to succeed in this world without lying; but now, as she recalled the grave air with which Wilfrid had received the hints that she was secretly working in opposition to her father, she grew first uneasy and then angry; though why she should let Wilfrid's opinion trouble her was a question that found no answer in her mind. There the fact was: her attitude towards her father, now, for the first time, appeared in an unfilial and hateful light, and it was mainly Wilfrid that had made it look so.

Another circumstance, though in itself absurdly tri-fling, added to her annoyance. Hitherto, she had been accustomed to regard the Czarovitch as her ideal of a hero, handsome and brave, courteous and charming; and lo, here was an Englishman handsomer and braver — had he not, even at the risk of his life, refused to bow to a tyrant? — more courteous and more charming, and, above all, truth-speaking, the last epithet being *not* always applicable to Alexander, as history can testify. She grew vexed with Wilfrid, as if it were a fault in him to be better than Alexander!

This odd frame of mind prevented her from obtaining her usual amount of sleep; and when she arose in the morning she started at sight of the wan face and heavy eyes reflected in the mirror.

Summoning her maid, Pauline proceeded to make her toilet, selecting her prettiest and daintiest attire; and never did Vera find her mistress more hard to please than on this particular morning. She was positively more critical of herself than on the day of her receiving the Czarovitch!

On her way down stairs she chanced to meet one of her father's oldest secretaries, who had been out for an early drive, and she stopped for a moment's chat with him. They might have been in England; they talked of the weather!

"A most remarkable thaw, this," observed the secretary. "The oldest inhabitant of St. Petersburg cannot remember one so rapid."

"When did the change begin?" asked Pauline.

"The thermometer began to go up a little before midnight, and has been going steadily up ever since. The Troitzkoi Bridge has been carried off by the moving ice."

"Then Count Baranoff, if he's in his Citadel, will not be able to do any mischief this side of the Neva for some days to come."

"His isolation will not last long," smiled the secretary. "In the opinion of experts, the river, before the lapse of many hours, will be passable for boats."

"Then we shall be having the ceremony of the Golden

Goblet," said Pauline to herself, as she continued her way down. "A quaint custom, which I would like Lord Courtenay to see; but here we are, debarred from going out."

Pauline moved onward and was passing through the entrance hall when she stopped short in surprise upon seeing Benningsen suddenly enter. He wore a somewhat haggard look, having, in fact, the jaded appearance of a man who has spent the night out of bed; and Pauline was quick to notice that, though his step had been steady enough on the previous evening, he now walked with a slight limp.

"What! General," she cried. "Not gone to Finland after all?"

"Pahlen persuaded me to stay," said Benningsen, with a smile that set Pauline's heart bounding; for it was a smile that augured good things. "He and I, with a great many of the ministers, went to the Michaelhof last night to have that long-meditated interview with Paul."

"To get him to abdicate?" she said breathlessly.

"Just so."

"How did he take the proposal?"

"'Tis a world of surprises," said the General. "We might have spared ourselves the visit. Paul had already abdicated."

"You are jesting," she said, angrily.

"Fact!" smiled the General. "Abdicated in favour of Alexander."

"Why this graceful act on his part?"

"Well, to be plainer —— "

Here Benningsen bent his head and whispered a short sentence. Pauline received it with a keen, cold, steady look that seemed somewhat to disconcert him.

"A fortunate ending for us," she remarked drily, "seeing the strait we were in. It matters little now who has found our lost document."

"The finder will be well advised to burn it," said Benningsen. "Alexander won't thank him for making it public."

"When is the event to be proclaimed?"

"Within an hour from now. Alexander himself is to make the announcement from the balcony of the Winter Palace. The people are already gathering in the square."

"How? They know?" she asked, in some surprise.

"They know nothing except that Alexander with his own lips is going to make public some great event. Hence, there is great excitement in the streets. The Foreign Ambassadors are already assembling at the Winter Palace. Where is Monsieur le Marquis? I must tell him the news. He must not be absent while others are tendering their congratulations to the new ruler."

"My faith! no," returned Pauline. "*Mon père* will be found in his study at this moment, inspecting his morning's correspondence. Louis shall take you to him," she added; and addressing a lackey she bade him conduct Benningsen to the Ambassador's study. "But stay, General," she continued, with a laugh that was not all a laugh, "what dreadful boots yours are, dropping mud and wet! Respect our carpets. You must leave those great Hessians behind you."

Benningsen stared oddly at her, hesitated for a moment, and then, perceiving that she was in earnest, he laughed, slipped out of his boots, and followed in the wake of the lackey.

"He did not limp like that last night, though wearing the same boots," thought Pauline, as she watched the General ascending the staircase. "It is the right foot that seems to be hurt."

As soon as Benningsen was out of sight, Pauline, much to the surprise of her maid, lifted one of the long boots and, for better inspection, held it up to the light.

Her next act was more surprising still. Drawing forth her handkerchief, she carefully wiped from the heel its caking of mud and snow. And there, in the leather just above the heel, was a double row of perforations, obviously caused by something sharp that had penetrated the leather from without.

"Vera," said Pauline, with a strange look, "tell me what you think was the cause of these marks?"

The maid regarded them attentively for a moment, and then said, "They seem to me very like teeth-bites, my lady. See!" So saying, Vera slipped off her pretty little shoe, and by giving the heel a hearty bite, produced in the red leather a double row of marks, very similar in appearance to those in Benningsen's Hessians. "He had strong teeth who bit this boot," she added.

"My God!" murmured Pauline. "What has happened?" And the boot dropped from her trembling hand.

"My lady, you are ill."

She had reason for her remark in Pauline's sudden pallor. But the Baroness made no answer. She stood, silent and motionless, deep in thought; and when, after an interval of five minutes, Benningsen reappeared, she regarded him with a look so strange and repelling that he intuitively felt that his secret had become known to her.

"Now can one keep a thing from a woman?" he thought, as he drew on his Hessians.

"General, what Bible-verse did Paul hit upon yesterday?" she asked in a careless manner; and the General, off his guard for the moment, replied —

"'Thou shalt bruise his heel.'"

"There has been a quick fulfilment of that text."

"True," said Benningsen with a side-glance at the maid, who stood by, wondering what it all meant, "and the less said about it before others, the better."

There was in his manner something approaching to the nature of a threat, that caused Pauline's eyes to blaze angrily.

"You have brought dishonour upon a noble enterprise," she said. "Henceforth, we are no longer friends. Pay no more visits to the Embassy, or I'll have you whipped forth."

"L'Ambassade, c'est moi!" said Benningsen, with something between a laugh and a sneer; and striking a Louis Quatorze attitude as he spoke. "But if the Marquis chooses to receive me —— "

"I'll have you whipped," she repeated, making the last word sound like the lashing of a thong, "like the savage that you are. As for *mon père* — have you told him the whole story? No! you dare not. You have lied to him, as you have lied to me. *Mon père* is a gentleman, and when he hears the truth, he, too, will forbid your presence here. Go, coward!" she added, with a stamp of her foot, and pointing to the door.

Benningsen's great face reddened as he saw that two clerks of the Embassy, passing through the hall to their daily duties, had stopped to listen to this piquant dialogue between a brother-in-law of the Czar and their chief's daughter.

"Coward?" said Benningsen, repeating the word. "But bah! one is a fool to bandy words with a woman. If only you were a man ——!" he added, turning away.

"Stay a moment, General," she said, sweetly, "I'll bring you a man."

He knew that she meant Wilfrid, whose sword he durst not meet; and without more ado he stalked off.

Almost at the same moment the Marquis de Vaucluse was seen descending the stairs in a state of perturbation very unusual with him.

"Has Benningsen told you?" he began. "Do you know that ——"

"He has told me, *mon père*," replied Pauline. "I know — more than you think," she added to herself.

The Ambassador was too much excited to notice how dejected his daughter was looking.

"Horses to the door!" he cried; and while the order was being executed he walked to and fro, muttering, "This event, I fear, will bring no good to the First Consul."

And it was with a very rueful look that he drove to the Winter Palace. If the Ambassador were gloomy, so, too, was his daughter. Wrapped in moody thought, she remained standing where her father had left her, till Wilfrid's voice put an end to her reverie. And very curious it was to notice how quickly Pauline's face brightened as soon as she became aware of his presence.

"Dare you venture abroad with me this morning?" was her first question; in the circumstances, a surprising one to Wilfrid.

"Is not this a somewhat rash act on your part?" he objected. "In rescuing a prisoner of the Czar, you made yourself amenable to arrest."

"The Czar," replied Pauline, without naming *what* Czar, "is about to issue an amnesty to all political prisoners."

"And we come under that term?"

"I believe so. At any rate, we may go forth without fear of arrest. I have received this assurance from — from an authoritative source."

"Good. The Czar is not such a bad fellow, after all."

"No, indeed he is not," said Pauline, with a laugh, perplexing in its merriment; "though you spoke somewhat hardly of him yesterday."

In his own opinion, Wilfrid had not spoken half so hardly as had Pauline.

"What has caused this sudden change in him?"

"Come with me, and you shall learn," said Pauline, with a charming air of mystery. "I could tell you now, but I prefer to be dramatic with you. The Czar himself shall proclaim what the Czar will do."

And Pauline, having ordered her carriage, retired to put on her hat and mantle, while Wilfrid, attracted by an unusual hubbub outside the Embassy, went to the door.

The Nevski Prospekt was alive with a throng of men and women, all moving in one direction, all animated by the same impulse.

The crowd was composed mainly of the lower orders, but now and again there appeared the stately equipage of some lordly boyar.

At times there would trot past little bands of Cossacks, who, carrying immensely long lances and mounted on shaggy ponies, sought to quicken the pace of the people by crying, "To the Winter Palace! To the Winter Palace!"

"Now, I wonder what all this excitement is about?" said Wilfrid, re-entering the Embassy.

"You do? Well, then, let us go to the Winter Palace, and discover the reason," answered Pauline, who had returned, looking more charming than ever in her handsome furs.

As for Wilfrid, having no choice in the matter of attire, he was wearing the same Austrian uniform as on
the previous day. Pauline, studiously critical, noticed
that he was without the ornament of a sword, and thinking it a pity that he should go forth without his full
equipment, procured a handsome weapon from her
father's collection, and even went so far as to help him
in girding it on.

Having assisted Pauline into the carriage, Wilfrid was
about to take his place by her side, when she cried, with
a little gesture of impatience —

"There! I have left my vinaigrette in the hall."

While Wilfrid went back to fetch it a troop of guards
came riding by. At their head was Prince Ouvaroff,
looking, so Pauline thought, pale, ill, and melancholy.

"Now what is troubling *him?*" she murmured.

No sooner did Ouvaroff catch sight of Pauline than
his melancholy seemed to vanish. There came upon his
face a smile, never seen there except when she was in
view.

He halted his troop, drew near to Pauline, and, saluting her with his sword as though she were the Czarina
herself, said: —

"Like the rest of us, you are bound for the Winter
Palace, I presume?" And on learning that such was
the case he continued, "You must permit me to be your
escort. Place your carriage amid my gallant band and
we'll clear the way for you through the crowd."

"I thank you, Prince, but my escort is already chosen,"
replied Pauline, pointing to Wilfrid, who at that moment
was descending the steps of the Embassy.

Wilfrid cast a smile at his old friend, the very man he
wanted to see. There was much that Ouvaroff could
tell him about the mysterious Grand Duchess.

"You and Lord Courtenay are friends, I understand,"
said Pauline.

"We used to be."

The Prince's air was so cutting and contemptuous that
Wilfrid, whose high spirit could ill brook an affront,
compressed his lips ominously. The cause of Ouvaroff's
disdain was plain enough to him. That Prince must

have seen him stealing from the Duchess's bedchamber. Wilfrid's face darkened, and his hand sought the hilt of his sword, but recognising the unwisdom of entering into explanations he turned his back upon the Prince and waited till Pauline should have finished her talk with him. In troubled surprise she glanced from one to the other, wondering what Wilfrid had done to alienate his old friend.

"Do you know, Prince, that when you frown so you remind me — yes, of Paul."

This remark, spoken with no ulterior motive, produced a very strange effect upon Prince Ouvaroff. As if detecting a hidden meaning in her words he started sharply, as a man may start who is unexpectedly confronted with his guilt, glared at her for a moment with a wild eye that made him look more like Paul than ever, and then, putting spurs to his steed, he suddenly set off at a gallop, leaving his astonished troop to follow or not as they chose. Pauline watched him with a troubled face. She knew something now unknown to her a moment ago.

CHAPTER XII

A GRIM BEGINNING OF A REIGN

"WHAT are we to do now?" asked Pauline of Wilfrid, when, as their carriage drew near to the Imperial Square, they found approach to the Winter Palace impossible by reason of the dense crowd. "We can't expect these good people to open a way for us to the front, and yet, as we are, we shall see nothing!"

Her situation at that moment contrasted singularly with that of her father. While *he* was within the stately palace and occupying a high place among the Imperial *entourage,* she was outside in the open square upon the skirts of a tumultuous swaying crowd.

Her glance, wandering around, rested upon the façade of the Hôtel de l'Etat Major, the seat of various governmental departments. Situated upon the south side of the Imperial Square, its front, nearly two furlongs in length, sweeps round in a magnificent arc, and faces the south side of the Winter Palace. The windows and balconies of this vast edifice were occupied by groups of well-dressed men and women, whose elevated position gave them a good view of all that was going on.

"That's where we'll go," said Pauline, glancing up at one of these windows.

She drove up to the chief entrance of the hotel, and, being well known to those in authority there, soon obtained for herself and Wilfrid a place among a little group upon one of the upper balconies.

As Wilfrid gazed downwards it seemed to him that all the city's five hundred thousand inhabitants must be gathered together in the space fronting the Winter Palace. They were prevented from getting too near the Imperial edifice by serried ranks of cavalry and infantry, whose numbers were being increased minute by minute.

Wilfrid, with his semi-military tastes, took pleasure in watching the advent of the various regiments that from different points kept continually debouching into the square. Ever and anon from some new quarter the rolling of drums and the wild strains of martial music heralded the approach of some fresh band, till it seemed that not only must all the civilian population of St. Petersburg be there, but the whole of the Czar's vast army as well.

And the variety and oddity of the uniforms!

Circassians were there, whose burnished helmets with steel veil falling upon the shoulder, shirts of linked mail, and long lances, seemed to recall the days of mediæval chivalry; Polish heydukes, whose upper lips were adorned by triple moustaches, the first twisted upwards, the second quite straight, and the third twisted downwards; Zaporogian Cossacks, whose trousers were smeared with tar to show the wearer's contempt for the costly scarlet cloth of which they were composed.

"A soldier's pride should be in his arms, not in his dress," remarked Pauline in reference to these last-named warriors, adding that this strange practice was permitted by the government.

The marchings, wheelings, and evolutions of these troops were all directed towards the formation of three main bodies, the first extending along the entire front of the Palace; at each end a shorter division was thrown forward at right angles to the main body, so that the arrangement formed three sides of a rectangle.

The fourth side of the rectangle was formed by the front ranks of the people, who were kept from pressing into the interior space by mounted Cossacks, who, whenever the crowd was pushed forward by the pressure from behind, did not hesitate to ply their whips with merciless vigour.

Upon the open ground thus kept clear by the lash of the Cossacks were numerous mounted officers, who rode leisurely to and fro, now conversing with one another, now issuing some order.

Conspicuous among these was General Benningsen on his famous black steed Pluto; and there, too, was Prince Ouvaroff in comand of the Preobrejanski Guards.

These two, being the only officers known to Wilfrid, came in for a good deal of his attention, and watching them for some time by the aid of a lorgnette, he observed that though Benningsen seemed to have a word for nearly every one among his equals and subalterns, he paid no attention whatever to Ouvaroff, who, on his part, seemed to ignore the General. It was evident that there was some estrangement between the two men, who, till the previous day, had been on good terms; and Wilfrid could not help wondering to what it was due.

Of the three divisions, that on the right hand, which stood, as previously said, at right angles with the main body, consisted of infantry, whose snub noses and up-turned moustaches proclaimed them to be the Paulovski Regiment.

"I don't see my friend Voronetz among them," muttered Wilfrid. "I trust he has not been cashiered."

Surveying these troops through his lorgnette, he observed that the face of each, without exception, was marked by a sullen expression, a fact to which Benningsen was keenly alive, for he eyed them from time to time as if apprehending some disturbance on their part.

"The Paulovski Guards seem dissatisfied this morning?" remarked Wilfrid to Pauline.

"Naturally, seeing that they are about to be disbanded."

"Paul's favourite regiment to be disbanded! Why?"

"Because they are too faithful to his interests."

Wilfrid elevated his eyebrows.

"Fidelity is an extraordinary reason for disbanding a regiment."

"Nevertheless it is the true reason," replied Pauline.

Though somewhat annoyed at this mystification on her part Wilfrid curbed his curiosity.

From the crowd his gaze wandered to the rear of the Winter Palace where flowed the Neva, a broad winding stream of vivid blue. On its surface floated miniature icebergs, varying in tint from white to rose colour. Carried along by the current, and assuming every conceivable shape, they crashed, and dived, and mounted one upon another as if they were trying each to be first in the race to the sea.

The sounds produced by the collision were like the sharp rattle of artillery, and could be heard above the hubbub of the crowd.

On the other side of the river, and grimly grey in the morning sun-light, rose the Petropaulovski Fortress, an object of interest to Wilfrid as being the place in which he would at that moment have been a prisoner but for Pauline's bold rescue.

On the waters of the river before the principal gate of the Citadel floated a sort of state barge, rich with gilding, and gay with coloured flags. This Bucentaur was being rapidly filled with officials from the Citadel, conspicuous among them being the Governor, Count Baranoff.

As soon as he had taken his place in the barge a puff of white smoke issued from the ramparts, accompanied by salvos of artillery, that were repeated at regular intervals.

"That gun is a signal that the river is becoming passable for boats," said Pauline. "We are about to witness an interesting ceremony."

"Of what nature?"

"On reaching this side of the river the Governor will proceed to the Winter Palace, taking with him a goblet containing water from the Neva. No matter upon what business the Czar may be engaged, custom enjoins that he shall come forth and drink from the goblet in sight of all the people. He then returns the cup filled with gold pieces. The ceremony is a kind of homage paid to the Neva, an acknowledgment of the advantages to be derived from the free course of commerce."

"Petersburgers think a good deal of the Neva, then?"

"So much so that I have seen a youth welcomed home from his travels, not with champagne or the like, but with a goblet of Neva water."

Wilfrid watched the progress of the Bucentaur. While its rowers plied their oars, men stationed at the prow and provided with poles kept the passage clear from the floating ice. In the wake of the state barge followed a long train of boats, filled with merchants and citizens clad in gala attire.

Count Baranoff, in his seat of honour, was in a jubilant mood that morning, as became a man who saw the elements conspiring to favour his interests. A break-up of the ice in a single night was a phenomenon almost without parallel in the history of the Neva.

He carried with him a secret, the disclosure of which would remove all enemies from his path, and open a way for him to the highest offices in the State. Fondly refusing to believe that any ill *could* have happened to Paul — though his brother who sat in the boat with him, was troubled with doubts — he purposed after the Czar should have performed the customary ceremony in the matter of the goblet, to ask for a private interview, in the course of which he would put the treasonable document into Paul's hands with the words, " Read that, Sire."

Eager for the coming of this moment, Baranoff urged the rowers to greater speed, and as soon as the barge grated against the steps of the granite quay he sprang hastily ashore, and taking his place among the detachment of military sent to escort him, he moved onward to the Imperial Square.

His coming drew a satirical smile from Pauline.

" There are surprises for you, Sir Count," she murmured.

He had now arrived at the principal entrance of the Winter Palace, an entrance lofty and arched, and surmounted by a spacious balcony, upon which Paul, whenever the humour took him, was accustomed to show himself to his people. Against this archway there had been set a staircase, covered with scarlet cloth, leading to the balcony above it.

Assuming an air of dignity suitable to the occasion, Baranoff ascended the staircase, bearing in both hands the historic golden goblet filled with water taken from the Neva.

As he slowly mounted aloft he became the mark of all eyes in and around the square. His appearance was greeted with a loud *"Hourra!"* from the crowd.   Their long waiting was over.   Usage prescribed that the Czar must come forth without delay to drink from that notable cup.

In truth, before Baranoff had gained the top stair the troops were presenting arms, and a military band, stationed beneath the balcony, broke forth into the soul-stirring music of Russia's national anthem.

A tall window giving access to the balcony was flung wide, and there stepped forth a lofty and majestic figure, arrayed in a rich uniform.   Behind him came a train of magnates, civil, military, and ecclesiastical; among this last and bearing in his hands a tall golden cross was the Archbishop Plato, conspicuous by his long snowy hair and beard, his stately person and majestic flowing robes.

The train paused while the figure in the rich uniform advanced to the edge of the balcony, and bowed to the populace, who greeted the action with thunders of applause.

But though the figure was far distant Wilfrid, without having recourse to the lorgnette, could tell that it was not Little Paul.   Who was it that thus assumed to himself all the honours of Czardom?

Wilfrid's feeling was one of surprise merely; that of Baranoff's was absolute, overwhelming dismay.

First on the list of conspirators to be denounced by him came the hateful name of the imprisoned Alexander, and lo! it was Alexander himself that faced him and put forth his hand for the goblet!

"None but the Czar can drink from this cup," said Baranoff huskily, drawing back a pace or two.

"True, and the Czar is before you," returned the other.

"Yesterday it was Paul."

"And to-day it is Alexander.   To-morrow it may be — who can tell?   Is Fortune ever constant?"

Mechanically Baranoff surrendered the goblet to Alexander, who, turning to the now silent people, cried with a loud voice —

"To the health of the Russian nation!"

He drank, and returned the goblet to Baranoff, first calling upon one in attendance to fill it with gold coins in conformity with ancient usage.

The populace looked on in silent wonderment. What mood had come over Paul that he should depute this duty to the Czarovitch? Was any explanation to be given? Yes, there was. Hush! little Sasha is speaking.

"People of St. Petersburg, my father Paul ——" His voice shook with emotion. He stopped, and turned to a minister in his rear, as if desiring him to act as speaker. Count Pahlen, for he it was, proceeded to make the momentous announcement.

"People of St. Petersburg, it is my melancholy duty to state that last night our little father Paul was seized with apoplexy, and died at a quarter to twelve." He made a pause, and then added, "The Czar is dead" — and, pointing to Alexander — "Long live the Czar!"

For a moment the people were dumb with surprise. The news seemed too good to be true. Then a mighty shout rent the air.

"Long live little Sasha!"

The cavalry spontaneously waved their sabres in an ecstasy of loyalty; among the infantry helmets danced aloft upon the points of bayonets; a remark, however, not applicable to the Paulovski Guards, who, in spite of the addresses of their officers, could not be made to show the least token of enthusiasm.

The civilian crowd, however, were wild with delight; it seemed as if their cheering would never cease. There could be no doubt as to the popularity of Alexander with the great mass of the people, and the ministers upon the balcony, who, for reasons best known to themselves, had feared that the news of Paul's death might provoke a very different feeling, began to be relieved, a relief somewhat discounted when they noticed the demeanour of the Paulovski Guards, many of whom, having grounded their rifles, were leaning upon them with a sullen and moody air.

Their action was, of course, unseen by the greater part of the people, who, after the fashion of crowds, began to make comments upon what they had just heard.

" The great Catharine was right. She said that Paul would not long outlive her."

" True. He hasn't reigned five years."

" A terrible blow this — to the Empress Mary."

" A blow! Say rather a piece of good luck! But yesterday, so 'tis said, Paul threatened to put her into a convent for life."

" Lucky, too, for Alexander. To think that he was a prisoner yesterday, threatened with death, and to-day the Czar!"

There was no disputing the fact that Paul's departure from this world had been very opportunely timed for Alexander by that particular angel who has the arrangement of such matters; very opportunely indeed — so opportunely that, perhaps, it may not have been an angel at all, but ——

There was less cheering now. Men began to stare suspiciously at one another. But what each thought he kept to himself, mindful of the Muscovite saying, " If three persons be seen conversing, one of them is a spy." How many spies must there be, then, in a crowd so vast! In Russia the wise man is the silent man.

Wilfrid's remote situation had prevented him from hearing the announcement made by Count Pahlen, but he quickly became apprised of it by the thunderous shouts of " Hourra, Alexander! Hourra, the new Czar!"

" Paul dead!" he exclaimed, turning to the Baroness. " So this is the secret you have been keeping from me? When did he die?"

" Late last night, suddenly of apoplexy, so Benningsen says. We shall see a full account of it in to-day's *Journal de Petersbourg.*"

Wilfrid, aided by the lorgnette, took a long and critical survey of the new Emperor.

He beheld a man as different in appearance from his father Paul as the day is from the night. Alexander exhibited in his person all the beauty of the Romanoff family. His figure, over six feet in height, was well proportioned and graceful in movement; his hair, light brown in colour, with a tendency to curl. His face was singularly handsome; he had eyes of a dark blue, a profile purely Grecian, and a complexion as clear and almost as colourless as marble. In short, it was no wonder that all the ladies in St. Petersburg were in love with him, for, externally, he was just the sort of man to captivate a woman's imagination. To add to his attractiveness the graces of his mind were, according to Pauline, far superior to those of his person. His conversation was lively and charming. In scholarship he far surpassed his equals in age; indeed, his grandmother Catharine had kept him to his studies so closely as somewhat to impair his eyesight.

Wilfrid listened with some indifference as Pauline ran over the list of the Czar's accomplishments. Truth to tell, Wilfrid felt a latent spirit of antagonism to the new ruler, finding — somewhat absurdly it must be confessed — a ground of complaint in the very fact that he should owe his recovered freedom to the action of this Czar, for the power to set free implies likewise the power to imprison. That the liberty of an Englishman and a Courtenay should depend upon the irresponsible will of an autocrat of twenty-three was galling to his high spirit. That young man, without consulting either judge or jury, could banish Wilfrid from his dominions, and, if he chose, could order Pauline to receive the knout. There was nothing in Russia to stop him. The wealth, the liberty, the lives of sixty millions were at his absolute disposal.

When Pauline went on to speak of Alexander's swordsmanship, and of how, in that art, he excelled every officer in his army, Wilfrid became more than ever critical and depreciatory. Empire might belong to the Romanoffs, but when it came to a question of swordsmanship, let them not presume too much.

"Can beat every officer in his army, can he?" muttered Wilfrid. "Humph! I shall never be happy till I have crossed swords with his Czarship."

Alexander did not retire immediately upon his proclamation as Emperor, but remained upon the balcony for the space of two or three minutes, possibly with the object of giving the people time to take a good look at their new ruler.

And then came a grim and significant incident, never forgotten by those who witnessed it.

Just as the Archimandrite Plato was preparing to pronounce a benediction upon the people, and with this view had raised his hand, an action which produced a solemn hush over the vast assembly, there came a sound like the shivering of glass. The panes of a window in the lower part of the palace were falling outward by reason of blows dealt from within, and through the opening thus caused there leaped forth a wild figure.

Alighting upon all fours in the rear of a squadron of horse, he sprang to his feet immediately, and though hands, and even sabres, were put forth to stay his progress, he contrived, by adroitly turning and twisting beneath the horses' bellies, to elude capture and to gain the open space fronting the palace, thus becoming visible to the Czar and his staff upon the balcony. The incident was not lost upon Wilfrid, who turned his lorgnette upon this sudden apparition.

Some twenty hours previously Wilfrid had seen the man's face, but now, disfigured all over with medical plasters, it was barely recognisable.

" My God! it's Lieutenant Voronetz! " said a lady sitting next to Pauline.

" And who's Lieutenant Voronetz? " asked her companion.

" The officer whose duty it is to guard Paul's bedroom at night."

Lieutenant Voronetz it was, and a more ghastly figure was never seen.

Moved by some overpowering impulse he had evidently escaped from the bed in which he had been put by the kindly, or perfunctory, care of the physician. He wore no clothing except swathings and bandages, which, criss-crossed all over trunk and limbs, suggested the idea that he had been hacked and slashed by sharp weapons from head to foot. The exertion of moving had caused his wounds to open afresh; his linen swathings had lost all their whiteness — from neck to ankle he was one red hue!

There was death in his face, death within a very short time; why then, instead of remaining peacefully on his bed, had he chosen to come forth in this startling fashion?

Voronetz, casting a wild glance around, had no sooner caught sight of the group upon the balcony than he raised his right arm and fiercely shook it at Alexander. With a thrill of horror Wilfrid perceived that the arm thus raised was without a hand — it had been severed at the wrist!

Those who at that moment happened to be looking at the Czar whispered afterwards that he trembled and turned pale. The benediction that the Archimandrite was about to pronounce died upon his lips.

Turning from the balcony the grim red figure ran, or, to put it more correctly, reeled forward in the direction of the Paulovski Guards. Trotting quietly in his rear, as if to keep an eye upon him, came Benningsen upon his black horse Pluto.

"Men of the Paulovski Guards," gasped Voronetz in a hollow voice, "do not . . . shout for . . . Alexander! Listen! I have a tale . . . to . . . tell . . . "

"Tell it, then, in hell!" growled Benningsen, as he whirled his sabre on high.

Men talked for days afterwards of that mighty stroke. When Benningsen lifted his sabre again Voronetz lay on the ground, cloven from skull to breast!

Angry cries broke from the Paulovski Guards. Many of them levelled their rifles at Benningsen, who, to do him justice, did not flinch at this critical moment.

"Eyes right!" he yelled.

So well had these troops been drilled that in a moment their eyes, in spite of their will, turned to the right.

There was no need for Benningsen to say more. The Guards saw what he wanted them to see.

A body of infantry near by had suddenly receded some six paces or more, revealing the startling fact that they had been posted as a sort of screen to mask a battery of twenty cannon, whose gleaming nozzles, obliquely turned, were trained full upon the whole line

of the Paulovski Guards.   Beside each piece stood a
gunner ready with lighted match.   If that battery should
be discharged it was certain that, though many civilians
in the rear would at the same time fall, the Paulovski
Guards themselves would be blown out of existence,
and with the recognition of that fact vanished, for that
day at least, all hope of revolt.

"Pile arms, ye snub-noses!— Paulovski Guards that
were!" said Benningsen with an insulting smile.

Slowly and sullenly the discomfited regiment proceeded
to obey, and defiled from the square, escorted on each
side by mounted Cossacks, who grinned rejoicingly that
an end had come to the favoured regiment with its high
privileges and high pay.

The young Emperor turned away, his face already
shadowed by that melancholy that was never to leave it.

"What a beginning to a reign!" he murmured.

"Sire, its future glory shall make men forget its beginning," said Count Pahlen.

CHAPTER XIII

THE TRIUMPH OF BARANOFF

FROM the balcony the Czar withdrew to a stately hall to receive in audience his late father's ministers.

As they advanced, one by one, Alexander with gracious air bade each continue in the exercise of his office. When, however, Baranoff approached, the Czar's countenance underwent a change, and the Count recognised that his dismissal was at hand. The Franco-Russian Alliance had been mainly due to him, and it was no secret that Alexander had viewed it with disapproval.

"Count," the Emperor began, "your policy in the past —— "

But at this point Baranoff, though it be contrary to all Court etiquette to stop a sovereign in the middle of a remark, boldly made interruption, recognising that if his dismissal were once pronounced Alexander could not, without loss of dignity, revoke it.

"*My* policy, Sire," said he, emphasising the first word. "Your Majesty errs in ascribing to me a policy of any character soever, other than this, 'The King's will is the highest law.' He surely is the best minister who obeys his sovereign without questioning."

Alexander wavered. There could be no doubt that the war with England had been the policy of his father.

Baranoff took courage from Alexander's hesitancy.

"Let me retire from office. I stipulate only that you shall write across my *congé,* 'Dismissed for being faithful to a Czar.'"

"Fidelity to a sovereign may be carried too far," said Alexander, who had not forgotten the lessons of his Republican tutor, La Harpe.

"True, Sire," replied Baranoff, who knew how to

trim his sails to meet the changing breeze. "And, therefore, when fidelity ceased to be a virtue I withdrew my allegiance."

"Since when did you withdraw your allegiance from Paul?" sneered Benningsen.

"Since yesterday at three in the afternoon," retorted Baranoff. "Sire, in dismissing me you dismiss the man to whom you owe both life and throne."

"Why, this is the language of treason," said Benningsen, fingering the hilt of his sabre and much regretting that he could not deal with Baranoff as he had dealt with Voronetz.

"Speak on," said Alexander, mentally contrasting the Count's deference with the General's *brusquerie*.

Benningsen and Pahlen were both disposed to play the master; it might be well, then, to have in the ministry a counterforce in the person of Baranoff.

"Seeing that your father Paul," continued Baranoff, addressing the Czar, "imprisoned you and the Grand Duke Constantine for a trifling breach of military etiquette, to what point would his anger have risen had he known that you were at the head of a conspiracy formed to deprive him of his crown?"

The ministers interchanged significant glances.

"I repeat it, Sire, that you and all here present owe your lives to my forbearance."

"Explain."

Baranoff drew forth the document containing the signatures of the conspirators, and laid it upon the table before the Czar.

"This paper came into my hands yesterday at three in the afternoon."

As a matter of fact he had not seen it till eight hours afterwards, but he wanted to make the best of his case.

"Had I shown this to the Czar Paul, what would have been the result?"

"Why *did* you suppress it if you were so faithful to him?" asked Alexander, toying with the paper.

"Consider, Sire!" returned Baranoff with an air of lofty disinterestedness. "Had I so acted, your life as well as the lives of the other signatories, would have been forfeited. I shrank from filling the city with the noblest blood of the State. And yet, to throw in my lot with your party would have been ingratitude to my Imperial master. Hence I took the only course consistent with honour. I remained neutral."

"Among the Athenians," remarked Pahlen, "he who remained neutral received punishment."

"The usage of an ancient heathen city is no precedent for a modern Christian state," was the reply, a reply that drew a secret curse from Pahlen, who saw that the Czar was being won over by Baranoff's tongue.

"Yes, Sire, the triumph of either side being distasteful to me, I held aloof from both. Happily, the course of nature has prevented you from lifting an unfilial hand against your sire. Who is so dull as not to see the hand of Providence in this sudden demise of his Majesty?"

While speaking, Baranoff cast at the ministers a covert smile, that caused Pahlen to murmur in Benningsen's ear : —

"This fellow suspects."

"What matters, so long as the Czar condones."

Baranoff was an accomplished hypocrite. None who saw his bearing in the presence of Alexander would have suspected that only two hours before he had set off from the Citadel, intent on destroying the very Prince whose favour he was now so anxious to win.

Entirely deceived by Baranoff's air of sincerity, Alexander was more than half disposed to retain him among his ministers, though well aware how displeasing this would be to the rest.

Baranoff, growing more elated as he beheld the disconcerted looks of the ministers, now ventured upon a very bold stroke indeed.

"How faithfully I have watched over, not only Paul's interests, but your own, I can clearly show, if your Majesty will permit me to speak with you only."

A murmur of protest arose from the Ministry.

"Let what you have to say be said openly," remarked Pahlen.

"The matter is for the Czar's ear only," retorted Baranoff, with an air of dignity. "It is for his Majesty to disclose it afterwards if he pleases. I trust your Majesty will grant me this favour, the last perhaps that I may ask."

There was in Baranoff's manner something that convinced the Czar that he *had* an important matter to communicate, that were better heard secretly, too.

"We will humour you," said Alexander, who proceeded to make good his word by calling upon the rest of the Ministry to retire to the ante-chamber.

"What tale hath that knave to tell?" muttered Pahlen. "His subtle tongue will be our undoing. He'll keep his place, and we shall see a continuance of the war."

In which forecast the chancellor was destined to prove a true prophet.

"Now, Count," said Alexander, as soon as the door had closed, "we are alone. What is it you would say?"

"The matter is one that concerns your honour, Sire. Hence my reason for this secrecy."

"Be brief."

"It is with pain and regret, your Majesty, that I bring an accusation against one of the Imperial house."

For a moment the Czar looked as if he doubted his own hearing.

"Accusation?" he exclaimed haughtily. "Of what nature?"

"Ah! Sire, I fear to say, knowing what a blow it will be."

"Tush! Am I a child? The weakling king who desires to hear nothing but what is pleasant will never hear the truth. What is this accusation?"

"It concerns the honour of a lady, who — how shall I say it?"

"Go on," said Alexander sharply, as Baranoff paused again.

"Your Majesty will surely understand me when I say that she whom the Czar loves should keep herself sacred to the Czar."

His Majesty didn't seem to understand, to judge by his perplexed looks.

"What would you imply?"

"Knowing, Sire, how great is your love for the Grand Duchess Marie — your pardon, I ought to call her —— "

"Is this a time for titles?   You would accuse *her?* Of what?   Speak out, and speak the truth; for, as there is a God above us, you receive a stroke of the knout for every false word."   He spoke in real anger, but beneath it all it was easy to see there lurked a fear that what Baranoff would say might prove true.   " Of what would you accuse her? "

"Of letting her love wander from the Czar."

"To whom? "

"To an Englishman."

"His name."

"Lord Courtenay."

It seemed as if the name were familiar to the Czar; at any rate he asked no question as to who Lord Courtenay might be.

"Your proofs? " he asked, affecting a disdain that did not deceive Baranoff.

"She wears at her heart a locket containing his portrait."

"Natural that she should preserve some souvenir of a man who once saved her life."

"Sire, a fortnight ago she obtained Paul's sanction to leave St. Petersburg for a few days.   Why? "

"For prayer and meditation in the Convent of the Ascension."

Baranoff smiled satirically.

"In returning she stopped at a wayside hamlet, named Gora, and stayed for the night at an inn called the Silver Birch."

"You are telling me what I already know."

"Do you know this, Sire, that Lord Courtenay was at this inn on that self-same night? "

No, the Czar did not know that, if one must judge by his startled look.

"Did they see each other? "

"Sire, in the dead of the night he was seen stealing from her bedchamber."

"A lie as black as hell! " cried Alexander in a sudden blaze of wrath, the more striking from his previous enforced calmness. Unable longer to control himself he sprang to his feet, at the same time half-unsheathing his sword, as if with the intention of striking the other dead. Then, as reason asserted itself, the weapon slid from his relaxed fingers down into its scabbard again, and the Emperor resumed his seat, glancing at the door as if fearing lest his voice should have reached the ears of his ministers in the antechamber.

"If it be a lie, ascribe it not to me, but to Prince Ouvaroff, from whom I receive the story."

"I will hear Ouvaroff. I will examine him — by torture if necessary. If you and he are found to be liars, you die. If you speak truth —— But I'll not think *that*, yet. Where is this Lord Courtenay at the present time?"

"In St. Petersburg, Sire, at the French Embassy."

"The French Embassy! How comes he to be there?"

Baranoff explained the circumstances.

"What was the Baroness' motive for this act?"

The Count shrugged his shoulders.

"Mischief, pure mischief! Pauline de Vaucluse is sometimes a woman, and sometimes a girl. As a girl she delights in offering defiance to established authority. 'Twas unwise of the Marquis to countenance his daughter's action, for whatever secret this Englishman happens to pick up at the Embassy will soon be transmitted to his own government."

"How? You think him to be a spy?"

"I *know* him to be such," replied Baranoff, who, always able to lie like truth, was on this particular morning quite surpassing himself. "This Lord Courtenay, who wanders about Europe, ostensibly in search of adventure, whose rank procures him admission to the highest circles, is in reality a secret agent of the British Government. Young, handsome, accomplished, and of noble birth, he is the very person to take a woman's fancy. By some means he has got to know of the Duchess Marie's infatuation for him, and he comes to St. Petersburg with the subtle view of using her as a medium for acquiring State secrets. Be sure, Sire, that whatever matters you communicate to her will soon become his, to be transmitted to his master, Pitt."

"That same Pitt," said the Czar, darkly, "with whom Pahlen bids me make peace!"

"Bids, or — advises?"

The Czar compressed his lips significantly. Baranoff smiled to himself. It was clear to him that Pahlen was disposed to play the master over the youthful sovereign, and that the youthful sovereign did not like the yoke.

"I have shown you, Sire, the infamous methods to which an English premier resorts. And yet you will make peace with him, merely because Pahlen urges you? — An ill precedent to set at the beginning of a reign! The ministers of a Czar are his servants, not his counsellors. The sovereign who accepts advice is not the ruler, but the ruled."

And then, in defiance of his own words, Baranoff proceeded to give advice.

"Will you reverse your father's policy all in a moment? despatch a courier to the First Consul to break off the alliance, even before your royal sire is laid in his grave? Will this be decent?"

Much more to the same point flowed from his lips. His specious pleading, but especially his lies concerning Wilfrid, began to tell upon Alexander, causing his young and plastic mind to waver from its friendly attitude towards Britain. Why not let the war continue — for a time at least, if only to teach his peace-advising ministers that the Czar's will must be supreme?

Wilfrid's love-affair was a matter unknown to the European chancelleries of that day. It would have surprised them — it certainly would have surprised Wilfrid — to know that it was a potent factor in shaping the foreign policy of the Czar. Another proof that great events spring from trifling causes. Did not all the wars of the Grand Monarch originate in a dispute about a window?

At this juncture there came a knock at the folding-doors followed by the entrance of two chamberlains, who, bowing low, announced that the new Czarina desired to speak with the Czar, whom she had not seen since his accession.

Alexander received this message with a frown.

"I am occupied on matters of State, and cannot see her now."

In the ante-chamber, arrayed in deep mourning that enhanced, rather than detracted from her beauty, stood Alexander's wife, the youthful Elizavetta, receiving with a gracious air the congratulations of the ministers on her accession to Imperial rank.

Upon this little circle the Emperor's cold and curt message fell like a bolt from the blue.

Too proud to venture into Alexander's presence after such a rebuff, the Empress turned away, affecting an air of unconcern, though in her eyes could be seen the glitter of tears.

"The devil!" growled Benningsen. "Baranoff has the laugh on us. He has become of more moment than the Czarina herself!"

CHAPTER XIV

On the second night after the death of the Czar Paul, it happened that Wilfrid was sitting over a newspaper in his private room at the Hôtel d'Angleterre, when a sound caused him to look up.

There, a few paces off, stood a young man, wrapped in a long cloak that glistened with the moisture deposited, apparently, by a heavy fog. He was perhaps not more than twenty years of age, singularly mild and placid of countenance, and with light blue eyes marked by a somewhat odd expression; they appeared to be looking straight at Wilfrid without seeing him.

" Do I address Lord Courtenay ? "

His voice was like his looks. He had a subdued air altogether.

" My name, sir," replied Wilfrid, somewhat resenting this sudden intrusion. " And yours? "

" Alexis Voronetz."

" Voronetz, Voronetz," repeated Wilfrid thoughtfully. " Any relative of a certain lieutenant of that name? "

" His brother."

" That cannot be."

" Why not ? "

" I understand that the man who killed him still lives."

" I am blind," answered the stranger with a sigh.

" Your pardon, good Alexis. I was not aware of that."

Wilfrid guided the stranger to a chair, and offered him wine. " And what does the brother of Lieutenant Voronetz want with me? " he asked, when the other had set down his glass.

" My errand is a strange one. I am sent by a certain

137

person, whose will is that I should escort you to a place, not far hence, where your coming is awaited."

"What place?"

"I am forbidden to reveal its name. You will learn, if you come."

"Without doubt," smiled Wilfrid. "But why should I go to this person? If he wish to see me, here I am, easily accessible."

"It is impossible for —— " he hesitated for a word — "for the person to visit you."

"Why not? Is he on a sick bed? Dying? In prison? Who is he?"

"I am on oath not to reveal the name of my principal. You are suspicious, I see; and your suspicions are, perhaps, natural; but in the name of God " — and here the speaker lifted his hand — "no hurt is intended you."

Wilfrid knew that when a Muscovite swears by the name of God, he may usually be trusted. Still ——

"I don't doubt your word, good Alexis, but I strongly suspect the motives of a principal who clothes himself with such secrecy. It is now close upon twelve o'clock. Why may I not go with you to-morrow, and in daylight?"

"To-morrow will be too late."

"Too late for what?"

"That is the answer I was told to give. It must be to-night or never."

"You do not know, then, for what purpose I am wanted?"

Alexis signified that he did not.

Wilfrid mused. Was it safe to pay a visit at midnight to a strange house for the purpose of meeting a man who declined to state beforehand either his name or business? It was certain he had in the city one enemy, Baranoff, if not more; and this errand of Alexis might be the initial step for putting him into that enemy's hand. A little reflection, however, caused Wilfrid to dismiss this theory. Why should Baranoff employ all this secrecy? If he wanted to remove an enemy he had simply to sign an order for that enemy's deportation to Siberia, and the thing was done.

Then there occurred to him an idea that set his blood tingling with a pleasurable excitement.

" So," said he to Alexis, " you will not give me the name of *the lady* that has sent you? "

It was a chance statement, but it found verification in Alexis' sudden look of surprise.

" I have not said that my principal is a lady."

True, but he had shown a scrupulous avoidance of the masculine pronoun, and hence Wilfrid's conclusion. Who was this lady, if not the mysterious duchess?

The atmosphere of peril in which she moved had doubtless left her no other way of seeing him except at midnight and in secrecy.

She wanted him, and that at once: to-morrow would be too late! Was it to give warning of some danger that threatened him, or her, or, possibly, both?

" Had the lady any reason for selecting you as her messenger? "

" My brother's death was mentioned, and I was told to be earnest in persuading you to accompany me, for it might lead to the punishment of his murderer."

As Alexis spoke he set his sightless eyes appealingly upon Wilfrid. There was something pathetic in the picture of this youth, whose infirmity rendered him unable to avenge himself. The brutal slaughter of Lieutenant Voronetz had filled Wilfrid with disgust, a feeling that, in a degree scarcely less strong, included the Czar likewise, when that ruler, instead of punishing the savage, gave him a place in the Ministry. Wilfrid hesitated no longer when he heard that his going with Alexis might bring about the downfall of Benningsen, against whom Pauline had whispered certain dark hints. In what way this was to be brought about, Wilfrid did not stop to inquire. Arming himself with a sword and a brace of pistols, he declared himself ready for the journey.

Sallying forth from the hotel, Wilfrid found the city wrapped in a fog so thick as to prevent him from seeing anything distant more than an arm's length.

No voices: no footsteps: no wheels: not the faintest sound anywhere. There was something weird in the silence that hung over all. Petersburg was like a city of the dead.

Wilfrid soon began to see that he was with a guide of peculiar excellence; the real reason, perhaps, why he had been selected for the trust. On a foggy night blindness is better than sight.

In walking down the staircase of the hotel Wilfrid had guided Alexis; in the street it became the turn of Alexis to guide Wilfrid. Linking Wilfrid's arm within his own he walked forward with no more hesitation than an ordinary man would have shown in traversing the street in broad daylight. It was marvellous to mark the ease with which he steered his course, now to right, and now to left. To him darkness was no darkness at all.

Twenty minutes of silent walking, and then the two were brought to a sudden standstill by a startling challenge. "Who goes there? Halt!"

Barely discernible, there loomed up out of the fog a figure clad in a long grey coat with cross-belt, and armed with a bayoneted rifle.

Alexis whispered something that Wilfrid did not catch, and the soldier, apparently satisfied, melted into the fog again.

"A sentinel, and a watchword," thought Wilfrid. "Either a Government building or an Imperial palace. I incline to the palace."

The two went forward, treading upon a wooden flooring that gave forth a hollow sound. Moved by curiosity, Wilfrid drew forth a coin and flung it sideways in air. Its descent, as he had expected, was accompanied by a slight splash.

"A bridge and water," he thought. "The Fontanka Canal, or the moat round the Michaelhof? The moat, I fancy."

At the end of the supposed bridge they were challenged by a second sentinel. Alexis whispered, and, as before, the two were permitted to pass on, walking now over a pavement of flagstones.

"The courtyard of the Michaelhof," murmured Wilfrid.

Presently Alexis stopped and put forth his hand; so did Wilfrid, who found his fingers touching damp stone, doubtless the actual wall of the palace itself. Turning to the right Alexis began to follow the course of this wall, stopping at last before what seemed to be a small arched entrance, and producing a key he applied it to the lock of an iron-studded door. Unlocking this, Alexis passed within, followed by Wilfrid. The place was as black as night.

"Make as little noise as possible," said Alexis in a low tone.

He moved forward through the darkness, and Wilfrid followed in silence, his hand and foot telling him that he was traversing a passage whose walls and floor were of stone.

In a few moments they had come to a wide staircase of oak, dimly visible in the faint light proceeding from some unseen point above.

This staircase gave access to a long and broad gallery, decorated with tapestry and paintings. A few lamps, ranged at regular intervals along the wall, did little more than make the darkness visible.

With the belief, right or wrong, that every corridor in a Czar's palace is tenanted by an armed sentinel, Wilfrid wondered to see this gallery left unwatched, till it struck him that perhaps this absence of a guard was due to some secret manœuvring on the part of those employing Alexis. Half-way down this gallery Alexis paused, and, opening a door, said : —

"My orders are that you wait here."

The "here" was a lofty apartment, very richly furnished, its recesses piled high with books, showing that it served the purpose of a library. A handsome reading lamp of bronze with a very bright flame stood upon the central table.

But why it should be ordained that night must for ever rest upon this apartment was a mystery to Wilfrid; yet such was the case. Windows there were none, the spaces that had once let in daylight being now closed with masonry, a walling-up that, judged by appearances, had taken place but recently. Alexis offered no explanation of this singularity; perhaps, being blind, he was not aware of it. Wilfrid could not help noticing how odd was his manner at this moment; he seemed to be under a spell of nervousness, if not of actual fear, his eyes being riveted upon a certain door at the far end of the apartment, as if, blind though he was, he could see something that the other could not see. Turning away, he said: —

"I must leave you for a time. I go to announce your arrival."

With this he stepped from the apartment, closing the door behind him.

Too much excited to spend the interval in sitting down, Wilfrid paced to and fro for a few minutes.

Suddenly, he stopped short in his walk, and, without knowing why, shot a suspicious glance at the distant door. What lay on the other side of it he did not know, but he felt a sense of satisfaction in having come equipped with sword and pistols.

He resumed his pacing, though more slowly now, and even when his back was turned to the door, he moved, as a Spaniard would say, with his beard upon his shoulder.

That door haunted him!

It was in vain that he tried to divert his mind from it by examining the objects of art contained in the room: a rectangle of wood, seven feet by three, proved a greater attraction than oriental alabaster or porphyry vases. Many minutes had now passed, yet Wilfrid still remained the only person in the apartment.

Growing impatient at this long delay he went to the door by which he had entered, and peeped out into the gallery.

He could not see anybody, nor could he hear the sound of coming footsteps. No sound at all, far or near.

"Truly, they are quiet people in the Michaelhof," muttered Wilfrid, as he closed the door again.

The midnight hour and the deadly silence, the mysterious character of this chamber, with its windows sealed against the light of day, but above all, the strange door, began to tell upon Wilfrid's nerves.

Was it fancy merely, or did he catch a glimpse of it in the act of closing, just as he was withdrawing his gaze from the gallery?

The more he dwelt upon Alexis' oddity of manner, the stronger became his suspicion that the door gave access to something strange, something that was a matter of fear to Alexis.

If the mystery were one to be solved merely by opening the door, then Wilfrid would solve it; if the door were locked, his curiosity would, of course, be baffled; even *his* boldness would hardly proceed to the length of breaking the lock of a door belonging to the Czar's palace.

Lifting the lamp, the only one in the apartment, from the table, Wilfrid, albeit somewhat slowly, went forward, fancying as he did so that he saw the door vibrate, an illusion due, perhaps, to the oscillating lamp.

Reaching the door he stood there for a time, hesitating, for all his boldness. He held his ear close to the panels, but failed to detect either sound or movement; he applied his eye to the keyhole; darkness was upon the other side.

He drew his sword as a precaution against he knew not what. As it is somewhat difficult for a man holding an object in each hand to turn the knob of a door, Wilfrid resolved to place the lamp on the floor in such a position that its rays would illumine the room beyond as soon as he should have swung the door open.

As he stooped to lower the lamp, his eye was caught by some dark stains, varying in shape and size. He raised the lamp again, and looked round about. The stains were nowhere else, only there, just around the door, and along one side of the wall at the foot of the arras.

Something had happened there, and it was the knowledge of that event that had put fear upon the mind of Alexis.

Setting the lamp upon the floor, Wilfrid rose to his full height, and placing his fingers upon the knob turned it, and at the same time with a push of his foot he sent the door flying wide.

The next moment a cry of vexation broke from him, as he realised when too late his want of foresight.

The sudden opening of the door had produced an indraught of air sufficiently strong to extinguish the flame of the lamp before he could catch even the briefest glimpse of the chamber. Being without flint and steel he was unable to rekindle the flame.

As a precaution against being transfixed by hostile blades Wilfrid, on opening the door, had recoiled a few steps, and he now stood with his sword on guard, half-expecting to be attacked, or at the least to be addressed, by some unseen foe. There was neither movement nor speech; the chamber was soundless, its darkness seeming to be not the ordinary darkness of night, but something far blacker, an effect due, Wilfrid intuitively felt, to the fact that the windows of this place, too, were walled up.

Now, while he was hesitating whether to go forward a few paces, just to ascertain whether this supposed chamber might not be a corridor, his ear was startled by the sound of something coming through the doorway, something moving low down, a slow, gliding rustle along the floor at the foot of the wall. Wilfrid did not doubt that some one was stealing into the chamber with some deadly design against him, else why this secret and voice-less action?

Wilfrid put no question; he gave no warning.

Swift as the electric flash his sword descended edge-wise upon the quarter whence came the sound, and he had the grim satisfaction of knowing that he had not struck in vain. His sense of feeling told him that the edge of the blade had not only cut the tapestry, but had also passed through some fleshy obstacle, severing it in twain.

But the strangeness of the thing! — the victim had uttered no cry!

A sensation, such as he had never before known, passed over Wilfrid. For a moment he hesitated; then, impelled almost against his will, he stooped, not neglecting, however, to keep on guard against a possible attack, and, feeling with his left hand in the place where his blade had struck, he grasped something that he immediately relinquished on realising what it was.

A human hand!

And the man thus maimed had endured the pain without a groan! an apathy so utterly opposed to human nature that Wilfrid recoiled with an eerie thrill.

And there he stood, staring at the place where he knew the hand to be, fancying he could see it looking ghastly white through the darkness. If that, outlined beside it, were really a human shape, and not merely a figure woven upon the tapestry, there could be but one solution of the mystery. The victim must be a dumb man, belonging perhaps to the class of those tongueless eunuchs often to be found in the seraglios of the East, though seldom, if ever, in the palace of a Czar.

Was he writhing in silent agony?

Wilfrid listened for any sound indicative of human presence. But there was no movement; there was not even a breath audible in the place where the handless man should be.

Recovering from his spell of fear, Wilfrid came slowly forward and passed the point of his sword along the foot of the wainscotting without lighting upon the owner of the hand. What had become of him? It was impossible to believe that the man, on receiving the sword-stroke, had risen to his feet and glided off without a sound. Where, then —— ?

Once more Wilfrid stooped, and, repressing the natural repugnance engendered by such a task, he began to search for the severed hand, which he was not long in finding. His gloved fingers could not tell whether the hand were warm or cold, but a touch of the mutilated member against his cheek told him that it was icy-cold. When held to his nostrils, it emitted a decaying odour, thus proving that some hours, if not some days, must have elapsed since its severance from the parent limb.

It had been lying near the door at the foot of the wall, hidden, perhaps, by the fringe of tapestry, and Wilfrid, when aiming the downward stroke of his imaginary foe, had, by a singular chance, lighted upon this dead hand, the keen edge of his blade slicing a part of the wrist. The sound mistaken by him for a stealthy human movement had perhaps been nothing more than the return of a hungry rat towards a meal that had been disturbed by the entrance of himself and Alexis.

Resisting the temptation to fling the ghastly relic from him, Wilfrid laid it upon the table, with the words: —

"This may have been the hand of a brave man."

He had just closed the door of the supposed inner chamber and restored the lamp to its place, when his ear caught the sound of footsteps in the gallery.

"Friends or foes?" he muttered, keeping the table between himself and the door, and laying his hand upon his sword. His eyes, so long in darkness, blinked with a sudden radiance, as the door opened.

"In the dark!" said a sweet voice in a tone expressive of reproachful surprise. "Did you leave Lord Courtenay here without a light?"

"Your Highness, no," replied Alexis.

The voice of the first speaker sent a thrill to Wilfrid's heart, for it was the voice of the lady he was longing to meet.

Graceful in figure, and stately in bearing, she moved forward with all the dignity of an Imperial princess. In Wilfrid's eyes she seemed more beautiful than ever, attired as she was in a clinging robe of the richest silk, her face and hair framed in a dainty lace wrap. Radiant and youthful, what did she want in a chamber so grim with suggestions of tragedy? He was glad to note that at that moment the dead hand lay in shadow. Beside the Duchess on her right walked Alexis, as faithful a servitor as his blindness would permit; in the rear, and carrying a small silver lamp that shed a soft glow around, came a third person, whom Wilfrid took to be a lady-in-waiting.

"Remain here," said the Duchess, addressing her two attendants, and with that she moved forward towards Wilfrid. Her reason for keeping her attendants in the room was obvious. When a youthful duchess holds an interview with a man in the dead of night it is well to have a witness by to prove that such meeting is all that it should be.

The Duchess's first question was personal, and to the point.

"Lord Courtenay, have you learned yet who I am?"

"Am I wrong in concluding that you are a Grand Duchess?"

She hesitated, an odd smile on her lips.

"I was — once."

"Once? Yet your attendant has called you Highness!"

"Alexis forgets that ——" And then she stopped. "No matter. Call me by that title. 'Twill do as well as any other."

A duchess no longer! What did she mean? Had the jealous Alexander deprived her of the title conferred by Paul? *That* he could do, but he could not take away her Imperial descent, nor the regal beauty that accompanied it. It was clear that, so far as Wilfrid was concerned, she wished still to remain *incognita*.

"Were you," said the Duchess — to call her still by that name — "were you expecting to see me to-night, when you accompanied Alexis?"

"Presumptuous of me, perhaps," smiled Wilfrid, "but I was not without hope that the summons *might* have come from you."

It was with a certain touch of hauteur in her manner that the Duchess replied: —

"Learn, then, that it was not *I* who called you to this meeting." — Wilfrid's hopes fell. — "Not till an hour ago was it told me that you had been sent for." Wilfrid's hopes rose. Her coming to see him immediately on hearing of his arrival was proof that she took *some* interest in his fate. "Is it likely," she continued gravely, and speaking more as if to herself than to him, "that I should invite you to a meeting like this, when death would be your lot should you be seen here by my enemies?"

Her enemies? Wilfrid wished he could have them all in line and fight with them, one by one, from sunrise to sunset, with due intervals for rest and refreshment. He'd have left none alive!

"Then, since you did not send for me, will your Highness condescend to tell me who did?"

"The Empress."

"Elizavetta?" asked Wilfrid, naming the youthful wife of Alexander.

"No, Paul's widow. The Dowager Empress, I should have said. She was desirous of seeing you in person, but circumstances preventing her, I act as her ambassadress."

Wilfrid breathed a silent benison on the head of the ex-Czarina for her choice of ambassadress.

"And what is the will of the Empress with me?"

"To do a work that — but your question will best be answered in that room," replied the Duchess, pointing to the door of the mysterious chamber. "Countess, bring the light."

CHAPTER XV.

THE lady addressed as countess came forward with the lamp, and the little party moved towards the ante-chamber — for such it was — Wilfrid himself opening the door.

The Duchess, as if claiming precedence, was the first to enter, and Wilfrid noticed that as she passed the threshold she looked downwards, seemingly careful as to where she stepped.

Wilfrid followed. The Countess and Alexis stood by the door, and as before, beyond earshot.

The chamber was one that had no exit save the door by which they had entered. As in the other apartment every window had been walled up. A plain camp bed in the middle showed that the place had been used as a sleeping-chamber. The rest of the furniture was of the simplest kind, quite in keeping with the bed.

"You are treading," said the Duchess, solemnly, "where, after to-morrow, the foot of man will never tread again."

"Then this is ——?"

"The death-chamber of the Czar Paul."

Then did Wilfrid remember that it is a usage in the Russian Court on the death of a Czar to wall in the windows and to seal the doors of his private apartments, a process which, if repeatedly carried on, must in course of time expel the living Czar from the palace of his ancestors.

"To-morrow will be too late," had been Alexis' argument for inducing Wilfrid to accompany him. A true remark, if applied to the seeing of this chamber, but wherein lay the necessity for his seeing it?

"Yes, Paul died here," said the Duchess. "But why

149

do I say 'died?' That is not the word. Died! **They** do well to shut the light from this room! Let there be perpetual darkness; it will be a fitting symbol of — of the work done here. If these walls could speak!"

She was silent for a moment, and then turning to Wilfrid with eyes that spoke of an inward horror, she said,

"Do you know how Paul died?"

"Your words lead me to suspect **the** official account that he died of apoplexy."

"It is false — false!" she cried with a vehemence that surprised Wilfrid. "Paul was murdered in this very chamber — cruelly and barbarously murdered. And they that did the deed still live. Live, do I say? They are the Czar's ministers, highest in the State, honoured of all men! And Paul's physicians are not ashamed to sign lying proclamations that he died of apoplexy; they are posted all over the city. And editors print the story, and people believe it — all save a few, and these dare not open their mouths, for it is a crime against the State to speak the truth. It is only in Russia that such things can be."

Overcome by emotion she sank down upon a chair by the bedside. Wilfrid thought she was going to faint, and made a sign for the Countess to come forward. Her help, however, was not required.

"Whence did you learn this?" asked Wilfrid.

"From one who, till his dying day, will be haunted by the memory of the deed — from Prince Ouvaroff."

"Will not your Highness tell me the story?"

"It is the will of the Empress that you *should* be told it."

Wilfrid could not help wondering why Paul's widow should honour him, of all persons in the world, with this confidence, seeing that, only two days before, he had given dire offence to her husband. Doubtless he would receive an explanation ere long of a circumstance that at present was altogether inexplicable.

Pausing for a time before she began her narrative, and often pausing after she *had* begun, the Duchess proceeded to describe Paul's death, one of the grimmest stories in the annals of Czardom.

Two nights before — to tell the tale more connectedly than it was told by the Duchess — upon the stroke of eleven, twenty cloaked men presented themselves at one of the gates of the palace. They were the ministers, relatives, and friends of the Czar, among them being Count Pahlen, the chief of the conspiracy; General Benningsen, a savage when roused to anger; and Prince Ouvaroff, a patriot actuated by the best and purest of motives.

The soldier on guard permitted them to pass, never suspecting that treason lurked beneath those brilliant uniforms and the decorations that attested rank and dignity. Once within the palace they silently ascended to the Emperor's apartments.

On guard before the bedroom door stood Lieutenant Voronetz. Guessing their errand, he shouted "Treason!" and, faithful to his trust, he drew his sabre, though well knowing that resistance meant death.

"We have no quarrel with you," said Benningsen. "Stand aside from that door! You will not? Well, then, if you prefer to die —— "

A dozen blades were stabbing and slashing at Voronetz; his hand was hewn off; mutilated and moaning he fell.

The door was fastened on the inside; a violent kick burst it open, and in rushed the conspirators.

The Czar was not to be seen.

"He cannot have fled far," said Benningsen. "His bed is still warm. Ah! Yon screen!"

From behind the screen there stepped a little figure clad only in a dressing-gown.

The conspirators, about to rush forward, checked themselves. There was in the figure a certain air of dignity that awed them in spite of their resolve. However insignificant in person, he was nevertheless the Czar, descendant of a long line of Czars, only son of the great Catharine, and nearest in blood to the mighty Peter himself. His picture hung in a million homes; tyrant though he were, ten million persons would weep if hurt befel the Little Father; ten million voices would demand vengeance upon the slayers!

Appalled at the magnitude of their intended deed some of the conspirators shrank back, and with averted faces stole towards the door.

But the master-spirit of the scene, Benningsen, intercepted them with drawn sabre.

"No weakness, or I slay you."

The figure spoke.

"By whose authority do you come here thus?"

"By the authority of the Czar Alexander."

Paul's eye flashed.

"Alexander is not Czar."

"He will be when — you have signed this," said Benningsen, holding forth a paper. "'Tis your act of abdication."

"I will never abdicate!"

"Sign!" said Benningsen, menacing the Czar with his sabre.

Paul defied them. As often as they repeated their demand so often did he refuse. At last he seemed to yield.

"Give me the paper."

The document was handed to him. He rent it to fragments and tossed them at their feet.

The smile of triumph accompanying the act provoked Benningsen to fury; in a moment of forgetfulness he smote Paul upon the face. Too late he realised what he had done.

"I have struck the Czar! We are all lost — *if he does not die!*"

The conspirators shuddered; there was now no retreat.

Flinging himself upon the Czar, Benningsen brought him to the floor. Emboldened by his example the others crowded around. There was a flash of steel.

"Hold!" cried Benningsen. "No bloodshed. No disfiguring mark on the body. A sash, some one!"

Paul, not realising till that moment that resistance might end in death, suddenly lost courage. His words were no longer threatening, but supplicatory.

" Spare — me — I will — abdicate — ! "

He could get out the words in gasps only. Benningsen's great hand was pressing upon his windpipe.

" Too late! Will no one lend a hand? " said Benningsen, for the Czar was making desperate efforts to fling his adversary off. " Must I do the work alone? "

Several knelt and pinned the struggling Paul to the floor. Benningsen rose, and directed their movements. A sash was slipped loosely round the Czar's throat, but in his deadly agony he succeeded in getting his left hand through the noose, and drew it across his chin.

" Give me time — for God's sake — a minute only — to say a prayer! "

His misty glance, wandering around in search of pity, suddenly fell upon Prince Ouvaroff, who, with a troubled look on his face, had come forward, bent, even at the cost of his life, on making an attempt to stay the deed.

" Ouvaroff — *my own son!* — among these men! — will you see your father — murdered? "

The Prince, his mind absolutely frozen with horror at this sudden and unlooked for revelation — a revelation that he felt to be true — stared with ghastly look at the Czar. The assassins, in the surprise of the moment, stopped in their work. Then the Prince, with a wild laugh like that of a man who has suddenly become insane, swayed feebly forward and fell senseless.

" I didn't know we had a woman among us," laughed Benningsen. " Good Lord! " he continued, apostrophising the struggling Czar, " did ever man yell so? "

He set the sole of his great boot upon the mouth of the victim; the heel slipped between the jaws of the Czar, who bit with such fury that the teeth penetrated the leather and entered the flesh. With a snarl of pain Benningsen withdrew his foot. Till his dying day he carried on his heel the mark left by the Czar.

They got the noose around his neck at last, and two men, one on each side, tugged at the loose ends. The work was hard and long; fully ten minutes passed before they rose from their knees.

And now that the deed was over their courage fell again, and they stared at one another in a sort of stupor. There would be a tribunal to face, namely, the nation, and what would it say to this deed of darkness?

Benningsen still maintained his hardihood, at least outwardly.

"Who'd have thought the little ape had so much life in him?" he sneered, looking down upon the body. "We have damaged him a little. But some paint and the doctor's art will soon make him presentable to the public. You are all witnesses that he died of apoplexy."

As they stole from the dimly-lighted chamber leaving Ouvaroff to awaken beside the body of his murdered Sire, they caught the faint moaning of the prostrate Voronetz.

"A lad of brave spirit!" commented Benningsen. "'Tis a pity he should die. We'll send Dr. Wylie to him to see whether he can be mended. But he'll have to hold his peace."

Making their way to another quarter of the now alarmed palace the ministers sought the chamber where the two Grand Dukes, Alexander and Constantine, were confined — under sentence of death, so it was believed — and setting the two brothers free gave them an account of their father's *execution,* seeking to pacify their grief and indignation by the argument, doubtless a true one, that since Paul would not sign the abdication, no alternative was left but killing. For let them but retire from his bed-chamber, and Paul would at once have called upon his guard to slaughter them; and, having now learned that his two sons were parties to the conspiracy, he would doubtless have included them in the slaughter. It was Alexander's death or Paul's, and they chose it should be Paul's.

"And thus," said the Duchess, concluding her story, "thus did Paul die. His body lies in state in St. George's Hall. A solemn mass is chanted twice a day — and twice a day the murderers bend in prayer beside the bier! The mockery of it! Does God sleep that such things can be?"

The Duchess's narration, correct in the main, as the

historian can testify, set Wilfrid's nerves a-quivering with a variety of emotions. Horror was followed by indignation, and indignation by loathing. The deed itself was black enough in all conscience, but blacker still were the cowardice, the hypocrisy, the lying employed to conceal it.

"In England," he remarked, "these assassins would be swinging. In Russia they are ministers. Truly, Alexander the Amiable merits his name. He *is* amiable — very — towards his fathers' murderers!"

The Duchess seemed to resent this disparagement of Alexander.

"Consider his position," she answered. "Is he to begin his reign by degrading the men who have put him on the throne? They who slew one Czar may slay another."

"And can a man die better than in the attempt to avenge his father's murder? If fear of the assassin's dagger keeps Alexander from doing an act of justice then have the Russians a Czar, but scarcely a hero."

"You are bold, sir, in the absence of Alexander."

"Nay, I would say the same in his presence."

And the Duchess did not doubt it when she remembered how Wilfrid had faced the fiery Paul — nay, had half-drawn his sword upon him.

Wilfrid ventured at this point to remind the Duchess of an earlier remark of hers.

"You said, I think, that the Empress had a work for me to do?"

"True. The Empress, well knowing your character, appeals to you to do what the boldest in St. Petersburg would shrink from doing, namely, to make known to the world the truth respecting Paul's death."

"I am indeed honoured, but in doing her will I shall be trenching on the Czar's ground. It is his duty, not mine."

"The Czar remains silent from a mistaken sense of honour. Looking upon Paul's death as a regrettable accident, Alexander would deem it a breach of faith on his part were he to denounce those with whom he was equally a conspirator. He had pledged his written word that the ministers should retain office. That word he will not break. But he must be made to break it. And the Empress sees but one way. There is something greater than even the power of a Czar, and that is, the will of a united people. Why do the ministers conceal their crime? Because they fear the people. Let the millions of Russia learn how Paul came by his end, and there will arise a flood of indignation strong enough to sweep the ministers from power. But that day will not come till a man be found bold enough to proclaim the truth."

" And does the Empress invite *me* to be the avenger of that Czar who, for no fault at all, would have had me knouted to death?"

" Yes, for she judges that Lord Courtenay is too noble to refuse an act of justice to a fallen foe."

" Humph!" said Wilfrid, immensely flattered; " is Alexander a party to this scheme?"

" No. It is of the Empress's own devising."

" She leaves it to an Englishman to teach her son his duty?"

The Duchess winced.

" How hard you are on Alexander!"

He was, and that because he wished to disillusion her of her idea that Alexander was a hero. " Women are all alike," he thought; by " women " meaning the Duchess and Pauline. " A crown dazzles them. A king can do no wrong."

" Has her majesty," he continued aloud, " any plan for me, or am I left to follow my own devices?"

" In view of the peril attendant upon the enterprise — for those who slew a Czar may not hesitate to slay the man who publishes their crime — the Empress has thought of a plan that can be carried out with secrecy, and yet with effect. What you did once, the Empress bids you do again."

The Duchess proceeded to make clear her meaning by words spoken in a subdued key. The communication, whatever its nature, caused Wilfrid's eyes to brighten and his lips to take a smile as of coming triumph. He accepted the office, not so much because justice required

it or the Empress wished it, as because he saw that success would give pleasure to the Duchess.

"You understand, now," continued she, "why the
Empress has summoned you to this death-chamber. It
is needful that you should see it with your own eyes, and
to-morrow would have been too late."

"Not a feature of it has escaped me," said Wilfrid.
And, indeed, he was confident that if he should live for
a century the aspect of the little bedroom would never
fade from his mind.

"Besides the ministers," she continued, "there are
others to be made a mark for public hatred."

"Among them being ——?"

"Pauline de Vaucluse."

Wilfrid turned upon her a look of wonder.

"The Baroness was not with the assassins."

"In spirit she was. She was the very soul of the plot.
The conspirators, aiming as they thought for a better
Government, were in reality dupes, ministering to her
selfish and wicked ends."

Wilfrid frowned. Selfish and wicked? He did not
like to hear such terms in connection with Pauline, whose
character he thought he understood much better than
did the Duchess.

"I fail to see what she has personally gained by Paul's
death."

"Her reward, so she hopes, is yet to come."

The Duchess, as she spoke, compressed her lips with
an air which plainly said that the reward, whatever it
might be, would not come if *she* could prevent it.

"I greatly fear," said Wilfrid, taking a decisive stand,
"that even were I persuaded that Pauline de Vaucluse
was the wickedest of all the conspirators, I could not
treat her in the way you suggest."

"Why, you must love her!"

Her tone implied pitying scorn for any one who could
be captivated by a Pauline de Vaucluse.

"My sentiment toward the Baroness is not love, but
friendship. Caring nothing for Paul's anger she rescued
me from the hands of his soldiers. Shall I then requite

her good deed by holding her up to the people's hate? No, I cannot do that, your Highness."

"She ran no risk. It suited her to play the heroine, knowing that Paul was to die that same night. But I speak to deaf ears, I see." And then abruptly changing the subject, she added: —

"Lord Courtenay, the Empress bids you ask a reward for your coming service."

It somewhat piqued Wilfrid to think that the Empress should hold him as one incapable of doing a just and generous deed without hope of payment. She was forgetting that he was an Englishman, and a Courtenay.

"Ah, yes! my reward," he murmured, wondering what answer to make. Then, all in a moment, a romantic and daring idea suggested itself.

"The reward I claim — nay, insist upon — is one that the Empress cannot give. It must come from you."

"From *me?*" she said, in a tone that somehow thrilled Wilfrid to the heart.

"It is that if I succeed in deposing the Ministry, you will give me —— "

"What?" as he hesitated.

"A kiss."

Strange that it cost Wilfrid a greater effort to say these two little words than it did to face the fiery Paul.

But the Duchess!

First she drew a sharp breath; then she started back, in her eyes a look of anger so deep that it made Wilfrid almost regret his bold request.

"Do you think because Catharine has reigned that there is no modesty left in Russia?"

"How can I think that, your Highness, when I look upon you?"

"Ask, instead, for fifty thousand roubles; you shall have them."

"I prefer something more precious."

"You — prefer — a — kiss — to — fifty — thousand — roubles!" she said, pausing in surprise between each word.

"If the kiss come from you."

"It shall never come," she said breathlessly.

"Your highness, 'tis yours to refuse; 'tis mine also."

"You mean that you will decline the Empress's wish."

Wilfrid's grim smile implied that he would; and at this the Duchess's face assumed a look of dismay, for she knew Wilfrid to be the only man qualified for the task required of him.

"Why do you ask this — this silly thing?" she faltered.

"That I may return home with the knowledge that I have kissed the fairest lady in Russia."

There was silence for a brief interval, during which the Duchess seemed to become reconciled to the enormity of being kissed.

"And nothing but a kiss will content you?"

"I will add a second condition; you must at the same time tell me your name, your rank, your history, and how it happened that I could save your life, as you say I did, and yet retain no remembrance of the event."

"To gain my ends I must consent to your humour. Thus then do I pledge my word. Rid the Czar of his wicked Ministry, and " — her eyes drooped, and a beautiful colour stole over her cheek — "and . . . you . . . shall . . . take . . . a . . . kiss . . . from . . . me."

"Pardon me. There must be no taking on my part. The kiss must be freely given by you."

"You are a hard taskmaster," she smiled. "Well, it shall be as you wish."

CHAPTER XVI

THE FALL OF THE REGICIDES

It was a usage of the Russian Ministry, in 1801 at least, for each member to present himself at the Winter Palace once a week on a stated day for the purpose of reporting on the affairs of his office.

Count Pahlen's hour for meeting the Czar coincided with that of General Benningsen, and hence, on the forenoon of a certain day in early summer, seated in a three-horse car, they were making their way towards St. Petersburg after a night spent at Strelna.

Upon entering the suburbs the two ministers were immediately struck by the unusual number of people abroad. Like other cities St. Petersburg has its artisan class that rises early and works till late. On this particular morning, however, the toilers had apparently taken leave of work, and were standing in knots about the streets and squares.

As the day was not marked in the calendar as a feast, some affair of great moment must have caused them to suspend their labours. They looked, by their grave air and subdued voices, as men look when hearing of the death of a king.

As the Petersburgers caught sight of the carriage, their whisperings ceased, and they eyed the ministers with an air that sent misgiving to the heart of the timid Pahlen; for, if ever hatred was seen in the eyes of men, it was seen in the eyes of the Petersburgers that morning.

On the previous day their appearance in public had elicited cheers and other tokens of good-will. Now all was changed; in one night they seemed to have toppled from the height of their popularity.

Interpreting this in his own way, Pahlen concluded that in his absence some ill news must have reached the city; that devil of a Nelson — he was known to be in the Baltic — had perhaps been bombarding Revel.

When Pahlen turned into the Nevski Prospekt, he met with a fresh shock. As high minister of the Czar, he might surely look for recognition and respect from the fashionable and wealthy crowd, whose daily habit it was to drive to and fro along that grand thoroughfare. But no!

A boyar of princely rank, seated in a splendid equipage, drew near. He was well known to Pahlen, who waved his hand in greeting. Looking straight before him, the boyar drove past, altogether ignoring the presence of the chancellor and the general.

This disdainful indifference towards men with whom lay the power of banishment to Siberia, kindled the anger of the two ministers, anger that increased as they continued their way.

They smiled at this fair lady; they saluted that grandee, but met with no recognition whatever. It was clear that the *élite* of St. Petersburg had made up its mind to ignore them. Why?

Fallen ministers have no friends — in Russia. Was it possible that the Czar had made up his mind to dismiss them, and that his determination had somehow become known to the people?

Glancing ahead Benningsen saw coming along the Prospekt a mounted colonel of his own regiment.

" Muscovitz," muttered he, fingering his sabre. " Let the fellow fail to salute, and I'll run him through.'

However, Colonel Muscovitz in passing brought a hand up to his helmet, though in a somewhat perfunctory manner.

" Halt! " yelled Benningsen; and the colonel, with a somewhat queer look, reined in his steed.

" Are we still ministers of the Czar? "

" I have heard of nothing to the contrary, General."

" Then will you tell me what has happened during the past twenty-four hours to cause everybody in St. Petersburg to look as black as the devil? "

"Pardon, General; I carry a message from the Czar, and may not tarry in his service. The answer to your question is to be seen at the Orphan Asylum."

So saying, Muscovitz saluted with the same indifferent air as before and rode off quickly, much as if it were a disgrace to be seen talking with the two ministers.

The Orphan Asylum? The two looked inquiringly at each other. The edifice in question was a foundation of the ex-Empress Mary, and the ex-Empress Mary, as both well knew, had good reason for hating the existing Ministry.

"Now, what devilry has that old bedlam been up to?" said Benningsen. "Drive to the Orphan Asylum," he cried, turning to the coachman.

"Better not," murmured Pahlen. "A crowd may be there, and I like not the people's looks this morning. They would do us mischief if they dared. Besides, the Czar awaits us."

But Benningsen scoffed at the other's fears, and swore he would go there though the place should contain ten thousand devils.

Arrived within sight of the building, they found the space fronting it filled with a vast throng, drawn mainly from the lower orders, a throng jostling, excited, garrulous. Women and children were there, as well as men, all animated apparently with the one object of pushing their way to the fore, in order to obtain a glimpse of something exposed to view behind the railings that guarded the façade of the Orphan Asylum. Everybody in the crowd was talking at once, making it impossible for the ministers to gather anything intelligible. The hubbub was loudest in front where those in full enjoyment of the view clung to the railings, refusing to give place to their fellows in the rear.

"A nice disorderly mob!" growled Benningsen, standing up in the carriage and surveying the crowd as it swayed to and fro like waves of the sea. "Where is the Governor of the city or the Chief of the Police? Asleep?"

"If the object behind those railings be to our hurt,

Baranoff and his brother will not be over-eager to disperse the throng."

Pahlen's suspicion was well founded. The Governor of the city and the Chief of the Police, having a foreknowledge of what was to take place, had arranged that the people were not to be interfered with.

At this point a man on the outskirts of the crowd suddenly caught sight of the two ministers.

" See, see! — Pahlen and Benningsen," he cried excitedly, extending his forefinger towards them.

Those beside the speaker turned, and, observing at whom he pointed, took up the cry —

" Pahlen and Benningsen! "

There was a wild rush of feet over the pavement, and before the terrified driver could set his steeds in motion the carriage was surrounded by a crowd of fierce-eyed men. Pahlen, his cheeks blanched, shrank back. Benningsen, familiar with the rush of bayonets on the battlefield, lost nothing of his presence of mind.

Whipping out a brace of pistols, he pointed them, the one to the right, the other to the left.

" I'll make a dead man of the first that comes within a yard of the car."

Those advancing with a fell purpose instantly stopped short, and strove to stem the pressure in their rear. They knew that, happen to him what might, Benningsen would keep his word. Had he not cut down a soldier in the very teeth of a hostile regiment?

Benningsen took advantage of the momentary lull to single out with his eye a young man whose dress showed him to be a student of the university, a youth distinguished likewise from the rest of the crowd by his bold, not to say defiant, bearing.

" Hearken, sirrah, your name? "

" Nikon, son of Andreas."

" Well, Nikon son of Andreas, you seem a more sensible sort of fellow than those around you. Just tell us in a few words to what all this excitement is due? "

" To the picture."

" What picture? "

" The picture placed at dawn before the Orphan

Asylum by command of the Empress Mary. Does that
picture tell the truth?" he added with a threatening
look.

"How the devil should I know when I haven't seen
it."

"Come and see it then," said the student.

This was deemed a good idea by the crowd, who
seemed to have taken fresh courage from the student's
bold attitude.

"Yes, yes!" they cried. "Bring them face to face
with it. Show them their wickedness."

The student gave the ministers no alternative. Forgetting or ignoring Benningsen's threat to shoot, he
took hold of the horses by the bridle, turned their heads
in the direction of the asylum, and motioned the by-
standers aside with his hand, crying, "Way there for
Pahlen and Benningsen."

The voice and gesture of the student caused the crowd
to open a path, and thus the ministers passed slowly
through a lane of people, who received them with a running fire of threats.

"Down with the regicides!"

"Death to the murderers of the Czar!"

"The liars who told us that Paul died of apoplexy!"

"Pull Benningsen from the car!"

"Stamp on his mouth, as he stamped on Paul's!"

And but for the dissuasive words of the student the
crowd would have made good their threats.

The student, having arrived at the railings that
guarded the front of the Orphan Asylum, halted and
cried —

"Behold your work!"

Pahlen gave a strange gasp. Benningsen looked on
with an air of scornful indifference.

If the Ministry had hoped their crime would never be
revealed to the public, that hope was now gone. For
there, exposed to view behind the railings, was an expanse of canvas, twenty feet by ten, painted with a
tableau, vivid and grim in its realism. It represented
the interior of a dimly-lit bed-chamber with furnishings
of the simplest. Within this chamber were human fig-

ures, drawn to life-size, their faces limned with a fidelity that made them instantly recognisable. Benningsen, gazing, saw himself standing with the heel of his boot planted upon the mouth of a struggling figure held down by four grim-faced men, two of whom were drawing the fatal noose around the throat of their victim.

The artist had dealt fairly with Prince Ouvaroff, who was making an attempt to stay the deed. Count Pahlen, more scrupulous, or more craven, than his agents, was represented as standing outside the chamber listening at the partly-opened door, at his feet the wounded body of the faithful Voronetz.

The helplessness of the victim, and the brutal strength of the assassins, formed a contrast that would have moved the least emotional to a sense of horror, pity, and indignation; and, as if to drive home the moral of the picture, there was written at its foot, in Russian, what were erroneously supposed by the crowd to be Paul's last words, words well adapted to quicken the blood of the coldest Muscovite —

"I LOOK TO MY PEOPLE TO AVENGE ME!"

Whatever weakening of the sentiment may take place in the twentieth century, certain it is that in the early part of the nineteenth the feeling towards the Czar was a sort of religion with the Muscovites of the lower classes. Rule he never so ill, still a Czar *was* a Czar and his murder the greatest of crimes. So at least the crowd seemed to think, if their looks and words meant anything.

"This is true," said the student, pointing to the picture, "for the good Empress would never put forth a lie. Ye are murderers! And what saith Holy Writ of such? 'Whoso sheddeth man's blood, by man shall his blood be shed.'"

"It seems, then, that this is a court of justice," said Benningsen.

He could afford to sneer, for he saw at that moment what the other apparently did not see.

"It is an assembly of the people, who adjudge you

both to be worthy of death. You shall be hanged from these railings."

"Lying prophet!" said Benningsen with a sardonic grin. "Look there!"

"The soldiers! the soldiers!" was the cry that suddenly rose from all sides.

And the student, looking in the direction indicated by Benningsen, saw glinting over the heads of the people the plumed helmets of a posse of cavalry, who, laying about them with the flat of their sabres, were endeavouring to open a way to the spot where the ministers were.

There was a moment of irresolution on the part of the crowd, and then, with a howl, they rushed at the carriage.

Well was it for Benningsen that disguised police existed, otherwise he would have made a tragic ending then and there.

It so happened, however, that a number of these secret agents of the Government had been slowly edging their way to the front, with the result that the crowd suddenly found the carriage girt by a ring of men, armed with batons and pistols, who, in the quickness of their appearing, seemed to have sprung from the ground. Their resolute attitude cowed the mob as if by magic, and as the trampling of horse-hoofs and the waving of sabres were now close at hand, to be far from the ministers and not near them, now became the object of the crowd.

Benningsen made no attempt at taking reprisals. At a word from him the cavalry closed in order round the carriage, and, escorted thus, the two ministers made their way to the Winter Palace.

Here, in the ante-chamber where it was their custom to await the pleasure of the Emperor, they found the rest of the ministers assembled, Count Baranoff alone excepted, a very significant exception. They had all received a special summons to attend the Imperial presence, and were looking somewhat downcast, an aspect due to the belief that the coming interview would end in their dismissal.

From the vast crowd that had gathered in front of the palace there came with regular iteration, the cry of

"Down with the Ministry!"—a cry plainly heard by those within the ante-chamber.

"Alexander will throw us to the wolves to save himself," said Plato Zuboff, an old lover of Catharine's, and one of the two actual assassins that had drawn the fatal sash around the throat of her son Paul.

"Think you that he will listen to the cry of the *canaille?*" said Pahlen. "That were to show himself a weakling—to set a premium upon future disorder."

"But the intellectuals, too, are clamouring for our downfall," answered Zuboff. "What! have you not seen to-day's issue of the *Journal de Petersbourg?* Read that."

And producing a copy of the newspaper he directed Pahlen's attention to a column containing an article to the effect that the continuance in office of the regicidal ministry was a public scandal, certain to alienate the sympathies of the European chancelleries. In any other country but Russia, concluded the writer, with a boldness rarely found in the Muscovite press, the ministers would now be on their trial for murder.

"What was the censor doing," frowned Pahlen, "to let language like this go forth to the world?"

"Doing! The will of the Empress Mary," replied Zuboff, in a lower tone, glancing, as he spoke, at the door of the presence chamber, where, as he knew, the ex-Czarina was sitting in conference with her son Alexander. "Her one aim is to send us to the gibbet. Since Paul's death she has never ceased intriguing against us. The picture is her latest weapon. Before daybreak this morning her hirelings were traversing the city with the cry, 'Go, see the picture at the Orphan Asylum.' And when the Black People had seen, and were cursing us, then her agents raised the further cry, 'To the Winter Palace, and shout for the downfall of the Ministry.' You hear them singing her tune."

"And when you remember," chimed in another minister, "who the Governor of the city is, and who is the Chief of the Police, you can understand why the people have been allowed to march at will through the streets."

"Then the hand of Baranoff is in all this," said Pahlen, biting his nails.

"Without doubt," returned the other. "The picture-idea emanated from him, and was eagerly adopted by the Empress. We should have made him a partner in the abdication-plot. We thought to exclude him from the Ministry; it is he who is excluding us. To-day Baranoff triumphs all along the line. We go; he remains."

As the speaker ended, the chamberlain appeared to summon them to the Czar's presence.

Entering the chamber the ministers stood in a respectful semi-circle at a little distance from Alexander, who was seated at a table. Beside him was his mother, the ex-Empress Mary, whose presence was a new feature at ministerial meetings. She scarcely deserved the disrespectful term "beldam," applied to her by Benningsen, for she had not yet reached her forty-second year, and still retained much of the magnificent beauty of her youthful days.

Alexander's face wore a troubled look; it was evident that he and his mother had been divided upon some question, and her barely suppressed smile of triumph showed in whose favour the dispute had ended.

For a few moments the Emperor did not speak. His head was turned to a large window that commanded a view of the vast crowd outside, whose voices had all joined in singing the national anthem.

The Czar's eyes kindled as he listened. His people were with him — whom, then, should he fear?

"'Tis a loyal crowd," said the Empress-mother.

"Loyalty to the Czar," broke in Pahlen, "should also include loyalty to the ministers appointed by him. I make request, Sire, that a certain picture be withdrawn from the front of the Orphan Asylum."

"For what reason?" said the Empress. "Does it not tell the truth?"

"It has made us ministers odious in the eyes of the people. They have attempted our life."

"Terrible!" said the Empress. "One may kill a Czar, but when it comes to killing a minister ——"

She paused, as if unable to express in words the enormity of such a deed.

"But," continued she, "this is a matter over which the Czar hath no jurisdiction. The Orphan Asylum is my own private property, and if I choose to decorate its exterior with a historic picture, who shall say me nay?"

"My mother speaks truly," said Alexander. "If you would have the picture withdrawn, it is to her you must address your persuasions."

"You will choose, Sire," said Pahlen, "between the removal of the picture or the resignation of your chancellor."

- The Empress laughed contemptuously.

"Chancellors are cheap enough!"

The singing of the national anthem, having now come to an end, was superseded by various cries, the most frequent being, "Down with the Ministry!"

"The voice of the people is the voice of God," said the Empress. "Go forth! Show yourself! Give them the answer they desire. Tell them that Czar and justice are the same word."

Her authority over the Emperor was great, and she seemed pleased that the ministers should see it.

He rose, walked to a window and, opening it, stepped out upon the balcony. No sooner was he seen than the air rang with cries of greeting.

The lifting of the Czar's hand was like the lifting of a magic wand. An instant hush fell upon the crowd.

"Good-day, my children."

Like a roar of thunder came the answer —

"Good-day, Little Father!"

"What is your will with me?"

Almost before the words had left the Czar's lips a man, evidently desirous of shaping the people's answer, cried —

"Justice on the regicides!"

The cry was immediately taken up; it rolled from mouth to mouth through the length and breadth of the crowd, and was repeated again and again —

"Justice on the regicides!"

Then, as if surprised by their own boldness, the crowd

became quiet again, waiting for the Czar's answer. Would he grant the request thus irregularly made?

Alexander hesitated for a moment, as if reflecting, and then replied: —

"Depart quietly to your homes. The Czar will do justice."

With simple and touching faith the crowd accepted this assurance of the Imperial tribune.

"The Little Father will punish the murderers! Hourra! Hourra! Now let us go. He will not let his word fall to the ground."

Alexander, believing that his own withdrawal would accelerate the departure of the crowd, turned and entered the council-chamber.

He seemed to have derived fresh courage from this brief interview with his people. His air of restraint had vanished; he spoke with authority and dignity.

"*Messieurs les Ministres*, it must ever be the aim of a ruler to hold by the good-will of his subjects. You see for yourselves that I shall forfeit that good-will by retaining you in office. It behoves me, therefore, for the sake of public peace, to dispense with your services. Perhaps," he continued, as if desirous of softening the humiliation of this dismissal, "perhaps, at some future day — it may be — that —— "

Here he paused, not willing to make a rash promise.

"In thus dismissing us," said Pahlen, "you break your written pledge."

"Not so. My pledge to retain you in office was made dependent upon my father's deposition. But you took from him not his crown only, but his life. As you have broken faith with me, I count it no wrong to break faith with you. Gentlemen, you will retire from the city to your country seats."

"No greater punishment than *that?*" said the Empress.

"And there await my further pleasure," Alexander added.

The discomfited ministers withdrew.

"The slave of his mother," sneered Benningsen.

"Our power is over. Dismissal to-day; to-morrow Siberia, if that old hag has her way."

The ministers gone, Alexander turned a gratified face upon the Empress.

"Mother, you have done well," he said, stooping to kiss her. "Thanks to a picture I enjoy a sense of freedom unknown before. Who is the artist that has done us such good service?"

"The Englishman, Lord Courtenay."

The Czar's face fell. His new-found pleasure vanished as he heard that name.[1]

[1] It may interest those readers, unversed in Russian history, to know that the murder of Paul took place in a manner differing little from that described in Chap. XV., and that the fact, concealed at first from the public, was made known by means of a picture painted by the command of the Empress Mary. The downfall of the Pahlen Ministry immediately followed.

CHAPTER XVII

A VOW TO SLAY!

ON the day following the dismissal of the Pahlen Ministry Wilfrid received a visit at his hotel from Pauline; a welcome visit, for he was not so foolishly enamoured of the Grand Duchess as to be altogether insensible to the charms of other fair ladies, and Pauline with her bright smile looked very charming indeed at that moment.

"I have been on a two days' visit to Peterhof," said she, "and returned only this morning to find all the city talking about you and your pictorial feat. I offer you my congratulations. You are a maker of history," she continued admiringly. "*Ma foi!* if some of the ladies of St. Petersburg could only see me now! How they would envy me my friendship with *le brav' Anglais!*"

Wilfrid's mind turned to the one lady. Would *she* feel envy, he wondered, could she have seen Pauline at this moment in confidential chat with him?

"Now, at last," continued Pauline, "I have learned why for three months you have lived an unsocial life, working mysteriously in an attic at the top of the hotel, any why, whenever I have called, you have looked cross at my coming, and glad of my going; and ——"

"I assure you, Baroness," began Wilfrid, laughing, "that ——"

"Hush!" said Pauline, raising her forefinger playfully. "Don't say it wasn't so. I am not blaming you. You were engaged on a noble work."

Naturally Pauline was all curiosity to know whence he had learned the true account of Paul's death. Wilfrid enlightened her; but, desirous of keeping his love-story a secret, he referred to the Empress's intermediary as "a lady whose name I do not know, because she declined to give it" — herein stating nothing but what was true.

"The Empress Mary," he explained, "was very desirous that I should repeat the feat done by me at Paris. There, though my paint-brush failed in upsetting a government, it might succeed here in upsetting a ministry; and, you see, it has done so."

"But how came you to hit off the likenesses so well, for I am told the faces are perfect portraits?"

"That's easily explained. You know that for the space of a fortnight Paul's body lay in state in St. George's Hall. Twice a day the Court and the ministers heard mass beside the bier. By favour of the Empress I was provided with a coign of vantage where, unobserved, I could take surreptitious sketches of the ministers, to be reproduced on canvas. When the picture was finished, I placed, by preconcerted arrangement, a blue lamp in my attic window, and that same night the picture was fetched away by two men. Now you know the whole story," he said in conclusion. "My patroness, the Empress, I have never seen; and, as for her fair intermediary, I have seen her but once only, namely on that strange night in the Michaelhof."

"But," objected Pauline, "if you attended the masses held in St. George's Hall, you must have seen the Empress Mary every day."

"Doubtless, and the young Czarina as well, and the Imperial Duchesses. But I don't call it seeing a woman when her face is covered with a mourning veil."

In truth, Wilfrid, from his secret place of espial, had breathed anything but a blessing upon the heavy veils worn by the Court ladies on the occasion in question, since the wearing of them prevented him from identifying the mysterious Duchess who, he doubted not, formed one of the group.

"And Ouvaroff, you say, is Paul's son?" remarked Pauline. "A natural son, of course? It was long suspected — the likeness between the two was so remarkable — but Ouvaroff himself appears to have been almost the last to learn it, and that at a dreadful moment. Poor Ouvaroff! No wonder he looked so ghastly and wild next morning! Do you know he has not been seen since that day?"

"A pity that, for there was a matter I would fain discuss with him," said Wilfrid, thinking of the night at the Silver Birch.

"No one knows where he is. Some say that in penitence he has turned monk." And then, coming back to the subject of the picture again, she continued, "And you didn't fear to set your name to the picture?"

"Fear! Do you take me for Alexander?"

Pauline thought it prudent to ignore this reflection upon her hero. She could not help inwardly acknowledging that while Alexander had walked in darkness, assenting to a course of deceit in the matter of his father's death, Wilfrid, though well aware that grim fortresses and Siberian mines awaited those who should give umbrage to ministers, had not shrunk from proclaiming the truth in the light of day.

"Three months' toil!" she said, her eyes round with wonder. "Did you do all this without hope of reward? from a mere abstract love of justice?"

"No—o! not exactly. I am to receive a sort of — of *douceur*," said Wilfrid. "Very much *douce*," he added, with a smile. "It's nature? Your pardon, Baroness. You shall know, but not yet. After it has been received."

Pauline thought Wilfrid was becoming very mysterious all at once. It was hard for her to put a curb upon her curiosity. After a short pause she murmured with a glad light in her eyes: —

"Well, thanks to you, Benningsen and Pahlen have had to go."

"True," grumbled Wilfrid, "but it's rather mortifying to find that one result of my work is to confirm in office the very man whose confusion both you and I desire to see. Count Baranoff, having had no part in Paul's murder, is not included in the list of disgraced ministers, and still retains his post."

"But not for long," replied Pauline. "His power is on the wane. His counsels are already being ignored by the Czar."

"In what way?"

"As regards the war with England. What! you do not know? Ah! I am forgetting. The story is not in the newspapers, since our editors must publish only what is pleasing. Of course, living at an Embassy, I often learn matters unknown to the outside public. Well, here's a secret for you. Our Russian admiral, knowing himself to be no match for the hero of the Nile, has declined an engagement, and is coming fast to Cronstadt. 'Tis the old story; leaky ships, cracked cannon, and an unpaid crew, sullen to the verge of mutiny. The result of this flight is to place all the towns on the Finland Gulf at the mercy of the English guns. Nay, the very gate of the city, Cronstadt itself, is liable to bombardment. Hence, let Baranoff protest as he may, the Czar is bent on making peace. So magnificently sure were your Government that victory would crown their arms, that along with their fleet they sent an envoy with plenipotentiary power to arrange the terms of a treaty. That envoy will arrive at St. Petersburg in the course of a few days. Should peace be established, and there is little doubt that it will be, the envoy remains here in the character of British Ambassador."

"Who is this envoy?"

"Lord St. Helens. What! you know him?" asked Pauline, observing Wilfrid's peculiar smile.

"My uncle."

"Your uncle?" she repeated, incredulously.

"My mother's brother. Baroness, you are indeed the bearer of good news."

The uncle in question was one who held, among other views, that the only business worthy of an English peer is the study of diplomacy; and hence he had often growled at his nephew's taste for painting and swordsmanship.

It would be pleasant now to show the old gentleman that his nephew's swordsmanship had defeated the policy of Baranoff at Berlin, while a painting had largely contributed to the downfall of a Russian Ministry. And both these events within the space of six months! Could the most accomplished diplomatist have done more in the time?

"With the coming peace," said Pauline, "the first half of my work is accomplished: Czar and Consul fight side by side no more. I call it my work, because it *is* mine. If you have wrecked the Czar's Ministry, I have had the chief hand in shaping his war-policy. How? Ah! that is my secret," she continued, with a peculiar smile. "The second and more difficult part of my task now remains — namely, to set the Czar in arms against Napoleon."

Wilfrid longed to give her a severe lecture, but refrained, convinced of its uselessness. It was clear from her words that she was still pursuing her course of working in secret against her father's policy, an undaughterly action on her part, and one with which Wilfrid could not sympathise.

"But a truce to politics!" exclaimed Pauline. "Have you received your ticket yet from Prince Sumaroff?"

"I have yet to learn who that grandee is."

"Here's ignorance, forsooth, from a three months' resident in St. Petersburg! Why, Prince Sumaroff's palace and gardens by the Nevka are one of the sights of St. Petersburg. A fortnight from to-day he gives a fancy dress ball, to which you are certain to be invited, by reason of your rank."

"How so?"

"The Prince's aim is to gather to the ball every titled personage in St. Petersburg, whether native or foreign, ranking from baron upwards. 'I am perhaps prejudiced,' he is credited with saying, 'but for me, mankind begins with the rank of baron.' So, you see, the ball is to consist of the *crème de la crème* of Society. To add to its splendour, Alexander himself and the young Czarina have consented to be present."

"And the Court ladies?"

Pauline replied in the affirmative, wondering at the quickness with which Wilfrid put the question. Then divining the cause, she added with a smile —

"So, possibly, you may meet your fair *incognita* there."

This was the hope that had just entered Wilfrid's mind. Since the Duchess was one of the Court ladies, what more likely than that she would be present at this fête in company with the Czarina? What woman, especially a Russian woman, can resist the attraction of a dance? Now that the Pahlen Ministry had fallen, it would be a matter of honour with her to redeem her word by bestowing upon him the promised kiss; and since every guest must be masked, such disguise would enable him to approach the Duchess without attracting attention or creating suspicion.

To this fête, then, it behoved him to go, and next day he received a ticket of invitation.

At nightfall there came something still more agreeable, in the shape of a visit from the blind Alexis Voronetz, who brought with him a pretty blue scarf embroidered with silver.

"Wear this at the masquerade."

And without any more words he withdrew, ignoring Wilfrid's request for an explanation, though, in truth, one was scarcely required. From whom did this favour come, if not from the Duchess? It was a proof that she intended to be present at the approaching fête, and was desirous of fixing some token upon Wilfrid to enable her to distinguish him from among the crowd of masked dancers.

Thirteen days yet before he would meet her! How was he to live through them all?

The first four, measured by Wilfrid's feelings, seemed more like four months: on the fifth, however, came a welcome diversion in the arrival of Lord St. Helens, the British plenipotentiary, sent to consider the peace proposals of the Czar.

There was assigned to him and his suite a stately mansion on the Nevski Prospekt, at the point where it is crossed by the Fontanka Canal.

Wilfrid lost no time in calling upon the old gentleman, who was delighted to see his nephew, and proud likewise of his late achievements in the political arena.

"Ah! my boy," said he, "since you can do great things in an unofficial capacity, what would you do as a diplomatist?"

"Much less," replied Wilfrid drily.

Lord St. Helens had frequent interviews with Count Panine, the new chancellor of the Empire, and from each interview he returned more hopeful. He condescended now and again to favour Wilfrid, under the seal of secrecy, with the course taken by the negotiations.

"Peace is agreed to," he remarked, upon the seventh day after his arrival. "Nelson will be disappointed at having to take his ships home again. The Russians think so much of Cronstadt that naturally our admiral is burning to show that their much-vaunted fortress is not impregnable. Its capture would be the crowning-piece of his life."

But a man in love has no sense of historic perspective. Living in a pleasant day-dream Wilfrid paid little attention to his uncle's political remarks. A single golden hair from the head of the Duchess had more interest for him than the departure of the British fleet from Revel. It was often in his mind to tell his uncle the story of the Duchess, but yet somehow he forbore. Supposing, in spite of the diplomatic caution upon which he prided himself, Lord St. Helens should, through some inadvertence, let fall a remark concerning her in the presence of any of the Czar's ministers, she might receive from Court circles a supervision not at all agreeable to her. Her going to the masquerade, for example, might be stopped.

"Two days more," he thought, "and from her own lips I shall hear her name and story. I shall know then whether the case warrants the taking of my uncle into confidence."

On the morning of the day fixed for the masquerade Wilfrid, calling upon his uncle, found the latter looking so grave that he thought at first the peace-proposals must have fallen through. He soon found that the envoy's gravity was due to a very different cause.

"Is your swordsmanship as good as ever?"

"I shall be happy to meet the man that questions it," replied Wilfrid.

"You are likely to do so. Have you seen Prince Ouvaroff since you came to St. Petersburg?"

"Once, and that for a moment only, on the morning of

'Alexander's accession. The Prince has not been seen since that day. Taken to a monastic life, some say."

"Nothing of the sort. He has been living quietly at his country seat in company with two or three of the best fencing-masters in Europe. During the past three months he has spent the greater part of every day in nothing but sword-practice. Yesterday he returned to St. Petersburg."

"With what object?"

"To kill you."

Wilfrid's smile implied that the Prince was welcome to try.

"He evidently imagines he has some grievance against you. I don't ask for confidences, but I suppose some woman is the cause of it all?"

"It's probable. He thinks that — but no matter what he thinks," muttered Wilfrid, with a dark frown, as he recalled the night at the Silver Birch. If Ouvaroff could believe *that* of the Duchess, there would be a pleasure in slaying him.

"Well," continued Lord St. Helens, "Ouvaroff now considers himself sufficiently skilled in his art, and it's his intention to be present at this masquerade with the object of forcing a quarrel upon you."

"You seem pretty well versed in his movements."

"I have learned all this from a friendly minister, whose name I am not at liberty to disclose. He was not aware that you are my nephew, and referred to you as that eccentric Englishman, Lord Courtenay. He seems to have a kindly feeling towards you, for he suggested to me that to avoid a possible scandal, it might be as well if I were to exert my influence in persuading you to leave St. Petersburg secretly."

"'Twas very kind of him! And your answer?"

"Can you not guess it? — 'Our house does not breed cowards, Monsieur le Comte. It is not our fashion to run away from any man. My nephew has no quarrel with Ouvaroff, but if Ouvaroff be bent upon forcing a quarrel with him, he'll find he has the devil to deal with.'"

"Precisely my sentiments," commented Wilfrid.

CHAPTER XVIII

THE night, long-looked for, had come, and Wilfrid, throwing a cloak over his fancy costume, was driven off in a covered carriage to the French Embassy, in fulfilment of a promise to escort Pauline to the masquerade.

While waiting for her in the entrance hall he was somewhat struck by the oddity of the situation that he, the nephew of Great Britain's representative, should be awaiting the daughter of one who stood for a power hostile to Great Britain, a thought quickly cut short by the entering of Pauline, fresh from the hands of her maid.

Naturally the first thing each did was to look at the dress of the other.

Pauline showed over Wilfrid's costume the simple delight of a schoolgirl. And in truth he presented a majestic figure, equipped, as he was, in a lofty silver helmet with silver wings, a corselet of silver mail, a rich baldric, a horn, a sword, and all the accompaniments of a Norse warrior; his look and bearing gave proof of his descent: he was the very ideal of a Viking chief.

Pauline was moved with a thrill of pride at having for her escort one so handsome in person and dress as Wilfrid, while he in turn felt a similar pleasure as he viewed Pauline's graceful and stately figure. She was dressed to represent Night, in a dainty robe of darkest blue glittering with stars, a silver crescent gleaming in her raven hair.

Conscious of Wilfrid's look of admiration Pauline coloured with secret pleasure, becoming somewhat pale again as she noticed his eyes resting upon the figure of an Imperial crown embroidered upon her sleeve.

" A secret token by which you are to be known to some favoured one? "

Her smiling assent gave Wilfrid a momentary pang of jealousy, a feeling strange and illogical; for, seeing that he had his own lady to meet, what did Pauline's doings matter to him?

" I am as you are," said she, touching the scarf upon his left arm. " That is not worn without a purpose? "

Offering his arm Wilfrid escorted her to the carriage, and they drove off to the masquerade.

On the northern side of that river-arm known as the Great Nevka, and fronting the Aptekarski Island, there now stands a long line of Government buildings, whose site in the opening years of the nineteenth century was occupied by the Sumaroff Palace and its beautiful gardens, gardens ample enough to furnish a camping ground for all the Czar's armies.

On this particular night, a warm lovely night in July, the halls and gardens of the palace were gay with a throng of picturesquely-clad masqueraders, drawn from the noblest blood in the land.

Some good people had affected to be scandalised at the holding of such a fête, with Paul but four months dead. Their criticisms vanished, however, when it became known that Prince Sumaroff had not only obtained Alexander's sanction for the fête, but a promise also that the Imperial family itself would be present.

" There is a time to mourn and a time to dance," had been the Emperor's remark — so it was said — and the time for mourning might be considered as fairly past.

On arriving at the palace Wilfrid and Pauline, both closely masked, entered the reception room, where their cards were scrutinised by liveried officials, after which the two were free to go whither they would. Their steps were immediately directed to the famous ballroom, known as the Hall of Mirrors, the glory of the Sumaroff Palace. Crystal columns sustained the roof of this hall, a hall that seemed far more spacious than its actual size, due to the fact that its walls consisted of mirrors, whose multiplying reflections created the illusion of endless vistas of twinkling lights and swaying dancers. Rare flowers glowing from porphyry vases perfumed the air with their fragrance. Here and there were fountains that diffused a refreshing coolness around. The tall windows, ranged along a colonnaded wall, were left open to the night, revealing the moonlit gardens, fair with marble terraces and statuary, gleaming white amid the dark foliage.

Wilfrid, familiar as he was with the various capitals of Europe, had seen nothing to rival the splendour of this ballroom, which, filled as it was with a crowd of masqueraders, all dressed in fanciful costumes, made a picture full of colour, brilliance, and movement.

The gigantic bronze chandelier, hanging from the middle of the ceiling was a superb work of art, radiant as a sun, a mass of flowers and foliage, and — what? Wilfrid turned his ear to listen more attentively: yes, from it came the orchestral music that regulated the steps of the dancers. The chandelier was large enough both to hold and to hide the musicians!

"Big as it is," said Pauline, "the one in the Hermitage is bigger."

The dance — it was the first of the night — had come to an end, and while a few couples had seated themselves, the greater number were slowly promenading around the ballroom. As they passed by in gay talk Wilfrid scanned the shape of each fair masker, and tried to catch the sound of her voice in the hope that he might hear the Duchess speaking; nor did he neglect to hold his arm in such a position that his lady's favour might be clearly seen.

Now, during this promenading, Wilfrid's attention was struck by a tall gentleman — he was more than six feet high — clad in the glittering dress of a Crusader. This individual, while going by, fixed a keen glance both upon Pauline and Wilfrid. Through the holes of his mask a pair of steely blue eyes seemed to flash anger; the next moment their owner had passed by.

"Prince Ouvaroff, or my name isn't Courtenay," murmured Wilfrid.

"Which is Ouvaroff?" asked Pauline.

"He in the dress of a Crusader," replied Wilfrid, indicating the receding figure.

"Yes, that is Ouvaroff."

She spoke with a sort of hesitancy that gave Wilfrid the impression that while she herself did not really believe that it *was* Ouvaroff, she was desirous that Wilfrid should! An odd impression, certainly, but there it was.

The music, suspended after the first dance, now started again. Eager as Wilfrid was to begin his search for the Duchess, he nevertheless realised that it would be unmannerly to escort Pauline to the ball without offering to tread one measure at least with her.

"The second dance is beginning. It is a waltz. Shall we —— "

Pauline's manner was odd, not to say perplexing. She hesitated; nay, Wilfrid fancied he could detect a look of fear in her eyes; then she gave a grateful smile, and the next moment to the sound of sweetest melody she was floating around in the dreamy mazes of a waltz, the very dance in which Wilfrid had no superior.

The waltz is the most voluptuous of dances, and Pauline drank fully of its charms. She had no need to look where she was going. Wilfrid's touch, strong yet tender, steered her gracefully and lightly through the moving throng. The ballroom, the lights, the dancers — all seemed to vanish. She and Wilfrid were the sole beings in a Paradise of their own. With her lips parted into an unconscious smile she yielded herself to the delicious spell of intoxication; her eyes half-closed, she rested on his arm, swaying to and fro on a billowy sea of pleasure. Could her wish at that moment have had its fulfilment this dance would have lasted for ever.

Wilfrid, to his shame be it said, felt little of this fascination; his pulse beat, perhaps, two or three above the normal; no more. His attention to Pauline was more apparent than real; his mind was dwelling on the Duchess, and whenever any lady, golden-haired and blue-eyed, floated past, she was sure to receive from him a scrutinising glance.

Then came a sudden surprise.

"*Baroness!*"

The word, though but faintly whispered, was nevertheless heard not only by the person for whose ear it was intended, but also by Wilfrid. The voice was a man's, and it was marked, so Wilfrid thought, by an intonation expressive of reproach at her evident pleasure in the waltz.

Wilfrid looked around, curious to discover who had been the speaker. Among the masked forms circling about them was that very Crusader whom he half-suspected to be Ouvaroff. Doubtless it was he who had spoken; at any rate, the voice was not unlike that of the Prince.

..He glanced at his partner, but Pauline, though conscious that Wilfrid had heard the name, made no remark, and Wilfrid, responsive to her mood, refrained from comment. It seemed, however, a safe conclusion to draw that the speaker, whether Ouvaroff or not, was the man in whom Pauline was interested, and that he had recognised her by the sign upon her sleeve.

The name had roused Pauline from her dreamy state; she continued dancing, but its pleasure was gone. The little hand within his own was trembling very much. The waltz over, he led her to a seat.

"I will release you now; it is time you looked for — for *her!*" said Pauline, indicating the scarf upon his arm. "Please, go," she added, as he hesitated.

There was something odd in her manner, a sort of defying and scorning of herself, and yet withal a touch of sadness in her voice, as though, in spite of her command, she was reluctant to part from him.

"Farewell, Baroness — for a time," said Wilfrid, and with a bow he turned away, leaving her seated upon a lounge.

He did not at once quit the ballroom, but, making his way to one of the open windows that gave egress to the gardens, stood there in a somewhat conspicuous position, his embroidered favour clearly showing, to the end that if the Duchess should be in the ballroom, it might certify her of his presence.

While standing there he could not help wondering what had caused Pauline to take so strange an interest in Ouvaroff — that is, supposing the Crusader to *be* Ouvaroff. What was implied by his whispered word, "Baroness!" so meaningly emphasised? Reproach that she should be found dancing with one so dishonourable as Wilfrid? Had he seen Pauline recently and given her *his* version of the affair at the Silver Birch, openly avowing that he would take vengeance upon Wilfrid? Was Pauline going to use her influence over Ouvaroff with the object of getting him to desist from the attempt? If so, she had chosen a strange time and a strange place for endeavours that, however well-meant on her part, would not be very acceptable to Wilfrid, who much preferred to punish with a little blood-letting the presumed traducer of the fair and innocent Duchess.

From time to time he turned his eyes in the direction of Pauline, who, seated where he had left her, seemed intent only on watching him.

Then it suddenly struck him that, so long as he stood there, Pauline would not be approached by Ouvaroff. Not wishing, therefore, to deprive her of the desired interview, Wilfrid walked slowly out upon the terrace, thinking that, if the Duchess were really in the ballroom, and had seen the embroidered scarf, she would perhaps, after a reasonable time, follow in his wake.

From the terrace a flight of steps descended to the palace gardens, now in all the glory of their summer foliage. Voices and laughter from near and far showed that many of the masqueraders preferred the purer air of night to the atmosphere of the ballroom. And then, too, the gardens with their shady walks, winding here and there beside silver lakes, formed an ideal place for love-making.

As he did not appear to be followed by the Duchess, Wilfrid resolved to make a tour of these gardens in the hope of meeting her.

Rapidly traversing this or that path, as chance directed, he came in the course of his search upon a terrace over-hanging the Neva. A little group was looking down upon the smooth-flowing water.

"There goes my fan!" said a fair masker, lamenting

the loss of that article, accidentally dropped by her into the river. " A hundred roubles floating away."

" Ask the Baroness Runö to restore it you to-morrow," said a gentleman beside her.

This chance mention of Pauline's name caused Wilfrid to listen for a moment.

" I don't understand —— " began the lady.

" Why, look you," replied her companion, " she goes to-morrow to her summer residence, the castle on her little island of Runö, some three miles down the river."

" You mean that —— "

" The current of the river strikes directly upon the eastern side of Runö, upon the shore called the Silver Strand. Things carried down by the river are always — "

" Always? "

" Well, say usually, cast ashore upon this same strand. There's a romantic story that a former Prince Sumaroff, being in love with a daughter of a former Baron Runö, used to communicate with her by putting a letter into the cleft of a stick and throwing it into the river. An hour afterwards the lady would be reading the message. So, perhaps, your fan —— "

An interesting anecdote, but as it had nothing to do with the whereabouts of the Duchess, Wilfrid passed on, coming finally to a lonely and quiet spot, a spot as far as he could judge, the most remote from the palace. Just as he was on the point of turning back, his ear was suddenly caught by the sound of voices coming from the other side of some shrubbery against which he was standing.

" The Neva's waters are deep! "

It was not the oddity of the speaker's remark so much as his voice that attracted Wilfrid. That voice he could have sworn to out of ten thousand. The speaker was none other than Izak, the driver, the companion of his long wintry journey from Kowno to St. Petersburg. What was he doing in these gardens upon a night when entrance was denied to all save persons of rank? Perhaps he had left off his profession of driver to become one of the many servitors of Prince Sumaroff.

Peering warily through the shrubbery Wilfrid caught a glimpse of four men, three sitting upon a rustic seat and a fourth, Izak, standing in the attitude of addressing them. All were masked, and all clad in the chocolate-coloured velvet and gold lace that marked the livery of Prince Sumaroff. But something told Wilfrid that, in spite of this attire, Izak was no lackey; the dress was assumed for that night only. The man no longer carried himself with an obsequious and servile air. He spoke with authority, and even with dignity, leading Wilfrid to suspect that he was a spy of the Government, and one occupying as high a post as is bestowed upon these agents. Desirous as Wilfrid was of finding the Duchess, there was something in the talk of these men that fixed him to the spot.

" The Neva's waters are deep ! " repeated Izak.

" Hush, speak low," said one of the men.

" We are safe enough here," returned Izak. " No one will wander so far as this from the palace. That is why I have chosen this nook for our little meeting. Now, what would you say if I were to talk of a thousand roubles to each ? "

" That you are lying ! "

" I guessed you would say so. You see what I am lifting with my hands ? "

" Earth ! "

" Earth it is, our common mother. I place it upon my head, and what does that signify ? "

" That you are on oath."

" So; the most solemn oath known among us. By this, then, know that I am speaking the truth when I say that, if we do it, a thousand roubles to each will be our reward."

An interval of silence followed this promise.

" How did he find out that she was here ? " asked one of the men presently.

" Her mask accidentally slipped off."

" But if it's now on her face again how are we to recognise her ? "

" By her dress. There are five hundred ladies here

to-night, so I'm told, but only one with her costume.
She wears a grey domino ——"

"So do many other ladies."

"Let me finish. There *are* many grey dominoes here
— true, but look well at them, and you will see that their
material is velvet, silk, or something equally costly,
whereas hers is modest serge trimmed with silver cord,
the simplest costume of the whole ball. Her mask, too,
is of grey silk."

"What made her venture here to-night."

"She wishes to see the Czarina."

"And she may be having her wish at this moment."

"Hardly. She must wait till the supper-hour comes."

"Why so?"

"O silly! Aren't all the ladies masked? No one
knows who's who till the general unmasking at supper-
time."

"And when she sees the Czarina — what then?"

"She's bent on giving her a letter. It's our business
to see that it be not given, and the sooner we set about
our work the better."

Thus advised, the three men rose and moved off, Izak
leading the way, bent, as his words showed, on preventing some girl or woman from giving a letter to the
Empress; but how was it possible to stop its presentation
without the employment of questionable methods?

Wilfrid by chance had evidently lighted upon some
sinister plot. Ever ready to oppose knavery, he put aside
the Duchess for a time, determined to follow the men,
and to defend, at the sword's point if necessary, the
woman against whom this plot was directed.

Now, had the men's way lain parallel with the course
of the shrubbery, it would have been an easy matter for
Wilfrid to shadow them; but it so happened that they
turned off in a line almost at right angles to this thicket,
which was too densely set to permit the passage of a
human body. Wilfrid ran, now to the right and now to
the left, and when at last he *did* come upon a gap the
men were out of sight.

With no clear idea as to the direction taken by them,

Wilfrid, nevertheless, hurried forward, but his attempt to discover them proved a failure.

His good fortune took him again to the terrace fronting the river and there, a few paces off, with one hand lightly resting upon the marble balustrade, stood a graceful figure, dressed in a simple grey domino, with silver cording. Silent and motionless she stood, as if absorbed in the beauty of the night.

Wilfrid's mind felt a sudden relief. Thank heaven, the knaves had failed, so far, in their purpose; the lady, whoever she might be, was still safe, and would continue to be so, as long as his trenchant blade swung by his side.

At Wilfrid's approach the lady turned her head, and, as her eyes fell upon the blue scarf, she gave a start as of recognition.

That start raised a sudden hope in his mind, a hope confirmed as he received through the holes of her grey mask the attentive glance of a pair of dark blue eyes.

Wilfrid thrilled, first with pleasure, and then with amazement, as he recognised that the lady, sought for by Izak and his confederates, was none other than his own duchess!

CHAPTER XIX

THE PRINCESS'S KISS

"Fair lady," said Wilfrid, bowing as he spoke, "you are alone, though it be the unwritten law of a masquerade that every one must have a companion."

"Then are you breaking that law," replied the lady; "for you, too, seem alone."

"A Courtenay is ambitious, you see; he will have for his companion none but the fairest."

"And have you not found her in Pauline de Vaucluse?"

Her tone was slightly satirical. Had she seen him in the ballroom, he wondered, and recognised with whom he was dancing?

"Your highness, it was not for Pauline de Vaucluse that I wrought for three months in a solitary attic."

"No; it was for a wronged and widowed empress," replied the Duchess, feigning not to see his meaning. "Lord Courtenay, the Empress is unspeakably grateful for your good work. The one desire of her heart was to see the fall of the wicked Ministry, and, thanks to you, she has been enabled to see it. You wanted no reward, but the Empress prays you to name one."

"Why, I thought I *had* named one."

"Foolish Englishman," she murmured, averting her head, "have you not forgotten *that?*"

And then, as if wishful to divert his thoughts from herself, she said, with her eyes set upon the river: —

"Have you any scene like this in England?"

Patriotic as he was, Wilfrid was fain to confess that his own land could never at any time show a scene so fairy-like as that presented by St. Petersburg on a midsummer night.

It was now on the stroke of twelve, and though the glow of the setting sun had scarcely faded from the western sky, yet the eastern horizon was already becoming shot with golden streaks. This intermingling of dusk and dawn illumined by the glory of a full moon, produced a light soft and clear, poetic and dreamlike.

The river flowed, silent and majestic, breaking here and there into silver ripples. Its long line of quays and palaces, fading away in dim perspective, seemed like the fabrics of a vision too lovely to be real.

Enchanting as was the scene, it was made still more so to Wilfrid by the presence of the young Duchess, attractive both by her beauty and by the romantic air of mystery surrounding her.

It filled him with pleasure to learn that while he had been seeking *her,* she had been seeking *him.*

"I saw you leave the ballroom," she observed, "and as soon as I could conveniently do so, I stole away. Not finding you in —— "

She paused. They were no longer alone. Merely a gallant and his inamorata in close conversation, and apparently so enwrapped in each other, as to be oblivious of everybody else. Nevertheless, the Duchess turned her face riverward again; and, evidently fearing lest her voice, if overheard, should lead to her recognition, she refrained from speaking till the two had fairly passed by.

"I fear a spy in every one I see to-night," she murmured.

"Is our meeting, then, a crime?"

"My enemies would endeavour to make it such."

"Let me know who these enemies are, that I may make them mine, too."

"Shall I take you at your word?" she said gravely. "Yes? Then mark. The one whose enmity I have most cause to dread is the woman with whom you have danced to-night."

"Pauline de Vaucluse."

"None other."

"That is a hard saying."

"But a true one."

"That Pauline de Vaucluse would use this meeting to

your hurt, and to mine? Nay, I cannot so think of the Baroness. I would that I could bring your highness face to face with her for a few minutes. I feel certain that such interview would end in your becoming the best of friends."

"Having full proof of her guilt, I have no desire for such an interview," she answered coldly.

It seemed clear from this that the Duchess must be known to Pauline. What act had Pauline committed against the Duchess that it should be called by the strong term "guilt"?

"That your Highness *has* enemies," he said, after an interval of silence, "is, alas! but too true. They, or rather their agents, are here to-night."

"How do you know this?"

"Concealed behind some shrubbery I overheard four men talking."

"Of me? But not knowing my name how could you tell I was the person meant?"

"Because they spoke of a lady wearing a grey mask and a grey serge domino trimmed with silver cord, such as I see yours to be. One question will show whether you are the lady meant by them. Tell me, are you not seeking to present a letter to the Czarina?"

The Duchess looked a little oddly at Wilfrid, as if surprised at this knowledge on his part.

"It is true. I have upon me a letter addressed to the Czarina," she murmured, speaking with a certain hesitancy.

"At this very moment these four men are looking for you, determined to prevent you, by means fair or otherwise, from giving that letter to the Czarina."

"Lord Courtenay, you must not leave me till I am safe in the ballroom again. This letter must not be taken from us." — The "us" thrilled Wilfrid. — "I say us," she continued, with a smile, as pleasant as it was mysterious, "because the letter is of vital consequence to you as well as to me."

"Your Highness is safe with me; have no fear. But since you seem to live in an atmosphere of peril, why not seek to escape from it?"

" How ? "

" There is a way open to you," said Wilfrid, with a sudden and bold inspiration. " The British Embassy is about to be re-established at St. Petersburg. Let that be your asylum. Come with me this night. Tell the Ambassador your secret history. Make him the guardian of your person. Under the protection of England you will be safe."

" Lord Courtenay," she said decisively, " yours is an impossible remedy."

" I will believe so only when you have proved it to be such."

" Were I to take refuge there, the Czar would demand my surrender."

" Very likely; and my good uncle, the Ambassador, would meet the demand with a refusal."

" I think not. Let the refusal be given, however; that would not prevent the Czar from entering with his troops."

" Not so. Such an act were an outrage upon the law of nations. The Czar would have to face an immediate renewal of the war with England."

" And he would be ready to face it, were I to act as you suggest."

Was she really a person so great in the political world that her detention at the British Embassy would be a sufficient cause for war between two empires? It was an amazing statement, and yet her air, quiet and grave, somehow carried conviction with it.

" Your Highness," said Wilfrid, with a sort of reproachful despair, " have you not mystified me long enough? May I not know who you are? You promised at our last meeting to reveal to me your name and history."

" Let me redeem my word, then."

She sat down within a hemicycle that formed part of the parapet of the terrace, and motioned Wilfrid to a place beside her.

At their back flowed the shining river; before them, and bordering the whole length of the terrace, rose a grove of dark pines whose leaves rippled to the night-breeze. From the far-off ballroom came the faint sound of the orchestral music.

Though attentive to every word spoken by the Duchess, Wilfrid, mindful of the four men in the chocolate-coloured liveries, kept a watchful eye upon all sides, though he doubted very much whether the quartette would show themselves so long as he was with her.

Now and again groups of laughing masqueraders would make their appearance; and, at their approach, the Duchess either suspended her talk or continued in a whisper till the revellers had gone by.

"I am at your service, Lord Courtenay. Question me."

"First, then, explain the puzzling mystery of how I came to save your life without retaining any remembrance of that event."

"That is easily answered. More than eight years ago — I was then a girl of fourteen — my sister and I were staying at the Castle of Silverstein in Saxony. One evening, among other diversions, there happened to be a series of *tableaux vivants,* in one of which my sister and I took part, each clad in the garb of a forester; and," added the Duchess, with a touch of vanity, "if all that was said of us be true, we made a pair of handsome lads. — The next morning, before breakfast, my sister, always full of mischief, proposed an especial piece of daring. 'Let us put on the dress we wore in the *tableau vivant,* and take a walk outside the castle grounds.' I laughingly consented; and, escaping the eyes of our elders, we two girls sallied forth in male garb. The keeper of the lodge, past whom we boldly marched, failed to penetrate our disguise, and doubtless wondered why we laughed so, when at a safe distance from the gate. It was a sunny morning, and we turned our steps to the forest that lay eastward of the castle. Forgetful of time, we wandered onward till at last it began to dawn upon us that we were a long way from home, and were, perhaps, doing a foolish thing, for we now suddenly remembered that a bear had recently been seen in this wood.

"Scarcely had the thought seized us when we actually

came upon two little black cubs rolling over each other at the foot of a hollow tree. The sight turned our blood cold, for one glance showed that this hollow trunk was a bear's den, and we did not doubt that its savage tenant was not far off. Then came a heavy pattering upon the fallen leaves, and a moment afterwards the mother bear appeared, growling and making directly for us. Too terrified to move, my sister and I clung to each other, uttering wild screams."

Wilfrid himself could now have related the sequel, but preferred to hear it from her lips. It was a pleasure to listen to her voice. The Duchess saw his smile, and smiled in turn.

"Need I tell you what happened? The report of a musket rang out, and the bear rolled over dead. The shot had been fired by a young man who came forward with a smile in which I fancied there lurked a trace of contempt. Of course, Lord Courtenay, you took us for what we seemed to be, namely, two youths, and as such, we doubtless looked very silly, screaming and making no attempt to save ourselves; and yet, perhaps, if you had been without a musket, you might not have looked so brave as you did just then."

"Quite true, your Highness."

"Naturally, we did not like to say that we were girls, and so, after thanking you, we hastened off and reached Silverstein without our escapade having become known.

"Now, in our confusion we had forgotten to ask the name of our deliverer.

"'We must try to find out who he is,' said my sister, 'and show our gratitude by something more than words.'

"So, later in the day, and this time dressed in a manner suitable to good girls, we drove forth in our carriage accompanied by our duenna.

"Fortune favoured us, for as we were proceeding along the high road that skirts one side of the forest, my sister pressed my arm with the words, 'There he is.'

"Sure enough it was our rescuer coming out of the Kronprinz, a pretty little hostelry by the roadside. He mounted a phaeton that had been standing at the inn door, and drove off. The innkeeper was known to us, and from him we learned that the stranger was an English nobleman, Viscount Courtenay by name, who had been staying in the neighbourhood during the previous fortnight. He had received the Prince's permission to shoot upon the castle lands and to fish in its waters.

"We hesitated to put further questions, lest our duenna should ask us the reason for our interest in this stranger; but as soon as we returned to the Schloss we got from the library a book on the British Peerage, and learned what little we could concerning Lord Courtenay, his family, and his ancestry.

"We went on the following day to take a look at the bear's den; this time armed foresters accompanied us. While I was walking round the spot, my eye was caught by a sparkle amid the fallen leaves. I stooped, and picked up a golden locket. We knew at once by whom it had been lost when we found within a miniature of yourself."

Wilfrid had often wondered what had become of that locket, a locket he had ordered to be wrought after a special design, intending it as a gift to his mother.

" 'The restoring of this locket,' said my sister, 'will give us an opportunity of speaking with Lord Courtenay. We will take it to the "Kronprinz," and tell him that we are the two youths whom he saved from the bear.' But on coming to the inn we found you had that very day left for England; so the locket remained with me."

"And you have kept it ever since?"

For answer, she pointed to her throat, and Wilfrid saw the long lost locket hanging from a slender gold chain.

"Is it necessary at this late day to restore it?" she asked, making as if to detach the locket from its chain.

But Wilfrid gently restrained her.

"It could not be in a fairer place."

The Duchess's story cast light upon some matters hitherto dark; it explained, for example, her recognition of him at the inn of the Silver Birch.

And she had kept his miniature for more than eight years, ever since she was a girl of fourteen! It was upon her breast now! Was that its usual place? If so, and if the fact had become known to Baranoff, it would explain why that minister had concluded that the Duchess must be in love with Wilfrid; if love, a seemingly hopeless case, since it was not probable that she would ever meet again the man that had saved her life. Did she often look at the portrait within the locket? he wondered. And now that the original was beside her, with what sentiments did she regard him? Gratitude for saving her life? gratitude deep and sincere, but nothing more? Wilfrid made up his mind that he would find out that very night.

"Question one having been answered in full," he smiled, "there comes question two — your name?"

"I should like first to hear whom you think me to be? You must have formed some notion."

"Am I right in supposing that you are a granddaughter of the Czar, Ivan VI.?"

The Duchess received this question with a merry laugh, the first Wilfrid had heard from her, a laugh so rippling and sweet that he was sorry when it had ceased.

"What gave you that idea?" she asked.

"A paragraph in the English *Times*," replied Wilfrid, repeating the passage; for, under the belief that it referred to the Duchess, it had been no task, but a pleasure, to learn it by heart.

"And you took me to be the lady meant? She never had any existence. If you had seen the *Times* just a week later you would have found that same correspondent withdrawing the story as an idle rumour, and apologising to his English readers for having led them astray. A grand-daughter of Ivan! I have not a drop of Muscovite blood in my veins. I am as you are — a foreigner in Russia."

Somehow Wilfrid was pleased to think that she was of a nationality other than Russ, although her statement increased his perplexity since, as she was not connected by blood with the Imperial house of Romanoff, how came she to be politically so great, as she undoubtedly was, according to the account both of herself and of Baranoff? Was she a member of some other royal house of Europe, and being, for some reason or other, viewed with jealousy by the reigning head, had she been sent into a sort of quasi-banishment to the Russian Court, whose orders were to exercise a strict surveillance over her conduct, and, above all, to see that she did not fall in love? Why would she not explain, and end all this mystery?

"I was born Princess Marie," she continued, "and Princess Marie is the name I love, and the name my friends still call me by."

"Then you shall be Princess Marie to me, and —— "

He paused. The clock-tower of the Sumaroff Palace chimed the hour.

"One o'clock!" said Princess Marie — to use the name favoured by her — speaking with a sort of dismay in her voice. "I have stayed too long. I must return, Lord Courtenay, will you escort me to the ballroom, and there — there we must part."

"Part! We have but just met. If we part, when are we to meet again?"

"Never, I fear."

"Never is a hard word."

"Do you think it is not hard for me to say it?" murmured the Princess, as she rose to her feet, evidently bent on going.

"Stay, Princess. You have not yet redeemed all your promise. There is your present name, and — the — the kiss."

"You will not let me off?"

"I kept *my* word, Princess. Will you not keep yours?"

As Wilfrid rose to his feet she receded a pace or two, with hands put forward as if to keep him off.

"What pleasure will you have in a kiss given on compulsion?"

"Shall you give the kiss, then, from no other feeling than to get rid of the duty?"

"In what other spirit should I give it?"

"If the Princess can give only a reluctant kiss, let her give none at all."

Princess Marie hesitated for a moment.

"I . . . I will keep my promise," she said. "But not

. . . not here . . . on the open terrace. There . . . in the shadows. It is death if . . . if we are seen!"

Wilfrid took her little hand — how it trembled! — within his own, led her across the terrace, and stood beside her under the gloom of the pine trees.

"It was not stipulated that you should wear a mask," said he.

She withdrew her vizard, revealing her beautiful face, made more beautiful by the sweet colour that mantled it.

She looked round on all sides to make sure that no one was within sight. Satisfied that they were alone she turned to Wilfrid. Never had he so trembled as at this moment when the Princess set her hands lightly upon his shoulders and looked him full in the face with eyes that, striving to be bold, were yet full of timidity.

Her lovely face drew near to his; he caught the fragrance of her breath; their lips met in a kiss, given on her part with a warmth that could spring from but one feeling. The tender glance of her dark-blue eyes told him, as plainly as words, what place he held in her heart. Moved by an uncontrollable impulse he clasped her in his arms. She did not resent the action; on the contrary she clung to him in that wild, sweet, thrilling embrace that comes but once in a life-time.

"Princess!" he whispered in a voice trembling with emotion, "you love me — is it not so? I will not let you go back to your old life. You must come with me — "

"Oh no, no!" she gasped, seeking to unwind his arms. "My God! what am I doing? Lord Courtenay . . . let me go . . . Do not tempt me . . . This . . . this cannot be!"

"Why not?"

She gave a wild laugh.

"You would not ask, if you knew me. I am the — "

The words suddenly froze on her lips. Wilfrid, gazing upon her face, saw its loveliness distorted by a terrible change. With blanched cheek and open mouth she was staring at something or somebody behind him. Her strange set expression almost suggested the wild fancy that there had risen from out the foliage the head of Medusa, whose chilling stare could turn the beholder to stone. Something of her feeling communicated itself to Wilfrid; for a few seconds he stood, still holding the Princess in his arms, scarcely daring to turn lest he should see at his elbow some awful apparition.

CHAPTER XX

WHEN at last Wilfrid *did* turn his head he beheld a tall masked figure, motionless, silent, watchful; the very Crusader who had glanced angrily at him in the ballroom.

Now when one gentleman comes upon another in the act of kissing a lady, politeness suggests immediate retirement on the part of the first. But this was a course the intruder did *not* take; instead, he kept his ground as if he had come there for no other purpose than to watch the pair, manifestly indifferent as to whether his presence caused embarrassment or not.

Wilfrid could have slain him without the least compunction.

Here was a lovely princess, clinging to his embrace, listening to his love-avowal, and lo! the charming situation must come to an end — for a time at least — by reason of the new-comer's clownishness!

As he withdrew one arm from the Princess she made a movement as if to flee.

"Stay, Princess," he whispered. "Do not go. You are safe with me. Do you know this man? Who is he?"

She seemed too frightened to make reply; she glanced, now to the right and now to the left, along the moonlit terrace, apparently deliberating which way to flee; finally, with a strength born of despair, she suddenly broke away, and before the surprised Wilfrid could stop her, Princess Marie was lost to view among the darkness of the pines. For a moment he hesitated whether to follow or not, but as running off might look like cowardice, he chose to remain, and turned upon the Crusader, with whom he was now doubly angry.

The new-comer moved forward from the shadow of

the trees, and, with an air of dignity, now stood in the clear moonlight, looking at the other as if requiring from him an explanation of his recent conduct.

"Qualifying for the spy service, sir?" Wilfrid asked. "I am told 'tis a remunerative profession."

"In dealing with dishonourable persons," was the reply, "nice rules of courtesy must be laid aside."

Wilfrid was convinced that the speaker was Ouvaroff, and that, for some reason or other, the Prince was seeking to disguise his voice.

It was not so much the voice, however, to which he gave heed as the words. Dishonourable? As Wilfrid recalled the Princess's sweet face and innocent eyes, still greater grew his anger against the man who thus ventured to charge her with wrong-doing.

"Dishonourable, my eavesdropper?" he repeated with a dangerous gleam in his eye.

"I said the word, sir."

"To whom do you apply it — to me or to the lady?"

"To both."

"'Tis a word you shall withdraw, or justify."

"The lady's last action justifies it. If innocent, why flee? She knows me, and knowing, dares not face me."

"In knowing you she has the advantage of me. Let me declare myself. I am an Englishman, Viscount Courtenay; my face you may see," and as he spoke Wilfrid removed his mask. "May I ask for a similar return on your part?"

For though Wilfrid had little doubt that the other was Ouvaroff, still the lifting of the mask would bring certainty.

"Is it possible that you do not recognise me?"

"Can *your* eyes see through a silk mask?"

The Crusader hesitated for a moment.

"You do not know me? It is well!" He seemed to derive satisfaction from Wilfrid's failure to identify him. "To-morrow morning you shall see my face and learn my name."

"And why not to-night, my Crusader?"

"It is my pleasure for the present to reserve my identity."

" But how if it be mine to know it now? How if I do not choose to wait till the morning? How if I take off your mask, and compel you at the sword's point to reveal your name? "

" You are welcome to try," responded the other, moving backward a pace or two to prevent Wilfrid from snatching off his mask.

" Good! got the right sort of stuff in him," thought Wilfrid as he saw the other grasp his sword-hilt and prepare to defend himself.

" In the morning," continued the stranger, " when you shall have learned my name you will readily acknowledge that I have valid reasons for preserving to-night my *incognito*."

" Egad, you are very mysterious, my one-time friend," thought Wilfrid.

" Nothing would give me greater pleasure," continued the other, " than to cross swords with you here and now, but that in so doing we should be abusing the hospitality of our princely host, Sumaroff. Moreover, the clash of our steel is certain to draw around us a crowd who would seek to stop our fighting; and," added he, with a grim and deadly earnestness, " when we have once begun there must be no stopping till we make an end."

In Wilfrid's opinion Ouvaroff must have attained considerable proficiency in swordsmanship to hold language such as this. Always having a respect for the man willing to fight, he replied with a bow —

" Be it so; since you wish it, retain your mask and your *incognito,* which," added he to himself, " is no *incognito.*" Aloud he continued, " Your desire to cross swords with me meets with a ready response. May I point out, however, that it is somewhat unusual to invite a man to a duel without assigning due cause. You have not yet justified your reflection on my honour."

" Honour! " sneered the other in a voice quivering with suppressed passion. " Honour! Are clandestine meetings consistent with the honour of an English gentleman? You meet — " He looked cautiously round as he spoke — " Let her be nameless, for who knows what ears may be within hearing? You meet her

secretly at midnight in the Michaelovski Palace; you
meet her with kisses and embraces at this masquerade;
you are seen leaving her bedchamber in the inn at Gora.
You, who have brought shame upon her — do you talk
of honour?"

Through the holes of his mask the man's eyes glowed
like fire; a great rage seemed to hold him. He fingered
his sword-hilt, as if longing to hurl himself upon Wilfrid
and end his life there and then, without troubling to wait
for the morning.

As for Wilfrid, the words of the other fell upon him
with the shock of a thunderbolt, filling him with a
dreadful dismay, not so much on his own account as on
Marie's. What had hitherto been a haunting suspicion
was now converted to a black truth; the bedchamber
incident was known to Ouvaroff, might be known to
others! All innocent as the Princess was, the finger of
scorn would now be pointed to her as one fallen from
maidenly purity. And the bitterest thought of all was
there seemed no way of refuting the slander. Vain
would it be for him or for her to deny. The mocking
nobility, reared in the tainted atmosphere of Catharine's
Court, and accustomed to measure others by their own
standard, would accept as true neither his word nor that
of the Princess. She was branded with the mark of
shame, and the cause of it all was himself — Wilfrid
Courtenay!

Well, he could have one satisfaction at least, the satisfaction of seeing the original traducer fall dead at his
feet, for he would give him no quarter in the morning.

"The fight cannot come too soon," he said, between
his set teeth. "You have cast a black slander on an
innocent lady, and by Heaven! you die for it."

"Innocent! Am I to take the kisses and embraces of
to-night as proofs of innocence?"

"Why should *not* the lady kiss me if she choose?"

The other drew a breath as of amazement, and for a
few moments stared, as if he doubted whether there were
not something wrong with Wilfrid's mental calibre.

"You speak thus, knowing who the lady is?"

"Your pardon, I do not know who the lady is. I am

under no obligation to offer explanations to you, sir, but
thus much may be tendered, that I know the lady only
by the name of Princess Marie — a name that conveys
no meaning to me."

Wilfrid did not ask the other to enlighten him in any
way respecting the Princess; in his present haughty
mood he would take no favours from him.

The Crusader looked at Wilfrid as if doubting his
statement.

" Can this be true? " he muttered.

" It might not be, were I a Russian prince."

As if confronted with some new and startling problem, the man turned aside and took a few steps to and
fro before he spoke again.

" Your statement sounds so improbable that I may
well hesitate to accept it. If the lady has *not* told you
her name, if you have been acting in ignorance of her
rank, then is the guilt hers, and not yours. Nay," he
added in a milder tone, " I am ready to withdraw my
reflections upon your honour."

" You are very good. But if I am honourable how
can the lady be dishonourable? "

" That will be seen in the morning."

" Before the duel, I trust? "

" Why, truly," said the other with a significant smile,
" you will hardly be in a condition to apprehend an
explanation *after* the duel."

" That's to be seen. But methinks you are somewhat
inconsistent, for, surely in admitting — as you have
admitted — that my honour is stainless, you have, from
your point of view, removed all cause for the duel? "

" So one might think," returned the other, who
seemed to be growing more calm, " but it is not so.
Matters are in a fairer state than I had thought them.
This scandal may yet be kept quiet; it need not become
the talk of Europe. None the less, Lord Courtenay, you
must pay the penalty of your daring. You have done —
unwittingly it is true — that which can be atoned for
only by death."

" Where shall the place of our meeting be? " asked

Wilfrid with some impatience, for he was eager to hasten after the Princess.

",You know the Viborg Road running northwards from the city? Good! A little way beyond the eight verst-post on the right-hand side of the road is a path leading to a small glade. At eight o'clock — seven hours from now — I shall be there, attended by a friend. And you?"

"Will not be a laggard in seeking the spot. 'And our weapons?"

"The choice belongs to you as the challenged."

Wilfrid, mindful of Ouvaroff's recent devotion to swordsmanship, and willing to accommodate him in the matter, made the reply:—

"What say you to swords of three feet?"

"Accepted," said the other with evident satisfaction in his tone. "My second shall bring the weapons with him. A doctor," he added significantly, "we shall *not* require."

"If you will put that last remark in the singular," said Wilfrid, "I will have no fault to find with it. Why, then, matters being thus arranged, we need not prolong this interview. The rendezvous, a glade near the eighth verst-post on the Viborg Road; the time, eight o'clock. Till then, farewell."

With that Wilfrid turned away, in an agony of suspense as to what might have happened to the Princess should she have come within view of the four liveried hirelings. And now for the first time he began to realise what a tool he had been in the hands of Count Baranoff. He had done the very thing that Baranoff wanted. His coming into Russia with the chivalrous purpose of defending a lady from the wicked intrigues of that minister had ended in compromising her name and imperilling her safety! She had given him the kiss of love in spite of her belief, "It is death if we are seen!"

And they *had* been seen, and that by an enemy!

Death might perhaps have been Wilfrid's lot a few days earlier, but the re-establishment of the British Embassy put a different complexion upon matters. The

Czar, the Court-party, the ministers, or whoever Marie's mysterious enemies might be, could not very well arrest the nephew of Great Britain's representative for a fault which, at its worst, was merely an irregular *amour;* still, bent on compassing his end, they sought to dispose of him in a manner speciously fair and open, by getting Prince Ouvaroff, the newly-expert swordsman, to challenge him to a duel to the death.

Well, *that* part of the plot should fail; the combat had no terrors for Wilfrid.

But what of Marie, the Princess of the sorrowful eyes, who in the presence of a witness had given unequivocal proof of her love for an Englishman? She was not a British subject; her liberty and life were at the mercy of the Russian authorities.

Would the royal house to which she belonged, pleased rather than otherwise, enjoin that the penalty for her fault must be seclusion for life in a fortress or a nunnery?

Wilfrid's immediate object was to find the Princess again, and he determined, when he should have found her, not to leave her side till he had seen her to a place of safety; and the safest place he could think of just then was the British Embassy. True, she had already refused that asylum, but fear, occasioned by the recent incident, might cause a change in her resolve.

Not more than fifteen minutes had passed since she had fled from the terrace, but in fifteen minutes one may do much in the matter of hiding one's self; and the Princess had hidden herself so effectually that Wilfrid could not find her, though he several times traversed the gardens as well as the ballroom.

Although tormented by the fear that she *might* have fallen into the hands of the four hirelings, Wilfrid adopted the more probable conclusion that the Princess had retired altogether from the masquerade. Was it likely that she would remain to run the chance of another meeting with Prince Ouvaroff, of whom she evidently stood in fear? But no sooner had Wilfrid formed this opinion than he dismissed it. The Princess had with her a letter meant for the Czarina. Did she still adhere to her intention of presenting it? Then, unless she knew, the secret of the Czarina's costume, she would have to wait till the Empress had publicly disclosed herself at the general unmasking, which was timed to take place at two o'clock.

And here again Wilfrid was met by a perplexing thought. Why should the Princess, presumably a member of the Court circle, choose the occasion of a public masquerade for presenting a letter which, one would think, might have been more suitably presented in private? And that letter, so she had averred, contained something of vital interest, not only to her own welfare, but also to Wilfrid's. It was strange — passing strange — but then so was everything else happening that night. Wilfrid had never known a more mystifying time.

When the hand of the clock was upon the stroke of two he repaired to the Hall of Mirrors, and, ascending a gallery, looked down upon the crowd of masked revellers. He hoped in a minute or two more to obtain a view of the Czar, and what was of more interest to him, of the Czarina, in case the Princess should be by to present her letter.

But at the general unmasking, when everybody was looking expectantly around for the imperial pair, Prince Sumaroff mounted the dais and gave out that the pressure of State affairs had prevented the Czar from honouring the masquerade with his presence; a slight touch of illness had likewise kept the Czarina from attending. Wilfrid was, perhaps, the only one present that did not hear this disappointing announcement, his attention at that moment being absorbed by a fact of no importance whatever to the thousand and one guests, but constituting for him a startling discovery.

A moment before the unmasking he had caught sight of Pauline, recognisable, of course, by her costume. She was leaning upon the arm of a tall and majestic figure clad in the glittering mail of a Byzantine warrior. Earlier in the evening when first entering the ballroom Wilfrid had noticed the man, and had called Pauline's attention to his splendid and striking costume.

The lifting of his mask gave Wilfrid a sort of shock.

The Byzantine warrior was none other than Prince Ouvaroff!

Clearly, then, unless Ouvaroff had changed his costume — a most unlikely event — he could not have been the Crusading knight whom Wilfrid had met upon the terrace.

What man was it, then, with whom he had to fight at eight in the morning?

CHAPTER XXI.

"YOUR OPPONENT IS AN EMPEROR"

THE unmasking of the guests was followed by a simultaneous movement toward the supper-tables, set forth in an adjoining room, a room scarcely inferior in size and grandeur to the Hall of Mirrors.

Tormented by the thought of the Princess, Wilfrid was in no trim for eating, even when the far-famed Sumaroff *cuisine* offered its temptations.

Having satisfied himself that neither Marie nor the Crusading knight was among the guests, he withdrew from the palace, having first sent to Pauline a servant with a brief note, in which, without stating the cause, he expressed regret at finding it impossible to escort her home.

It was now past two o'clock. He had by eight of the clock to be at a spot distant six miles from the city, and in the interval he must find a second, and try to snatch a short repose. He had no time to waste.

Making his way to the entrance of the Sumaroff Palace he procured a car and drove to his hotel, where he changed his antique garb for one more modern, and this done, he went off at once to the British Embassy, with a view of getting one of his uncle's secretaries to act as his second.

"Unless indeed the old boy himself will volunteer, which isn't very likely," thought Wilfrid. "He'd be compromising his diplomatic office."

On reaching the Embassy Wilfrid learned that, late as the hour was, the "old boy" had not yet gone to bed, but was sitting alone in his study.

Making his way thither Wilfrid found the Ambassador seated at a table, upon which, in addition to cigars and wine, was a very large parchment with seals attached thereto, and bearing every appearance of being an important State document.

"Pouf! windows closed and curtains drawn this hot July night?" said Wilfrid, glancing at the heavily-draped casements.

"Put your head out of the window, and you'll soon scent the reason. Fontanka Canal below. What do the Russian Government mean by putting me in this malodorous hole? Damme! they'll have to find me fresh quarters. See my new Diana over there? Winkelman! Bought it yesterday. Cost seven hundred roubles — think it's worth it?" And then, seeing Wilfrid's eyes attracted by the document upon the table, he continued, "Ah! the editor of the *Journal de St. Petersbourg* would give much for a copy of this."

"It is, I presume ——?"

"A duplicate of the secret Anglo-Russian Treaty of Peace. I am studying it for the twentieth time. Must leave no loophole for the enemy to creep through."

"The Czar hasn't signed it yet?"

"He signs to-morrow night, or rather, as it's long past midnight, to-day. And yet," continued the Ambassador, a queer look coming over his face, "and yet — who knows? — he may never sign it."

"His autocratic Majesty is so changeable?"

"No, but life is. The Czar may be dead by to-morrow."

"For the matter of that so may I," remarked Wilfrid, thinking of the coming duel. "So may you; so may all of us."

"Ah! but in the Czar's case there is special cause for fear. But there! I'm talking too fast. I mustn't betray State secrets."

This assumption of reticence was a mere preliminary to disclosure, as Wilfrid very well knew. The Ambassador had a tale to unfold, and was burning to unfold it, and, anxious as Wilfrid was to get to the subject of the coming duel, he was not unwilling to be a listener, impressed by his uncle's air of subdued excitement.

"It was told to me in confidence," continued Lord St.

Helens, "but I see no reason why I should not tell you.
The story is certain to be made public property within
four and twenty hours. Well, here it is then. Like the
rest of the diplomatic body, I received an invitation to
this Sumaroff fête, and looked in for a short time just
before supper; and am not sorry at having gone, for
there, in spite of his mask, I recognised my old friend
Panine. He was in a state of great agitation, caused by
something he had just heard from Alexander."

"Alexander was at the fête, then?"

"Of course he was."

"Prince Sumaroff publicly announced that he wasn't."

"Never believe public announcements — in Russia.
He *was* there, but retired before supper-time. As you
will see he had very good reason for wishing to be alone
with his thoughts. Talking of Alexander, I suppose you
know that he was married when only sixteen years old —
that is, at an age scarcely capable of forming a just
judgment. As a matter of fact he had no voice in the
choosing of his wife; she was chosen for him by his
grandmother Catharine, and our poor Alexander had no
alternative but to obey.

"It is obvious that a marriage of this sort, contracted
for political reasons merely, cannot yield that happiness
arising from a union based on mutual affection. Far be
it from me to speak one word adverse to the young
Czarina Elizavetta; she is beautiful, she is charming,
she is good; but still, you know the remark of the old
Roman to the persons who were praising his wife: ' This
to you may seem an excellent sandal,' he said, taking it
off. ' I alone know where it pinches.' So of the Czarina.
To us she may seem an ideal consort; Alexander alone
knows where the sandal pinches."

"It is easy to see to what all this is preliminary."

"Just so. The usual result when kings are forced to
mate from policy. Our Alexander looks round to find a
companion more to his taste."

"And the lady's name?"

"Is a secret unknown to Panine, and therefore to me."

"Has the intrigue reached a guilty stage? — but no,
it cannot have."

Lord St. Helens wondered at the husky voice and at the strange look with which his nephew put this question.

"Panine thinks not. In fact, judging from what happened to-night at the masquerade, it must be inferred that the love is on the Czar's side only."

"Why, what *did* happen?"

"A masquerade, as you know, affords excellent facilities for an intrigue. The Czar, aware that his inamorata would be at this fête, determined himself to be present. He came without state, masked, and costumed, and sought eagerly, as we may suppose, for his lady-love, and at last found her."

"Alone?"

"Hardly. She was with another man, and — one can scarcely refrain from smiling — the pair were in the act of kissing each other as the Czar came upon them."

"How did you learn this?"

"It was witnessed by Panine."

"By Panine!" repeated Wilfrid.

"He was meditatively walking amid a grove of trees when he happened to see the lady bestow a kiss upon a gentleman, no unusual occurrence at a masquerade, but this affair began to assume a serious aspect when there stepped forth into the moonlight a figure whom Panine recognised to be that of the Emperor. At sight of him the lady instantly fled as if in fear, leaving the Emperor and the man together.

"An animated conversation followed, inaudible to Panine, who, out of respect, kept his distance, nor did he venture forward till the man had left the Czar's presence.

"'Count,' began Alexander — I repeat Panine's words to me as nearly as I can remember them — 'Count, you know that in the abstract I am opposed to duelling; but occasionally it may happen that a gentleman has no other way of defending his honour. Now there is a certain man who wishes to fight a duel to-morrow. As his cause is just, will you do him the favour of acting as his second?'

"Panine, naturally concluding that the Czar's recent interlocutor was the man referred to, made reply: —

" 'Your Majesty's command is my pleasure.'

" 'You promise to be this man's second?'

" 'Most certainly, Sire.'

" 'Look to it, then, that you keep your word,' said Alexander with a face sterner than Panine had ever before seen it, ' for *I* am the duellist. Honour leaves me no alternative but to fight. Stop! no words, I pray you. I know beforehand what you would say; that, if any one offends me, it is within my power to banish, to imprison, to execute the offender. Granted: but that were an ignoble vengeance. None hereafter shall say that Alexander took advantage of his position in order to slay a rival. The man must die, and his death shall come by my hand in fair and open fight. I waive my imperial prerogative, and meet him as one gentleman, when affronted, should meet another. My opponent's name? — let it remain a secret. The rendezvous? Well, that you'll learn when we set out. Be at the palace at seven this morning ready to attend me. And, as you value your life, not a word of this to any one.' And with that the Emperor strode away."

" Did Panine tell his tale to any besides you? "

" When I left him he was in doubt whether or not to communicate it to his fellow ministers."

" And he doesn't know who the Czar's opponent is? "

" Hasn't the least notion. The man was masked, you see."

" But his costume should serve to identify him."

" It would, if Panine could remember what the fellow wore. I should very much like to know the name of the man. To cut the Czar out in love, and then to stand up to him in a duel! Gad! the fellow must have the audacity of the devil! "

" Audacity, my dear uncle, was always the mark of a Courtenay."

For a moment the Ambassador stared blankly at Wilfrid; then the truth burst upon him.

" Good God! " he gasped. " You don't mean that — that ——! "

" The Czar's opponent is distant from you by no more than the length of a table."

It would not be true to say that Lord St. Helens's hair rose on end, but it very nearly accomplished that feat.

"I accepted the challenge to-night," continued Wilfrid, "from a masked stranger, whose anger apparently had been kindled at seeing me receive a kiss from a certain lady. The fellow refused his name, but from his voice I took him to be Prince Ouvaroff. It seems now that I was wrong, and that my opponent is a much more august character."

Overwhelmed by the startling news the Ambassador could do nothing for a few moments but gaze in a sort of speechless terror at his nephew. Finding his voice at last he said: "This is a devilishly awkward affair. Let me know how it all happened?"

Wilfrid related the whole story from his first meeting with Baranoff in Berlin down to that night's scene at the masquerade, adding: —

"How was I to know it was the Czar? He talked exactly like an ordinary mortal. You told me yesterday that it was Ouvaroff's intention to pick a quarrel with me, and as the stranger had a voice very like Ouvaroff's I naturally concluded —— "

"Alexander and Ouvaroff are half-brothers, as you know. Their voices *are* very similar. Now, what's to be done in this matter?" continued the Ambassador with a thoughtful regard for his nephew's safety.

"My first care must be to communicate with Panine. It will relieve him to know that the duel will not come off."

"But why shouldn't it come off?"

"Your opponent is an emperor."

"And are not we Courtenays the descendants of emperors? 'Equal to Cæsars,' is not that our motto?"

"Come! this is mere bravado. You cannot really be serious in saying you will fight the Czar."

"The Archangel Gabriel himself, if he came between me and the woman I love. It is easy to see how matters stand with the Princess. She hates the Czar's addresses, but does not know how to repel them. And diplomatists like you would bid me stand aside and let him work his libertine will with the sweet lady who loves me, because, forsooth, he *is* a Czar, between whom and me an awful gulf is fixed! Czar me no Czar! On this condition only will I withdraw, that he hands the Princess over to me; if not, he fights."

Lord St. Helens became full of dismay, as he realised that Wilfrid was perfectly serious in his utterance. If Alexander were equally determined there was no power on earth to stay the duel; and since Wilfrid had no peer in swordsmanship, what but ill would befall the Czar in a mortal combat? In cooler moments Wilfrid might not wish to kill the Emperor, but in the hot excitement of the duel, when he saw before him the man who was persecuting the Princess with unwelcome attentions, there was no knowing what might happen, especially if Wilfrid's anger should be aggravated by the smarting of a wound.

"And pray, sir," said the Ambassador after vainly expostulating with his nephew, "pray, sir, who is to be your second in this infamous business?"

"I am going to ask *you* to officiate in that capacity."

The Ambassador felt as if he were choking.

"Go to Gehenna!" he yelled.

"You won't? What will the family think when they hear that you have refused to stand by me in an affair of honour. Who's to conduct my funeral if I fall?"

"I'd be most infernally happy to conduct your funeral at this present moment. Cease this foolery, and talk sense — if you can. Should this freak end in the wounding or it may be, the killing of the Czar — which heaven forbid! — to whom do you intend to look for safety?"

"To you, of course."

"To me?"

"Most certainly. Doesn't the nation pay you £10,000 a year to look after British subjects in Russia, of whom I am one?"

"*I* to protect you?"

"If you don't the British public will want to know the reason! Remember that the duel is not of *my* seeking; he challenged me, not I him. In an autocratic realm what can a man do when its ruler insists on fighting him? It's useless to go against the will of a fellow who can send you to Siberia for disobedience. And if he fall, whose is the blame?" "Well, I must be off," continued Wilfrid, glancing at his watch; "but before going I should like — of course, with your permission — to see young Mulgrave," naming his uncle's chief secretary. "He is a man of spirit, and will stand by me in this affair."

"Do you think ——?" began the Ambassador angrily, and then broke off as if hit by some sudden thought. "Well, I'll send for him, and you'll hear what he thinks. Perhaps you'll listen to him, if not to me."

He pencilled a few words upon a card and touched a hand-bell, whose chime immediately brought in a servitor in livery. Handing him the card, and pointing to the name upon it, the Ambassador said with a meaning look,

"Tell him to come at once."

The man had no sooner set eyes upon the card than he gave a slight start, glanced oddly at Wilfrid, and withdrew without a word.

"Oho, my uncle," thought Wilfrid, who had observed this little by-play, "why did you give a written message, when an oral one would have sufficed? There is something on that card you do not wish me to see. Very good! Forewarned is forearmed."

After a brief interval there came a tapping at the door.

"Wait a moment, Williams," cried Lord St. Helens. "Stay outside till I call."

"Williams? Why, I thought it was Mulgrave you sent for?" said Wilfrid in mock surprise.

Ignoring this question, the Ambassador said with a stern air: —

"I am to take it, then, that you have quite made up your mind to fight this duel?"

"Certainly."

"Well, I have made up my mind that you shall not."

"And how do you propose to stop me?"

"You are not in Russia now, remember. This Embassy is Great Britain, or rather, a part of Great Britain in Russia. As the representative of His Majesty King George, I am, so long as you are in this house, your sovereign, and you are my subject. In the exercise of my lawful authority —— "

"You'll put me under arrest," said Wilfrid, smiling amiably. "Yes, I thought that was the idea when you sent out that little note."

Somewhat disconcerted at Wilfrid's guessing his intention, and uneasy, too, at his air of unconcern, the Ambassador called out: "Come in."

At the summons there trooped in five athletic men, lackeys apparently. Their attire, consisting of shirt and breeches only, showed that they had been hastily roused from sleep. They advanced a little way into the room, and then stood still, awaiting orders. Wondering what the trouble was about, they glanced alternately from the flushed uncle to the cool nephew.

"This madman," said Lord St. Helens, indicating Wilfrid, who bowed sarcastically, "my nephew, I regret to say, is an enemy to Great Britain. In the name of the King, I call upon you to arrest him and to take him to the Green Chamber, where he must remain till he has renounced his treasonable designs. Sorry, Wilfrid, my boy," he added, in a side whisper; "but I've no other course. Go quietly, like a sensible fellow," he added, as he saw the fighting spirit gleam from Wilfrid's eye. "You can't contend against five men."

But Wilfrid, having formed his plan, proceeded to act. The only light in the room came from the six tapers in the chandelier above his head. As the five men moved slowly forward, Wilfrid, with one swift bound, sprang aloft and hung his whole weight upon the chandelier. Down it came in an instant, and almost before it reached the floor he had extinguished the six lights by the easy process of flinging the table-cloth over them.

By this action, the work of not more than four seconds, the room was plunged into sudden darkness.

"Look to the door," screamed the Ambassador.

Tumbling over each other in their haste the five raced back, and ranged themselves in fighting order before the door, the only exit from the room.

In the dead silence that followed, the Ambassador and his satellites strained eye and ear, endeavouring to discover by sight or sound what Wilfrid's next movement would be.

They had not long to wait.

From the far end of the apartment there suddenly darted intermittent rays of light, apparently caused by the wavering of a heavy curtain that draped one of the windows overlooking the canal. Simultaneously all were seized with the same idea. Wilfrid was going to —

Crash!

The sound was like that of a sheet of glass shivered to atoms by the impact of a heavy body, and was instantly followed by the splash of water.

"Good God! He's leaped into the Fontanka, through glass and all," cried the Ambassador.

Men falling into that shallow canal have been known never to rise again from its deep deposit of mud!

The Ambassador ran to the window, thrusting the heavy curtain on one side. Moved by a common impulse, the five men ran too.

The Ambassador unfastened the catch, flung open the window, and, with his body half out, looked down upon the water, whose surface had upon it a rippling ring that grew wider and wider each moment, a ring obviously caused by the fall of a body.

The watchers kept their eyes fixed upon the centre of this ring, waiting for Wilfrid's head to appear. The circle spread outward farther and farther, till it became imperceptible to the sense of sight. The surface of the water grew smooth again; one minute passed, two, three, and still Wilfrid was not to be seen, nor any trace of him.

"By God! he's gone! Caught in the mud at the bottom," said the Ambassador in awe-struck tones.

"Still alive, dear uncle!" said a voice, coming from the direction of the door.

So deep was the amazement of the Ambassador and his lackeys at hearing the voice of one whom they had just taken for dead that for the moment they were powerless to do anything except to stare, vacant-eyed and open-mouthed, at Wilfrid's smiling face, which in the dim light could be seen peeping in at them from the other side of the half-open door.

"I knew that crash would fetch 'em from the door.

Your attempt to imprison me, dear uncle, has cost you seven hundred roubles, for your marble Diana is lying at the bottom of the Fontanka. Well, good-bye! I'm off to that meeting!"

Recovering from their stupor, the five men, mortified at being thus fooled, rushed forward, too late, however, to repair their blunder.

During their three minutes' watch at the window, Wilfrid had quietly removed the key from the inner side of the room to the outer, and before his foes had time to reach him, he shut the door, locked it, put the key in his pocket, walked downstairs, and escaped safely to the street.

CHAPTER XXII

WILFRID'S statement that he would face the Czar in duel was no boast, but who should be his second?

Having no very high opinion of the Czar's honour, Wilfrid considered it advisable to have a friendly witness to see fair play. But who would care to be his companion in a venture so perilous? He rapidly ran over in his mind the limited circle of friends, or rather of acquaintances, he had made in St. Petersburg, and knew full well there was not one upon whose spirit he could rely. Second the Czar's adversary! · The very idea would take away their breath.

Without knowing it he had stopped short before the French Embassy, a fact of which he was made aware by observing a covered carriage whose panels bore the armorial device of the Marquis de Vaucluse.

A moment afterwards the French Ambassador appeared, descending the steps of his mansion.

" Ah ! " murmured Wilfrid, an idea striking him. " Perhaps M. de Vaucluse can recommend a man bold enough to act as my second."

The Marquis, about to step into his carriage, stopped on seeing Wilfrid, and advanced with outstretched hand.

" I must apologise," said Wilfrid, " for returning from the masquerade without the Baroness, but a grave event has called me away. Can you favour me with a word in private ? "

De Vaucluse led the way into the entrance hall, and thence into a small cabinet.

" To be brief, Monsieur, I have been challenged to a duel. It is to take place within four hours, and at some distance from St. Petersburg. At so short a notice I have a difficulty in finding a second, especially as I have but few friends in this city. Can you recommend a gentleman, one of resolute courage, inasmuch as my adversary is a high political personage?"

"Supposing that I cannot name one?"

"In that case I must proceed alone."

"That shall not be. It shall never be said that a *seigneur* of old France was lacking in chivalry. Permit me to have the honour."

"The honour is mine; but will you not be compromising your own character as ambassador?"

"Hasn't Pauline told you what has happened? No? France has at the present moment no representative in St. Petersburg. Two weeks ago I forwarded my resignation to the Consulate. It was accepted, and my successor will arrive within a few days. My resignation," he continued in answer to Wilfrid's look of inquiry, "has no connection with politics. It has been made on purely personal grounds. I desire Pauline to leave Russia, and I see no other way of accomplishing my end than by leaving it myself."

While speaking he glanced keenly at Wilfrid, as if to mark the effect of his words, and seemed to derive satisfaction from Wilfrid's blank look; for, the Princess excepted, there was no one in St. Petersburg whom Wilfrid liked better than Pauline, and therefore he heard the news with deep regret.

"Your offer to be my second is extremely generous, but you will do well to refrain till you shall have heard the name of my adversary."

"A *seigneur* of France knows not fear. I am your second whoever be your adversary. A high political personage? Humph! One of the Czar's ministers, I suppose?"

"Higher than a minister."

"*Ciel!* Surely not a Grand Duke?"

"Higher than a Grand Duke."

The Marquis looked hard at Wilfrid.

"There is no one higher than a Grand Duke except the Czar."

"Incredible as it may appear, my adversary *is* the Czar!"

The Marquis showed surprise, yet that surprise was not so great as Wilfrid had expected. There was about him an air of satisfaction, as if he were pleased at the situation.

" With what weapons do you fight? "

" With swords."

" And you are deadly with the sword, I understand," said the Marquis. " As most duels are caused by a lady," he went on, " I presume yours is no exception to the rule? "

" No exception."

He begged for a little light on the matter, and Wilfrid accordingly gave a hurried account of the events that had brought him into connection with the Princess Marie, making no mention, however, of the compromising adventure at the Silver Birch. The Marquis was deeply interested, and — a puzzling point to Wilfrid — even pleased. He seemed to brighten more and more as the story reached its climax.

" I thought I was well acquainted with all the personalities of the Russian court," he remarked at the close of Wilfrid's narration, " but I must confess that this Princess Marie is to me an unknown person. And the duel is to be to the death? "

" So said the Czar."

" Then I hope you will kill him !"

" Monsieur ! " said Wilfrid, surprised at the vehemence of the other's utterance.

" I hope," repeated the Marquis, slowly emphasising each word, " that — you — will — kill — him ! "

" You have suffered a wrong at his hand? "

" Not yet, but it is certain to come if his life continue. It were better for — for some of us that he were dead. Therefore, as I have said, I hope you will kill him."

" He mayn't give me the opportunity," smiled Wilfrid. " Should I find myself his superior, I shall just show him what I *could* do with his life if I chose; but as to killing him, what would Paul — the Baroness say if I were to slay the Czar? Is he not her hero? But, monsieur, on reflection I will ask you to withdraw from this affair. Though Alexander may pardon my wounding him his ministers may not prove so chivalrous. Should the Czar be brought home injured there will be a hue and cry for his assailants. Why should I imperil your life as well as my own?"

"In asking me to be your second you have conferred a high honour upon me. This affair is certain to be famous. We shall live in history — you and I. You see," he went on with a smile, "that vanity has something to do with my motives. Now, as your second, let me urge you to leave St. Petersburg at once, lest your uncle or Panine should communicate this matter to the police. The Czar they dare not meddle with, but they would not hesitate to seize his opponent. Did you tell your uncle the place of the rendezvous? You did not? And Panine does not know it? Good! Set off this minute. Take my carriage; it is drawn by my two fleetest horses. A little beyond the eighth verst-post you say? Ah! that is very fortunate, since near that same verst-post, but on this side of it, lives Ruric, the charcoal burner. He is one of Pauline's freed serfs. You have but to mention her name, and there is nothing he will not do to serve you."

"I do not understand."

"To meet the Czar you must be near the rendezvous, but not too near."

"Why so?"

"Supposing the secret of the rendezvous has become known, what more likely than that a band of Cossacks will be despatched to the spot to carry you off before the Czar arrives? Now this Ruric resides a little way past the seventh verst-post in a hut not visible from the road, which at this point is bordered on both sides by dense forest. He dwells on the left side of the road; the appointed glade, you say, is on the right. While you remained concealed within his hut, he can reconnoitre for you without exciting suspicion. Should he report the presence of police or soldiers, you will know that you have been betrayed, in which case you will do well not to show yourself. As for me, I will join you later, not leaving the city till the last moment to mark if anything suspicious takes place. When you are passing the seventh verst-post Ivor will drive the carriage close to the trees, and when opposite the path spring out without stopping the carriage, and by following the path you'll come to the hut. Meanwhile, the carriage will drive on, returning to the city by a circuitous route, so that should any mounted spies be following, they'll be thrown off the scent. For the present, farewell, and good fortune attend you."

With that the Marquis wrung Wilfrid's hand and accompanied him to the door, and having first taken a precautionary glance along the street he pushed Wilfrid into the carriage.

"I am unarmed, monsieur," observed Wilfrid. "A sword would be —— "

"No, no! Don't play into the enemy's hand. They'll do no hurt to a nephew of the British Ambassador if you yield quietly. But offer resistance, and that'll be a convenient excuse for putting a bullet through your head. Your single sword will be no match for a dozen carbines."

He whispered a few words of instruction in the driver's ear, and Ivor set off at the furious gallop common to all Muscovite coachmen.

"So he intends merely to wound him," murmured De Vaucluse as he walked slowly back to the cabinet. "Ah, but accidents may happen! It were better for Pauline that he were dead. It is the only way to save her from —— "

The sound of light footsteps came tripping along outside the cabinet, and the next moment his daughter appeared.

On seeing her father Pauline sprang forward to kiss him. Full of a pleasurable excitement, she did not notice that he gave her but a cold reception.

"Ah! *mon père,* why were you not at the masquerade to-night to witness my triumph? See, I bring home the tiara given as the prize for the daintiest costume. Do I not look beautiful?" she added, placing the ornament upon her dark hair and glancing with pardonable pride at her image in the mirror.

"'Twere better if you were less beautiful!"

There was in his words an intonation that caused Pauline to look hard at him as if she were trying to read his thoughts. He returned her look, and for a few moments they stood gazing at each other.

Pauline did not, however, seem at all disconcerted.

"*Mon père*, how grave you are! I will show you by and by that you have reason for joy."

"Pauline, my mind is made up. Within a few hours we set out for Lovisa."

"Lovisa! In Finland?"

"And thence to Sweden. You and I are leaving St. Petersburg for ever."

"For ever! That is a long time, *mon père*, especially when I have the best reason in the world for remaining in Russia."

"Your reason — I know it well — for remaining is the very reason that induces me to remove you."

A smile of triumph appeared on her lips.

"I fear that you misapprehend the situation. Nay, I am sure you do. When you hear all I have to say you will change your mind."

"Nothing that you can say will induce me to change my mind. You will set out first; I will follow later. Lord Courtenay will perhaps accompany us: at least, I will do my best to persuade him. It will not be safe for him to remain any longer in Russia."

"Why, what new piece of mischief has that knight-errant been doing?"

"This morning at eight o'clock he commits the most daring deed of his life."

Pauline elevated her pretty eyebrows in surprise.

"A daring deed! He did not tell me of it to-night. You are more in his confidence than I am. You have a story to tell, is it not so? Eh, *bien*, tell it me. See, I am listening. I am, as the English say, all ears."

"Had you returned two minutes earlier you would have met Lord Courtenay."

"What! has he been here?"

"He was in this room with a story that should interest you — you, perhaps, more than any other person," said her father drily. "At the masquerade Lord Courtenay chanced to meet a certain lady."

"I was hoping that he would."

"A lady whose true name he has never been able to learn."

"Her reticence on that point is a high tribute to his sense of virtue. She knows very well that on his hearing it he would have no more to do with her."

"What! you know this lady?"

"My enemy. Siberia would now be my home could she have her way."

"Who is she?"

"That's a surprise I'll keep in reserve. You shall learn by and by. Continue your story, *mon père.*"

"Do you know that this lady is loved by Alexander?"

"You should put that remark in the past tense," said Pauline with an odd smile.

"This favourite of the Czar was so gracious as to bestow a kiss upon Lord Courtenay, and, unfortunately for her, the Czar himself witnessed the act."

Pauline laughed softly.

"The very result desired by me," she said.

"You are pleased. Yes, I can quite comprehend your motive in wishing that this lady should forfeit the Czar's regard. You will not find the sequel so pleasing. The Czar and Lord Courtenay came to words."

"Over the lady! Strange, when matters were taking a course acceptable to all three! And I suppose that Lord Courtenay, so bold before Paul, was equally bold with Paul's son?"

"He did not know at the time that he was speaking to Paul's son, since Alexander would neither remove his mask nor disclose his identity. But Lord Courtenay has learned his name since."

"And what was the end of the affair?"

"The end comes this morning at eight, when the Czar and Lord Courtenay cross swords!"

In a moment Pauline's airy manner was gone. She rose from her seat, trembling in every limb, but sank down again apparently powerless.

"A duel!" she gasped.

"To the death! Such is Alexander's determination."

"A duel!" she repeated in hollow tones. "Between those two! Oh, it can't be! You say this to frighten me. Emperors don't fight duels."

"Alexander acted, perhaps, on the spur of the moment in giving a challenge to the finest swordsman of the day, but having given it he will keep his word."

"Lord Courtenay must be persuaded to withdraw."

"Pshaw! As well bid the sun not shine! That his opponent is the Czar lends added zest to the fight."

Pauline shuddered.

"He dare not kill the Czar."

"Not purposely, perhaps, but in the hot excitement of ——"

"Speak the truth, *mon père*," interrupted Pauline with an indignant flash of her eyes. "Say that you are hoping to see the Czar killed!"

"That *is* my hope."

"Why?"

"Can *you* ask why?" returned the Marquis. "To preserve the honour of Pauline de Vaucluse. And that is the reason why I, her father, am acting as Lord Courtenay's second. Can he have a more suitable one?"

"Your daughter's honour was never at hazard," said Pauline haughtily, rising to her full stature and facing her father. "Do you think that I would ever consent to become the Czar's mistress? You doubt my word, I see."

Taking from her bosom a small scroll of parchment, she unfolded it, and held it before the eyes of the Marquis.

"Perhaps this will convince you. Here you have the reason why I have consorted so much with Alexander."

The Marquis took the scroll in both hands, which trembled with suppressed agitation. Though there was not much writing on the scroll he had to read it several times before he could grasp its meaning. And when at last its meaning *was* grasped, his face wore a ghastly smile, the half-believing, half-sceptical smile of the pauper, when suddenly told that he is heir to stores of gold.

"You see what a traitress I have been to your diplomatic policy? But you forgive me, *mon père;* is it not so? You give up Bonaparte from this day henceforth. The Bourbons must be your friends now as they once were."

"Can this be true?" murmured the Marquis hoarsely, lifting his eyes from the document to his daughter's face.

"There is the signature. You have seen it many a time, and should know whether it is genuine."

Bewildered, the Marquis sank upon a sofa. A new feeling stole over him as he contemplated his beautiful daughter — a feeling of admiration bordering upon awe.

"Then," said he, "who on earth is the lady whom Lord Courtenay met at the masquerade?"

"Did you say that Lord Courtenay has been here?"

"Yes."

"In this room?"

"Nowhere else."

"And didn't notice that?" said Pauline, pointing to a lady's portrait hanging upon the wall.

"My God!" gasped the Marquis, more startled than ever. "Is *that* the lady?"

"None other. Now you see why this duel must not be."

CHAPTER XXIII

It was past five o'clock when Wilfrid sprang from the coach on the Viborg Road and disappeared down the narrow path that wound through a forest of pines, while the vehicle continued on its way northwards.

After a few hundred paces the path opened out into a little clearing, in the middle of which stood a rough log cabin, such as the Russian peasant raises with his own hand. Ornamental carving marked the eaves and door-posts, and on the straw thatch rested heavy stones, placed there to prevent the cottage from being unroofed by tempest.

The tenant was already at work preparing a pile of timber for charcoal burning. Wilfrid liked the look of the man, and felt that any trust placed in him would not be betrayed.

First hailing the fellow with a cheery " Good-morning," Wilfrid went on to speak of the Baroness Runö, at the mention of whose name the peasant's eyes glistened with a grateful light. It was clear that if he could do anything to serve her or her friends he would do it. So Wilfrid in a few words explained the object of his visit, without, however, mentioning the name of his august opponent.

" Now, good Ruric, you understand my position. The Baroness's father, who is my second, advised me to leave the city before him lest the authorities should stop the duel by arresting me."

" Surely, surely," nodded the man. " 'Twas wise."

" To keep a clear head and eye I must have two hours' sleep. But while I sleep what is to prevent my enemies from coming upon me?"

"Little father, they shall not do that. I will keep watch for you."

"Good! Well, then, while I rest in your hut, do you from the shelter of the trees keep an eye upon the road near the eighth verst-post, and should anything suspicious occur come at once and rouse me. You shall have roubles for your trouble."

"It is enough reward for me," returned Ruric, "to know that I am serving a friend of the Lady Pauline."

He led the way into his hut, which consisted of one room only, with furniture of a primitive type. Ruric lived all alone, it seemed, having neither wife nor child.

Left to himself Wilfrid sat down upon a wooden bench and soon dropped off into unconsciousness.

He was roused from sleep by the touch of a hand upon his shoulder. Lifting his head he was startled to see, standing around him, nine men. Their flat features and peculiar dress seemed to bespeak a Finnish origin, a remark not applicable to the one who acted as chief, for he was a man of handsome and aristocratic appearance, middle-aged, and wearing a costume that might have belonged to a French gentleman of the old *régime.*

"You are Lord Courtenay, I presume?" said this gentleman, bowing politely and speaking in French.

"That is a name I never deny."

"I am Dr. Beauvais, physician at one time to his late majesty Louis XVI."

"And why this visit? 'They that be whole need not a physician —' You know the rest."

"Pardon me, monsieur, it is my humble wish that you accompany me to a carriage that stands hard by."

"And how if I decline to come?"

Dr. Beauvais shrugged his shoulders.

"Monsieur will surely not oblige us to use force?"

Force? Oh, why had De Vaucluse refused him a sword? With that in his hand he would have faced the nine. But without a weapon he was entirely in their power. Good-bye now to his hopes of a duel with the Czar! He saw that some one, friendly to Alexander, had got to know of the coming fight, and, with a view of preventing it, had sent these men to carry him off.

"Use force," he said, repeating the other's words. "That may bring trouble upon you. I am here to meet the Czar by his special desire. Remove me, and you make a mock of his majesty."

"It is because we know the nature of this intended meeting that we are here to prevent it."

"You are prepared to face the Czar's displeasure?"

"We are prepared to do the bidding of the person that sent us. Time presses; I must ask you to accompany me."

Vain would it be for Wilfrid to threaten Beauvais with the name of his uncle, Lord St. Helens. If the doctor cared little for an emperor, he was likely to care still less for an ambassador. Physical resistance was certain to end in his humiliation, at least in the hut; but outside in the free air it might be possible to break through the ring of his captors and escape by fleetness of foot.

But the doctor had read his thoughts.

"You must pledge your word of honour as an English gentleman that you will not seek to escape; that when in the coach you will raise no cry for help, make no sign to passers-by; nay, that you will not venture even to peer through the blinds. Of course, if monsieur, instead of travelling pleasantly and comfortably, prefers to be corded and gagged —— "

Wilfrid gave the required pledge, adding, with a hard smile: —

"Lead on. At present you are master of the situation; ere long I may be; in which case, Dr. Beauvais, a mere apology will not content me."

The little procession moved out of the hut into the open sunshine, traversed the winding path, and came to the high road, where stood a covered carriage with drawn blinds. Wilfrid stepped into the vehicle, followed by the doctor only, who closed the door after him. It seemed that the eight men were not accompanying them, a fact that showed Beauvais' faith in Wilfrid's word of honour. The horses' heads were set in the direction of St. Petersburg, and since the carriage moved off without turning round, Wilfrid concluded that he was being taken back to the city. After half an hour's riding the sound of other

vehicles blending with the hum of human voices convinced him that he had now reached the outskirts of the
capital. Noting the slant of the sun's rays as they came
through the carriage windows he was of the opinion that
the vehicle was going due west. If it continued in this
direction long he would soon be out of the city again
and in the district known as " The Islands," or delta of
the Neva, a region of groves and waters, adorned here
and there with bungalows. These islands, left in winter
to snow and wolves, become, in summer, flowering and
leafy paradises, the favourite resort of the fashionable
world of St. Petersburg.

The coach stopped at last without having deviated
much from its westerly course. Beauvais alighted, and
Wilfrid following suit, found himself in a quiet spot upon
the northern shore of the Neva, close to the water's
edge.

Westwards, as far as the horizon, stretched an expanse
of blue sea, the bay conducting to the island-fortress of
Cronstadt, distant about eighteen miles. Southwards,
and separated from them by a channel not more than a
furlong wide, was a small isle consisting of green lawns
and pine woods; and, rising prettily above them, a castle,
built in true Gothic style.

Wilfrid recognised the edifice in a moment as being the
original of the needlework picture that hung in Pauline's
boudoir. He was casting eyes for the first time upon her
island and Castle of Runö, the insular demesne that
furnished her with the title of baroness.

A real old feudal castle, with Pauline for its queen,
would have been welcomed at any other time; but, as
matters were then, Wilfrid was possessed by a feeling of
bitterness towards its fair owner, for it scarcely admitted
a doubt that he had been carried off by her orders. On
her return from the masquerade she had learned from
her father of the intended duel, and had planned this
abduction for the purpose of preventing it.

On the river bank, waiting for Beauvais and his companion, were two sturdy Finlanders in charge of a small
rowing-boat. It would have been easy for Wilfrid to take
to his heels; but, honouring his plighted word, he stepped

with the doctor into the boat, was rowed across the channel, and was soon treading the green turf of Runö.

Entering the castle, Wilfrid was led through several corridors and apartments, till his conductor stopped at last before a certain door, at which he tapped thrice.

"Come in," said a sweet and familiar voice.

Beauvais drew aside, and Wilfrid entered the room alone.

Of the size, character, and furnishings of this apartment, he took no note; his eye rested on one object alone, the figure of Pauline, the sole occupant of the room. She had risen to receive him, and stood looking somewhat paler than usual. Her half-smile of greeting died away as she beheld his stern glance.

"So it is to *you*, then, that I owe this abduction?"

"Am I not acting for the best?" she said, in a faint voice.

"I compliment you upon your new greatness," he continued sarcastically.

"My new greatness?" she faltered.

"Yes. If the Czar may not fight a duel when he is so disposed, then it is not the Czar that rules, but the Baroness Runö."

She looked at him with a sort of fear in her eyes, as if detecting some hidden meaning in his words.

"Do you know that you have made me lose my honour?" he continued.

"In what way?"

"You have caused me to break my word to be at a certain spot by eight this morning. My absence will be attributed to fear."

At this point Pauline's pent up excitement bubbled over in a quick agitated flow of words.

"You have no right," she cried, "to undertake this duel. A chance slip of your blade, and all might be over with Alexander. And how would you save yourself from death? Whither would you flee? To the British Embassy? Do you think that the people of St. Petersburg, roused to fury by the death of the Czar, would care anything for the law of nations? You, and the uncle that gave you protection, and all the English within the build-

ing, would be dragged forth into the streets and mas-
sacred. Think of others, if you will not think of yourself.
The Czar, in condescending to waive his rank and to
meet you in duel, is acting like a gentleman, but you are
not acting as such in taking advantage of his condescension. Indifferent as to whether you kill Alexander,
indifferent as to whether the Peace Treaty be signed,
indifferent as to whether you plunge an empire into
mourning, or cover European politics with inextricable
confusion, you wish for the duel merely to boast of being
the only man in history to cross swords with a Czar,
merely to be talked about. Not honour, or truth, or
justice, calls you to this duel, but sheer vanity, and vanity
alone."

She paused, completely out of breath, with her rapid
speaking. Never had Wilfrid seen her looking so angry;
and he was fain to confess that her lifted hand, the
unstudied grace of her figure, the sparkling of her eye,
and the colour that burned on her cheek, gave a new
aspect to her beauty.

"I want to be talked about?" said he, taking up her
words with a feeling that he had been somewhat hard hit
by them. "Well, and what if I do? Call it vanity, if
you like. The poet will style it fame; the soldier glory;
the statesman ambition. As to this idol of yours, this
unclean thing called a Czar, the craven who shrank from
punishing his father's assassins, who let a printed lie go
forth to the world, who continued his father's war, and
then made peace as soon as he heard the British fleet was
coming — whether he be worthy of your fiery defence
is a question I shall leave to the judgment of history."

At the word "unclean," the scarlet glow of anger on
Pauline's face gave way to a deathly white. Wilfrid
could see that her teeth were set, and that she breathed
hard. Her look of anguish was so keen that he almost
regretted his use of the word. And yet, was it not
applicable?

She was silent for a few moments, and when she spoke
it was in a humbler key.

"The one desire of my life, as you know, is to see the
Bourbons restored to the throne of France. Alexander

has advanced a step in this direction by breaking with the First Consul, Napoleon; his next will be to declare war against him. If, then, Alexander should fall by your hand, and such accident *might* happen, that barbarian Constantine would be Czar, and then, good-bye to my bright hopes, for he favours Bonaparte. No, Lord Courtenay, you shall not imperil my plans. For this seizure of your person I have the sanction of the British Government —— "

"What?" cried Wilfrid incredulously.

"That is, if Lord St. Helens be the representative of the British Government, as I suppose he is. I had a ten-minutes' interview with him early this morning, and he approved this plan of mine."

"He did, did he?" muttered Wilfrid, a little confounded to find that Pauline was acting with a sort of quasi-legality. "And pray, how long do you propose to detain me here?"

She hesitated; and then, adopting a gentler tone, she said, with a persuasive look: —

"Promise me — promise that you will give up all thoughts of this duel, and you are free now."

"Such promise I will never give."

"Then here you will remain," she said firmly, "till you be of a better mind."

"That answer cancels all friendship between us. Baroness, I have said my last word to you."

With a look that cut her to the heart, he turned his back upon her; and then, seized with the sudden hope of being able to force his way from the castle, he made quickly for the door by which he had entered, only to find that it had been locked on the outside by Beauvais. He turned back just in time to see Pauline disappear through the only remaining door. Ere he could cross the room she had closed this door and turned the key in the lock.

Foiled in his attempt Wilfrid looked angrily round upon the place appointed for his detention. It was an apartment dainty with pictures and tapestry, with velvet carpeting and costly furniture. The bookcase contained the works of those English authors for whom he had once expressed a preference in Pauline's hearing. Upon a table was an epergne crowned with fruit of different kinds. Various sorts of wines glowed in decanters, and Wilfrid, reading the silver labels, saw in them another tribute to Pauline's memory. A box of fragrant Havanas was likewise to be seen. It was evidently the aim of the Baroness to make his captivity as pleasant as possible.

To avail himself of these luxuries would, to a certain extent, placate Pauline; for this very reason he resolved to abstain from them.

After a long and careful scrutiny of the apartment, with its barred windows, locked doors, solid walls, and flooring of oak, Wilfrid sat down to think out some plan of escape; but whatever shape the attempt might take, its execution must be deferred till night-fall. The numerous servants, moving in and around the castle, would make his flight in the face of day difficult, if not impossible.

His natural longing for freedom was intensified by the wish to see the Princess again, the desired of the Czar! As he contemplated his position, nameless terrors for her safety seized him. He was tormented with a mixed sensation of love and jealousy, fear and despair; in this mood he sprang to his feet again, and paced the apartment, inwardly raging against the Czar, Lord St. Helens, Beauvais, and above all, against Pauline, the originator of his present misfortune.

The grating of a key caused him to sink quietly with folded arms into a chair that faced one of the open windows, through which came a pleasant breeze.

He did not even turn his head to notice who was entering, but the rustle of silken skirts showed that the newcomer was a woman, and he supposed that it was Pauline. He would abide by his word, and treat her with silence.

Pauline — for it was she — suddenly stopped. The fruit and the wine had been arranged by her own hand; she saw that neither had been touched. She turned her eyes to the bookcase; not one volume had been lifted from its shelf. With a strange sinking of heart she realised that he would take no favour at her hands.

Though well aware that Pauline was standing by his

chair, Wilfrid took not the least notice of her, but continued to gaze fixedly through the window over the Cronstadt Bay, whose waters glittered in the rays of the afternoon sun.

"Lord Courtenay," she said, with an air of humility, very rare in her, "I regret that this — this state of affairs should have arisen between us. Promise that you will not seek to renew this duel, and I will let you go."

The colour of shame tinged her cheek as she spoke. What right had she to detain him a prisoner against his will? Even the sanction of that great potentate, Lord St. Helens, was proving but a sorry salve to her conscience. Her cheek paled again when she found that Wilfrid remained indifferent both to her presence and to her words.

"Give me your parole not to attempt escape, and you are free to wander at will through the castle and the isle."

There was no reply. With a fresh sinking of heart she recalled Wilfrid's utterance that he had spoken his last word to her.

"You are angry, I see; but I, too, have cause for anger in your resolve to do hurt to the Czar. Give me credit for good intentions. I am acting for the best interests of both parties. Why should two good men seek to slay each other?"

Still Wilfrid sat staring stonily at the sea.

Observing in what direction his eyes were set she drew near to the window, ostensibly to arrange a curtain, in reality to come within the sphere of his vision. It would be a pleasure if only she could attract his look. His glance fell on her form, apparently without noticing it; his eyes seemed to look through and beyond her.

Humiliated beyond measure Pauline turned away, and with a quick step quitted the apartment.

The moment she had gone Wilfrid allowed his hitherto grim face to relax into a smile.

"You are not so hard in grain as I thought, Mistress Pauline. You are beginning to feel remorse, and that remorse, if I err not, will work for my good."

Time flowed quietly on. The sunlight stole from point

to point along the tapestried wall, till finally it took its leave of the room altogether, and still Wilfrid sat in silent meditation.

Again the grating of the key and an opening of the door; and again Wilfrid showed his indifference by not turning his head.

This time it was two prettily attired maids who entered, each bearing a tray laden with hot dishes, which they proceeded to arrange upon the table.

" Will the little father be pleased to dine? "

The little father paid no attention, though being mightily hungry he had secretly to confess that the savour arising from the dishes was very appetising.

The maids repeated their words. Receiving no reply they glanced in surprise at each other, whispered together for a moment, and then withdrew.

" They will tell their mistress that the Englishman refuses to eat. She will come here again."

Nor was he wrong. Ere the lapse of an hour Pauline was again in the room, and saw that the repast was cold and untouched.

" You cannot live on air."

Wilfrid sat, the same impassive figure as before; to her eye it looked as if he had not moved a muscle since her previous visit.

She contemplated him with secret terror. This grim silence, the silence of one who seemed to have taken a vow upon him; this abstention from food, served vividly to bring to her mind an anecdote he had once told her of a certain Viking ancestor of his, who, enraged at some insult, went home, sat by his fireside, refused to take food, and so died! Was Wilfrid going to do the like?

Though secretly piqued, grieved, angered — there is no one word to describe properly her strange feeling — by Wilfrid's manner, she could not refrain from addressing additional remarks to him, remarks whose tenor showed an interest, and even a tenderness, in his welfare.

She might as well have talked to a statue. Animated by a spirit of despair she at last put the question point blank : —

" Lord Courtenay, will you not speak? "

No! he would not; and to hide her vexation and tears, she flung herself from the room.

"The woman is yielding," was his thought. "Her next coming will be to set me free."

An opinion that proved correct. From the moment when she had first locked the door upon Wilfrid, Pauline had been miserable. She could not see him mortified without being mortified herself. What her head bade her do, her heart bade her not do. All day long this struggle had been going on in her mind, and when night came the struggle was too great to be borne any longer.

The key turned in the lock, the door swung wide, and Pauline entered. With timid steps she drew near to Wilfrid.

"Lord Courtenay," she said humbly, "forgive me for carrying matters with so high a hand. It has been done with good intent, to avert bloodshed; but it — it pains me to keep you a prisoner. See! the door is open. My Finland henchmen are withdrawn. You are free."

Then, overcoming a sort of shame that had hitherto kept her from the act, she knelt before him.

"Say that you forgive me, for I — I have been most wretched all the day."

Hard indeed would have been the mortal who could have resisted the wistful light of her dark eyes when added to the pleading tone of her voice.

Moved by a sudden and natural impulse, Wilfrid took her hands within his own and carried them to his lips; and by that act Pauline knew that she was forgiven.

CHAPTER XXIV

THE FIGURE IN THE GREY DOMINO

"I HAVE tasted nothing all the day," said Pauline, "I could not eat while you were fasting; but now, if you will give me your arm, Lord Courtenay, you shall conduct me to a chamber below, where there is a dinner set forth for us."

Wilfrid, who received this news with a good deal of pleasure, for he happened to be terribly hungry, escorted Pauline to the room in question.

The two maids who were preparing to station themselves at the table, were dismissed by their impulsive mistress.

"Let me be your serving maid," she whispered to Wilfrid.

There was about her an odd yet pretty air of penitence, an air that gave place at times to soft laughter when some jest fell from Wilfrid; then, as if conscious that gaiety did not become her so soon after her ill-treatment of him, she would become grave again; and so, what with her obvious desire to please him, and what with her winning glances, the last trace of resentment faded from Wilfrid's mind.

He could not help thinking it strange that Pauline, who had evidently learned from her father all about the proposed duel, should betray no curiosity as to the lady that had caused it, but so it was; and, since she was silent on the matter, he himself maintained a similar reserve.

"Can you tell me," he asked, "if the Czar attended the rendezvous?"

"Not if he believed in the lie of Lord St. Helens."

"What was that?"

"A lie to which — what will you think of me? — I gave my sanction. At six this morning your uncle was to repair to the Czar with the news that Lord Courtenay, having discovered his opponent's identity, had not only retired from the combat, but was travelling post haste to Narva, intending to take ship for his own country. In fact, it is your uncle's plan that you be kept here under my care while he arranges to have you shipped and carried off to England. And in so doing he thinks he is consulting your best interests. *My* part of the plan," added Pauline, with a mock-mournful air, " has broken down. Now that you are free how do you intend to act?" she added, a little nervously.

" The Czar must learn that I have not played the coward. I shall go to St. Petersburg and somehow let him know that I am still in his capital, ready to meet him in duel, if he be so disposed."

Pauline sighed over Wilfrid's romantic obstinacy.

" The Czar will learn," said she, with a rueful little smile, "that you were spirited away by Pauline de Vaucluse."

" No, Baroness, no. I will suppress your name. You shall remain hidden under the title of a — a — ahem! a misguided patriot."

" You are not going to set off for St. Petersburg to-night, I presume, seeing that it is now past ten o'clock?"

" No, I'll defer my journey till the morning."

Pauline sat in silence for a few moments, and then an odd light came into her eyes, and she smote her forehead with a pretty little gesture.

" *Ciel!* how stupid of me!" she exclaimed. "Strange, is it not, that ideas the most obvious never seem to strike one at the time they should."

" And what," smiled Wilfrid, " is the obvious idea that you have overlooked?"

" That I need not have taken the trouble to imprison you when a sentence, one short sentence, would extinguish in you all desire for this duel."

She spoke with a confidence such as half-disposed Wilfrid to believe her statement true. But though pressed as to her meaning, she refused just then to satisfy his curiosity.

"I will explain in the morning. You have had gloom enough for one day. Let me not act the part of a kill-joy to-night."

The dinner being over, Pauline sent for Dr. Beauvais, — her steward, as well as physician — who, on entering, seemed surprised at beholding the two on friendly terms again.

"Now mind, sir," said Pauline to Wilfrid, with an air of mock command, "no duelling with Dr. Beauvais, for I hear that you threatened him with one this morning."

"Dr. Beauvais, as a loyal servant of the Baroness, is a man for whom I have the highest respect."

"Then, in that case," she smiled, "I can leave you safely with him. You will pardon my retiring, but I have not closed my eyes since the masquerade."

Upon her withdrawal Beauvais proposed a cigar, and the pair sallied forth from a portcullised archway.

"I did not expect to see a feudal-looking castle in this part of Europe," remarked Wilfrid.

"An architectural whim of the first Catharine," returned Beauvais. "Built in imitation of one in Livonia, that she had often admired when a peasant girl."

Before them in that faint, lovely twilight, which is the only night St. Petersburg has in the month of July, lay a smooth, verdant lawn, fringed by a dark pine-wood, whose vistas terminated in a distant shimmer of blue water.

"If you are hesitating which way to go," observed Wilfrid, "let us turn to the Silver Strand."

"Ah! Good! The view from that point is particularly fine."

It was not the view that Wilfrid was thinking of, but the remark overheard at the masquerade that the lady's fan that had dropped into the river would be carried by the current to this strand; and an unaccountable impulse came upon him to verify the statement.

Smoking and conversing, the two men strolled leisurely onward through a woodland path that finally opened upon a beach of glistening grey sand.

The view from it, as the doctor had said, was very fine, so fine that Wilfrid forgot all about the fan.

Pauline's island of Runö was situated near the entrance of one of the deltoid arms of the Neva. Standing upon the Silver Strand and looking eastwards Wilfrid had before him a long perspective of broad water, its shores on each side dark with woods of birch and pine. Amid this night of groves gleamed many a white villa, whose twinkling lights were mirrored in the water. The beauty of the night had drawn the dwellers forth; gondolas glided to and fro; the laughter of men and women, mingling with the sweet strains of the guitar, came, mellowed by the distance, over the smooth, blue water.

"A midsummer night's dream," murmured Wilfrid.

Turning to his companion he found that *his* eyes were set, not upon the river-view, but upon a part of the Silver Strand itself, and following the direction of the doctor's gaze, Wilfrid saw, some distance away, and a few feet from the water's edge, a recumbent figure bearing resemblance to that of a woman.

She was lying at full length upon her left side, her face being turned from them, lying in a somewhat singular attitude, Wilfrid thought; for both arms were extended behind her back in such fashion as almost to suggest that they were tied at the wrists; distance and the twilight prevented him from seeing clearly whether such were the case.

"One of the Baroness's girls asleep?" said Beauvais, taking the cigar from his teeth. "*Parbleu!* she chooses an odd hour and an odd place for sleeping."

Thinking to rouse her, he gave utterance to a shout, loud enough, one would have thought, to awaken the soundest sleeper.

The woman did not stir.

The doctor looked at Wilfrid; Wilfrid looked at the doctor. There was something weird in the sight of this lonely figure as it lay there, silent and motionless, in the ghostly starlight, with the river plashing faintly at its feet, above its head the night-wind sighing through the pines.

Strange that both men hesitated to take the few paces necessary to solve their doubts!

The doctor perhaps would have been puzzled to give

his reason. Far different was it with Wilfrid; he hung back from facing the truth. All the fear he had ever known, gathered up and sublimated into one tense, over-whelming sensation, would have failed to equal the dread that fell upon him at this moment as he discerned that the figure had fair, sunny hair and a costume whose silvery grey colour was scarcely distinguishable from the sand it touched!

What if it should be —— ?

Suddenly the doctor, throwing away his cigar, set off at a brisk run in the direction of the figure, an action that caused Wilfrid to run likewise.

He was the first to reach the silent woman, and saw that her ankles and wrists were bound with cords. The face was hidden by a mask of grey silk that had lost its crispness, apparently by saturation in water, for it adhered to her features like a second skin. It had slipped downwards a little, so that the eyes and mouth were hidden.

Wilfrid stooped and lifted the mask.

And it was the Princess, cold and dead!

CHAPTER XXV

THE DOCTOR'S PLOT

WHEN Wilfrid saw the Princess manifesting every sign of death, there came over him that strange feeling that often follows a fall from a great height, a numbing of the limbs and a dulling of the senses.

He could hear the melancholy lap-lap of the water upon the sands and the distant strains of music, without understanding the origin of the sounds; he knew that he was supporting the head of the Princess, not because his arm felt the weight of what he was holding, but because he could see the arm performing the task; he knew that he was looking down upon a face, beautiful and still, but could not for the moment tell why the sight of this face should cause him to feel a gnawing pain at his heart.

As for Beauvais, he, too, looked quite confounded when the mask was lifted; indeed, his expression of fear at the sight of the dead countenance seemed somewhat out of place in a physician, especially in one who, having lived through the September Massacres and the Reign of Terror, should have grown familiar with death in whatever shape it came.

Wilfrid, wrapped in stupor, saw nothing of this strange perturbation on the part of Beauvais.

The latter, becoming suddenly conscious of his professional duty, drew forth a penknife, severed the cord that bound Marie's wrists, and applied his trained fingers to the pulse, while Wilfrid, dimly comprehending what the other was about, waited in a state of suspense more dreadful than any he had ever known.

" She is past my art," said Beauvais, in an awe-struck tone. He rose to his feet, and eyed Wilfrid curiously, as if wondering what effect the statement would have upon him. One might have thought that he knew something of the relationship previously existing between Wilfrid and the Princess.

As Wilfrid realised the fell meaning of Beauvais' words, there broke from him a cry of anguish; his arm relaxed its hold, and the Princess's golden head slid gradually down on his arm to the sands again.

Brought by the swift-flowing river to the Silver Strand, she must have reached it alive, for the body was too high upon the beach to have been cast there by the current.

"Syncope!" murmured Beauvais. "The joy of having escaped from the waters proved too much for her, and she dropped dead upon the sands."

Wilfrid, who had never once removed his eyes from the Princess's face, suddenly thrilled with a new sensation. For the first time in his life he found it a struggle to speak. He could get his words out only in husky, staccato tones.

"Doctor . . . she's . . . not . . . dead . . . I . . . saw . . . this eyelid . . . quiver."

Beauvais dropped like a stone upon his knees, lifted the lid, and scrutinised the eye while holding her pulse again.

"The *rigor mortis,* and yet not dead? Catalepsy, by heaven!" he cried. "She's just rousing from it. There's life in her. But — but, it may ebb. Brandy, hot water, chafing — without delay."

"Will it do hurt to carry her thus?" asked Wilfrid, tenderly lifting the still form.

"Not at all."

"Then in heaven's name run on first to the castle, and rouse the women-folk."

Beauvais required no second bidding; he set off with fleet feet, while Wilfrid, bearing the Princess in his arms, followed as fast as he was able.

At the castle-entrance he was met by a wondering-eyed maid, who, apprised of his coming, asked no questions but at once led the way to a bed-chamber that was being rapidly prepared for the reception of the patient. Two other maids were there under the doctor's directions, getting ready the necessary restoratives.

"Now, girls, to work!" said he cheerfully. "It's a

struggle betwixt life and death, and we're not going to let death be the winner."

Leaving the still comatose Princess to their ministrations Wilfrid withdrew to the corridor, and there met Vera, Pauline's chief maid, and, it may be added, confidante.

" My lady is in a sleep so sweet that it would be a pity to awake her," she observed. " Still, if you think — "

" Let her sleep on. Why should we disturb her? She can do no more good than is being done. Besides —— "

But Wilfrid thought it best to let his next thought remain unspoken. He recalled the Princess's expressed aversion for Pauline, and though he doubted whether that aversion had any real justification, still it might tend to retard her recovery if, upon opening her eyes, the first person seen by her should be the one whom she regarded as her deadliest enemy.

So Pauline was permitted to continue her sleep in ignorance of what was happening.

While the doctor was busied in his work, Wilfrid, sitting in the corridor without, tried to picture the circumstances that had brought the Princess to the shores of Runö.

Though her clothing had felt quite dry to his touch, it bore the appearance of having been saturated, proof that the body of the Princess had been carried to the Silver Strand by the current of the Nevka.

That her plight was due neither to accident nor to attempted suicide was shown by the fact that her hands had been fixed behind her back in such a fashion as to preclude the possibility of their being self-tied. As she was still wearing her mask and domino, it scarcely admitted a doubt that, falling into the hands of the four hirelings, she had been flung into the river from the terrace of the Sumaroff gardens before the *bal masque* had come to an end.

Her white satin shoes, he had noticed, were deep stained with black ooze, matter not to be found on any part of the Silver Strand; hence her feet must have touched the bed of the river, once at least. As the Nevka is remarkably deep, it followed, in Wilfrid's opinion, that her feet could not have descended so far, unless they had been attached to some heavy weight; this must have somehow slipped from its fastenings, with the result that the body of the Princess rose immediately to the surface. She was evidently versed, to a greater or less extent, in the art of swimming, for though bound hand and foot, and weighted by heavy clothing, she had contrived to maintain her breathing during a course of three miles. Swimming or floating as she best could, her head now above water and now below it, blinded by her mask that had slipped down over her eyes, battling desperately for life, she was borne along on the broad bosom of the rushing river till, by happy chance, she found her feet touching ground, and making her way through the lessening depth of water, ended her course by crawling up the shelving shore.

The sudden revulsion of joy at this escape from death proved too much for her; catalepsy supervened.

So, by a singular destiny, during the whole term of Wilfrid's captivity, and for some time before and after it, the Princess had been on this island, separated from him by a distance of less than a quarter of a mile!

While he had been anxiously wondering what had become of her, there, upon the warm sandy shore, the Princess had lain all day long, nature alone attentive to her. The sunlight had dried her clothing, the breeze had played with the tangles of her golden hair, but till nightfall no denizen of the isle had drawn near. As for passing boats, their occupants, unless they had come very near the shore indeed, would have been unable to distinguish the silver grey of her costume from the silver grey of the hollow in which she lay.

Such was the train of thought pursued by Wilfrid during the suspense of waiting.

By means of Vera he was kept informed as to the state of the patient. After a lapse of two hours a turn for the better was announced; each succeeding report became more and more favourable, till at last, his work apparently over, Beauvais himself made his appearance, his face expressive of pleasure at having come off victor in his wrestle with death.

"A tough struggle," he said, "but we've won it. Talk? No, she didn't talk much. Wanted to, but I enjoined silence. She's sleeping peacefully now, a natural, healthful sleep. She'll wake up as bright as a new silver rouble."

This was all Wilfrid wanted to know. With a sense of relief he bade the doctor good-night, and, under the guidance of one of the maids, repaired to the room appointed him.

Upon Wilfrid's departure Beauvais went back to the Princess's bed-chamber and dismissed the second maid, by which act Vera was left the sole attendant. Standing at some distance from the bed the doctor beckoned her to approach. She came forward on tip-toe. Keeping a watchful eye upon the sleeper, Beauvais said in a whisper :—

"I saw that you recognised her, and cannot sufficiently commend your prudence in keeping a silent tongue. Those who attempted her life may attempt it again, should they find that their plan miscarried. Hence we must exercise caution, and keep her name and whereabouts a secret. So far you and I are the only two to recognise her. The Baroness will make a third, and perhaps we shall have to admit Lord Courtenay into our confidence, but that's my business; yours is to be mute and to know nothing. It may be that our patient herself for reasons of her own will wish to keep her identity a secret, even from Lord Courtenay. In such case not a word to him. You may be quite sure that I should not give you this advice were it not for the good of the Baroness. Now show me where you have put our patient's clothing."

Vera indicated the place, and the doctor, walking thither, proceeded to examine the Princess's garments. Discovering a pocket within the domino, he placed his hand within and drew forth a sealed envelope, crumpled and discoloured. Its exterior was a blank.

"Now what does this envelope contain?" muttered Beauvais pressing it between his fingers. "I must know its contents. Perhaps it's the key to the mystery. It may — or may not — explain how she came to be in the

river. Vera, should our patient or Lord Courtenay
question you on this point, you will be pleased to say
that you searched the clothing and found — nothing."
He moved towards the door as he spoke. " I will send
you a companion, and as soon as our patient awakens let
me know, for I must have a talk with her before the
Baroness or Lord Courtenay sees her."

Having summoned another maid Beauvais betook
himself to his own room.

" In the Baroness's service," he remarked, " everything
is lawful."

And without the least hesitation he broke the seal of
the envelope, and read the letter it contained.

" A very useful document," he observed with a smile
of wonder and delight. " The one thing wanting to
round off my plan and make its success sure."

He laid the missive aside. Its contents had set him
thinking, and so absorbed was he that he let the hours
pass without taking any rest.

A message coming from Vera caused him to repair
once more to the Princess's bed-chamber, from which,
after the lapse of half an hour, he emerged with a
triumphant smile.

" Better and better ! " he murmured. " Who'd have
thought it ? Why, there's little need to plot. Matters
are taking of themselves the very course I want."

An hour later, when Pauline issued from her dressing-
room, beautiful for the day, she was surprised to see
Beauvais waiting for her in the corridor.

" A story for you, Baroness," said he. " One that you
must hear without delay."

His air brooked no refusal, and so with a little shrug
of her shoulders she took a seat within an embrasured
window.

Her look of indifference vanished with his first sentence, and as he proceeded her interest finally passed into
vivid horror.

" Consider who she is," concluded the doctor, " and
then picture her lying alone on that shore for nearly
twenty hours, and a whole castleful of people close by."

" Tied hand and foot, and flung into the Neva ! "

Pauline gasped. " My God! This must be Alexander's work! "

" Not so, Baroness."

" But I say yes. Who would dare lay a finger on *her* except by his order? "

" Be calm, dear Baroness. Alexander is guiltless. The truth is, the assassins made a terrible mistake. Did you not tell me that she went to this masquerade in gold-brocaded silk? Just so! Well, when discovered by us she was wearing a grey domino of common serge, which is a clear proof that she must have exchanged her costume with some other woman, her aim probably being to conceal more effectually her interview with Lord Courtenay, and I strongly suspect that this other woman was one Nadia Borovna, of the Inn of the Silver Birch. It is easy to see how one woman might meet the fate intended for the other. In fact, the ruffians appear to have made so sure of their victim that they did not even remove her mask. This letter, written by the said Nadia and found upon the dress of the victim, will partly help to prove my theory."

Pauline took the missive and read it slowly.

" It must have been Baranoff's doings " she remarked, looking up from the letter, intensely relieved to find her suspicions against Alexander groundless.

" Seemingly. At any rate he is the one most interested in seeing that both the letter and its writer are destroyed. When he learns what a mistake his hirelings have made he'll be ready to cut his throat. The Czar will show him no mercy."

" I never believed in Lord Courtenay's guilt at the Inn of the Silver Birch," said Pauline, glancing over the missive again, " and this letter vindicates my opinion."

" True, but you'll be unwise to show it to him."

" Why? "

" Because if that event is allowed to receive an innocent interpretation, it will be still easier to explain away the kiss given by her at the masquerade. It was simply a reward for service done to the State. No, no, Baroness; it must be our duty to see that her return to Alexander is made an impossibility, and as matters are at present the way is still open for a reconciliation between them."

" What, then, do you advise?"

" Why, this. Let her remain here for a time in concealment. She'll not object. She is evidently in love with Lord Courtenay; he with her. Let matters, then, take their natural course. Isn't it to your interest to promote this love affair?"

" Didn't you tell Lord Courtenay last night who she was?"

" I kept it a secret for — for reasons."

"Lord Courtenay is a man of honour. When he learns the truth his love will cease."

" Just so, and therefore we must not let him know the truth, till — till it be too late."

" You talk foolishly. How can he be kept any longer in ignorance?"

Beauvais smiled mysteriously and triumphantly.

" My dear Baroness, everything is working beautifully for our ends, so beautifully that I am tempted almost to think that Providence —— "

" Providence! " she repeated significantly.

" I'll say fate, to please you. Fate must have had a hand in bringing her and Lord Courtenay under this roof."

" You are not answering my question. How can we keep him from learning her name, if she chooses to reveal it?"

" There's the point, the very point in our favour. She can't reveal it."

" In heaven's name, why not?"

" Because, though her intellect be otherwise as clear and as bright as your own — and that's saying a good deal, Baroness — it is accompanied by one defect. The awful shock occasioned by her sudden plunge into the waters of the Neva has had the effect of depriving her, not of her whole memory, but of a part of it — that part relating to her personal identity. She cannot recall her own name. You don't believe it, I see," smiled the doctor, noting her look of scepticism, " but you can soon test my words. Go and see your rival. She won't know you!"

CHAPTER XXVI

WITHOUT A MEMORY!

WHILE Pauline repaired to the Princess's chamber, the doctor went off to Wilfrid's room to acquaint him with the strange news.

Being new to mental phenomena of this sort, Wilfrid received the announcement with every token of unbelief.

"Do you mean to say," he asked in amazement, "that she cannot tell how she came to be in the Neva?"

"Has no recollection whatever of the event. Her mind is a complete blank as to her past: cannot recall the name of a friend or the name of any place where she has dwelt."

"In what mood is she. Sad?"

"Not at all. Smiles at her own perplexity — in fact, her loss of memory seems rather to amuse her."

"And how long is this state likely to last?"

Beauvais shrugged his shoulders.

"One cannot say. A week: a month: a year. Perhaps for the rest of her life."

"And you have no idea who she is?"

"Not in the least; nor has the Baroness. Am I justified in supposing from your agitation last night that she is the lady that set you and the Czar at feud?"

Wilfrid replied that such was the case.

"Ah! Then of course you give up all thoughts of this duel?"

"Honour calls me to it."

"But the lady's safety calls you from it. Now that, thanks to your uncle, the name of the Czar's opponent is known to Count Panine, your appearance in St. Petersburg will be instantly followed by your arrest and deportation to the frontier. In such case what help can you give the lady, should her enemies discover that she is still alive? Her state calls for a protector, and your past relations with her entitle you to assume that rôle."

This way of putting the case modified Wilfrid's views, and — " Postponed indefinitely," became his decision on the question of the duel.

The Princess's loss of memory filled Wilfrid with extreme disquietude. When he last saw her she had been in a vein bordering upon love; this new state of mind on her part would now cause her to be ignorant of his very existence. He would have to begin his love-making all over again, and might — fail!

He breakfasted with the doctor, who, the meal ended, paid another visit to his patient, returning almost immediately with the good news that she was strong enough to be up and dressed.

So, as soon as word came that the Princess's toilet was completed, Wilfrid sought her presence.

Attired in a dainty sarafan of soft muslin, supplied from Pauline's wardrobe, she was reclining in a deep *fauteuil* with the Baroness by her side.

Although she had occupied so large a space in his mind Wilfrid had seen her but four times, and, by a singular coincidence, at night only. Her beauty underwent no diminution by day; on the contrary it seemed to be enhanced by the soft morning light. Her delicate pallor was the only evidence of her recent grapple with death.

It was the same Marie, and yet different. The pensive melancholy hitherto marking her aspect had vanished; a new and happier light glanced from her eyes; the passing of her memory seemed to have brought with it the passing of sorrow.

As Wilfrid recalled the bitter language which the Princess had applied to Pauline, it was with a somewhat odd feeling that he now beheld the two conversing with the familiarity of old friends. It was difficult to believe that the sudden return of the Princess's memory would be accompanied by hostility to Pauline again.

A slight movement on his part caused the Princess to lift her head and look at him.

It was with a sense of disappointment that Wilfrid met

her calm, quiet gaze. He had been fondly hoping that whomsoever else she might have forgotten she could not have forgotten *him*. But alas! her dark blue eyes betrayed no sign of recognition; their expression was simply one of curiosity to know who he was. Her manner differed in nothing from that of a woman meeting with a stranger, a manner that Wilfrid felt to be genuine on her part, and not assumed.

"This is the Lord Courtenay of whom I have been speaking," said Pauline.

Wilfrid bowed gravely. That he should need an introduction to her!

"I am sorry," smiled the Princess, "at having to meet you in the present circumstances. You must think me a very stupid person not to be able to recall my name and history; yet so it is. Try as I will I cannot carry my memory farther back than this morning. That I awoke a few hours ago in a certain bedroom of this castle is all I know of myself. Unless I have dropped ready-made from the skies I must have lived for twenty years and more, and yet of this long time I can remember nothing! Is it not absurd?"

So absurd that she broke out into a laugh; and one more sweet and silvery never rippled from woman's lips, at least in Wilfrid's opinion.

"The Baroness has been telling me that you can perhaps help to revive my memory, as you have seen me amid other surroundings."

"You have been known to me as the Princess Marie."

"Yes, but on looking into the Court Register," she answered, pointing to a book at her feet, "we cannot discover that there is a Princess Marie."

"Whose suggestion was the Court Register?" asked Beauvais, who had accompanied Wilfrid to the presence of the Princess.

"Mine!" answered Marie.

The doctor tapped his forehead significantly at Wilfrid to intimate that, however defective her power of remembering might be, that of reasoning remained intact. Indeed, but for her own confession no one would ever have supposed that any faculty of her mind lay dormant.

Princess Marie was now all eagerness to know on what occasions she and Wilfrid had met, a request that put him in a somewhat embarrassing situation. Was she to be told, for example, that he had once spent an hour in her bedroom? — that she had kissed him at their last meeting? and that she had always expressed enmity towards Pauline?

He looked at Pauline for guidance, who in turn looked at the doctor, while the Princess herself looked from one to another, wondering why there should be such hesitation in telling her a plain story.

" It will be as well," said Beauvais, addressing Wilfrid, " to tell all you know, while the Princess follows you in mind, striving to recall the situations in which your story places her. Such effort will perhaps stimulate her memory."

So spoke the hypocrite, hoping that her efforts would do nothing of the sort.

After a moment's reflection Wilfrid proceeded to relate not all, but as much as he thought needful, for the Princess to know; and it was with a strange sensation of pleasure that he found her eyes fastened on him with a wistful attention, that never once wavered during his recital. Leaving out Baranoff and his infamous proposal Wilfrid began with the bedroom incident; then went on to tell how he had been requested by her to paint his now historic picture, saying nothing, however, as to the reward he had demanded; and coming finally to the masquerade, he led Marie to suppose that the meeting was merely a formal one on her part to thank him for his services. As for the Czar and his presumed aim towards her, Wilfrid suppressed this part of the story altogether.

" How long ago is it since this fête in the Sumaroff Gardens? " she asked.

" Only two nights ago."

" Only two nights ago! " she repeated with breathless incredulity. " And I have no recollection whatever of it! "

She closed her eyes, knitted her brows thoughtfully, pressed her forefinger hard upon her forehead, evidently making a strong effort to recall the past, but could not succeed.

She was silent for a few minutes, pondering her mental state, which was not only inexplicable to her, but also to Beauvais, the student of psychology. For, observe the contradictory nature of the case: her struggle in the water had formed a dividing-line in her history; over this dividing-line she was able to bring into her new life all, or most, of the knowledge acquired in the old, and yet she was unable to bring with it the knowledge of her own personality. Why her mind, able to retain so much of the past, should become an absolute blank upon one point — there was the mystery that humbled, nay, frightened her. Better for her to lose, say, her knowledge of languages or of music, than to lose the knowledge of herself. A gulf seemed to separate her from her three companions; they could carry *their* minds back to childhood's days; for her life began with that morning only. Her previous history lay hidden behind a black curtain. A native from the planet Mars, new-dropped upon the earth, could not have felt less at home than did Princess Marie at that moment.

"What is this that has come upon me?" she murmured with fear in her voice. "If I lose my memory, what is to prevent me from losing my reason?"

"Now you are distressing yourself unnecessarily," said the doctor, cheerily. "Why did I ply you this morning with so many questions upon this, that and the other topic, but to ascertain whether there is any ground for what you fear. And the result? My dear lady, if all the heads in the Czar's cabinet were half as sound as yours, Russia would be well governed. Your mind is perfectly sane, have no fear upon that point. As to your loss of memory — humph! I'll call it a misfortune, to please you. But there are many persons, Prince Ouvaroff for example, who would be glad to obtain an oblivion as complete as yours. Patience, my good lady, patience. Time will restore your memory."

These optimistic remarks, and many more of the same sort from Beauvais, combined with Pauline's caresses, gradually brought the distressed Princess to a calmer state.

"I am justly punished," she said with a sad smile, addressing Wilfrid. "I have so long kept my name a secret from you that it is now a secret from myself. And you say I was found last night lying insensible upon the shores of this island? How did I come there?"

Pauline and the doctor could both have answered this question more fully than Wilfrid, but for reasons of their own they chose to be silent, leaving him to tell as much as he knew of the matter. To his story Marie listened with a troubled air.

"Have I enemies so malignant that they seek to murder me?"

"It would seem so," replied Wilfrid, adding for her consolation, "but since they must now look upon you as dead they will molest you no more."

"It is not for me," said Pauline, "to dictate your course of action, but in view of the recent attempt upon your life, you will do well to remain in hiding here, for a few days at least, until we learn what is best to be done. In the meantime you must look upon the castle and the isle as your own."

A proposal that found a warm seconder in Wilfrid, who foresaw the facilities it would afford him for pushing his suit with the Princess.

So it was settled that she should stay at Runö.

Now, although Marie's companions were three in number, it was to Wilfrid principally that her remarks were addressed, and Pauline and the doctor, well pleased to have it so, presently withdrew to another part of the room, and had a little *tête-à-tête* on their own account.

"Our plan promises to work smoothly," said Beauvais. "She favours him as much in the new state as in the old."

"Yes, but how long can we keep her here in concealment? She has now been absent from the palace for more than a day. By this time the Czar's agents must be swarming everywhere on the look-out for her. Not a spot, not a house, in and around St. Petersburg will remain unvisited."

"We must keep them from visiting Runö," said Beauvais.

"How can it be done?"

"Very easily. Will not Count **Baranoff** and his brother Loris, Chief of the Secret **Police,** have the direction of this affair? And have we not in our possession a letter containing matter enough to hang them ten times over? We must go at once to St. Petersburg and make this compact with them, that unless they are prepared to do our bidding we shall reveal their guilt to the Czar. And our bidding is that they instruct their subordinates to let this island alone. We need not shrink from stating the reason. Has it not been Baranoff's aim to make yonder pair fall in love with each other? What are we doing but pursuing the same plan, though for a different reason? Freed from the intrusion of police agents Runö thus becomes a sacred asylum, an enchanted garden, in which our two wards may make love to their hearts' content without the knowledge of the Court."

"And the end of it all?"

"When her love is sufficiently strong she will be willing to fly with him from Russia. Cronstadt harbour is distant by water but eighteeen miles. A swift boat and a dark night, and they are on board a vessel bound for England."

"But should we in the meantime be detected in our plot by Alexander —— "

"What then? Will he be very much vexed when we are supplying him with the pretext he wants?"

Pauline sighed.

"Ah me! If only I had told Lord Courtenay yesterday who his inamorata is, it would have prevented me from beginning this course of deception. Not till nightfall did it suddenly occur to me that knowledge of this fact would have been the best way of making him cease from the duel; and then from very pity I refrained from the telling, knowing what pain the revelation would bring him, and now — now it is too late! What will he think when he learns — as learn he must — how basely I am deceiving him?"

"Pooh! what matters what he thinks?"

"Much — to me," she answered moodily.

At this point the pair found themselves appealed to by Wilfrid.

"Was there not a letter in the Princess's dress-pocket?" he asked, giving his reason for the question.

"I can of myself testify that there was not," said the unabashed doctor, "for I examined her clothing in the hope of finding some clue to her identity. If it were the object of the four ruffians to get hold of a compromising letter we can scarcely expect them to leave it upon her person."

A specious argument that answered the purpose intended.

The Princess here put to Wilfrid a very sensible suggestion.

"This Prince Ouvaroff, who as you say acted as my escort from some unknown place to St. Petersburg, must surely know who I am. Is it not possible to communicate with him?"

"You echo my thoughts," said Pauline. "Dr. Beauvais and I will go to St. Petersburg this very day for the purpose of seeing the Prince upon this matter."

This proposal on the part of Pauline was more acceptable to the Princess than it was to Wilfrid.

"Supposing," he whispered to Pauline, "that Ouvaroff suspects the motive of your questioning, and springs to the conclusion that Princess Marie must be at Runö?"

"Why, in that case," whispered Pauline in turn, "she would be restored to her old surroundings. But have no fear. I'll approach the matter so cautiously that he shall suspect nothing. I must not delay, however, lest I be too late, for he told me at the masquerade that the Czar was about to send him on a diplomatic mission to Berlin."

So, accompanied by Beauvais, Pauline went the same day to St. Petersburg, but made no attempt to see Prince Ouvaroff.

While the doctor was transacting some private business, Pauline visited first the British Ambassador, and had an interview with him, which terminated with these words on her part: " Never mind how he was persuaded to give up the duel; you have my word for it that St. Petersburg and the Czar will see him no more. *That* surely ought to content you."

And it did, the Ambassador breathing a sigh of relief that the awkward business was over.

The bureau of Loris Baranoff, Chief of the Secret Police, was the next place to receive a call from her, and to judge by her smile as she quitted his office the result of her mission was a complete success.

CHAPTER XXVII

THE CZAR'S PORTRAIT

WHILE Pauline was absent on her mission to St. Petersburg Wilfrid was spending a pleasant time with the Princess, who, avowing herself to be quite well again, refused in defiance of the orders left by Dr. Beauvais, to remain any longer confined to her chamber, but went forth, under Wilfrid's escort, for a ramble around Pauline's insular demesne.

It was a still summer day, and the island with its pine-groves and green lawns lay like a lovely garden upon the bosom of the Neva, whose waters were tinted with the delicate sapphire of the sky.

Wilfrid was certainly a fortunate fellow. Resident at the fairest season of the year in a picturesque old castle upon an island lovely by day, more lovely perhaps by night, with a beautiful young Princess for his companion — what more could he desire?

The pair had reached in their rambling a blue tarn, so smooth and beautiful as to have received from Pauline the pretty name of the Fairies' Mirror. By the water's edge was a rustic seat, and here the two sat down.

"Lord Courtenay," said the Princess, turning her deep serious eyes upon him, "let me hear again the story you told this morning. I am naturally curious to learn all I can about myself."

Compliant with her wish Wilfrid repeated his narrative, finding a pleasure in the telling of it, partly because he loved to dwell upon everything connected with Marie, partly because it was pleasant to have so fair and interested a listener.

"You seem to have remembered my words very well," she murmured, noting that he had repeated her utterances with little or no variation.

"I trust you do not impute that to me as a fault?"

"And have you told me all? Have you kept nothing back?"

Just a trace of embarrassment appeared upon Wilfrid's face, but, faint as it was, it did not escape her quick glance.

"I can see it! No, do not equivocate. You are hiding something from me."

Wilfrid's manner confirmed the Princess in her opinion. What was he to do? Tell her that she was suspected of being the Czar's favourite? No, much as he hated deceit he would rather tell a downright lie than let a thought such as that rankle in her mind!

"Why do you hesitate to tell me all?" she asked.

"In telling all, I must tell of my own folly."

"Folly in which we were both participants? Yes? Then I must know it. It is not fair to hide my past doings from me. What was this folly?"

"Well, since you will have it. In asking me to paint *The Death of Paul,* you made offer of fifty thousand roubles, which I declined in favour of a sweeter guerdon."

"And that was —— ? "

"Perhaps you will show as great anger now as you did when you first heard the proposal."

"Tell me, and you can judge."

"I declined to paint the picture except on promise of — a kiss from you."

"And what was my answer?"

"You gave the promise."

The colour stole over Marie's cheek. Was ever woman so unfortunately circumstanced as she — compelled to accept whatever this Englishman said about her? If he should go farther yet and say that she had promised to marry him, how could she refute his statement?

"Did I redeem my promise?"

Wilfrid assented.

The Princess's colour deepened. She longed to deny the action attributed to her, and yet — and yet — the story brought with it a certain relief to her perplexed mind. With drooping eyes, and speaking in a low tone, she said:—

"I am glad you have told me this. It seems to settle a — a certain question. Seeing that I must be twenty-three or twenty-four years old, Pauline has — we have both — been wondering whether — you must not smile — whether . . . I . . . am . . . married. And now I think I know. Were I a wife, a true wife, I could not have acted as you say I did."

Wilfrid thought this reasoning just, and was very glad to think it such.

"You speak," he smiled, "as if a husband would be a calamity."

"He might be — in present circumstances. You forget there are two Maries, the old and the new. The new, through no fault of her own, may turn her face from what the old one liked. Would it not be dreadful to be claimed as wife by a man whose appearance, in my present state of mind, might fill me with aversion? And I . . . I . . . kissed . . . you? We were alone, I trust?"

"Humph! I regret to say that in the very act we were surprised by no less a dignitary than the Czar, who, for reasons best known to himself, appears to have been playing the spy."

Here Wilfrid proceeded to relate how he had been challenged by the Czar, and how the duel had been averted by Pauline's action; and to every part of the story Marie listened in wonder mingled with regret that she should have been the cause, however unwitting, of such trouble to Wilfrid.

Vainly did she try to force her mind to recall the incident in the Sumaroff Gardens, and as Wilfrid saw her knitted brow and pained look, and guessed their cause, he urged her to cease troubling herself over the loss of her memory, but to leave its recovery to Time's remedial hand.

He himself tried his best to divert her thoughts, and by resorting to a string of pleasantries, he succeeded after a time in moving her to smiles, and once or twice to laughter, laughter so soft and sweet as quite to captivate Wilfrid, and to make him wish — for he never for a moment forgot the person of his great rival — that the Czar had been present to hear it.

On betaking themselves to the castle again they found Pauline and Beauvais just returned from their visit to St. Petersburg. Great was Marie's disappointment to learn that Prince Ouvaroff had, on the previous day, left for Berlin, being sent thither on some diplomatic business by Alexander.

"So Princess Marie," smiled Pauline, addressing her guest, "must remain a mystery to us for some time longer. It is unfortunate, but patience: Time reveals all things."

As the two guests had not yet seen all that the castle contained, Pauline proposed to spend an hour in saunter- ing through its apartments, a proposal to which both readily assented, and so, with Beauvais accompanying them, they set out on the round; and as the doctor kept close to Pauline's side, it of course fell to Wilfrid's lot to escort the Princess.

As became a place that had once been the residence of an empress, and that had seen little change in its furnish- ings since her death, Castle Runö contained much to interest the new-comers.

With dramatic reserve Pauline kept to the last her fairest surprise, namely, the Hall of the Czars, a gallery so called because its walls were decorated with all the procurable portraits of the Russian emperors. To Catharine's original collection additions had been made by the castle's successive tenants, including Pauline herself, whose contribution was represented by two pictures, one being the likeness of the late Paul, and the other that of his son Alexander.

Of the many portraits the last-named was naturally the one to attract most attention. Very keen was the look bestowed both by Pauline and the doctor upon Marie as she gazed at the face of the reigning Czar. To judge from their manner one might almost have thought them imbued with the belief that the sight of this portrait would effect the instant restoration of Marie's memory, and they felt a sense of relief on find- ing themselves wrong. Certainly the Princess stayed longer before this portrait than any other, but her lin- gering was due to the story told her by Wilfrid. This

was the Czar who had challenged him to a duel for a
fault — if fault it were — that was hers and not Wilfrid's.   Thinking of this, she felt more than ever
drawn towards the daring young Englishman who
had gone forth to vindicate her honour with his sword.
She contrasted Wilfrid's countenance with the Czar's
as portrayed on the canvas before her, and unhesitat-
ingly gave the preference to Wilfrid's.   If the character
of a man is to be learned from his personal exterior,
then in her opinion Wilfrid's disposition was frank and
open, Alexander's secretive and ambiguous.   A similar conclusion forced itself upon Pauline, for she, too,
had been making a mental comparison between the two
men.   Her sigh, noticed only by Beauvais, drew from
him the whispered comment: —

"You are repenting?"

"Never!" she exclaimed emphatically.

"For the sake of *la belle France,*" murmured Beauvais encouragingly.

"What," said Pauline, addressing Marie, "what is
your opinion of Alexander's face?"

"It is a handsome one, but — but there is something
about it I do not like," she replied, speaking in a somewhat lower tone as if afraid that the portrait, over-
hearing the remark, might do something to show its
resentment.   "See how cold the eyes are!   It — seems
to be frowning at me," she continued timorously.   "What
do you think of it, Lord Courtenay?" she added, turning to Wilfrid.

"Our hostess," he replied, bowing towards Pauline,
"has so high an opinion of Alexander that in her presence I hesitate to say anything derogatory even of his
portrait."

To this Pauline did not reply, but continuing to
address Marie, she said with an odd smile: —

"Then I may take it that you would not like to be
his wife?"

"His wife!" echoed Marie, opening her eyes wide,
as if it had been seriously proposed to marry her to
Alexander.   "What a strange question!" — To judge
by his quiet chuckle it was one in which the doctor

seemed to find some amusement. — "After what I have said of his portrait you can guess my answer. Besides, has he not a wife already?"

"A wife whom he is ceasing to love," remarked Pauline quietly.

"Why?"

"A childless empress is always a disappointment both to her husband and to his people. Hence the reason, according to this morning's newspapers, of her visit this week to the Convent of the Holy Madonna, not the first of such pilgrimages. There, prone upon the cold stone pavement, before the picture of Our Lady, she will spend nights of devotion, praying that her husband's desire, her own, her people's, may be answered. If Heaven will not take pity on her tears, then will the Czar grow colder and colder."

Marie shivered all over with sudden fear. If the Czar's alienation from the Czarina should reach a point such as to cause him to obtain a divorce, he would be free to set his love upon any woman he pleased. What if he had already made her his choice? What if his anger at the masquerade was prompted by a jealousy that saw in Wilfrid a successful rival? How could she, one weak woman, offer resistance to the will of the mighty Czar? She glanced again at his likeness, deriving from it a more distasteful impression than before. During her course round the hall she had surveyed more than twenty portraits, but none of them had exercised so strange a fascination over her as this one. It seemed to defy her to remove her gaze from it. Whether she stepped to the right or whether she stepped to the left, its eyes, like those of a living being, would follow her movements with the stare as of a person reproaching her for some wrong suffered at her hands; and the longer she gazed, the more this fancy grew upon her.

"Perhaps," said Wilfrid, in answer to Pauline's remarks, "it is as well that Alexander should have no children."

"Why?" asked Pauline, with an intonation so sharp as to show Wilfrid that he had said something

to offend her, and he wondered wherein lay his offence.

"There must be a touch of madness in his blood,"
replied he.

"Why *must* there be?" asked Pauline, looking almost
as much concerned as if it were her own mental state
that was in question.

"If the father Paul were mad is it reasonable to
believe that the son Alexander can be altogether sane?"

"And so you think that if Alexander should have a
son ——?"

"That son might develop the madness that may be
dormant only, not extinguished, in Alexander. Such
a fear would ever be present to the Empress. Picture
her, in the long, slow course of months and years,
hanging over her child, studying every look and every
word of his, every mood and every act, watching and
waiting for the fatal sign ——"

"That might never come," interrupted Pauline, in
her voice a touch of contempt, very unusual with her,
at least when speaking to Wilfrid.

"Quite so, but to a mother's heart this suspense
would be almost killing, and the Empress Elizavetta
would do well to consider this point."

These words seemed to put Pauline in a state of
uneasiness.

"M. Beauvais," said she, "there is a portrait, in
feature and in expression faithful to the original. Can
you, as a physician and disciple of Lavater, read
insanity in that face?"

"One cannot judge of a man's sanity merely from
seeing his portrait," replied the doctor. "Let it suffice
that Alexander, now in his twenty-fifth year, has so
far shown not the faintest sign of a disordered intellect."

Marie was disposed to regard the Czar's quixotic
challenge to Wilfrid as a sign pointing in this direction, but perceiving the theme to be a distasteful one
to Pauline she refrained from expressing her opinion.

As they had now seen everything contained in the
Hall of the Czars they withdrew. Marie could not
resist the temptation of casting a backward glance at

Alexander's portrait, and observed that it seemed still to be following her with eyes of reproach; in fact, so strange an impression did this picture make upon her mind that she resolved for the future to keep out of the Hall of the Czars.

CHAPTER XXVIII

PAULINE REPENTS

'A' MONTH passed, during which Runö remained untroubled by visits from police or soldiery, nor did anything occur to create a suspicion that the isle was under espionage.

This month had been a time of the purest happiness both to Marie and to Wilfrid. Their intercourse was not confined to the walls of the castle; they went out daily, keeping, for safety's sake, to the woods and never venturing within sight of the shore. These walks were necessarily circumscribed, but, as Pauline remarked, they suffered far less hardship in that respect than the voyagers on the deck of an East Indiaman.

The loss of her memory had ceased to trouble the Princess: nay, she was now apprehensive lest the revelation consequent upon its recovery should cause a return to her former life. With very little knowledge of that former life she had, nevertheless, a profound belief that it fell far short of her present happy state. At any rate it had been a life apart from Wilfrid, and Wilfrid was now the chief, if not the sole, object of her thoughts. It was no secret to her that she was loved by him, for though he had not said it, his homage showed his feelings as plainly as if he had spoken.

It was sweet to have such power over him; a source of pride to her that she should be preferred to all others. It was wonderful, for example, that he had not fallen in love with the beautiful Pauline, but it was certain that he had not. In his eyes Pauline was a friend — the dearest, staunchest friend, it might be — but still no more than that. At least, that is what Marie usually thought, but, once or twice, when she was sitting close to Wilfrid, Pauline had drawn near, in her eyes a wistful look, as if yearning for the affection that was being bestowed upon another.

One day when Wilfrid was in the armoury teaching Beauvais some secrets in swordsmanship, Marie ventured to question the Baroness on this matter. And she came to the point without any skirmishing.

"Pauline, do you love Lord Courtenay?"

The Baroness gave a start.

"Have I ever shown that I do?"

"No," answered Marie, not altogether truthfully.

"Then why should you ask?"

"Because," said Marie evasively, "Lord Courtenay is so brave, so handsome, so — so winning — that's the word — that — that —— "

"It is difficult for woman to avoid falling in love with him. Is that what you would say?" smiled Pauline. "Well, you see, it would be foolish to love one that does not love me."

"Ah, but you are not answering my question!"

"Would it please you if my answer were, 'I do love him?'"

Marie coloured and was silent.

"Ah! you are not answering *my* question," smiled Pauline. And then after a pause she continued: —

"Lord Courtenay is never likely to ask me to be his wife, but if he were to ask, my answer would be, 'No.'"

She spoke in a tone that carried instant conviction to Marie's heart.

"Why?" she asked simply.

"Because I have promised myself to another."

This was indeed a surprise to Marie — a welcome one, as her looks testified. Pauline was not her rival, then.

"I am willing," said Pauline, "to tell you his name, on one condition."

"And that is ——?"

"That you will keep it a secret, especially from Lord Courtenay."

Marie thought it hard that Wilfrid must not be permitted to share this new knowledge with her.

"I should not tell the name, even to you," continued Pauline, "but that it will prove beyond a doubt that I am not aiming at the affections of Lord Courtenay."

This remark decided Marie; she consented to observe secrecy as to the name.

"Learn, then, that I am pledged to marry the Czar Alexander!"

If Pauline had said that she was pledged to marry the Archangel Gabriel, Marie could not have been more startled. Her bewilderment was at first too great for words. The fact that Pauline was not of royal blood did not make her statement doubtful, for had not the great Peter mated with a peasant girl? But — but ——

"How can that be, when the Czar is already married?"

"An emperor can always find an archbishop willing to pronounce sentence of divorce."

Marie, unconsciously perhaps, drew away from the speaker.

"You are trying to steal a husband from his wife! You would put an innocent woman away in order to gratify your ambition! Oh, Pauline!"

There was on Marie's face a look that went directly to Pauline's heart.

"Listen, Marie, and see whether there be not some justification for me. It is some months ago since I first guessed Alexander's feelings towards me. Knowing the love of a wedded Czar to be dishonour I avoided all places where I was likely to meet him. But one night, quite by accident, we met at a masquerade. No, not the Sumaroff fête; this was one that took place a few days before Paul's death. — Before I had seen Lord Courtenay," she murmured to herself. — "He came upon me when I was alone; he held my hands in his, and asked why I had of late avoided him. Then all in a moment he uttered a flow of wild passionate words that — that — well, I will not deny it, they were sweet to me. But, remembering from whom they came, I strove to put them aside. 'Your love must be given to Elizavetta,' I murmured, 'and to her only.' Ah! if you could have seen his look of sorrow. 'Elizavetta,' he answered, 'has already taken to herself a lover.' If this be true, if the

Czarina be faithless to her husband, is he justified in retaining her as his wife?"

"You are dealing in 'ifs,'" replied Marie. "Have you any proof that the Czarina is false?"

"The Empress has been under espionage for some time; her conduct is very equivocal. When she has given clear proof of guilt her divorce will come."

"In other words you and Alexander are waiting for her to take the irrevocable step?"

"Something of the sort."

"And will she?"

"I think so."

"And you will be pleased when it is taken?"

Pauline was silent.

"She is gliding on towards wrong, and you are letting her! You can stop her by a word of warning, and yet will not! Pauline!"

Marie could not have spoken with more touching earnestness had she been pleading her own cause. Involuntarily Pauline turned from the look of disapproval in those grave, innocent eyes.

"If the Czarina," said Pauline — and none knew better than she the sophistical character of the self-justification she was now attempting, "if the Czarina knew that a hundred eyes were secretly on the watch for her fall, she would of necessity be virtuous. But why should she, more than other women exposed to similar temptation, be put on her guard? Respect for her fair name, the memory of her altar-vows, the imperial diadem itself, should each be a sermon to her. To warn her would be to put her into a state of enforced virtue. Why should Alexander retain a wife willing to go wrong but kept in the right only by the fear of discovery? No! let her be tried by the fire of temptation. She must fulfil her destiny, as I must fulfil mine."

The Princess was silent, not knowing very well how to refute what she felt to be sophistry. No wonder Pauline was anxious to keep the matter a secret from Wilfrid! The knowledge of it might lead him, with his sense of honour, to decline any longer the hospitality of a hostess so questionable in her ways.

"You may gain a crown, but you will not gain a hero," said Marie with a touch of scorn. "A man who sets spies to watch his wife, and, before his suspicions are verified, promises to wed another woman, cannot be a very honourable character."

In her haste Marie forgot that the same charge was equally applicable to her hostess. Pauline felt the point of the rebuke.

"I cannot imagine Lord Courtenay acting so," continued Marie proudly.

Nor could Pauline. Wilfrid was a man of very different stamp from Alexander.

"How can you trust one that acts so dishonourably?" continued Marie. "What guarantee have you that Alexander will fulfil his promise?"

"I have here his written pledge," said Pauline, taking from her bosom that same scroll of parchment whose contents had evoked such emotion on the part of her father.

This secret document would certainly have sent a thrill of amazement throughout the various European chancelleries, for it was nothing less than a statement to the effect that, in certain circumstances, the Empress Elizavetta should be divorced in favour of Pauline de Vaucluse! The document was signed, "Alexander Paulovitch, Czar and Autocrat."

That her friend Pauline might one day wear the diadem did not appear to afford much gratification to Marie.

"You aspire to a crown," she said. "Remember the fate of the Hungarian King Bela; his throne one day broke beneath him and its pieces crushed him in their fall — an apt illustration of the dangers attending a throne. It will bring you more sorrow than joy, especially if gained by the means you contemplate. Pauline, will you let me destroy this?" she continued, seeming as if about to tear the document in two.

The Baroness hastily recovered the scroll.

"Why," asked Marie, "did you not destroy it on first receiving it?"

"Why should I have done so?"

"To show your trust in Alexander. What sort of love

is it that needs a written guarantee? Pauline, you dare not burn it, and that very fact shows you have no real faith in him."

It was true, poignantly true. Though it had not appeared to her in this light before, Pauline began now to realise that the satisfaction arising from the posses-sion of this document and the care with which she guarded it, were but so many proofs of distrust in Alexander. Nor could she help reflecting, at the moment, that she could have implicitly trusted Wilfrid's spoken word.

As Pauline contrasted the English peer and the Muscovite Czar, a pang of jealousy seized her that Marie should be the chosen of Wilfrid, while she her-self, though the chosen of an emperor, could find little joy in the fact. The diadem that had looked so splen-did, when viewed from afar, seemed a bauble now that it was well-nigh within her grasp.

"What have you been saying to Marie?" said Wilfrid later in the day, on finding himself alone with Pauline. "She is quite grave and pensive."

"She is wondering, perhaps, whether Lord Courte-nay's attentions to her are to be interpreted merely in the light of friendship. Are all Englishmen so cold and tardy in their wooing? You love, and yet you hesitate to say so to her, who would be but too willing to listen."

"It is precisely because I *do* love her that I hesitate to say it. Her present state of mind is not normal. Supposing that with the recovery of her memory there should come a reversal of her sentiments towards me?"

"You are over-scrupulous," answered Pauline. "A return to her former state should not be so very un-favourable, if she voluntarily kissed you in the Sumaroff Gardens. The fairest woman in Russia is waiting for your love, and by your hesitancy you are adding to her suspense. See, yonder is your Princess taking her way to the woods. Go with her, and on your return let me hear that you have said the words that will gladden her heart."

Wilfrid went off, bent on following this advice, and

Pauline, knowing this, watched him, at her heart a pain such as she had never before known.

Turning, she saw Dr. Beauvais by her side.

"There was a time," she said to him, "when I hated her, or thought I did; you know for what reason. And now —— "

"And now?" repeated Beauvais as she paused in her utterance.

"And now, during the past month, she has won her way to my heart and this makes my task difficult. I have been telling her of my ambition, and she has been pleading prettily with me to save the Empress Elizavetta from dishonour, little thinking that she was pleading for herself! What a shock when she learns how I have deceived her! when she realises the guilt from which a word of mine could have saved her!"

"Her own fault. If blame is to be apportioned, she must take the initial share; for, to her encouragement of Lord Courtenay is due our present imbroglio. We are but helping her onward in the path she entered of her own accord."

"True," assented Pauline, glad to snatch at any argument in justification of her wrong-doing. "And to-day the goal is in sight, for to-day she entrusts herself and her future to his keeping."

"That's good," murmured the doctor. "I have all but completed the arrangements for their departure, and her flight will prevent the Empress Elizavetta from ever returning to her husband."

"The sooner they go the better," observed Pauline, "or I shall be repenting my share in the plot."

She turned from him and, entering the castle, proceeded to a little oratory which, originally Byzantine in character, had been altered by Pauline to a style more in harmony with Latin art.

The sunlight, coloured as it passed through stained glass, slanted upon an altar surmounted by an ivory crucifix, a symbol forbidden by the Greek Church.

To this place came Pauline in a devotional spirit. For, as Italian bandits put up prayers to the saints for a successful haul, and as Cornish wreckers of old went straight from church to kindle beacons on the cliffs, so did Pauline attend daily to pray to the Virgin for the furtherance of a scheme that required for its success a continuous course of deception.

She was about to light a candle in honour of the Madonna, when a voice seemed to whisper, "Hypocrite!"

The taper dropped from her hand and she sank trembling upon a seat, her gaze wandering slowly around as if expecting to encounter some speaker.

For the first time she became conscious of the incongruity of her devotions. There broke in upon her mind a light that revealed her past doings in their true character. She was at the parting of the ways. If she must pray let her cease deceiving; if she must deceive, let her cease praying.

Her eyes, moving slowly round as if in the hope of receiving guidance from some object in the oratory, rested finally upon the western oriel, whose stained glass showed a divine face, lit up by the setting sun. She had seen this face many a time, but never before had it exercised so potent an attraction. The eyes seemed to be looking at her with infinite pity. Pauline thrilled.

Her intrigue for the diadem of empire was receiving a silent rebuke from a crown of thorns!

Vera, her face white and her eyes full of fear, came flying along the corridor that led to the oratory.

She tapped at the door once — twice — thrice.

Receiving no answer she entered and found her mistress in a swoon on the marble floor. Vera stopped short, her hands partly raised.

"She must have seen! But no! She could not from these windows."

She flew to Pauline, dropped at her side, and, happening by good fortune to have her *vinaigrette* with her, employed it with such effect that before long Pauline opened her eyes and smiled faintly.

"Dear Baroness, what has happened? You are looking like the dead."

"It is nothing," replied Pauline as she rose with the help of her maid. "Only a swoon."

Vera could see that for herself; she wanted to know its cause.

"Your coming has been so timely," observed Pauline, "that I must not scold you for disobedience. Tell me why you are here when I have said that I am not to be disturbed at my devotions?"

This question reminded Vera of her mission.

"My lady, if I tell my news you will swoon again."

Pauline's face became transfigured with a smile, such as Vera had never before seen, a smile that perplexed and awed her.

"Speak on, Vera," she said gently. "Nothing that you may say can alarm me now."

Vera hesitated, and then, taking courage from her mistress's manner, said: —

"My lady, the Czar is in the castle!"

To Vera's surprise the Baroness did not faint. True, she gave a great start, but grew calm again in a moment.

"Is this an answer to my prayer?" she murmured to herself. "An invitation from heaven to speak the truth and fear not?" Aloud she said, "What brings him here? Does he suspect that ——?"

"I think not, my lady. He is taking a quiet sail on the Neva in his gondola with his equerries, Princes Ouvaroff and Volkonski, and has pulled up off Runö for the purpose of paying his *devoir* to the Baroness. He is in the entrance hall awaiting ɪ ⌡ lady."

"Where is Lord Courtenay· ᴀnd — and —?"

It was with a ghastly smile that Vera replied —

"Lord Courtenay is by the ɪake making love to the Czarina!"

CHAPTER XXIX

WOOING A CZARINA

WILFRID and his Princess occupied their favourite seat by the Fairies' Mirror. Marie was musing upon her kinsfolk — she supposed she had such — and, with a mind dominated by her love for Wilfrid, had come to the conclusion that should they now appear with intent to restore her to her former life she would be disposed to resist their action. Her life at Runö had been so happy that she felt that any change must be for the worse.

"You saw me in my old life," she remarked. "Tell me, did I seem very happy in it?"

"Truth compels me to say you did not."

"How did I appear?"

"You looked like — like — well, like the moonlight, beautiful, but sad."

"And now ——?"

"Now I may liken you to — to the sunshine."

"Radiant and happy?" smiled she. "Yes, I feel so. The difference must be due to changed conditions," she continued, "and I am resolved not to return to the old state. What I lose by this resolve, I do not know; therefore, I do not grieve. I — heaven forgive me, if my act be a wrong one! — but I am bent on separating myself entirely from the past."

Prompted by a sudden thought, she rose to her feet.

"Which way does St. Petersburg lie?"

Wilfrid pointed to the east.

"St. Petersburg! city that was once my home, you are my home no more."

And she flung out her arms as if casting something from her.

"Friends and relatives, if such there be to me, you are discarded."

She repeated her action.

"My old life, farewell! I turn my back upon you."

Suiting the action to the word, she turned upon her heel and stood facing the west. Wilfrid being an artist could not help admiring the curves of her graceful figure. Her hat had fallen off and some golden rays glancing obliquely through her hair seemed to illumine it as with an aureole. Wilfrid saw in this last attitude a happy augury for his hopes; she was facing the west, and the west was the direction of his home.

Though her words and gestures were not in any way meant to influence Wilfrid, being entirely spontaneous on her part, they none the less appealed to his sense of chivalry. Her new state required that she should have a protector; and who should that protector be, if not Wilfrid?

"If you are really bent on severing all connection with your former life," said Wilfrid, as Marie again sat beside him, "we must not leave this spot without settling what your future course must be. For, to remain at Runö is to run the risk of being drawn back again into those old surroundings that you seem to dread. Now, I am going to suggest a plan that I trust will be for your welfare."

He certainly *had* a plan, a delightful one; the difficulty was to find courage enough to put it into words. A delicious sensation of expectancy stole over Marie. Her eyes dared not meet his.

"Well, what *is* this plan?" she murmured, after waiting for a while.

"I am beginning to think that you might not accept it."

"How can I say till I hear it?"

"Cannot you guess its nature?"

"I might guess wrongly. *Please* tell me," she said, stealing a witching glance at him from beneath her dark eyelashes, and encouraging him with a smile that showed a dazzling set of teeth.

Wilfrid still fenced with the question, making it a matter of wonder to Marie that he, who had never been lacking in courage, should show such hesitation with her. How sweet to have such power over him! but how much sweeter it would be if he would only say the words she was longing to hear!

"You said just now," he remarked, "that you have been happy here. What has made you so?"

"Many things. The malicious joy of being alive, when my enemies think me dead; the beautiful summer air; the waving woods of Runö; the quaint old castle, with its books and antiquities; the sweet doing-nothing all day long; the sense of freedom and irresponsibility; above all, Pauline's kindness."

"Nothing more?"

"Your — your friendship."

"You put that last, I see."

"No, Lord Courtenay, I put that first," she said softly. And then —— !

Who made the first movement towards the other neither ever knew. Certain it is that Marie suddenly found herself returning Wilfrid's passionate kiss and clinging to his embrace as if she meant never to part from it.

In the stillness that followed, she could hear the wild beating of her heart above the ripple of the forest leaves.

"And do you really love me?" asked Marie, breaking the long spell of silence.

"Do you doubt it?"

"No, but you have not yet *said* it. It will be sweet to hear it."

So Wilfrid said it, not once, but many times.

"And is this," she asked, with a significant pressure of her arms, "is this the plan you were speaking of?"

"Yes; that you will entrust your future to my keeping: that you will come with me to England and be the Countess Courtenay."

The sound of this name gave her a sweeter sensation of pleasure than any she had yet felt.

"And you will marry me, knowing so little of me?"

"I see you to be beautiful, and I know you to have a sweet, lovable nature — what more can I desire?"

He turned her happy glowing face upward to his own, kissed it again, and softly stroked her hair. She thrilled at his caresses, finding it the most natural thing in the world to nestle in his arms.

"I never realised till now," he said, gazing downwards upon her face, "the full force of the poet's words —

> ' When I lie tangled in her hair,
> And fettered to her eye.' "

"What a pretty hand yours is!" he continued, taking it in his own. "Snow, thou art not so white, after all. Will you hold it up for me?"

And Marie the next instant found her finger encircled with a ring.

For a moment she was dumb with a new pleasure, all her soul sparkling from her eyes.

"Now I am linked to you," she said, kissing the gift.

"For ever. The ring was my mother's. The stones are amethysts. See how they mock the violet lustre of your eyes!"

Marie laughed softly.

"Am I the first woman you have ever loved, Wilfrid?"

"The first and the last. Why do you ask?"

"Because you seem to speak so well for a novice."

She accompanied her words with a smile, but the smile soon gave place to a pensive expression.

"Dearest, why that sorrowful look?"

"You have made me so happy," she said, "and yet, amid my happiness there comes a thought that fills me with fear. I am not mistress of my true mind. Supposing I should recover my memory and forget my present self, I — I —— "

Wilfrid finished the sentence for her.

"You might not regard me in the same light as now? Is not that what you would say? Well, I am willing to take the risk. But ease your mind, dearest, on that point. I do not think that in your former state you viewed me with indifference. Is not your kiss at the masquerade a proof?"

Though Marie took courage from this last incident, she was still troubled with doubts of another sort.

"I have cast aside all former ties. I want to be yours, and yours only." She clung to him as if he were her life itself. "But supposing a father or a guardian should appear, forbidding our union?"

"They may forbid: they won't prevent!"

"Or one saying that I had betrothed myself to him?"

"He must resign you."

"You will not hand me over to any one who shall claim me?"

"Not even to the Czar himself if he should want you."

"Remember this promise," she said, raising her forefinger with a pretty air. "You do not know how soon you may be put to the test."

And so in happy talk they sat, drawing bright pictures of the future, till the coming-on of twilight reminded them of the passing of time.

"Shall we return to the castle?" said Wilfrid. "I am eager to present Countess Courtenay to Pauline."

Marie rose and took Wilfrid's arm. As she quitted the dell she cast a backward lingering look at the spot, now rendered sacred in her eyes by reason of Wilfrid's love-vows there.

They emerged from the wood to the open space surrounding the castle, from whose windows twinkled numerous lights, more numerous than usual, Wilfrid thought.

Upon entering the castle they soon learned the cause. A very distinguished visitor was beneath its roof. The Czar had paid the Baroness Runö the high honour of an unpremeditated visit, and was now holding converse with her in an apartment that, from the colour of its upholstery, was known as the Blue Chamber, while in the entrance hall his equerries Princes Ouvaroff and Volonski were discussing some excellent wines with Dr. Beauvais.

Wilfrid was one of the very few men who are not dazzled by titles, a sentiment arising, perhaps, from a magnificent faith in his own lineage.

"The Czar!" he whispered to Marie. "The very

gentleman I am wanting to see, since he can explain who you are. You do not fear to face him?"

"Not if you are with me."

As it would be contrary to Court etiquette to enter the Czar's presence unbidden, or to send a message into the Blue Chamber while he was conversing with the Baroness, Wilfrid's plan was to wait till that interview was over, and then, when the Czar should return along the grand corridor to the castle entrance, step forward and ask for the favour of a few words.

"And then," he remarked in philosophic vein, "we shall see what we shall see."

With a view to keeping an eye upon departing majesty Wilfrid chose as his place of vigil a chamber whose door opened upon the corridor.

Among other ornaments decorating the walls of this chamber were several sabres. Carefully inspecting these he selected one, and girded it at his side, while Marie tremblingly asked his reason for this act.

"One may as well be prepared for emergencies," he smiled.

Beneath the mask of his light and careless air Marie could see that he apprehended there might be danger, and she began to realise more vividly the nature of the coming ordeal.

What if the Czar, on seeing the man who had mocked him by not appearing at the rendezvous, should order his attendants or Pauline's to arrest Wilfrid? Wilfrid, she well knew, would fight for his liberty against any odds. Or supposing the Czar should be tempted to renew his duelling proposal, what could Wilfrid do but respond to the challenge? Or what, too, if the Czar, in the exercise of his legitimate authority, should insist upon her returning with him to St. Petersburg?

Wilfrid, true to the promise she had exacted from him, would endeavour to prevent this; but what could his single sword achieve against the power of the Czar? Her lively imagination began to picture scenes of altercation and fighting, of bloodshed and death.

Let the mystery of her origin remained unsolved for

ever if its attempted solution must bring danger upon the head of Wilfrid.

Her quick changing colour, the trembling of her hand within his, spoke eloquently of her fears.

Folding her within his arms Wilfrid tried both by words and caresses to infuse her with some of his own spirit.

"It is for you I fear," she said, as she clung convulsively to him. "Let us leave the castle till the Czar be gone. Nothing but harm will come of this meeting." All in a moment that frowning portrait in the Hall of the Czars rose vividly before her. If a mere picture could fill her mind with a nameless terror, what would be the effect of the living original? "Oh, Wilfrid, don't — *don't* make me face him!" she gasped. "I dare not — I don't know why, but I dare not! If he sees me . . . there is something . . . something at my heart . . . that tells me this embrace . . . will be our last! Let us . . . My God! he is coming . . . it is too late!"

CHAPTER XXX

BEHIND THE CURTAIN

THE door by which Wilfrid and Marie had entered was not the only one giving access to the room; at the opposite end was a second, partly open, and along the corridor leading to this came the sound of voices, two in number, a woman's and a man's.

Pauline and the Czar were approaching. A moment more and they would be within the room.

Marie's terrified air alarmed Wilfrid. She must be kept from the trying ordeal of facing the Czar. As it was too late, however, to escape from the room, he hastily drew her behind a curtain that hung across the entrance of an alcove, and, seating her in a *fauteuil* that happened by good fortune to be there, placed his finger upon her lips as a warning for her to be silent, a warning that was scarcely needed.

A moment afterwards the Czar and Pauline were in the room.

The drapery of the alcove consisted of two curtains, hung so as to leave from top to bottom an opening of about an inch in width, that enabled Wilfrid to see the Czar.

Tall and handsome, Alexander was endowed with a presence that, majestic in itself, was rendered more so by a grand and brilliant uniform. Wilfrid, despite his prejudice, was compelled to admit that here was a *man* as well as an emperor. His stately aspect seemed to breathe a sort of challenge to Wilfrid, upon whom there stole that elemental feeling that made the old heathen warrior raise his clenched fist to the skies with the cry of, " I defy thee, O Odin! Come down from heaven and let us try which is the better man ! "

But Wilfrid's desire to try conclusions with the Czar was immediately lost in a new interest as he viewed that monarch's manner towards Pauline.

As she entered, her hand resting lightly upon his arm, he was bending over her with eyes that plainly spoke of love, though her reserved air showed that she did not return the feeling.

Wilfrid's gorge rose. Not content with making love to Marie, this imperial libertine sought to lure Pauline also to his arms! Was this the business of an emperor? Fortunately he seemed as little likely to succeed in the one case as the other.

On seeing the two entering, Wilfrid thought that the Czar's visit was over, and that Pauline was conducting him through this apartment as being the shortest way out of the castle. He was wrong. The two had come to this apartment for a private talk, for the Czar, having led Pauline to an ottoman, took his place beside her.

This was a development which Wilfrid had not anticipated. To continue longer in concealment would be to play the spy, yet remain there he must, on Marie's account, since there was no way of quitting the alcove except by revealing himself.

At first, with an odd sense of preserving his honour, Wilfrid tried not to listen, endeavouring to fix his attention on other matters. But the attempt was a failure; against his wish he was attracted by the words of the speakers, and as the dialogue grew, so, too, did his interest.

"You were praying in the oratory," said Alexander to Pauline. "Did *my* name mingle with your prayers?"

"Yes, Sire," answered Pauline gravely. "I prayed for you more earnestly than ever I prayed before."

The melancholy, seldom absent from the Czar's face since his father's death, brightened into a smile.

"And what was the petition on my behalf?"

"That your Majesty might have a right judgment," replied Pauline with a meaning plain enough to Wilfrid, though not to the Czar.

"'Sire!' 'Majesty!'" repeated Alexander, with what in a woman would be called a pout. "Leave this formal

style to ministers and courtiers. With you I am Sasha.
Ah! shall I ever forget the night when first you called
me by that name? Never did it sound so pretty as when
coming from your lips! And you said that your name
to me must be no more Baroness but Pauline. Do you
remember?"

"I remember," she answered with a sigh.

Becoming conscious of this restraint in her manner,
Alexander eyed her wistfully, failing, however, to divine
the reason for her altered demeanour.

He was not much more than a youth and a somewhat
simple-minded one to boot, but he had a high sense of
his sovereignty, and it never occurred to him that the
gallantries of an emperor could be other than acceptable to the object of them.

"Pauline, how beautiful you are!" he murmured after
a moment's silence.

Time was when she would have thrilled at such language. But to-night his words had lost their old charm.

"Your Majesty must not speak thus."

"'Majesty' again? But I let it pass. Why must I
refrain from speaking the truth?"

"You must reserve such language for Elizavetta only."

"Elizavetta!" said Alexander, his face darkening with
a noble but mistaken scorn. "Elizavetta! A wife who
from her wedding-day never loved her husband."

"I think your Majesty is wrong."

"Nay, I will prove myself to be right. Do princesses
ever marry for love? Is it not their duty to take the
suitor whom political interest prescribes? Princess
Marie of Baden was only fourteen when her parents bade
her prepare for her wedding. The Empress Catharine
desired that she should be the wife of her grandson
Alexander, then a youth of fifteen."

Princess Marie! The title dropped lightly from the
lips of the speaker, but upon the woman behind the
curtain it fell with a shock more startling, perhaps, than
if it had been the voice of the archangel calling her to her
final doom.

In one swift moment all the sweetness and brightness
of life was extinguished for Marie by the ghastly revela-

tion that she was already a wife. What booted it that her consort was a Czar? Better, far better, so ran her wild thoughts, had she gone down in the waters of the Nevka, or died on reaching the Silver Strand, than live to see this sudden mockery of all her sweet hopes.

Her fingers were still locked within Wilfrid's, but as she realised that her love for him was now a sinful thing, that henceforth she must live apart from him, that she must be handed over to a husband, who, at that very moment was playing her false, a husband, who, in her present state of mind was a stranger to her, nay more, utterly abhorrent, there broke from her a low wail of anguish, which the Czar and Pauline would surely have heard had not their attention been absorbed in each other.

As for Wilfrid, he, too, was completely stunned, as much by the thought of losing Marie, as by the discovery that, purposing to deliver a beautiful princess from the attentions of a too-amorous Czar, he was really guilty of attempting to steal a wife from her husband. In the matter of the duel it was now clear that the right had been on the side of the Czar, a mortifying and humiliating thought for Wilfrid. Still, his position was a blameless one, as far as he was concerned, being due, not to intentional wrong-doing, but to ignorance.

"How could a girl of fourteen," Alexander continued, "be expected to love a man whom she had never seen? She married me because she was told to do so. Without a murmur she accepted a new religion, the Greek; a new name, Elizavetta. In the same way she would have accepted the Sultan and Islamism."

"In blaming her you blame yourself, who were equally submissive to Catharine's will."

"For her submission I blame her not, but for — you shall hear.

"We married and at first were happy: — at least *I* was. Her beauty, her sweetness, charmed me. Yes, I truly loved her till — till I discovered that I held only the second place in her heart."

"I think your Majesty errs. How did you discover it?"

"In the early days of our betrothal she spoke to me of a certain Englishman, Wilfrid Courtenay, and earnestly begged that she might be permitted to continue wearing a locket containing his portrait on the plea that he had saved her life.

"As heaven is my witness, I bore this man no jealousy: nay, I told her I would love him for her sake, that when I was Czar I would invite him to my Court and pay him high honour as one who had preserved for me a sweet and fair bride.

"But mark the sequel.

"One night — it is now about two years ago — I entered her bed-chamber at a late hour, and found her fast asleep. As I bent over her, admiring her beauty, a smile curved her lips, and from them came a word softly spoken. That word was — 'Wilfrid'!

"I started back as from the hiss of a serpent. The Englishman was in her thoughts, his name was on her lips, his image within a locket lay upon her breast!

"That night was the beginning of my suspicions."

"Suspicions which Baranoff did his best to fan," interjected Pauline.

"Baranoff has been the zealous guardian of my honour. 'Twas he who bade me observe. And I observed. I watched and waited and found my suspicions verified. Her guilt at the Inn of the Silver Birch rests on the testimony of others, but at the Sumaroff Masquerade I had the evidence of my own eyes. In a retired part of the gardens I surprised her, wrapped in Lord Courtenay's arms, submitting to his caresses. Detected in the very act of guilt she durst not face me: she durst not return to the palace. She fled that very night. Lord Courtenay disappeared at the same time. Is it not plain that they went together?"

"Is that the talk of St. Petersburg?"

"Neither St. Petersburg nor the Court itself is aware of her flight. Would you have me make my humiliation the theme of every gossip's tongue? No! the matter is kept a secret. The public journals have received notification that the Czarina is spending a few weeks in religious seclusion at the Convent of the

Ascension. Meantime the police agents have received
their orders — to make diligent search for Lord Courtenay. Where he is, there will Marie be found."

"And when they are found?"

"For her, the nun's cell; for him, the headsman's
axe."

"Your Majesty is somewhat severe upon them.
Seeing you have resolved that Plato shall pronounce
your divorce, why should she not be left free to go
with Lord Courtenay, if she will?"

"An ex-Czarina to re-marry! That were to put a
premium upon adultery and set a dangerous precedent.
Let her have her lover? Give her the prize she has
been guiltily striving for? Let him parade Europe
with an ex-empress for his bride, boasting how he had
won her from Alexander? That were a humiliation
too much to be borne. No! Death for him; for her,
life-long penitence in a convent. — She has chosen to
forfeit my affection and my throne; let me think no
more of her."

He took Pauline's hand; she did not resist, but let
her fingers rest passively within his.

"Pauline, you know our compact?"

She knew, and the memory of it troubled her.

"I have not forgotten," said he, "your sudden start
when first I confessed my love to you, your grave look,
your pleading for Marie, your little homily on virtue:
'I may be the wife, I will never be the mistress of a
Czar.' I loved you all the more for that saying. It
was then I told you of Marie's secret longing, and you
agreed that if guilt should be found in her, and I should
put her away, you would be my wife. Was it not so?
To prove how much I was in earnest did I not commit
my promise to writing?"

"You did, Sire. It is here," she replied, withdrawing her hand from his and taking the document from
her bosom. "Let me return it to you. Or, better
still —"

She rose from the ottoman and, placing one end of
the scroll to a lighted taper in the chandelier, let the
parchment burn till the flame all but touched her fin-

gers. The charred fragment floated from her hand to the floor.

"It was a dishonourable compact. It shames me to recall it."

The writer of the document had watched her action with a troubled look.

"Pauline," he said gently, "in what have I offended? What has caused this difference in you? Why are you so cold to-day? Speak, as you spoke at our last meeting, or I — I —— "

His voice trembling with emotion, he rose to his feet and, taking both her hands within his own, strove to look into her averted face.

"Nay, do not turn from me," said he. "It is a Czar that offers you his love. Among the royal princesses of Europe is there one but would thrill with pleasure to be as you are to me? All that I have is yours — palaces, gold, jewels. You will be above queens. At my coming coronation you shall sit beside me on the throne amid a blaze of glory, admired and worshipped by all. Ten thousand swords will flash from their scabbards, ten thousand of the noblest in the Empire will swear to shed their last drop of blood in your defence. My ministers shall be nothing to me; it is your sweet counsel I shall follow. Your policy shall be my policy. Do I not know that the dearest wish of your heart is to see the exiled Bourbons restored to the throne of France? That wish shall become a reality; at your word armies shall march to overturn this Corsican adventurer."

Pauline caught her breath at this last — of all his arguments the only one that had power to move her. But her hesitation lasted for a moment only. Strengthened by prayer, purified in mind, she had come forth from the oratory a new creature, armed with a power that enabled her to set aside the ambitious hopes that had dazzled her during so many months.

"It is useless to tempt me, Sire," she said firmly, seeking to withdraw her hands. "It must not·be."

"Why not?"

"I will not wrong Marie. I will not deprive an innocent woman of a husband's love, of an imperial diadem, to gratify my own ambition! Once — with shame I confess it — I desired her to walk in the ways of guilt; nay, I have plotted for that very end; her fall should be my stepping-stone to glory and power; but now my eyes have become opened. Equivocal as the Empress's conduct may have seemed, I do not believe that her love has ever seriously wandered from you. If your Majesty will sit calmly down and listen to me, I will so prove her innocence that —— "

The sentence was never finished.

Marie, overwhelmed by emotion, at this moment clutched at the *portière,* and the curtain fell.

The fabric, though light, made a swish that caused the Czar to turn his head toward the alcove. And there, clearly revealed in the brilliant light, stood Wilfrid and the missing Czarina!

CHAPTER XXXI

THERE was a spell of terrible silence, followed by an impulsive cry from the Czar.

" Marie ! "

More dead than alive the Czarina leaned against the side of the alcove, her eyes set with a dreadful stare upon the face of the man whom she could not think of as her husband. To her he seemed a veritable stranger. And yet he had the right to take her from Wilfrid and do with her as he listed; and as her dazed mind realised this there broke from her bloodless lips a shivering mournful cry, like water reeds when thrilled by the evening breeze.

As for the Czar, his mind was filled with consternation, rage, and embarrassment. Though he saw before him his missing wife secreted in an alcove with her lover, he was conscious of the ludicrousness of posing as an injured husband, seeing that he was himself caught in the very act of making love to Pauline.

The latter was scarcely less agitated than Marie herself. The deception practised by her during the preceding month was now laid bare to Wilfrid. She had hoped, by making a voluntary confession that night, to dull the edge of his anger. Too late now! After her first hasty glance at the alcove she stood with averted eyes, fearing to meet his reproachful gaze.

Of the four Wilfrid was the least embarrassed, though he scarcely knew how to act in this dilemma.

By the law of God and of man Marie belonged to her husband. Yet a rapid review of the facts — in particular the Czar's illicit love-making — made Wilfrid hesitate to resign her unconditionally to a man whom she abhorred, and who had vowed his intention of immuring her for life within a convent.

The Czar was the first to break the silence.

"An interesting tableau!" he said with a bitter sneer. "The guilty wife and her paramour hiding from the husband's gaze."

Wilfrid's eyes flashed dangerously, though he was compelled to admit that the accusation was natural in the circumstances.

"A word of caution, Sire. We Courtenays are not accustomed to take insults, even from emperors."

"Brave words from the hero that fled the duel!"

"There was no fleeing on the part of Lord Courtenay," said Pauline. "He would have met your Majesty, but when on his way to the rendezvous he was seized by my orders and brought to Runö."

"An act of treason!" commented the Czar, the autocrat asserting himself above the lover.

"It was the saving of your life," was Pauline's answer, a tacit assumption of Wilfrid's superior swordsmanship that galled Alexander's vanity.

"Stand aside from my wife!" he cried angrily to Wilfrid.

"Your wife! How can that be when but a few minutes ago you disowned her?"

The charge was true and the Czar could not deny it.

Scarcely knowing what to say or do in his embarrassment he looked hard at his wife, she at him. Usually so loving she now seemed a veritable piece of marble. It was impossible to understand so strange a change. Pauline in refusing his love had shown some pity for him, but Marie, in holding aloof, displayed not a trace of affection or regret; her manner was as though she had never known him.

As he looked, a new feeling stole over his heart. Four weeks' absence seemed to have made her more beautiful. With that inconsistency characteristic of human nature he now began to desire what but a short time before he had been willing to discard.

Whether this change of feeling was due to Marie's very coldness, or to Pauline's rejection of him, or to jealousy of Wilfrid, or to all three causes working together, certain it is that Alexander found his affection, long-suspended, beginning to revive; if Marie had made but one step towards him he would have been willing to receive her. It was hard to believe that he had lost her for ever. He wished that Pauline and Wilfrid were not present that he might take her by the hand and speak the tender words of the old days; surely, then, her hardness would relent?

An impulsive step forward on his part caused the Czarina to cling shudderingly to her new protector.

"Wilfrid!" she gasped. "Remember your promise! Do not — do not give me up to this man. I shall die if he touch me! God forgive me . . . if I do wrong! I cannot . . . I cannot let you go. I am yours . . . yours only."

The rigid moralist, reasoning from a distance, will say that it was Wilfrid's duty to retire immediately in favour of the husband: but let that moralist be in the like situation, with a beautiful woman clinging to him, her lovely eyes appealing for aid, the perfume of her dress casting an intoxicating spell around her, and he would do as Wilfrid did, who, casting aside nice ethical consideration, silently vowed that Marie should not be led off against her will.

The Czar stood perfectly confounded at his wife's declaration.

"She calls him 'Wilfrid'! Says she is 'his alone'! My God! is this the language of innocence?"

"She is not in her right mind," intervened Pauline hastily. "She —— "

But the emperor cut her short before she could make the necessary explanation.

"It is easy to see that. He has corrupted her nature."

"The Czarina," said Wilfrid, though it grated upon him to use the title, "has lived at Runö as purely as a vestal maiden. My word of honour upon it."

In view of Marie's attitude at that moment the Czar might be pardoned for declining to accept Wilfrid's statement.

"Your word! Yours!" he retorted with ineffable disdain.

"Mine," returned Wilfrid. "And never yet did Courtenay speak falsely, or — sign a placard that his father had died of apoplexy!"

"By heaven, you die for that saying!" cried Alexander, clapping his hand upon his sword-hilt.

"Faith! 'tis hard if one must die for speaking the truth!"

"Get you from the side of that lady," said the Czar, his eyes blazing with wrath.

"Do not leave me, Wilfrid!" murmured Marie.

"The Czar bids, but the Czarina forbids!" returned Wilfrid. "Honour enjoins me to obey the lady."

"By what right do you constitute yourself her champion?"

"By the right of every man to protect a woman, even the wife of another, from injustice."

"Injustice?"

"You have threatened an innocent lady with life-long imprisonment in a convent. From such fate it shall be my duty to defend her."

Emboldened by these words, and moved by a sudden impulse, Marie kissed Wilfrid, placed her arms about his neck, and, facing the Czar, said, with a proud light shining from her eyes: —

"I belong to Wilfrid, not to you."

She was never dearer to Wilfrid than at that moment as she stood with her arms about him — to the Czar, proud and defiant, to him, all tenderness and trust. However questionable the nature of his triumph, Wilfrid would have been more than human had he not felt a thrill of pleasure. His dashing audacity could rise no higher: henceforth it must descend; he could never hope to surpass the feat of hearing an empress declare her love for him in the very presence of her husband.

Alexander drew his sword with intent to wreak vengeance upon the man who had stolen his wife's heart.

Pauline, trembling all over, threw herself in his way.

"No, no! — for God's sake — your Majesty — you are risking your life! Consider your rank — *Sasha!*"

WILFRED DREW HIS OWN BLADE AND ASSUMED AN ATTITUDE
OF DEFENCE.

"*By Neva's Waters.*"

Page 299.

Putting aside her detaining grasp Alexander, his blade gleaming in his hand, advanced towards the alcove amid the screams of the two women.

With a movement, as swift as it was gentle, Wilfrid detached himself from Marie's arms, placed her behind him, drew his own blade and assumed an attitude of defence.

" Leave this apartment to me and to the Empress! " cried Alexander, pointing with his sword the way Wilfrid should go.

" If the Empress bids me," replied Wilfrid.

But no such bidding came from the white lips of the Empress, who had sunk half-fainting upon the seat within the alcove.

Wilfrid's words, the Czarina's attitude, put the finishing touches to the Emperor's fury. With a cry of " Look to yourself! " he rushed upon the defiant Englishman, but, on the very point of making a savage lunge, he stopped short; his sabre dropped; and then, his face flushing purple and his eyes rolling in their orbits, he fell prostrate on the floor.

CHAPTER XXXII

FLIGHT

STARTLED at the strange turn of events the three spectators stood, staring in doubt and fear at the unconscious figure. Was this collapse the stroke of death?

Before they had time to ascertain for themselves there came an insistent knocking at the door, as of someone attracted by the screaming.

Wilfrid walked forward and, opening the door just wide enough to ascertain who the new-comer was, beheld Beauvais standing without.

"The very man we want," he said, pulling the surprised doctor within and locking the door. "The Czar requires your aid."

Beauvais, being a wise man, spent no time in asking irrelevant questions. Hurrying forward he knelt down, and examined the body of the fallen emperor.

"An apoplectic stroke. Takes after his father Paul," said Beauvais, as he loosened the Czar's military collar and bade Wilfrid bring him a carafe of water.

"Is it serious?" asked Pauline.

"I think not, but one never knows."

"How long will it be before consciousness returns?" she continued.

"I cannot say. He may recover in an hour; in two hours; five; perhaps more. It is impossible to tell. Let me have help, Baroness."

With Wilfrid's aid Beauvais laid the Czar upon the ottoman, while Pauline summoned two maids to assist the doctor's ministrations.

This done she gently drew Wilfrid and the Empress to a small anteroom and, with downcast eyes and humble air, knelt before the latter.

" Your Majesty —— " she began.

" Majesty! " exclaimed the other. It frightened her to see Pauline suppliant at her feet.

" Yes, for you are in truth the Czarina —— "

" Is this a conspiracy to mock me, or is it really the truth? I cannot — I *cannot* believe it. It is so strange that I — that I should be — Ah! would to heaven that I were not! What do I gain by the change? — Would that I were dead! " she murmured with a look of unutterable anguish. " O Wilfrid, Wilfrid, we are lost to each other."

If Pauline ever felt remorse, she felt it at that moment as she contemplated these two, with whose affections she had wantonly sported for the sake of her own ambition.

" Yes, reproach me," she said, observing Wilfrid's grave eyes set upon her. " I deserve your bitterest censure. My only excuse is that it was done for France — for France. I have acted wickedly, yet I repented, but — but it was too late! And I, too, have suffered — "

She swayed and would have fallen had not the Czarina held her up by the wrists. For a few moments they continued in this attitude, till the Czarina, pitying Pauline's unhappy look, stooped and kissed her.

" I forgive you," she murmured, raising the other.

" Alas! I cannot forgive myself," murmured Pauline bitterly.

An embarrassing silence followed, broken at length by Marie.

" If I am Empress," she said with a sad smile, addressing Wilfrid, " show your loyalty by doing my will. Aid me to escape. When the Czar recovers he will order your arrest and mine. I will not lose my liberty. I must fly at once."

Wilfrid was quite alive to the necessity for her immediate flight. Her relation with the Czar was, in his opinion, a question to be decided at some other time; for the present she must not remain at Runö while the Czar's anger and jealousy were still hot upon him.

Yet how could he give her aid when police and spies — as the Czar had said — were everywhere on the look-out for him? Should he be recognised, not only his own flight, but that of the Empress would be frustrated.

"Your Majesty," said he after awhile, "the only asylum that I can think of is the British Embassy, which we can reach by water along the Neva and Fontanka Canal, and thus perchance elude the police. Lord St. Helens will be honoured by your confidence. Within the Embassy you may remain concealed till some plan be devised for your escape, or till friends shall have effected a reconciliation between you and the Czar." — Marie shivered. — "Even supposing your presence at the Embassy should become known, you cannot be removed by force, nor can the Czar enter without leave. You will, in fact, be able to treat with him on equal terms."

Marie caught eagerly at Wilfrid's suggestion. To get away at once was her one desire. Pauline, too, approved of the scheme.

"A boat shall be ready at Silver Point within ten minutes," she said, and gave an order to that effect.

It now occurred to Wilfrid that to accompany the Empress would give a tongue to scandal, and confirm the Czar in his suspicions. He whispered this much into Pauline's ears.

"I have thought of that," she murmured, "and the Czarina's brother-in-law shall go with you, to see," she added with an air of shame, "that there be no more love-making between you."

"The Czarina's brother-in-law!" said Wilfrid.

"I refer to Prince Ouvaroff," explained Pauline, "who is now beneath my roof."

"Ouvaroff will be more likely to intercept than to assist her flight."

"Because he misjudges her. But I will undeceive him. Escort the Empress to the Silver Strand and wait there for me."

Wilfrid, taking the Empress under his care, stepped through the French window and set off for the appointed place, while Pauline made her way to the entrance hall.

Here the Czar's equerries, Princes Ouravoff and Volkonski, were whiling away the time over a game of chess.

Upon her entering the two arose and bowed.

"The Czar ——?" began Volkonski.

"Is taking a short sleep," answered Pauline. "Prince Ouvaroff, may I have a word with you?"

The Prince was only too pleased at such an honour. She drew Ouvaroff, much to Volkonski's surprise, from the entrance hall to the moonlight outside and began to whisper her tidings.

"*She* here!" muttered the Prince, confounded, "and preparing to fly."

"She has been living in concealment here since the night of the Sumaroff Masquerade. Now before you pronounce her guilty read this." — She handed him a letter. — "It is a confession written by Nadia, once maid at the Inn of the Silver Birch."

By the light of the harvest moon Ouvaroff rapidly ran his eye over the document. His face wore at first an expression of surprise that finally merged into joy.

"This establishes her innocence," he said looking up from the paper, "at least as regards the affair at the inn." And then, with a look of deep dismay, he added in a stammering voice, "And I — it was I who accused her to Alexander —— "

"Well, you can atone for that error by helping her now."

"But — but," exclaimed the perplexed Prince, as he handed back the letter, "since she can now prove her innocence what need is there for flight?"

"Because the Empress has lost her memory, and — But we've no time to lose. Come with me and I'll explain matters as we go along."

He followed Pauline, and, as they went, she put him in possession of the chief events of the story, finishing her recital just as they reached the Silver Strand.

Close to the shore with which it was connected by a broad plank, lay a handsome gondola, *The Pauline*, capable of holding eight or ten persons. Within it and resting upon their oars were four sturdy Finlanders, ready to undertake any charge, however perilous, at the bidding of their mistress.

Marie had no more recollection of Ouvaroff than she had of the Czar, and gazed wonderingly at him as he knelt before her upon the sands.

"Prince Ouvaroff," whispered Wilfrid for her enlightenment.

"Your Majesty," said the Prince, "I — I have done you a grievous wrong, for which I know not how to atone. If the taking of my life can afford you any satisfaction it is yours to take."

The Empress put forth her hand and raised the Prince.

"Aid me to escape, good Ouvaroff, and you are forgiven."

The Prince vowed that he would do all he could to further her wish, for he perceived that, till the recovery of her memory, it would be unjust and cruel to force her return to the Czar. For his part, zealous to retrieve his error, he desired nothing better than to die in her service.

"As I am of like mind with you," said Wilfrid, addressing Ouvaroff, "what is to prevent us from being the best of friends as once we were?"

The Prince grasped Wilfrid's outstretched hand and thus the two, so long estranged, were at one again.

"Are you not coming with us?" said Marie to Pauline.

The Baroness shook her head.

"Have you the courage," continued the other, "to face the Czar's anger when he awakes and finds us gone?"

"I must try to repair the wrong I have done. I remain to act as conciliator between you and the Czar."

The Empress shook her head, kissed Pauline and, turning away, was guided across the plank by Ouvaroff and Wilfrid. She seated herself beside the latter in the bow of the boat, while the Prince took his place in the stern and busied himself with the tiller. The oars dipped, and the next moment the boat was shooting forward into deep water.

As Marie silently watched the castle fade in the distance and thought of the happy time spent there, her eyes suffused with tears.

Wilfrid, too, was silent. He was glad of the presence of Prince Ouvaroff and the four Finlanders; there could be no love-making so long as they were by. A beautiful woman is a beautiful peril and she becomes doubly perilous when in distress. Wilfrid, in spite of the claims of honour, felt that he durst not trust himself alone with her, lest passion should usurp the place of reason.

" *Wilfrid,*" said the Czarina softly. " How is this to end? "

" Your Majesty —— " he began.

" Majesty! " she repeated reproachfully. " It was Marie once."

" A treasonable word, for which I humbly ask your pardon."

" Pardon, for giving me pleasure? "

There was fire in Wilfrid's blood when she spoke like that, and he was gladder than ever that they were not alone.

" It must be our aim to do the right," he remarked. " There is something higher in life than love — there is honour."

" That means that you have ceased to love me," she said; in her voice a pathos that thrilled him to the heart.

" Your Majesty, I would gladly resign life itself to ensure your happiness."

" I know it and am grateful. But," she faltered sorrowfully, " that feeling is loyalty, not love." There was a brief interval of silence, and then she resumed: —

" The Czar loves Pauline; he will obtain a divorce and then — then — what is to prevent us from being — happy? "

" That were to justify men's suspicions of our relations. Your fair name would be gone. No, your Majesty. You are an Empress and shall remain such. The Czar will forget his fancy for Pauline when he finds that she is set against him. He shall believe in your innocence — how, I do not at present know, but all will come right in the end."

Deep down in her heart Marie was fain to confess the justice of what she felt was Wilfrid's final decision, but — the hardness of it! Without Wilfrid the future seemed black and joyless. What was the diadem of an empress without Wilfrid's love?

Under the vigorous strokes of the four oarsmen *The*

Pauline moved onwards at a fair pace, Ouvaroff keeping to mid-stream, the better to escape notice from the shore.

Heavy with thought the Empress took little heed of external things, but was roused from her reverie by a sudden whisper from Wilfrid.

" The Sumaroff Palace."

With some show of interest she turned her eyes towards the broad extent of gardens stretching backwards from the river and gazed at the long marble terrace from which, according to what had been told her, she must have been flung on that dreadful night exactly four weeks ago. For the hundredth time she thought how strange it was that her mind should preserve no memory of that event.

With his eye still upon the terrace Wilfrid observed a tall figure standing at the head of a short flight of steps leading down to the water. He had an impression that it was none other than Prince Sumaroff, a personal friend, and a very great one, too, of the Czar. He had just taken leave of a gentleman, wrapped in a long cloak, who had entered a small boat that was now being vigorously pulled by two men, not in a transverse, but in an oblique line, that would bring them within a few minutes across the bows of *The Pauline*.

As the gondola drew near, the two rowers in the other boat, without any apparent reason, suddenly changed their course. With a warning yell Ouvaroff swung the rudder round as far as it would go. All too late! A snapping of oars and a grinding crash of woodwork, cries of men and a woman's scream — and the next moment both boats turned completely over, their occupants being precipitated into the Neva, not, however, before Ouvaroff had recognised the cloaked figure in the other boat.

It was Count Baranoff.

Wilfrid, seated in the bow of *The Pauline* talking with Marie, had not noticed the proximity of the other boat till roused by Ouvaroff's shout. Turning his head and seeing the danger, he made a sudden clutch at Marie, but at that very moment came the shock of collision; her form eluded his fingers, and he went down into the water without her.

Being an excellent swimmer he rose at once to the surface and looked about for her. The two boats, keel uppermost, were a few yards away, moving off upon the fast-flowing current. Two of the Finlanders were clinging to *The Pauline;* the two others were struggling desperately in the water; so, too, was one of the rowers in Baranoff's boat. The five, unable apparently to swim, were uttering piteous cries.

These five were all that Wilfrid could see. There should be four more. Then, near by, arose the dripping head of Prince Ouvaroff. Like Wilfrid, a swimmer, it was no trouble for him to keep afloat.

" The Czarina! " he gasped, treading water and staring around.

" I'm looking for her. She hasn't risen yet."

Seeing that Marie, though tied hand and foot, had yet contrived to drift safely all the way to Runö, Wilfrid did not feel any alarm for a few seconds, but as the moments passed without sign of her, his easy feeling vanished.

Was she held a struggling captive, under one of the upturned boats? Hardly, he thought; so good a swimmer as she could surely extricate herself from such a position, unless she had been struck and rendered senseless.

Filled with this fear he was about to dash off after the two boats when a cry from Ouvaroff stopped him.

Looking where the Prince looked he saw a face, ghastly in the moonlight, the face of Arcadius Baranoff.

" Save me," he gurgled, his mouth full of water. " I cannot swim; I'm drowning! "

" The Count must take his chance," thought Wilfrid, and he was on the point of turning away when he caught a gleam as of floating gold locks beneath the hands of Baranoff. It was a sight that filled Wilfrid's heart with horror and sent a cry of vengeance to his tongue.

The coward Count was clinging to the struggling Empress! Unable to swim, he was seeking to gain a foothold in the water by resting his hands upon the head and shoulders of the Czarina, indifferent as to *her* fate, provided *he* might be rescued. But for this grip Marie could easily have made her way to the shore.

She slipped from his grasp and rose above the surface, fighting desperately for breath. A moment only was her white face visible; Baranoff had caught her again by the shoulders and the two immediately sank.

"The coward! He'll drown her!" cried Wilfrid.

A few strokes brought him to the place of their disappearance. Fearing that she might rise no more Wilfrid swam downwards without coming upon either of them. Unable to hold his breath longer he rose to the surface and saw Baranoff, a few feet away, drifting with the current, still clinging to the Czarina.

"I'm drowning! I'm drowning!" he screamed in a paroxysm of terror.

In another moment Wilfrid and Ouvaroff were by his side.

"Let go your hold, or I'll kill you!" said the furious Prince, and, clutching the Count by the back of his collar, he forced his head under the water, a diversion that caused Baranoff to relax his grasp, while at the same time Wilfrid seized the unconscious Czarina and holding her head above the surface, struck out immediately for the shore.

Prince Sumaroff, who had witnessed the catastrophe without being able to render any aid, descended the steps as Wilfrid drew near with his burden.

"I trust the lady lives," he said preparing to assist her from the water.

"If not, Russia will mourn its Empress," replied Wilfrid, revealing the Czarina's face to the gaze of the petrified Prince.

CHAPTER XXXIII.

FOR three hours the unconscious Czarina lay as one dead; then life began slowly to return, news received with feelings of intense relief by Wilfrid and Ouvaroff, who, seated by the cheerful light of a log-fire — Prince Sumaroff, it seemed, hated the national stove — were discussing the situation.

"It's satisfactory to know that Baranoff has gone to his long account," remarked Wilfrid.

"It's impossible to be sorry," returned Ouvaroff, "though I would have saved the unworthy wretch if I could, but he sank like lead, and never rose again."

The entrance of Prince Sumaroff put an end to this conversation.

"Gentlemen," he said, taking a seat between them, "that the Empress has been spending a month of religious seclusion in the Convent of the Ascension, a story I have hitherto believed, is evidently untrue. You, I think, can clear up this mystery. As you shall see by-and-by, I do not ask this from idle curiosity."

Thereupon Wilfrid frankly told the whole story of his dealings with the Czarina, beginning with Baranoff's offer at Berlin, and ending with the events of that very night, Ouvaroff confirming him in such parts as he was able.

When Wilfrid had finished, Sumaroff rose to his feet.

"Pardon my absence for a few minutes. When I return I shall have a pleasant surprise for you."

Wilfrid and Ouvaroff resumed their interrupted talk.

"And your suspicion of me ——?" said Wilfrid.

"Was the prompting of Baranoff. Long before I met you at Berlin he had assured me that the Czarina, the

Grand Duchess Elizavetta she was then, had a secret
lover in some Englishman. He refrained from giving
the name, however, till the night of that ball. ' To-night,'
said he, ' I will point out to you the favourite of the
Grand Duchess.' "

" And he did it," said Wilfrid, " by writing my name
upon a card and sending it to you as we sat together.
And you could believe him! Serge, my boy —— "

Wilfrid stopped on seeing the Prince enter, leading by
the hand a girl who seemed reluctant to come forward.

It was Nadia of the Silver Birch, as pretty as ever, but
deadly pale and so timid that after one glance at Wilfrid
she averted her eyes, and did not look at him again.

" Now, Nadia, tell your tale," said Prince Sumaroff.
" It is the only way to set matters right."

So Nadia told how, bribed by Baranoff with the price
of her own and her father's freedom, she had introduced
the Englishman into the bedroom of the Czarina — whom
she then only knew as a great lady. Immediately upon
doing so she had apprised the Czarina's maids, who
(themselves in the plot) were awaiting her summons.
Then, having done the work assigned her, Nadia had
fled to a room above, where the removal of a knot of
wood in the flooring had enabled her to observe all that
passed in the chamber below. She could thus testify
to the lady's innocence and the Englishman's honour.
Her father having died shortly afterwards, Nadia
had come to St. Petersburg and entered the service
of Prince Sumaroff. One day when she was on the
Nevski Prospekt there rode by in state a lady, whom
she recognised with fear and trembling, and who, she
learned from a bystander, was the new Czarina. After a
long struggle with herself she resolved to confess her mis-
deed and chose for the occasion the night of the masquerade. Putting her statement into writing and having
incidentally learned from the Princess Sumaroff in what
costume the Czarina intended to appear, Nadia had
watched her opportunity to present the letter to her, saying no more about it than that its contents would
exonerate her and Lord Courtenay from a false charge.
The Czarina eagerly took the missive, but said she would

reserve the reading of it till she should have returned to the Winter Palace. "'And,' she added, 'since I am known to you by my costume, I may be known to others, and therefore, good Nadia, in order that I may be *incognita,* you and I in this quiet nook here must exchange costumes for a time.'" It was agreed that they should meet again in the same spot an hour after midnight; and so the two parted, the Empress in the plain grey domino and Nadia in the rich brocaded silk. The Czarina, however, failed to appear at the time and place appointed, a fact that puzzled Nadia very much. The Empress during a whole month having taken no notice of her and her writing though the matter was one of vital interest to her good name that very day, Nadia, moved by some indefinable fear, had revealed all to the Prince and Princess of Sumaroff.

"And you are willing to tell this story in the presence of the Czar himself?" asked Ouvaroff.

Nadia expressed her willingness, even though the telling should end in her exile to Siberia.

"I will answer for it that no hurt shall befall you," said Ouvaroff. "The Czar will be more pleased than angry to hear your tale. But it's as well for Baranoff that he has gone to his account."

At a sign from Prince Sumaroff, Nadia disappeared.

"I invited the Count here this evening," he said, "and in Nadia's presence taxed him with his guilt. Unable to deny it and rendered craven by fear, he implored me to keep the matter a secret from the Czar. Moved by his entreaties, I said, 'Write me out a confession and I'll give you three days within which to get out of Russia.' I little thought when he stepped into the boat that the hand of Death was already upon him. Heaven, you see, would not let him escape."

"He met with a just doom," commented Wilfrid, "dying by the very death he had appointed for another."

For it was evident now that the four liveried ruffians at the masquerade were Baranoff's hirelings and that it was not the Czarina's life they sought, but Nadia's.

"I think," mused Sumaroff, "that we are now in a

position to effect a reconciliation between the Czar and Czarina."

"I would give much to see it," remarked Wilfrid. "Through me," he added moodily, "an empress seems destined to forfeit both husband and crown."

"You have nothing to reproach yourself with," said Sumaroff cheerfully. "You have acted throughout as an honourable man. Let us review the points in your favour. First, there's the affair at the Silver Birch. *That's* satisfactorily explained."

"The kiss in the garden witnessed by the Czar," said Wilfrid.

"Merely a reward for a great service to the State."

"She lingered very much over it."

"Still the Czar must overlook it. Doubtless," he added, with a twinkle in his eye, "he, too, has lingered considerably over the kisses he has bestowed upon the fair Pauline."

"The four weeks of love-making at Castle Runö?"

"To be pardoned, when the circumstances are considered. *She* had forgotten her identity; *you* believed her to be an unwedded woman. The Baroness can testify to the truth of this — is testifying, perhaps, at this very moment."

"All very good," returned Wilfrid. "But there's another difficulty — the greatest. The Czarina herself is opposed to a reconciliation. In her present state of mind, Alexander is an object of dread to her."

"He'll soon cease to be so," replied Sumaroff with a mysterious smile. "But the hour is late; let us to bed. If the plan I have in view succeeds, by this time to-morrow all will be in harmony again."

And so ended the most memorable day in Wilfrid's career, a day in which he had won and lost the love of a wedded empress! It was a pleasure to think, as Prince Sumaroff had remarked, that through it all his honour had remained stainless.

Late in the forenoon of the following day Wilfrid was summoned to the presence of the Czarina. At first he demurred. Better, he thought, for the interests and happiness of both that they should never meet again.

"You had better see her," said Prince Sumaroff, appreciating Wilfrid's hesitation. "The sequel will, I trust, prove the wisdom of this advice."

So persuaded, Wilfrid was conducted to a small cabinet where, the Prince retiring, he found himself alone with the Czarina.

She was seated, pale and stately, in an antique high-backed chair, her eyes grave and sorrowful. Her manner was in singular contrast with that of the previous evening. She was no longer the "Princess Marie" of his love-dream; she seemed to have waked up to the consciousness that she was an empress, between whom and Wilfrid was an impassable gulf. He had been hoping that she might forget her love for him, and yet, now that his wish was realised, it sent a pang to his heart.

"Be seated, Lord Courtenay."

Grimly contrasting this formal title with the caressingly spoken "Wilfrid" of the previous evening, he sat down and waited for her to proceed.

She set her beautiful eyes upon him and said in a tone approaching almost to awe :—

"Do you know who it was that came upon us last night in the Sumaroff Gardens?"

Last night! The event was distant by four weeks, yet she spoke of it as occurring but a few hours previously. For a moment Wilfrid stared blankly at her. Then the truth flashed upon him, and he realised the cause of her altered manner.

There had happened to her mind one of those phenomena which, by no means rare, are yet extremely puzzling to students of psychology.

The shock of her second immersion in the Neva had nullified the effects of the first, and had caused the return of her memory, with this defect, however, that the intervening period was a complete blank. She had no recollection whatever of the love episodes at Runö.

Wilfrid's silence, due to his surprise, drew from the Empress a reiteration of her question.

"Do you know who he was?"

"I shall be pleased to learn his name from you."

"He was my husband — the Czar, Alexander Paulo-vitch!"

She watched him keenly as if to mark the effect of her words. Wilfrid, therefore, endeavoured to simulate amazement.

"You are the Czarina Elizavetta?" he said in a tone of feigned incredulity.

"I am," she answered proudly. "And you have dared to address words of love to me, words heard by — by *him!*"

"He will surely pardon on learning that I was ignorant of your name and rank?"

"You he may pardon; will he forgive me — me, who listened to you? It was but for a minute, I know. For a minute only I was tempted to forget my duty to him, when I remembered how he was neglecting me for the smiles of Pauline de Vaucluse. One brief minute, yet I fear it will be a fatal one for me!"

It was with a keen sense of anguish that Wilfrid marked her mournfulness.

"Why," she murmured, "ah! why did I withhold my name on first meeting you at the Silver Birch? It would have prevented many complications. But, believing that I should never see you again, I deemed it best to keep my identity a secret. And when I met you a second time, on that night in the Michaelovski Palace and would have told you my name, you spoke so hardly, so contemp-tuously of Alexander that somehow I shrank, foolishly shrank, from telling you that I was his wife."

"Your Majesty, had I known that, I should have re-frained from all comment, still less would I have dared to exact a kiss from —— "

At this point he was interrupted by the Empress, eager to learn the result of the interview between Alexander and Wilfrid.

"The Czar spoke to you," she said breathlessly. "What did he say or do?"

"He did precisely what I should have done if I pos-sessed a wife and saw a stranger kiss her. He challenged me to a duel."

The Czarina's face showed signs of the liveliest disquietude; in her agitation she half rose from her seat.

"Oh, but you did not fight! You have not accepted!"

"Your Majesty, do not distress yourself. The duel has not come off — never will. Now, may I make so bold as to ask your Majesty what strange event befell you after leaving me. How came you to be in the Neva?"

The Czarina trembled, partly with fear, partly with indignation.

"The recollection turns me cold. I, the Czarina, to be handled so! They could not have known who I was. They could not have meant to kill their Empress. I was seized by four men; one pressed his palm upon my mouth — the others tied my hands and feet. It was the work of a few moments; then I was lifted up and flung into the river. I have a faint recollection of rising to the surface, of battling for life; but everything at this point fades away into oblivion. It seems like a dreadful dream." She shuddered and added, "I am told by Prince Sumaroff that my life is due to you."

"I — I had a hand in saving you," said Wilfrid, referring to the second immersion, while she, of course, was thinking of the first — to her the only one. "I saw you floating on the water and brought you ashore."

"Then this will be the second time you have saved my life," she said with a sort of resentment in her tone. "It makes it harder for me to say what I *must* say. Lord Courtenay, you must leave Russia at once. You are anxious to serve me, I know. It is a cold saying, but the best service you can do me is to put a thousand miles between us. Your continuance in St. Petersburg exposes me to suspicion. You have been the means, though innocently, of setting the Czar against me."

Around her throat she still wore the gold chain with the locket attached, containing Wilfrid's miniature. She hesitated for a moment and then detached the locket.

"The original cause of all the misunderstanding," she murmured softly. "But for this Alexander, prompted by Baranoff, would never have begun to suspect me."

She held forth the locket though her eyes told Wilfrid that she parted from it with sorrow.

He rose, took the locket and remained standing, perceiving that her interview with him was all but over. That pledge of his ill-starred love, the gold ring that he had given her on the previous day, was not now on her finger, and he wondered what had become of it.

"You will leave Russia without delay?"

"Your Majesty, I will."

He had barely given this promise when he suddenly caught sight of a startling apparition behind the Empress's chair. Alexander himself! — no longer the furious being of the previous night, but mild and gracious of aspect: nay, with a half-smile upon his lips.

Secreted near he had heard every word freely and spontaneously uttered by the speakers unaware of his presence, and thus had received convincing proof that Wilfrid's relations with the Czarina had been, from beginning to end, of an honourable character.

The Czarina, apprised of strange happenings by Wilfrid's stare, turned to ascertain the cause and beheld — her husband!

Startled, she shrank back, hesitating, shivering, terrified, as she recalled the kiss and the embrace in the garden; then, re-assured by his tender and forgiving look, she gasped —

"Sasha!"

"Marie," he whispered bending over her, "I have come to take you back to my heart!"

Trembling with wild joy she rose to her feet and fell within the arms that opened eagerly to receive her.

"Plainly I'm not wanted here," thought Wilfrid, and he vanished from the apartment.

He had not gone far before he met Prince and Princess Sumaroff, to whom he gave an account of his interview and its dramatic termination.

They received his tidings with smiles of satisfaction.

"So my innocent little artifice has succeeded," said the Prince. "Early this morning I went to Runö and saw Alexander. The lapse of a few hours had made him more amenable to reason. The Baroness had already half-persuaded him of the Czarina's innocence. I brought him here and he listened to Nadia's story

and read Baranoff's confession. That convinced him.
'If you require further proof,' said I, ' why not secrete
yourself and watch Lord Courtenay as he takes his
farewell of the Empress? You will be able to judge
by their language whether their relations have been
guilty or not.' For I knew, Lord Courtenay, that you
would say nothing to the Czarina but what would become an honourable man. You have vindicated my
opinion of you, with the happiest results.

"All's well that ends well," remarked Wilfrid phil-
osophically.

"But the end has not *quite* come," said Princess
Sumaroff with a peculiar smile. "You must put the
finishing touch to this reconciliation by making it impossible for Alexander's thoughts ever to wander again
towards the Baroness Runö."

"And how can I do that? "

The Princess laughed sweetly.

"By making her Countess Courtenay, of course!"

Wilfrid started. Such an idea had never before
occurred to him. How could it, with his mind full of
Marie? But now that love had become part of his
nature, who more capable of satisfying that sentiment
than Pauline, in whom he had always taken an interest
bordering on affection? Her recent course of deception, censurable as it was, had done little to diminish
his regard for her, seeing that she had not sought her
own aggrandisement, but the supposed welfare of
France.

Princess Sumaroff drew forth a gold ring, set with
amethysts, and gave it to Wilfrid.

"Yours. I took it last night from the Czarina's finger while she slept. She might have been asking
awkward questions about it, and it will be better for
her to remain in ignorance. Now, why not bestow this
ring upon the Baroness? She loves you, — not that she
has ever said so — at least to me. I judge by the
warmth with which she speaks of your bravery, your
honour, your good looks, your accomplishments, your
heaven-knows what. It is my firm belief that you are
the cause of her refusing an empress's crown when it

was within her grasp. Don't let her make the sacrifice in vain. The Baroness is walking in the gardens at this moment, miserable because she thinks she has lost your good opinion. Seek her, and on your return let us have the pleasure of greeting her as the future Countess Courtenay."

Wilfrid, his heart beating with pleasurable sensations, walked out into those gardens which four weeks before had been the scene of so much mystery and romance.

He found Pauline alone, walking on the terrace that overlooked the river. Her face, sad and pensive, brightened at his approach; and still more when she learned the result of his final interview with the Czarina.

"That is good," she murmured.

Side by side the two slowly paced the terrace in silence.

Wilfrid was thinking of the words spoken by Princess Sumaroff, Pauline of Wilfrid's coming departure. He had told her of his intention to leave Russia within a few days; she received the news with a strange sinking of heart. How desolate her future if deprived of his presence! Yet what had she done to deserve his companionship? Nothing! but much to forfeit it; and yet, if the true working of her mind could be known to him, he would see that she was not *quite* so bad as he perhaps thought her.

"And you have no word of reproach for me?" she said gently.

"It was wrong of you, but I am willing to forgive you on one condition."

She looked at him, uneasy in mind as to what his next words would be.

"The condition is that you consent to be Countess Courtenay."

Greatly daring, he put his left arm around her, and, taking her left hand within his right, drew her towards him.

He had need to hold her: but for his strong grasp she would have fallen to the ground in sheer amazement at words so unexpected.

Recovering somewhat, she strove to put aside his

arms, saying many times over, what she sincerely believed, that she was not worthy of him.

"Do you *really* love me?" she said at last, raising to him eyes in which tears were glittering.

"You are the dearest woman in the world to me — now," he replied, encircling her finger with a ring that had once adorned the hand of an empress. "It would not be true to say that you are my first love, but then, perhaps," he added, thinking of Alexander, "neither am I yours."

But Pauline repudiated this with warmth.

"I have never loved any one but you."

And with this answer Wilfrid was content.

THE END.

www.ingramcontent.com/pod-product-compliance
Lightning Source LLC
Chambersburg PA
CBHW022210010726
47493CB00002B/505

I0563607

THE EXILES OF DAMARIA

Borgo Press Books by ARDATH MAYHAR

The Absolutely Perfect Horse: A Novel of East Texas (with Marylois Dunn)
The Body in the Swamp: A Washington Shipp Mystery [Wash Shipp #2]
Carrots and Miggle: A Novel of East Texas
The Clarrington Heritage: A Gothic Tale of Terror
Closely Knit in Scarlatt: A Novel of Suspense
Crazy Quilt: The Best Short Stories of Ardath Mayhar
Deadly Memoir: A Novel of Suspense
Death in the Square: A Washington Shipp Mystery [Wash Shipp #1]
The Door in the Hill: A Tale of the Turnipins
The Dropouts: A Tale of Growing Up in East Texas
The Exiles of Damaria: A Novel of Fantasy
Feud at Sweetwater Creek: A Novel of the Old West
The Fugitives: A Tale of Prehistoric Times
The Heirs of Three Oaks: A Novel of the Old West
High Mountain Winter: A Novel of the Old West
How the Gods Wove in Kyrannon: Tales of the Triple Moons
Hunters of the Plains: A Novel of Prehistoric America
Island in the Lake: A Novel of Native America
Khi to Freedom: A Science Fiction Novel
The Lintons of Skillet Bend: A Novel of East Texas
Lone Runner: A Novel of the Old West
Lords of the Triple Moons: A Science Fantasy Novel: Tales of the Triple Moons
Makra Choria: A Novel of High Fantasy
Medicine Dream: Being the Further Adventures of Burr Henderson
Messengers in White: A Science Fantasy Novel
Monkey Station: A Novel of the Future (Macaque Cycle #1; with Ron Fortier)
People of the Mesa: A Novel of Native America
A Planet Called Heaven: A Science Fiction Novel
Prescription for Danger: A Novel of the Old West
Reflections; & Journey to an Ending: Collected Poems
A Road of Stars: A Fantasy of Life, Death, Love, and Art
Runes of the Lyre: A Science Fantasy Novel
The Saga of Grittel Sundotha: A Science Fantasy Novel
The Seekers of Shar-Nuhn: Tales of the Triple Moons
Shock Treatment: An Account of Granary's War: A Science Fiction Novel
Slewfoot Sally and the Flying Mule: Tall Tales from Cotton County, Texas
Soul-Singer of Tyrnos: A Fantasy Novel
Strange Doin's in the Pine Hills: Stories of Fantasy and Mystery in East Texas
Strange View from a Skewed Orbit: An Oddball Memoir
Through a Stone Wall: Lessons from Thirty Years of Writing
Timber Pirates: A Novel of East Texas (with Marylois Dunn)
Towers of the Earth: A Novel of Native America
Trail of the Seahawks: A Novel of the Future (Macaque Cycle #2; with R. Fortier)
The Tulpa: A Novel of Fantasy
Two-Moons and the Black Tower: A Novel of Fantasy
Vendetta: A Novel of the Old West
Warlock's Gift: Tales of the Triple Moons
The World Ends in Hickory Hollow: A Novel of the Future
A World of Weirdities: Tales to Shiver By

THE EXILES OF DAMARIA

A NOVEL OF FANTASY

by

Ardath Mayhar

THE BORGO PRESS

An Imprint of Wildside Press LLC

MMX

Copyright © 2003, 2010 by Ardath Mayhar
The first half of this novel was previously published in 2003 as
Riddles and Dreams.

All rights reserved.
No part of this book may be reproduced in any form
without the expressed written consent
of the author and publisher.

www.wildsidebooks.com

FIRST EDITION

CONTENTS

BOOK TWO: SHIPS AND SEEKERS

FOREWORD

Some years ago, an editor asked me for a book that would continue the Tolkien story of the elves' retreat to the Western Isles. That didn't happen, but the concept of exile kept niggling at me until I wrote this book. It was great fun to write. I hope it is as much fun to read. Half it was published in 2003 as *Riddles and Dreams* by Imagesco, a small press. This is the first print version containing the entire story.

—Ardath Mayhar
Chireno, TX
November 2009

PROLOGUE

THE PASSING OF A KING

"A time has come when even Kings must die."
—From *The Songs of Riddle the Poet*

The King of Damaria braced himself against the back of his chair, feeling the fatal bubbling in his lungs. He knew he was dying; the man who stood across the table from him had thrust him through the back and lungs, and soon he would drown in his own blood.

He was not afraid, for one who has lived for more than two thousand years must be willing to die, when the time comes. Yet now he had regrets. Why had he not gone again into the south to his kin, when his niece-wife died childless? He now left no offspring of the full blood to take his place and to avenge his death.

His brother's offspring, sole heirs to his throne, were not likely, he knew, to survive to inherit it. If he had done as his fathers did, he would have children—one at least—safe with a mother in the homeland. Now the weight of rule in Damaria rested on whichever of those nephews managed to survive.

It was almost incredible that one of his kin had achieved four children, for the Ancient Race was not fecund. Yet now the question was irrelevant. He closed his eyes in grief, knowing they were probably all dead at the hands of this power-mad half-cousin.

The man now staring at him with hard, pale eyes was his son, true, but not of the full blood. Armor had outlived dozens of such sons, begotten on the short-lived kind his race had raised to sentience from the lower orders they found when they came north.

He gasped, holding himself upright with effort against the pain and the growing weakness. He should have a son—a true one of the Ancient Race—and that had been denied him.

There seemed a strange balance in nature: the long-lived races had very few young. The short-lived ones regularly produced numbers of offspring, though many of those were not viable. It was ironic, he thought, as the wave of pain receded. The breeding program his people had instituted was not completely successful; the numbers of new people had not increased as expected. Now he was all but certain this was a part of the problem that had led to this terrible rebellion and caused the end of his family in Damaria.

Armor closed his eyes, feeling about him his beloved rooms, glowing with subtle shades of rose and gold and blue. Lorbek was astonished, he could tell, at the plainness of his surroundings and at the unpretentious house in which his father the King seemed content to live.

Returning from his long years in the southern lands, the young man had expected to find his father living in state, it was evident. Armor thought of Lorbek's almost-forgotten mother, who must have told him tales of grandeur, there in her southern exile. He could not even recall her face, but Armor suspected she had spun fantasies for her son as he was educated in the arts and skills of his father's people.

"Do not smile!" The words came almost as a shriek. "Where is the Orb, old man? We will have that from you, and then we will let you die!" That was Nikol, who had led the rebellion here in Damaria when Lorbek returned.

The King braced himself against a stab of agony, keeping his gaze resolutely turned from the paneling above the mantel over the low hearth. He would never reveal the hiding place of the Sealed Flame that allowed him to peer into other places, other times, and even the workings of living bodies.

Now he knew, too late. Its use in deliberately breeding sentient creatures for specific traits was in itself a major error. Even though he was dying, his mind seemed clearer than ever before, and he suspected that to be the source of this disaster to his family.

Lorbek bent over the table and stared into his eyes. "Tell us where you keep the Orb. My mother told me it is the source of your power."

Armor tasted blood on his tongue, but he held it back, swallowed, and said, "Your mother did not understand us. How could she? We bred your people up from their lives as primitive savages who roamed the forests, as your cousins the Lirfolk still roam the northern hills." He swallowed again, feeling his strength draining steadily from his sturdy body. "She could not comprehend what she saw here." He coughed, seeing bright spatters of blood stain his snowy beard.

His knowing eyes discerned the gray tint, inherited from his maternal ancestors, still apparent in the fair skin of his son. The pale hair, the gray eyes came from those savages. He recalled with horror that they had eaten their own kind until tamed by the breeding programs and the teachings of his people.

"I wonder why you returned here," he said, his tone soft. "My father and his brothers came because they were called to free this land of a dreadful sickness. They were the only ones among all our kind in those distant lands to dare the perils of the journey."

"I understand all this too well," Lorbek said, a contemptuous set to his narrow lips. "I saw the laziness, the cowardice of those very distant kinsmen of mine who reared me. Not one had the strength of will to seize power in that rich land. Not one even considered crossing the quaking volcanic mountains to the north, although I had come that way with my mother as a child."

And a strong party of attendants accompanied you, the King thought. Armor almost groaned, but he held his control. "Peace and contentment are the attributes of our forebears. My grandfather was one of the last to go away from our own place into another, more dangerous country. Those still there will never leave, now. Only the children of the Damarian Kindred go north from the Old Land. Why did you return, Lorbek?"

"I came because my childhood friend called to me," said Lorbek, glancing aside at Nikol. "I came because I am the heir to the throne—if you can call that miserable chair a throne—of my country. When the unrest became unbearable and my kinsmen took action, they sent messengers to me. Of the dozen, only one arrived alive and able to speak, for they were caught when the burning mountains belched molten stone. I took that dangerous path northward to fulfill my destiny, Father." His narrow face was bleached white with his anger, his coloring untouched by any trace of the golden-brown skins and dark hair of his father's people.

Nikol, like all the new people of pure blood, was still a very pale gray, skin, hair, and eyes, but there was a similarity between the two in slender bone structure and narrow skulls. They looked far nearer in blood than did he and his son.

Armor choked back another cough. He felt light in the bone, as if he might drift up from his chair and float free. But his untiring mind still held questions. "Why...." He turned his gaze to Nikol. "...did you rebel? Have we ever mistreated your people? Have we not met your needs?"

The man's gray gaze met his for an instant before he lowered his eyes. His tone gruff, he said, "You met our needs, perhaps, but you bred others to replace us! Do you not know that we see and we think? You took the tree-swingers out of the forest and led them upward, as you had done our own kind. You made the Turnig think! They had farther to go, being animals in the beginning, but we knew you intended for them to supplant us, for they have more young that live.

"You taught them to do things for which we have no skills. They were to become your new people, and we were to be destroyed or left to our own devices."

Armor's mind recoiled, refusing to accept such a wild belief. He ran his hand down the satiny grain of the chair, knowing his life had been as smooth as the polished wood. The lives of those before him, here in the north, had been gentle. Now he saw that he had been blind, and his fathers before him had refused to see.

"We are so few." It was a moment before he realized he had spoken aloud. But what did it matter now? The man searching the room was moving toward the fireplace.

"Three half-brothers came north together, with their wives. Breeding slowly and scantily, as is natural for our kind, we never numbered more than a dozen here in Damaria, once the family of Blade moved north to the City in the Mist, facing upon the sea." He coughed again, the blood coming more freely.

"We need little, and only because this rich land required hands to grow crops, as well as herdsmen and metalworkers and weavers, did we interfere with the development of your young race. Those waning people whose need originally called us here were old, the species depleted, and they died away, as this new kind took their place."

One of the armed men was poking at the walls, probing between panels, nearing the hiding place. Armor kept his gaze on his son and Nikol, willing the searcher to pass the mantel without investigating the wood above it. If he could keep them thinking about his words, rather than their search, he might keep the Orb safe.

"For three thousand years there has been unbroken peace in Damaria. War is a footnote in the history even of those in the south; almost impassable mountains separate our coastal lands from the interior of this continent, whose grasslands are scantily populated. Those whose lands lie beyond the seas do not come here at all. They voyage only as far as the City in the Mist, on the western shore."

The blade with which the man was testing the panels was moving toward the spot behind which the Sealed Flame burned. He must keep their attention. "The Goremin living in those mountains were older and wiser than we, even then, and posed no threat to anyone. How could I have known I might need soldiers, here in the twilight of my life? Against my own son?"

Lorbek was only half listening, his expression grim as he watched his man search the room. Armor sighed, feeling he had lost everything, here at the end of his life. His Companions, chosen and trained individuals of the new people who lived in his house and served his needs, had gone down before an angry mob of their own kin. They had tried to fight with fists and teeth and hastily improvised weapons, but sudden need cannot replace skill. They had all died.

He tried again to gain their full attention, this time directing a question toward Nikol. "Do you truly believe we would nurture you, only to abandon you?" he asked the gray-skinned man.

Nikol did not reply.

"You have done what you intended," the King said. "We are all gone, I take it, from this land. I suspect the simian-descended men also will not survive. But do you believe you will rest untroubled in Damaria?"

His son curled his lip. "I know the Ancient Race in the south. They will never move from their indolent lives, their philosophies and their dreams. They cannot leave, now. Vengeance is a thing they cannot understand, so they will not come to punish me. We may, indeed, move southward ourselves. We are young and strong enough to survive the perils of the journey, and there are things there well worth the taking. Your kin will not defend them."

Armor braced himself again against the pain and the slow filling of his lungs. Worse than his own plight was the thought that he had sired a son so apt for being manipulated and compelled by the ancient force whose will had tainted these lands in ages long past—Dinorm—he pushed the thought away.

Amid a burst of agony, he longed for the book his kind had made, setting into its pages the secrets of ruling well, of harnessing the natural world, and of controlling those ancient, unpredictable wills that waked, from time to time, beneath the roots of the world. So potent had been the content of the volume that its very presence filled its holder with unexpected abilities.

But the book was lost. He had never dreamed that loss might become so terrible! In the rule of the second King of Damaria it was stolen, and no trace of the thief had ever come to light. The Goremin had a grim tradition of a violation that degraded it for terrible purposes, but even in its polluted condition it had not been traced.

Armor shook away the thought. That was only the lesser of the two powerful things his people possessed. The Orb, which was so close, now, to that searching blade, was the last and most important. He must endure whatever came without revealing its hiding place.

"You will tell me where you keep the Orb," said Lorbek, leaning close enough so Armor saw the mad glint in his eyes. "We must have it to hold the new people together, for already there are factions demanding we spare your life and that of Riddle, your nephew. We must not yield to weaklings."

The pale eyes were close—too close. "I need the power my mother revealed to me. Where is the Orb?"

Armor did not speak, for his breath was all but at an end. He stared up into the eyes of his son, knowing the man was controlled by forces he could not understand. Those would use him without pity and discard him without thought, once their purpose was fulfilled.

Then, to increase his agony, there came the screech of wood against stone as the searcher pried away the paneling above the fireplace. There, glowing with subdued light, was the sphere of colorless crystal set upon a golden pedestal.

At the center of the Orb burned the Sealed Flame, which had been brought from the south three thousand years before. It had helped Armor's grandfather to battle the creators of the evil from the north and to heal the creeping blight that threatened to destroy the land, corrupting all the living beings in Damaria. It had helped with improving the strains as the new people were bred for intelligence and ability.

Despite his resolve, Armor groaned. His son turned to face him, those pale eyes glittering with triumph. The long-fingered hands reached to take the pedestal with its bright burden from the niche in which it rested.

The thing shone through his flesh as if he, too, were made of crystal: his bones showed as shadows when his hands clasped about the Orb, which was the size of two fists, smoothly turned from a single piece of flawless quartz. Its interior flame was a cold, clean blue, motionless and filled with vibrancy.

Lorbek set the Orb before his father, and Armor stared into it. What he saw gave him great pain, but it held also a hint of hope, visible only to his trained gaze. He gulped down a surge of blood and spoke for the last time to his son Lorbek.

"Orm...Dinorm.... You know...of them?"

Lorbek shook his head, looking puzzled. "I do not. Save your breath, old man. You have served your purpose. Now it is time for you to die."

"You...will...learn." And Armor, King of Damaria, loosed his hold upon his ancient body, letting his spirit go free.

BOOK ONE

RIDDLES AND DREAMS

CHAPTER ONE

"The forest hides more kinds than animals...."
—Riddle

Chark, who considered herself a leader of the Turnig of Damariste Forest, was readying herself to go and tend the hidden gardens beyond the brook. Grumbling in her gruff voice at having to work by night to avoid encountering hunters or trappers in the forest, she raised her head and smelled the evening breeze. Someone familiar was walking on the road.

She had thought this one dead, with almost all the rest of his kind, when the Other Men took control of the land. She scurried to the fringe of the forest to see for herself that her senses had not deceived her. Her black eyes, circled with rings of dark brown fur, opened wide in amazement to see Riddle, the Poet of Damaria, still among the living.

* * * * * * *

The poet walked away from Damaria, avoiding the road until he was well clear of the last house. He never looked back, though he could see with the eyes of memory the city rising, like the mountain it was, against the tender blue-green of the evening sky. Cut from the stone of the upthrust eminence, fanciful grillwork, delicate balconies, and intricate gables made lacework against the glazed windows and pale walls.

All had turned red-gold in the last light, and here and there a pane winked into a different glow as lamps were kindled inside the houses against the coming of the night. He sighed at the thought.

The end of his world had come unexpectedly, in the midst of a song. He sat at a feast at the house of his brother, entertaining the family with his lute and his verse, when the door of the house boomed under the impact of a ruthless fist.

He shuddered, reliving the terrible night. He had, of course, drawn his seldom-used sword, but his brother held up a hand, even while drawing his own blade. "You are our only poet," he said. "And I would trust you to save my smallest son, for the other children are old enough to stand with their mother and me. If we hold them for long enough, perhaps you can bring Lute to safety."

A ram was crashing, now, at the solid wood of the door.

"Go, Riddle. You arrived after dark, and nobody expects to find you here. They will not search for you. Get Lute from his nursery and leave by the kitchen gate. I doubt we are surrounded, for everyone knows that we of the Ancient Race know nothing of warfare." His tone had been wry and sad and desperate, all in one.

The taste of his tears was still on Riddle's lips, as were those of his sister-in-law, his other nephews, and his niece. All were now dead, he knew without question, except for the child he carried. His own tears ran down his face, as he remembered his flight with small Lute.

Fortune had been with them, for they were caught by a smallholder of the new people who had been his friend. His suggestion to his companions that the poet be allowed to sing of their victory had gone down well. Once they were apart, Kollek had freed him and sent him running to save the child, who might well now be the King, concealed in his pack.

The rebels would never have allowed the tiny Heir of Damaria to escape, if they had known he was there. Riddle hoped Kollek would not suffer because of his generosity, but he had no doubt that he would. The rebels were filled with a thirst for blood, though he could find in his heart no memory of any abuse that might have kindled such hatred.

He walked steadily, his long legs sending his boots forward in puffs of dust. On his back were all the beloved things he had left in the world, and in the crook of his arm he sheltered his harp. It was the last of the gifts of his father to his poet-son, before the old man died.

Hidden in the pack, heavy and warm against his shoulders, was the child. He felt, with every fiber of his body and mind, that they two were the last of the Ancient Race who survived here in the northern realm.

As he went, he could feel hostile eyes watching him, though he knew he was beyond identification, so far along the road. It saddened him to think these whom his own kind had nurtured, teaching them arts and skills needed for living in a sane world, should have gone mad so suddenly and without warning. It was as if some evil will had turned its attention upon Damaria, shaking the old pattern awry and sending the colored threads flying.

Now, after three thousand years of peace and kindness, his old race was reduced to himself and his nephew, and set to wandering the world. They could not help those who might protest this new rule, and his heart grieved for those he knew to be still loyal to the King and his family.

These new rulers did not hesitate to kill, for mercy was one lesson they had refused to learn from their teachers. Lorbek—he had heard a murmur from one of those who captured him that Lorbek had taken the King and forced from him the secrets of the Sealed Flame.

He wondered how they had been able to accomplish such a seemingly impossible feat, without help from powers he had believed to be safely controlled and hidden away. Yet now he was unsure they had been contained. The Mover from the North was subtle and unresting. After so many generations, even of the Ancient Race, had he found his opportunity at last?

What other force could have driven these primitives so desperately against those who had provided only good things for them? What else could have enabled them to prevail over those whose wills helped to shape the world about them?

Never had he felt so orphaned and alone, though he hoped others of his kind might live still in the City in the Mist, far to the north and west. There ships had for centuries been built to bear travelers across the western sea to the islands that were a myth and a dream to all his kind.

Better death in seeking out a dream than at the hands of people capable of hunting out devices for destroying men, or of hurting Turnig for their fur! If Oakbeam the Builder still plied his trade, and if Riddle lived to find him, he would commission a vessel capable of carrying all who were left of his own people away to those kinder lands to which, for generations, certain of his kind had traveled.

As if his thought had conjured her out of the deepening twilight, he saw a small round face with dark-ringed eyes staring at him from a clump of vines at the edge of the forest ahead. He did not indicate that he noticed her, for someone might be watching. The new people paid a premium for Turnig fur to trim their robes of state!

But once he was past the first deep bend in the road, surrounded by tremendous trees, he paused. "Chark? Is it you?" he called softly into the screen of vegetation at the edge of the road.

The deep ferns trembled, their fronds showing the motion of something moving within their shelter. Two brown-furred hands parted the last clump, and Chark's face again stared into his. Even as she opened her mouth to speak, she stiffened with alarm and gestured for Riddle to join her in the concealment of the ferns.

He did not hesitate. More than once, in his years of wandering the forests and roads of Damaria, keeping watch over the many kinds of beings and singing their histories into immortality, he had found this small person to be one whose wit and instinct could be trusted. He dived into the ditch among the green billows and burrowed forward until he found the fringe of the wood. There the bushes and vines were too thick for any mortal eye to penetrate, and he crawled out into a clump of redberry and sat beside Chark.

Hoofbeats thundered on the road behind him, rounding the bend that had concealed him. He thought for a panic-stricken moment of the tracks he had left in the dust, ending at the spot where he jumped into the ditch. Chark tugged at his sleeve and pointed.

There were, of course, chinks in the wall of greenery. Through those the road could be seen fairly plainly. As he stared at the mounted man galloping northward along the dusty way, Riddle heard a warning hiccup at his back. He shrugged off the pack and unwrapped the disturbed child, just before a hearty howl might have betrayed them.

Hugging small Lute, he watched the long-legged beast pass the spot he had left, obliterating his own tracks with its heavy hooves. The man on its back wore the symbol he had noticed on those who caught him near his brother's house. It was, he thought, the sigil of the Mover from the North. Even as he thought it, the rider went out of his view, leaving the echo of hooves and a cloud of dust behind him.

He sighed with relief, although a faint chill touched his nerves. This was the way of the new people. Hurry and hurry, trample and trample, and never pause to think or to observe. Which was, of course, very fortunate for him and those of every kind who still survived.

Chark turned to him, her bright little eyes examining his nephew with interest. "Child? Whose?" she asked, her whiskers twitching with intensity.

"My brother had four children. This is the very last of them all. My brother and all the rest died at the hands of those who attacked their house. Lute, this is Chark." He turned the small boy so that he could see the Turnig.

The child was brown-eyed, brown-skinned as a berry, his small body square and strong for his age. He held out his hands to this new kind of person, and Chark put her furry fingers into his. Even at the age of four, Lute knew the rules for meeting other kinds. The Ancient People had practiced that etiquette for so long it was a part of their very blood. The child did not squeeze her hands or try to grab her bushy tail, but waited until the Turnig nodded.

Then the two put tentative fingers upon each other's faces, leaning to sniff the characteristic scents by which they would know one another again. Riddle sat back, trusting to the training of his nephew, as the ritual was completed.

But then he rose to his feet. "We had best get away from the road. I suspect someone back there sent a runner to Damaria to tell the new rulers I took the northern way. It may be they have changed their minds about letting me go free. Quite possibly, the honor of having the song of their conquest composed by the poet of the Kings of Damaria has been outweighed by the danger of having any of my line left alive. So, Chark, if you will lead us away, it will be very intelligent of us to go."

She disentangled herself from the child and turned her nose back toward the depths of the wood. Her whiskers twitched again, as she sniffed the air.

Riddle had found a bit of oatcake in his pack, and he set the boy on his shoulders to nibble the morsel and drop crumbs down his collar. Then he turned to follow the Turnig, as she led him along dim trails, among thickets and tangles of vine and long straight vistas amid huge tree-boles. Even one as used to finding his way through the wild as the poet soon found himself completely disoriented.

But the Turnig knew the wood as a housewife knows her kitchen. Soon Riddle heard the chuckle of a stream, and he hurried after his guide down a long slope of moss-covered roots and overgrown boulders to find a brook bubbling, cold and sweet, at its bottom. He knelt and cupped his hands, filling them with water. Lute drank thirstily, and then Riddle satisfied his own dry throat.

Chark bounded over the brook and ducked through a screen of bushes. "Chrrrk!" she said.

Riddle rose and lifted the child once more. "I'm coming. Where are you?"

The bright eyes stared up from a bush near his knees. "Chrrrk!" she said again, pushing aside the undergrowth to show the man a narrow path made by very small feet in the debris of the forest floor.

As he stepped forward, Riddle felt something touch his face, lightly, tenuously, and yet he knew this was something powerful. He stopped in his tracks. The strands, not material and yet strangely real, were still clinging against his skin.

"Chark?" He barely moved his lips. "What?"

"Trap," she said. "Not bad trap. Not good trap. Just trap. Big thing sleep in ground. Keep trap up here...know who comes. You wait. You see."

That did not, for some reason, reassure the poet. The child wriggled on his shoulders, kicking his heels into his uncle's chest. "Go! Go!" he insisted.

"Not quite yet," he said, still motionless. "A big...animal...is about to come. You want to see it, don't you?"

"Umm." Lute was overly fond of animals. For once, Riddle blessed his inclination, for the boy subsided to an occasional kick at his chest or tug at his ears.

The wait seemed endless. Chark did not go on into her garden, as she had intended, but waited with him, sniffing the air constantly, looking about the wood, pricking up her pointed ears at every sound.

Above them, there came a pure burst of song. Riddle almost smiled against the tug of the trap, for that was the call of the blue warbler. He had walked many a weary mile to the accompaniment of that song, making up his own counterpoint as he fitted words to its burbling cadences.

"A bird!" cried the child. "Bird!" He clapped his hands, almost tumbling down his uncle's back in the process.

The song grew louder, as the bird came down to a lower branch. But it was suddenly cut off, and the blue-winged shape darted away with a discordant squawk.

A bit of the forest floor began to rise, a round trapdoor of soil, matted with roots and covered with dead leaves, moving upward on invisible hinges. The smell of cinnamon filled the air, and Riddle felt his heart thud into his boots. He had heard of the Groundbears. He had seen the huge skins of Groundbears. He had never had any wish to see the beast itself, alive on its home ground. But now it seemed he was going to, like it or not.

Chark darted into the undergrowth, for the creatures were fond of small furry animals, which they ate with much enjoyment. Lute gave a final kick of his heels and went still on his uncle's shoulders. Riddle sighed with relief, for who was to know if the beast might not think the boy a sort of small animal, too?

The cover of the lair was completely open, and the animal climbed into the shadowy wood, raising its blunt head to sniff the air. "Huroo?" it said, its tone gruff.

Riddle ventured to speak, though he knew the Groundbears were not among those beasts who had grown to think like human-kind. "A traveler. Riddle, of the Ancient People. I mean you no harm, trapper of the forest."

With a heave, the creature moved onto the surface and stood up-right, its bulk black against the dark trees. Its breath came in deep "hurffs" as it approached the trap it had set and ran its paws over the body of the poet, who stood quite still and silent while that was done.

"I am truly not anything you would use for food," said Riddle, hoping his words were true. "While the new rulers of this land use the hides of Groundbears for rugs, my own kind have never troubled them in their forest burrows."

Lute whimpered softly, deep in his throat. Riddle thought the thick scent of cinnamon was choking the child, and he ventured to move his hand to pat the sturdy leg beside his cheek.

The beast moved around him, sniffing at his clothing, nosing the little boy, touching the pack with inquisitive paws. Riddle prayed that Lute would remain still and that the animal would not take it into its head to try the taste of either of them.

The forest was now black shadow against blacker shadow. It was almost impossible to see the creature, but it was still close, its fur occasionally touching him, its snufflings clearly too near for comfort.

He needed to sneeze. He needed to sit down and rest his weary legs. He needed to run, fast and far, but he stood still and waited. Even Lute seemed frozen by the nearness of such a huge creature.

The bushes rustled, though he felt no breeze against his face. There came a rush of small feet on dried leaves, a gruff war-cry, and the Groundbear, now on all-fours, leaped convulsively, brushing against his legs. With snorts of pain and frustration, the beast moved back toward its burrow, its paws crashing through the undergrowth.

What now? Riddle wondered. And then he felt small hands tug-ging at his cloak, and he sank to squat on his heels. "Chark?"

"Come now! Stick that thing with rake, but it know soon what hit it. Then it come back. Come quick!"

The poet rose, wondering how such a small creature dared to at-tack one so many times her size. But he didn't wait while he won-dered. He reached down, caught the small furry hand, and followed Chark through the night-bound wood toward her unknown destina-tion.

CHAPTER TWO

"...but for the mesh of pain that binds me fast."
—Riddle

The manacles chafed her delicate wrists, and the damp chill of the stone cell made her bones ache. Moonlight sighed patiently and eased herself against the wall, trying for a position that would put less strain on her shoulders and her back. Beyond the iron-studded door, she could hear the voices of the guards, who were gambling for her cloak and her small packet of clothing she had managed to snatch as she ran from the burning house of her grandmother. The thought made tears come into her eyes, though she blinked them back with grim determination.

She had left her grandmother to burn, though the old lady had been dead. She kept reassuring herself about that, for any other thought would have sent her mad, she was sure.

The axe the barbarian had whirled over his head, before burying it in the fragile skull beneath the coiffed silver hair, had gone deep. The ivory-skinned hand had loosed the Jewel of the Nairneks. Moonlight had snatched it up, along with the basket of clean things, as she ran, ducking beneath the hairy arm, the stinking cloak, of their attacker.

His awkward attempt to catch her had been useless, of course. She would have got clean away, if the raiders outside had not been alert for escapees. But even then, she had managed to conceal the Jewel, which was small and colorless when not in use. Tucking it down through a hole in her pocket, she had made certain it caught in the hem of her tunic. There it would have to wait until she found an appropriate time to retrieve it, or until those jailers outside gambled away her present tattered garments, stripping them from her corpse.

Not that her gem would be of help to a prisoner or a warrior. What possible good could the Jewel of a Dreamer do, in such circumstances as she now faced? Even as she wondered, the bars outside the door scraped and rattled, and the heavy leaf swung inward.

The man standing in the doorway surprised her; he did not look like either a barbarian or a murderer. He was obviously of half blood, his pale hair and skin like that of the new people, his length of bone and his delicately formed skull hinting at a heritage from the race of the Kings. His features were so fine and aristocratic she thought at first he must be a friend, come to rescue her. But the events of the past days had warned her against too ready a trust. The end of her own House, the day before, made her cautious.

This was a kinsman, of course, for her people the Dreamers were also of half blood. But where this man had the human eyes and the coloration of his kin, those who were born to Dream were of a different, a definitely feline look. She gazed at him from eyes slitted like a cat's, and her hair hung in tangles of russet braids about her shoulders. Only her fellows had that Dreamer look. The combination of certain of the new strains with that of the Ancient kind had produced, some centuries ago, a different breed entirely.

Only the common people valued her kind or even noticed them, she understood. The Kings took note of little that numbered less than a thousand years to its history. In time, they would have learned to value her people, but that time had been cut short.

She said nothing, though she kept her gaze fixed on that pale face as he approached her. A traitor? Possibly. A rescuer? The closer he came, in the light of the torches just outside the door, the less she believed it. There was an air about him that made her skin crinkle with distaste.

"You are of the Nairneks? A Dreamer, they call you." His voice was musical, soothing...deceptive, she felt instinctively.

"I am Moonlight." That would betray nothing, for her skills and her lineage were of no interest to the new rulers of the lands east of the Ocean.

"You are very beautiful, Moonlight," he said. His hand came forward to touch one of her ruddy braids. He ran a finger down the golden tan of her cheek. "I did not think, as I lived my life in the south, that there might be such beauty in my home country. But what is a Dreamer? Do tell me. I was taught nothing about your kind of crossbreed." His fingers strayed down her neck.

"I dislike overly familiar men," she said, her tone brisk. Inside she was quaking, but for the honor of her family she must show neither fear nor submission.

He laughed, and now she could hear a wicked note in that smooth voice. "Your preferences are no concern of mine. I crave your company, for a time. If you please me, you may possibly live.

If not, you will be thrown to the guards, who will make short work of you, I assure you."

"Ah," she said, looking straight into his eyes. "I see that you are a man of subtlety. One who is skilled in the courtly and gentle arts." Even he flinched at the sarcasm in her tone.

He turned without another word and gestured to someone outside. A guard entered at once, unlocking her shackles and freeing her from the wall. He caught her elbow in a harsh grip as she staggered, trying to regain her balance along with her strength. So many hours hanging chained to a wall did strange things to the body, she noted with interest.

"Take her to the baths. Then send her to me!" That was the voice she had already grown to loathe, echoing back along the crooked passage.

She was half carried up flights of stone steps, along damp corridors, and at last into a round chamber centered with a pool that steamed gently in the chill of the day. Two women stood beside a heap of towels and clothing, and they came to assist her, as the guard turned and left.

"I need no help," she said. "I prefer to bathe alone. You may leave until I call you." Into her voice she put all the authority of the generations of Nairneks who had sung dreams for farmers, herdsmen, and hunters. The women withdrew without argument, leaving her alone to transfer her Jewel from the seam of her tunic.

She knew clothing was too temporary to risk as a lodging place for the gem. She must swallow it, and hope it did not work its way through her system to be lost later. As long as it was with her, no matter how, the focus would work, and her dreaming gift could be transmitted. A stream of cool water purled down a stone chute into the pool, and she cupped her hand beneath the rivulet and drank, gulping down the Jewel easily. Then she removed her clothing and sank gratefully into the bath.

She did not dally, however. She had an intuition that her captor was an impatient man, and she wanted no incident to mar her approach to him. He would be comfortably aware that she was entirely within his power, and this was an illusion she wanted to foster.

When the time was ripe, she would make her escape, but until then she did not intend to alarm him.

There was a thick velvet robe with white draperies that went beneath it. She clothed herself and tied the golden sash tightly. The robe went over the filmy draperies, and she was glad of the warmth, as she looked about and found that sandals had also been provided. They were too thin-soled for escaping in, but anything would be better than bare feet.

She longed for her own stout boots, but they were gone, burnt with everything all the generations of her House had accumulated. Again she wondered why her people had been slaughtered, their home ransacked and destroyed. They had never threatened anyone, in all the time of their existence. It was remotely understandable if the new people had envied the power and the long, long lives of the Ancient Ones. But it was unlikely they had ever known anything but good from the small clan of Dreamers. This Lorbek had been reared in the south, which must explain his disregard for the attitudes of others of his kind.

Dreams, as she knew well, could heal the sick, comfort the troubled, and strengthen those who faltered. They were a subtle exercise of Will, which shaped the world she knew and was the instrument of those who ruled it. By use of her own will, she could create, within a waking mind, a dream so real the dreamer believed it fully, allowing his body and his mind to heal as he lived the vision.

Those who came to her House had been of all kinds, and none had ever been turned away. If they brought gifts, those were welcome, but if petitioners had nothing, they also were served. Only in the most secret elements of her training was there any hint of a darker side to her inherited gift.

No, she could not see the commons taking part in this destruction of her kind. It had to be a private act on the part of this man who commanded the keep that had been one home of the King himself. Indeed, there was something of Armor in the look of Lorbek....

She hoped to find out, before she was done with him, just what the truth might be. But for now she slipped the sandals onto her feet and rang the silver bell hanging from an ornate loop. As she had suspected, the two women returned and took their places on either side of her.

"The Lord awaits you," said the smaller of the pair. Her voice trembled. Her skin was even paler than it had been, as she pushed aside the draperies that concealed one side of the round chamber and opened the door beyond them.

"We wish you no ill, Lady." The young voice trembled.

Moonlight took no comfort from her words, for they promised dreadful things. She knew she should be terrified; one as slight, as seemingly helpless as she could not hope to resist the Lord, whatever he might propose to do to her. Yet she had hope, even when her hands were shackled before her and her feet attached to each other by a long silver chain, the end of which was in the calloused hands of one of the guards.

There was an atmosphere in the house that chilled her, set her skin to crawling. She controlled the trembling of her hand that the smaller girl took into her own. But she knew she could control what was to come as well, or at least her own reaction to it, if she kept her head. She might have to compromise her principles, but she could keep her life and her sanity.

Raising her chin high, she clinked along between her captors toward the chamber of Lorbek, wondering all the way if her delicate gift could be of any value to her in such a desperate situation.

CHAPTER THREE

"Seismic stresses
have warped me awry,
heaving my obdurate spirit upward...."
—Riddle

Gorghoz of the Mountain Hold had never left his lair without protest. In the old days, the Kings sometimes summoned him to consult with them concerning strange weathers or unusual problems with beasts or men. They had wondered, he knew with some amusement, at his ability to understand the workings of a world into which he seldom ventured.

The common folk feared him as well. Not the Kings, of course, or the Dreamers, but many even of the Ancient Race made the Circle with thumb and forefinger when they saw him stalking along the streets of Damaria.

He was, he knew, of another breed than men or even the Ancient Race. His great face, craggy with lumps and bony protrusions, and his huge, hairy body, struck terror into them. Which was as well. He lived alone by choice, lacking even one other of his species with whom to converse. He was far too old to think of searching for a mate among the mountains that lay in snowy splendor to the east. His own mountain, his own carefully worked complex of caverns, suited him best, and he needed only infrequent company there.

He did wonder, from time to time, what was happening past the barrier of rough foothills that lay at the foot of his own peak. The Kings had not been heard from for a very long time. Though he seldom admitted it to himself, he had developed, over the aeons, a certain affection for the small people who valued his advice. Indeed, over the past months he had become a bit concerned about those who were his friends.

There was a taint of something in the air, even here in the cleanliness of the mountains, that filled him with unease. Something stirred down below, and he felt he should busy himself to investigate it, for it seemed dark and troublesome, when he allowed himself to think of it.

So it was with well disguised pleasure that he saw a climber on the steeps below his house. He was still very far below Gorghoz's front porch, which to another would have looked like an outcrop of granite, but someone was coming from the world below with news. He hoped it was nothing that would require him to leave his deep couch or his scrolls of history, carefully compiled over the generations in the ornate script of his kind.

He watched for a long while, as the sun went to rest behind the distant edge of the sky, where the forests rolled to the sea. Then he went down into his kitchens and set a soup kettle to boiling. From personal experience, he knew that clambering about those shockingly inhospitable foothills was hungry work. The climb to his front door was worse. His visitor was going to be famished.

It took half of the next day for the climber to come to his portal, but his kettle was patient, simmering a haunch of mountain ram with a toothsome mess of vegetables from his patch of garden. The meat was falling from the bones, and the steam alone was enough to nourish a hungry man, when the rope was pulled, and the sonorous clang of the big bell sounded through his chambers and along his halls.

Gorghoz put on his cleaner robe and smoothed his wild locks of fine-spun gray hair with both hands. He was not vain, but he did like to make as good an impression as possible upon those sensitive souls from Damaria. But when he opened his heavy door, which needed no locks or bolts (for no army of small ones could hope to stir it on its pivot), he forgot his appearance.

This was not a man who had come to his door. Though it had something of the size and shape of one, it was covered with coarse fur which peeped from openings in its garments. Its face was flat, with a blunt snout poking from its middle, and its eyes were set far back under protective ridges of bone.

He had watched from a distance the development of the hairy men who had once been animals. This, however, was the first he had seen face to face. The creature staggered as he beckoned it into his house, and he set his great hand beneath its elbow to keep it from falling.

"Well, now," he rumbled, "it is a good thing to find a visitor on my doorstep. Come in and eat. And then you will be able to tell me what brings you so far to talk with old Gorghoz the Goremin, who has never before met one of your kind."

"No time," gasped the creature, almost inaudibly. "They hunt...

me!"

That brought the great Goremin up short. Hunting intelligent beings was a thing so foreign to anything he knew that it took a moment for him to comprehend just what the creature had said.

Though men must hunt, in time of hunger, the small and dim-minded beasts, they had, in all the time he had known them, never thought of hunting those who were like them in intelligence. The thought was disturbing. But he controlled his curiosity.

"You must eat," he said. "You are so worn that you cannot tell me anything, as you are. Come. Then we will talk."

"Killeli thanks you," said the hairy man. He followed, stumbling a bit, as Gorghoz led the way to the kitchens and set him a small billet of wood to sit upon, using a stool for a table, so he could reach his food.

He tucked into the big bowl of meat and broth with an intensity that told the Goremin he had not eaten lately. It had been desperation alone that gave him the strength to climb so far. He wondered what was happening down there to cause such strange happenings, but he held his tongue until his guest finished his meal.

"Now," he said, "we will go and sit beside my fire in the library, and you will tell me what brings you here. How can one old Goremin help you?"

Once he had settled the weary Killeli on cushions beside the fire, he took his own favorite seat, poured each of them a bit of the wine with which the Kings had paid him, over the years, for his advice, and leaned back to listen.

Killeli sipped the wine cautiously, which was as well. It was potent stuff, made stronger by its years in the cask in his wine-cellar. But the hairy man seemed to recognize that, and he did not drain the cup. Setting it beside him on the floor, he stared up at his giant host.

"There is death down below. The Ancient Race have been killed or driven away. The Kings are dead, and upstarts from the New People sit on the throne in Damaria. They have burned the houses of the Dreamers. They kill the Turnig for their meat and their fur, and my own kind they slaughter simply because we look too like them, and yet not like enough.

"I escaped by accident. I had been working in the shop where my family made useful things from wood to trade in the city. When I came back to my home, I saw smoke, before I could see the house itself. That alerted me, for I knew the New People were beginning to turn their eyes from the Ancient Race to the other thinking kinds.

"I turned aside into the forest and crept near enough to see my home was in flames. Not a living person could I see, though my father lay dead outside the door. His hair was matted with blood, his skull crushed. I could see that, even from the shelter of the trees." His voice wavered, and he paused for a moment before going on. "The Kings are gone. The Dreamers are being killed—I saw a house in flames and a prisoner being taken away as I came through the lands north of Damaria.

"Who will help me now? Those Other Men will kill all my kind, leaving me homeless and without kin, helpless against them. But I thought of the tales I heard from my granda, when I was a small one. I came to you."

Gorghoz stared into the flames of his coal fire, feeling a chill that the blaze could not touch settling in his heart. This was the end of the world he had known for centuries. The Kings, his friends, were gone, their line ended, and their kindred, if any survived, probably fleeing from their old home.

"Even the Dreamers?" he asked, pain in his gruff voice.

"Even they." The hairy man was now relaxed, full and warm and safe for the time, but his eyes were filled with sadness beneath their ridged brow. "And what being did a Dreamer ever harm, in all the history of Damaria?"

"We will go down," said Gorghoz. "We will find a way to get you to the City in the Mist with some honest traveler who will take you along. You would not be happy remaining here with me. Indeed...."—his eyes opened wide with wonder—"...I may not remain myself. For I cannot live, I see, in a world that holds no friend to visit me.

"Perhaps I can be of use to someone down there below. I never thought before, but that has been my pleasure over the years. I have enjoyed helping the small ones who live in the valleys and the forests."

* * * * * * *

He slept that night very poorly in his giant bed. Before dawn paled the sky, he was stirring about his quarters, packing a roll of belongings. Unwilling to leave behind all his work, he made sure that a part of the pack was filled with scrolls, rolled tightly together and situated so as to be unharmed by the items that were to join them.

Tools and clothing, a bag of cut gems that had been a gift from a King long dead, a long cloak that could hide, to some extent, his vast and unlikely body, went into the pack. By the time Killeli woke, the Goremin was ready, and breakfast was waiting for them both.

It was still cold and shadowy on the western side of the mountain, when the two of them began the long climb downward. The wind shrilled about the Goremin's ears, and something about its note filled him with apprehension. When he paused on a ledge beside Killeli to rest, he took the smaller person inside his cloak for warmth.

"Long ago," he said, above the whine of the wind, "I was told a tale about dark forces that used to walk free on all the lands we know. They preyed on beast and man and every kind alike, and they blasted the forest when it pleased them. Crops withered at their whim, and cattle sickened and died, and the people lived in dread.

"But when the first of the Kings came out of the south, pushing into a country that was being desolated, they joined with my earlier kinsmen and other, greater powers to confine those destructive wills and to free the world of their power. I have not thought of that in many generations of men, but now, hearing the whispers that lie below the voice of the breeze, I wonder.

"In their arrogance, have those Other Men listened to hidden voices and loosed their dark powers again into the world?"

Killeli did not reply, and the voice of the wind was not reassuring.

CHAPTER FOUR

"...down in the safe, the dark, the interior places...."
—Riddle

The Turnig's tribal home was dug into a complex of hills, which had been covered with forest for centuries. The tunnels and chambers, bolt-holes and entrances were so well concealed beneath the covering of stone and soil and tree-roots that no one coming there without a guide would ever have suspected a flourishing community existed beneath his feet. Even after their ancestors had begun to learn new skills at the hands of the Ancient Race, they had kept to their old homes and many of their old ways.

Riddle had visited Chark and her people from time to time over the years of his travels, but even he, coming to the spot in the night from an unfamiliar direction, found himself puzzled when she stopped and called sharply into the darkness. Blackness had settled into the forest as they traveled, and from its depths came a gruff Chrrrrk! in reply to her signal, startling the poet.

His movement woke his nephew, and Lute began to whimper in the confines of the pack. "Sssh!" hissed his uncle. "You will be out in a bit. We are about to see a lot of animals."

This satisfied Lute, who began audibly sucking his thumb, though that was a baby habit he had long discarded, before his world came apart. In a moment, a rift of light shone between the roots of one of the tremendous oaks, as the stone door was pushed aside. A black shape, rimmed with a nimbus of fur, stepped through the opening to consult briefly with Chark.

Then it turned to Riddle. "You be welcome, Poet of Kings. We be glad one still walks the world; even more glad you come to us. We have great troubles; perhaps you help us, even as we help you. Come into home. You be safe there...for a time, at least."

He turned and dived into the rough doorway, and Riddle, knowing the method for entering a Turnig burrow, dived after him, holding the pack straps tightly to keep Lute from bouncing. The hole into which he fell was a deep one, but he managed to land undamaged, with his burden only then beginning to shriek.

Before he could dig his nephew out of his wrappings, the door was moved into place, and by the time he had Lute free, there were half a dozen Turnig surrounding them. The child forgot his complaint, as he found himself staring, in the red torchlight, at such a wonderful array of furred people. When Chark handed him over to an elderly female, Lute went with a chuckle and trudged away beside her to be fed and put to sleep.

Riddle was led in the opposite direction, finding to his surprise that he could stand upright in the corridors down which Chark led him. In the past, he had been forced to bend double in order to negotiate the halls of his furred friends.

He gestured toward the groined roof, dimly seen in the torchlight. "You have been busy. But why take the trouble?"

She glanced up at him, her small eyes sparkling. "Dirt roof fell. We fix—find stone above. Think maybe better so. But we didn't think you come here like this, afraid and hunted. Bad thing. For all, bad thing!"

Riddle ducked to avoid a looping tree-root the thickness of his body. Beyond it was a rounded chamber so large in circumference and so high as to roof that he suspected that it might be a part of some ancient house, buried for millennia beneath the wood.

A fire burned in a stone pit at the center, and some well-planned system of vents and draughts carried the smoke away in a straight column that added its soot to the darkness of the upper reaches. Near the blaze was a pile of moss on which lay two rotund shapes, and Riddle realized with delight that Chark's grandparents, Chirrik and Jree, were still alive.

They rose from their positions as he came out of the shadows of the corridor. They seemed, except for silver tips to their fur, no more feeble than they had been years before when he visited here. They came to meet him, their fur-rimmed eyes shining with pleasure—and relief? He thought he recognized the look. As he settled onto their mossy couch, other Turnig arrived from different doorways and grouped around the fire.

"You are troubled," he said, thrusting his feet to the flames and relaxing for the first time in a very long while. "You are, I know, being hunted. So am I. This is not going to be a place for thinking people to live in now, and it is time for me to leave it. I suspect that you are thinking of that yourselves."

Chirrik, Chark's grandfather, smoothed his face-fur as he stared into the fire. "We think of that," he said. "We go—but where? Other places be ruled by the New People now. Some Turnig go already, from other burrows. They go west, where Old Ones tell us is water. We think we follow them there, for east there be mountains. We not know how to live in mountains. You come to us now, and we know you. Where you go? You let us follow you? Give us your word, Poet, and we listen."

There was no sound among the other furred people. Jree rose to meet a young Turnig, who came with a bowl of steaming root vegetables and a cup of herb tea. "You eat while you think," she said, in her usual abrupt fashion. "We wait for long time. Wait some more. You think, and then we talk."

Riddle ate with good appetite. He had walked hard and worried a great deal. He had been frightened by the Groundbear, and he had found over the years that fear made him hungry. Now that the child, last of the line of the Kings, was safe for the moment, he felt the easing of a great burden. Where there was no longer a kingdom, how could there be a king? He himself must serve as such for a time, leading these vulnerable people to safety, for they looked to him for guidance, but when that duty was done he might possibly find rest.

He sipped the last of the tea, mopped the vegetable broth with a scrap of seed-bread, and sighed. The fire had warmed him through, and the food had given him new energy. He knew that it was time to consider the plight of his old friends, and he already was forming a plan to meet it.

He touched Chark's silky shoulder as he leaned forward to stare around the circle. "How would you like to go with me?" he asked the assembled Turnig, "All the way to the City in the Mist?"

Chark turned sharply to stare at him. "Why we go? Nothing there for Turnig. No place to run away, when they hunt us to sea."

"Ships go westward," he said, his tone almost dreamy. "The Westward Isles have been the goal for the restless ones of my people and their companions for centuries. Why could you not go there with me?"

"In ship?" That was Jree, and she sounded both dubious and wary. "On water?"

Riddle remembered suddenly that the Turnig were highly suspicious of rivers and streams. Even rain was something they seemed to think was aimed directly at flooding their homes and discommoding their lives. But what else could they do? He had heard the new rulers at their planning. Unless they fled into the wild western forest or north to the coastal city, there was no refuge for any of them.

"The New People will cut down the trees of the forest and plow all the land," he said. "I have heard them say this. What forest they do not need for firewood, they will burn, so as to drive out all living things that shelter there. They will skin and eat what they want and leave the rest to rot. They boasted to me about their plans. How can you stay here to face that?"

He glanced around into the many eyes sparkling in the firelight. "Can anything that may happen to you on the sea be worse?"

Chark sighed, her breath ragged in her throat. Her grandparents said nothing, but their furry faces seemed blank with shock.

"I will rest now," said Riddle, "while you think of what I have said. When I reach the City in the Mist, I will find Oakbeam, who builds stout ships and houses of wood and stone. I will have him build for me a great vessel, large enough to carry with me all those who agree to travel out of these tainted lands and into the west."

He paused and felt compelled to add a warning. "There is only one road northward, and if the New People keep watch at the ford over the river, we will be in danger. There are other ways to cross the river, I know, and if we keep to the trees, out of sight of the road, we may come to a spot where we may find the chasm passable. Yet I can only say that we will be in great peril all the way. There will be only one direction for us to take, and we must hurry, for winter will come soon to the northern lands and if it catches us without shelter, we will all die."

Without commenting, Chark took his hand and led him through one of the doors into a long corridor. This one was low and the air was warm, as she turned into a nook furnished with a pile of moss and a felted cover. "Sleep now," she said to him. "When you wake, we know what to do. The child already sleeps."

Riddle accepted the torch from her hand. When he thrust it into the sconce waiting for it, he saw that Lute was bundled into a basket-like crib, sucking his thumb, his face flushed pink. A great sorrow filled him at the thought of the merry parents this child would never know, the happy world into which he would never venture, and the people who would never live under his kind and effective rulership. He had been taught, so far in his short life, in the way that had sustained many thousands of years of Kings in their wisdom and justice.

The long tale of the Ancient Blood was in his veins. He would grow into a wise man, wherever he was and whatever happened. But what a waste it was that he could not carry forward the work of his ancestors!

* * * * * * *

The poet dreamed. Voices rode the wind, speaking to him in almost understandable words and tones, but no matter how he tried he could not comprehend the things they said. Nevertheless, he was filled with foreboding, and he turned on his mossy bed, frowning and speaking in half-syllables.

He sank deeper into sleep. He felt himself being pulled along the currents of dream, and he was suddenly cold with dread. An icy shape rose before him, darkness on darkness and yet completely visible to his mind. It shone with a black intensity, and its sheen was that of a glacier under a night sky—shuddering, he recognized the Mover in the North, of which he had been told grim tales as a young man. Facing it was a shape even darker, its features outlined in silver. He felt a terrible fear for the small image opposing the cold one, slight and terrible and filled with dread.

"No," he said aloud, almost rising from his dream. "No!"

But the greater shape split into many, wisping into veilings of smoke-gray and midnight, trailing chill fingers along his face and whispering terrible secrets into his shrinking ears. The other was gone as if it had never been. He struggled to awaken, to pull himself from the grip of the nightmare. At last he rose like a drowning swimmer, up from the tides that gripped him. When he opened his eyes, he stared at the curved rock above him, the chisel-marks outlined in shadow by the light of the dying torch.

That was an ill-omened dream. It told him things he did not want to learn. With the death of the last of the adult Kings and his legitimate adult heirs, the old enemies had been loosed. As a poet, Riddle had not been trained fully to deal with them. As a small child, his nephew had not yet been taught the things he would have had to understand. There was nobody left alive who was capable of saving Damaria from the frozen wave of terror that would sweep down upon it from the north. The people his kind had loved and nurtured for millennia were going to suffer worse than death, because of the ill judgment of the New People who now ruled his unhappy land.

CHAPTER FIVE

"...there is a magic word, among our many,
that can shatter locks...."
                                    —Riddle

Moonlight felt the girl on her left shaking. Was this Lord so cruel that she felt endangered, even as she led someone else to his chambers? In order to distract the child, she asked, "What is the name of this great conqueror Lord? If I am to please him, at least I must know what to call him."

Without slowing her pace, the girl whispered, "He is the Lord Lorbek, whose mother was of my kind and whose father was.. "— she glanced about at the guard and spoke still more quietly—"...the King." The Dreamer shivered. Had Armor spawned such a cold and treacherous child?

"He came back to lead his mother's kind to victory. He will be King now, and he will rule Damaria with a harsh hand, I think." The whisper died as they neared the doorway.

Moonlight said nothing; her feet, in those inadequate sandals, stepped firmly forward as a door opened at the end of the corridor and she glimpsed the wide chamber beyond.

Lorbek reclined on a crimson couch. Before him on an inlaid table was spread a display of fine porcelain ware, the dishes filled with fruits and confections, the goblets waiting for their burden of wine. On a cushion at one end lay the modest crown of Damaria, which was a plain circle of silver. Lorbek smiled as she entered but it was not the smile of a friend. His face was that of a predator. The young women closed the door behind her, and Moonlight moved forward still, until she stood at the foot of the couch.

"So I am here. What is it you want, Lorbek? Something of the talent that your ancestors possessed? Something of the awe and love with which they were held for generations? Or is it raw power you desire?" Her tone was cool and unafraid, which seemed to irritate him. He rose to his feet and faced her.

"It is better to keep silent than to annoy me," he said. He reached to take her elbow in a harsh grip and drew her down to sit beside him. Her chains clinked as she moved, and he laughed as he loosed her hands, playing out links until she had enough slack for eating. He did not, she noted with interest, completely secure the lock.

"There is food here. Wine. Eat. And then...." And now his smile was even more wicked, with a hint of cruelty that told her much about the treatment those other women must endure at his hands. "...Then I will remove your shackles—and other things, as well."

Moonlight smiled, willing herself to seem calm. That seemed to disturb the man. He leaned forward and poured wine into a goblet. When he straightened again, he set his fingers into her hair and jerked her toward him, pouring the red liquid into her mouth, spilling it down the velvet robe.

"Endure!" She heard her grandmother's teachings inside her mind. "There will come a moment when his attention turns aside, and then you will feel for the Jewel. Then...only then will your gift be of use to you."

For a fleeting moment, Moonlight recalled the other, darker lessonings she had learned from her people, but she pushed aside the thought at once. Even this degenerate man, evil as he hoped to become, did not deserve to see the other side of Dream.

His hand swung, and her cheek stung with the blow. She did not whimper. Her will, steely with a lifetime of training, did not allow a single tear to rise to her eyes. She set her face into marble hardness and stared into his eyes, uncowed and untouched in her innermost self. That seemed to drive him frantic. He rolled onto her, but she managed to tumble both onto the floor, and he soon tired of banging his elbows and his back against the heavy table as he groped for her.

When he pulled himself up again, she took the opportunity to scramble backward and heave herself to her feet. His eyes were wide, fury and madness blazing in their depths. There was no time to wait for a better chance; unless she wanted to risk immediate rape and death, she must find the Jewel and form a Dream.

She fingered her shackles as she felt inside herself for the presence of the Jewel. A warm tingle grew within her, and colors flickered behind her eyelids; she began to build a Dream. His hard hands, battering her face, did not disrupt her concentration as she poured the distillation of will that was hers as a Dreamer into the illusion she formed.

The room changed, for her, into a vast chamber centered with fountains beneath an open skylight. Roses bloomed on trellises beyond the dancing waters, and the scent of their blossoms filled the warm air. The harsh voice of Lorbek dimmed from her perceptions. A woman of exquisite beauty was bathing in the basin filled by the fountains, her pale skin gleaming with wet, her silver-blond hair flowing over her shoulders as she rose to step out into the blue towel held by a handmaid. As she turned, Moonlight felt the man, whose hands were now at her throat, go stiff; she knew that he saw and was frozen with astonishment.

She must turn the desire he had felt for her toward that waiting woman, and she Dreamed more intently. The towel dried away the wet, and the woman stood naked as the handmaid laved her with scented oil. Moonlight put into her vision all the things she had avoided in the past, for her people were not interested in arousing the passions of those they served, but in helping them to solve their problems and soothe their pains. The use of such debased arts disgusted her, necessary though they might be in her present situation.

Yet she knew just what motions would most titillate her companion, what textures and tints would catch his senses and focus his desires. And when he was fully in the grip of her Dream, she placed him, too, into that picture inside her mind. He moved in her vision toward the fair woman, his face alight, his hands extended toward her. She looked up and smiled. With a motion, she sent away the woman, and then she turned, arms outstretched, to Lorbek, who came swiftly to meet her.

He was caught, now, within that Dream. He would live it to its ending, leaving her free. Moonlight loosed her attachment, letting the vision float like a bubble within the mind of her companion, who lay back on the couch, an expression of ineffable bliss on his narrow face. She sobbed deeply, just once. Then she dropped onto the couch and worked at her chains, using a slender fruit-knife from the bowl to pick their locks. Once free, she turned her attention to securing weapons and supplies. She must flee through the forest, and for that she would need more than a velvet robe and flimsy sandals.

She unfastened the sheath of the dagger hanging from Lorbek's belt. It was not much, but it would serve until she could do better. There was a vast armoire filled with clothing. She found a hunting outfit that would serve her well, along with a great leather cloak lined with wool. That would keep off both cold and damp, and as winter was on its way, she knew she would need its warmth.

The tunic was too long and wide, but she belted it closely and fastened the dagger's sheath to the hooks provided for that purpose on the belt. The trousers were too long as well, but she tore off strips at the bottoms of the legs to make them fit. All the boots were far too large, though there were stockings that she could make do. As she searched again, she found, far in a back corner, a pair of leather-soled shoes. Some unhappy victim of the new King must have left them behind when she was taken away. They were a bit too long and too wide, but she folded the woolen socks about her feet and made them into a fair fit, blessing her luck in finding them.

There was a great chest at the foot of Lorbek's richly hung bed. She opened it. Perhaps there might be a sword there, or something else that would serve her need. What she found was a box, carefully wrapped in a length of silk, that drew her hand to its bulky shape. She unrolled it, finding inside the folds a thick book, bound in some soft leather that made her fingers curl with distaste at its touch. When she put both her hands upon it, they jerked with the shock of that contact. What sort of creature had given its skin to provide the pale leather? She thought she knew, and she shivered at the notion. A thinking being had been skinned to cover this book.

She overcame her aversion and opened the thing. It was lettered in a scrolling script in the language of the Kings, she was sure. She could decipher it, she knew, when there was the time and opportunity. Moonlight was certain to the depths of her soul that Lorbek would be more than anguished to lose it. This was something important and dangerous, and the breath of terrible power hung about it.

"We are not thieves, we Dreamers," she said over her shoulder to the dreaming man. "You have taken from me my home and my kin. This will be some repayment for that loss, for I feel it is something you will be more than reluctant to lose. I hope when you find it gone you will remember me with fury."

He groaned with ecstasy, and she smiled grimly. He would wake in a mood of euphoria, her grandmother had told her long ago during her training, but such erotic dreams carried with them an aftertaste of despair. That would grip him quickly, leaving him in a state of disorientation and anger for hours afterward.

She made a pack of a length of wool and wrapped the book, touching the thing gingerly and wrapping it in many layers of the bolt of silk. To the store she added more stockings, the sandals, and a selection of fruits and sweet cakes, folding them separately in silk before depositing them in the bundle. She took another cloak to use as a blanket for sleeping and rolled the pack inside it, making a manageable burden secured to her shoulders with sword-belts she found in the chest.

She was now, to some extent, provisioned for a journey. It would have helped if she knew where she must go or what must be done when she arrived, but as that could not be, she would make do with what she had. Now she must escape from this house, past guards and servants, before the master woke from his enticing dream. She crept to the door and laid her ear against the thick panel.

The sound of steps in the corridor told her these new troops, ill-trained after so short a time, patrolled the house as well as its grounds. A soft giggle indicated that the women were waiting outside their master's door.

So. She must go another way. She gazed around the room, which showed only hangings over the walls. There had to be windows behind them; she began feeling her way around the chamber. On the wall opposite the bed, she found shutters closed tightly. They were secured with metal locks, and it took her some time to remove one set without making too much noise. The shutter opened reluctantly, and she muffled its creaking with the draperies about the window. Beyond it was yet another barrier, this one an outside shutter. It was locked only with an interior latch, which was soon freed.

She wondered what time of the day or night it might be. She had hung upon that wall in the dungeon for what seemed like days. By now she was completely unsure whether it would be light or dark outside. Were there guards below, who would give the alarm if the Lord's window opened to show light?

After turning the lamp as low as possible, she drew a deep breath and pushed gently. The wooden barrier swung outward an inch, and she saw to her relief that only darkness lay beyond it. Not even the ruddy glow of torchlight colored the night in that direction.

She pushed the shutter wide and climbed onto the window-sill. Starlight spangled the sky, and she waited until her eyes adjusted to its faint glimmer. When she could see, she found there was a drop of two stories beneath her precarious perch. So. She clambered into the room again and found another roll of silk, this of midnight blue. Very appropriate, she thought, as she tied off the end around a heavy chest and flung the rest of the roll out the window. It was invisible in the starlight, but she hoped it reached fairly near to the ground below.

Then, securing her pack to her back and ignoring her bruises and her cut lip, she swung herself out of the window and climbed cautiously down the wall, pushing off with her feet as she swung and slipping the silk between her hands as she moved along it. She had only to drop a couple of man-heights when she reached its end.

She found herself in a garden, sheltered enough still to hold the scents of spicy blossoms. The starlight shimmered faintly from drifts of flowering shrubs and lines of pale autumn lilies. Moonlight could see its wall dark against the stars; she moved carefully among the hedges and the statue-lined walks that were rayed outward from the pool she could hear rippling at the center of the garden. She made her way noiselessly until she reached the trees that stood at intervals along the inner side of the wall.

Behind her there came a shout. Lights began to bloom in unshuttered windows on the lower floors of the house, and that one from which she had escaped was suddenly flung wide and more brightly illuminated. Lorbek was awake, and his women had discovered her escape. She only hoped they would not look for her as intently as he would have done. He had, she thought, done a complete job of knocking all spirit and wit out of them.

She could not wait to see but went up a slender tree trunk with the agility of an arboreal, her damaged muscles protesting all the way, and found the top of the wall studded with spikes. Moonlight sighed. Nothing was going to be easy, it seemed. But, then, she was free, when she might still be shackled to that wall.

She climbed higher in the tree, a fragrant conifer with flexible branches and a springy top. Finding a secure hold, she began swaying back and forward, until the top whipped partway over the wall with every oscillation. When it was at the limit of its movement, she sprang free and dropped to the ground beyond the spikes.

She rolled, but her breath was partially knocked from her lungs, and she had to recover it before she could move again. As she gasped for air, she heard many feet trampling in the garden beyond the wall. The tops of the trees were red-lit with the flames of many torches. Surely the searchers would not notice the vibration of that single treetop. She sprang up and checked her pack. Then she darted into the hem of the forest, which rose some rods distant from the garden wall, for she must be gone before anyone thought to search outside.

Once she was well within the tree line she began to think. Which way should she travel? She had no destination, no friend left in all the world. North or south, east or west, there was no help to be had. Yet to the north and west, along a difficult and limited route, lay the sea, and there were always ships.

Other continents of her world were not unknown to her kind, though those native to Damaria did little trading and less traveling. Only the family of the Kings had ever gone west over the sea from the misty City. She would go northward! She found a small clearing and stared up at the sky. The Yoke lay to the west, the Crown to the north, at this time of the year. If she kept her course set somewhat between the two, she would find the river, perhaps at a point she could cross, and the sea at last, near enough to the great port city to find a ship.

As she tramped along, she began to consider her situation. For the first time in all her life—indeed, in the lives of any of her kindred—she was free to go where she would and to do what she might find to do.

Amid her grief and her anger, her fear and her uncertainty, she found to her surprise there was a hint of excitement. She was about to have adventures, and none of her unique kind had ever had the time or the opportunity for that.

Feeling just the smallest twinge of guilt, she moved toward the northwest, wondering what she would find to be and to do in this new and intriguing life she was about to begin. The wind was in her face, the stars bright above her, and she felt exultation and a strange sort of joy.

She moved into the night, and only caution kept her from humming as she went.

* * * * * * *

Keeping the stars in sight as well as she could among the arching treetops, Moonlight trudged along through the forest. She had no torch, nor would she have used one if she possessed it. Light might betray her to those who would search for her, and she felt convinced Lorbek would rattle the very foundations of the world to recover the thing she carried in her pack.

But this was the forest near her own home, and she had roamed it all her life. When she was a child, she and her young cousins, secure under the rule of the King, spent days, sometimes, exploring these aisles of great trees, finding streams among the boulders that lay in long drifts among the hills cloaked with forest. They slept at night upon piled leaves, and they drank the unsullied waters and ate the plentiful fruits of the wood.

She knew this land as she knew her grandmother's house, although she had not roamed its ways since growing old enough to take upon herself the work of a Dreamer. Her feet knew the contours of the ground. She knew when she was about to come to a hill before she began to climb, and she found streams whenever she thirsted.

She did not intend to stop until day sent her into hiding. No matter how her chafed wrists and ankles pained her, how much her muscles quivered and balked with the pace she forced upon them, she was going free. No one sent after her would take her alive and she had no intention of being forced to die.

The pack-roll was heavy on her back, and she constantly shifted it from side to side. The book inside it seemed to burn through the wrappings, irritating her skin and making her mind wander. Moonlight began to wonder, before she had gone many miles, if the thing were not trying to force her to turn back, confusing her so she forgot her direction.

That, of course, might be the effect of her confinement in the dungeon or of seeing her people die, but she thought not. That book was an entity. It was resisting her, every step she took away from the hold that had been in the keeping of Lorbek. She could almost feel it wriggling like a stubborn child, trying to force her to obey its impulses.

But she was not a Dreamer for nothing. Her will had been honed in a discipline that few other thinking beings could endure. She kept to her course, as the stars turned over her head, and she was left to move by her own instinct for direction. She had been walking in the dark for a long while, for the trees above her were thick conifers that shut out the stars, when she caught a glimpse of light, far away through the forest. It was the merest hint of fire, an orange glimmer all but hidden among the trees.

She stopped, listening hard. There was no sound of a step or a voice, although the wood was busy with small creatures that had not gone into their winter sleeps. A bird overhead "chip-chipped" in a treetop. A scatter of dried bark fell about her shoulders, as it moved on its perch.

Far to the east, a howl stilled all the motion about her. She shivered, as she waited to see what might come through the trees. The sharp noses of the wolf-kind could find the scent of Man over miles of forest, and that was their favorite meat, she had been told. The flesh of a Dreamer was no different from that of any other, and she had no wish to become dinner for one of the over-intelligent beasts.

Before the howls grew too near, there was a change in their cadence, and she knew some unfortunate beast had taken flight before them. She must move quickly, before they caught their kill and hungered for more. Veering in a wide arc to avoid that distant fire, she kept going, resenting the time required for the roundabout way, yet unwilling to risk meeting those who built it. In these troubled times, nobody could be counted as a friend, and almost anyone who roamed Damaria must be an enemy.

Her new course took her into a hilly country of hardwoods, with clean mats of dead leaves underfoot. The boles of the trees were tremendous and far apart, their autumn leafage smothering away the sun from anything that might grow about their roots. She was walk-ing quickly, her caution focused on those beside the fire. Her step into nothingness came as a jolt of terrified surprise.

Even as she fell, she wondered if this was a trap or a naturally occurring hole leading into a system of tunnels formed by long-dried underground streams. She had known many such in her youth, and they could provide excellent hiding places, as she and her cousins had found in their games.

Yet even as she slid downward amid a tumble of leaves and dust and grit and brittle twigs and branches, she knew that was no untenanted place. She could smell the odors of life here. Rank scents, not unclean but disturbing, all but stifled her, as she rolled out at the bottom of the opening into which she had fallen. Ending up on her face, she lay for a moment, getting her breath again. Then she pushed up onto her two hands and sneezed several times.

When the echoes of the sneezes died away in what seemed a maze of passages, she could hear breathing close by. Snufflings, small grunts, and little hiccuppy sounds surrounded her, and she could feel the vibration of footsteps through the palms of her hands, which were still flat on the floor of the cave. Even the cat-eyes of a Dreamer could not pierce the gloom of the tunnel in which she found herself.

Again, she found that a twinkle of light was visible, coming from around a bend in the passage in which she lay. As the illumina-tion came nearer, she found herself staring up into a circle of smooth gray faces, long-snouted, silver-eyed, that were smoothly attached to long, silken-haired bodies shaped for burrowing.

That circle of silver eyes shone like coins in the light that now seemed very bright, after the total darkness. The small lamp, a tor-toise-shell filled with oil and wicked with a tuft of fiber, was held high to reveal her, as she sat up and looked into the eyes of its bearer.

A Pazmi! She had never thought to see one of the shy diggers, and now here she was in a veritable town of them. They were not friends of men, she knew, but neither were they enemies. The two kinds had little need to cross paths, but now they had, and she won-dered just how she might deal with these unknown people.

Moonlight rose to her feet and brushed away the dust. She would have to think quickly, reading their actions and their inten-tions as well as she could in the darkness of their buried home. After the events of the last days, she felt she could manage to do even more, if she were called upon.

She smiled and waited for the Pazmi to make the first move.

She rolled over to sit. After dusting herself a bit, she stood, her head coming just higher than those of the adults. "I am Moonlight," she said in the common tongue, her words as distinct as she could make them. "I beg your pardon for intruding into your home. I fell into a hole in the forest and could not help myself."

There was a chittering and whistling and clicking all around the circle. Then, somewhat to her surprise, the large specimen with the lamp lowered his flame so he could observe her face. "Dreem'r?" he asked, the word quite understandable.

"Yes, Dreamer. One of the last. All are dead that I knew. Killed."

There was a sudden intense silence, as if the creature had ceased breathing. "Kill...Dreem'r?" It was unmistakably a question. "Who kill Dreem'r?"

"The New People. The hairless ones. They have killed the King and his family. They have killed the Ancient Race."

The Pazmi listened closely. Then he stood still for a long moment, thinking about her words, obviously translating them into his own language. When he was satisfied, he chattered and whistled to his people, and there came a gust of moans and gurgles that sounded like pained protest.

"Can you show me to a door into the forest? Perhaps one farther north than the place where I fell? There was someone in the wood. A fire was burning, off to the east. I would like to miss the ones who built it, if possible. They may be New People."

The one with the lamp nodded and turned up a passage. The rest melted into the dimness, and she could no longer hear their breathing as she followed her guide between the twined tree roots that roofed and walled the tunnel. Rocks twinkled with mica in its sides, and the packed floor was lined with neatly cut paving stones. Now and again another round tunnel forked off from the main one, and she began to have some notion of the pattern of waterways that had once run beneath the forest. The Pazmi had taken advantage of an existing system to use as their highways and streets.

As she pattered after her guide up a long series of twisting ways, she tried to talk with him, but he seldom replied to her comments. At last she fell silent, simply setting her feet in the prints of his and thinking hard about what she might find when she emerged from the tunnels.

Surely by now Lorbek was beginning the hunt for her and for his book. His people would soon be ready to spread out over the countryside, searching for her. The thought made her shiver, as she moved along the damp corridors, where tiny red eyes twinkled from crevices, and occasional draperies of webbing curtained the way ahead of her guide. This was not a route taken often, she guessed, as she stooped beneath a dusty tangle of cobweb and found herself noticing a draught against her face.

This was air scented with the needles of the conifers and the mellow richness of leaf-mold beneath old hardwoods. An opening into the outer world. The tall Pazmi set his lamp in a nook that hid its light from anyone above. He moved close to Moonlight and pointed toward a dark splotch above her head. There was no trace of light there, but it was through that opening the fresh air flowed.

"I lift Dreem'r," he said. "You come." He bent and allowed her to climb upon his back. When he stood upright, she could feel the steely strength of him as her weight was lifted by his steady motion. When he was straight, she found she could reach a sort of plug of dead leaves and moss, which had been woven intricately upon a network of slender branches.

This cover pushed aside easily, and she found she could set her elbows into a bracing of tree roots. She levered herself upward, and the Pazmi lifted her about the knees once she was clear of his back. She found herself lying on the forest floor, as a trace of light touched the sky above.

He thrust her pack after her, and she leaned down to touch his smooth head softly. "Thank you," she whispered. "Good luck to you and to yours. Take care, for men will come to hunt you, I think."

The silver eyes twinkled below as they stared up. "Men come, already. We kill. No place safe, Dreem'r." He lowered the lamp and turned into the dark passages behind him.

Then he was gone, and she stood in the forest, listening to the dawn. Far at the edge of hearing, she thought the sound of howls echoed, but she was not sure of that, as she turned her steps northward, guided by the growing light over her right shoulder. As she went, she thought of those strange people down there in the dark tunnels. How did they kill that hunter who came after them? She wished them well, as she moved away into the night.

CHAPTER SIX

"This was the final Autumn, gold on blue...."
—Riddle

Autumn was dying in the valley below the mountaintop. A sharp wind blew from the west, shifting to the north at times, then gusting again over the western forest. It brought with it the scent of old leaves and wood smoke. Not for a long while had Gorghoz breathed other air than the clean, acid wind of the snowfields, and he sniffed this distant and yet familiar scent greedily.

It was long since he had climbed down from his aerie. He wondered if his acute senses and his ancient wisdom might have warned at least a few of the Ancient Race in time to avoid their fates, if he had been in Damaria when the rebels were making their plans.

The New People had never had the audacity to cross wills with him, over all the generations of their climb to civilization. It was possible that if he had stood beside Armor as an obstacle to their ambitions, they might have backed away and let the old order remain in place.

He said as much to Killeli, but the furry man shook his head. "They would not have paused for the Great King himself, if he had returned to life and come up from the south," the monkey-man replied. "Something aided them that I do not understand. The man they call the King now is an outlander, though somehow akin to the old King. He is cold and cruel, they say, and you would have died, it is likely, though perhaps not as easily as the Ancient Race did. I think you are not as trusting as they."

Gorghoz chuckled deep in his throat. This might be one whose ancestors had swung by their hands in the trees, far back in the innocent days before they began thinking, but he was now a shrewd person, capable of making sharp judgments.

"Anyone can be attacked in his sleep, for all living creatures must rest. Anyone can be ambushed, no matter how cautious he may be. But you are right—they would have taken me down, at last, along with those whose ancestors were the allies of my own.

"It saddens me that I was not there, just the same. I would have defended the King and his family, even though I will not take the lives of small people willingly. Did they all die?"

"All," said Killeli. "Or that is what the new rulers insist. I have heard a whisper, while my own people remained untouched, that the Poet was spared."

Gorghoz stopped in his tracks in the middle of a sheep field, staring down at his companion. He ignored the querulous baas of the animals about them. "Riddle? He lives?"

"I have not seen him." Killeli's tone was cautious. "But it is said the New People wanted the tale of their conquest set into verse by the poet of the Kings. No one among these people can sing a note or rhyme one word with another. But it may be they changed their minds, after, and he now lies with his fathers."

The Goremin turned his great, lumpy head to stare at the sky. He breathed deeply of the scented air, savoring the forest smells as if they were some fine wine he had just encountered. Then he sighed and turned back westward, his course set to intersect the northward road that led, at last, to the City in the Mist.

"Living or dead, I wish him well. He sang truly, did Riddle, in the days when he was a youth at the court of his father the King." He took the fields before them in stride, and when Killeli, panting behind him, begged for rest, the great Goremin lifted him to his back as if he were a child.

The two of them moved forward as the sun went down and the sky reddened over the distant and invisible sea. Even when darkness covered the fields they did not stop. For several hours the great creature persisted, striding over the stubble fields of grain or the mown hayfields, where a few late sheep or goats grazed, untended now their new owners were not required to tend their flocks by knowing masters. They seemed glad to greet the travelers through their pastures and sad to see them go.

When the Yoke and the Crown hung in the sky, Gorghoz stopped in his tracks, stiffening with a shock that was not of the flesh. Something terrible was freed into the world—he felt it with all his senses. A source of power that had been working quietly and in secret had been brought into the open, touched for the first time in a very long while by hands that were not tainted with its own darkness. It reacted silently to that touch, but the vibrations of the reaction spread ripples of sensation to anyone able to feel them.

Gorghoz sniffed the air again, as if some hint of that disturbance might ride the wind, but he could not detect it there. His skin prickled as if he were near lightning, and his great muscles bunched and relaxed by turns, trying to control his reaction to this unexpected intrusion.

Even Killeli, riding on his back, felt his alarm. "What troubles you, Goremin?" asked the furry man. "I can hear nothing. I feel nothing. No one walks the fields by night."

Gorghoz rumbled, deep in his chest, something between a growl and a groan. Then he said, "I would that you were right, furred man. Yet I believe something or someone else stirs tonight. A thing that has been hidden has been found. Something that was quiet is now moving across the land."

He said nothing of it to Killeli, but he felt as if hands had touched his own skin, paler gray beneath the grizzled fur that showed his great age. Long ago, there had been a book. He knew the tales of it, the power of it. The Ancient Race had used its help in pushing back the corruption out of the north, and his ancestors had aided them in their task.

The book had been a part of the spell binding the powers that had troubled Damaria and the surrounding lands. Its secrets had secured the locks guarding the realm from intrusion. But it had fallen into the hands of a thief long ago, lost before he had been born. That was a thing that had always filled his people with unease, although it seemed all was well for almost a thousand years.

Now he recalled from his voracious readings a thing that had so disgusted him he hid it away in the deeps of his mind. His own father had spoken of it when he was small, and the nightmares those words brought to him had troubled his dreams ever since, making him speed through the history that told of it.

A Goremin had been lost, back in those days when there were others of his kind in the Damariste Mountains. A young female, fair and wise, had gone down into the valley, and she had never been seen again. Yet her kin knew, in the wordless way they had of feeling what happened with their own, that she had been taken, even in her young strength. Tortured, flayed alive, she had died at last, and her skin had been used to rebind the Book of the Kings, twisting it from its purpose into a degradation all the more powerful for its roots in the writings of the Wise.

The men who lived in the lowlands knew nothing of those who did that deed. The Kings had searched and questioned, and the Goremin themselves had sent their instincts to look where bodies could not go. Yet no hint had come of what kind of being had done so terrible a thing. Now Gorghoz had a premonition—faint and ghastly—that the Mover from the North had been involved from the first theft of that powerful talisman.

It became a tool of evil, the Goremin histories said. Thinking of the dwindling of his kind, the slow withdrawal of the younger generations eastward, he wondered if that act, the twisting of the book's nature, had been a reason why he was now alone in this part of the mountains.

Gorghoz, remembering now after so many years of willful forgetfulness, suddenly knew those lost words were true. Someone had found the Book of the Kings. Someone had taken it from a hiding place and into the air of the world. He shivered violently, almost shaking Killeli from his back.

"It is growing very cold," the furry man agreed, huddling against the big back. "We should stop soon, for you need rest, no matter how strong you may be."

"The forest is ahead. We will take shelter there for a while. I must think. Something moves, Killeli. Something is happening that will have a great impact upon our future. I can see it with the inner Eye all my kind possess, and yet it is not clear and sharp in my mind. We must hurry—that is all I know. And to hurry, I must first rest."

They were almost to the fringe of the trees now, crossing the last of the mown hayfields and striding into the shelter of the wood. The stars twinkled mockingly through the twined branches to which some leaves clung stubbornly. Gorghoz, using their light, found a nook beneath the edge of a slantwise boulder and bent to let Killeli slide to the ground.

"We must have fire," he said. "You pile dead leaves, and I will go to find deadfall. I must get warm and eat well, for tomorrow will try me greatly. We must find the road. We must go northward. I feel it north and west, toward the road leading into the hills. There are travelers there. I feel them moving."

CHAPTER SEVEN

"We seek the ocean and the westing sun...."
—Riddle

Lute woke his uncle with his usual morning conversation in the language he had brought forward from his babyhood. Riddle lay for a time, listening to the child's voice, his occasional chuckles and chirrups. What a joy it was to know that at least one other of his kind was left to go forward into the future! Perhaps there were others, children of his father's younger brother, making their way toward the only haven left to them. He hoped that was true, and he knew that he must surely find kindred in the City in the Mist, for at least two families had taken up residence there centuries before.

Lute, discovering that his uncle's eyes were open, crawled down from the cushion on which he lay, and came over to demand his breakfast. Riddle laughed and rose to dress. Then he lifted the child and went out into the passageway, returning to the chamber in which he had met with Chark and her grandparents.

Today they must make decisions that would disrupt the lives of the Turnig for generations to come. After learning the fate of the clan in the southern forest, he knew they must go. He, though one of the youngest of the Ancient Race, remembered when they were animals in this place, before they began to develop greater intelligence and ability under the breeding program and guidance of his kind.

He handed Lute over to a small female, who led him away giggling, and dropped to sit on a cushion beside the renewed fire in the pit. When he looked into the circle of furry faces, there in the glow of the fresh flame, he knew his hosts had come to the same conclusion. They must leave their only home. Some of the furry faces were unhappy, but he saw no disagreement there.

"Riddle, son of Kings, will you take us with you, as you go?" asked Chirrik. "We have talked through the night. It will not be easy for us to take all our people, for some are old and stiff, some are tiny and must be carried, and some are ill.

"We will leave behind all the beautiful things we have made over our generations of work here. But we understand the danger. If our kind is to survive, it must be in a different place."

The poet turned his gaze toward the fire, feeling a terrible sadness at the waste of all their generations of patient labor. The rock carvings about the walls were lovely, and he hated to think of their being left in darkness while their makers went away. Then he looked up. "I will take you with me. But you must be ready quickly.

"Time is of great importance. Winter will soon walk down from the north, and we should pass through the hills before the snow falls. That is stark and difficult country, and vicious people live there. If we are caught there for the winter, it will go hard with us. We must leave by night. Tomorrow, at the latest."

"We be ready to go tonight, as soon as full dark. We already thought this; we know we move soon. Rest today, Riddle. Tonight we go." Jree's husky voice was filled with sadness.

* * * * * * *

The day passed slowly for the poet, who rested in his nook while the Turnig packed what they could take, and stored in deep tunnels and wells the things they could not carry, but could not bear to think might be taken by intruders. The stone carvings of flowers and birds that decorated the rooms were hidden there, along with the delicate weavings their people made from cobweb, their own shed fur, and plant fiber. Their books, which were carved onto splits of wood, were too heavy to carry, and they, too, were put away, carefully oiled and wrapped.

"One day, children return. If so, there be home here waiting, records of us to teach old ways." Jree looked sad as she peered in at his doorway. Her small hands were folding something tightly, and as he watched she fitted it into a packet.

He smiled at her. "One day it may be that Damaria will be clean again, safe for those unlike the new people. They, too, will grow old in time, and then perhaps they will realize that mind is not a thing that is shaped by outer appearance."

As she hurried away, he added to himself, "But perhaps not. I think they have meddled with dangerous matters that may destroy them before they mature as a race." Then he turned on his side and slept deeply until a soft touch on his shoulder woke him.

"Is time," said Chark. "Boy has slept, is fed. We ready to go.

Will you carry nephew, or shall I?"

The poet rose and again donned his boots and his cloak. His pack was waiting beside him, and he arranged his possessions to make a place for Lute. "He is used to riding on my back. It will be best so, for his legs are too short to keep up with us in the forest. He knows to be silent, when he is packed into my bundle."

The child seemed to agree, as he was put into his riding place. He settled down quietly, and it was time to go.

The forest was dim with twilight when the stone door was slipped aside for a last time. No light shone behind the shapes that crept out into the wood, and when the stone was replaced, many hands set moss into the cracks about it in order to conceal its purpose.

Riddle watched, feeling cold and empty as he thought of the care with which his kind had nurtured Mind among creatures unlike themselves. They had shaped these and other kinds with love and attention, finding the work a worthy thing over the generations. It was a deep pain inside him to think that one of those carefully nurtured species had turned upon their teachers so cruelly.

He had never suspected, in his youth, that it might be a disservice to those beings who had increased their abilities through that nurturing. Would the Turnig have been safe, unknown in their animal obscurity, if they had never dealt with his kind? Or would their skins and their tender flesh still have made them victims of the madman now ruling Damaria?

As if she read his thoughts, Chark touched his arm. "They hunt us for fur, for meat, whatever inside our heads," she said. "We would not lose understanding your people gave us. Things not different, Poet, no matter what."

He followed her away down a trail that was invisible in the dimness, after the rest of her people. How far they had come, these furred people, from their origins. Chark had the understanding and the perceptiveness of the Wise, and he knew he would exert himself fully to save her and her kindred from the fate the new rulers of his country intended for them.

* * * * * * *

Gorghoz woke with a start and lay listening to the night. It was late, for the stars had moved across the sky, and now the Shears and the Loop rode above the bare branches that curved to shelter the nook where he lay. The fire had died to a few single coals, and Killeli was sitting beside them, his body hunched as if in pain. The

Goremin thought of what had happened to the furry man's people, and he understood; the pain Killeli bore was not that of the body.

He groaned softly and sat, trying to unkink the soreness in his bones. "I am too old for such things," he muttered. "Centuries of sleeping in my own great bed and sitting in my library have made me unfit for running about through forests and sleeping on the ground."

The skinny fellow turned to stare at him. "Complain as you will, Gorghoz, you are still the strongest and the greatest living person in Damaria. No man could have come the distance you covered yesterday. When you grow weary, you may ask me to carry you, but I will refuse. Very politely."

The Goremin grinned. It took great troubles to remove the humor entirely from one of the simian-descended people. That hint of teasing told him Killeli was deliberately mending himself of his hurts in the ways he knew best.

"Then cover the coals with ash and dirt and dead leaves," he said. "But let us eat before we move, for my size and my exertions require nourishment."

They laid a few twigs on the coals again, just for the little warmth while they ate. Then they doused the fire and concealed the place where it had burned. They were not pursued, as far as Gorghoz knew, but in these new and troubled times, who could ever determine what inimical eye might see traces of their passing and follow them to their harm?

When they set out again, it was still dark, but the indefinable feel of dawn was in the air. Before they had gone more than a few miles, light touched the sky above the treetops, and Gorghoz knew the tops of his mountains were pink with the rising of the sun. He felt a sharp twinge of loss, as if he would never again watch a sunrise over the mountains from his own doorstep.

He shook himself and strode onward, hearing the determined pattering of Killeli's feet behind him. He would find a traveler who would take the little fellow northward. Then he would do what he could for the victims of the new rulers before returning to his own place. Who among the new people would dare to trouble him, whose kind had been wise and powerful before ever theirs emerged from the forest on two legs?

He was not satisfied with the thought. It was all very well to live alone, savoring it. It was far different to be alone forever, without contact with minds from other places, people who came with news or problems for the solving. He had no wish for such isolation. He suddenly knew he had never intended to go back. Not so long as these troublemakers were in place in Damaria. He would go, along with Killeli, with whatever traveler they might find. He would see, for the first time in too many years of his life, the north country, perhaps even the City in the Mist.

He would smell the sea and hear the cries of the water birds, as they swooped and quarreled among the fishing boats that cast out their old bait. The thought brought back to him the long swells, rolling endlessly from the horizon, which had captivated him as a very young Goremin on the first of his few journeys with his elders among the haunts of men.

Even as he thought, his great strong legs strode forward, and his keen ears searched the forest for any hint of danger. So it was that he heard the voices of the Gyrduk long before the wolf pack came into sight.

He stopped, and Killeli, behind him, came close, as if his size and warmth comforted his fears. "The hunters of the night!" whispered the small one.

"They make a last sweep before going to their dens," the Goremin agreed. "Their hunt tonight was not a good one. They are still hungry—can you hear it in their cries? And they have scented us. 'Meat!' they are thinking, in those cold little minds."

Yet, though he did not mention it, the Goremin sensed something else among those distant hunters. A colder, sharper mind, housed in a body as strong and dangerous as those of its companions.

Killeli shivered, and Gorghoz lifted him and set him into the low-swinging branches of a nearby tree. "You wait there. I do not like to worry about others while I confront vermin. You will be safe until I am done. Then we will go on."

"But there are many of them," the furry man objected, through chattering teeth.

"Do not worry. And keep still!"

They waited in the darkness, while the sky above paled still more, and the howls of the Gyrduk came nearer and nearer, racing the dawn after a last morsel to fill their lank bellies. The Goremin stood motionless in the space between two great nut-trees, and Killeli clung to his perch. The great being felt the approach of the leader of the pack with interest and a chill of distress. This thing seemed to hunt for specific prey. He did not think it hunted for him or his companion, and he pitied the object of its pursuit.

The first of the beasts, the leader, came with a rush, his paws a scutter in the leaves, his breath a foulness in the clean morning air. Behind him poured a dark river of bodies, low to the ground, heads up to scent the wind, mouths already filled with saliva at the thought of food.

Gorghoz braced his legs and straightened himself to his full height. The first light from the sky penetrated into the wood enough to show his waiting shape, and the leading beasts faltered, only to be overrun by their impatient pack-mates.

The Goremin smiled into the fresh light, feeling his thick lips peeling away from his layers of needle-like teeth, forming the triple-ranked square that was the grin of his kind. Few creatures, human or animal, could endure the smile of a Goremin.

The howls of triumph turned to plaintive yips and yelps, as the foremost hunter skidded in the leaves and turned aside from that terrible adversary. In a moment's time, the pack changed from an efficient hunting machine into a tumble of terrified individuals, each doing its best to escape into the remnants of darkness beneath the trees. The purpose of that leader had evaporated into instant panic.

Gorghoz raised his head and cried out, a long, deep shout that filled with dread those still thinking to find a meal. With a last scatter of whimpers, the predators made off in all directions, their precision undone and their bellies unfilled.

The Goremin stared after them, his eyes thoughtful and a bit sad. It was often convenient to be so huge and fearsome, but sometimes it was a lonely thing as well. Then he took Killeli down from his tree and turned his steps, once again, toward the west and the road leading to the river crossing. It would be a long journey, he feared, and even his strength might be tested and found wanting before its end.

INTERLUDE

"Unguessed creatures lie in deep places."
—Riddle

Orm stirred uneasily. His ages-long sleep had been good, and his dreams had fueled those of the other kinds who lived above him in the world beneath the sky. He had dreamed of Kings who ruled well and wisely, of beings smooth-skinned and furred, winged and scaled, who grew toward control of thought and mind.

In the uncountable millennia since he burrowed deep for his nap, forests had grown and died and grown again over his sleeping shape. Cities had weathered to dust and been rebuilt by other kinds and again fallen. Damaria was only the most recent of his dreams, although it was one of the most pleasant.

He had, in some strange quirk of his sleeping mind, even dreamed of Dreamers, whose skills, in a very small way, resembled his own. Realities shaped by thought and made perceptible by will— those were the matters in which Orm excelled. Will, in his world, was the force that brought things into being.

Yet he knew, also, that his dreams reflected the living histories that took place overhead. They shaped each other, in some strange way, his mental images and that concrete world.

Yet now a chill seeped down through the layerings of geological ages, through stone and soil, through leaf-mulch and tree-root and his own wrinkled hide, to creep into his sleeping mind. Something stirred, up there beneath the sky in the fall of the year, on the lands that he had shaped when he was new-made and energetic.

Orm opened one of his many indented eyes a bit, peering into the darkness that was his cave. He willed light, exerting pressure on the layered stones, and they began to glow, very slightly, with their own piezoelectric energies.

His own body began to phosphoresce, as well, as he shook himself and sneezed violently. A mist of dust rose in the narrow chamber.

He moved one forearm, stretching it outward. The other seemed to be asleep, and he worked for a time to make it function. When both gray-green limbs were workable, he heaved upward onto his hinder legs, his thick, blunt tail helping to balance his slug-like body.

He yawned, his round mouth going wide, his phosphorescent eyes glowing more brightly as sleep left him and his senses came to life. The slow surge of his vital juices quickened, and his mind began to function in its waking mode.

He went still, as he felt again the cold message that had reached his sleeping brain. Something moved, there in the upper world. The thing that was his twin and opposite, the force of disorder and destruction set against his own need for creation and order, was again alert.

It had troubled the dwellers here in the past, but before he could wake and do something about it others had come to his summoning will and controlled it. The Kings had arrived from the south, and he had welcomed them, from his deep room, for they saved him the effort of waking fully.

But now there was a fatal feeling about that creeping chill. Something evil moved on the land. Wicked energies were loosed in the north, telling him that his dark twin was waking.

The world above him was again at risk, and this time there were no Kings to come to its rescue. He knew he must begin the long task of rousing himself to his full potential.

Orm sighed gustily, stretching his limbs, moving his tail, getting ready to leave his napping place. There would come a time when he must be active again, must take part in the battle to come. Such things came with discouraging regularity in the struggle for control of the lands between the mountains and the sea.

CHAPTER EIGHT

"...a forest, rough with lichen...."
—Riddle

The Turnig moved through the forest as softly as mist over water. Riddle had thought himself a fair woodsman until he began his long journey with these people, but soon he admitted himself to be bested. Their short legs were unfaltering when even his long limbs grew tired.

Lute rested on his back, a welcome burden, his small body heavy with sleep and comfortingly warm. As long as it was dark, the child would drowse, which was convenient. The thought of this youngster who was the last hope of his kind kept him moving to keep pace with the others.

Around him, the forest moved with breeze in the dying leaves, small beasts scurried in the undergrowth, hunting and being hunted, and night-birds cried lonely calls into the darkness. He had walked for many leagues in his life, traveling for his own enjoyment or on errands for his uncle the King, but never before had he felt himself hunted, threatened to the point of exhaustion.

The sounds that had seemed friendly at other times now set his ears turning to the wind. He paused from time to time, feeling the night around him or locating the nearest of the Turnig in the long line of furry people, who went silently over the dead leaves and the dried branches, disturbing nothing as they moved. Their ability to understand their own kind, without words and without conflict, was admirable, he thought. His ancestors had done their work well when they brought these burrowers up to the level of thinking beings.

Despite the lack of any signal to the contrary, Riddle felt there must be other movement in the wood. Not close by—he would have detected any presence at once—but at a distance some other two-legged creature moved, for birds called warning signals, the far-away shrilling audible to his sensitive ears. Besides his woods-sense, he felt that some other force was stirring as well. The abilities of the Ancient Race were convenient at times, but they were so vague and unspecific that they often left him more irritated than enlightened

On this night, it seemed that a stronger, slower, more powerful mind had waked and begun to search out the countryside, drowning Riddle's intuitions in the flood of its awareness. A name floated from deep inside him, where his early teachings were stored.

Orm. When had he first heard that name? Orm. It was a name he had learned as a child three hundred years before, but he shook his head in frustration and went forward.

So it was that when he paused he sent a signal up the line of Turnig ahead of him: "Be cautious! Step carefully! Watch and listen for anyone in the forest."

* * * * * * *

The night passed slowly, but the fleeing Turnig and the wary poet moved with swift precision, heading straight north, toward the passage through the hills beyond the forest. They knew winter was waiting, just across those stony outcrops, to ambush them in their journey. They hoped to pass through the hill country before the snow began to blow.

The road to the sea was a long one, and only the City in the Mist provided ship-building facilities. They must pass through the dangerous country now or later, and the sooner they crossed that widespread barrier of round hills and flat stone slabs, canted perilously toward the sky, the better it would be for all of them. The Lir-folk hunted in winter, and they had always been a cruel and all but mindless people, beyond even the capabilities of the Ancient Race to raise them above their old levels.

The travelers rested from time to time, gathering into a clump of furred bodies and bundles wrapped in felt and woven mesh. It was already growing cold at night, and they huddled, sharing their warmth. Riddle, buried among his companions, was glad of that, for Lute whimpered and squirmed from time to time. His uncle knew he was not warm enough, even amid the fur of the Turnig.

When the time came, he added layers to the boy's wrappings, and the journey continued. Night crept past, and first light touched the sky, making the webbed branches above him lace-like against the pewter and pale blue of the morning clouds. As the sky warmed with dawn, he stopped in his tracks, whistling a signal to the line of Turnig. The signals of birds told him someone was near. A familiar presence moved in the forest to meet them.

* * * * * * *

Gorghoz had been thinking of the Gyrduk, wondering what had made the predators so bold and from what source their leader had come. Usually it was deep winter before they began running so close to the fields of Damaria. But since Killeli had come to his door, his entire world seemed to be changing, old rules crumbling and new situations rising almost before his eyes. So when he found himself staring at the road through a thin screen of bushes, it took him by surprise. He had not dreamed the two of them had come so far.

He dropped to hands and knees as the pounding of hooves echoed between the ranks of trees along the road. While he had no fear of the new rulers of Damaria, neither had he any immediate desire to confront them. First he must put Killeli into safe hands. Then he would turn his attention to those who were disrupting their country.

Six riders thudded past, beyond a screen of bushes and vines, leaving a thin veil of dust behind them. They were flogging their beasts cruelly, which told the Goremin they were on some important errand. They were, strangely, dressed alike. Uniforms were a fashion that had never made its way into the Damarian way of life, and only old books about lost cultures beyond the sea told the Goremin what he was seeing. No sensible traveler would walk the road with such messengers abroad.

He knew his best hope was to cross the thoroughfare and try the forest beyond it, where trails paralleled the way northward. Before he could cross, another group came galloping back toward Damaria in the dawnlight, their steeds lathered, their cloaks dusty in spots and muddy in others, as if they had traveled far in desperate haste.

What had happened to arouse such frantic activity? In the old days, one might sit beside this road for hours, even on a day in summer, and see only a farmer's cart or a woodsman with a bale of fagots for the fires of the villagers. Now, in the space of a hundred heartbeats, he had seen some dozen riders, all of them full of haste and anxiety. All were, he had no doubt, in the service of the killers of the King.

Before he stepped into the track, Gorghoz looked about him with his keen senses alert. No other traveler was on that road for some distance, but in the wood beyond it he could hear a faint rustle, as many creatures moved in the morning's dim light.

One of those was a man—he sniffed the scent into his nostrils— indeed, one of the Ancient Race, and he felt almost certain it was the poet of the Kings. Surely this would be a fitting companion for the furry man to follow northward! He was sure that Riddle would agree to help the hairy man find safety.

He beckoned to Killeli, who came after him across the narrow way, stepping in the tracks of the Goremin so as to confuse any trail they might leave. When they moved across the ferny ditch beyond and into the thick wood, Gorghoz turned, lifted his companion, and began to stride through the trees at a tremendous rate, careless of noise or traces left behind. No being in its sane senses would pursue a Goremin, he knew all too well.

So, as Riddle and his Turnig were settling for a brief rest, the great Being approached from the south and east, coming toward them amid a sprinkle of sun through autumn branches. As he neared the waiting group, Riddle came to meet him. Gorghoz felt something in his chest ease as he recognized the poet. A world without this man would be sadly impoverished, and he was filled with gladness to see him still among the living.

"My friend!" he called, as the two came face to face. "I did not know what was happening, here in the lower world, until it was too late to act. This one, Killeli, brought the word to me as he fled from those who had killed his people. Will you take him north with you?"

"I go northward, yes," replied the poet. "But after that, I go west, across the seas to the islands of which my people dream. Will your friend go so far with a stranger?"

The furred man, now on his own feet and looking up from face to face as the two spoke, stepped forward. "I will go anywhere, Lord Poet, to escape those who slaughtered my kind. The fear of death will send one, I have found, farther than he would have dared to go without it.

"You do not know me—indeed, I was a tiny child when last you visited my village. You bought a carven bookstand for your brother, and it was my father who made it. I remember you well, and you could never seem a stranger to me."

Gorghoz stepped back while the pair renewed their acquaintance, but he was not thinking of that. He was thinking of those western islands, to which so many of the Ancient Race had gone. He had said goodbye to dear friends as they set off for the City in the Mist. Not one had ever returned to stay, only a very few coming back to attend to business or to visit their kin and then to hurry again to their beloved islands. Now he might go there, too, and renew acquaintances he had thought forever lost. He began to feel a dim excitement building inside his hairy chest.

As Riddle beckoned to him and his friend to come into the circle of Turnig, the great Being sighed. His eyes brightened with new hope. As he sank onto the ground beside Chark and her people, he turned to Riddle. "I will go as well."

Satisfaction filled him as he spoke. He had never dreamed he would travel again, here in the twilight of his lifespan. "I had thought to remain here and do what I could to help those left behind. But what can one do, even if he is a Goremin? Against so many, I would be merely an irritation. I could save some who might perish, but I could not stay the progress of this new history that has over-taken Damaria.

"I have never seen what may lie beyond the City in the Mists. I have dreamed, too, of those islands to which so many of my friends have sailed away. Allow me to go as well, for I would travel over water before I die and let my gaze rest on the dream of the Ancient Race."

The poet's face seemed to glow in the morning light. The joy in his eyes was echoed by that in the heart of Gorghoz, as they took their places amid the sleeping Turnig. "It is good that the route north lies along such a narrow way," he said. "Otherwise we might have had to travel alone, and in the north, at this time of year, that is a dangerous thing to do." Lute stirred in his cocoon of wrappings as he lay between Chark and Jree.

Gorghoz reached absently and took up the boy, remembering a time, lost in the past, when last he held a human child. The sleepy warmth against his chest was a thing too precious to believe. He cuddled the small one as he squirmed to find a new position and sank again into sleep. Riddle smiled drowsily as he, too, lay back and closed his eyes. Killeli, weary after scrambling to keep up with the long legs of his champion, was dozing already.

In a while, as the autumn sunlight slanted through the trees in dim splendor, only Gorghoz sat erect among the sleeping travelers. The child was on his lap, content against the warmth of his great body. Soon they must all rise and go forward on their journey, but for now he was filled with contentment.

He was among friends. He had almost forgotten the wonder of that. Here there were no tainted hearts who found fear in the awk-ward contours of his face and body. The kindness the Ancient Race had bred into those they nurtured formed a kind of strength of its own, capable of withstanding, he hoped, stresses that would have set other kinds of beings at each others' throats. Before this journey was done, that would serve them all well. Perhaps, in his waning years, Gorghoz the Goremin had found the home he had lost with the dwindling of his kind, over the ages in which the Kings of Damaria had held the land in their spell of grace and peace. It was strange, he thought, that it had been cruelty and killing that brought him to his own fulfillment.

But even as he sat in a haze of unwonted contentment, he was listening to the forest, in his Goremin way: Small feet scurried frantically in the distance. The ever-present birds called with increasing anxiety. There was another abroad in the forest, one worth saving, his instinct told him.

When Riddle woke, he would suggest someone be sent to find who this might be and to guide that other fugitive to their route. When hunters were abroad, there would be safety in numbers. if every one of that number were a person of courage and determination.

Keeping a watch to match that of the sentinel Turnig, the great Goremin sat through the morning. When the others woke, it would be time to act.

CHAPTER NINE

"For wisdom can be bound into a Book...."
—Riddle

The forest was strangely still, as Moonlight stretched herself and breathed the clean air of morning. She sneezed three times in rapid succession, broke off a tuft of needles, and brushed away the remnants of cobweb and dust from her stolen clothing. The pack was dirty as well, and she took the time to beat the debris from it, before pulling the belt-straps over her shoulders and taking up her course.

Her long detour below-ground had disoriented her, though she felt it had put the Gyrduk off her trail, if they still ran hungry. She cast about for familiar landmarks, but this was now beyond the haunts of her childhood; nothing seemed recognizable. The sun was now up, however, and she set off toward the north, knowing that before she went too many leagues she would find the road, which curved northeastward in order to take the easiest route across the river bordering Damaria on the north. She had no intention of following it, for she knew Lorbek would have his people watching every road leading away from the city, but she could use it as a guide from a distance.

The birds of summer had flown south weeks before, and the branches above her were quiet, except for groups of small black-capped chatterers and the rustle of drying leaves in the breeze. From time to time a group of birds flew up as if at some prearranged signal, leaving her to wonder if someone else might be abroad in the wood.

That made her even more cautious. She had not escaped from captivity only to be taken back to face Lorbek's wrath. She kept to low-lying tracks sheltered by bushes and vines, pausing often to listen for any sound that might tell her what stirred among the trees; nothing betrayed a presence.

The book, wrapped carefully and stowed in her pack, grew hot against her skin, as she trudged along amid the crackling leaves. Some force she could not locate or explain seemed to be interacting with the contaminated volume, and its influence dragged at her. She grew weary and sweaty, despite the breeze that blew chill from the north, and her feet became heavier as she went. At last she stopped entirely and took off the pack, laying it aside on the carpet of leaves at the foot of an ancient tree.

Perching on one of the big roots, she opened the roll of cloaks and dug out the volume. The silk in which she had folded it was crumbling. The pale leather of the cover shimmered with a ripple of heat, and Moonlight was afraid to touch it with an unprotected finger. Folding a thick layer of cloak about her hand, she took the book out of the pack and laid it on a knob farther along the root on which she sat. There came a sizzling, and the tough bark began to smolder. A tendril of smoke rose into the air, and she stared in dismay.

She didn't want to set the forest afire. Where could she put this cursed thing so as to be safe?

She rose and looked about for a stone on which to set it, but nothing of the kind could she see in any direction. The ground beneath her feet heaved slightly. She thought for an instant that she was dizzy, but the roots of the giant tree seemed to writhe like serpents, as a ripple of motion heaved below.

Something deep in the earth stirred. Closing her eyes, she centered herself in the Great Will, hoping that would keep her calm until she could find what troubled the land. She could think of only one way to learn what she must know: focusing on the Jewel in her body, making a picture of a dark space beneath the forest where that stirring took place, she drew upon the ancient resource of her kind, the Will that shaped the world. But instead of creating her own vision, she left her mind empty, to be filled by another will, if such a thing existed below.

She saw Orm, outlined in his own phosphorescence and the light of the stones in his deep place. He was of no shape she knew, but something inside told her that this was—must be!—the shaping force that had been in place here long before the Kings came from the south, long before even the ancient evils had traveled down to Damaria from the cold wastes in the north. It was, she understood with sudden clarity, the Will that had helped the Kings to shape the Dreamers from their feline ancestors.

The blunt, seeking head turned as if to look into her eyes. The round mouth moved, and though she heard no word, a chant came into her mind. Words of the oldest of the kinds to live in these forested lands filled her mouth:

"Ekeria tepar. Ekeria tepora. Ekeria tepederium noletesste."
Her voice was strange to her own ears, holding timbres that echoed with other kinds of life than her own. Her instinct echoed the words in the common tongue—"Be cool! Be cold! Be frozen to quietude!"

The line of smoke thinned to nothing. The bark, black beneath the book, ceased to smolder. The shimmer died away, leaving the binding strangely limp and lifeless, though it had seemed almost a living thing before. She tried to open her eyes, but the vision was not yet finished. That glowing head still stared at her, its many eyes closed and yet terribly aware. Its powerful will encompassed her, and her conviction grew.

This book was a thing of awesome potency. Created as an instrument to aid a good purpose, it had been altered terribly by wicked wills, reshaping it to their own ends. She must take it away from Damaria, the forest, and the stony hills beyond, as far as she could manage to go. The ocean must roll in all its strength and fury between this defiled creation and those who ruined it for their own purposes and sought it to retain their present strength.

She must keep it in the possession of trustworthy people, and for that she must find help. Help was near! She must fold the book away again and go at once to the north and west. The Dreamer opened her eyes at last, staring blankly at the sun-streaked branches of the wood and the dappled leaves beneath her feet. What had she seen, there beneath the forest's floor? What was Orm, the Ancient Will that her ancestors had sensed and worshipped?

But she was a Dreamer. She knew duty and honor, if nothing else. The order she had been given was of grave importance; that impression still lingered in her mind. Orm, whatever he might be, was not evil, though he surely had his own purposes. She knew she must obey his wordless command.

So she rolled the book in the remnants of the silk and again made up the pack, putting the uncomfortable burden into its center. When she stood, she faced northwest, some inner compass telling her exactly when she reached the proper course. Then she began to walk very quickly, ignoring any threat the wood might hold.

If help was near, she knew that she must find it soon, for she now had more cause to avoid the searchers of Lorbek than she had known before. The book was more important than her life; she must find a way to take it beyond the sea, if it required her death to accomplish it.

She did not stop to rest or to eat. From time to time she sipped from the bottle of wine she had taken from Lorbek's table, though she longed for sweet water. But there was no time to hunt out a stream. She almost stumbled into the road, so quickly did she plunge through a tangle of ferns and vines and berry bushes. Pausing to listen again, she detected no hint of movement along the way; she hitched up her pack and darted across, diving into the growth beyond the track and going deeply into the trees before she stopped again.

Behind her, she heard the dim mutter of hooves against the packed ground of the roadway. Someone was coming, as if the thing she carried were drawing her pursuers after her. Moonlight ran desperately among the trees, dodging deadfall and stump holes, trying to gain distance. That rider could not know she had crossed, no matter what sent him there or compelled him onward. Perhaps she could lose him, if she kept running.

As she pelted along, she thought she saw something ahead in the sun-dappled reaches of the wood. A line of Turnig? There was, as well, something huge and unhuman, yet oddly unfrightening. She did not slow her pace, for she felt, behind her, the compulsion of pursuit. "Help!" she called softly, as she came nearer. "Oh, help me!"

The big creature turned its lumpy face toward her, and she gasped at its hideousness, though she knew at once this must be the legendary Gorghoz from the mountains. His great head cocked downward to survey her, the eyes, bright as coals in the grayish face, seeming to recognize her. The wide mouth stretched into a square grin filled with pointed teeth that hinted at more layers behind them.

"So," came the booming reply. "We have found each other, Wanderer. I felt you moving in the forest, and we were coming to look for you."

"Someone...is...on the road!" she gasped. "I think he...wants... the thing I carry with me!"

"Indeed?" The great being moved past her. "You wait here," he called over his shoulder.

"Wait with Riddle and the Turnig. I will deal with any pursuit."

She stumbled to a halt and went down to her knees, her lungs heaving, her throat burning with effort. Someone came and took her pack from her back. When she made a gesture of protest, he laid it before her, beside her protecting hand.

At last she could see through the red haze that had obscured her vision for a moment; to her astonishment, this was one of the Ancient Race. She searched her memory for that wide-browed face, the dark eyes, the tangle of brown curls.

"Riddle! The Poet of the Kings!" she said, rising to her feet. "I am glad you still live. Was that a truly a Goremin?"

The poet looked past her toward the road, which was too distant, now, to see. "That is the last of the Goremin in Damaria. He will...deter...the one who might pursue you."

She felt a twinge of guilt, for Dreamers were careful not to cause injury or death to anyone who did not threaten them directly and repeatedly. She shivered to think of that terrible figure confronting her pursuer.

"Will he kill him?" She thought she recalled a tale from her youth, but she could not bring it clearly to mind.

Riddle looked at her searchingly. His dark eyes seemed to read her, down to the deepest of her thoughts and her secrets. "You are a Dreamer," he said. "Your people are kindred of my blood, though new-sprung on that ancient tree. I have never heard ill of any Dreamer, and I will trust you with a secret no other must know."

She nodded, wondering, as he looked about to make certain no Turnig was within earshot.

When he turned back, he bent close to speak into her ear. "Goremin will not harm any living thing. Their only power, other than wisdom and strength of body and will, is the power to paralyze with fear almost any ill-intentioned being they choose to confront. They have no need to kill. Only the most desperate of dangers could compel such an act on the part of his kind.

"He will not kill that one who came along the road. But he will frighten him so that he will ride for the city as if death itself ran behind his mount, lashing both beast and rider with cold terror."

She felt herself relax. She was again, unexpectedly, among people of her own kind. Her days and nights of captivity by those who lived by threat and pain and fear had chilled her spirit. She had almost feared herself to be contaminated by that experience, unable to return, even in part, to the innocent world from which she had been taken.

But now she knew she had truly escaped. Whatever came, after this, these new companions would help her to shield the thing that was in her charge, once she explained her need to them.

For the first time in a very long while, she felt safe.

CHAPTER TEN

"A smile can frighten evil men to flight."
                                        —Riddle

The Goremin reached a foresters' track in the wood and hurried along it toward the roadway. Ahead, he could hear the scuffling of hooves in the soft litter of leaves strewn across the way, and he knew the young woman's pursuer had turned from the road to search the forest. Her paleness, beneath her golden skin, had told him her danger was great, for he read her as a brave woman. This must be a henchman of the new King, bent on mischief.

He turned aside toward the sound of the horse's slow progress through the tangle of the wood. Slipping through the shadowy ways, as he had learned to do many centuries ago in his boyhood, the great creature set his course to intercept that of the rider.

When he saw the man at last it came as a shock. He was clad in the brown and green of Gem, the brother of the poet, though the cut of his clothing was strange and awkward. He had the pale gray skin and the straw-colored hair of the new people, and his face was at once cruel and weak.

The narrow jaw was set and grim. An aura of fury hung about him, even as he whipped his reluctant mount into the insecure footing of a streambed and spurred him up the other side. His cloak was secured with a brooch, and as the struggling beast heaved itself onto the soft bank just beyond the spot where the Goremin hid, Gorghoz recognized the symbol set into its glinting metal.

His great heart chilled. Not for many millennia had his kind seen that symbol, which was noted into their histories with a warning. A scorpion grasped a human heart in its claws. Dreadful as that might seem, even worse were the powers represented by the thing. This was one of the henchmen of the Mover from the North, he had no doubt.

Another look at the man's expression, now that he was very

near, beyond a cloak of grapevine but quite visible, told him all he needed to know. There was no question but that this one's heart was, indeed, held within those terrible claws.

As the horse panted and the man surveyed the surrounding wood, Gorghoz pushed aside the tangle of greenery and stepped from his concealed spot behind the vine-draped tree. He made no sound, of course, but the beast sensed his presence immediately. Goremin had a devastating effect upon horses.

Feeling his mount tense, the rider turned his head. His eyes widened beneath the shadow of his helmet, and his hand went to his side. The Goremin smiled at him pleasantly, knowing the effect it would have upon any human being who was unprepared to meet one of his kind.

There was a harshly indrawn breath, echoing the terrified whinny of the horse, which was already wheeling. The face beneath the helmet paled to the shade of whey, and the spurred heels clapped together against the mount's heaving sides. With a snort of panic, the beast responded, leaping the runnel he had so recently crossed and tearing away toward the road with desperate speed. No rein would stop him until his panic subsided, the Goremin knew.

Gorghoz followed, although he knew it was a waste of effort. Even as he gained a point from which he could see the way, he heard the frantic hooves reach the hardened ground and go pounding away toward Damaria and the debased master the rider served.

The weapon of the Goremin seldom failed, although it was a painful one for the user, for his kind felt what their opponents suffered. Gorghoz turned away from the road. Although the terrified retreat of the horseman was amusing in its haste, still the reactions of other sorts of thinking beings to his appearance always saddened him. Among Goremin, he was considered rather comely.

* * * * * * *

When he came again to the spot where he had left his companions, he found Riddle sitting beside the young woman, who was talking very quietly, gesturing from time to time toward the pack she had borne strapped to her back. He called to warn them of his arrival. Riddle and the Turnig had accepted him easily, but others were not so quickly accustomed to his appearance.

Riddle gestured for him to approach, and the Goremin hurried his silent steps to the spot where the two waited. He looked down into the eyes of the young woman, and his gaze met one of dark amber, slit-pupilled and assessing, in an oval face. He smiled again, and even that did not disturb her calm.

"You are a Dreamer," he said. He saw her clothing fitted ill, that her russet braids were in a tangle that hinted at the lack of a comb, and her shoes were too large for her slender feet.

From behind him came a timid voice. "If I do not mistake, this is the child of the Nairneks. Did I see you taken captive, some days ago, as the home of your people blazed and men shouted and dragged you away?" Killeli peered around the tree beneath which the others were sitting.

The girl looked keenly at the furred man. Then she nodded. "I am Moonlight, granddaughter of the Nairnek. My grandmother died and her body burned, but I cannot hold those responsible to account. Lord Lorbek was the one who gave the order. I cannot imagine why. I escaped from the farmhouse of the King, where he was in residence."

Riddle rose to his feet, and Gorghoz reached a long arm to touch him lightly on the shoulder. "Be calm, poet. You know your uncle and your brother are dead, with all except the child. What does it matter that a villain lives in his house? It is the wrongful death that wounds you."

Killeli was looking from face to face as they spoke. When the Goremin paused, the furred man stepped forward. "Is it permitted that I sleep, Gorghoz, while you talk with these others? I feel the need."

Of course that smaller person would be exhausted, even after a night's sleep. He had pushed his weary limbs for too many leagues in too few days.

Gorghoz nodded. "Take the blankets from my pack and rest well, Killeli. I will wake you in time to eat something before we proceed."

As Killeli trudged toward a group of drowsing Turnig, Moonlight whispered, "Do you suppose he heard what I said? About the book?"

Riddle shook his head. Then he motioned to Gorghoz to sit beside Moonlight. "Tell him about it," he said. "I want to think a bit, before we decide what to do next."

So Gorghoz listened as she recounted her discovery of the book in the chest at Cairnstone. "It is very dangerous, I think," she said at last. "The dream I had in the wood filled me with dread, for the responsibility is terrible. What do you make of it, Gorghoz?"

He leaned back against the rough bole of the tree and closed his eyes. His hand rubbed at the lumps on his forehead as he thought hard about the situation.

At last, he opened his eyes again and said, "I can decide nothing until I see the thing. If it is what I fear it may be, then we have a dreadful task ahead of us. But I must be sure.

"Orm has moved beneath Damaria—that is the thing that makes me feel the chill of age and death in my bones. Unwrap the book. Everyone over there is asleep. Now is the time."

Riddle, who had been watching from a distance, returned at once when Moonlight unrolled the cloak-blankets and pulled aside the darkened silk from the volume. Gorghoz ignored him, for now he felt the source of the strange mood that had gripped him since this thing had come into the forest. This was the book bound in the skin of Gorezha, the Goremin.

He shivered, as the girl pushed the thing toward him, using a fold of the cloak to keep from touching the smooth leather that bound it. But he knew he must touch it, open it, and examine the letters on its pages. Only then would he be certain this was the thing whose troubling he had felt as he moved through the forest with Killeli.

He touched it with a hesitant finger. The leather, which had seemed limp and lifeless, sent a tingle through his skin, up his bones, down his spine. Gorezha, something mourned deep within his racial memory. A darkness spread across his mind, blotting out his thoughts, blackening the world around him as if thick clouds had covered the sky.

Gorghoz began to tremble, his great teeth chattering against each other with the sound of clicking pebbles. A fear, the like of which he had never dreamed, filled him. The solid foundations that his kind had always understood to underpin the world were shaken and destroyed, and even the innocent breeze that stirred the dead leaves of the trees was cold and threatening.

But Gorghoz was no coward. He took up the book in both his huge hands, holding it as if to keep it from flying from his grasp. He opened the covers and laid the thing flat on his knees, staring down at the rusty ink of the script that flowed across the pages.

The words of those ancient Kings were there, powerful and compelling, but their message was subtly tainted. A sickness entered his heart, as he read, for the wisdom of the Kings, which he knew to be that of the forces his own people served, seemed twisted and darkened. The formulae for binding evil wills seemed foolish, and questions rose, unbidden, into his mind.

This was, indeed, a thing of wicked intent, which had at one time been a tool of enlightened protection. Those who had bound it in this skin, cruelly flayed from its owner, had with that act contaminated everything the book stood for, everything that it taught, and every mind that now looked into it.

Even he, whose people had been forces for order before the influence of the Scorpion Sigil ever tainted this land and brought the Kings to Damaria to give battle, was touched by the dark aura. But he turned the page and read on, trying to wrest the true meaning from the written lines.

His mind could do that—yes. But his heart could not accept those glowing words as anything but tarnished and trite. He sighed and closed the book, wrapping it again in scraps of silk.

"It is, indeed, dangerous," he said. "The man from whom you took it was, you said, calling himself King, here in Damaria. But who rules him?

"That is the question that haunts me. The evil breath that came from the north many thousands of years ago now wants to return. Its forces are returning, if we can trust the things we see and hear. And this is their tool. I wonder...."

"What do you wonder?" asked Riddle.

"I wonder where Lorbek found it. Or was it given into his hands? And, if that, by whom?"

They sat, the three of them, staring at the bundle Moonlight had rolled again into her cloak. Above them the wind became more brisk, the chill deepened, as the hem of a storm from the north penetrated even those southern forests.

Gorghoz rubbed his hands absently against his rough cloak, trying to remove the feel of the awful binding of that even more terrible book. He had felt, for an instant, a sense of the lost Goremin, a hint of her agony, and a bit of her spirit, still lost in the chaos that had been her death.

"I will take it," he said, "if you will permit. My people understand such things and have dealt with others, over the years. It is the skin of one of my kind that forms the binding, and I believe she will be more at peace in the hands of another Goremin. It affects me, but I can, to an extent, control it. I wonder if either of you younglings would be able to, if its master compelled it to use its power.

"You would resist, I know, but I dread what the effort might do to you. However, I believe I might, in time, learn to master it."

The bundle quivered as if the breeze had stirred the cloak. But Gorghoz knew it was another power that moved the book. He sighed. "Or if not to master it, at least to keep it from mastering me."

Moonlight looked up at him, her amber eyes filling with tears. "If you would take from me that burden—not the responsibility, for I have accepted it and will carry it through to the end—but the thing itself, I will be able to go forward. Thank you, Gorghoz."

Riddle, who had sat silent and thoughtful through the entire proceeding, rose again to his feet. "It is time to go. The wind grows cold, and the hills await us. Damaria is young, as yet, in wickedness, but we are moving northward.

"That, if you will remember, is the direction from which evil things have traditionally come. We would do well to go quickly and to cross the hills before winter sets in fully. I do not relish the thought of a season spent in their snows and winds."

Gorghoz shivered, nodding. With one accord, they moved to wake the Turnig, to wrap Lute more snugly, and to take up the trek northward. The Goremin tried not to think of the Lirfolk, who now would be driven from their normal places by the need for game.

To those primitive people, even mankind was meat.

CHAPTER ELEVEN

"... not one instant's agony would I spare...."
—Riddle

As if to slow their progress, the cold blast from the north shifted to the west, bringing heavy rains from the distant sea beyond the wood. The forest paths ran with water, wetting the feet of Turnig and man and Goremin alike. Even Killeli, who seldom complained, began to droop.

But Riddle, carrying the last of his line on his back, was worried about the child. Lute was shivering, his teeth clicking with the damp chill of the morning. An unusual warmth was coming through the bag and his own clothing, telling him the boy was feverish. To tend a sick child in a forest in the rain was a task he felt himself unfit to do.

When they paused to rest and nibble a bit of dried fruit in the shelter of an enormous conifer, he turned to Chark. The little Turnig had always seemed eminently practical, and he felt that if anyone in the group might know what to do, she was the one.

There were many small ones in the Turnig group, and they seemed to be traveling well. Surely another sort of child could do it, too.

"Lute is shivering," he whispered to his old friend. "His teeth chatter, and I think he has a fever. What should I do?"

He had bent to speak into her furry ear, and that put the boy's head within reach of her short arms. She pushed back the top of the bag and felt his forehead, her expression thoughtful. Then she nodded and motioned for Riddle to give the child to her.

"He needs the tea we give our own. And he needs to travel in one of the baskets with our little ones. That will keep him from being lonely, and the tea will warm him and take away the fever. The boy has known too many terrible changes, Poet, in too short a time. Even an infant understands loss and fear, and he is well beyond infancy. Let him travel with the Turnig, and I believe you will find him mended very soon."

She took Lute into her short arms, and he sighed and snuggled against her as she turned away.

Riddle sighed, too, hoping desperately that Chark was right. He felt if anything happened to his brother's only surviving child, who might one day reclaim the throne, he would have failed at the most important task of his life. But he could only hope, and he hurried ahead to catch up with the Goremin, whose long-legged strides carried him well ahead of the rest of the travelers. Moonlight was not far behind Gorghoz, and when he reached her he slowed his pace.

"Your nephew—he is well?" she asked. "I dreamed he had a fever, and nightmares were terrifying him."

Riddle had known Dreamers all his life, but never in a very close and intimate fashion. His people had tended to discount their talents and to think of them in the same light as other crossbreeds. Now he stared at her, surprised, although he should not have been, at the accuracy of her Dreaming.

"Can you dream him well again? He is shaking with chill. I had not thought of it, but you might give him the illusion of health, until he mends. The Turnig are dosing him with their own medicines, and I trust their judgment, but I would also like to ease the little one's feelings."

The young woman stared at him for a moment, and he felt she was seeing, instead of his own image, something deep inside herself. Then she smiled. "I believe I can do that." Her smile grew even wider. "I had never thought of doing it before, but it seems very possible. Let's go and see!"

She turned and ran, sending sprays of water with each step, toward the group of Turnig who were carrying the large baskets in which their children rode.

Riddle hurried after her, wondering what effect the intervention of a Dreamer might have on illness. He felt he was about to learn something interesting, and he arrived just behind her, to find that Chark thought the idea might have merit.

"Which basket carries Lute?" asked Moonlight.

Chark indicated a particularly large and heavy one, and the girl moved alongside the carriers and laid her hand on the wickerwork top. She began to hum softly to herself, and Riddle saw her eyes close, as she followed the line of Turnig through the wet ways of the forest.

* * * * * * *

Moonlight Dreamed a spring wood, with sunlight striking down through branches laden with new leaves and starred with small, fragrant blossoms. On a mossy spot sprinkled with tiny white flowers, she set Lute and two Turnig children, bringing them sharply into focus as she remembered meeting them the night before.

Into the circle she moved a round-eye, one of the small burrowers that sometimes prowled the forest in spring, looking for a mate. His fur-trimmed ears perked up when he saw the young ones, and he showed no fear as Lute reached to stroke his gray-striped silver fur.

Moonlight strode forward, unmindful of the splash of her feet in the wet, the runnels of rain that poured down her face. She was living in a warm, bright circle with the three younglings.

How long it lasted she never quite knew, but there came a moment when something dark and cold entered the field of her Dream. A black shape, like a great bird, came between the spot of warm moss and the sun; a shiver of revulsion and fear shook her.

She had never before known any outside influence to enter her Dream, but now she felt the intrusion of a dark will. The children, who had been laughing and petting the round-ear, fell silent, and their small faces grew still. Turnig and child alike, they seemed to understand they must not attract the attention of the thing that was alighting, like a huge black bird, in the tree above.

Moonlight looked up into deep pits of night that stared down at her with unhuman indifference. The thing raised its great wings and flapped them, sending petals fluttering downward, darkening the light, shriveling the leaves on the branches.

She knew with sudden conviction that she must take the children away at once. This was nothing her talent could resist or repel. Flight was the only answer. In that instant, she reached with her Dreaming sense and snatched the three young ones away from the mossy circle, out of the spring wood, and set them again in their tight basket. So intent was she upon what she was doing that she didn't hear the outraged cry Lute gave as he found himself once again sick and shaking.

Moonlight, still inside her Dream, faced upward toward that ugly bird-shape. The wings beat the air, stirring a stench that grew worse every moment. The lightless eyes searched the moss-bank, as if the disappearance of the children had not yet penetrated its dim mind.

She struggled to break the Dream, to return to her body, still walking beside the basket, but she found she was incapable of leaving the vision. She tried feeling her feet as they splashed along, her hand as it lay on the rough weave of the basket. Visualizing that scene, she could not pull her vital self back from the place she had created for the children.

Moonlight, more even than when shackled in Lorbek's house, felt trapped and terrified, as the crook-beaked bird head came slowly around from its last sweep of the ground below and the pit-like eyes focused again on her. This was a physical representation of a power so great it might well destroy her—or change her, past all redemption, into something similar to itself, a tool for the hand of the Mover in the North.

As if from far away, she heard a despairing shriek. The bird launched itself from the branch, sailing down toward her purposefully.

In the instant before his filthy claws would have touched whatever part of her went into her Dreams, an alien will shook her, snatched her away, took her from that scene into a darkness so intense that she felt it to be tangible. She welcomed it, for whatever it was, the alternative was far worse.

And then, for a long while, she knew nothing more.

* * * * * * *

Riddle held the limp shape of the Dreamer, covering her with his cloak against the rain, which seemed to pelt down even harder than before. He had no inkling what it was that had sent her into such a state.

He suspected from the fretful voices in the basket beside him that she had taken the children away from the pleasant place she made for them. He could not imagine her reason for doing it. When she screamed, Gorghoz came pounding back along the path, sending Turnig tumbling out of his way.

It had been the Goremin's great hands that grabbed the Dreamer and shook her fiercely, as if to awaken her. But she had not waked. Instead, she seemed now to be in a sort of trance, incapable of rousing.

Even as he thought it, Riddle felt the ground tremble beneath his soggy boots. He stared up at Gorghoz, who was standing still, eyes closed, his lumpy brow furrowed with concentration. In a moment, the motion ceased, and Riddle began to think he had imagined it.

"What is the matter with her?" he asked, rousing the Goremin from his efforts. "And why do you look so grim?"

"You did not feel—but of course you could not. That is not one of the talents of the Ancient Race. I was too intent on moving quickly past the hills or I might have saved her this. She was attacked, inside her own vision, by something from outside. Something wicked and ancient and very powerful.

"When she cried out, I knew she was in mortal peril, and I ran. But it was almost too late. Instead of bringing her back here, with us, I was forced to cast her into...into...I cannot find words for it. It is not a place of evil, nor of good. It simply is, and she must rest there in limbo until we find shelter and stop for a time.

"If we try bringing her back without her being strong and rested and well, we may sentence her to something far worse than any death we know. Carry her, Riddle, until you tire. Then I will carry her to the end. It is my fault. I should have been on watch, for I saw and understood the Scorpion Sigil. That might well have warned me there are worse enemies abroad on our road than winter and Lirfolk and the servants of the new rulers."

He said nothing more. Riddle, carrying the Dreamer, followed at his heels, keeping an eye on the basket in which Lute rode. Whatever happened, he would be there, his strength and his will ready to defend his nephew and those who traveled with them toward the sanctuary of the West.

CHAPTER TWELVE

"...over perilous, ice-paved paths...."
—Riddle

When the rain paused, the wind shifted again. This time it brought harsh blasts of hail, along with sleet and gusts of snow. The forest's shelter thinned, as the group struggled northward, moving more and more slowly.

Gorghoz, carrying the still unconscious Dreamer, led now, trampling out a track for the shorter legs of the Turnig, Killeli, and Riddle. Even his great stamina was beginning to flag when he came to the steep banks of the stream that flanked the hills forming the northern boundary of Damaria.

Below the spot where the Goremin paused, the river flowed, its deep waters rolling in oily turbulence and specked, already, with ice. The embankment was too steep to attempt in the storm that now raged, and Gorghoz looked upstream and down, trying to remember his distant childhood and the last time he had explored this part of the country with his peers.

He was chilling, now, his shaggy coat of grayish hair damp and beginning to freeze into clumps. His brain seemed slowed by the cold, and he huddled behind a bastion of rock while he thought. About him, his companions gathered into a close group, out of the wind somewhat and sharing their body heat. In his arms, Moonlight had begun to shiver as his own warmth faded and failed her.

Against his back, in the pouch where he carried the few necessities needed by his kind, he felt a stinging pain. Not warmth—that would have been welcomed. Instead, a nervous prickling of his skin, making the roots of his hair seem to twinge, was spreading from the spot against which the book now lay.

That woke the Goremin fully to his senses. He had been lulled by something, he now knew. The wind carried from the north an ill will that could influence even one of his own kind—because of the binding of that evil book, he suddenly knew. That was going to be a burden past anything he had expected, when he relieved the Dreamer of its weight.

He shook his lumpy head and breathed a long draught of icy wind. It cleared his mind even more, and he knew what it was he had been trying to recall. There was a way across the river, hidden, perilous, highly unlikely. It had been shown to him as a child by the older Goremin who supervised the ramblings of the young ones.

"Only in extreme circumstances should anyone take this route," he remembered Gorlushta saying. "It is too dangerous to take without excessive caution, and it is best that nobody know of it who might use it recklessly."

Its day had come at last, after many lifetimes of men, even those who were members of the Ancient Race. It lay there!

He growled a command and turned downstream, toward a place where winged buttresses of stone jutted over the water. It looked totally impossible and impassable, but his companions followed him, their feet crunching on the sleet, their breathing harsh in his sensitive ears.

It took hours to reach the place that was his goal, for progress was slow, and often they had to pause and take shelter when the wind, swirling out of the deep cut of the river, threatened to sweep them off the ledge they now followed. Luckily, there were crannies in the stone, deep enough for some protection, and Gorghoz managed to fight his way to one or another of them, as blasts howled along the cliff.

He found his way, at last, to a narrow cut in solid rock, leading back away from the precipice along the river. They retreated into the trees, now stunted and gnarled, that guarded the edge of the Forest Damariste.

There, out of the wind, his splayed feet picked up a familiar path. Invisible as it was to his eyes, it was there for his memory, and he followed it around convolutions of stone, down into a tunnel running below the winged rock that soared high above the current.

He emerged onto a shelf of granite, his feet submerged in running water but aware of the solidity of his footing. He turned to Riddle, who was just behind him, carrying Lute again, for on the ledge arms were safer than the cumbersome baskets.

"There is, beneath this wild water, a ledge of rock that crosses to the other side. When the ice locks up the headwaters, the level will fall, and we will be able, I think, to take that route. Night will bring great cold to the uplands from which the river runs, and in the morning we should make our attempt.

"It will not be easy, even then. I must cross first with a line, for the Turnig are too short in the leg to go safely in even a diminished current. They must have something to which to cling. Killeli will go with me, riding on my back, for he is agile and clever, and he may be able to help those coming after us.

"But for tonight, we can take cover inside the tunnel, if we can find a way to block the lower end of the passage, stopping the draught that pulls through it. There is wood for fires, above us.

"We should be able to warm ourselves, to cook hot food, and to rest enough to allow us to travel more comfortably, when dawn brings the deepest chill to the waters above."

He deposited Moonlight in a washed-out nook, along with the Turnig young and Lute, whose cough was less harsh, since taking the tea Chark had given him. Once they stopped the tunnel's end with robes and rocks and woven branches, the dark channel warmed somewhat, and the night passed in some comfort.

All too soon, however, the Goremin felt the approach of dawn, and that woke him from a sound sleep. Before he was quite ready to make the attempt, he found himself standing ankle-deep in water amid the icy wind that purled along the surface of the stream.

All the young and Moonlight were left in the tunnel until it was time to take them across, but the rest of the travelers were there, ready to help in any way they could. That was little comfort, as the Goremin set one wide foot into the water, feeling the bite of it through all his great body.

The level had lowered, and that was a comfort. Killeli, on his back, said nothing as he waded through the still swift current, holding his place on the stone ledge and digging in his icy toes with great difficulty.

No lesser being could possibly cross without help, and he felt again for the rope, which was uncoiling from his shoulder. He hoped it was stout enough to sustain the people who would come after him.

The river seemed far wider than it looked from the shore, but he persisted, leaning against the push of the water, curling his prehensile toes about the stone beneath them. At last he reached a sheltered spot behind an outcrop of rock, and Killeli scampered onto the bastion to relieve him of his weight.

The Goremin found a spur of stone to which to anchor his end of the rope. Killeli leaped into the water, his long hands clinging fast to the taut line, and scurried over the stream to the middle. There he found purchase and stood, his teeth chattering audibly, to steady the middle of the line.

A chain of Turnig moved onto the crossing, linked with more of the invaluable rope that Chark had brought. Riddle anchored the other end, watching closely as those carrying the small ones struggled to the other side. Then he went into the tunnel and brought out Moonlight, who still lay, pale and cold, in her trance.

He slung her on his back, securing her with strips of cloth, thus freeing his hands for the rope. Gorghoz watched, his body tense, as the poet made his slow way along the ledge, buried to the knees in rushing water. Killeli, holding fast, steadied him as he passed.

Once Riddle staggered ashore, chilled and exhausted, the furred man sped to the other shore and loosed the line. Then, holding and coiling as he came, he battled the waters as he moved to join his companions.

But that tingling presence in the air was growing again in intensity. Gorghoz felt the book, once more in the pouch at his back, begin to radiate its power once more, and it filled him with unease.

He shouted, "Hurry, Killeli! Hurry! Something is...." Before he could finish his words, a great floating log came rushing around the bend above the crossing and bore down upon the helpless Killeli. With a roar, Gorghoz surged into the current and hauled on the line with desperate strength, jerking Killeli out of the path of the tree trunk.

When they pulled him from the water, there was blood on his narrow head, and a flap of fur hung loose from one shoulder. Red drops sprinkled the wet stone as they hurried him up the all but invisible track leading away from the river, and Riddle, staggering along behind, took the time to scuff them away with his wet boots.

The will that had sent the log needed no guide, he knew, but there were other things that might follow a blood trail. Other things might also follow the book in Gorghoz's pack, and the thought made the poet shiver as he walked.

* * * * * *

Moonlight stood on insubstantial feet in a stranger place than she had ever Dreamed. Pillars of ice, their sharp angles catching the pale light and forming prismatic gleams inside them, sprang upward from a frozen floor, which shone like black glass. From some invisible source, illumination shone in diffused radiance from the pillars and from the frozen sculptures that were the groins of the roof, high above.

She moved forward, not walking but drifting effortlessly over the reflective surface. The place was like a temple, and yet it filled her with dread and chill. She tried to turn her gaze toward the sides of the long aisle down which she went, but some powerful will had caught her, holding every facet of her mind and body in an unbreakable grip.

Moonlight fought, deep inside herself, to regain control of this Dream. Surely she could shape it to her own will, moving herself back into her physical body, wherever that might be. It was not the way of a Dreamer to walk abroad clad only in the spirit. But no matter how she tried, still she was moved against her wishes toward the end of the crystalline chamber.

There was a series of ascending angles there, like a stair formed of glassy ice, cut into facets and glowing with all the colors of gems. A glow shone through the stuff, now rosy, now palest blue, now delicate green, and she could see that a shape hovered at the top, staring down at her with invisible but compelling eyes.

It was not, itself, a physical body. She was certain of that, for the glow refracted through the surrounding ice-jewels struck through its shadowy form.

She drifted against the base of the plinth, through it, and into the interior, which gave her the feeling of being inside a huge gem. The guiding will pulled her upward, slowly and inexorably, toward the waiting figure. As she neared the misty shape, which though tenuous and gray was well defined, she found her gaze locked onto the sphere of fog that served as a head. A point of brilliant light speared out of it, once she was on a level with the being.

That ray seemed to pierce her mind to its roots. She had never before had her thought invaded by that of another, and it seemed to her the ultimate in violation. She gasped, as a tendril of mist reached out from the center of the creature and curled about her.

"No!" Every atom of her Dreamer's strength and courage surged within her, resisting that clammy touch. The probe within her mind flinched with the shock of her resistance.

"Yes!" The word formed inside her, melting the hard core of resolve that seemed her last resource. Avid hunger ran through her, having its source in the voracious will of that other.

"Oh, yes!" And the tendril sank through her, chilling her to the heart. Moonlight braced her own will against it, set her mind on the warmest, kindliest things she could recall from her childhood, and set herself to endure, as her grandmother had taught her to do.

CHAPTER THIRTEEN

"There is a hunter whom the hunters fear...."
—Riddle

The land beyond the river was unforested, the hills thrusting higher and higher, like swells in some troubled ocean of stone and barren soil. The wind, once Riddle had followed the Goremin past the outlying barriers of rock outcrops, swept down without hindrance, freezing the moisture clinging to his clothing from the river passage.

He could hear the Turnig's small teeth chattering, and Lute, even wrapped in layer after layer of protecting felts, was shivering in his arms; Riddle regretted the warm baskets, lost in the stream. If they could not find shelter, they would all die, he was certain, of exposure and the coughing sickness.

Chark, struggling along ahead of him, turned her head to stare up at him through the thickening blast of snow and sleet. "We find hole soon, or we die," she said. Her tone was untroubled, for the Turnig accepted death as they did life: both were things over which few people had much control.

Riddle felt somewhat the same, but Lute was another matter. He must survive, or his nephew would die. That was a thing the Poet could not accept or allow, without making a fight of it. He nodded to Chark and handed her the child. Then he plowed ahead through the drifts alongside the path the Goremin had made. In a moment, he caught up with Gorghoz, who was helping the wounded Killeli, now bound about with bandages from Chark's supply, and limping forward with much determination.

"There is a valley, up ahead. House there! Trees, too, for fuel. Used to be..."—he gasped for breath, as his lungs chilled—"...farm. We may find help there! This way!"

Gorghoz nodded. His covering of long hair was trailing fringes of ice, and his knobby face was bluish with chill. He turned after the poet without protest, and the line of Turnig came after them, carrying their burdens of young ones and supplies. Their short legs were moving slowly, and their small furred faces were frosted with rime. Exhaustion was dogging their footsteps.

Riddle forced his aching legs and his numbed feet forward, breaking the trail now for everyone. He was facing directly into the wind, and the snowflakes stuck his eyelashes together as tears froze on his cheeks. He couldn't see where he was going, but his feet, in some strange way, knew the path to take, even buried beneath the deepening drifts.

The world dissolved into a swirl of ice and wind, of snow and fogged vision, but he trudged on, his head bowed and his back bent to force his way forward. Although he had wrapped himself in his heaviest cloak and hood, with a scarf wound about his chin, he felt his skin stiffening, his cheeks turning to marble.

Abruptly, he topped a ridge of snow-covered gravel; below there was a cupped valley, dark with conifers. As the wind gusted, a rift in the snow allowed him to see his goal.

The farmhouse stood, sturdy and dark, amid its circling trees, but no smoke rose from the chimney, and he could smell no hint of any on the wind. Still, it was shelter, and that was the thing most needed by his troop at the moment. The trees would provide fuel, and there was, he remembered, a great fireplace in the central hall of the house. Merely getting out of the wind would be a tremendous relief.

Gorghoz came up behind him and his sigh of satisfaction rose even above the whine of the wind. "Come, Poet," he said, pushing past the reeling Riddle, "Let me lead, now I can see where we must go. We will survive yet, if we can gain those walls."

Killeli, following close behind the Goremin and seeming much stronger than he had since his accident, touched the poet's arm. "I will help," he said. "You are very tired." He put a wiry shoulder beneath Riddle's armpit and it helped, as they made their way down the slope, skidding in the snow, finding their footing with difficulty. When they moved beneath the shelter of the valley's rim, the force of the wind was lessened; this allowed the following Turnig to force their half-frozen legs toward the waiting house.

Riddle knew the family whose ancestors built that house. For four generations of Men he had befriended them, as they struggled to farm the patches of fertile soil in their tiny valley. A stubborn sort of independence had kept them at their chosen work, though they knew he would have welcomed them in Damaria and given them other work to do there.

He respected them, was fond of them. And now he feared for them. In such weather, they would have had a huge fire roaring in their fireplace. Lights would have blazed through the crannies in the shutters, as the sun, hidden behind the turbulent clouds, had gone down behind the circling hills.

Riddle staggered momentarily, pulling Killeli off the track of the Goremin's huge feet. Stumbling over something buried in the snow, he fell into a drift, pulling the furred man down with him. He put his hands down to help in pushing himself upward, but what they touched was not frozen soil. He was touching a cold face, there beneath the layered white.

"Killeli!" The furry man turned and rose. Then he bent to help the freezing poet to his feet. "Killeli, there is someone under here. Dead. I felt his face."

There came a sharp intake of breath. Then the other called shrilly into the gusts of wind that found a way into the valley. "Gorghoz! Come quick!"

The Goremin was almost to the house, now, but he turned, gesturing for the Turnig to carry the Dreamer and go into shelter while he investigated this new call. In a moment, his long legs had brought him back to the spot where Riddle knelt beside the body in the snow.

"What?" he asked, as he dropped to his own knees beside the poet. Riddle was digging with both hands. Instead of replying, the poet pushed aside a layer and revealed a face, pale even against the snow. "This was Fergid, the son of Regusson. His family should live in that house. If he is dead, unburied, then all of his people must be. Killed by what?" He stared into the Goremin's face in the dimness of the snow light and the last reflected glimmer from the clouds overhead.

Gorghoz breathed a long sigh. "Again the old powers have come down with the north wind," he said. Riddle could see that even his huge strength had been depleted by the cold and the effort of making his way through the drifts.

"I had not thought they could arrive so quickly, but as soon as your kind lost control of Damaria, they evidently began to move. Perhaps even before. That one who captured the Dreamer was some extension of the Mover, I am certain. Even the weather, I think, is dancing to his piping. It should not be so harsh this early in the winter. He is slowing us, preventing us from crossing the hills and finding sanctuary in the City in the Mist."

"But he—the Mover..."—Riddle felt his heart congeal at the thought of that power, believed to be contained and rendered harmless so very long ago—"...does not leave his own place. What has he sent here to do this? Or is it the work of the New People, who have removed from their hearts any kindness we tried to instill in them?"

"Who can tell? The Lirfolk are wild and cruel enough for such work, without much encouragement; whoever it might be who drove them, there is no one here now. I could feel a living presence, if one lingered. I can feel nothing but the small lives of the trees and the living cold." He rose to his feet and pulled the poet up after him.

"We must go inside and make fire. This poor man will not come to more harm, here in the snow. We will bury his body, when we can, but if we freeze we will be unable even to do that much for him." Again he pulled at the poet's arm, and Riddle allowed himself to be led, his eyes still blurred, his bones creaking with the chill, toward the dark house.

The Turnig had not waited. When the three crunched their way across the drifted porch and into the building, closing the heavy door behind them with both latch and barring beam, they found Chark sparking a flame into tinder.

Already the fireplace was filled with carefully arranged sticks and splits of wood, laid ready for the burning. As the tinder flared up, the dried fringes of bark on the smaller sticks blazed into sudden life, curling and twisting in the flames. The spicy scent of aromatic wood filled the place, driving out the damp smell that tainted the rooms.

Riddle found Moonlight lying on a pile of felts beside the hearth, and the young ones, including Lute, were a series of bundles beyond her. They were just beginning to wake and protest at the lack of the motion that had lulled them to sleep during their long journey.

Removing his snow-dampened cloak and hood, Riddle shook them briskly and hung them in the kitchen, where another fire had been kindled in the cooking hearth. Many garments of all sizes and shapes were drying there, for even the Turnig had been forced to supplement their coats of fur with outer ones of felt in the blasts of this storm.

The small people were rummaging in the pantries of the old house for anything of use to them, and soon they found that the winter's food stores garnered by the lost family were untouched. Squash and other dried vegetables, grain for the grinding, and fruit, both dried and stored in jars and covered with honey, were there. Regusson's family had been well found for the winter.

Riddle found himself wondering, as he smelled the stew of vegetables simmering in the iron pot over the kitchen fire, where the others were. Strong Lant, laughing Deri, dour Brend, teasing Myrta—were their bodies, too, lying out there in the snow?

Regusson and Tyrza, stout as ancient oaks, would not have died easily. Surely there must be some trace, out there in the blizzard-ridden gardens, of the battle the family had made. For there was no hint, inside the house, of anything amiss, though there had been no time for a thorough search of the place.

Those who dwelled there might have gone out for a morning's tasks, leaving their table set for the nooning. Handwork had been laid aside to be taken up again in the evening; even an ancient book, in which the history of their lives was written, sat waiting for another day's records to be set down.

He carried a bowl of steaming broth back into the main chamber and knelt beside Lute. The small boy was sitting, awake at last, staring into the blaze as if unable to believe in it. Nearby, Chark was already feeding sips of the liquid to Moonlight, taking care not to strangle the unconscious woman as she fed her.

"Where are we?" asked Lute, catching his uncle's sleeve as if for reassurance. "Fire!" He turned and pointed to the flames.

"Soup," said Riddle, presenting a spoonful. That caught the child's interest at once, and he finished the hot broth quickly.

About them, the Turnig children, fed and warm, were beginning to tumble about the floor in playful heaps, and soon Lute joined them, his cough only an occasional problem, as he rolled and wrestled with the others.

Riddle, his own hunger satisfied at last, returned to the fire and sat watching Moonlight's pale face return to a more normal coloring, as she warmed through. Gorghoz came to join him, and they sat in silence, seeing faint hints of expression move across the features of the unconscious Dreamer.

For a long while, she had seemed to be in a trance, her mind far removed from her helpless flesh. But now, as they observed her, Riddle saw a struggle begin, behind that pale face. Doubt. Fear. Anger. Determination. Despair. All were visible to the intent watchers.

He touched the Goremin lightly. "Look!" The word was the merest breath, as he saw a frightening change beginning in the face that had become so familiar.

CHAPTER FOURTEEN

"Gaze into a rose of icy flame...."
                                                    —Riddle

Even as the misty tentacle began drawing her toward the core of that shape, Moonlight found something stirring within her. Words her grandmother had spoken, long ago, seemed to form in her mind. The fine, pale face, the earnest eyes—those were growing in clarity behind her eyelids.

"You may find, Child, that you must deal with those who are cold and cruel. I pray this never happens, but should it, there is a way to chill our Dreaming warmth to an icy edge that can counter such forces. Remember, Moonlight! Remember...."

The Dreamer felt, for the first time, a bit of confidence return to her. She could not battle this power in any way she had ever used. But there was, in her training, such discipline, such strength of will, and such rigorous skills that she felt she might possibly be able to deal with the foggy image which was sinking into the rosy gem on which it stood, bearing her Dream-body with it.

Moonlight ceased her resistance to the motion and to the will that caused it. She drew inside herself, deeper and deeper, past the concern that made her people Dreamers, past the love she had borne for her kin and her new comrades. She went beyond fear for herself and her own life, going into a cool, clear place she had almost forgotten existed.

"You must be colder, more cruel than those who confront you." That was her grandmother, speaking to the child she had been. "And you must do this without letting it contaminate you, making you insensitive to others who are not evil. Be swift and chilly as a sword to any who threaten those under your care. And when you turn from that task, put it away and close the door into that part of you. Grow cold, Moonlight! Grow cold!"

The tendril helped her, as she began doing the thing she had almost forgotten was possible. She froze, feeling every part of her mind crystallize into gemlike angles to match those now moving about her. Hard edges, knife-like angularities—those were what she needed now.

She went willingly with the guiding tentacle, deep into the cluster of colorful ice. On either side, congealed into the formations, she could see shapes, some human, some animal, some even Goremin. They seemed agonized, even in that frozen sleep, and she pitied them.

She pushed that feeling away, for it was not a part of the cruel self she was becoming. She slipped silently through the pile, and something inside knew the nearness of a thing more evil than any she had ever thought to face. The chamber of ice was an expression of its own nature, although that was far colder than any natural thing could become. She felt something inside her curl away in revulsion, but she forced it back into focus.

I am colder than you, she thought, knowing that her words would reach the sensing of the Mover. She went through a facet and found herself confronting something that had no face, no body, no tangible part at all, and yet which was appallingly real. More real than any creature she had ever Dreamed.

Strangely, she was no longer afraid or despairing. Now she was, most truly, her grandmother's heir and the Dreamer she had been trained so stringently to become. She felt as if she might glitter with her own internal chill, as she confronted the vision of the Mover in the North.

"Dreamer...." The voice was a whisper and a wail, the rushing of wind and the grating of ice floes against glaciers.

"Verrainig." She waited to see what effect that would have, for few knew the name of the Mover from the North, and even among Dreamers it was almost unknown. She had been probably the last member of her kind who could have called its name.

The shadow pulsed with rosy light, and she felt certain she had surprised him. She had hoped to shake him...but that was unlikely. If only she could hold against him, that was all she asked.

"Moonlight." The breathy gust carried her own name to her ears. She was not disturbed. "Do you think me a witling, to be frightened by my own name?" she asked. Her tone was as cold as even her grandmother could have asked, and that, at last, disturbed the thing within the shadow.

The mist quivered, very slightly. The frozen facets glowed and faded, glowed and faded, as if some heartbeat had become visible. "Take care. You are toying with your death."

Aha. This was the first sentence spoken by the thing, and she felt that might be a good omen. If she could irritate it, anger it, make it grow warm with its own wrath, while she remained frozen and inviolate, perhaps there would be a way to escape.

"Death? Do you fear death, Cold One? I am astonished. The Immortals should be above such petty things. I am merely mortal, and I find it trivial. I prefer it, indeed, to the sort of existence your kind must endure, living only at secondhand through your puppets and your tools, or in Dream, as you appear to me now." She waited, cold and amused, for the result of that jab.

Suddenly the interior of the gem was gone, and she was suspended in a yellowish fog. Shrieks and moans echoed through the muggy clouds, and she could make out words of despair, words of anger, words of hopelessness.

"These are those whom I have possessed and discarded. Those who have defied me are in far worse case than this. Dare you risk that, Dreamer?"

She managed a frozen laugh. "Do you think to imprison a Dreamer? Whatever you do, in time I will form my own reality, which will bear no resemblance to your intention, I assure you. While you think of me screaming in agony, I will be walking in a wood or playing in a fountain. You cannot affect a Dreamer more than a very little, Verrainig."

She was back inside the ice, and the shadow was now pulsing scarlet. She felt a surge of hope, for surely the Mover was becoming too moved, himself, to sustain his control over her Dreamer's will. Moonlight could feel his anger changing the light to red, and she regained enough volition to turn and look out through the crazy angles into the chamber behind her. The soaring pillars glowed crimson; the vaulted roof, far above, seemed afire. Even the black floor was aboil with scarlet reflections.

But she went deep again, into the place her grandmother had shown to her. She remained cold and composed, her spirit armored with frost and her mind sharp-edged as glass.

"You are easily disturbed," she said, and now she could hear her own voice echoing from all sides. "How secure you must have felt, in your hiding place. Else you would have kept your wits and your skills sharper than they seem to be. Or have you grown lazy, as you grew old?" There came a grating breath, as if heralding a reply. But she laughed again, suddenly feeling herself gaining control, able to shape this terrible Dream.

She envisioned a wall of diamond glass, rising between herself and Verrainig. The pulsing red light reflected from it, distorting his misty shape, locking his will away from hers.

"I am free of you, Verrainig. You cannot entrap a Dreamer, and even you should have understood that. You have been apart from the warm-blooded kinds too long, or you would know better. Now I will go, and if you again enter one of my visions, I will battle you on your own ground."

Now the grating roar filled her mind. "Do not think to escape again, Dreamer! I learn quickly!"

Now she moved out through the crystals, into the long nave of the frozen temple. Around her, colors leaped like flame inside the pillars of ice, and the floor shimmered with orange and black, as if she walked over coals of fire. The air shuddered with the roars of the voice behind her, bellowing with awful impact.

The columns shivered, and a tinkle from above marked the fall of a delicate sculpture against its curved support. She saw, beneath her Dream-body, the surface of the floor melting, the skim of water rippling in the vibrations that now seemed about to shake down the place.

"I control this Dream!" said Moonlight, and into her mind came a vision of a big farmhouse, a chamber filled with firelight and tired travelers. The shape of Gorghoz dozed, leaning against a cushioned corner, and Riddle lay beside the small figure that was Lute.

"I control my own vision!" Now her voice was firm and sure, and as she spoke she found she no longer drifted between the columns of ice. Now she whisked out and away, through snowy winds, although she could not feel their chill.

She was warm. She was safe. She opened her eyes, and there was the fire she had Dreamed, though for a moment she could not be certain this, too, was not a vision, instead of the reality she had felt it to be.

There came a small whimper to her ears, and she rose on an elbow and saw that one of the Turnig young was waking. Chark was up in an instant, wriggling across the floor to check on her charge. When she looked up and saw the Dreamer watching, she gave her chittering chuckle. "Welcome back, Dreamer," she said. "You be hungry?"

At that Moonlight laughed aloud. It was so like the Turnig, that practical attention to immediate needs. But she found that she was, indeed, ravenous.

"I am very hungry," she whispered, taking care not to waken the many sleepers who had put down bedding in the room heated by the great fire.

Chark beckoned, rising to her furry feet and pattering away toward the kitchen. The girl managed to rise also, finding, after a moment, that her legs steadied. She followed the Turnig through a wide hallway, which was hung on both sides with tools and harnesses, drying onions and herbs.

The kitchen was almost as large as the great chamber they had left, and Chark motioned to her to sit at a table that seemed made for a very large family. Benches made of split and smoothed logs extended down both sides, and generations of use had polished their surfaces to a rich patina that felt like satin to her hand.

"Is everyone all right?" she asked, as Chark ladled soup from the big pot over the fire and held it out to her. "I was...busy and could not keep a focus on what was happening to you and the others."

"We crossed river, after you fall. Killeli was wet through...log almost finish him, but he is very strong, that one. Riddle know this place and family who lived here. We find one dead in snow; no trace of rest."

Moonlight sipped the soup from the big horn spoon, thinking hard. Something had entered her Dream and threatened the young ones she had taken there. As if a great hand reached after her, she had been jerked out of the path of the thing that searched for her, and for a long while she had been outside anything she knew.

A step sounded in the passage, and Gorghoz entered the warm room. He looked into her eyes and nodded, as if satisfied.

"Was it you who pulled me away from that...being?" she asked.

"I cast you into a place of unbeing, for the time, until we could do better. I thought you might remain there until we could wake you. How did you return to us without help?" Gorghoz was taking a bowl of soup for himself, but he kept staring at her, as if puzzled.

"A Dreamer does not react as others do. And someone pulled me away from that limbo into which you set me. Verrainig took me to his icy realm, and he almost overcame me before I learned how to deal with him."

The Goremin gasped, setting down his spoon with a splash of hot liquid. "Verrainig himself?" His deep voice almost quavered.

"Himself. But I managed to disturb him. I made him angry. Only my grandmother's teaching saved me, and I do not claim I could have done it alone. I used that old training and it worked. I left him roaring with rage. His temple of ice was clashing and crashing as the noise brought down icicles from high above."

Gorghoz sighed. "That was well done. And yet it will mean we must take care more than ever. The Mover from the North will be set upon destroying us, every one, and he will want to take back the book more intensely. We must take care, Moonlight. How can we travel through the hills in such weather, with that searching spirit trying to spy us out?"

She looked into his eyes, appalled. She knew with sudden conviction that she should have allowed the terrible will to absorb her, to swallow all she was, if that would have kept it busy and allowed the Goremin to carry the book away from the lands now subject to the will of Verrainig.

She had made a terrible error. Her own arrogance had hidden from her the probable result of damaging the self-esteem of Verrainig, the Mover from the North.

CHAPTER FIFTEEN

"And all around the snow lay blanketed,
While winds from northward sang their frozen songs."
—Riddle

Chark did not like the houses of Men. She had visited them, over the good years, oftener than most Turnig did. She had bartered herbs and wild fruits and nuts from the forest, as well as special vegetables from her gardens, with the farm wives living in the fields bordering the Forest Damariste. The woven cloth of wool and the iron pots had been things the Turnig had no skills for making, and her people found them useful. But she had never become used to the smells of Men or to their activities, and this new house was no exception.

Still, she knew, deep in her Turnig instincts, that there was no turning back. The forests where her people had crept from their holes under the guidance of the Ancient Race were closed to them, now. The teachings that had brought her kind so far from its origins were not any part of the new men. Enemies were at that moment, she felt certain, hunting small groups of Turnig in their burrows in Damaria, or would be when the weather turned again. The thought saddened her.

She set fresh sticks beneath the simmering kettle, scrubbed the bowls for future use, and stared about the kitchen. A female who has loved to prepare food for her kin knows a place where one of kindred mind has worked. This was such a place. Of all the rooms in this house, she felt most at home cooking over the fire or standing on a stool at the washing-up pan.

She set the metal fire-wall before the flames to keep stray sparks from setting the place afire, took up a candle, and moved up the dark passage toward the room where the others slept. As she went, something troubled her; a sense of that other woman was like tiny voice inside, warning her that something important had been left undone. A finger of chill, distinct from the cold of this unheated part of the house, ran up her furry spine.

"We have not searched the house above the stair!" she said softly. That was a mistake, she felt. So strong was the feeling that Chark went carefully among the sleepers to wake Riddle.

He was her friend, the one she had known for much of her life, and now he was the one she chose to help her investigate the intuition that troubled her mind. The Goremin and the Dreamer were new friends, but she did not turn to them in an emergency.

She touched the poet's shoulder gently, and Riddle turned and stared up at her. Chark put her finger to her mouth in the old gesture for quiet, and he stood and followed her out of the room. There in the passage, at the spot where the cold had stopped her, she paused and looked up at the tall poet. "There be someone up there, perhaps? We go to see?"

Riddle's summer tan was fading, and now he seemed paler than usual. His gaze swept up the narrow stair leading to the bedchambers above. "I did not search there. Who looked?" he asked the Turnig.

"I look. Not good, just glance about. See nobody. Call very loud. No answer. But now I think we need look there."

"Yes." There was no doubt in his voice, and he bent to take her small hand. "Yes, we must. Something may be there still, and it might be dangerous."

* * * * * * *

Riddle had been so terribly weary when he came into the house of his old friends that he had been forced to rest before wondering too much about their fate. Now he had eaten and slept. He was warmed and once more filled with the concerns that befitted one of the Ancient Race. A search must be made, and he had a feeling that it might result in painful discoveries.

He squeezed the hand of the small person beside him. Then he mounted the stair, motioning for her to follow him. As he went upward, he felt something might well be waiting...something he did not want to see.

The first bedroom was empty. Each of the other four also held no one, alive or dead, for the pair of them rummaged in cupboards and beneath the beds, missing nothing. But at the end of the upstairs passage was a door that could not be opened. Its lock was frozen fast, and it seemed to be barred from within, when he tried to shake it. "Did anyone try looking there?" he asked Chark.

She shook her head. "Too much hurry. We look, see nothing, go back to build fire, make food."

"It must come open. Can you feel the cold seeping out from around the edges of the door?" He shivered, feeling a different sort of chill reach out from the hidden room beyond the closed panel.

Chark's dark eyes widened, and she gave a great shudder. She backed away slowly, as if pushed by unseen hands. "Bad thing, there. Bad thing!"

Riddle moved to her side and put his hand on her furry head. "No need for you to look. Go and fetch Gorghoz, will you? He will be able to open this with one heave, I suspect."

As her little feet pattered away down the steps, he found himself feeling terribly alone. He had faced evil things before, had fought unjust men in his travels about the continent upon which Damaria existed, but never had he felt so terrified.

Waiting there in the cold corridor, lighted only by the candle that Chark had left with him, Riddle stared at the door, dreading what they might find behind it. He had loved generations of this family he had known, helping them when he could, comforting them when he could not. Now he had a sick certainty that he was about to look upon the dead faces of Regusson and his kin. Everything that made him one of the Ancient Race protested against the thought.

The great feet of the Goremin thumped solidly up the stair. The huge head, gray and lumpy, came within the feeble glimmer of the candle's rays, and the pale eyes gleamed as he looked questioningly at Riddle.

The poet gestured toward the door. "Something is behind that. Can you feel it?"

Gorghoz stood as if frozen, and Riddle knew that the Goremin's greater powers of perception were probably reeling under the impact of the sensation that had reached out to bring them there. Only his exhaustion had kept the Goremin from sensing this much earlier, for his kind was sensitive to horrors.

"Yes." It was the merest breath of a word, and Gorghoz moved with it to the door. He tested the panels with both huge hands, shaking it against its hinges, but it was solidly set and hinged on the inside. With a sigh, the great being splayed one wide hand against the carved wood and pushed. With a splintering and crackling, the wood gave way, leaving an irregular hole in the middle of the door. Riddle reached through the sharp fragments with his smaller arm and found the bar, which he managed to unfasten and slide aside.

Another push from Gorghoz broke the tang of the lock. The door creaked open dolefully, letting the faint gleam of candlelight into the dark space beyond it.

"We need torch," came a small voice from behind the Goremin. And there stood Chark, holding two pitch-soaked torches of the sort farmers use when attending to outside emergencies at night. They lit the first from the candle. Then Riddle, taking his courage in both hands, accepted one and thrust it into the room.

For a moment, the flame seemed smothered, the light dimming, the pitch sputtering fitfully as if the fire were about to die. A gust of staleness, tainted with another, worse odor, fled through the door as if pursued by the light. The draught from the window, which had been broken, did nothing to help the atmosphere of the place.

And then Riddle saw the family of his old friend. Deri, Myrta, Lant, and Brend were skewered to the farther wall with many small flint knives, thrust through the skin of arms and sides, hips and legs. Their frozen faces did not hold the peaceful expressions of death, but were agonized, teeth bared and eyes wide, as if protesting the last thing they saw in life.

Sick, grieving, he touched one stiff hand, to find it hard and cold. He turned, holding up the torch. On the facing wall he found his old friend and his wife Tyrza. They were not pinned with knives. They were frozen to the paneled wall by a sort of slime that had turned to ice. Regusson's dead eyes stared straight into his own, and there he read a plea.

"If it can be done, I will avenge you. And if that cannot be done, I will help to take the burden with which we have been entrusted beyond the power of the Mover in the North. I promise that, Regusson. You will live in my memory, with your people, for as long as I am alive."

He did not realize he had spoken aloud until the Goremin touched his arm, nodding agreement. "If we can take that...thing... out of Damaria, beyond the ocean, it will hurt the one responsible for sending this death more than anything else."

Chark, to Riddle's surprise, interrupted them. Her eyes gleamed red in the torchlight, and she was sniffing the air, all her animal instincts aroused fully.

"Cannot stay here!" she said. "Put them other place, burn house. Bad thing come here now. Any time, can come here. I smell watcher, somewhere close by; Turnig have good nose. You say too much, if there be listener, too!"

Riddle, bringing himself out of his preoccupation with his own grief, realized she was correct. Where the hand of the Mover had come, no matter which of his minions had done the deed, it could reach again at will. And now it might know they had the book, for there could have been nothing else implied in his promise to his old friend. If some unbodied intelligence stood guard over its victims, it now knew what they carried with them.

He stared into the eyes of the Goremin, and they reflected his sudden understanding. They turned together and chipped the bodies loose from the walls. In the bedrooms, they laid each corpse upon a waiting bed and covered it with the blankets that Tyrza had woven from the wool of her own sheep.

Then they closed the door at the top of the stair and went heavily downward to give this terrible news to their companions.

CHAPTER SIXTEEN

"Lost wayfarers go struggling through the snow,
fleeing the hunters howling at their heels."
                                        —Riddle

It was now well after midnight, and the Turnig slept as if drugged, exhausted with their struggles of the day before. After considering the situation, Riddle and Gorghoz decided not to wake them or Moonlight, who was now sleeping naturally. All would need every bit of strength they possessed if they were to go out into the blizzard, which still roared about the eaves of the house and puffed ash and smoke down the chimney into the room.

They lay down, after feeding the fire, and tried to sleep, but Riddle found it difficult to forget the new peril that hung, literally, above their heads. Those who had died at the hands of the Mover's tools were vessels, now, of his will. Their spirits had fled safely, but the bodies formed a toe-hold here for the sensing of the Mover.

He turned and sighed, there before the fire, thinking of the hundreds of things that must be done in the morning. They must take out of the house every blanket left untainted, all the stored food, extra torches and pots and weapons. There had been barrows in the out-sheds, in the old days; he hoped they were still there, for the burden would be far more than even the many Turnig could manage to transport.

Still, they must have the supplies, if they were to survive this unseasonably cold winter in the hills. If they could have sheltered in this stout house over the cold months, that would have served them well, but the hand of the Mover had touched it, and it would be no shelter but a trap, if they remained. He dreaded telling the others the dreadful news, when they woke.

At last, when he knew he would not sleep at all, he rose and crept from the room. In the cellar was a great store of wood, dry and waiting for use. He found his way into the midst of the orderly piles and checked the positioning of the fuel. Then he laid trailers of logs from one to the other, knowing the intense heat that burning would generate would consume the house above.

Not a bone or a tooth must be left of those pitiful victims in the bedrooms. No one knew the extent of the powers of the Mover, but he dared not risk leaving anything that might serve him, when the party turned their faces away from Regusson's home. The house must burn, with its lawful tenants. He would have Fergid brought in from the frozen garden, to go into the Afterward with his kin.

There was tinder in baskets, and he tucked wads beneath the stacks, getting them ready for the kindling. As he moved about, he heard quiet steps on the stone stair from the kitchen, and he paused to see who came.

Moonlight stepped into the cellar, her candle held high. "I thought you might do this. It would have been too easy, too simple for us to find a haven so quickly. Gorghoz told me about—those above. I am sorry. But I am here to help, if I can."

He smiled, finding it something of a struggle, yet feeling warmed by her solid good will. "I am almost done, but if you like, you might hold the light so I can finish laying the wick to set this ablaze. It is hard to do in the dark, and I daren't risk trying to keep my torch about me."

He worked quickly, and she said nothing, merely holding the candle to let him see. Then they looked about the cavernous space, where black shadows danced beyond the piles of wood and the great casks of wine that Regusson had fermented from his own fruit.

"That will burn well," said Moonlight. Her words were simple, but her tone held a deep sadness.

Riddle turned and looked down into the Dreamer's eyes. "Thank you for coming," he said. "Yes, it will burn well, taking with it a long span of my life and something of my heart. I kill reluctantly, yet if there were a way to slay the Mover from the North, I would set my blade to his throat and slice deep. I think I would never feel one moment of regret."

She nodded. "Even Verrainig is not flesh, unfortunately. I have seen his shadow, and that has not made me want to see his substance. But perhaps we can hurt him in ways he did not expect, as we go forward toward our goal. He does not respect those who walk in flesh, Riddle. He finds us trivial and helpless." She smiled fiercely, and he saw her amber eyes were shining with anger.

He took up his torch from the sconce where it had waited and turned toward the stair. "At the last, I shall cast this down onto the wick. Then we shall run as fast and as far as we are able, before we find shelter or die in the cold."

"We will not die!" Her tone was harsh with determination, and as they regained the kitchen he found himself agreeing. They were tough, all of them. They were bent upon escaping the evil here, and they might do some damage to their enemies, in the course of that journey.

* * * * * * *

Gorghoz knew that when they left the shelter of walls it would be his strength that must save most of his smaller companions. The wind, now howling with increased fury about the house, bore on its blast chunks of ice, as well as blinding snow. His directional sense would keep them from staggering in circles until they fell into the drifts and died. His great legs could tramp out a path amid depths of snow that would stop the others in their tracks.

Beyond his concern about his own ability to hold out until they located some shelter, there was another worry. Who had used those tiny flint knives? Surely the Lirfolk would not venture out into such weather, unless they were driven by a terrible need—or, perhaps, a more terrible will. Still, he found the thought returning to his mind, as he welcomed the poet and the Dreamer back into the circle of warmth. As they took their quiet places beside him, the Turnig began to move and make noises that said they were about to begin waking.

Light was touching the sky above the storm clouds, Gorghoz knew. His old bones felt the sun, distant and cold now, about to rise beyond the mountains.

"We will go as soon as possible," he said to Riddle. His hand went out to touch Lute's round bottom lightly, as the child snuffled against his felts and sighed again into sleep.

Riddle stared into the fire and thrust a fresh stick of wood into the glowing coals. "Who was it?" he asked. "Who did the actual killing?"

Gorghoz had known he must be wondering that. It saddened him that he must answer with worse tidings still. "The Lirfolk, I think." He waited for the effect of his words.

Moonlight stiffened and sat straighter. Riddle reached to take a hand of each of them, holding tightly, as if for comfort. "But they have been quiet since the Ancient Race came up from the south!" the poet protested.

"That is the tale told in the firelight at evening by grandams," the Goremin agreed. "But so are other things. The book you carried,

Dreamer, was such a tale among my folk.

"Orm, whom you sensed beneath the wood, is stirring now, and in the north, beneath the temple of Verrainig, his opposite and equal is awake as well. Orm is the oldest of tales, thought to be mist and moonshine for ages of Men and even of Goremin."

Riddle shivered, and Moonlight turned pale in the firelight. "Are all the myths, then, true? If that is so, then we face a far worse journey than any of us suspected, when we began it."

"We may well be hunted by worse things than cold and sickness," Gorghoz agreed. "To shiver through the snow with the hunters of myth at our heels is not a thing that makes for pleasant travel. We must go, and it is time to wake our fellows and to secure the small ones. The Lirfolk love to steal the young of Man. Or so I have been told."

Shuddering at the thought of his nephew in the hands of those fierce hunters, Riddle rose. Before the sun had cleared the mountains or the morning blast had begun grating about the eaves, he and his companions were once again outside in the snow.

CHAPTER SEVENTEEN

"The tall gray hunters of the north...."
—Riddle

Although he knew they should be moving away as quickly as their legs could carry them, Riddle stood with the group of wayfarers at the gate beyond the orchard trees, staring at the house that had welcomed them and saved their lives. There was not one, Riddle knew, who did not grieve at what must happen now.

He had stood at the head of the stone stair and flung a torch onto the tinder he had left ready. Then, last of all, he had gone from the wide door, leaving it open behind him to the dawn wind. And now he found himself locked into place, as were the others, waiting to see the funeral pyre of Regusson and his people. It seemed the least he could do to honor them.

It felt like a very long while, there in the chill wind and the gritty beginnings of a new snow, before warm light began to shine through the windows. That light turned from gold to orange and from orange to scarlet; the burden of snow slid from the roof in a hiss of steam. As the slates of the housetop cracked and shattered, the heat of the flames reached out to touch his face. Riddle knew the bedrooms where his friends waited were now wreathed in redder funeral blossoms than any he could have picked for them in summer. Somehow, the notion comforted him.

They would go out in a blast of heat, countering the cold will that had caused their deaths. Their clean ashes would mix with the soil they had loved, and where they rested real flowers would bloom, in time. Perhaps, in distant seasons to come, Damaria would again be clean and wholesome, and others would tend the soil and the fruit trees. Another house might rise, in time, to stand where this had stood.

Now the windows shot gouts of fire into the blizzard, and even in the blast of the wind Riddle felt too warm. A dull roaring accompanied the death of the old home, as if the building itself groaned.

Gripping Lute tightly, his small face uncovered to let him see the fire, Riddle said to the boy, "Remember this, Lute. The people who built that house were good friends to our family. Will you remember?"

"Fire!" said the child, his voice small in the howling wind. "Friends? Fire!"

"Yes," said his uncle. "Friends and fire. But I think you will remember."

The roof sank in a gush of sparks and smoke, and the walls sagged outward, buckling and falling at last. Even the storm seemed to pause for an instant as the heat gusted outward. Riddle's eyes streamed as the smoke stung them, and Lute began coughing again.

A hand caught Riddle's elbow. "Come!" said the Goremin's deep voice. "It is time and past time!"

Killeli came up on his other side. "I will carry the child for a bit," he said, extending his long, thin arms. "When I tire, you take him again. I have recovered from my injuries, I think. Your legs are longer, and if you go behind Gorghoz, it will be easier for the small people."

It seemed a good plan, and Riddle set off in the footsteps of the Goremin, trying his best to stamp out a trail between the big prints. It seemed much better than trying to lead the line of travelers, for he had only to keep his gaze fixed on the broad back ahead of him, letting Gorghoz's keen perceptions hunt out a way.

All too soon, his legs ached with cold and weariness, however. The Goremin slowed, and at last he stopped in the lee of one of the hills. "Look back," he said. "The Turnig are struggling already. We must go more slowly, or we will leave them behind."

When the last straggler had caught up, they passed around padded pottery jugs of soup, and the warmth put new life into the travelers. Then it was time to move again, and Riddle knew that however much his own limbs protested, the Turnig were in worse condition.

They wore out the day, resting when they must, eating cold food when they rested. When the pewter sky faded to dark gray and the snow lessened a bit, they had gone deep among a tumble of round hills overgrown with scrubby conifers. Everything was covered with snow, but Riddle was too old a traveler to be frustrated by that.

He led the way around the southern side of a tall hill and found a bluff sheltering a space beneath the level of the wind. A huge drift had piled against the stone, and the poet and the Goremin dug into it, stamping out a series of round rooms.

Behind them came Killeli, who had entrusted Lute to Chark. The three packed the snow hard to make wind-proof walls. It took some time to make enough space for all the Turnig to shelter there, but in time they had a tight chain of bubbles beneath the snow. They poked holes in each for ventilation, before they stopped their work. Extra blankets and felts were used to line the spaces, and the presence of so many furry bodies, once they shook off the accumulated snow, soon began warming the air. A glaze of ice formed on the inside, making the chambers even tighter.

They slept warmer than they had dreamed they could, that night, and Riddle found time to bless his many years of wandering and making do in harsh conditions. Huddled against Gorghoz and Chark, with Lute curled in his arms, he passed the night without any feeling of alarm.

When light shone through their frozen roof, he joined Gorghoz in forcing a way through the new accumulations of snow blocking their entryway. The Turnig, gathering up the robes and felts, waited patiently, but now their eyes were brighter and their small bodies seemed better able to attack the snowy hills, after their rest.

They burst out into a morning of blinding sunlight. The countryside had undergone a change so drastic Riddle hardly recognized even the largest of the juniper-crowned hills about them. The cold still held. The drifts were not melting, but he knew that before noon in this latitude they would be walking in the wet.

They plowed out of their sheltered spot behind the hill and made their way toward the north and west, guided by Riddle's knowledge of the land and the Goremin's unerring instinct for direction. The sun blazed down, and soon they were pulling off scarves and mittens, hoods and cloaks, and bundling them into their packs. Their efforts, in addition to the warmth of the sunlight, made them glow. As it turned out, that was a very good thing, for just as the sun stood overhead, Riddle heard a thump and a smothered shriek.

He stopped at once and turned, with Gorghoz at his heels, to find what problem had beset those at the rear of the Turnig line. Chark, who had brought up the end of the group, checking those ahead of her for exhaustion, was lying flat, gesturing frantically for the others to hurl themselves face-down against the snow.

Although he had no idea of the reason for it, Riddle flung himself down and crawled toward the little Turnig, whose pack, he suddenly realized, seemed strangely decorated. Once he came near enough, he understood her anxiety.

A short arrow, fletched with the feathers of the checkered grainbird, had gone through a corner of her pack. The felt blanket stuffed into it had kept it from penetrating her side, as well. He could see the chipped flint of the point showing through the exit hole. A scratch beneath the fur of her pelt dripped a single scarlet drop into the snow.

The Lirfolk were on their track.

* * * * * * *

Moonlight, still weakened by her long trance and her encounter with Verrainig, saw at once what was taking place. As Riddle helped Chark, the Dreamer motioned for those carrying the little ones to huddle behind an outcrop of stone. Then she looked about for an avenue of escape, though in the blanket of white all ways looked the same.

Gorghoz came crawling toward her, his odd shape and great size looking very strange and forbidding as he swam through the snow. "We must go due west," he said. "There are buildings there, a city built long ago, before even the time of my people.

"Take the Turnig! Go fast, keeping the shadow of the sun behind you, once it goes down a bit. I will help Riddle. We must..."— he grimaced, which made his usual forbidding expression grow positively frightening—"...hold them back...."

"...or they will pick us off, one by one, as we move," she said. She did not like the situation, but nothing could be done except to try getting the Turnig and the children to some sort of safety.

She found Killeli at her elbow, his arms full of Lute again. "I go first," he said. "You come behind and see if any need help." Then he plunged off in a spray of displaced snow, heading between two pudding-basin hills whose toes almost touched, leaving a narrow gap through which they might pass.

As she took her place behind the last struggling Turnig, Moonlight felt a pluck at her sleeve. She saw another arrow caught there, and she almost touched its point, which thrust through the fabric. But a shout from Riddle, now well behind them, stopped her hand. "They use poison!" he cried. "Chark is already feeling it, even though her wound is tiny. Pull it out by the shaft, whatever you do! Never touch the flint!"

Shaking inside, she gingerly tugged the thing out of her felted sleeve, making a considerable hole in the process, and looked about for a safe place to deposit it. As her head turned, she saw a glimpse of motion behind a tumble of rocks to her right. Without thinking she flipped the arrow toward it.

There came a doleful cry across the snow, and a gray-clad figure leaped to its feet behind the sheltering barrier, clutched its right eye with both hands, and slumped forward over the biggest of the boulders. Moonlight realized with horror that her instinctive gesture had killed one of the Lirfolk, which was not a thing she had intended. Even though the gray people wanted nothing more than her own blood, a Dreamer did not kill.

She went on again, shivering, yet keeping a close eye on her charges. She knew she must put that act behind her, for she had lives to save. The narrow gap between the hills, as she drew nearer to it, took on a more threatening look. Killeli, now well ahead of his short-legged companions, seemed to think so, too. He turned back and stopped those just behind him.

In the distance, there came a war-cry, shrill and disturbing. Gorghoz's deep voice bellowed, and Riddle's shout rang against the hills. They were being attacked from behind. It made no sense to risk walking into an ambush in front as well.

The Dreamer caught Killeli's arm. "Is there a place ahead, like that one where the Lir died? A sort of barrier of rocks? We could crouch there, while the battle behind is resolved. And if the force to our rear comes up, we will have rocks to heave at them, if nothing else."

The shelter they located, in their desperate hurry, was nothing much, but it held all the Turnig. Moonlight and Killeli huddled behind individual boulders, keeping watch on the track along which they had come.

It was as well their barrier was some distance from the hill behind it, which was covered with a growth of tall conifers. When Moonlight turned to check on the waiting Turnig, she shouted instead. "Above! Watch!" And then she rose, taking the staff she had used in walking, and ran to their aid. For a half-dozen Lir were leaping down the hillside, bows laid aside, their hands filled with stone axes and knives of red metal.

CHAPTER EIGHTEEN

"Sing now of war and death amid the snows!"
—Riddle

Somewhere, Moonlight found the strength to fly among the descending Lir, battering them with her staff, shouting with all her might, as the Turnig left their shelter and fled toward the gap between the hills. The bones of the gray people crunched far too easily beneath her blows, she realized as she fought.

Killeli was shouting, too, but she did not turn to see what he was doing. Instead, she began backing after the last fleeing Turnig, feeling every step, for a fall now could mean her death. The eyes of the Lirfolk were wild and bloodshot, as if they had taken some drug that made them careless of their own deaths, but something held them back from killing her. They were intent on capturing her, she grew certain.

She crushed two skulls before she realized that their bones were even lighter and more brittle than she had thought. Sickened, she belabored their ribs and backs, managing to slow their pursuit of her charges.

A rock zinged past her shoulder from behind, and another of the gray people dropped, a red mark showing where the stone had struck between his deep-set eyes; a raw socket held the missile in place. Killeli was staying with her, holding back the attackers while the Turnig passed through the gap.

"Now," he panted. "We go, too!"

The Dreamer felt she had lost all strength and will. Her arms were too heavy for her shoulders, and her feet moved reluctantly. "You go," she cried, keeping her face toward her enemies. "Save the young ones!" She heard, above the yells of the remaining three Lir, the sounds of his feet crunching away through the snow.

Again she backed, moving cautiously. The gray people fanned out, trying to find a way to approach her without risking their bones to her staff. A stone came at her head, and she only just avoided it. There were more of them up there among the trees. Why had they not shot her with their poisoned arrows?

Or did they—or their master—want her alive? Verrainig must find her small victory rankling, there in his frozen temple. Was he anxious for revenge?

She backed again, setting her feet firmly, keeping a stout grip on her staff. She found, as she knew many had before her, killing to be a thing that grew easier with practice. She was grieved, even as she prepared to kill again.

Then the long faces, striped with ash and clay, grew tense. Something approached from the rear, and she could not turn to see. But even as she prepared to die, the voice of the Goremin roared over her shoulder. The Lir turned and fled around the hill, joined by those above, who leaped away as if pursued by something too terrible to face.

She turned and leaned against his warm bulk for a moment, trying to regain strength. Her encounter with the Mover had drained her more than she thought, and there had not been time to overcome that weakness.

Gorghoz lifted her with one great arm, and as she looked up she saw his teeth grinning in the sunlight. For the first time, she realized why the Goremin did not need to kill. He had only to smile at his enemies, and they flew like chaff before the wind.

"We will go to the City of Light," he said, his deep voice rumbling against her side. "The Lir will not dare to go inside it, for those who built it were their masters and their shapers. We will have peace, for a time, if we can make it so far."

Riddle spoke, startling her. "I have never set foot there. I was warned—"

"There comes a time when warnings must be disregarded and old dangers preferred to new," said the Goremin. "This is such a time. If we remain unprotected by walls, all the small folk will die. Lute will die. Another blizzard is over the horizon, and this welcome sunlight is a mere pause between trials.

"Even if the weather should hold, which it will not, the Lir will return, again and again. Once they understand that I cannot lift a hand to harm them, they will overcome you and Moonlight and Killeli, and if this should happen I dare not guess what fate they and their present master might have in store for you."

"Then we will go. But I have heard many tales sung over campfires and beside hearths that do not make me long to see the City of Light." The poet sounded doubtful.

Gorghoz forged ahead on the track of the Turnig, half carrying Moonlight in the crook of his arm. "Yet it is the ancient counterpart of the City in the Mist, which you desire so ardently to reach. I have not walked those crystalline streets or heard the wind singing among the facets of the towers, but my people knew it well. I believe I will be able to safeguard you all, if we can only reach its shelter and find harbor among its great and shining cliffs."

Now the sun was shimmering silver instead of gold, as a thin, high haze of cloud groped across the sky. The storm Gorghoz promised was beyond the horizon still, but its outriders were moving into the hills, filling the air with the tang of snow to come.

The travelers, once they regrouped and again set up a line of march, set out westward, moving determinedly through the drifts and across treacherous places where smooth blankets of white-covered, bone-breaking tumbles of rock and scree. The hills grew taller still, and the trees dwindled to shrubs and bushes, which grew in odd circles and spirals on the slopes. Glints of something bright, like stone streaked with mica, sometimes shone from the hilltops.

Moonlight, now walking steadily on her own feet again, wondered what strange towers or watch points had been placed there by the lost people Gorghoz had mentioned. There was no tale among the Dreamers of such a city or of such a people.

The snow was not as deep in the long valleys they now entered. Planes of unbroken white swept on either hand to lap at the feet of the hills. At the distant end, where the slopes came together in purple shadow, it seemed the way was lost and the travelers might be forced to climb those slippery hills.

But Moonlight was too weary to think of it now. She put her mind to setting one foot before the other, time after time, yard after yard. Only the broad track stamped out by the Goremin and Riddle enabled her to go forward, as they traversed that seemingly endless valley and came to the curve that blocked the view of the way ahead.

* * * * * * *

Riddle again carried his nephew, holding the child closely against the cold and against the fear of loss that had overcome him while he battled the Lirfolk. He hated battle with all his poet's heart, and that had been a nasty one. He had been sickened at the ease with which those tall gray people died. But worse was the unheeding manner in which they kept coming to his hand to meet their deaths.

He put that memory out of his mind and kept watch on the long line of people marching ahead of him toward the ravine ending the long valley. Gorghoz was no worry—the Goremin was capable of caring for himself and far more. But he was concerned about Chark, who was being carried between two of her kin. Her small legs were still trying valiantly to walk, from time to time, although the poison had numbed her, spreading outward from the puncture wound in her side.

Ahead of her were those carrying the young Turnig. And behind Gorghoz, at the head of the van, Killeli kept a watchful eye on Moonlight, whose effort was plain as she moved behind their guide.

He kept thinking of her account of meeting with Verrainig in his temple of ice. Only a Dreamer, he thought, could have survived that encounter unscathed—a Dreamer or one of his own kind, who were armed against the cold of that evil will by the fires of their training and the teachings of their fathers.

He found himself drifting, from time to time, as he followed, followed along that endless valley. But he came to himself at last, finding Gorghoz had disappeared around a bend, and the line of Turnig was rapidly dwindling as they, too, passed that point. The valley had come to an end at last. Beyond, he hoped with sudden fervor, would be their goal.

For the wind, which had been gentle and fitful, was now stronger, coming from the north beyond the walls of the valley and sweeping over the snow with chilling effect. Even the shelter of the ravine had not helped, for the currents funneled through the cut, carrying pellets of blown ice on their blasts.

At last he came to the turn, and when he passed it, he found the land beyond had opened out, dropping into a rounded cup many leagues across. Great fir trees and junipers and dark-leaved evergreens made clumps of black-green against the snow, as the path descended. He suspected that tilled fields had run from hill to hill in days long lost.

But it was not the trees that fixed his gaze and all but stopped his heart with wonder. It was the City, standing in the center of the cup, its bold towers soaring columns of light against the sky, great crystalline formations of palest green and gold and rose, which almost staggered him with wonder and delight.

His fellows had gathered in a clump, the ten hands of Turnig, with Killeli, Gorghoz, and Moonlight, and all were staring down the way, their eyes shining with amazement. But when Moonlight turned to meet his gaze, he was amazed to see she was shaking with terror, as well as fascination.

"That—that is like the place where I was. Where Verrainig makes his home in the frozen gems of ice. His is smaller, far colder, but the arrangement is the same; the colors are similar."

Gorghoz grunted, his lumpy face furrowed. "That is not surprising," he said, and his voice boomed away down into the cup and echoed as tiny barks of sound against the towers and the farther slopes.

"Verrainig is not the designer of such strange loveliness, but only its imitator. Those who made these towers grew them from elements in the soil, which they tended like gardens, nourishing them with their skills and their care. Those people were as unlike the Mover from the North as this place is unlike that one.

"He is a shallow reflection of a great reality." Gorghoz sighed, staring with rapt eyes at the glowing city, whose angled heights refracted every remaining bit of light, striking through the beginnings of new snow.

Riddle felt his heart grow warm. This was a marvel the like of which he had never thought to see. Why had he not ignored those old warnings and turned his steps westward, when he wandered the hills over all those years of his travels?

He shook Lute gently. "Wake, Lute. See the bright towers?"

The child opened his eyes and stared at his uncle for a moment, caught between sleep and waking. But he turned his head obediently, as Riddle pointed into the cupped valley.

"Fire!" shouted the boy. "Are friends there?"

Moonlight broke into laughter. "He does not forget," she said. "And I hope he is right!"

The Goremin was moving forward again, setting his great splayed feet on the snow-covered track. "That is as may be," he said, over his shoulder. "But we must get under cover, for there is another storm on the wind. Night and heavier snow will arrive together; the sun is touching the horizon, beyond those clouds."

Riddle waited for the Turnig to follow, and then he carried Lute along in the wake of the band. He hoped the bright glimpse of wonder had not been entirely misleading. But Gorghoz seemed concerned with something, and he knew by now that the Goremin did not worry himself needlessly.

CHAPTER NINETEEN

"Cold things sleep beneath the rock,
dreaming awful dreams."

—Riddle

Change was in the wind, although the deep burrow of Dinorm was far beneath the snows carpeting the lands above. The worm had slept for many ages, there in its chill stone crypt. It woke reluctantly, squirming uneasily for a long while before the sensing pits that were the eyes admitted to its mind any hint of the glow caused by its own phosphorescence.

Something stirred in the world above. The hated twin, there in the southern lands, was again awake and aware. This was a thing that disturbed the ancient being. Had its distant kin upset the delicate balance holding their realms apart? Or had something else disrupted its rest?

It felt outward for the first time in ages, seeking the mind of that One who had been so apt for its teaching. Left to his own devices, had Verrainig managed to disturb forces best left to sleep?

The upper world had changed somewhat. The long stretches of countryside had drifted so deeply with snow that the rock beneath was cracking and shifting. Ice welled up from frozen springs and rivers, pushing apart the clefts through which they rose and forming crystalline mountains. Where the stone house of Verrainig had been, when last Dinorm had turned attention toward him, nothing was to be seen.

A stab of alarm energized the gray-glowing length, and the glow brightened. Through all the conduits of power that served as veins and nerves, Dinorm sent a peremptory summons.

"Verrainig! Verrainig!"

For too long there was no answer. It willed again, compelling the impulse of that sending so strongly it felt ice-packs cracking on the lands and waters above. The vibration of the summons could shake the northlands into rubble, if the Mover did not reply. Having shaped it in the beginning, simply by an act of will, Dinorm would not hesitate to shatter the countryside above its slug-like head.

Glowing, now, with anger, the great being flexed its thick body, tried ancient strength against the stone that surrounded the crypt. It crumbled into gravel about the sticky skin, and the worm felt at last that its long sleep had augmented its internal power, making it, after so many aeons, the fit equal of Orm.

* * * * * * *

Riddle watched the last light waver among the facets of the towers, as he followed Gorghoz down the winding way leading into the valley. Even the fresh gusts of snow-laden wind had not dulled their splendor, and the light cast over the entire depression by the reflections and refractions of the crystalline structures was strange and beautiful.

But as they went he could feel tension growing in the Goremin. The great head was up, the eyes searching the tree-lined way, the snowy fields beyond, the distant canyons marking the streets of this most ancient city. Moonlight now walked beside him, and he could feel her shiver, from time to time. He knew it was not the renewed assault of the wind that shook her. She recognized those towers, and he could read her heart enough to know she was terrified of their likeness to the stronghold of Verrainig, although she did not allow it to show to the others.

He found himself wondering, as they came beneath the arches and angles of the city, what kinship there might be between this place and that in the north, where the Mover had made his lair. What linked the two? But he caught himself and came to the alert, as the Goremin turned aside from the main way into a narrower one.

In a city of men, it would have been an alley, perhaps, but here it was a cleft of white and saffron light. The towers above were pulling the last of the day down long shafts of crystal into the deeps of even the least of the streets.

Riddle found himself wondering if starlight and the faint glimmer of the distant moons also brightened the buried places here. Was there no night here, even when clouds hid the stars?

Gorghoz turned again, this time into a way so tight his hairy elbows touched the walls on either side. As if energized by brushing against the crystalline stuff, the Goremin's coat began to glimmer, his coarse gray hair rising beneath his cloak and shining faintly.

He was counting, and Riddle found himself counting too. Three four—five—and at the sixth angle in the shining wall Gorghoz turned to face the smooth facet. He reached to touch it, two fingers, one finger, five fingers, three fingers laid against a spot of silver set into the crystal.

The wall evaporated as if it were ice melting away or mist dissolving in sunlight.

"Here we can rest in some safety," said the Goremin, motioning the line of Turnig into the building. "Unless things have changed mightily in the past millennium or so...."

Riddle found the words did not comfort him, as he held Lute close and stepped after Moonlight into a room that must have been vacant for many lifetimes even of his own long-lived kind. He moved through a tenuous sort of light to stand beside the Turnig against the farther wall of a circular chamber.

There was no dust. That was the first thing he noticed, as he glanced about the polished curves of the walls, the immaculate circle of the floor. Set at regular intervals about the perimeter were curved benches of black stone, each holding a cushion of prismatic material seemingly spun from glass and starlight. What could have endured for the millennia at which Gorghoz had hinted?

Something in the air made his hair tingle, as if trying to stand on end, and he noticed the fur of the Turnig and of Killeli seemed to be unusually thick and bushy. There was a potential here for power, though of what sort he had no clue. Crystal, he knew, could generate a certain force, and he thought that might be reacting with the living bodies now inside the room.

Those who were carrying Chark laid her down on a cloak spread over one of the cushioned benches. She was breathing roughly, her eyes glazed.

Gorghoz bent over her, his lumpy brow furrowed. "Killeli, take from my pack the small box. In it is a stone vial; give it to me."

He took the dark tube and pulled its cork with his teeth. Chark's small jaws were clenched tightly, but the Goremin carefully poured a drop between her lips and stroked her throat until she swallowed, her eyelids fluttering open.

Riddle felt a cold lump in his breast begin to melt. He had feared the Lirfolk's poison had killed his small friend, but she sat, now, painfully but with determination, and leaned against the wall. He could see the signs of tension easing from her furry body.

"Here we will rest," said Gorghoz. His face was grayer than usual, and Riddle thought the efforts of the past days had told upon him. "Out of the wind, out of the reach of the Lirfolk and the thing that has set them upon our track. Who will watch first?"

The great Goremin had been plowing the way for everyone, all day. He had faced enemies and quelled them with his terrible face. He was weary past enduring, Riddle knew with sudden clarity, and no reasonable man would sleep in such an alien place as this without setting a watch.

"I will watch," he said, handing Lute to the Dreamer and checking his blade and his harp. "Sleep, Gorghoz, for I will keep my eyes open and my wits sharp. I hope it will not keep you wakeful if I touch my harp from time to time."

"It can only lull me more deeply into rest," came the reply.

With a minimum of bustle, the Turnig laid their felts and settled for the night, too exhausted even to eat. Moonlight lay on her cloak near Lute and not too far from Riddle. She stared at the wall for some time—he could see the gleam of her eyes in the dim light—but at last she, too, was asleep.

Riddle was left to ponder this strangest of days. He sang softly to himself, from time to time, in order to stay awake. When Lute began turning and whimpering, he took the child and carried him to the other side of the great room, away from the sleepers.

He strummed softly upon his harp. Lute quieted, staring up at his uncle until he slept, once again, his round cheeks colored by the tints brought down from the snow clouds by the towering structures above.

Killeli relieved the poet after some hours, and Riddle rested at last, to wake amid a bustle of Turnig. The small people were rolling away felts, as well as taking dried fruits and nuts from the food supplies. Once Gorghoz roused, he pulled from the wall a sort of brazier, filled with thin metal bars.

The Goremin moved the thing until it matched grooves sunk into the sides of the slot; once it was set into position, the bars began warming, though Riddle could not imagine what source supplied the heat. Soon they glowed red; pots of soup and of herb tea were set to heating for the famished travelers.

While they waited, Riddle turned to the Goremin. "Tell us what you know, Gorghoz. There was no time yesterday, and we were weary. Now we are curious about this place.

"How is it that you understand the way to enter these houses and to make the cooking place work? There is a long, strange tale here, and I would understand what it is we face, here in the City of Light."

Leaning back against the wall, the great creature sighed. "It is a tale old before my father's father was born, and among Goremin that counts in thousands of years, for we live long. But my people have visited this place over long spans of time, and when I was very young I listened to their tales with interest.

"I determined that before I died I would visit it, too. Little did I think it would be under such circumstances, but seeing the future is not a trait my people possess."

Lute crawled into Riddle's lap, and the Turnig sat in a circle on the floor, which held a warmth that seemed to have no source. Riddle waited while the Goremin settled himself comfortably and thought for a moment. This would be a tale worth the hearing!

CHAPTER TWENTY

"Long ago, when time was bright and young...."
—Riddle

This is the story told by Gorghoz in the City of Light:

The Goremin must relate this tale, for it is from my kind that all records of those lost people must come. Indeed, some of my earliest ancestors think those who caused the towers to grow in this valley also caused my own people to become what they are, shaping them by the force of their wills from who knows what elemental animal, as your own people did with later beings.

You must remember that not even my grandfathers saw the Litati with their own eyes. Their grandfathers' ancestors did, but the memories of my kind are long, and our records are accurate.

They were, according to the ancient accounts, a small people, frail in appearance and yet strong as the fragile-seeming towers they raised, which yet stand and defy wind and time with seeming ease.

They did not look like Goremin, or even like men of the Ancient Race. I cannot visualize them, though I have tried for many years, for they were unlike any beings our world has seen since. That is stated as fact in our records. But it was not their bodies that were their pride and their strength. Their minds were filled with inventions, for they could remember things that had never happened and see things that did not exist. And what they envisioned they brought into being, if they found it interesting enough. It was from them, I think, that the potencies of Will, in our time, originally came.

Where they had their origin is not even hinted in Goremin lore, but they did not come into being on this continent. They left some distant home and journeyed to find this very valley, which contained the elements needed for their City.

None now understand the ways they used to make this great

complex grow upward from the earth, dividing itself into rooms and streets. Yet they assured our earliest ancestors who were capable of understanding that it was in such a manner they built their new home. Yet it was not only with metals and crystals that they were skilled at shaping with the force of their willing.

They could change living flesh, warping it from its natural shapes into others that seemed to them more beautiful and more useful for their needs. They began the long process that has resulted in Killeli's kind, as well as my own. The Turnig might be only small furry beasts, if the Litati had not helped to form them, at the beginning, giving them hand-like paws and flexible jaws that could, after aeons and with the nurturing of the Ancient Race, learn speech.

They put into the grasslands the scanty-furred creatures that have now become men who think themselves wise enough to rule Damaria. They shaped the Lirfolk, who had no help from the Kings in order to evolve into thinking people, like their cousins in Damaria, but are frozen into their half-animal state.

But they had no part in the making of the Ancient Race, there in its distant southern homeland. Unless Riddle knows his own history, this is a tale that is lost. There must have been other forces than the Litati at work here, in those forgotten times.

The mountains where I lived were young, still surging upward with the forces of their internal fires, in the time of which I speak. The forests were great, and those have died and their saplings' distant offspring have come and gone many times since the Litati disappeared from our perceptions.

And yet I feel now the truth of my ancestors' conviction. Entities the Litati created and set in motion still live, affecting everything and everyone on this shore of the Circling Sea. For my longfathers wrote that the Litati formed a pair of beings to their design, making them most powerful and very wise, giving them all they knew of shaping and altering, of growing and destroying. They put into their creations a portion of their own potent Will.

They made two, equal and yet opposite, although they did not at first realize it. One they sent south into the land we now know as Damaria. My people call him Orm, and he is a strong bastion of positive force in the world his passing will shaped as he moved across the country. It is Orm, we believe, who sent the call that brought the Kings to preserve his country.

The other went northward, into the frozen waste. Dinorm, we call it, for it has no gender as does its twin. Gender is a thing wedded to creative impulse, and only destructiveness followed that grim creature. As it went, the shapes of the lands it traveled changed inexorably, stone shattering, rock splitting, the hills and the northern waste becoming what we know now.

After ages of slow, thoughtful travel, one twin making the graceful country we know and pushing the mountains up to guard it, the other forcing the north into the harsh contours it still possesses, the pair burrowed into the stone beneath the soils of their assigned places. Weary with creating, they slept for millennia.

We are certain they have waked, from time to time when affairs above their heads disturbed their rest. More than once Dinorm has sent troublesome forces southward into Damaria, and each time its twin has managed to oppose it successfully.

Orm, beneath Damaria, has stirred within the past months, disturbed by emanations from his distant sibling. I felt his movements as we passed through the Forest Damariste, many days ago.

This means that Dinorm, there in the Mover's frozen country, has begun another assault against the lands it hates and fears, for the two are paired in perceptiveness, although their impulses seem terribly different.

Orm has held our lands in peace for all the time since the Ancient Race came to save us from the devastation sent by his twin, in our far past. Orm has created the ability to Dream in some of those who came from the mating of the Ancient Race with the new, and he has strengthened the power of will in those who mean well for his country.

Dinorm, there beneath the throne of Verrainig, has locked the northern lands in ice, along with the heart of his puppet, whom we call the Mover from the North. He uses that one as an instrument of his purposes, though it is doubtful if Verrainig realizes that.

We believe the Litati did not understand, completely, what it was they had made and set into motion. They were used to manipulating the creatures they shaped, using them to work their will upon the lands about their city. But the Ormin were made from elements of the earth and the rock. They were given life in some way no one now living can understand, and in that giving they attained wills of their own, in addition to the small quantity the Litati granted to them.

Where Dinorm found Verrainig, no one knows. Perhaps the Mover was also a construct of the Litati, an experiment that went woefully wrong.

Only the fact that the Ormin sleep for aeons at a time has saved our world from constant struggle and devastation. But Dinorm found one who did not sleep, and he instructed him in all he knew, keeping back only those matters that might give his creature too much power of his own. And then began the creeping attacks from the north. Those have been beaten back, time after time during the existence of my people, only because Orm wakes and wills the coming of those who are able to give them battle and, so far, to push them back. Or that is what my people believe, and generations of philosophers have spent their lives unriddling the puzzle.

The Ancient Race came northward, we have always known, because Orm called to them from his stony crypt. But now the new men have killed them all or driven them out, and there is no one ruling Damaria with will or wit enough to counter the manipulations of the Mover from the North.

Dinorm has, at last, found a time in which his twin is weaker than he. Damaria may be lost to us and to all thinking beings who long to live in peace and conduct their lives in harmony.

"But how do you still know how to get about the City?" asked Moonlight.

Because my people have visited it often—or often in terms of Goremin lives—over the past ages. Each generation has sent a group to study this place, to learn as many of its secrets as possible for outsiders.

My grandfather was one of such an expedition. He sat in this very room, once, musing about the glassy chips that were the books of the Litati, trying to find how to read them, though without success.

Although neither he nor any Goremin ever deciphered the writing of the lost race, he did learn how to open the doorways, how to cook, using the devices here, and how to find his way about. He wrote everything into his journals, as well as telling me and my siblings the tales, time after time. For we were always intrigued by this lost city, and we asked for his stories again and again.

"But when did your people learn that the Litati were gone?" That was Riddle.

The oldest of our tales deal with our early interactions with our teachers. The elders of the Goremin, in those lost times, came twice a year to the City, bringing herbs the creators wanted from the forests and the fields and the mountains. They also brought their infants, who were taken away into the City by certain of the Litati.

When they were returned to their anxious parents, they seemed brighter and stronger than when they left, and we have wondered often what it was that was done to them during those visits. That, we believe, was when our intelligence was augmented by those who made the city.

There came a time in spring, generations after the earliest records, when those who approached the city saw no activity among the towers. The intense inner lights that the Litati kept always glowing were quenched, and only the sunlight struck through the faceted shafts. When they called among the streets and sounded the crystalline chimes at the doorways, no answer came except the singing of the wind among the angles of the towers. Then my people learned that not a single Litati was left in all the city, nor in the lands they knew. They searched for years, seeking for any trace of their going.

The city was left as if for a short time, all the furnishings, although they are hard to recognize, still in place. The libraries are still here, in their sealed chambers, their chips glowing with contained energies, the writing still as impenetrable as it was when first my grandfather investigated it. If they had intended to leave forever, I cannot believe the Litati would have left their records. We have pondered this puzzle for millennia among my kind, and we have made some guesses as to what occurred.

For the time in which the Litati disappeared was aeons after Orm and Dinorm had taken their places beneath the ground. There had been time for those powerful minds to grasp the realities of their world and to think about what they might do with their abilities.

Did they turn their thoughts toward those who created them? Did they fear, there in their hidden lairs, that the Litati might in some manner decide to unmake them or to frustrate their freedom of will?

Of all the creatures living here at the time, only the Litati, the Ormin, and the Goremin were thinking beings. And the Goremin have never injured anything, great or small, for it is not in their nature to hurt others.

The Litati were creators, not destroyers. They would not, we have always been certain, knowingly have worked their own doom or that of other kinds.

Which leaves only the Ormin with the capabilities for endangering those who made them and taught them and freed them to go their own ways. Of the twins, we have studied Orm, of course, most closely.

While that creature is inaccessible to anyone from the surface, his mind ranges outward, when he awakens, and explores thinking creatures when he finds them. The Goremin are not among those whose thoughts can read those of others, but when such a powerful force as Orm comes among us, we can be examined by him. In the process, some of the reality that is his being enters our minds as well, and so we know something of him. It is through those interactions that we have come to understand what we know of occurrences far in the north concerning his twin.

We do not believe that he would think of destroying those who made him. And that leaves Dinorm, bitter and cold, far in a vacant and harsh environment, to turn its mind toward revenge against those who sent it there. That has been the will for destructiveness plaguing our lands since we have been thinking beings. It, I feel, was the will that destroyed or drove away the Litati, because of Dinorm's anger.

I cannot say how it was done, or if it only succeeded in sending them fleeing. Yet this is the only explanation that satisfies logic and seems possible to generations of my kind.

And that is the tale of this City of Light, as it has come down to me. It is incomplete. Much is guesswork, though based upon some sound knowledge. It is a puzzle without a solution, and we sit, this moment, in the midst of a struggle having its roots in lost times and a vanished race.

CHAPTER TWENTY-ONE

"There are songs that entangle the ear
and make the senses reel...."
                                    —Riddle

When the tale was done, the food was ready. Once fed, the group felt inclined, now there was some safety, to explore this great City, of which few had ever heard so much as a tale in winter. Riddle, more than most, was intrigued by the thought of the library, unvisited and unread for so many ages. He asked Gorghoz to show him the way, following the directions in his grandfather's journal.

The others, once they tested the edge of the wind that sang through the streets, chose rather to go into the tunnels connecting the towers beneath the ground. For some distance, Riddle and the Goremin accompanied them, before turning away into a rose-shot tube of light that led straight toward an arched doorway at its end.

As they went, Riddle marveled that this wonder had lain here in the north and west for so many aeons without his people exploring it. He could see through the walls of the way they traversed; granular soil and fragments of flint were quite visible, and yet the veil of crystal colored them with its own shade of warm rose.

Gorghoz went silently, his great brow wrinkled. As they came to the doorway, he hesitated for a moment, staring into space as if thinking. Then, with a deep sigh, he put his hands against the round spots on either panel of the paired doors and allowed them to rest there, warming the opaque stuff until it glimmered with streaks of gold.

There came a quiet breath of motion, and the doors swung back on either side, allowing a gust of strangely scented air to touch Riddle's face. For a moment he felt stifled, as if that dead breath had paralyzed his lungs, but after a moment he was able to breathe again.

Gorghoz, too, had stilled, and Riddle knew he had encountered the same problem. Soon, however, they turned together toward the opening and stepped into the chamber that led into the library of the Litati.

This lay at a long slant upward, and along the walls of the narrow room stood indescribable figures shaped of glass. As they moved along, Riddle studied the sculptures, wondering if they represented animals or abstractions—or were they the Litati?

"You said you had never visualized them," he said to Gorghoz. "Might those tangled groupings of limbs and torsos, sinuous branchings and hemispheres, be living beings?"

"Yes," said the Goremin. "And if those are they, I do not wonder that my ancestors could not describe them in words. 'Like spiders,' some said. 'Like eels in a bunch,' said others. I would say both are correct, and yet both are strangely wrong."

If the shapes were hard to decipher, their activities, frozen into sculpture, were impossible. Whatever those weird beings had pursued as tasks or play, as crafts or studies, were things outside the realm of human thought, the Poet decided.

But the library, once they arrived at its tightly sealed doors, told him that in one way, if no other, the Litati resembled his own kind. As the Goremin palmed the locks once more, Riddle peered through the crystalline wall, able to see glimmering ranks of hand-sized chips laid on long trays set in tiers, filling the room. The Litati had reveled in the written word, he thought, whatever it was they found to write there.

As the doors opened, he found Gorghoz at his elbow, and for the first time he saw the Goremin truly excited. His deep-set eyes glowed like coals beneath his overhung brows, and his great head was lifted as if in triumph. "Here my own ancestors stood, and here they studied the books of their teachers, trying to learn to read that cryptic writing. I would wish we might succeed, as they did not. They tried feeling of the chips, singing to them, tapping them with tiny hammers. Nothing worked for them, so my longing is only a wish and cannot be fulfilled. Yet we are here, where I never thought to come."

Riddle moved forward, strangely timid now that he stood in this enchanted place amid these enigmatic writings. He found each of the trays to be made of a different shade of translucent stuff, which lent its color to the glassy chips lying there. Approaching a rosy rank, he touched the endmost chip, which was a square plate the length of his hand.

Its depths contained scrolled symbols in intricate and beautiful patterns. His gaze seemed to follow the inscription deeper and deeper into the glass, tangling his thoughts into a meaningless knot. He wrenched his mind away and closed his eyes for a moment, re-orienting himself. A thought rose in him like a bubble from the depths of a bowl of wine. He turned to Gorghoz. "Do your people sing well?" he asked.

Gorghoz laughed, vibrating the nearest tray of chips. "There is no music in my kind," he said. "Our voices are deep and gruff, but we did the best we could."

Riddle nodded thoughtfully. "I think your ancestors may have had a useful notion, but they were not equipped by nature to use it. What if these are not meant to be read with the eye at all? What if they are sound, somehow trapped by means of those scrolls in crystalline stuff, requiring certain tones to bring them out?" he asked.

The Goremin stared at him. Excitement dawned in his deep-set eyes. "You are a poet and a musician. You have a harp, and my kind has no gift for music or its instruments. I have heard you sing, and your voice is clear and true." He moved to pick up one of the chips, holding it awkwardly in his huge hands.

Riddle reached to bring his harp from its strap over his shoulder. "Perhaps in some manner these might respond to sounds at my command, if they contain spoken words. I will try a few notes, perhaps some chords, and we will see, though we will not understand the language if this should succeed."

He tightened the pegs, tested the tension of the strings, and plucked a random note. It rang, clear and true, through the chamber.

The nearest of the chips began to glow and to hum in tones that harmonized even as they rose in volume. Others began to take up the harmony. Hastily, the Poet muted his string, quelling the invading sound, and the chips quieted.

"So now we know!" he said. "Your kind could not produce the correct notes. And yet, even if we could hear every one, how could we translate their music into meaningful words?"

"We can only try," Gorghoz replied. Now his face was blazing with triumph. "Not in a thousand generations of my kind have we gained even so much. Surely we will be able to understand something of what we hear! Strike the strings boldly. Play the wind-song you sometimes sing for the children!"

Riddle nodded, touching the strings gently. "Down the valley, the wind blows free," he sang. "The grasses roll like a deep green sea."

Into Riddle's mind came a quiet picture of fields in which unusual flowers nodded to the breeze. Across those stretches moved two distant shapes, wriggling away in opposite directions, their pale skins distinct against the green. Blunt heads rose from time to time, as if testing the wind. Without turning to each other, the pair moved away, and around them the fields heaved and wrinkled, the grass parched and the sky itself darkened. Orm and his twin, moving to their homes in the time of their creation?

A soft chime of cool tones joined his notes and his voice, rising with the intensity of the song. "The storm comes trampling field and tree." The stronger notes crescendoed. He heard stone shattering, as the shapes heaved and flowed out of his sight.

His hand dropped away from the harp. Now a storm of notes chimed and hummed and moaned about the two of them, there amid the trays of singing books. The sounds did not lose their momentum with the dying of his song. This time the muting of his strings did not dim the storm of tonalities he had roused. Some one among the notes he had struck had found the harmonic key to most of the chips—or perhaps to the trays holding them. Even, it was possible, to the crystalline walls of the library. The tonalities grew stronger with every passing instant.

Riddle felt his brain go numb, his hands loosen, so that Gorghoz had to catch the harp as it fell from his fingers. Caught in a whirl-wind of notes, which rose in intensity until he felt every nerve vi-brating near the snapping point, Riddle knew he would fly apart like a shattered vase if nothing quelled the wild music he had waked amid the books.

Something inside him whirled with the storm of sound, rose with the harmonics now making the chamber tremble and the trays add their castanets to the symphony. Without help, he would break free of his imprisoning flesh and fly up with the words of the Litati to whatever undreamed-of ending they promised....

But a hand grasped his arm, and he was pulled away from the singing chips, out of the wide doorway and into the antechamber. Dimly he knew that Gorghoz was laying him against the wall, out of the direct range of the tumult inside the library. The Goremin laid his harp in his lap and moved to the portal.

He caught the panels of the doors and slammed them together so violently the translucent material went dark, shutting off the vi-sion of those chiming crystals, which now were vibrating so in-tensely on their trays they seemed to dance to their own music.

That muted the tones reaching the Poet's sensitive ears, and he lay for a moment, struggling to regain some mastery of himself. Then he shuddered, for the wall against his back was beginning to hum its own song, rising in pitch as if to a shattering climax.

The Goremin gave him no time to think of it. Lifting him effortlessly, he slung him over his back and ran down the long slope of the chamber, toward those other distant doors.

"Why—the—hurry?" Riddle asked, his words jolted out in abrupt bursts.

"Listen to the tower!" said Gorghoz, and he added even more speed to his headlong rush.

Riddle's ears still rang with the song of the library, but he tried to focus his hearing more sharply. Once he had done it, he began trembling again, for about them the shafts of the towers were beginning to hum, too. Up the long planes and angles from their roots, they were adding their own notes to the music from the depths.

The tunnels were like the stems of flutes, carrying the sounds along their tubes, intensifying them with every ell. As Gorghoz gained the tunnel and closed the second pair of doors, the Turnig appeared, wide-eyed, from those passages they had chosen to explore.

"What?" asked Chirrik. "We go fast! Towers shake!"

"Gather the supplies and run!" shouted the Poet, from Gorghoz's back. "Moonlight, please find Lute and make sure he is cared for! Get all the young ones out first! Hurry! I think I have brought down the City of Light!"

If they had any doubts, a new vibration, rising beneath their soles in the floor of the tunnel, would have persuaded them. They ran, every one, taking the infants and the small ones ahead, helping the hurt.

They paused in their original haven to bundle Chark and the others who were ill or exhausted into their winter wrappings. Then the group streamed through the narrow doorway and into the alley beyond.

All around them the towers sang fiercely to the wind, the notes growing higher and more wild. As if the sound generated power, the colors rising along the shafts grew in intensity, flaming in scarlet and deep gold and vibrant orange, purple and sapphire and emerald against the low clouds overhead.

Gorghoz carried as many of the slower Turnig as he could, as did Moonlight and Killeli. Riddle, now on his own feet, hugged Lute and two Turnig children close as he angled his way through the streets toward the rising land just visible between the shafts of the buildings, at the other side of the valley.

The Turnig in the lead turned and beckoned, and within a few strides Riddle found himself outside the complex, dashing for the shelter of the trees that lined the road leading away on its farther side. He ran desperately as the city behind him sang its death-song;

he struggled up the slope at last and over the rim.

Beyond that, the land leveled a bit, and then there came a gentle drop toward a streambed. Only when they were safe in the shelter of the land itself did the group pause. And then, once Lute was safely placed with the young and the helpless, Riddle turned back to lie in the snow at the rim of the valley with Gorghoz and the others.

He found Moonlight at his right side; Killeli lay on his left. They stared down at the shining city, now lit by daylight as well as its own luminescence, and it was glowing as if fires raged inside the towers, shooting streams of color into the air, ringing so loudly with harsh melody that he could not hear when Moonlight spoke to him.

Gold and green, purple and blue, rose and amber were the mingled shades now fluttering within the City of Light. The sound of the dying crystals was so great that his ears rejected it as the first of the towers burst into long shards of burning glass, which fell outward slowly, great ribbons of colorful flame that sliced through the surrounding structures.

Now the city was shattering, its crashes interrupting the terrible harmonics he had wakened to life in that buried library. But it was too late—there at the roots of the city those vibrations were bringing to an end the place the Litati had grown from the crystal-bearing stones of the valley. Even as he watched, it sank into bright heaps of faceted rubble, still glowing with color like the embers of a colossal fire or a treasury of living gems, dropped by some giant robber in his flight.

Behind him, Riddle heard a muted groan. Alarmed, he turned to find Gorghoz standing there, his gaze fixed upon the ruins. "We were greedy for knowledge, and we brought it down. We wanted too much—more than we were capable of using or understanding—and that was the death of the City of Light. But we saw! We saw the Ormin, in the day of their setting out. What other wonders were there among the crystals?

"Oh, the books! Oh, the books!"

Tears rose to Riddle's eyes, as he thought of the great loss he and the Goremin had brought about. But nothing could be done, and they were, at the least, still alive and moving toward their goal.

"Do you have the book?" he asked, his tone as quiet as possible.

Gorghoz stared down at him for a moment as if he did not understand the question. Then comprehension dawned in his eyes, and he nodded.

"I have the book. We must go, for the Lirfolk will see this blaze of color from far away, and they will come. They have yearned for generations to enter the City of their creators. Only its secrets have kept it safe. Now they will see it in ruins, and they will blame us for the downfall of the place that is the only holy thing in all their barren lives. When they arrive, we must be far away, no matter if the snow is deep and the wind bitter."

Riddle rose and followed him toward the others, who were already gathering their hastily retrieved supplies for another journey into the teeth of the wind. Once more, they were cast out into the terrible winter.

CHAPTER TWENTY-TWO

"Sing the death-songs now!
Mark your faces with ash; tear out your hair
for grief!"

—Riddle

Gorghoz sent the Turnig ahead with Killeli, Moonlight, and the children, for he felt Riddle shared his need to watch the death of the City of Light to its last glimmer. The poet seemed glad to turn back with him, watching from behind stones and the bushes as the multi-colored shards flickered into spurts of brilliancy or dulled to pale glows of pastel blues and greens.

As they lay there, the snow sliding into their cloaks and down their necks, there was movement on the road beyond the city, down which they had come the evening before. A trickle of individuals crept toward the mass of shattered crystal, followed by a thick line of more timid ones, who seemed to be waiting to see what happened.

The Lirfolk, pursuing their prey, now seemed staggered to find the City of Light in its death throes. They halted and stared, raising their hands, throwing down their weapons, tearing hair from their long heads.

Instinctively, Gorghoz flattened himself in the snow behind the ledge that lipped the valley.

Those who now were standing in shock, watching the play of light and color where the towers had stood in impregnable splendor, had not expected to find the thing that now confronted them.

He remembered the tall Lir in the pale fur cloak. He had faced him, back in the hills, and only his roar had kept the warrior from removing Riddle's head with one stroke of his broad-axe. Now the big fellow was beginning to move forward toward the flaring colors of the crystalline piles, which played fantastically upon his cloak, his hairy face, and the blade of his axe.

"Surely they could see the glare from beyond the heights to the east," Riddle whispered. "Why are they so surprised?"

"The Lirfolk are not great thinkers, according to my teachers. They are so little above the beasts that some must touch a fire in order to understand it will burn. Even if they saw the glow, they would not put that together with the City, making a pattern of assumptions. Only in fighting each other and attacking passing strangers are the Lirfolk to be considered efficient."

But he was thinking about the tales his grandfather had told concerning those wild people. "They eat the flesh of their own kind," he had said, horror in his deep voice. "They attack without warning or reason, and those who are captured are never seen alive again."

There were rumors of torture and slavery and things even darker. It made Gorghoz wonder if their nearness to the lair of Dinorm might have darkened the minds and the hearts of the Lirfolk, making them more bestial than they might otherwise have been. But he said nothing of that to Riddle.

Instead, he pointed downward, where the mass of those following their leaders now surged forward. To his surprise, the big Lir fell to his knees, scooped up handfuls of snow, and poured it over his head.

An agonized cry came across the valley to the ears of the watching Goremin. "Ahhhhhiiiiiieeeee!"

Riddle turned questioning eyes toward him, and he shivered. "This was their holy place," Gorghoz said. "Look at the others!"

There was a rush of fur-clad bodies toward the edge of the mass of crystalline embers. As he watched, a thin female, taller even than the leader of the group, flung herself among the razor-edged shards and rose again with a shining spear of green glass in her hands.

With that she sliced at her cloak, her skin, wound her hair in one hand and cut it off, letting the thick tail of gray-streaked strands drop into the burning colors, where they flared up into a bright yellow pulse of light. She was wailing now, her voice joining that of the first to cry out, as others added wild, grief-stricken notes to the din.

A long line of mourners spread along the edge of the bright rubble. Most seemed to be imitating the female, and soon long ribbons of blood glimmered in the morning light, staining the trampled snow with scarlet.

It was a wrenching sight, and the Goremin found himself saddened by it. His people had revered that City as well, and his internal grief was a more civilized match for that of the wild hunters of the hills.

"The books," Riddle was whispering. "All those books! If only I had been more cautious! If only we had tried one note at a time, carefully building a melody that would evoke the visions those books contained!"

"It is too late," said Gorghoz, "to think of that now. The Lirfolk are grieving. But even they will, in time, begin wondering if those they hunted here might not have had a hand in destroying the City. If that happens, I would like to have us all many hours farther along our road, whether or not this snow grows heavier and the wind sharpens. I would not promise that my war-cry could stop them again, after this loss of their holiest place, when they come after us."

"They might not put it together." Riddle did not sound as hopeful as his words. "But if they do, you are right. We must follow the others, sweeping out the tracks as we go."

As they moved away, the long wailing cries pursued them, and Gorghoz still saw, behind his eyes, the blood-streaked mourners kneeling beside the piles of glowing crystal. Would there be a change in the Lirfolk now? Would the death of their holy place force them to use their minds more than they had done in the past? Or would they become beasts altogether, without a focus for their thoughts and their spirits?

But he did not slow to ponder the question. He sped along the trail left by the others, as Riddle came behind, sweeping the snow with a broom made of bush-tops.

* * * * * * *

Moonlight carried three small ones, following in the tracks of Jree, who was, in turn, stepping in Chirrik's. The elderly Turnig seemed able to trudge forward endlessly through the snow, ignoring the bitter wind now blowing from the north and the stinging gusts of sleet that punctuated the snowfall.

Moonlight concentrated upon keeping to her feet in the buffeting wind and holding onto the young ones she carried. Killeli had taken Lute, who was far heavier than the Turnig young, but she held an infant in her left arm and a squirming toddler in her right. The third bestrode her neck, and she knew a misstep on her part would send him headlong into the drifts walling in the line of travelers.

She found herself drifting, at times, into a sort of dream-state. She wondered at herself, but she kept moving, and when the attack came she hardly knew what had happened for a single vital moment.

Then it was too late. A line of Lirfolk rose from the drifts ahead and beside them and came yelling down upon the chilled and weary

Turnig.

She threw her toddler into the arms of the nearest of his kin, shrugged her rider into a soft hummock of snow, and set the infant carefully into Killeli's hands. She turned to face the attackers, and the broad-faced and bearded Lir leading them lifted his hand to strike her down.

With every ounce of her strength, she formed a Dream about her fellows on the track. A bubble of transparency surrounded her, and the Lir, who had evidently intended to brush her from his path as if she were a dead leaf, suddenly froze.

She looked out of that bubble of intense energy and turned each of his fingers, as he perceived them, to serpents. They raised irritated heads, flicking forked tongues at the bearded face above them. The sinuous necks waved back and forth, as if the heads consulted. The tiny black eyes glinted into those of the one whose hand they now tenanted.

She left a fraction of her attention to keep this one occupied as she created another Dream, this one large enough to encompass all the Turnig, as well as herself and the furred man. If it must be a Dream at all, why not a warm one? She thought of scenes in the books the Ancient Race had brought from the south, picturing the tropical lands from which they had come.

The Turnig had retreated to surround her when the attack came; she traced about them a latticed wall made of pale golden stone. Through the lacework spaces, she could see the Lirfolk staring wildly at the exotic landscape forming about them, as she Dreamed.

Trees with rustling leaves in long fronds trailed over the wall, and inside the garden she enclosed beds of bright flowers. A fountain poured streams of water from the flutes and horns of sculptured musicians, and it trickled away down mosaic runnels, beneath graceful bridges arching over the brooks.

About her, the Turnig were beginning to babble, spinning about to see each new wonder as she created it. The children stopped wailing and began to struggle to get down from the arms that had carried them so far. Instantly, they were among the flowers, sniffing delicately without tearing petals or picking the bright blossoms.

But outside the perforated wall the Lirfolk were beginning to turn their gazes toward those who had been their prey. The wonder of their present situation did not seem to enter their primitive minds. They only saw aliens and enemies. Of the fifty or so who had attacked the column in the snow, at least half now headed for the wall, spears and bows and long blades at the ready.

She had, of necessity, released the hand of the leader from his illusion when she created a vision for the minds of so many. Now he was halfway up the wall, setting his toes into the stone niches.

Sighing, Moonlight conjured from her mind a pack of Gyrduk, hungry and hunting. She saw the line of beasts come into view beyond the last of the attackers, and she urged them forward relentlessly. There came a long howl, and the leader of the Lir stopped atop the wall and looked back at his warriors.

The pack snarled and snapped as it lunged into the grouped Lirfolk; Moonlight could hear the snapping of bones and the tearing of flesh. She shivered, even as she fed the vision from her Dreamer's well of energy, remembering the false Gyrduk that had hunted her.

The leader of the Lir leaped down again, his now snakeless hand raising his staff to strike the Gyrduk springing at his throat. The rest of the Lir were milling about, and the Dreamer caught the coppery taint of blood on the warm and scented breeze with which she had supplied her vision.

The Turnig were now gathering at the wall, watching the carnage with fascinated horror. The narrow muzzles of some of the beasts were thrusting into the openings, trying for the Turnig faces beyond the barrier, and Moonlight forced the predators to turn back to attack the Lir instead.

She knew she could not hold this Dream for long. If Riddle and Gorghoz did not come soon, she would use the last of her strength. The vision would pop like a bubble, leaving the Turnig to face Lirfolk, unarmed and unskilled.

She gritted her teeth and clung to the Dream. She would maintain until she fell, and then what happened must happen. She could do only as much as was possible.

Even as she fell at last, she heard the terrifying growl that was the war-cry of Gorghoz and the clang of steel that was Riddle's blade.

CHAPTER TWENTY-THREE

"Then let the bubble break in rainbow shards,
the Dream evaporate into a mist."
—Riddle

Riddle found himself stepping on the heels of the Goremin, as they hastened through the snow. Those grieving Lir, back in the valley, were relatively few.

Many more were left elsewhere, who might well trouble their companions, now forging through the snow. He suddenly felt a compulsion to know that all was well with his nephew and Moonlight.

Gorghoz paused and he plowed, nose-first, into the felts protecting that hairy back from the thickening snow. The Goremin's head was up, his eyes closed, his flared nostrils quivering in his lumpy nose.

Riddle felt a chill of apprehension send prickles up his back. What was the great creature sensing amid the increasing bluster of the wind? He found himself, somewhat to his surprise, as concerned about the Dreamer as about his own kind, as he waited for some sign from the Goremin.

One great arm reached back and down, lifting Riddle as easily as the poet lifted his young nephew. Then the wide feet plowed forward, sending sprays to either side as Gorghoz ran through the piled snow, cutting across the bends taken by the short-legged Turnig in avoiding the worst of the drifts.

Riddle, squeezed beneath that iron arm, did his best to breathe. He was too compressed and snow-blinded to worry, as he was carried forward. But he found a sudden spark of comfort in his heart. He found that he had developed a certain confidence in the strengths of the Dreamer.

Moonlight was with the Turnig. Her skills had, it seemed, unexpected aspects. Those of his family who had considered such gifts useless except for healing and amusement among the lesser peoples had not seen warriors suddenly cast into a Dream that became their reality.

He had watched, once in earlier years, as armored men struggled desperately against foes that he, outside the scope of the Dream, had not been able to see. The unprepossessing little man, cat-eyed and auburn-haired like all his kind, had been with Riddle's group by accident, and by his efforts they were saved from being forced to kill and, perhaps, to die. A mission had been concluded because he was there.

Some of those warriors he had ensnared had died. So powerful was the impact of the Dream upon their minds that they bore wounds as deep as if they had been inflicted with weapons of metal instead of imagery.

That had influenced Riddle's thinking drastically, for it is a poet's function to create images that become so real that they move thinking beings. But only he, among his people, had paid more than passing heed to the crossbreeds who Dreamed.

As Gorghoz plowed toward the group ahead of them, he wondered, suddenly, what Moonlight's true name might be. Dreamers were secretive folk, and he suspected that the *nomen* given the infant Dreamer was not the use-name by which he knew her. One day, it might be vital that he have that key to her inner self. Indeed, he wondered as much for himself as for the welfare of their fellows.

If they all survived, he would learn that *nomen*, for he was, after all, her King for the time, as long as Lute was a child. He might have need of the power that could evoke, in tandem with talents such as hers.

This journey was going to demand all the potencies the lot of them could produce, before it was done. He felt it in his intuitive bones.

Gorghoz went through the middle of a giant drift that could as accurately have been called a hill. Riddle closed his eyes and felt snow trickle into his ears and around the neck of his cloak. But they pushed through the frozen skim on the other side and he felt the wind against his face.

Gorghoz halted, but this time he set the poet on his feet. "See!" the deep voice commanded, and Riddle opened his eyes.

Lirfolk raged beyond the perimeter of an invisible circle in which their companions had sheltered. He and Gorghoz were, of course, outside the scope of the Dream, unaffected by the willing of Moonlight, and even as he watched he could see that the perimeter of the circle of power was telescoping inward as she used up her resources, her energies weakening.

The Turnig were gathered into a loose clump, which had unoccupied eddies amid their cloaked shapes, as if to their senses crevasses or pools might lie in the space where they sheltered. And yet there was no shelter there: the wind blew over them, flapping their cloaks and yet seeming not to disturb them in the least.

Their attention was focused in one direction, the side away from that on which he and Gorghoz stood. There the Lirfolk leaped and howled, threw spears and used arrows as daggers, as if there were no room for drawing a bow. They fell backward, some of them, holding hard to invisible attackers that seemed to be trying to tear out their throats.

Riddle could almost see the Gyrduk, so strong was his sense of their presence. He smiled.

Moonlight knew the most effective images to call into the minds of her victims. But he could feel that she was flagging, and he looked about, trying to see her.

She was standing somewhat apart from the main body of Turnig, facing toward the Lirfolk. Her hands were clenched at her sides, and her eyes were tightly closed.

He could almost feel on his skin the force of her will, projecting the Dream she had chosen for the defense of her charges. He was beginning to glimpse the vision she was creating, even at that distance.

"We must send them flying before she falls," said the Goremin. He was gathering up his felt cloak and bundling it aside. His great staff was freed from the tangle as he turned to the poet.

"I am afraid that once again you must bear the weight of our battle. There are times when I regret my inhibition against injuring the smaller kinds. But I will do my best to frighten them out of their wits." He sighed heavily.

"Kill, if you must, but if you can avoid it, withhold the fatal thrust!" His deep-sunk eyes were sad in his warty face.

"Now!" Riddle leaped forward, to find himself inside the vision at last.

It was warm there, and the Lir were still struggling with the Gyrduk, almost one-to-one. He strode into the fray, knowing that the beasts were only specters, which made him immune to any attack from them so long as he did not forget and believe in their actuality.

He sliced apart a Gyrduk that held a Lir by the throat. The freed warrior looked up at the one who saved him, saw the bared blade swinging for his neck, and rolled frantically to escape.

His yell distracted the animals from their business and got the attention of his fellows. Even as he cried out, Riddle raked his back with steel. Two warriors sprang to their feet, facing him with flint knives in hand.

He feinted at one, spun on his heel, and slashed the cheek of the other to the bone. Both turned and ran, as he prepared to confront the remaining thirty or more still left on the field. As they stared at him in shock, he saw vividly their resemblance to their evolved cousins in the south. But for the Kings, the new people would be just such primitives.

They seemed to lose their taste for battle, as his bloodied blade came up and he strode nearer to the center of the group. More began backing away, retreating toward the edge of the illusion.

It was one thing to attack a line of unarmed Turnig, who were less than half their own size. It was quite another to risk facing one of the Ancient Race, blade in hand. Their fragile bones could not withstand the assaults of those their own size.

When Gorghoz rose from behind a hilly drift, his square of teeth snarling, and opened his arms wide as if to grasp and crush them all, the Lirfolk broke. His deep roar of rage vibrated the very air, and the nerves of the leaders broke free of the compulsion driving them.

One after another, they disentangled themselves from their snarling adversaries and dashed across the hot pebbles over which they had fought—only to find themselves, Riddle knew, suddenly enveloped in the fresh blizzard that raged outside the illusion Moonlight had sent into their minds. He hoped that the abrupt change would not shock them into a realization of what had befallen them.

But Gorghoz had been correct. They were not capable of much coherent thought. Flight was the only thing in their hearts as they ran, freed by blind panic from the hold of the Mover from the North.

As they left the scene, the bubble of the vision collapsed. Moonlight sank slowly onto her knees amid the Turnig.

The small people found themselves blasted by the bitter wind, as they hurried to gather the small ones again into huddles of felts and blankets. Riddle saw that Lute was well wrapped and uninjured, and then he turned to the Dreamer, his heart thudding with concern as he checked her condition.

Her amber eyes were dull with fatigue, and even the strand of bright hair escaping beneath her hood seemed limp with exhaustion. She was paler, even, than before, but her blood beat steadily in her wrist, and he thought that she was not physically injured.

She, of all the group, was expending the most energy in keeping the travelers safe from harm. If this went on, she would wear herself away past mending. The thought filled him with pain.

He turned to find the huge shape of Gorghoz, who was bending over Chirrik, listening to something the small one said. When he straightened, Riddle gestured for him to come.

"We must safeguard Moonlight, if she is to last to see the Western Isles. You can see that she is draining herself.

"Can you carry her for a time, Gorghoz? We must move away from this spot, in case the Lir behind us decide to come this way. She cannot walk."

She was lying against his shoulder as he knelt there, her translucent skin almost as pale as the snow beneath her knees. Her eyes had closed again, this time in instant and necessary sleep.

Without speaking, the Goremin lifted her, wrapped her against him in his felted cloak, which Chirrik had brought to him from its hiding place, and stood erect. Her weight was nothing to the great creature, as he strode away toward the north and west.

Riddle fell in behind him, and the Turnig, their goods and their young hastily gathered and loaded onto their backs, came after them. Lute wriggled in his pack against his uncle's back, and Riddle knew again how lucky they all were that the Dreamer had joined their company. Once more a vital task was depending upon the talents of one of her breed.

Even as he thought that, he saw the Goremin stagger. Something had impacted upon the great one, and he moved up beside him.

"What was that? You winced, as if an arrow had struck you."

Gorghoz shrugged Moonlight into a better position and dug into his pouch after something. He brought out the wrappings concealing the book.

"The Mover watches. His power shows him that we move over the lands, carrying this thing that is a key to his desires.

"He is thrusting through this tainted book, trying to hinder us or to kill the one who carries it. If one of the small ones bore it, he might have succeeded. Not easily, however, does one touch a Goremin to the quick...we are older and tougher than any others now walking the lands."

Riddle held out his hand. "I will carry it, while you bear Moonlight in your arms. The Ancient Race conquered those old forces before, and I think that I may be able to bear the prying of that power, if it comes again."

"Then let Killeli carry your nephew. I would not have this injure the child, as it might easily do. I am confident that you will be able to turn aside any attack. Take the thing, keep it close, and never loose the wrapping."

He handed over the swaddled lump, and so thick was the snow that not even Killeli, at Riddle's side to take the infant, knew that anything had gone from hand to hand. But as the volume was stowed in his pack, taking the place of Lute, Riddle felt as if his feet had grown heavier, his view of the snow-swept landscape less clear. A burning pain settled into his muscles, which he could only control. He could not eliminate it.

Around him the snow swirled with particular fury, and the wind seemed to be trying to sweep him off his feet. He gritted his teeth and followed Gorghoz, hearing the crunch of Killeli's feet just behind him.

The Ancient Race of Kings had strengths of their own, and no dark will from the north would sway him from his task. No delusion sent by Verrainig or the deep-buried worm of the north would be allowed to distract him.

But, against his back, the book sent out that cold burning that did nothing to lessen the impact of the blizzard. It was a burden, indeed.

CHAPTER TWENTY-FOUR

"In a frozen chamber let me wait
to learn the dreadful lessons I must know."
                                        —Riddle

The storm worsened. Every one of the travelers was now weary, disoriented, and dismayed, for there seemed no refuge nearer than the City in the Mist itself. Riddle knew that many of his companions would fall soon, never to rise again, unless some shelter could be found.

He had not imagined in his worst nightmare what shelter they would come to, there in the snow-swept hills, amid the vicious blasts from the north. He had dropped to the end of the line, making certain no Turnig fell without being caught up and carried along. He had learned to shut away the nagging of the book in his pack, as well as the chill of the wind.

Far ahead, Gorghoz's huge shape was lost in the blowing snow, and only the half-dozen nearest of the furry figures were visible to him. He tried to check the snow on either side of the trail as he went, hoping to find any who had fallen without being seen.

He thought, at first, that the land had taken a sudden slope downward. Those ahead were descending abruptly out of his view, and his own feet seemed ready to slide from beneath him.

Yet the tilt grew steeper. He knew with sudden clarity that the ground beneath the drifts was giving way, cracking apart to let his entire company fall into the guts of the world. He tried to brace himself with his staff, but there was no solid footing for even its narrow tip.

The book burned through its wrapping, searing his side and back. A force akin to that tainted thing was troubling the soil and the stone, tumbling the travelers into its own buried place.

Dinorm! It could only be that twisted twin of Orm, lying in its crypt beneath the northern lands, using its strange powers and directing the will of the Mover from the North.

And then he was falling free, twisting in the air as he tried to slow his fall by dragging his hands against the walls of snow on either side. He landed safely enough in a pile of snow that had fallen before him, but his staff snapped beneath him as he crunched to a stop.

The drift trembled beneath his weight, and a furry head thrust up and began shaking snow from its ears.

"Chirrik?" he asked, beginning to dig after other buried Turnig. "Are you injured?"

The Turnig grunted wordlessly, sending up a flurry of snow as he, too, began to dig. Soon they had a handful more of the furry ones digging too.

Seeing that they had this group well on its way to being freed, Riddle crawled along the cranny, whose top was now leaning together as if to bury them all alive. But even as it groaned together, pebbles and grit falling about him, he saw that it left a passageway, which led down into the deeps of the frozen soil and stone.

"Gorghoz! Moonlight! Killeli!" he shouted, the vibrations of his voice bringing even more debris from above. "Are you hurt? Where are you?"

"Here," came the reply ahead of him, in the Goremin's deep voice. "All together and well enough. The fall waked Moonlight, if nothing else."

The poet scrambled over the rough passageway, finding more Turnig to help along as he went. In the darkness, it was hard to tell that he was nearing his goal until he tripped over something at last and fell, head-first, into Killeli's lap.

Lute gave an irritated grunt.

Riddle crawled to one side and set his back against a wall of rough stones. "I have a lightglass in my pack, if it hasn't broken," he said. "That might help us find what to do."

"It will make us feel more comfortable," rumbled the Goremin, "but I think that we are not the ones who will decide what is to come. We are in the lair of Dinorm, or I am badly out in my reckoning."

Riddle found the device, drew it from his pack, and thumbed the flints. A spark leaped to the oily wick, and the reddish light, usually so dim and smoky, was brilliant in the darkness.

"You are right," he said. "I felt it, just as my feet slid. I will face it, Gorghoz, if you will take the book again. I dare not go into its presence with the thing, for I cannot know surely that I will be able to resist its will. My own is trained to shape my world, but that is a far older will than mine."

Gorghoz laid Moonlight carefully against the wall, propping her up until she got her balance. She still seemed disoriented, dizzy, perhaps even unaware of their present situation.

That was just as well, Riddle thought. Let her rest before she must take up her burden of worry again.

But the Goremin was shaking his great, lumpy head. "I think you misunderstand the way of it," he said. The despair in his voice was foreign to anything Riddle had ever heard from the Goremin. Something here in the deeps was affecting him drastically. He gestured down the tunnel toward the unguessed end.

"Dinorm was the first, long before the Mover came into being. He was shaped by the Litati, as the tale says, in the time before the mountains rose or the ocean walked its present shifting paths.

"Dinorm came from the hands of those ancient people and existed long before any other living being was here in the north. Perhaps it shaped the Mover with its own will; Verrainig is its puppet far more than the Mover dreams.

"No, you will not face Verrainig, when you walk down this dark way. You will confront one of the ancient mysteries of the world, and the thought of it makes my heart freeze." In the reddish light, Gorghoz looked almost shrunken, so drawn was he into a fearful huddle.

"I would not tell you to go. I cannot go, myself, for my kind has a deep-rooted horror of Dinorm. That would render me helpless before the thing.

"It is your free choice, Riddle. I will care for the child, if you do not return. If you choose not to go at all, we will remain here until we find an escape route or until we die." He closed his eyes and leaned against the wall as if he, too, were exhausted with the terrors of the day.

Riddle felt his own heart chill. He reached to take Lute from Killeli's lap, and the child opened his eyes. His small hands gripped his uncle's cloak for a moment before relaxing again into sleep.

Riddle felt a surge of determination, as he set the child again in Killeli's lap and rose stiffly, feeling the bruises from his fall up and down his back and legs.

"You are right. It is my free choice, Gorghoz. I did not ask or want to be King. Many lives lay between me and that estate, and now my nephew is the true King of Damaria.

"Yet the responsibility has fallen onto my shoulders, and I must deal with it as best I can. Even so, it is better so than for others, less able, to be left helpless in the grip of terror."

He set the lightglass beside Moonlight. He took off his pack and laid it aside as well, and his cloak he spread over Killeli and the child.

Standing there in his tunic and breeks, he felt the endless cold of this northern soil and rock striking through to his bones, but he ignored it. He might soon be colder, still, in the grip of death.

"Care for them all, Gorghoz. Get them to the City, if you can. Ask for Oakbeam, the builder.

"My family has entrusted funds to his for generations, and he will build you a ship. Give him this, as my warranty." He took from his wrist a thin chain of dull silver links, set with a pale blue medallion the shade of a spring sky.

Gorghoz's great hand closed about the thing and he tucked it away in the belt that held his pouch and supplies. Then he gripped the poet's hand tightly in his.

"We are with you in spirit," he said. "Go with all Good, Riddle. Your ancestors stand behind you, dead though they may be, in all their power and pride."

Riddle nodded, turned on his heel, and, before he could change his mind, he strode away down the rough tunnel toward the lair of Dinorm.

* * * * * * *

Lorbek stared into the Orb, his pale eyes straining to see some image in the flame trapped within the crystal. He had waked from troubled sleep, compelled by the will that now shaped most of his thoughts and feelings. He had been driven to take the Sealed Flame from its hiding place and set it before him on the table in the King's room.

Why? He had only jumbled perceptions, filtered through the alien emotions of that distant Immortal. There was victory within his grasp; that came clearly enough through the surge of gratification. But there was also danger of some unspecified but perilous nature. He could feel the tension of the Mover across all the leagues, and if he had dared he might have called that emotion fear.

He bent forward, his face almost against the glowing crystal, seeking to take into his own mind the blue-green glow of the flame. Something moved there. He should be able to will it, shape it, force it to do his bidding, but he was not of the full blood of the Ancient Race.

With desperate effort he tried, but he knew, at last, that only the true King or his heir could force his will upon the lands and the beings upon them, using that as a focus of power. Lorbek was, after all, his mother's child, and only enough of his father looked through his eyes to recognize that there was the potential for purpose, there in the burning Orb.

He was, his innermost thought admitted with pain and frustration, half a primitive, as well as half a King. And that was not enough.

* * * * * * *

Alien feet walked upon Dinorm's lands, ignoring the blizzards its will sent down upon them. Alien voices spoke and cried aloud above its head, frightening the vermin with whom it sometimes amused itself.

Dinorm woke more fully than it had in ages, the cold glow intensifying, its sticky length straightening from the thick curl that was a favorite position for dozing. It felt a touch at the doors of its mind, a question forming, but it ignored that.

The arrogant creatures who lived above and wondered at the shaking of the lands were irrelevant now. It was Dinorm's own will that had been flouted by the presence of those intruders. Now the ancient Shaper had no time to mislead Verrainig into thinking that he was the Mover, instead of the Moved.

The thing moved its powerful length against the rock of the lair, willing the stones to shake, the soil to crack, the ice to shift. It set its mind upon bringing those bold interlopers into its presence, and it was not long before Dinorm felt the fulfillment of its will.

There was no place in the cold mind of the creature to hold satisfaction or amusement, but something within it responded to the despair that those trapped surface-goers must feel. It had learned much from Verrainig concerning the two-legged beings that crossed the lands in summer, when the warmth drove it deep into the rock to sleep most deeply.

It waited without impatience. Waiting was the thing it did best, after all, there in the wastes of the north. But in time Dinorm heard steps echoing down the tube of stone that it had caused to form between the trap and its chamber. It wanted to sense this new kind for itself, rather than accepting Verrainig's assessment.

Those steps, while they stumbled from time to time on the fallen stones and the ridges of debris lying in the passage, seemed filled with confidence. That seemed strange, after the assurances of Verrainig that those in the south were weaklings whose cowardice would make them easy prey.

"Once the intruders from the south are destroyed," the Mover had said, "We will sweep down upon those warm and pleasant lands and possess them. You will confront your weakling twin and devour him, and then we two will rule from the mountains to the sea."

Dinorm's aims were far different, but it had allowed the puppet to think what he would, using his own powers to achieve unguessed goals. When it no longer had use for the cold one above, Dinorm would devour him, along with that distant Orm.

Then nothing would move on the lands except the small, helpless beasts. And that would please the deep-dweller better than anything else could do.

The steps neared, and Dinorm raised a blunt head, moving all the sensors into position. The newcomer would find it in its own place, at the height of its powers. Before destroying him, the great worm would winnow out everything that he was and knew and thought.

That would help in the cleansing of the lands. It might even give Dinorm an additional weapon with which to torture that chattel in the icy temple, when the time came to make Verrainig grovel.

CHAPTER TWENTY-FIVE

"The fires of will can burn with awful power,
melting fears and holding fast the heart."
—Riddle

The tunnel was black, once Riddle passed the sinuous bends that separated him from the glimmer of the lightglass. The poet felt his way along, stumbling from time to time but managing to keep his balance and his goal equally under control.

After what seemed hours, he realized that he was seeing another faint phosphorescence, without warmth and something like the glow of fungus decaying in a dark wood, that touched knobs and angles of rock with subtle lines of gray. It allowed him to see his way more clearly, as it grew stronger, and he was able to hurry his steps.

The glow turned greenish-gray, as he went, and by the time he emerged into the bubble of space in the stone he could see quite well. Eyes accustomed to complete darkness adjust easily to even the smallest of lights.

His could not, at first, believe the thing they saw. Curved to fit the round chamber, the stubby length of fat gray flesh gleamed stickily in its own phosphorescence. Stubby arms and thick legs moved aimlessly on either side of the slug-like body. It stirred lazily, as if sensing his approach.

The raised head, spade-shaped and almost featureless, was dotted with dark patches, not the sensory organs his kind knew, but pits of darkness. Riddle knew with sudden clarity that those allowed it to sense its surroundings as accurately, it was probable, as eyes and ears and nose might do. The head turned toward him slowly, arrogantly, and he imagined feelers of those invisible receptors crawling over his face and his body.

He shuddered. But he stood his ground, facing the thing, holding his courage in both hands, and remembering the impossible matters that his kind had achieved over the millennia.

"Dinorm," he said, his tone quiet and untroubled.

The head moved slightly, dipping toward him as if some sense served it as hearing. A tingle formed in his mind, and he felt meanings that had no voice but held the impact of words.

"Intruder!"

That, at least, was true, though only through necessity and for as short a time as possible. "Yes. But not for long. We only travel toward the ocean and the City in the Mist." He hoped the thing understood.

He felt fury building inside the creature. There was an impression of hatred and frustration, and he suddenly wondered if this imprisoned being hated its confinement and felt envy and hatred for those walking free on the land or traveling on the reaches of the sea.

"Vermin!"

"Thinking beings of several kinds," he said aloud, though he suspected the thing could read his thoughts. "Your Mover has not told you the truth about us in the south, I suspect.

"He has faced one of us already, and he was the loser in that encounter. A Dreamer escaped from him, taking her spirit back from his keeping. And she took with her a certain book, which it seems that Verrainig hated to lose."

A sudden shock ran along whatever linked him with Dinorm, through his mind and into his body. The Mover had not told Dinorm about losing—even, perhaps, about capturing—the Dreamer. As for the book, it might be that the Shaper had no knowledge of it at all.

This was something the thing had not known, and he could feel it assimilating the new knowledge in some esoteric manner. The fury grew stronger.

Moonlight had used the anger of Verrainig against that frozen creature. Could he use the same weapon against Dinorm?

But he knew with sudden finality that he could not. Already, that cold and arrogant mind was controlling its reactions. The will inside the hideous body was as old and as strong as the stones of the crypt, and no words, however unexpected, were going to disrupt its focus upon its goals.

He sighed inaudibly. There was no trickery he knew that might disturb the creature enough to loose its hold upon his companions. He would have to face it, will to will, strength to strength.

Though his father or his uncle or his grandmother might have been the equal of this ancient force, his own strengths lay elsewhere. His training, while intensive, had not equaled theirs.

If he accomplished even so much as the opening of a way out of the tunnel for those behind him, he felt that it would be all that his own life could buy. He braced himself as he had learned to do when he trained with his father's Guard. He pulled all his attention from his body into the keep of his skull, and he sharpened it there, waiting for Dinorm to make another move.

That took a very long while. Time did not exist, here in the deeps of the world, for a deathless being. Its mind was moving with curdled slowness toward its next step in this encounter, and Riddle knew that he could only wait and endure until that came.

Anything he did, without guidance or training in dealing with such a creature, would probably be wrong and possibly destructive. But he pulled his thoughts away from such concerns. Worry could defeat one who might triumph, if he held himself under control.

His knees felt stiff as old iron. His neck and his eyeballs ached from staring at the inscrutable head looming above him. He had forced himself so firmly into a waiting mode that it took a long moment for him to realize that the creature was moving, when the great body shifted at last.

His mind sprang to the alert, and he unbraced his back, taking up a more flexible stance and subtly tensing and relaxing his stiff muscles. He would need every strength, every skill he possessed, as he met this challenge.

He opened an old window that his training had set into his racial memory. His inner vision shone with the light of lost suns, the shapes of faces that had long been dust. He saw his father's and his mother's, frozen in the sleep of death.

The ranks of his forebears existed inside him, as they did within every member of the Ancient Race. For generations, any of those had been able to call upon their knowledge and experience, when the need was great.

He could only wish that he had been trained more deeply in the use of that gift. But it was too late for concern now. The huge head was dipping toward him, the sensors pulsing, turning purplish in the gray light.

He focused his gaze on that featureless face, trying to read the purposes of the thing, trying to find a hint of its intentions. But it told him nothing, and at last he closed his eyes and called upon those stored memories for aid.

The creature's will attacked with the suddenness and the impact of a blow, striking at Riddle's innermost self, the things he dreaded and the weaknesses he knew. He felt himself defiled and exposed, a laughable pretense who thought to thwart the will of the one who had shaped the north.

It almost felled him, in that first instant of conflict, and he felt himself stagger, only to catch his balance and brace himself again.

But now he was warned. The shield that his forebears had forged, long ago, against such attacks rose into his memory, and he locked it into his mind as the blunt head came about, surveying him with all the pits of both its sides.

Another onslaught of the strength the last had held would have defeated him, he knew. But now, with his ancestral strengths in place, perhaps he might endure, holding for long enough to stir the creature to wrath.

Again the flail of compulsion struck, but this time he stood firm, and the steely will of his people met the stroke with a solidity that stopped the thrust of Dinorm as if a sword had struck an anvil. There was a moment of shivering tension, the vibrations of that silent impact ringing through Riddle, through the creature, and through the rock itself.

There was a surge of warmth through his body. A rosy spark leaped, as he opened his eyes again, along an invisible thread between his face and the head of Dinorm. Along that thread, he sent a filament of thought, a bit of the reality that was the Ancient Race from the south, rulers of lands Dinorm had not dreamed existed. Their unbending justice, their cool kindness, their contempt for the trappings of power darted into the mind of the ancient being.

The creature flinched; Riddle knew that something drawn from inside himself had touched it painfully, piercing its self-centered mind with rays of light kindled in other races untouched by the Litati.

He closed his eyes again, allowing the well of knowledge and power to flow upward through veins and arteries, through the channels of his brain and his nerves, into this strange enemy. He had a terrifying thought—what if this strengthened the thing, instead of shaking its confidence?

But he suppressed that. He might not understand the intricacies of the potencies inside him, but whatever it was that his ancient line intended, that was all he had as a weapon. If they must pour themselves into the mind of Dinorm, he would stand firm as the channel through which they moved.

He endured, as his nerves burned with the passing of that flood. He stood straight, letting it flow through him, out of him, lighting the worm with the rosy stream of its power.

Dinorm squirmed. Riddle could feel the pain that filled the creature, the unaccustomed energy that quivered in its lethargic muscles. He could feel the thing withdrawing into itself, confused by the inrush of alien concepts, alien perceptions. It began sliding backward toward a thick crack in the farther wall of the crypt.

The end of the blunt tail disappeared into the fissure, the sticky length thrusting itself backward, trying to escape the painful current invading its mind and its body. It was not defeated—far from it—but it had been too long since it had known discomfort. It was not used to dealing with things it had not created.

Dinorm had grown soft, there in the safety of its lair. For geological ages, it had lain in the security of the stone, touched only by the tentative thought of the Mover and its tenuous link with its twin.

This invasion of alien wills and ways was a thing it could not bear. With a sucking and sticking of its slimy body, it fled through the crack toward some even deeper and more secret burrow. Once it recovered its equanimity, it would be even more dangerous, but for now it was forced to retreat, to digest the flood of carefully selected knowledge that had engulfed it.

Riddle felt the link snap. The flow of the past was cut off suddenly, and the internal pressure brought a groan from him. Then, feeling vaguely triumphant and oddly sad, he felt himself slip to his knees. As the gray light faded from the crypt, he fell into a well of darkness and knew nothing more.

* * * * * * *

Moonlight rubbed her eyes, trying to regain her alertness. She was still exhausted, but her sleep, while Gorghoz carried her through the snow, had given her back some strength.

"Riddle?" she asked, her voice barely audible. She cleared her throat and sneezed, hard, three times.

Gorghoz reached to pat her arm. "He has gone to find the end of this tunnel."

The words were simple, but something inside her stiffened with alarm. This tunnel—she looked about, understanding at last where she was.

The snow-covered hills over which they had been traveling, and the oasis of warmth and safety she had Dreamed for her companions, had disappeared. She was underground.

If they were below-ground, it meant they had come voluntarily, which she doubted, or had been deposited there by some slippage of the soil and rock. That could only mean that the creature dwelling in the depths for ages, of which Gorghoz had told them, had moved, opening this passage beneath the blizzard-wracked hills.

And if that were the cause of their present position, then Riddle could only find, at the tunnel's end, the Dinorm. She sighed and stretched, feeling the pain of overused muscles and nerves.

"If he lives, he will not walk away from the thing he will find. And if he dies, I will not leave him there to freeze fast to the store," she said.

Even as she spoke, there came a subtle quivering in the walls and floor of the rift. Something was happening, down there in the darkness, and Riddle, she knew unerringly, must be its cause.

She caught a knob of stone and pulled herself upright, swaying for a moment before she regained her balance. Her cloak was a hindrance, even though the tunnel was filled with the endless chill of perpetual winter, and she dropped it over the nearest of the Turnig.

But Chark wriggled from beneath it and stood beside her. "You not strong yet. I go too. Gorghoz stay here, look after small ones. We go get poet together."

Moonlight smiled down at the sturdy figure, clad only in its own thick fur. "Welcome, Chark."

The Goremin looked down the tunnel, his great eyes shining dimly in the glow from the lightglass. "I would go, but my courage has gone. If Riddle is dead, I must take the Turnig and the child to the sea. Good luck be with you, Dreamer."

She caught the small square hand of the Turnig and they moved cautiously down the passage, stumbling once they were out of the light. But it was impossible to become lost in that narrow way, and they moved along with fair speed toward whatever end awaited them.

After a long while, she could feel something looming ahead of her, as a pressure of stalled air against her skin. She needed light, and there was a chance that a Dream of light might work as well as one of warmth and shelter had done.

"Wait," she whispered to Chark. "I will see if I can help us to see."

They stood close together, and she gathered her depleted energies for a last effort. Closing her eyes, she concentrated upon a gleam, the merest flicker, rising from the depths of the stones along the way. She knew she had succeeded when Chark's small hand tightened on her own.

"Look!" the Turnig gasped. "Look!"

She opened her eyes to find that the darkness had been alleviated by a pale yellow glow from certain of the layerings of the walls, just enough to allow her to make out the way and the wall ahead. A recumbent shape lay on the stone some strides from the spot where she had paused.

Chark was already moving toward the poet. Moonlight hurried

after her, seeing the ghostly illumination from the stone outlining his body.

She felt his forehead, which was chilly, and the pulse at his throat. A steady throb told her he still lived, though she could not guess if he would rouse again to become the person she knew. If he did not...but she shook away the thought.

"I help!" gasped the Turnig, setting her shoulder under his arm and trying to lift him.

Moonlight took the other side, exerting all her strength to raise most of the poet's length, so that only his toes dragged behind the unlikely trio as they turned back toward the waiting company.

As they struggled down the way, the light faded slowly. Moonlight knew she had no strength to create more illumination, and they went on in the dark.

That was unimportant, however. They had Riddle, and he was alive. If only they could find a way out of the rift Dinorm had made, they might carry him forward toward the City in the Mist.

In time they came again to the spot where Gorghoz waited, with Killeli and Lute and the Turnig. The lightglass still shone steadily, its tiny spark burning so little fuel that the oil would last for many nights.

The Goremin seemed not to hear their noisy approach, however. His head was turned away, toward the passage along which the group had moved after falling.

Overhead, something was grinding, groaning, gritting stone against stone like great teeth gnashing. She dropped Riddle carefully onto her cloak and stared, too, amazed.

The poet had done his work well. The crack was opening again, to expel these irritants from the awareness of Dinorm. The creature must, she thought, lurk someplace beyond the end of the tunnel, nursing its wounded pride and wanting only to rid itself of those who had fallen into its trap.

She caught up Lute out of Killeli's lap, jogged the elbow of the Goremin, and urged Chark into a crack that would shelter her from falling debris. Once that split was fully open, she intended to take herself and the others out of these deeps, if she had to Dream them all wings in order to accomplish it.

CHAPTER TWENTY-SIX

"To move into the sunlight is a thing to lift the heart."
—Riddle

Gorghoz shook his great head, feeling groggy and disoriented. What had happened to him, during this time below-ground? Something had reduced him, in that place and that time, to a shivering youngling.

He had never in all his long life lacked control over himself and his surroundings. But now he felt as if he had been cast adrift from himself for a time, his will and his energies lessened. He had half a memory of sending Riddle down a tunnel alone, to face a terrible enemy.

Again he shook his head, and Moonlight's touch on his shoulder brought him out of his daze.

"Gorghoz! The rift is opening. We must go now, or it will close again." Her tone was urgent, and he pulled himself up and wavered for an instant before the feeling of strangeness thinned.

What had Dinorm done that could make a Goremin lose confidence and courage? But there was no time for questions.

He strode forward to stand beneath the crack. Beyond it was a streak of sky, seeming almost clear except for a wisp of cloud and tinted with the pale rose-gold of dawn. Today the sun would rise unobstructed, he thought.

Had Riddle so discomfited the creature he faced that it had retreated into the depths, forgetting the people it trapped and the obstacles it had put into their way? He could only believe so, as he stretched upward, measuring the distance to the nearest hand-hold.

It was a good man-height above his reach, a knee of rough stone thrust out over the space below. Killeli was tall enough, he thought, to catch it. His monkey-like arms and hands were suited to such work, as well.

"Killeli," he called. "Can you go up there, if I lift you and push?"

There was a moment of waiting, while Killeli emptied his lap of its accumulated youngsters. Then the wispy shape appeared in the glow of the lightglass and the sky, staring upward. The sharp eyes measured the distance carefully.

"I believe I can. The rope from your pack, Goremin, will be needed, too. I can secure it above, and we can haul up those who cannot climb for themselves." His leathery mask of a face was squinched with thought.

Gorghoz reached to lift him, and he was astonished at how much lighter his companion was than he had been a few weeks before. Surely, he was still feeling the effects of this terrible journey as well as that drenching in the river!

But he went up with some ease, catching the outcrop with both hands and flipping himself onto its top without effort. The rope followed him, and he moved again, setting his toe into a niche and crawling out onto the surface they had thought was forever beyond their reach.

Once he had secured it, the rope slithered down again, its end curling onto the floor. Gorghoz made a sling of it and fastened it about the limp body of the poet. Moonlight reached higher and began to climb the rope to join Killeli.

The pair of them managed to pull the unconscious Riddle up without banging him against the rough walls of the rift. Gorghoz felt himself give a harsh sigh as the poet's body disappeared over the rim of the crack.

He watched that swinging shape with anxiety, dreading a motion that might dash out his brains against the wall of the rift. Riddle was a treasure too valuable to lose.

Then it was a matter of getting the multitude of Turnig and young ones to the surface, which was an easy matter, as none weighed enough to make a problem. It was the Goremin who would be difficult to raise to the top of the crack.

At last he stood alone in the dimness, having sent the lightglass up, extinguished, to be safely stored against further need. The rope came down a last time. Moonlight's head appeared over the lip of the crack.

"Gorghoz, make a sling for yourself, as you did for Riddle. Fit it securely.

"We are all going to pull, and if you can set toes or hands against the rock and help us, we will have a better chance of raising you. You weigh almost as much as the rest of us put together, and this is going to be hard."

He looked about, thinking of his earlier behavior. He felt shame at the memory. Even if they could not lift him, it would be a fair exchange, his life for those of so many. And he had put the book, once more, into Riddle's pack, so that would continue on its journey to the sea.

But he made the harness and secured it about his great hairy body. Then he tugged at the rope, peering up into the girl's face.

"Pull away. And if you cannot lift me, go on without me. I have lived for millennia. I will not grieve if this is the end of me."

She scowled at him. Then her head vanished, and the rope lifted, tightened.

He went onto tiptoe, higher, until his feet were clear of the floor. Reaching a long arm, he pushed downward against an outcrop of rock, helping as much as was possible.

He felt as if he were being squeezed into slices, for the thin rope cut into his ribs and his buttocks. But he continued to rise, pausing from time to time while those hauling away at the top rested. He felt as if he would emerge in pieces, sliced by the thin rope.

A hand's span at a time, the determined people above pulled his bulk upward, and once he got his fingers onto the knee aloft, the task was all but done. His great hand gripped the rock, and he managed to get an elbow onto it as well.

He rested as little weight as possible on the stone, as he reached for the edge above his head. His hand was caught by others, small but determined, and he heaved upward as the outcrop beneath his elbow began to move.

The rope tightened again, and the Turnig held him, as he and Moonlight and Killeli managed to bring his bulk onto the frozen soil. He lay there, panting, before drawing up his feet and legs.

When he was able to look about, he realized that all the rest were lying flat in the trampled snow, drawing in great gasps of the cold air. Bringing him from the deep had exhausted the entire troop of Turnig, as well as the others.

He turned onto his back, ignoring the slushy snow. It was good to stare into the eye of the sun again. No wind blew, at the moment, and he felt almost warm in the slanting beam. As the sun rose, it warmed him still more, and at last he sat and shook himself, grooming his coarse hair and smoothing out his crumpled cloak.

About him, the rest were reviving after their struggle. Moonlight bent over Riddle, and Gorghoz realized that the poet was again conscious.

"What?" came the faint query.

"We are out. Whatever you did, it made Dinorm open the rift

again. The thing wasn't there when we went after you, so evidently you injured it in some way.

"But it was there, back in the dark tunnels, for I felt it. It will remember us, in time, and we must be gone when it does, for it is going to be far angrier and more dangerous than any enemy we have known."

She caught his offered hand, and Gorghoz went to take the other. Together, they pulled the poet to his feet, where he swayed like a reed in the wind.

"I think that I am not very stable," he said, catching onto the Goremin's arm. "But I will walk. My knees are strong enough, I think."

The Turnig were gathering their packs and their young into travel mode, quietly and speedily. They, too, knew what lurked beneath their feet, and they had no wish for a closer acquaintance.

Lute was again entrusted to Killeli, while Moonlight watched the line of walkers. Gorghoz supported the poet, whose steps grew firmer as he moved along.

After a bit, Gorghoz lifted him onto his shoulder and carried him, for all now felt an urge to leave this place behind them while the sun shone and the wind was quiet. Dinorm was there. They dreaded risking another encounter with the ancient being beneath the snows.

* * * * * * *

Riddle moved in a fog, only half aware of the Goremin who carried him, of the snow, blindingly bright in the sunlight, or of the others moving along in Gorghoz's tracks. A part of him seemed to be lost in darkness, deep beneath stone and soil.

Buried alive? Who? He struggled to remember, closing his eyes against the glare and straining to recall what had happened, there in the lair of Dinorm.

But instead he slept, warmed by the closeness of Gorghoz's hairy body. It seemed a long while before he opened his eyes, finding that the troop had paused in its journey. The wind was moving again, for he felt it whipping at the loose bits of his cloak, and the chill had all but frozen his face.

He moved, and Gorghoz set him carefully upon his feet, holding him steady until he could stand. "We must rest," said the Goremin. "We began our trek already weary, and we have come many miles now.

"I think that Dinorm, if it would trouble us with its movements, would have to disrupt much of the hill country to reach so far. It does not waste its strength, that one."

Riddle suddenly caught at a memory. "It did not know that the Mover had taken Moonlight. Verrainig is keeping secrets from his master. Is that useful?" He knew that it must be, but his mind was still fogged and uncertain.

"Ah! I thought we had escaped too easily. You troubled the creature to its depths with that news, I am certain, whatever else you managed to do to it. It serves it out for bespelling a Goremin, making me timid and helpless as an infant.

"It will be long before I can forget that!" The deep voice was hoarse with feeling.

Riddle straightened, feeling a trickle of returning strength. And with that, he began recalling his visit to the lair of Dinorm.

"It is disturbed but not injured," he said, his voice gaining in clarity. "The thing retreated into the deeps, troubled and confused by the things that it found inside itself, but Dinorm will come out again, doubly determined to clean the lands of everything that walks aboveground. Even the small beasts, I think, will suffer, if the creature should gain the power that it wants.

"For I felt it, there in the cold glow of that sticky hide. I knew its aims, in part, and I read the hatred it felt for me, not as an individual but as a warm-blooded creature with a will of his own."

He saw that blunt head, as the dull patches turned purple and the sensors licked outward to feel and understand this new thing that had come into its trap. He felt the tingle along his skin and nerves as the thing attacked his mind.

He shook away the feeling. "I called upon my racial memory, for nobody, even the King himself, was ever trained to face such a thing as this and triumph over it. Yet the collective impact of all my ancestors, all their skills and strengths and minds, turned aside its will, filled it with concepts alien to its mind, and disturbed it so that it fled. That was when it ran, and I fainted."

The wind picked up strength, and a spatter of snow gusted over the hills. There was the faintest of tremors underfoot, as if the earth itself shivered.

Without another word, the travelers lifted their burdens, set down so briefly, and headed into the west, away from the cold hills and the colder beings who inhabited them. For Dinorm had come out of hiding and realized, Riddle knew, that the quarry had escaped.

The creature would not destroy its own habitation completely, as would be required for shaking them to their knees at such a distance. But Riddle understood now that it had other and less obvious ways of working its will.

He did not want to learn what they might be.

He caught Gorghoz's cloak and, pulled along by the mighty creature, he kept pace as again the Goremin broke trail for the following Turnig. Lute and the book must make their way to the City in the Mist, if not another did. He would walk until he dropped and then he would crawl, to see that the two found that sanctuary at last.

Behind them, distant and yet distinct, there came a howl. Gyrduk! Riddle jerked the Goremin's cloak. "The Gyrduk do not hunt the hills in winter!" he gasped.

Behind them there came a quiet voice. "One does. It hunts for me, and I dread to think what it may lead in its train." Moonlight took his other hand and helped him along, and now his feet moved faster still.

They were not yet safe from pursuit.

Chapter Twenty-Seven

"Great strivings can wound great hearts...."
　　　　　　　　　　　　　　　　　　—Riddle

As they moved forward doggedly, ignoring their exhaustion, the wind grew even sharper. More snow stung them, carried into their flinching faces by its gusts. Behind them the howls grew fainter, and the Dreamer hoped the weather, the new snow, and their time below-ground had confused their trail and delayed their pursuers.

Moonlight pulled her hood about her cheeks and over her eyes and walked, head down, into the gale, which had shifted from its original direction in the north to the northwest. Even as they wound about the hills, which now were lower and smoother, the wind managed to remain ahead, stinging their faces and blinding them with blown snow.

Behind them in the frozen hills, Verrainig knew their destination. He had, she suspected, stirred Dinorm to action again, intending to hinder their steps toward the City in the Mist. She shivered, feeling her knees quiver with weariness and her head pound with the cold, as well as her own tense nerves.

They were drawing near their goal. A few days, at the most, lay between the fugitives and the port city. To fail at this point, after coming so far and through such trials, would be unthinkable.

She shrugged her pack into a more comfortable position and trudged onward in the beaten track the line of Turnig had trodden behind their big leader. By now the snow was so dense she could barely see the form of the Goremin striding ahead, his cloak flapping behind him, half concealing Killeli.

A sudden compulsion sent her hurrying toward the Goremin, moving around the furry shapes in her way. The book! Even as she ran, she saw Gorghoz stagger and stop, his shoulders hunched in pain. The power channeled through the book was attacking their strongest, and she knew the time had come for her to carry through the mission she had begun with the theft of the volume. Lorbek was linked, she felt with much certainty, into a chain of will that was surging into the contaminated volume, set upon bringing down Gorghoz, then Riddle, and then herself, as they took up the book in their turns.

She must carry it now. The reason was unclear in her mind, but it compelled her forward on cold, dead legs. She bumped into Riddle without recognizing him until he caught her elbow and pulled her to a stop.

"Moonlight! What is the matter?" His eyes stared out at her from the shelter of his hood and the scarf wound about his face so thickly that it was hard to see just what sort of being he might be.

"The book." She found that her teeth were chattering. "I must carry it. I feel...I don't know what it is that I feel, but it tells me to take the parcel into my own hands and to carry it ahead of the rest of you, into the teeth of the storm.

"It is important, Riddle!" She stared at him, feeling the desperate compulsion of her need.

He set Lute into Killeli's waiting arms and took her hand. "Then we will go and get it from Gorghoz. I will walk behind you, making certain this is not some misguiding impulse sent to you by those who want the book. It might be a trap of some sort; Dinorm has tremendous abilities, and it was only the unexpectedness of my own strengths that allowed us to escape him."

She took his hand with relief, and he towed her forward, past Chark and her grandparents, to the heels of the Goremin. The big creature groaned at her touch on his back and turned his great head.

"We must hurry!" His deep voice had grown faint and weak from pain in the increasing whine of the wind. "I feel the thought of Verrainig turning toward us. I feel the wrath of Dinorm squirming below the soil, surging after us in growing wrath.

"I feel the distant will of Lorbek tangled into the weave that has been flung wide to snare us. Those wicked wills can pursue us to the very gates of the City, if they do not bring us down before we arrive there."

Moonlight felt her vision blank out, as darkness veiled her eyes. Yet upon that darkness was drawn a picture, in lines of silver and gray. She walked over snow, carrying the book, and a terrible and necessary goal lay before her. She faced an old enemy once more, and she shrank from the thought, terror deep in her heart.

She knew what it was she must do, but there were no words with which to describe it, nor was there time for them. She stared up into the lumpy face and the kind eyes below the grizzled brow ridges. She struggled to free her lips from the cold that numbed them, to free her mind from the thing that was pushing her toward her waiting task.

Riddle loosed her hand and set his own upon the Goremin's arm. "She needs to carry the book. Something compels her."

"A trap!" Gorghoz's eyes narrowed against the wind. "Dinorm again, trying to delay us. Surely you do not agree to her going?"

Riddle shook his head, his expression puzzled. "I should disagree, and yet something inside me says this is the way...the only way to reach our goal. No, Gorghoz, the book came first into her hands. It was her unerring instinct that took it out of the possession of those who might use it against the few who could resist the rebels in Damaria. It is her responsibility.

"She entrusted us with it because we are bigger and stronger than she, not because it is our task to carry it. The thing came to her, and she must be the one to follow her needs concerning it. She will protect it with her life, as she has been willing to do already. I say give it into her hands. I will follow her closely to prevent any treachery lying in ambush for her. We two will take the burden upon us and go forward, while you lead the Turnig onward toward the sea."

Gorghoz's heavy shoulders bent even more; his head bowed. But he reached into his pouch and pulled out the scorched silk that wrapped the book. He touched it lightly, as if his fingers dreaded the feel of the thing, and he handed it to Moonlight with a look of relief, able now to straighten and to draw breath without agony. In the distance there was a shrill cry, and he shivered as his fingers released the volume.

She took the thing from his big hands into her own slender, calloused ones. A surge of energy pulsed through her at the contact; it felt almost as if the tainted leather squirmed in her fingers. Despite the burning sensation that brought, she grasped it tightly and moved past the Goremin into the full blast of the returning blizzard.

She heard Riddle's feet crunching into the snow behind her, and his company comforted her. Yet she forgot he was there before she had gone ten paces. Something called to her. Something summoned at the same time that it repelled her. And yet, deep within her in the core of the heritage and the training that made her a Dreamer, there was a stability that kept her steps firm as she moved across the frozen soil toward one of the rounded hills, topped with a circle of juniper about a broken-toothed arc of stones.

Her dreaming Gift moved within her, roused and yet appalled at the thing she must do. And what was that? She could bring no vision clearly into her mind. Only a hint of the answer formed in her depths, and she shuddered at the thought.

To taint her Gift with a darkness akin to that which had sullied the book was a thing that made her spirit freeze inside her. Yet she knew all the generations of her Dreamer kindred were commanding her now, pulling her weary body and her resistant mind toward a task from which she shrank.

"Grandmother!" Her cry was lost in the wind, but she knew the teachings of her kinswoman had saved her from Verrainig. She had grown colder than the Mover and had from that stance forced him to make an error that cost him dearly. That seemed opposed to everything a Dreamer was or meant, and yet it had worked.

Another of the old teachings, imposed on her unformed mind when she was a child and then buried carefully beneath gentler lessonings, roused into life. Her memory winnowed it free, and for the first time in her adult life she looked squarely at the ability she had been taught to forget.

The Dreaming could become destructive and deadly. A Dreamer using such matters for her own gain would destroy herself, certainly and totally, leaving a ruined hulk to live out a twisted life.

One using it for the benefit of others, for what she perceived as a vital necessity or a positive good, would still be corrupted, rendered unfit for her calling ever again. She would be blinded in her abilities, made impotent. Perhaps she would die—it seemed a fitting punishment for such a misuse of power.

She would never again dream, she guessed, even the innocent visions of sleep. And that, for one of her kind, was far worse than any death imaginable. But still she went forward, passing the frozen clumps of rock and bush, the ridges and the ruts, without seeing anything except the hill that was her goal.

Dusk brought darkness, for the cloud was thick. She arrived at her goal after a time that seemed endless, and yet it was too soon, for this might be the end of her life.

* * * * * * *

Riddle was hard put to keep up with the Dreamer, as she all but ran into the teeth of the wind. Her legs, which had seemed almost unable to bear her weight, sped through the snow, carrying her some distance ahead of him, no matter how he hurried to catch up.

Her shoulders were pushed forward with the intensity of her speed. He could tell from the set of her head that she was seeing and hearing things invisible and inaudible to him. Something, it was certain, was pushing and pulling her on a course that lay on a straight line toward the north, angled away from the route of their companions.

He hoped desperately this was not some machination of the Mover or his master. If that were the case, their cause was lost and the book would come into the very hands least suited to hold it. Yet still his own instinct told him to follow, to watch, and to let the Dreamer be.

As they went, he found the wind on his left shoulder, freeing his eyes for watching the way his feet must take. So the enemies behind were still working to impede the larger group of travelers. Did they yet understand that two of them had split off from the rest and were going northward? He could only feel they would have set their best efforts toward stopping Moonlight, if they understood what was taking place. He prayed that her unexpected action might be, somehow, to the advantage of his weary and frightened troop.

A pudding-basin hill loomed ahead of them, this one crowned with a circle of scrubby conifers, prickly with needles. Moonlight moved, die-straight, up its side, her feet sinking into the snow and slipping backward from time to time.

Riddle found himself panting as he struggled after her. When he looked up at last he found she had stopped at the top of the hill, surrounded by the junipers that seemed to have been set deliberately in a ring edging a stone wall. At its center there was a slab of rock, angled upward to form a tall triangle that sliced through the blowing snow like the prow of a ship. It was a chill gray-blue, dark against the white pall in the air and on the ground.

Something told him to wait outside the circle; he huddled into his cloak, enduring the blast and watching the Dreamer. She moved to the stone, her hand going out to touch one sharp angle that could hold no snow on its all but vertical surface. Then she went behind it, out of the wind, and he moved around the ring of junipers, keeping her in sight. When Riddle found a sheltered spot from which to watch, she had already set her back to the soaring slab of stone and was standing, her face pale, her eyes closed, her hands clenched into fists.

What was it she intended? He had no clue, and even searching those internal recollections that lurked in his racial memory could not tell him what she was about to try. His people had never studied the Dreamers to any degree.

He was protected from the worst of the wind by the bushes and the bulk of the stone, and he crouched beneath his cloak, waiting to see what would happen next. He had a cold intuition that something was approaching out of the north and east. Something terrible and deadly was about to confront the Dreamer, who might well be forced to battle it with some even more terrible talent of her own.

Riddle shivered again, feeling helpless and impotent, as the evening drew on, darkening the sky even more than the blizzard had already done.

CHAPTER TWENTY-EIGHT

"Those who travel darkest roads
must reckon with the night."
                              —Riddle

The poet felt that he and the hill and the Dreamer, now only a blot against a darker blur that was the stone, were caught in some frozen eddy of time. They might circle here, helpless and lost forever, he thought, as the night drew in and he was held to the physical world only by the snow that whipped around the barrier of trees to sting his face.

He had wrapped his thick scarf even more closely about his chin, keeping only his eyes free of its folds. His teeth chattered, as much with cold as with fear, and he had no trouble with keeping himself wakeful. Time crept past, as he grew colder and more afraid. Yet, at some point in the frozen darkness, he knew something had changed.

He could feel a loathsome presence looming over the horizon, coming nearer all the while he waited, dreading its arrival. There grew upon his mind the impression that he could see, not by moonlight or snow light; a faint illumination was turning the drifted snow to gray. A baleful glow was filling the space in the circle with a cold, dead hue like that of old lead.

Riddle crept deeper beneath a juniper, hiding himself as well as he could while still keeping watch on Moonlight, who stood in the spot at which she had come to rest, her eyes still closed, her hands still clenched. The strange light had turned her skin a pallid greenish shade that made her look as if she were dead.

* * * * * * *

When her hands touched the slanting stone, Moonlight felt a jolt, as if some long-stored force had sprung out of the ancient slab and into her fingers. Still tingling with the contact, she set her back against the thing, hearing the wind sing across its top with vicious shrillness, and waited for the battle to come.

The change came so subtly that she was not, at first, aware of it. Then she understood that she was able to see—a leaden glow touched the snow, the junipers, and her own body, edging them with sickly gray-green. Her hands looked dead, and her burden was growing heavier by the instant.

She gripped the book more tightly still, as a voice dropped like a stone into the circle. "You cannot resist, Dreamer. You cannot keep the thing you stole from my inept servant. Drop it into the snow. Drop it and walk forward, away from the stone."

And then she knew she had chosen well. Something about this place, created by a race that might be even older than the Litati, lost before the records of the Goremin began, would hold her body fast. It would keep the book safe while she did the thing now welling up inside her, burning darkly behind her eyes, longing to pulse outward against that dead gray pall that was the presence of Verrainig.

She did not deign to answer. Instead, she pulled herself out of the chilled body standing against the stone, drawing at the same instant a well of total blackness from deep sources that her kind kept secret even from themselves. Concealed by that darkness, even from the probing spirit of the Mover, she hurtled toward the place in which she felt his physical presence and that of the Ormin.

As she went, she felt herself changing. The clarity of thought, the kindness of spirit that were the attributes of her kind, were winnowed away in the rush of wind and space. What arrived in the cold gray place where Dinorm lay beside his servant was something no Dreamer, no King, no Mover from the North had ever encountered, for it had never before existed in their age of the world.

She came to rest in a wide space, deep in the rock. Before her stood Verrainig, and at his side lay Dinorm, its sensor-pits pulsing with activity. It knew at once when she came, though she brought no physical self with her. Its spade-like head came up, towering above that of the Mover, and turned toward the spot where she stood on insubstantial feet.

Before either could react, Moonlight spoke. "I was colder than Verrainig, though he brought me helpless from the midst of my Dream into his presence, when I was not prepared to face him. His temple is melted with his own wrath, Dinorm. Did you know that?"

The blunt head moved, lowered, and the eye pits pulsed purple. It had not, she thought, known of their encounter at all—only of her escape, because Riddle told it.

"Though I am not an Immortal, not one shaped by those able to form the world to their requirements, I am, Dinorm, more evil than you!" She felt the boiling darkness that had risen to her call come pulsing from her spirit self, filling this larger hall in Dinorm's caverns with its black presence. She began to weave, from the negative aspect of her people's art, the Black Dream.

From ancient evils, lost in the youth of the world, from cruelties in the forgotten past, so thoughtless and automatic that they seemed almost innocent, she birthed a self that could confront Dinorm on its own terms. She was purest destruction, antithesis of all that existed.

Where she was, no created thing could remain, for all the primordial hungers and fears and angers from ages of evolving life were channeled through her spirit from the black wells in which they had waited through the millennia.

The big chamber was now in total darkness, yet the blackness pouring into it from her withering awareness glowed with its own sheen, and in that negative glare Moonlight saw Dinorm slither backward, and she saw Verrainig fall to his knees, his hands clasping his eyes. But she did not pause in her outpouring. These beings had failed, before, but they had returned to the attack too soon. She must quell them, making them require time to recover their confidence. A day—two days—so little time was needed for reaching the City in the Mist.

The Mover fell flat on the gritty stone and lay still, as Dinorm retreated against a farther wall, its sticky hide smearing against the rock, leaving a glittering trail in that black illumination. At last it, too, lay flat, and though she knew neither was defeated or even injured to any great extent, she had done what was needful. She had bought time for those waiting in the snow.

Releasing her hold on the deep fund of knowledge her people had understood but never used, Moonlight drifted back slowly, her mind dimmed with her efforts and with the ragged remnants of darkness trailing after her. In time, she found herself standing against the slanting rock, her hands dull and dead, so tightly had they retained their hold on the book that still was clasped between them.

* * * * * * *

Riddle watched, his heart freezing at the things he saw beyond the wall and the stiff shapes of the trees. The face and the body of the girl, as well as of the stone, were drawn upon that dark slate in lines of silvery-gray, sharpening all the while until he could see a sort of reverse image as clearly as he might have by day. And her face, in that negative light, was evil, ancient, worn with terrible things.

Even he, son of the Ancient Race, King—for the time—of his people, shuddered with fear at the destructive energy that poured from Moonlight's still body. He shrank into the shelter more deeply, rejecting the thing he saw.

Using such dangerous arts, those crossbreeds that his kind had discounted as Dreamers might have unseated even the Kings themselves. And yet they had not. They had helped where they could, healed what they might, and always been friends of all living things. He found himself awed at the strength such control required.

It was almost impossible for Riddle to believe the woman standing on the hilltop might be the gentle Dreamer with whom he had traveled for so long and for whom he felt a growing affection. This was one ancient in dark power, able to work terrible things upon any who stood in her way.

And then he felt, in his poet's perceptive bones, that with her stood, invisible and yet solidly real and present, someone else. Someone familiar with the black spaces within the earth and between the stars, with the power to blast this puny planet to rubble and the stars to dust. It was not the Dreamers' dark knowledge alone that empowered Moonlight—another will had joined hers, connected by the touch of that enigmatic stone.

The black light intensified, and the shapes limned upon it in silver-gray flashed brilliantly into Riddle's vision, striking through his eyelids when he closed them. The image of the book seemed to glow inside his skull. And then it was gone, and only the dwindling wind and the night, black with cloud and pale with drifted snow, was there amid the trees.

He rose from his crouch, straightening his cramped knees with difficulty. A sound came to his ears from the spot where Moonlight stood, and he stumbled forward, feeling his prickly way through the trees, to find her. The stone was black against black, and the Dreamer's dark cloak seemed a part of it until she sagged forward. A harsh sob was wrenched from her throat, as he touched her hooded head.

"Come," he said. "We must go back to Gorghoz and the others. We will freeze out here in the open."

He could hear the chatter of her teeth, but she would not take his hand. "Don't touch me," she whispered. "I am tainted now. This night's work, this tapping into the dark spaces of the world, has dirtied me to my soul.

"Lead me back, Riddle." Her voice was infinitely sad, holding a note of terrible loss. "But do not touch or look at me. I am no longer a Dreamer who might dare to love one of your kind, but an outcast, unable to do the thing I was trained for and unwilling to risk harm by trying others. Oh, take me back and let me rest!"

Her voice was hopeless, her tone dead, and Riddle ached for her as he went slowly back, following his best guesses at the direction. What a sacrifice she had made! And yet, given the ability and the choice, he would have done the same.

"You have accomplished your task," he reassured her, hearing the dragging crunch of her boots in the snow behind him. He paused and put his arm about her, helping her to move. "You have bought time for us that may save us all. And you have kept the book from the hands of those who would use it as a focus for the destruction of everything we value.

"Moonlight, the price you offered to pay is terrible. And yet do you regret making that choice?"

He felt her sag against him, hiding her face in his cloak. She shuddered violently before pulling herself upright again, but she made no reply.

* * * * * * *

Gorghoz had pushed his line of walkers until they could not lift one foot to set it before the other. Even Killeli had fallen into a drift and was unable to rise again. Twice the Goremin had gone back along their rapidly drifting track and shouted to drive back the hunting Gyrduk, knowing the alien beast leading the pack would never give up its pursuit as long as it lived.

As darkness fell, the Goremin cast about for a likely spot to make a defensible camp. Finding a small valley cupped between two hills, he stopped there. In this western part of the northern hills, juniper and scraggly pines grew with some frequency, and he was able to gather enough deadfall to build a fire, although in the snow it was very hard to kindle the wood.

Oil from Riddle's lightglass helped at last, though he hated to waste it. But when he struck the flints and the spark leaped into the shiny patches on the rough bark, his heart rose as much as did those of the Turnig huddled about him. The flames, crackling and sputtering in the dead wood and the snow-wet, seemed to revive the small people a bit. Some ventured into the upper parts of the hills, searching out more wood, so the fire could be kept roaring all night. With them went torch-bearers, armed with sharpened sticks or their stout staffs for beating away any persistent Gyrduk that might attack.

Others rummaged small pots from their packs and put dried roots and herbs and preserved bird eggs to boiling, making broth for the small ones and the elders alike. Soon the savory smells filled the little cup, and those returning with more wood sniffed appreciatively.

Moving through such cold drained the energies even of Gorghoz, and the smaller people had less bulk to supply strength for their efforts. But once all had been fed and fed again, and the youngsters were tumbling about on blankets set close to the fire, the Goremin felt more cheerful than he had in a very long while.

The others seemed to feel the same, particularly as the snow dwindled and the wind died to a breeze. There was no sound from the pack he had driven away, which was also a comfort.

The Turnig slept at last, and Killeli stretched his skinny frame beside his warm and furry friend. But Gorghoz did not sleep, though he rested deeply. He felt that Riddle and the Dreamer would come, and he intended to be awake to greet them.

Something had happened, out there in the snowy night, and he had an intuition that it had changed drastically an important element in his life. He was uneasy and unable to name the source of that unease.

When the two came through the drifts out of the darkness and moved into the firelight, he knew his dread had been based on fact. For the Dreamer was hidden completely within her cloak and hood, and her step was no longer that of a young and vital woman.

Riddle came ahead of her, carefully avoiding outpacing her weary limbs. His face, the scarf pulled away, was deeply lined, and not only with exhaustion.

Gorghoz set the pot more deeply into the coals to heat the fresh stew. "Come," he said softly. "It will take much to wake this tally of travelers tonight."

He ladled bowls of the steaming liquid and toothsome vegetables and handed them to the pair. "Eat. Do not speak of what has happened, if you cannot. But something has changed radically. I think that we will go to the sea, now, without the attentions of those you have faced, though their creatures still pursue us."

Riddle bent his face over his bowl, but Gorghoz could see that tears streamed down his weathered cheeks. The girl had taken her own bowl into cold hands that seemed bent almost into claws.

She turned away, so he might not see her face as she ate, and the Goremin had a sudden, terrible suspicion. What had she done, this Dreamer who had saved them? And had she brought some doom upon herself by her action? At what cost would their journey come safely to an end, beyond the last of those frozen hills to the west?

CHAPTER TWENTY-NINE

"A journey's end may seem a distant thing,
and yet, in time, it comes."
                                        —Riddle

Again the Mover and the worm had withdrawn their attention from the weather and the travelers in the hills. The snow ceased, the wind stilled, and the sun rose behind a thin screen of high cloud, turning the sky to silver and the snow to a glare of brilliance.

Riddle woke, feeling as if he had dreamed ill, taking his nightmare with him into his waking day. And then he remembered. He sat and set his teeth against a groan as he donned his boots again. Gorghoz, beyond the hairy shape of Killeli, was staring at him, his ancient eyes sad and filled with foreboding, which told Riddle that his nightmare was reality.

Around them the Turnig were waking, the mothers nursing fretful infants, the grandmothers and uncles and brothers tending the older children. Gorghoz had set fresh stew over the fire long before daybreak, and the odors rising from the pots quickly brought the sleepiest of them out of their dreams.

Chark came from her family group to stand beside Moonlight, who was folding her sleeping cloak, stolen long before from Lorbek in Damaria. The Dreamer's hands were steady, but her face was still hidden beneath her hood, for she had pulled down the face-veil that served to keep the snow out of her eyes.

The small Turnig, still thin from her own narrow brush with death, tugged at the edge of the Dreamer's cloak. "You well?" she asked, her gruff voice anxious. "Feel strange. You go—you come back different!"

The girl's laugh held an edge of hysteria. Riddle nodded to Chark, who came over to stand at his knee, staring up into his face. "What?" she asked. "Tell!"

Moonlight hunched over suddenly, as if an arrow had struck

into her heart. Holding herself with both arms, she stood for a moment, bent like an old, old woman. Then she straightened, her cloak falling back. With both hands, she drew back her hood, dropping it down behind her, and stood in the pitiless light of the morning sky.

Chark's indrawn breath shrieked between her teeth. Gorghoz groaned so deeply it seemed almost to make the ground beneath the snow tremble with his pain. Riddle closed his eyes as the hood fell.

But he knew he must look, must know what it was that had happened to the Dreamer he had begun to love in her encounter with the forces of the north. Feeling the tug of Chark's hand on his own, he squeezed her small fingers and opened his reluctant eyelids.

The oval face, the amber cat-eyes, the tumble of auburn curls were still recognizable. But the lines of the face had altered, coarsening. The eyes, ringed with cruel creases, were amber marbles staring half-blinded from the raddled countenance. Her curls were streaked with white, the pale strands glistening in the silver light.

Age and blurred vision and a terrible overlay of dark power had turned the Dreamer into the very spectre of a nightmare. Worse yet, Riddle felt a sick certainty that the stain went all through her, coloring her spirit as well as her flesh.

But she was still Moonlight, whatever she had paid to bring her people out of the grasp of Dinorm and his minion. Standing straight and still, she said, "Lead me to the City in the Mist. Find a place where I may sit in a corner and spin or tend young children or stir the pot over the flames.

"I cannot go with you to the west, now, for I carry within me the taint of the enemy. A ship upon which I set out to sea would founder and sink with the weight of my guilt.

"For I have misused the power of the Nairneks. I have betrayed all my training as a Dreamer. I am crippled not only in flesh but in mind. No dream will ever visit me again, and I will go into death expecting to become dust on the wind.

"But the King is alive and free. The burden I carry is safe. And the Turnig will survive to populate a new land, becoming what they may be in generations to come."

The Turnig were wringing their small hands, their fur-ringed eyes stricken with horror. Gorghoz was weeping, and Riddle understood at last that nothing in all the universe could be more heart-rending than hearing a Goremin cry.

Killeli stood, his monkeyish head cocked, surveying the scene. "It is hard," he said. "But do not waste her effort. We must go now, before the Gyrduk recover their courage and come after us again."

And that was the best sense Riddle had heard in what seemed a very long while.

He had visited the City in the Mist often, in his very long life-time. As a child he had looked forward to a trip there with great enthusiasm, and as a man he had found fascinating elements in the history of the people who had built the place, there in the arms of the sea.

His feet had no difficulty in finding the old track, buried though it was in the drifted snow. He led his troop out of the last of the hill country, leaving behind the stony soil and the scrubby trees. Before him swept a wide panorama of snow, which blended at its farther edge with the dun-colored fen country surrounding the port on its landward side.

Gorghoz, beside him, sighed deeply. "It has been a hundred generations, even of your long-lived kind, since I last stood here. I can see a glimmer of the sea—can you find that silver line at the horizon's edge?"

But Riddle's were not the eyes of a Goremin. He saw only the waste of the fens and the distant blur of gray mist that hid the city wall.

"Come!" he said, forging ahead. Even as he spoke, there came a cry from the end of the long line of Turnig.

Riddle turned, his hand on his sword, and ran back toward the small shapes struggling in the snow beneath a tumble of dark bodies. The Gyrduk had caught up with them once again.

Behind him, he could hear the flying steps of Killeli and the Goremin, but Riddle didn't look back. He hurled himself at the pack, slicing hairy paws from thin-boned legs, splitting narrow skulls.

Two Turnig lay bleeding in the snow. He stood over their bodies, facing the snarling creatures that now waited for a move from the alien Gyr that led them. The beast stood, its lip raised over long teeth now stained with red, and its eyes met those of the poet.

A shock ran through Riddle's body, making his hand shake on the hilt of his blade. This was no animal—not entirely. Purpose gleamed behind those slitted eyes. Almost human intelligence directed the hairy body as it leaped for his throat.

But another shape intervened, flinging itself between the poet and the flying shape of the Gyr.

Moonlight, her cloak swirling with her motion, caught the creature by the neck and went down beneath its weight, holding the red muzzle from her face with both hands.

Riddle felt frozen in place, unable to move, to swing his weapon, or even to stir to help the Dreamer. She gazed up into the green-glowing eyes of the beast, and it, too, seemed locked in place, staring down into the slitted amber eyes below it.

Riddle wondered, as her hands closed on the hairy neck, if some remnant of the dark power Moonlight had drawn upon in the night still lingered about her, for she sat, holding the Gyr, bending its backbone into a curve that ended with a snap that echoed sharply in the cold air.

The green eyes dulled, and the gaping jaws went slack. As if freed by the creature's death from their compulsive hunt, the pack wheeled, yelping, and fled away toward the more hospitable lands in the south, never looking back at the thing that had led them.

* * * * * * *

Lorbek bent forward in his chair, staring into the Orb. He had felt the withdrawal of his masters in the north, though he did not understand the reason for it. Angry at being left to direct his Gyr alone over such a distance, he now put every ability at his command into keeping the creature after its prey.

He had, over the weeks, learned to draw some insignificant but helpful power from the energies of the Sealed Flame. Now it burned before him, still and blue beneath his gaze as he forced his will upon that distant pseudo-beast, focusing his purpose through the sphere.

The bestial tool given him by his master must catch the Dreamer and regain the book! Only that would soothe the burning of his anger. Only that would save his spirit from the moods sent as punishment by the Mover from the North.

Even as he entertained that thought, he felt the Gyr die, far in the northern hills. It came as a shock, recoiling upon his mind in a burst of agony.

A flare of energy surged in the Orb, stabbing through his eyes into his brain, and he fell back, holding his hands over his face and moaning. All was lost! He had no way in which to follow the Dreamer and her stolen book. Only those who were in the north could save them from that loss, and they would not move, would not respond to his desperate need.

He opened his eyes and let his hands move down to lie flat on the table. Incredulous, he stared at the flame inside the crystal.

The cold blue light was gone as if it had never been. Now a tiny spot of scarlet glowed in the bubble inside the crystalline sphere, turning the white table cover and his trembling hands the shade of fresh blood.

* * * * * * *

Now the snow was less deep, the footing surer; before they had traveled half a league, there was only a thin blanket that barely covered the frozen soil. Those carrying the wounded Chirrik and the dead Jree walked more easily, their short legs no longer forced to drag half frozen feet through the deep layers.

Farther to the west, the poet could see wisps of steam, which told him that most of the fen had not yet been turned to ice, though the air was still very cold. He swept his gaze around the distant horizon, but to his great gratitude there was no sign of anything threatening at the moment.

Moonlight, walking to his right and holding onto his cloak, said nothing. Her clouded vision could not see clearly the colors that now were visible, and he wanted desperately to comfort her with the gift of his own knowledge and vision, despite his grief at the loss of his old friend Jree.

"The fens have protected the City in the Mist from all comers for generations," he told her. "The builders came from the west—possibly from the very islands to which we now are fleeing."

As if for comfort, Chark was on his other side, her small hand touching his wrist, and he nodded down at her.

"Masters of shipbuilding and seamanship, they carved out a hold on the rocky knob that guards the bay and the harbor at the mouth of the River Erste. It is their ships that have carried my kindred westward, over the generations. My uncle and my cousins live there and trade with distant continents beyond the ocean, under the reign of the seagoing people.

"Those have held that ancient city under attacks from many kinds. Some came, in ages long past and forgotten, from the far east, over the mountains and through those same hills we have crossed. I suspect those invaders were directed and motivated by no other than Dinorm and his henchman, but they died to the last man.

"Others came from Damaria itself, in the days before my ancestors traveled up from the south to set that land in order. The primitives who were ancestors of the Lirfolk and the new people were also driven here to howl before its wall, in the season when the fens dry up and large groups of warriors can travel their length and breadth."

He paused, feeling her clutch at his cloak ease a bit. She was interested, and that was something. She had seemed like one turned to stone, since she loosed the dead Gyr and rose again to follow him.

Gorghoz was staring seaward. "I can see the seabirds circling. I can smell the salt of the waves. "Once we have our charges safely inside those thick walls, there will be time to rest and to tell long tales of the past. But now we must hurry. I do not trust those who may be behind us."

Riddle did not realize his pace had slowed, and he set himself to match that of the Goremin. From time to time he turned to check on the Turnig and on Killeli, who was shepherding the entire line from its distant end. They, too, seemed determined to reach the city as quickly as possible. If the beasts had fled, there was no surety that the Lirfolk had also turned aside, and they were known to be persistent in pursuing those they hunted.

The pewter and green-gray and dead orange-tan of winter-killed plants now lay on either side of the raised track that crossed the fenland. The snow had been left behind, and there was a dank smell in the air, rising from the water-soaked vegetation now rotting all about them.

With the end of this terrible journey in sight, Riddle found himself thinking of the ending of his life in his old home. The Litati had created the Ormin, and it was likely Dinorm had caused their end or their flight. His kind had, in a sense, created the new people, who in turn had destroyed the Ancient Race in Damaria.

If there was a lesson here, it was one that he must learn well. Meddling with the stuff of life had penalties that the meddlers could not foresee. Even those meaning only good had achieved ill, down the long reaches of time when balances must be struck and accounts paid.

If he came at last to the Western Islands and those of his kind who had lived there for ages, he must tell them what he had learned. The same error must not be made again.

* * * * * * *

It was warmer, and the Turnig began taking off their felted cloaks and rolling them into their packs, but Moonlight wrapped herself more closely still. Riddle watched with pity as she hid her face beneath her hood and folded the veil about it.

What pain it must cause one who had been trained to help others to be forced to work within the dark power she detested! But he pushed that thought aside, for the wall of the City was now rising tall before his speeding feet.

Its heavy stones had been quarried from the rock on which the city sat, forming the defenses as well as the building blocks of the houses within. The gate frowned down at him, thick and business-like and all but impregnable.

The long train of travelers strung out over the track, lagging now, and weary. Riddle, however, was caught in a compulsion to reach the gate, to identify himself to the keeper, and to take his vulnerable companions out of the perils that now lay all but unbroken over the land that his fathers had ruled.

He forgot Moonlight, almost running now to keep up. He forgot Gorghoz, who had eased his pace and watched the approach of the first Turnig, checking that all were there. Five furlongs from the heavy gate securing the City from the outside world, Riddle stopped. A thin line of Lirfolk rose from the straggly weeds beside the road and faced him, their weapons ready and their faces ashen and determined.

This, then, was the price he must pay to get his people within the shelter of the walls. The poet, staff in one hand, blade in the other, charged the Lir, shouting the name of his uncle, the dead King.

"Armor! Armor and the Kings of Damaria!"

Metal met wood and flint. Sparks flew, as his blade hacked through a spear point and into a thin chest. Something struck his back, and he moved with the blow, whirling to meet the assault of another of the gray warriors. As he countered the thrusts of a metal-tipped spear, he felt the slow dribble of blood down his shoulder blade.

Something ground harshly, shaking the very soil beneath his feet. Were the guardsmen of the City opening their gate for these ragged strangers, without identifying them first? But there was no time to see, as he drove the Lir back and back, making room for his people to pass into the space near the wall.

Then there were armed men beside him, thrusting and hacking at the Lirfolk, who began to retreat, their line breaking as their people fell or fled into the fens. When the last was dead, his spine shattered by the iron-shod staff in a guardsman's hand, the poet leaned upon his own bloody weapon. His lungs heaved, as he wiped sweat from his forehead with a sleeve and felt the tug of pain across his back that was his wound.

As if they had never existed, the armed men left his side, withdrawing into the gate. When Riddle turned, the portal had ground shut again, and the heads of helmeted men showed over the walls on either side.

At his feet was a line of stones set into the graveled track. The mark—anyone setting foot past that without permission would be shot by archers stationed on the wall. There he stood, bleeding but upright, waiting until all his companions were ready. At last, he turned his face up to the watchtower that rose above the portal.

"Riddle the poet, now for a time King of Damaria, and his nephew, future ruler of that land, stand at the gate of the City in the Mist. With me are Gorghoz, the Goremin, last of his kind in the Damariste Mountains; Moonlight, last of the family of Nairnek, Dreamer; Killeli, of the hairy men, who worked side by side with those who now destroy his kind; and a tribe of the Turnig from the Forest Damariste.

"I call upon our ancient treaty and upon the friendship between my people, some of whom live in your city, and your own. As surety, you may call Oakbeam the Builder. He is a blood-brother to my father and a long-time friend."

Although no head appeared at the slitted window of the tower, a voice came down to them, pitched so as to travel no farther than their waiting ears. "And what name does the sometime King of Damaria carry, other than his use-name? One who cannot entrust his *nomen* to us cannot, in turn, be trusted."

Riddle stood proud and straight, ignoring the pain of the long slash across his back. He was no witchling to fear the use of his true name.

"Rhadalf Musicius, nephew of the former King of Damaria, uncle of Lute, the present King. Poet and traveler, historian and song-maker, I claim shelter in the city of the Sea Lords, for me and mine."

There was a long silence. Riddle could envision runners sent into the city to pound upon Oakbeam's tall door, which had the heads of snarling Gyrduk carved into its thick panels. He could see that stout individual puffing along the cobblestoned street toward the gates. He would hurry, but that bulk could not move speedily.

Feeling her presence behind him, the poet reached back and caught Moonlight's shrinking fingers in a close grip. After a moment, her hand relaxed and she moved closer to his shoulder. Her fingers grew busy, stuffing cloth against his bleeding cut.

"Mardilena Lunaria of the Damariste Nairneks," came the breath of a whisper near his shoulder. Not even Gorghoz, looming above them, heard her words.

He sighed and winced, as she put pressure on the wound. That was a fair exchange; now he knew her *nomen*. A day might come when that knowledge would serve them both very well.

As if for the first time, the great panels of the gates began to move, grinding back on their worn tracks just enough to let the newcomers enter the outer wall. Those who had come to his aid might never make themselves known, for such unannounced assistance was not the way of the Sea-Lords. The fact that they had come at all told him much about the situation those in the City understood to be facing them.

Riddle staggered forward, pulling Moonlight behind him. Gorghoz lifted Killeli, who was drooping with weariness. The Turnig trooped behind them all, murmuring in their gruff voices at this strangest of all the strange places they had seen since leaving their deep home in the forest, though some were weeping softly as they carried the limp body of small Jree into the refuge that had come too late for her.

The darkness of the maze that was the entrance into the city swallowed them all. Narrow passages angled to right and left, and Riddle remembered that sophisticated system, which would leave anyone forcing the gates at the mercy of small bands of archers and swordsmen who could appear from unexpected angles in tight places. They might drop from above or pop from a hidden chamber to one side or the other.

He had never walked here in darkness before, for always there had been torches and laughing people to greet those of his kindred who visited this place. He had never before, of course, entered this city wounded, leading those threatened with death in their own country.

He could hear the clank of metal and the sibilance of mail against stone from the hidden watchers along the way, keeping watch even upon one of his ancient family, who had fought their enemies at their very gate. That, more than anything else, told him the change in Damaria had reached even to the edges of his familiar world. And if the City in the Mist felt itself besieged, there was no place left to go, indeed, except over the sea.

Bleeding and weary, leading the blinded Dreamer and the exhausted troop of Turnig, Riddle walked beside Gorghoz and Killeli into the place he had toiled for so long to reach. Would he, wondered the poet, ever return to Damaria?

But that was a question which had no answer.

* * * * * * *

Orm curled in the deep chamber, feeling the motions of those walking the world above. That twin formed by the Creators, long, long before, had begun another assault there in the north. The vibrations of its will had brought Orm fully awake.

Evil things were done, now, in the lands he had thought secured

forever. Those who had been entrusted with the forests, the mountains, and the fields were dead, or they had fled.

The talisman that Dinorm caused to be made, and Orm shuddered at the thought of it, was now beyond the reach of its destructive will. That was a thing of which the great worm was certain, for
it had tracked the journey of those who carried it, even to the gates
of the Sea-City itself.

What went away from the land could return. Those who fled
might regain the ability to take their home out of the hands of those
unfit to rule.

Orm was old, and he was patient.

He had seen the very face of the world change shape from that
into which the twinned Ormin had formed it. Even the Litati, at the
beginning of time, had not been immune to their own works and had
disappeared even from the perceptions of their creations.

The single matter that did not change, Orm knew, was change
itself. Those sitting above in the stone houses of the Kings might
think themselves secure, might strut about, slaying the smaller kinds
or enslaving them, but that was a thing of passing interest.

Orm curled comfortably into the deep chamber, feeling that
twinned mind in the north settle again into something like repose.
Let Dinorm sleep. A time would come when they would match
strength against strength, will against will.

And that might not be as far in the future as the Mover in the
North and its master might think.

BOOK TWO

SHIPS AND SEEKERS

CHAPTER THIRTY

"Those calloused hands that work the wood...."
                                                        —Riddle

The builder sat at his drawing table, studying the plans spread before him on the polished wood. Absently, he stroked the amber and umber grains that showed through the varnish, while his gaze followed the lines of the blueprint.

Oakbeam the builder loved his crafts. A house was as dear to him as the swiftest ship that ever sprang from his nimble mind and his busy workshops. A new warehouse must be built for the timbers and the tar, the ropes and the caulking tow, that his shipbuilding enterprises required. While that was not the challenge a dwelling might be, it must be strong to resist the terrible winds that dashed across the headland from the ocean beyond. In winter the city was beset by the sea-storms as if by an armed enemy.

The City in the Mist had stood for centuries uncounted, simply because there were builders of the caliber of this one, working in stone and stout wood, anchoring their foundations into the bedrock of the granite-based arm of land on which the city stood. Sheltered by the cape though it might be, nourished by the trade flowing through the secure harbor of which the seaward arm formed another bulwark, the city must withstand assaults more violent than any armed men could mount.

Even now, Oakbeam felt in his middle-aged bones the approach of another storm, following those earlier ones that had pounded the coast and sent blizzards raging inland ahead of their proper season. This would be a bitter winter. The warehouse must be even more solid than the rest, standing as it did in the full blast of the wind, if the weather should continue as it had begun.

He drew forward a pad of rag paper and sketched onto it a line of baffles of stone angled against the prevailing wind, with another line acting as bulwarks on the opposite side of the proposed building.

But even as he did so, he shivered. Something more than weather was afoot in this strange autumn. While he had not the potencies claimed by those of the Ancient Race, no Orb with its Sealed Flame in which to descry what happened at a distance, no life measured in centuries and even millennia in which to assess the elements of his world, Oakbeam understood his own experience.

He had noticed, in his dealings with them, that the four members of the Ancient Race of the Kings of Damaria who now lived in the city were uneasy. Their usually acute minds were focused elsewhere, and Oakbeam found himself wondering what was taking place far to the south and east in Damaria.

Tulip and Silk, Blade and Wonder had not concerned themselves with the construction of their new garden wall. Before this unusual year they had noticed everything he did about their comfortable house, which was set in a bulge of land encompassed by the wall of the city and cornered by the stream that watered the eastern parts of the place. Yet their attention was distracted, and even Blade seemed not to know the reason. Though Oakbeam sent his best masons, supervising the work as often as he could, he realized they were not concerned, this time, with the quality of the stonework and ornamentation. They were obviously looking elsewhere.

He sighed and returned his attention to the warehouse, but it was not easy to keep his mind focused. Something was in the air; even enclosed in the stout walls of the city and the stouter ones of his own house, he could feel it.

The stories told by those who had come earlier in the autumn were disturbing. Even if Girnig Wind-Tamer, Lord of the City in the Mist, discounted those tales as the ramblings of disgruntled refugees, there had been something in them that set Oakbeam's teeth on edge. There was a core of truth there, a cold sense of impending disaster that made the builder shiver, even in his warm room, wrapped in layers of wool.

Girnig had been the heir to the greatest of the Sealords, plying the ocean to bring back goods from the distant western islands and the even more distant continent beyond its troubled waters. That, Oakbeam had found too late, was not the best qualification for one who must pull together the strange conglomeration of peoples forming the population of the City in the Mist.

Any question from a citizen Girnig regarded as potential mutiny. Only the efforts of Oakbeam and the other Councilors had saved the heads of several craftsmen and small tradesmen who protested taxes or ordinances that made their lives difficult.

He had, worse than anything else, a great antipathy for the non-human members of his citizenry.

Simian-descended people and other furred beings with the capacities of men were often oppressed for no reason. Oakbeam found himself often at loggerheads with the Lord over such matters.

With a sigh, the builder closed the folder of blueprints. His mind would not remain on his work. It was better to go out and let the wind blow the cobwebs out of his head amid the tall stone canyons of the city.

There came a thump at the study door, and he turned to find his plump wife puffing there, her face scarlet and her eyes wide blue pools of excitement. "A runner came, this moment. You are wanted at the East Gate!"

He stared at her, his chest tightening. Was this the thing he had felt approaching for months now?

"Here, you put on your cloak. The wind is bitter out there!" said Nilda, reaching for his fur on its peg and wrapping it about his square shoulders.

He put his arms about her warm shape and squeezed her hard. "Did the runner say anything about the problem?" he asked her.

She chuckled against his chest. "Not he. But seldom does Girnig send for you nowadays. Go quickly and then tell me. I am dying of curiosity."

He released her and pulled the fur close about him. At the rack beside the heavy front door, he took down his fur hood and tugged it over his wild red curls before venturing out into the wind.

The snow that had lashed the coast had dwindled a few days before, but the damp in the sea-wind searched out his bones, no matter how thick the clothing. As he strode up the street's stone paving, he felt flutters of chill slip their fingers about his ears and down his collar.

In the distance he could hear shouts. In his middle years his increasing weight was a problem, but he picked up his pace still more and arrived, his heart pounding, the breath singing in his throat, at the inner portal.

There Martig, the officer on duty, waited. When their eyes met, Oakbeam understood this to be a situation into which the soldier did not want Girnig intruding. A member of the Council must give consent for unusual actions, and Martig had been his friend since he was a sprout.

Something strange was in the wind, indeed.

"What is happening?" asked the builder, trying both to catch his breath and to ease the stitch in his side.

Martig gestured toward the first offset chamber in the complex that was the gateway itself. Once there he turned and put his lips close to Oakbeam's ear. "There are refugees at the gate. I sent a party to their relief, for the Lirfolk attacked them almost beneath the wall itself. I need your consent, even though it is late, for that action." The wide gray eyes were steady, but the gloved fists were clenched.

"You have it. But who stands outside? And why have they not been admitted?"

"The King of Damaria." Martig's lips tightened. "And an order came down from the Lord this week past that no one is to be admitted without direct consent of himself or one of the Council. If he could decently have excluded your name from the list, he would have done, but he could not. And you are here."

Oakbeam felt his fear relax a bit. "Armor stands in the cold wind, left out by this upstart Sealord?"

"No. The King of Damaria now is a tiny child, and his uncle, Rhadalf, holds the regency. He is accompanied by a woman, a rag-tag group of Turnig, a furred man, and even a Goremin. They are in bad shape, worn and wounded. Shall I admit them to the City in the Mist?"

"You shall, at once," said Oakbeam. "And I will stand above the gate and welcome them."

Together they climbed the interior stairways to reach the parapet along the inside of the battlements. And there, holding up a drooping woman on his arm, stood Riddle, the poet whom he recalled meeting when he was a child and Riddle a much younger man, in company with the King of Damaria.

Once they had been bidden to enter, Oakbeam hurried down the steps again and through the maze of narrow chambers and passages that led through the wall defenses to the gate. Anyone forcing that heavy portal would find himself lost in the darkness of the space, trying to fumble a path through the treacherous labyrinth that was the gate into the city. From either side—or from above, indeed—defenders could and would fall upon invaders and kill them in the darkness.

Before he was more than partway into the maze, he heard low voices, and he asked Martig to kindle a torch. By its wavering light, he saw the face of young Riddle, who counted his years in centuries and yet was a youth of his kind, now prematurely aged by loss and hardship.

"Greetings to you, quondam King of Damaria," Oakbeam said. He reached for the young man with both arms outstretched.

When he hugged Riddle, something that had been holding the man upright and intact crumpled, and he sagged against the builder. "Well met, old friend," he said, his voice ragged and breathless.

"Care for my people, I beg you. They have come far and through dreadful trials. And Moonlight—see to her. She has paid a terrible price for our lives." He turned his head, his tattered scarf twisting aside to reveal a drying runnel of blood down his cheek.

"Gorghoz! Are you all right?" he called to the towering shape of the Goremin.

When that being came forward into the light of the torch, the soldiers behind Martig gasped, their united breaths audible in protesting his incredible ugliness. But Oakbeam had known his kind before, though not those in the family of the mountains of Damaria.

He ignored the lumpy face, the many-layered shark-teeth revealed in the square of the creature's cautious smile. Oakbeam the builder reached for the gray-furred hand extended toward his own. A great relief filled him at having inside his own city one of that old race, which understood more of the world than the younger kinds had ever thought to question. As well, there was a member of the Ancient Race, young and strong—or at least strong once he had been tended who would make the odds far better, if a time came when the people of the City must face the powers that had disrupted Damaria's ancient and peaceful life.

When he glanced down at the woman beside the poet, he found she had her face swathed in her veil. She stared at the stones beneath their feet until he put his finger beneath her chin and lifted her face to his. Then he almost flinched backward. This was—or had been—a Dreamer. The eyes, their slitted pupils like those of a cat, said as much. And yet where in other Dreamers he had seen only firm wisdom and calm control, in this one he saw raw pain and a hint of something cold and cruel.

What had she done, this Dreamer, to buy the lives of her companions? She looked old and withered, her skin pulled tight to her skull, her limbs fragile as sticks. The ruddy braid peeping from beneath her veil was streaked with silver strands.

Oakbeam looked into Riddle's eyes, and there he saw pain almost to match the woman's. But there was no time, now, to learn their story. They were all but dropping in their tracks.

Indeed, some of the Turnig had sat on the flat stone of the corridor floor, dropping their round heads into their arms or onto their knees. This was a battered and dispirited group, needing every bit of care and kindness they could find.

He turned to Martig. "Find quarters for the Turnig; there should be others of their kind in the Quarter who will be happy to shelter them and give them suitable care. I will take these five with me." He gestured toward Riddle, the Dreamer, the Goremin, the fine-drawn furry man, and the child in the furred man's arms.

They went out into the windy street, finding that now a light sleet was tickling along the stones. Oakbeam put one great arm about Riddle and the other about Moonlight, while Gorghoz lifted Killeli and the child together and carried them against his warm chest.

Together, they went toward the long-sought haven of Oakbeam's stout walls.

CHAPTER THIRTY-ONE

"Long words spoken, old wounds reopened...."
—Riddle

Nilda met her returning spouse with a bustle of activity. Before Riddle could catch his breath or believe that his long trial was over, he found himself neck-deep in a hot bath, with one of Oakbeam's sons scrubbing his tired back and exclaiming over his wounds.

Those counted more than a few, for to his older batch had been added those acquired in the battle with the Lirfolk outside the walls. A long gash behind his ear, a cut down his thigh, a stab-wound in his left forearm were the worst, although he found abrasions and bruises too many to count.

Once he had been helped from the bath (and so weary was he that the strong hand of Efnild was more than welcome), he was stretched on the couch in the room assigned to him, Gorghoz, and Killeli, and inspected from head to heels by Nilda herself.

"You have been walking about the country with festering wounds," she scolded, as she applied unguents that both stung and soothed. "It is as well you came when you did, or it is possible one of these might have carried you off, Ancient Race or no. Your kind is as susceptible to infection as any of us from oversea-stock or even those of the new people."

Riddle smothered a yelp, for she was scrubbing the stinging ointment into a half-healed gash along his back. "So I arrive in a safe haven to find my old friend's wife is determined to finish killing me," he moaned. "What will Oakbeam say to you when he finds me dead?"

He felt her chuckles through the heels of her hard, capable hands. "He will say what he thinks is safe, for he knows me too well to risk my wrath," she said.

He felt something cool spread over his stinging skin, and a blessed relief filled him. "It works!" he said, astonished. "After all that pain, now I find the misery I have carried for so long has lifted almost altogether. You are a miracle worker, Lady."

"Not I," she said, wiping her hands on a towel and inspecting her work with satisfaction. "Merely an herbalist and tender of injuries. You would not credit the sorts of accidents my four sons, even now, can bring home to be healed. Not to mention my aging but active husband, who will fall from a roof beam, if he can find no other mischief to get into."

Riddle smiled drowsily. She reminded him of his mother, who was long dead and yet fondly remembered. Quince had possessed the same capable common sense, the same impatience with the antics of her menfolk. Thinking of lost days, the poet slipped into sleep.

He woke to the sound of someone extremely large and heavy trying to walk softly and be quiet. "Gorghoz?" he asked without opening his eyes.

"It is I," the Goremin sighed. "I had thought to let you sleep on, but my feet are too large for the space, even in this great chamber. Stools and tables and beds clutter it too much for me to avoid them."

Riddle heard the low couch Oakbeam had found to hold the creature's weight give a creak as that bulk sat upon it. "Gorghoz," he said quietly, "do you have the feeling there is something secret in Oakbeam's manner? Do you sense that we will not be welcomed by the Lord of this city, no matter how ancient our ties here may be?"

"I do," the Goremin replied. "The officer on the wall sent for Oakbeam, not for Girnig. That bodes ill, my friend. It may be that the deep workings of the Mover in the North and Dinorm, the Shaper, have long been at their subtle undermining of those here so near their northern realm."

That was what Riddle had been wondering, dimly before he slept, more sharply now. "Did you speak with the builder, while his son scrubbed me and Nilda tortured me?" he asked.

There came the rumble that was a Goremin chuckle. "I did. The Lirfolk have no strength to pierce my thick-furred hide, and I was not so weary as you of the smaller kinds. We sat and we talked before the fire in his study.

"He is not a happy man, Poet, even amid his lively family and his prospering business. He has been concerned for years now about this Girnig Wind-Tamer who rules here. The Sealord is no Armor, King of Damaria, dealing justly and living in peace with all.

"Indeed, Oakbeam says Girnig feels the Ancient Race in Damaria must have been weak fools to maintain three thousand years of peace and kindness among their developing species. He would have bred Dreamers to reinforce his own power, Turnig to labor in the forest, and the simian-descended men to work their crafts for his own enrichment.

"Girnig sees the world in terms of business and battle, and those are obsessions long lost to your kind." Gorghoz sighed heavily. "The newer kinds, mere children in the art of living wisely, think power over others, battle and heroics, raw force used to compel their wills on the world, comprise the meaning of life. Those old and wise enough to have put such things aside cannot be understood or respected by the new adolescents. Girnig, I am convinced, is such a one."

Riddle turned and sat, wincing as his cuts pulled. Yet he felt no fresh trickle of blood, and once he was still again, the pain was less than it had been in many days.

"When do we go before the ruler of the City in the Mist?" he asked. "Surely we must, for no Lord can have a King and his Regent living secretly in his city. Oakbeam would lose his head, along with those of his family, if I remember ancient laws correctly."

"A message has been sent. Oakbeam is no blockhead, work with wood as he may. He told Girnig he was nearby when we came, which is not much of a lie, for his house lies nearer the East Gate than does the Great House, when Martig needed a Councilor to give him orders as to the refugees.

"His position is an old one, and the sea-people, most of them, like and trust him, so Girnig will not be able to do more than post another grudge to his account. We go to the Great House tomorrow, after we have rested and our wounds have been tended. The runner came within the hour and put the summons into Oakbeam's own hand."

So. Tomorrow would see another sort of trial begin, Riddle thought.

* * * * * * *

He woke to find Killeli still soundly asleep and the Goremin lying awake on his cot, staring into the dim light of the room. When he heard Riddle move, Gorghoz turned to face him.

"I feel a storm, out there on the sea," he said. "I felt them in the mountains, over the forests, in the hills, and now I find I can sense them far beyond sight across the waters. Today will be cold and damp. Tomorrow will be terrible."

"Then it is just as well that we go outside today. I do not like taking Lute out into such weather, and Moonlight is not able even to face the sort of chill we found here yesterday." Riddle fastened his tunic and belted his breeches close about his depleted belly. He had an intuition that Nilda meant to fatten them all a bit before they left her hands, and he welcomed the notion.

"Surely the young King should not go out again so soon!" the Goremin protested. "He has withstood trials that would have pinched the life from another sort of child."

"He is the King," said Lute's uncle. "He must face his host, even though he is only four years old. We begin training our young very early, as you have probably noticed by his behavior. He will do what is expected, and Girnig will be surprised. Not pleased, I suspect."

They went down the wide, shallow steps into the welcoming warmth of Oakbeam's kitchen-sitting-room. He did not hold with formal reception rooms, and any guest he welcomed was glad of it, so hospitable was that chamber, with its deep settles, its cushioned chairs, and the constant smell of good food.

A long table, flanked by benches, ran the length of the inner wall. Already trenchers were in place, their contents steaming and sending savory odors to hungry noses. Platters of the light, flat bread favored by the sea-descended people were placed at intervals down the length of the board, and the members of the family were taking their places.

All the newcomers were there except for Lute and Moonlight, who was, Nilda said, too weary to rise. "She has suffered much, that young woman," said Oakbeam's wife. "I do not want to know how she saved you—such matters only trouble my mind. But I hope you appreciate what she has done, for she has ruined her spirit forever in order to do it."

She nodded to Riddle. "Oh, she is fed already and asleep again. Believe that I will look after her as if she were the daughter I never bore. Old as she looks now, she is a suffering child to me."

They dug into the meal with delight, and when they were done and wiped off and brushed up, Oakbeam said, "Now, like it well or like it not, we must visit our gracious Lord, Girnig Wind-Tamer. Come, my friends, and put on the furred cloaks I have rummaged from the stores for you. We must face the cold again."

Lute, who had been fed in the nursery with the children of Oakbeam's two older sons, was bundled into a bag made of fur and wool and put into his uncle's arms. From that familiar perch, he beamed out at the company as if he had never suffered that long march and those strange dangers. To be very young is to live one day at a time, and he was the better for it.

They went into the street to find a cold day with high, steel-gray cloud. Though no sleet slanted through the wind, there was the promise of worse in the bank of black hovering over the sea beyond the cape.

"We must hurry," said Oakbeam, squinting at the sky. "The weather will not hold off overlong, I think. And Girnig likes for his visitors to arrive panting with haste. It is a part of his character that I like little."

They came through the gusty streets to the Great House after turning innumerable corners, passing uncounted shuttered house-fronts, and being hailed three times by bold shopkeepers who knew who it was on the Council who saved their heads and their busi-nesses.

There was a tall guardsman standing before the door, and the blade he held unsheathed before him was one that had seen battle. Riddle, having traveled widely in his world, recognized the sheen of constant honing, the unavoidable nicks that came with use against armor and bone. Whom had Girnig found to fight, here on the peaceful edge of the eastern continent? The warring countries be-yond the all but impassable barrier of the mountains had not turned their eyes westward in many centuries.

The guard stepped aside and sheathed his sword. "The Lord will see you," he boomed from behind his closed visor.

The door behind him opened, and an ancient man, stooped and twisted by the years he had lived, beckoned them inside. His color-less eyes were extremely bright and knowing, though a tangle of white hair hung down, almost hiding them.

Riddle sensed in him a deep well of mischief that might well prove worse than active evil. Such men manipulated others simply for amusement. He had read of them in the old books of history, brought with his ancestors from the southern lands that were the home of the Ancient Race.

"Aha!" cackled the ancient. "So you come, arrogant Oakbeam, who dares to admit those whom our Lord wishes kept outside his walls. Come in, come in! It is too late now for mending!"

Oakbeam paid no heed to the twisted seneschal. He pushed past his swirling robe into the lamp-lit hallway beyond. The builder stalked away toward an arched doorway, where he tapped once, rather impatiently, and waited to be bidden to enter the room beyond it.

Riddle noted with amusement that the wait promised to be long. Girnig thought he could keep the Kings of Damaria waiting in the hall as if they were flunkeys!

He stepped past his friend and pushed the door wide. "It must be, Girnig Wind-Tamer, that you do not know who waits beyond your door," he said. "One does not in courtesy keep a King and a Regent, Lords of the land where your city stands, cooling their heels in his hallway."

The man sitting in the tall chair (as like to a throne as he could make it) rose abruptly, staring with angry eyes at the intruders into his audience chamber. He wore, Riddle noted with amusement, a linked chain about his brows, and it, too, was as like a crown as he could manage without rousing the laughter of his subjects. They stared for a moment, eye into eye, and Riddle knew this would be no ally. He might, indeed, prove to be a formidable enemy to one who wanted a ship built in his city.

But there was nothing to be done. He must tread warily and speak with wisdom and tact to this self-absorbed son of the Sealords.

CHAPTER THIRTY-TWO

"When strong opponents struggle silently...."
                                                    —Riddle

Girnig was angry. He woke, hot with fury in his wide bed shaped like a ship, beside his sleeping wife. Staring into the elaborate mural of clouds running before the wind that arched across his ceiling, he stretched silently, thinking about Oakbeam's insolent message, received too late for anything to be done about the advent of these intruders into his city.

He rose, swinging his long legs down the side of the high bed, and moving down the three steps to the thickly carpeted floor. The ornamented headboard of the bed loomed above him as he took his velvet morning robe and his furred slippers from their place in the armoire set into the wall beside it.

Once wrapped in the crimson folds, his narrow feet chilly even in the slippers, he went softly to the door opening into his private study. The draperies had been pulled, as was his invariable order, by the maid who started the fire of driftwood in the shell-shaped hearth.

A grim, gray day did little to augment the ruddy light from the fire and the fish-oil lamps. He scowled toward the window for a moment and turned to pull the bell that would summon his breakfast and his seneschal.

The Council might be the ruling body of the City in the Mist, but he had caught into his own clever hands much of the power the Councilors used to wield. He had no prime advisor chosen from that body, which disturbed them.

He chuckled softly. It would have disturbed them more if they had known he consulted with Arken. The warped ancient was not even of the race of Sealords, being one found adrift in wreckage as a child, far out on the waters of the ocean. His kind was unknown on this continent, for his skin was brown and thin, and his eyes were black as tar.

Girnig's grandfather, who had once been a Councilor and a Lord of the City, had pulled him from the sea with his own hands and adopted him as foster son. He had trained him, educated him, and infected him with the lust for power that had always plagued the family Wind-Tamer.

For decades he had conducted the practical affairs of the Great House. No one had ever suspected that he assisted two generations of the family of his benefactor in gaining the rulership of the trading city for themselves. Ability, not heredity, had always determined the descent of that authority.

Girnig's dour expression lightened as he recalled the way in which the ancient had falsified the records of his expeditions and had contrived to send those of his men who might have quarreled with the tallies off on voyages that would keep them busy for years.

There came a timid tap at the door, and he grunted permission to enter. A maid brought his breakfast tray into the chamber and set it onto an inlaid table. Watching him nervously, she arranged fragile dishes, golden utensils, and a great golden cup gemmed with rubies.

Fruit was set, just so, on plates, a thick slice of red meat on another. A steaming pitcher of mulled wine filled the cup. Then she sank onto her knees and put her forehead against the dark plush of the carpet.

"Lord, is all well?" came her muffled voice.

He grinned. This was the sort of servility that filled him with joy. But he controlled his expression and looked properly stern when she looked up again.

"It seems well. Send in Arken to me."

She backed from the room as warily as if she left behind a pack of predators. That was good—those who served him must live in fear of his displeasure.

He had, some years past, caused to be amputated the hands of a young woman who had dropped his breakfast tray. He passed her, from time to time, begging in the streets those streets far removed from the Great House, he was pleased to notice. She had, in a hand of years, turned from a plump and pretty wench to a withered hag. As well she should!

There came another tap at the door. He grunted again, his mouth filled with hot wine, and Arken shuffled into the study. His twisted neck made him look upward and sideways, and his skinny limbs were crooked as old branches, but those tarry eyes were bright and filled with intelligence. "You are not happy to have more of the Ancient Race within your walls," he observed, as he perched his skinny buttocks on the high stool reserved for him in this private place.

"Riddle is not one of the great ones of his kind, but any of those southerners can become stubborn for little reason."

He chuckled, as Girnig pushed a smaller cup of wine toward him. After a sip, the old man cocked his head at an even more perilous angle.

"I think his cousins will not take kindly to his presence, either. And to think the new king is a child—that will go hard with them. They are not the people I knew when your grandfather was alive.

"Something in this northern climate has changed them. Something has made them more...human?" He buried his long nose in the cup again, leaving the Lord to think over what he had said.

The Sealord nodded. He had noticed the same thing, though he had known Tulip and Silk, Blade and Wonder for only a handful of decades. In their long lives, that was nothing, yet even he had felt a change in them. They no longer gave the feeling of solid and unchangeable probity that was a part of their race.

Tulip, in particular, had begun to seem—shifty.

Girnig finished his breakfast and turned enigmatic green eyes toward Arken. "Is something in our delightful climate corrupting even the Ancient Race?" he mused aloud. "An interesting development, if true.

"But that will be of no help in dealing with this new-come Regent and his brat. Not to mention more of the furred vermin that the Kings bred and taught past their station. What must we do, Arken, about our uninvited guests?"

"Why, make them welcome, Lord," the seneschal said, his voice thin as the wind fingering the window frame. "Make them welcome, and then see if there be not a way to rid ourselves of them quickly."

"And if there is no such way?" he asked.

The black eyes twinkled. "Others have vanished without trace from the City in the Mist. Not, perhaps, members of the Ancient Race, but many who thought themselves important and even noble."

The Lord rose and went to the window to stare into the gloomy morning. Without turning, he said, "Did you know Armor, when he visited my father here?"

"I met that arrogant King," said Arken. "But he did not come to visit your sire, which was all too like his lack of respect for power. He came to visit his kin and the father of Oakbeam the builder."

The lines in the narrow face deepened. "You were at sea, and Riddle, if I recall, was young of his kind. I wonder if he shows any change, now—they age so slowly that mere men such as we age and die before they leave their youth."

"That is of no consequence. What sort was he—or did you have the opportunity to judge him?"

"A poet. Merely a poet, with a talent for music and a way with words. He cannot be much to fear, this last of his family. And the child is easy. Children die of many ills before they reach adulthood."

The two smiled, and Girnig nodded dismissal. Arken slid from the stool and limped to the door. "They will come early," he said over a withered shoulder. "Do you want me to greet them?"

"I do. And let them know, without being too bold, that they are not wanted. I am no hypocrite. I will not pretend with this—this poet!"

He stared at the door for a long while, once the seneschal had limped away. There was a disturbing feel to the damp air that managed to penetrate his thick stone walls. He did not want to meet these newcomers or to speak with Oakbeam, who held him in low esteem.

But he must, and to do that he intended to seem as regal as his wardrobe would allow.

* * * * * * *

There was a long silence. Riddle felt the tension about him, as he faced the ruler in his own chambers. Beside him, Oakbeam had gone stiff, his red beard curling aggressively over his fur collar and his mittened hands clenching about the head of his carven staff.

Then Gorghoz followed him into the room, and the green eyes of the Sealord focused on his huge shape, which blocked the door from side to side and from top to bottom. They widened, and a gasp came from the Sealord's throat. Evidently Girnig had not seen a Goremin before, and the sight of this one rendered him speechless.

"My friend Gorghoz, of the ancient mountain people," Riddle said in a pleasant tone. "Oakbeam you know, and my nephew is a bit too young to take formalities seriously. But this is Lute, King of Damaria."

He held up the child in his woolly bag, and Lute laughed, his voice clear and happy in the musty air of the Great House. Echoes chased themselves about the room and down the corridor behind them, and the ruler of the City in the Mist was barely able to keep from flinching.

"Greet the Lord of the City, Nephew," Riddle said. He lifted the child clear of his wrappings and set him on his sturdy legs, and Lute stepped forward, suddenly solemn and wide-eyed, his face framed by his velvet hood.

"Hello," he said. The word rose like a bubble in the stillness.

The child held out his small hand in the ritual gesture of a ruling King toward a lesser ruler, and Girnig, held and compelled by something inherent in the blood of the Ancient Race, bent his proud neck.

"We have taken shelter here in your City," said Riddle, "knowing that the old treaties made between my fathers and the earliest of the Sealords to reach these shores guarantee us that right. We will cause no disruption of your life, if we can avoid it."

Girnig made a strangled sound, cleared his throat, and managed to speak at last. "I have not read those treaties. Is this true?" He turned his gaze toward Oakbeam.

The builder bristled. "The Regent of Damaria does not lie, Girnig," he said. "Those treaties are in your own archives, under the care of Arken, unless he has gone through the musty shelves, destroying anything he feels would displease you. And if that should be true, we of the Council have our own copies, housed in our own place where important documents are kept safe."

"Then you may remain here. But what is your purpose? You cannot intend to live here permanently." The dread of such an eventuality tainted the Lord's tone.

"No. We must build a craft capable of bearing westward all those who wish to leave this continent and find the Western Islands, where my people have gone for generations. Oakbeam will design and construct the vessel, which will, in time, carry us all away from your city."

Girnig turned again to Oakbeam. "And how long will that require? Your workshops are busy with other projects; that I know, for you are building a ship for my own trading ventures."

"I will begin gathering materials at once. There are logs drying in the forests along the Damarian coastline. I shall send barges at once, before the storms of winter become worse, to bring enough for this new project. Then, given a reasonable amount of good fortune, we should have a seaworthy ship within three years."

Riddle saw in the Sealord's eyes the bitter realization that he would have to endure the presence of a King and a Regent for years to come. The trappings of royalty that the copper-haired Lord had donned for this meeting looked suddenly shabby, and Riddle understood the mind of Girnig. He could not bear the comparison with those from the south who had inherited the secrets of fair rule from generations of noble and honest forebears.

Suddenly, he pitied the man. He smiled and said again, "We will do our best not to disrupt your city or your life. You will not, I hope, know that we are here at all." Then he turned and left the room, holding Lute's warm hand and hearing behind him the thud of the Goremin's feet, the clack of Oakbeam's boots.

He had not, he thought, made a friend of Girnig, but he hoped that he had not made an implacable enemy.

CHAPTER THIRTY-THREE

"The pain of children wrenches fathers' hearts."
—Riddle

The house belonging to those of the Ancient Race was no palace. It was, instead, a large and comfortable home built of the gray stone forming the walls and the bedrock of the City in the Mist. The stream that entered the city through a conduit beneath its outer wall curved through the garden of the house and out again beneath its own garden wall, built of recent years by the workmen of Oakbeam.

Nothing there was ornate or pretentious, yet the shapes of the stones forming the house, the arches of the windows, the width of the doors, all served in harmony to create a place that quieted the spirit. Even the colors favored by the Ancient Race—rose and gold and blue—were muted and calming.

Blade wondered often why the effect achieved upon the others in the family did not work with his daughter Tulip. She alone of the household paced restlessly through the garden, treading the carefully chosen creepers and blossoming plants under her careless feet. Only she slammed the heavy doors, making the very carvings on their panels seem to wince.

His nephew Wonder and his elderly cousin Silk lived quietly, thoughtfully, calmly, as their people had always done. They devised intricate philosophies and mathematical puzzles and poetry of surpassing strength and rare delicacy. Yet for a century or more Tulip had stalked through their lives as a disturbing and disruptive element. Now, Blade was convinced, something of her own irritable temper and unsatisfied ambition had transferred itself to his other kindred. His household had lost its ancient peace, and he sometimes found himself longing for the dreamy contentment of his brother Armor's kingdom.

Pacing, now, along the terrace outside the glazed doors of his study, he paused to finger a rose, which dipped its golden head from a loaded vine. He had savored the beauty of this place, the contrast of the wild ocean winds and the bitter winters. But it was spoiled for him now. He felt the approach of something evil, something frightening, even to one of his long-lived and potent kind.

The early onset of this winter had warned him. A change was coming that might well shatter this tranquil life into irreparable shards. Even as he entertained that thought, brisk steps tapped over the flagstones of the garden walk. Tulip rounded the carved post overgrown with late-blooming vines, whose blossoms had been protected from the cold and still thrust feeble glimmers of gold into the gray day. A blast of chill wind came with her, like a portent.

"They have come!" she shouted, although she might have whispered, she was now so near her father.

Blade flinched at the hard edge in her voice, which had once been quiet and musical. Now her words cut him, wounded his ears and his spirit. "Who?" he asked, turning to the study doors and waiting for her to pass through before he tugged them shut against the resistance of the wind.

"The rag-tag remnants of our southern kin. The Damarians, Father! The runner told me Armor is dead, and a child is now the King. A rebellious half-blood now rules where our ancestors built their city, and a child is the heir. A mere infant!"

The bitterness of her tone hurt almost as much as the news of his brother's death. He turned away and found his cushioned chair, sitting heavily and staring at his daughter.

"My brother is dead? And you tell me so? What kind of creature are you becoming, Tulip, to feel so little for the wounds you deal to others?"

For a moment, she looked ashamed, the rose-tan of her oval face paling. She bent forward to run a finger down the map of the Eastern Continent, stopping it over the point marked with the star that was the City of Damaria. Her brown hair, smooth and satiny, swung forward over her shoulders, and Blade thought with pain that there was nothing so lovely as his daughter, or so cruel.

"Riddle, who visited us with his father years ago, has brought the new King..."—her tone was cutting—"...to this City. He has also brought a group of weird creatures with them, among them, if you would believe this, a Dreamer." She quirked a brow at her father, waiting for his reply.

"We seldom saw the Dreamers," he said, thinking hard of all he knew about this interesting cross-breed. "But what I have heard has been most favorable. They are useful and well balanced, and if they still in some ways resemble the cat-people who were their ancient ancestors, that is not surprising."

"This one is a hag, ugly and skinny, yet she clings to the poet as if he were her betrothed, the runner told me."

And now Blade understood his daughter's tone. So far from those of her own blood, destined, if no more suitable match were found, to wed her cousin Wonder, she was already thinking that Riddle was one whom she could substitute for her too-well-known kinsman. She had never favored Wonder, nor he Tulip.

She had already decided, Blade understood with sudden pain, to hate and to destroy this unknown Dreamer who threatened—however faintly—to thwart her quick-forming plans. The inclinations of her cousin Riddle were no part of her calculations, he knew.

"Daughter," said Blade, "I forbid you to fantasize in this fashion. Your cousin is a man in his own right. He is, if no one else survives, the Regent for his nephew. He has, I do not doubt, survived trials that would appall you, and he does not need a woman of the Ancient Race stalking him as prey.

"Do nothing. Say nothing. Make no move against anyone in his train or concerning his person. I promise you, if you should disobey me in this, you will suffer consequences that you cannot believe I would impose."

He found himself standing, looking down into that heart-breaking face, which was turned up to his, blank with astonishment. Never had her father spoken so to Tulip in all the three centuries of her life.

Without speaking, she whirled in a graceful flutter of fine woolens and slammed from the room.

Blade, knowing the full weight of his brother's death with her going, locked the door behind her and sat again in his chair, his face bent into his hands. Tears leaked between his long fingers, and he felt the weight of loneliness descend upon his heart.

Only they two of their generation had survived. Now only their children and those of their dead sibling, whatever of them might still live in hiding in Damaria, were left of the line that had come north, three thousand years before.

Tulip, he knew, was afire with the notion that her father should rule in Damaria. Her ambition had grown, in recent years, more devouring than any he could recall among the Ancient Race, for whom the ambitions leading to personal power were outgrown early. But Blade, his face resting in its own tears upon the palms of his hands, knew that no matter what happened to the infant King, he would never rule in his brother's place.

That would be an unthinkable thing to one of their blood. So long as kindred of the blood survived, anywhere, in the direct line, that was the true ruler of the old country to the south.

* * * * * * *

Moonlight had lived the past days as if in a lightless trance. Even reaching the haven of Oakbeam's house had not roused her from the state into which her wounded spirit had sent her, and she slept for a night and two days after being installed under the care of Nilla.

But something woke her at last, as dawn lit the edges of the draperies hiding the eastern windows. A stab of pain, a thrust of impatient curiosity forced her up to sit shaking in her bed. Her soft moan as she roused brought a quiet presence to her side.

Chark's furry face peered over the edge of the couch. "You sick, Moonlight? You hurting?" the little Turnig asked.

The Dreamer drew a shuddering breath, crushed her hands together until her fingers ached, and then forced herself to relax. "Call Riddle," she whispered. "There is something...."—but before she could finish, the Turnig pattered away to find the poet.

Sitting there, Moonlight realized that she had dreamed as she slept. Not what her kind considered dreaming, of course—this was no conscious construction of the imagination, made real to others. It was something sent into her mind by another mind, and that was a thing she had never experienced, in quite this way, even with Verrainig, the Mover.

Painfully, she swung her feet off the bed and pulled a velvet robe, waiting on the nearby chair, around her. She did not glance into the mirror, for she knew what she would find there, and the blurred sight of her own withered features, her streaked hair, still had the power to wound her. She rebraided her rumpled locks with stiff fingers, as she waited for Riddle to come. The thing in her dream had been something sent by the Ancient Race, and yet she had never known anything from their hands except kindness. This, however, reeked of ill will, and she wondered if even the poet could analyze it.

There came a tap at the door, and she opened it to the Regent. Chark backed away, gesturing for him to leave her outside, now that her mission was done; he entered the room and closed the panel behind him.

Moonlight sat on the edge of the bed again, feeling her legs wavering beneath her. "My friend," she said. "I have dreamed. Not in the way of my kind, but as if another will set a stamp upon my sleeping spirit. It felt like the touch of your people, although there was a taint."

"Tell me," he said, sitting on the low stool beside her. "There are those of my family here, but I do not know them well. I visited them in years past, but only my Uncle Blade became my friend. His daughter was busy with her own affairs, and the others seemed aloof and uninterested in a visiting poet."

"I stood in a garden," Moonlight said, closing her eyes so as to see the memory better. "Golden roses, touched by frost, were withering on vines clinging to stone walls and pillars. A fountain was still playing, though its spray formed icicles on the rim, and I could feel the damp and the cold to my very bones." She shivered involuntarily and pulled the robe still closer.

"A woman stood there beyond the fountain, half hidden in its chilly spray. She was staring at me with utter contempt, as if I were some verminous creature better destroyed than given house-room. She regarded my face and my shape, and she smiled. But she did not look deeper to find who and what I am. On the basis of one glimpse of my outer self, she sentenced me."

"Sentenced you?" Riddle's voice sounded strained. "To what, Dreamer?"

"'You will die,' she said to me. 'I shall see to that myself. And you will not meddle with my kinsman, or that death will not be a pleasant one.'"

The poet rose, pushing the stool over behind him. Ignoring its clatter on the tiled floor, he bent over Moonlight and took both her hands. "What did she look like?" he asked her.

Moonlight could see a terrible surmise in his eyes, but she could only give him the truth. "Her face was heart-shaped; she had large brown eyes, and smooth brown hair streamed like silk to her waist. If her expression had not been so cold, so arrogant, she would have been rarely beautiful. But she filled me with loathing, Riddle."

The poet righted the stool and dropped to sit on it again, his face paling. "My cousin, Tulip," he said. "She was never a friend to me, but I had thought all our people were loyal to kindred. It seems that the taint loosed upon our lands by the Mover and Dinorm has been at work here, so near the frozen hills.

"It seems strange that one of the Ancient Race should be corrupted, however. My kind has proven resistant to those alien wills for generations uncounted. Perhaps there was an inborn weakness in Tulip that opened her defenses to such influences."

Moonlight swayed, and he rose again, helping her to lie flat. He pulled up the warm woolens and tucked them about her shoulders.

"Sleep, Dreamer. We are two whose lives have been inevitably joined by destiny and by our shared dangers. Never believe that one of my house will be allowed to betray you into the hands of an enemy, no matter if she might be my own sister."

He drew the draperies closer over the window, shutting out the line of morning light. "I shall send one to guard you who will keep such dreams away from your defenseless mind. Gorghoz has strengths that few understand. He cannot read thoughts, but his will is ancient and potent, and he can fill this chamber with forces that will deflect any ill wish or sending, no matter who the sender might be."

"Thank you," she whispered. "I will sleep for a long while more, but if such dreams plague me, I think I might die."

"Yes." He opened the door. "That is what I think, and I suspect it may be what she intends. Rest well, Dreamer. Gorghoz will come at once."

Almost before she could wonder, he came, that great hairy shape filling the room with its presence. The warm fingers touched her face, smoothed down her eyelids. She could feel the atmosphere of the room ease, warming and losing the sense of tension left by her dream.

"Gorghoz," she murmured, and he bent close to hear. "I do not regret...the thing I did...there in the frozen waste."

His voice came from far away, as she slid down the well of sleep. "I know, little Dreamer. And I shall see that you do not suffer, if I must battle the Ancient Race itself. Goremin know their friends and they pay their debts."

But she was already deep in darkness.

CHAPTER THIRTY-FOUR

"Great timbers shape a hull to plow the seas...."
                                                    —Riddle

Arken the Seneschal wrapped himself well in his dark cloak, putting onto his scanty white locks a fur cap and onto his skinny feet the best of boots. Seldom did he venture out into the city, and never when the weather was inclement, yet he had an errand that he could entrust to none of his agents.

For almost three generations the old one had been the secret hand of the Lords of the city. His wit was subtle, and his wickedness knew no limits, when there was profit to be made or mischief to be invented. Now he found his designated task almost too easy.

He preferred more challenging games than this, and he grumbled, even as he stumped through the flagstoned streets, his pouch of gold tightly wrapped to keep it from jingling. The wind of the bitter night bit through his garments, and even the fur of his hood did not divert thin tendrils of cold from his knobby neck and his crooked ears.

When he came to the Merry Tarman, even its stench of spilt liquor and spittle did not make its warmth less welcome to his creaking bones. He slipped into the crowded room, lit dimly by tallow dips, and found a place on a settle, his back to the wall. In the Merry Tarman, a wise man always set his back against something solid, else he might find his life leaking out of his veins and his pouch missing.

No one seemed to note his coming. That was good, for secrecy was a game he played with skill and gusto. Only after he had sipped a second cup of ale did he so much as look up and scan what could be seen of the room through its haze of tallow smoke and alcohol-laden breath.

Orrig was there, standing beside a table near the long counter that served as a bar. He had one arm about a fur-covered woman, and the other hand in the pocket of a drunken sailor who was snoring with his head on his arms.

A wench came around the room, pitcher in hand and a tray full of clanking cups balanced on her arm. Arken gestured, and she clumped to the table before him and sloshed a stingy ration into one of the cups, which showed unmistakable signs of previous use. But the ale was strong enough to rout the Plague itself, and Arken did not hesitate to bury his nose in it, once she moved on.

A fight broke out in the corner of the tavern, and a slight figure went sailing across the room to land on the table flanking the one at which the old man sat. Everything went down with a crash as the flimsy legs of the piece gave way, dumping the burden of cups and platters onto the bruised Monkey-man lying amid the debris.

Few noticed the commotion, as the babble of talk and drunken song and loud argument had grown uproarious. Orrig, seeming to be a part of every group he joined, drank and sang and argued with the best of them and then passed onward.

Arken watched the man circle the room without haste. Pockets were picked along the way, for that was Orrig's profession. At last the thief nudged along the wall and pushed Arken aside. "Make room, old man," he muttered. "I must sit or I shall stand through m'feet."

The seneschal said nothing but slid along the settle, allowing the pickpocket to take his place beside him. The pouch bunched, hard and noticeable, between their thighs, and there came the faint chink of metal. With amusement, Arken felt it slip away as if evaporating into mist.

He dabbled his stained forefinger in spilled ale among the dirtied cups and drew random patterns on the tabletop as he said, as if to himself, "It would be best if Oakbeam finds no sailors or shipbuilders, this winter, for other work than he already has in hand. It would be a terrible thing if anyone perished in bringing back logs from the Damarian coast."

He sighed and drooped, as if overcome by drink. Orrig, beside him, snorted at some joke told farther along the table and nudged the old man's ribs. As if waked by that, the seneschal started up, looked about blankly, and made his feeble way out of the tavern. Behind him he heard guffaws, and he grinned, recalling the sort of ribald tale that Orrig told so well.

His message delivered and payment made, Arken made his way back against the wind to the small door at the side of the Sealord's house. Girnig would not be pleased if he learned of that delay, but Arken had ways of keeping secrets from his master. It was best for the shipbuilding to be slowed, he felt in his ancient bones, whatever Girnig might say.

Only devotion could take an old man out on such a night, he thought. Devotion—but to what?

He chuckled. His own amusement, more than anything else. Still laughing silently, Arken hobbled off to bed. His master might think himself the Lord of all creation, but if truth were known, Arken played his own hand always. No one knew his purposes, and even he might be hard put, at times, to put into words what it was that he proposed to do or what moved him to take action.

* * * * * * *

Oakbeam kept woodcutters busy, in summer, choosing and felling straight trees whose close-grained wood could be sliced and shaped to form his hulls. They laid the trimmed logs in ricks, braced to prevent warping, and the barges came across the bight of the bay, around the horn of protecting land, and onto the shore of Damaria to load the timber. Old agreements between the King and Oakbeam assured the builder of an endless supply of material.

Winter was time for work in the slip and workshops, when the wood was shaped with tension and water and steam to form the ribs of his tall ships. Buildings were shored up with new shutters and braces for their roofs. Every twig of wood was spoken for, when Riddle brought his people into the City in the Mist.

The barges must go out across the stormy winter waters for more wood. To waste the winter, when the ribs might be setting, the tholes and pins and sails and ropes, the caulking tow and tar, the brass and steel fittings of the poet's ship might begin taking shape, would be criminal.

The City was tenanted, principally, by descendants of the bold Sealords who had created this harbor town. There was never any hesitation, no matter how terrible the weather, when the sailors along the docks were approached by one needing their skills. The sailors of the Sealord breed were born to their tasks, and winter was a long and boring time for most of them.

That was why Oakbeam found himself staggered to learn that no seaman wanted to man his barges. It was as if some word had passed among the docks and taverns: no one is to bring wood for the ship to be built for the King of Damaria. No one is to shape metal or pick tow or twist rope for it.

Such a thing had never happened in all the years in which Oakbeam's family had been the greatest builders in the city. Every worker hoped to be employed in his shops, to set hand to shaping his vessels, or to sail on his decks. And now even the boys who melted tar seemed to be hard to find.

Girnig held his peace and said nothing to Oakbeam concerning his projected shipbuilding. No whisper of the source of the ban could be found, either by the builder or his sons, who listened in the taverns and the shops for any hint of its origin.

Arken, when asked obliquely by one of Oakbeam's associates, merely grinned maddeningly and said, "Those who put their own business higher than that of the Lord of the City may well find themselves uncomfortable with the result." Which meant nothing, as far as Oakbeam could tell.

But more than fifty Turnig had survived to reach the city, where a hundred or more of their fellows had already chosen to live when the northern forests fell under the influence of the Mover. They were not happy living amid stone and brick, but it was better than finding themselves skinned by the Lirfolk for meat and fur. These small people knew hard work, among other less obvious matters, and once the need was made known, many of them volunteered to haul timber, although manning barges was a bit beyond their size and abilities.

Luckily, there were only four of the awkward craft, and Oakbeam's four sons were true heirs to the seagoing tradition. Managing a barge in a stormy sea was nothing to any of them. The logs began moving, propelled by many small hands, onto the wharfs and into the sheds beside Oakbeam's workshops; and other Turnig learned the secrets of making rope and turning wood and shaping metals into useful brackets and bolts and hinges.

Oakbeam suspected that Girnig was not pleased to find these "vermin," as he considered them, capable of such work. There were harassments in the lower quarter of the town where the furry people lived, and Riddle himself stood a watch, from time to time, to protect those laboring in his cause.

Oakbeam kept a wary eye on Girnig, through his sons and the many workers who were his friends. Most of those owed him some debt, for he was one who helped when there was need, and even the servants in the very House of the Sealord kept him informed of the moods and the calculations of the ruler of the city. All of his friends, however, were already working either for the builder or for one of his subcontractors, who made barrels or ship's lanterns or fittings for the vessels he created.

The builder learned that the prospect of ridding the city of many of the Turnig had caught the Lord's fancy. Yet the resistance toward working on the ship for the King of Damaria did not lessen, and Oakbeam was puzzled. Why should Girnig put obstacles in the path of ridding his city of those he disliked having there?

Some interest, neither his own nor that of Girnig, seemed set upon slowing the building of that vessel.

CHAPTER THIRTY-FIVE

"...and people one has known can always change."
—Riddle

Riddle was weary. The stress of the terrible journey had taken its toll, but deeper even than that was the agony of his loss. Only this small nephew, of all his family, still lived. His brother, his nephews, his entire world had disappeared like smoke in the breeze, leaving the poet feeling bereft and bare to the winds of fate.

So it was that once he had settled his charges into the City in the Mist his thoughts turned to his kinfolk living there. It had been many years since he had spoken with Blade, who was the only member of this branch of the family whom he knew at all well, but he found himself longing to speak with one of his own breed.

Oakbeam, for all his tough practicality, was still a child in terms of the lifespan of one of the Ancient Race. The Goremin was alien in thought and history. And Moonlight—he could not bear even to think of her, until his exhaustion had healed somewhat. Her sacrifice had cost too dearly, and Riddle felt he might have done more or differently and saved her this agony.

The storm that had come with them into the city blew itself away over the hills toward Damaria and the mountains, and the sky settled again into its usual sullen winter hue. Once the streets were less painful to walk, Riddle set out for the house of his kinsman, feeling a warmth at his heart at the thought of that reunion.

He had new boots made by Oakbeam's cobbler to his measure, and his feet were warmed by hose that Nilda had knitted herself as part of the great store she kept ready for her busy-footed menfolk. The wind no longer knifed about his ears, though the air lay chill upon stone and flesh alike. It had been a long time since the poet had walked through this city to the home of his people. He found to his dismay that stones had fallen from house fronts and been allowed to lie, unmended, in the streets. Paint and mortar had been let to weather in too many cases, and only those new houses built by his host showed painstaking craftsmanship. The City in the Mist showed its age, and not gracefully.

When he came to the wall of Blade's garden, that was a different story. The stones were well cut, solidly set in mortar almost as durable as the rock itself. He followed the curve along the street to the gate, where the leaves were pulled together but not locked.

A silver bell hung in a loop of metal, its pull dangling below in a glitter of silver rope. Smiling, the poet caught the pull and gave it a long tug. The thin, high voice of the bell sang through the moist air, and in a moment the panel was pulled back and a weathered face peered through the crack between the leaves.

"And who be come to the gate of Master Blade?" came the question. The voice was younger than the look of the face promised, and its timbres woke a faint echo in Riddle's memory.

"Fladan?" he asked, staring into the eyes, which were almost hidden by their wrinkled lids. "Is it you, old friend?"

The gate was flung open in a single motion, and the wiry shape grabbed Riddle about the shoulders. "It be the young poet, indeed!" came the cry. Fladan danced about him, once he loosed his grip, as agile as a boy.

"Come'un within and see th' master! You've no changed, though I've gone from youth to age sin' we met. Come! Come! The folk are all agog to see you again!" And the shrunken shape of the ancient who had been a stripling when last Riddle laid eyes on him went dancing before him up the graveled path and into the wide porch of the house of the Ancient Race in the City.

Once they were inside the broad doors, standing within the low-domed chamber that was lit from above through glass, Riddle gazed about, enjoying finding something that was unchanged. The colored glass of the dome altered the gray light of the sky with something like the brightness of summer. The carpets underfoot had not faded, their flowers still blooming in shades of blue and rose and gold as clearly as they had the first time he saw them.

Fladan was out of sight, calling for his master along the corridor leading into the living quarters of the house. Riddle glanced about and chose a deep chair. He was just letting his weight settle comfortably into its embrace when he heard a small cough.

Startled, he jumped to his feet and stared toward the source of the sound. He had thought the wisp of color lying on the sofa to be a band of light refracted from the dome, but it was his cousin Silk, her ancient body even more slight and unsubstantial than it had been when last he saw it.

She reached a pale hand toward him, and the poet moved to bend over it. Holding her fingers lightly, he bent farther to kiss her forehead. She smiled up at him apologetically, and Riddle knew she was now unable to rise easily.

"Silk," he said. "It is so very good to meet you again, though we knew each other very little in the old days."

"Your father and I were of an age," she said. "Though I suspect he was not so frail as I, when his time came. I would as soon be taken at the hands of the rebellious as on the slow rack of illness."

And, indeed, she looked very ill. Her eyes were dark-shadowed, her lips thin, her neck scrawny. The hand he held was like a handful of twigs, easily crushed into splinters.

He sat beside her couch, finding a damask stool for the purpose, and talked of his journey, leaving out the more terrible aspects. When he showed signs of pausing, she would nod, her eyes shining as if with fever, and he would go on. But she fell asleep before Blade arrived, drying his hands on a cloth, his wide face beaming with gladness.

He glanced down at Silk, now dozing on her couch, and gestured for Riddle to follow him.

Tiptoeing, they moved away down the corridor and, at last, into Blade's study that opened onto the garden terrace.

A single yellow rose stood in a crystal stem, the last of the summer's lot, Riddle suspected. Blade had always loved blossoms about him. But now that rose seemed to sadden his cousin, and he pushed the vase aside and gestured for Riddle to take the chair on the other side of the round table.

"Ellever! Bring herb tea and cakes for our guest," he called. Then he turned and gazed at Riddle as if to absorb him bodily into his eyes and mind. "It has been long," he said. "Your great-uncle, my brother, was hale and well when last we met in this room. How did he die?"

Riddle shook his head and took the steaming cup the woman servant brought on a silver tray. "I do not know. I was with my brother and his family when the rebellion broke about our heads. It came to my ears that his own son Lorbek struck the fatal blow, and that does not really surprise me, if it is true.

"Lorbek is a proud and ambitious man. Even from the south, where he was taken for nurturing, word came to us about his nature, and it was not comfortable to hear. His father loved and distrusted him, with good reason."

Blade sipped his own cup and crumbled a cake between his long fingers. "The Ancient Race is not infallible," he said, his tone sad.

"Even here in my own household, there is dissension and, I fear, ambition without thought of other needs and wills. My daughter...."

"Yes?" came a sharp question from the terrace doorway. Riddle stood, setting aside his cup, to greet his cousin Tulip, who entered the room like a sunbeam, bright in golden silk and rose-colored slippers. In her hand was a withered rose from the garden, which she offered playfully, teasingly.

He felt himself smiling. It had been so long since he had seen anyone so completely, joyfully normal as this young woman seemed. Something about her brought out an answering playfulness within him as well.

He caught up the rose from the vase and came to a guard position, and the two crossed roses, stepped back with courteous bows, and fenced for a moment with flowers, amid a flutter of detached petals. He found himself laughing, relaxed, soothed more than he would have believed possible, upon entering this house.

Blade laughed, too, his deep boom filling the room. "When last you met, you were less compatible," he said, when they bowed again and sat at the table. "If I recall, Tulip thought you a very sedate sort of young man, and you paid no attention to her at all."

The girl's silver laughter rang out gaily. "So I did. I was a madcap in those days, I suspect. Adventure was my goal, and I suspect Father often despaired of rearing me safely to years of wisdom. But now he has succeeded..."—the wicked glint in her dark eyes gave the lie to her assertion—"...and I am the most sensible of women."

Riddle drained his cup and tasted one of the cakes, finding it, as he expected, both tasty and satisfying. He leaned back in his chair and gazed at Tulip admiringly. "You have grown even more beautiful, Cousin. I had thought you lovely, the last time I saw you. Now I wonder that your father has not sent you southward, for all the dangers of that journey, to find a suitable husband of our blood. It would be a pity to waste such a treasure here where none of our people come."

"But you have come," she said, her tone demure. She sipped her tea and glanced up at him through lowered lashes. "And perhaps I need not seek southward for a mate."

Riddle woke to himself with a start. He was no boy, unburdened by responsibility, to flirt with a winsome girl. He was, instead, burdened as none of his kind had often been, faced with tasks that wearied him to think of. His nephew would come to his throne, if ever, through the efforts of a single poet of the old blood.

Riddle smiled, sighing, and shook his head. "Sadly, Cousin, I cannot remain here. I must take my people beyond the reach of the

Mover in the North and of Dinorm. Those two are resting, but that is a temporary matter. They will wake again to their full power, and when that happens I must have my group beyond their reach."

"And who are these...people...who are so important to you that you must leave your own country on their account?" asked Tulip. Her father stirred suddenly, as if disturbed by her words.

"Why, my nephew, Lute, who is King of Damaria. My friend the last of the Damarian Goremin. Killeli, the furred man, a host of Turnig, and Moonlight, who sacrificed youth and beauty and the truth of her heart to save us all. Each of those is dear to me, and I must take them away from this continent to find the Western Isles."

Blade rose and went to the window, gazing into the gray afternoon.

Tulip stretched and smiled, her lips curving wickedly. "Perhaps I shall persuade you differently, Cousin. I am capable of great persuasiveness."

"Of that I am certain," Riddle said, though he felt inside himself a certain unease. Something was not well here, though a moment before he would have given much to be able to remain in this warm house with this charming woman.

He thought of Moonlight, standing before the powers of the north, tainting her spirit and spoiling her gift in order to preserve those for whom she cared. He wondered suddenly if this woman might be capable of such self-sacrifice.

Gazing into those brilliant eyes, Riddle found himself certain she would not. Tulip, daughter of Blade, would find what best profited herself, and she would pursue that course without giving thought to the welfare of anyone else. The thought dismayed him, for this was not an aspect common to his people.

Something had come into this warm, bright house to touch the spirit of one of his kind. Suddenly the poet was quite sure of that. Dinorm had never been able to touch the Ancient Race themselves, there in distant Damaria. But those dwelling in the City in the Mist were much nearer to the center of his power. Had the mind of that destructive principle loosed in the north by the Litati turned here, as well as southward?

Without making it obvious, Riddle withdrew gently from his encounter with his kindred. Rising, he said, "I must return to help Oakbeam find workers and barges for our shipbuilding. It is strange how difficult that has become, this winter.

"But I will visit you again, when I can remain longer. Kin-meeting is good. Give my affectionate regard to Wonder, with my regret at finding him away from home, and to Silk when she wakes.

I must be off about my business."

They went with him, of course, to the gate to see him off. As Riddle looked down into the face of Tulip, he saw behind her eyes a speculative gleam that unsettled him. This was not a woman who relinquished the thing upon which she set her heart.

Surely, in so short a meeting, she could not have set it upon him! But the thought lingered as he hurried away down the street, where once again the cold wind from the sea was gusting and sending spatters of sleet into his eyes and down his neck.

Uncomfortable within and without, he retreated to Oakbeam's house, and even when he was inside its strong walls, he was not completely at ease. He had roused something dangerous, he felt, with that visit to his people.

CHAPTER THIRTY-SIX

"A scarlet blossom blackens 'neath the moon...."
—Riddle

The house lay still about the sleepless girl. Her father had spoken sharply to her again, once her cousin had left, and so seldom did this happen that it struck her to the heart. And yet his words had not altered her resolution.

Tulip meant to marry her cousin Riddle. He was heir, after his nephew and her father, to the throne of Damaria. Her cousin Wonder she dismissed as a weakling, who would not reach out for power if it were at hand. She fancied being one of great consequence, although she had been taught all her life to disdain such brief and unimportant follies.

"Why should I risk myself on that terrible southward journey to find a husband, if there is one conveniently at hand?" she asked the image in her mirror.

Candlelight pooled beneath her chin, masking her eyes with shadow, turning her silken hair to a cloak of darkness. "I am beautiful," she said. "No man should be able to withstand me, if I remove the reasons for his leaving. And I shall remove them!"

She smiled, and her face in the glass curved into lines of light and dark like some demonic mask. She felt, for a moment, that the image she saw was more nearly like the person she felt herself to be than that which she showed to the waking world. There was a hard, dark core to her the rest of her kin seemed to lack.

"Strength," she mused. "I have the strength of will and body, the determination to do what I wish, without concerning myself with others. I shall keep the poet here. He is not strong, perhaps—not as strong as I—but I shall shape him to my will, once he is mine."

She turned, her pale robe a drift of light about her slight body, and paced up and down the room, pausing from time to time to place a lump of sea-coal in the flames blazing in her arched hearth. She could hear the wind tearing at the house, even here in the shelter of its garden wall.

There was a storm, tonight, to match her own mood. Both of them might work their will upon the world, she was certain, if they persisted. Even as she thought that, a loosened slate went clattering down the roof and shattered outside her window.

"Moonlight," she murmured, drawing back the drapery and staring out into the blackness of the wet night, "will shatter like that slate. I shall break her will and her strength, and she will die, even though something has begun blocking my sendings to her chamber in Oakbeam's house.

"Riddle must forget her, as he will, in time. We have that time, he and I, for we shall live when all those vermin in the city have been forgotten and their precious city is a heap of rubble and dust "

She moved back to the hearth and warmed her hands before the dancing flames. Warmed by her thoughts, Tulip turned at last to her bed and extinguished the candle.

Lying in the darkness, she relaxed at last and felt the approach of sleep. She smiled lazily, envisioning the withering away of that Dreamer who lay in the house of Oakbeam.

There are ways, she thought, to have things done which risk no exposure. There are people who carry out tasks for those disinclined to do them with their own hands. And I am clever enough to make plans and clever enough to hire them accomplished, she thought.

Then she slept, and no dream disturbed her rest.

* * * * * * *

Wonder had not been away when Riddle called. He had gone out earlier, but by the time the poet arrived, his cousin had returned and gone to his rooms over the northern portion of the house. These were isolated from the rest, and even the servants seldom knew if he came or went.

To Tulip's contemptuous amusement, he insisted upon cleaning his own chambers, claiming the servants disturbed his work. This, as far as it went, was true. They dusted and moved papers, they polished the floor and rearranged his paintings that leaned against the wall. They even cleaned his pots of paint and disturbed the order of his carefully made brushes. This made him furious.

For in Wonder the talent that wandered through his family showed itself in a passion for making pictures. Not a single one of his kin, there in the city, knew of his work, for he never showed a painting to anyone. Often he locked himself away for weeks at a time, sometimes remembering to eat from the trays left each day at his door, often forgetting food entirely.

He had returned on this particular afternoon with a new picture forming in his mind. He had walked the headland and the cape, watching the waves battering wildly at the offshore rocks, whose skewed contours shone with water and with the pewter light reflected from the sky. This was a stern and uncomfortable work he proposed to do, and he began it immediately after locking his door and taking off his cloak and hood.

He did not hear the silver bell when Riddle rang it. He lost himself in his work, and when at last the light dimmed too much for him to continue, the painting loomed against its stand like some alien landscape from a lost and sodden world. It reflected his mood, which grew darker with every passing year.

He found his tray waiting outside the door, as usual, and while devouring its contents, he continued to study this new work by the light of his crystal lamps. It was a frightful thing. Sometimes, now, he frightened himself, and he felt the need for drastic change.

Madness, he found himself thinking, was not a thing he could discount. And his cousin Tulip was no help, for when she could, she pushed him farther and deeper in that dark direction.

If he should, and he shuddered at the thought, be foolish enough to marry her, she would soon have him caged and controlled, a puppet dancing to her will. He was not one who could bear dissension, and he knew he would give in, just for the sake of peace.

No, he could not wed his cousin, and he was beginning to understand that he must leave this home where he had lived for over three hundred years. While he was still young, of his kind, he must find another way of living that would not destroy both his sanity and his talent. Absent-minded though he had become, he recalled hearing that the Damarian cousins had arrived in the City in the Mist. Riddle, he remembered, was far more determined and steadfast than he had ever hoped to be, and he wondered if this unknown cousin might have a suggestion.

Perhaps—perhaps Wonder might pack up his paint-pots and his panels of work and take ship with the poet toward those Western Isles that promised a haven to any of their kind arriving there! Staring at the new painting, he thought seriously about that terrifying step into the unknown.

He knew and loved Blade. Silk was a gentle balm for his spirit, when he found her awake and well enough to talk. Losing them would be a painful, a dreadful thing, and yet in the balance there was Tulip. Losing her would free him, he realized suddenly, from the element that was making his life a burden and a trap.

Rising from his small table, he packed the dishes back onto the tray. Instead of setting it outside the door, he dimmed his lamps and carried the remnants of his meal to the kitchens. On the way, he passed Tulip, who was wandering along the corridor, deep in thought. Disturbed at his appearance, she glanced up at him, and Wonder saw for the first time the hatred in her eyes as she looked at him.

Yet he knew all her expressions, for centuries of living in the same house made them all too familiar with family traits. She was plotting something, was Tulip, and Wonder shivered as he passed with a cool nod and went on to the kitchens. He pitied the person upon whom she set her will.

Once he rid himself of his tray, he went into the south wing of the house and tapped at Blade's study door. It swung open under the gentle pressure to reveal his cousin sitting at his worktable, staring into space. His expression was troubled, his dark eyes sad.

"Wonder!" he said, as the painter stepped into the room and closed the door behind him. "Seldom do you visit me. Welcome! Have you eaten?"

"I have," Wonder replied. Now that he was here, he found it hard to begin what he had to say. But he straightened, as if to take up a weight, and asked, "Was our cousin Riddle here today?"

Blade's eyes widened. "I thought you were out, or I would have sent a servant to call you. He was, indeed. And I am deeply troubled about Tulip."

They knew each other too well to pretend. Each understood all the implications of that cryptic statement, and Wonder nodded, comprehending the source of Blade's unrest.

"I am troubled, too, Cousin. I would like to go away when Riddle goes. I heard in the city that he will build a ship and sail west, and the notion haunts me. This place has become a prison to me, and Tulip seems to act as my keeper, tormenting me when she can, and ignoring me when she cannot. Would you consider it desertion if I went away with the Damarian cousins?"

Blade rose and moved to the window, though Wonder knew he could see only his own reflection in the shining glass; outside it was completely dark, and sleet pattered against the panes. He clenched his hands together behind his back and turned.

"It is a great temptation to me to go as well. If it were not for our precious Silk, who may live for decades yet in her sickness, I would join you. No, Wonder, I encourage you to approach your cousin. We are at a dead end here, without a future and without a task worthy of our strengths."

"You would leave your daughter?" Wonder found the thought shocking. "Tulip would never consent to go!"

"I would. I have come to the realization, dear kinsman, that my daughter is corrupted beyond my help and beyond my control. Her intention with regard to Riddle has been told to me, and I find it a shocking misuse of the abilities of the Ancient Race. Tulip might remain here, if she liked, or she might go south. If Silk were not to be considered, I would join you in petitioning passage from the Regent of Damaria."

Wonder had never dreamed his cousin knew what Tulip's nature truly was. Now he knew Blade had suffered as much from that knowledge as from his worry over the situation in Damaria or Silk's condition. He tried to smile and stretched out his hand to take that of the older man.

"I will go. And should Silk die beforetime, I shall ask Riddle on your behalf as well. It is time we try our strengths in appropriate ways, Blade, instead of hiding here on this cape among men who do not understand what we are capable of doing." He paused to think.

Then he ventured a thing he had never thought to do: "I have something to show you, Cousin. Will you come to my rooms with me? There is something there that I think you may be interested in seeing."

Shivering with excitement and dread, he led Blade through the house to his own door. He turned, after opening it, and looked into those dark eyes. "This is my life," he said. "Deal with it gently."

But Blade's awe-stricken gaze was sweeping about the walls, where paintings of all sizes and subjects leaned in brilliant shades and wonderful designs. He moved forward as if enchanted and bent to look closely at them, one by one. When he turned, there was amazement in his gaze.

"Wonder, you are truly named," he said softly. "But do not reveal these to my daughter. She would...destroy them. And you."

But Wonder knew that far better than Tulip's father would have believed. He nodded and smiled, reveling deep inside himself at this first reaction from one who would, no matter what the cost, give him only the truth.

CHAPTER THIRTY-SEVEN

"I will safeguard all those who look to me!"
—Riddle

Although Oakbeam offered the shelter of his house for as long as the Damarians needed it, Riddle knew it was best to find housing apart. The builder would be hindered less in his efforts if he were not so closely identified with the refugees, for one thing.

He had considered, before visiting Blade, asking for sanctuary in his kinsmen's home, but his encounter with Tulip had scotched that quickly. Putting Moonlight beneath the same roof with this brown-eyed serpent would be asking for terrible problems. He needed a house large enough to house the Turnig and Killeli, as well as the Goremin.

There were many empty houses in the City in the Mist, for the population of Sealords had dwindled, after its earlier surge, and even the influx of Monkey-men and Turnig had not occupied more than the lower-lying fraction of the homes built inside the walls.

The Poet set out, just as winter turned its edge toward spring, to find a place that could house his assorted charges in some comfort and privacy. Killeli, now recovered from his journey and even growing a bit plump, volunteered to go with him, and the two donned their great woolen capes that Nilda had dragooned her daughters-in-law into making for them.

The wind was less vicious now, and the sea beyond the cape was not pounding like drums at the rock formations at its edge. Indeed, as they trudged along the stone-flagged street, stepping into puddles of slush, the sky took on a rosy hue, as if the sun might break through at any moment.

Riddle had explored the city during the winter, when infrequent calm days allowed such expeditions, and he had a good notion of the section most suited to his needs. In addition, Oakbeam had provided a map, and on it he had marked the empty houses he could recall as being large enough for the motley group that must live there.

The street into which they turned lay along the upper wall, highest on the shoulder of the cape, and the houses that fronted on it had their rear gardens tucked snugly against the cliff that protected the city from the worst of the ocean's storms. These were great stone houses, built to last for a thousand years, Oakbeam had assured Riddle. Their porches curved outward from many-windowed faces, shuttered now for winter, and the square posts holding the porch roofs were carven with the shapes of animals and men, of Turnig and Goremin.

The street seemed lined with watching beings, standing very still as Riddle walked past. The fifth house was the one Oakbeam had recommended, though all stood empty, and the door yielded to the heavy brass key the builder had entrusted to him. A gust of musty air met him as he stepped in and held the great door for Killeli.

The central hallway was wide, with a fireplace at its end that could make it useful as a sitting-room. To the right a stairway curved upward into dusty darkness, and to the left an arched doorway opened into a series of chambers, all high-ceiled, paneled in wood, empty of any furniture except that too heavy for its former tenants to move.

The huge chair beside the grate looked wide and stout enough to hold even Gorghoz, Riddle thought, and the long settle could hold a tribe of Turnig, all at once. The rooms that led through a series of ample doors, going away toward the back of the house, were well proportioned and quite large enough to accommodate numbers of Turnig, sleeping, playing, or simply killing time. So far, the Poet thought, he was pleased with the place.

They returned to the hall and went through the door at the end, which led into a great kitchen, large enough for cooking even for the assortment of kinds and appetites Riddle would bring. Its great driftwood-burning cook stoves looked capable of roasting whole meat animals at once, and the worktables provided space for busy Turnig hands, for the long benches beside them would be just right for the small beings to stand on while they worked.

When they climbed the stair, the wood was solid underfoot, and the rooms above were lofty and well lighted by windows looking out onto the sheltered garden, now frozen to grayness but showing still the outlines of herb and flowerbeds and the long stretch that had to be a vegetable garden. Chark, once spring arrived, would be out and digging, planting, in her element.

"I like it," he said to Killeli, as the two stood at the head of the stair, looking down into the capacious hall below. "We can live here for the years it will require to build our ship, I think. Do you feel this to be a good place, Killeli?"

The wiry fellow smiled his thin-lipped smile. "Gorghoz will like it, too," he said. "We will be comfortable here, if it is to be had."

Riddle grinned as he strode down the stair. "Anything can be had, my friend, if you have wealth, and the hoard of my father and uncles has been invested here for many lives of men. The merchants who trade beyond the ocean call here, and those holding our wealth deal with them for things our continent does not provide. There will be gold enough, believe me."

That proved to be true. Indeed, the Poet found that the hoard of wealth held and added to by the traders of the City was great enough to do more than buy the house and build his ship. He looked about and saw the needs of the small people who had come here, and with the help of Chark and Gorghoz he managed to fill many of those without arousing the anger of Girnig.

His people, Turnig and Goremin, Dreamer and furry man, moved into their new home with delight at having their own place. Many hands turned to and made furniture from the wood scraps Oakbeam provided from his shops. Turnig cleaned and polished and sewed and painted, until the place shone with the color and cleanliness they loved in their own burrow-like homes.

Moonbeam, behind that stout stone wall, seemed to gain strength and sometimes left her room to lie on a settle before the great fire of driftwood and smile at the antics of Lute and the Turnig. As the year turned and spring greened the garden, sending the Turnig into ecstasies of digging, she often sat in the chair they built for her, beneath the shade of the sachal tree, breathing the salt air that now spoke of warm and distant lands instead of bitter cold and storm.

Riddle, working with Oakbeam to find workers for his ship, to bring logs from Damaria, to see that all went well, still kept a close watch on the Dreamer. He knew his people; though a really evil one of the Ancient Race had not been known for thousands of years, he understood Tulip would be as skilled at wickedness, if she turned fully in that direction, as her ancestors had been at kindness.

Gorghoz, in the strength of his age, yet had been tried by the severity of their journey. He was content to sit in that garden, holding squirming Turnig infants or helping Moonlight to wind yarn for the eternal weaving and knitting that provided clothing for their large family. With the Goremin there, Riddle felt Moonlight would be safe from the probings and sendings of his cousin.

Spring moved into summer, and there were enough workers for all they needed, for even the most fearful felt the need of work in summer, to save up for feeding hungry families when the cold months came again. Suddenly, the shipyard was alive with carpenters and rope-makers, tar-boys and cabinet-makers, and those who measured the yardarms and calculated the amounts of canvas that must be sewn into sails for this great ship.

Oakbeam was in his element, beaming and rosy as he bustled here and there, supervising everything, forgetting no smallest detail of his design and construction. Riddle stayed by his side, watching, learning, listening to the news of the town brought by those who came there from all parts of the city. There seemed no danger from Girnig, now, but he was not content to let his wariness relax.

Twice he returned to his house by the wall to find Gorghoz waiting. The first time, he looked grave at the Goremin's report.

"We sat in the shade, shelling the beans from the garden," he began. "When I looked up, the Dreamer had gone very pale, and her gaze was set as if some force had invaded her mind and frozen her in place.

"I knew at once what I must do, and I took her hands in mine and turned my mind's strength to shielding her from any outside influence. In time she sighed and looked at me again, and she does not remember. But your cousin has not forgotten her purpose."

So warned, Riddle kept his mind bent toward his cousin, and he turned his steps toward the house of Blade on a sunny afternoon, when the sky was beginning to turn scarlet and gold and purple in the west. Now the streets were as warm as they had been chill, and he breathed deep and thanked fortune that he had been able to bring his people here, through all the dangers that had beset them in their desperate escape from Damaria.

He was smiling when he pulled the silver rope that sounded Blade's bell before his gate. When the panel opened and the gnarled face of Fladan looked out, it split at once into a wide grin. Again the gate opened, and the keeper led him toward the house where his kin dwelt.

This time he did not find Silk in the sitting room, as he waited for Blade to come in from his own garden, where he loved to work among his roses. Instead, his cousin Wonder came hurrying in, not long after he settled himself into his chair.

It had been many years since the poet had seen this quiet cousin, who now came forward and held out a hand on which smudges of color betrayed his calling. Riddle grasped it warmly. "Blade told me you are an artist. I am so glad to see you again, Cousin," he said.

"There will be time," Wonder whispered, "to come and see my paintings, while Blade bathes himself from his labors. Do come, Riddle. And be quiet, for if Tulip hears she will be angry."

Surprised to find the man so uneasy about a girl with whom he had grown up, the Poet followed the slight shape, wrapped in a robe of sapphire and silver, up the stair. He felt a sudden desire to laugh at the strange stealth Wonder displayed as he crossed the landing and went up yet again to his own tower. But once inside his chamber, Riddle did not laugh.

Upon the walls were paintings that stirred his heart and made him feel like weeping or laughing or shouting. And, largest of all, in the middle of the wall he faced as he entered there hung a dark work, holding the essence of storm and winter and raging ocean. He could feel the wind in his teeth, taste the salt spray, feel the vibration as the rock formations shouldered into the pounding waves.

Looking more closely, he saw that on the very edge of the cape, standing against the wind, minute and yet steadfast as the rock itself, stood the figure of a man. The face was turned toward the sea, as if longing to become one with the tumult that possessed it.

It was a staggering work, and Riddle felt suddenly ashamed of his earlier internal laughter. Wonder was well named, indeed.

But his cousin was speaking, his voice so low that the Poet had to bend close to hear. "I want to go with you, Riddle. I must get away from Tulip. She comes here when I am gone. Lock the room as I may, she gets in. She has...she has destroyed some of my work that I will never recreate, for the mood is gone and will not return."

Riddle felt a flush of anger. Was Tulip truly akin to his people or some wicked changeling left among them? How could anyone dare to destroy work that so clearly and feelingly portrayed the world about them, the people involved in it, and the emotions roused by wind and sun, sea and City?"

He took Wonder's hand in both of his own. "You may come, Cousin, and welcome. You might, if your spirit is so moved, paint the tale of our crossing to the Western Islands. Whatever you choose to do, I am proud that you want to come with me. Our kin across the sea will welcome you, I have no doubt."

Wonder looked immensely relieved, as if he had thought this kinsman might reject his plea. Again he whispered, "I would like to come with you, when you go. I can have Fladan and his wife pack up everything and send it after us. I must go, Riddle. I must leave, for Tulip is plotting something.

"I know her look when she intends to do something that her father will not condone. She has it now, and Blade cannot watch her constantly. If I am safely away with you, in your house on the other side of the City, perhaps she will leave me out of her calculations, whatever they may be."

"Make your plans," the Poet said. "When I go, you will go with me. But are you not sad to leave Blade and Silk?"

He was sorry he had asked, for tears sprang to the man's eyes, and his dark golden skin flushed with emotion. "It will be a pain to me, no matter how long I may live, that I must leave them. But I am nothing, as a person. Only when I paint am I a useful part of the universe. And she will take that from me, Riddle, if I remain here."

They turned and embraced. Then Riddle went down the stair again, hearing the locks click into place behind him. What was Tulip planning that so terrified her timid cousin? Her attempts to hurt Moonlight had come to nothing. Who else could be her target? Surely not even she would attempt to move against the Regent for the King of Damaria!

CHAPTER THIRTY-EIGHT

"The child of Kings must be a king, in truth."

—Riddle

The ship grew steadily and was being readied for launch. Often Lute was taken to see it, amid the bustle of work surrounding the great land-locked shape in its slip. His uncle would climb up on a platform beside Oakbeam, where they gestured this way and that, studied rolls of parchment, and did dull grown-up things for far too long.

Chark, however, always went along, and she was Lute's best friend and companion. As the years passed, however, she became busy with her own work, and as Lute was older and larger he needed less supervision. By the time he was almost seven, and the ship was almost completed, lying in its slip like a beached sea-creature that longed for the waves, the boy was familiar not only with the dock area but also a complex of streets leading into the town.

Riddle had no fear for the child, for everyone kept an eye on him. Lute understood the reason why he now could roam at will, watching craftsmen at their work, talking with women scrubbing their stone steps or with the Watch, set to guard the ship basin.

He was a King, the child of Kings, and he had been taught from his birth to behave as a king should. On the infrequent occasions when he felt the urge to fling a tantrum, he pulled himself up short, remembering the dimming faces of his mother and father bent over his small form. They had taught him better, and so had his uncle.

So he roamed from the docks to the marketplace, sometimes even walking along the parapets of the wall with those who kept a watch on the east and the Lirfolk. Everyone was kind, and he felt he had nothing but friends in the City in the Mist. The dangers of the journey that he could now recall only in bits and pieces seemed remote and far in the past.

It was early summer, and there was talk that by midsummer the ship would be completed, loaded, and their long voyage would begin. The boy was bubbling with excitement, for he felt the ship would take him into adventures that would be the envy of the Seafolk's children who played with him in their own courtyards or followed him as he wandered restlessly up and down the streets. They didn't take seriously his claim of being a king, and that stung, for Lute never lied. But he comforted himself with the thought that while he sailed away beneath the triangular sails of the ship, they must remain behind, staring enviously after him.

On this day, his midday meal eaten with Riddle and Oakbeam in the dock area, he found himself at loose ends. His cousin Wonder would ordinarily welcome him into his room at the top of Riddle's house, allowing him to stare at the pictures there as long as he wanted. But today he had taken his painting things and gone away up the Cape to paint waterfowl and the sea.

Chark was up to her furry elbows in her garden, digging potatoes and planting beans in their place. The objection that Riddle made because they would be gone by the time the beans bloomed was ignored by that small person. "Someone will come and make my harvest," she said. "Those Turnig who intend to remain here will be glad of them by winter."

Even the small boys who had been his playmates seemed to be busy, for not one came when he whistled along their streets.

He might be alone, but Lute felt for the first time the lure of solitary exploration. He could go anyplace within the walls, for everyone assured his uncle that here, if nowhere else on this continent, those of the Ancient Race were safe.

He set out over the high cliffs edging the flats along the dock area, moving downhill toward the lower-lying houses along the stream that curved through the town. There he found more inhabited buildings, though few children were outside at play, and those regarded him with cautious interest but made no move to talk with him.

He poked and pried among the narrow streets, finding alleys leading into tunnels that carried off the winter rains into the little river. Those looked dank and echoed with hollow chuckles that were a bit frightening, so he turned back to the more populated ways.

The sun moved westward, until the long shadows of the steep roofs made a dark corridor of the street along which he moved. Lute began to feel extremely empty. Lunch was a long way in the past, and his small legs were growing weary as he trudged determinedly toward the ridge marking the cliffs. His uncle would be concerned, for he had never gone so far alone before.

He paused beside a wall to catch his breath. The easy downward way was much harder when he must climb it, and he began to feel very forlorn and abandoned. But at that moment, a door opened in the gate, and the most beautiful woman he had ever seen since his mother came through it.

She smiled down at him, and he felt his unease melt in the warmth of her gaze. "You look very tired, young one—you are Lute, the King of Damaria, are you not?" she asked.

He nodded, speechless with hunger and relief. She reached down and took his hand as the gate opened again. They stepped through into a garden filled with ranks of flowers, on shrubs, on vines, and in neat beds. The smell of them was intoxicating.

"I am your cousin Tulip," she said. "You can see that I plant tulips along the walk, though they are past their bloom now. But you are hungry, I know, and must rest before we take you back to your uncle Riddle. Come and I will feed you."

That was an offer that Lute could not refuse, and he lagged after her, his hand in hers, trying to see all the flowers as they passed along the walk and into the wide doorway leading into the house. A man so old that Lute wondered if he would shrivel away before his eyes met them there and led them into a small room.

There was a table beside a window, now covered with books and manuscripts. It was cleared swiftly, and before Lute could think of anything to say to this surprising new relation, food had sprouted magically on the table and he was burying his face in a cup of soup. That was followed by thin-sliced fillets of flounder and rounds of cheese with spicy bread.

It ended with a tart filled with fruit, which filled him so very full he knew he must take a nap before going anywhere at all. "Thank you," he said in his best company voice. "I was very hungry. And now I think I must sleep, if you will let me, before we go home again. I am awfully tired."

Her smile grew even warmer, and she led him into a passage, up a small stair, and into a room filled with books. There was a long couch beneath its window, through which came the songs of birds and the quiet breath of the evening breeze.

"You may take your nap here," she said, smoothing his hair back from his hot forehead. "And once you have rested we will talk of getting you home again. Wash your face and hands there…"—she indicated a pitcher and a bowl of water on a small stand in the corner—"…and sleep as long as you like. We will get word to Riddle, to keep him from worrying."

That was the right thing to do, Lute knew, and he nodded. He washed, half asleep, and lay on the couch. Instantly, he was asleep.

When he woke it was quite dark in the room, although he could see a faint light in the sky beyond the window, reflected from a haze of cloud. He remembered a lamp in this room, but he was not allowed to use flint and steel to make light, so he knew he couldn't light it.

Rising, the boy fumbled toward the door, hoping he had his direction right, and at last his hands touched the painted wood. There was the latch he pushed down on it, but it did not move. Stuck. He tried again, but the thing seemed fixed firmly, impossible to budge.

Lute leaned against the bookshelves beside the door and thought for a long moment. He had been trained all his life to think before he acted, and now he thought long and hard, remembering everything he could about his uncle's talk since they came to the City in the Mist.

There were those who were enemies. That he knew, for he could remember being tucked into his uncle's pack and carried away before those enemies outside his home could break in and kill him. On their journey there had been many more enemies, intent upon killing them. Were there enemies here?

He thought again, piecing together bits he had overheard as the grownups talked together before the fires in winter. Yes, even here there were enemies, he realized. But this was a cousin!

Tulip...he thought of the name, bringing from the depths of his memory a hint of something troubling surrounding that name. Moonlight. She had spoken with Riddle, when they thought themselves alone. But he had been playing Turnig, using the covered table as his burrow, and he had heard his uncle say, "Tulip!" with a world of loathing in his voice.

Why hadn't he remembered that when she introduced herself? It had been a very long time ago. He must have forgotten it, until this moment.

If she was Moonlight's enemy, then she must be Lute's, he knew. He straightened and took a long breath. There was no way of knowing what she intended.

Again he tried the door, knowing it would not open. He had been caught neatly and without fuss, and he wondered now, with the insight that belonged to his race, if his impulse to wander had been entirely his own. Had this beautiful Tulip led him here, in some way, making him believe he guided his own steps?

She had come to the gate when he was just there. She knew his name at once, without being told. Who else knew that he was here?

The servant, Fladan! Lute remembered his uncle laughing about his old friend who was Blade's gatekeeper, and he knew Fladan would get word to Riddle. That was a comfort.

And then, from the garden below, he heard voices. Tulip's he recognized at once, and then the rough tones of the servant.

"Yes, I sent him home with a messenger, before it was fully dark. It is good of you to think of it, Fladan, but you need not worry. The child is again at home, and I found him well-mannered. It was lucky he came to us."

Lute ran to the faint glow of the window, to find it had been closed while he was asleep. The pane would not slide up or out or sideways, and he pounded on it with his fists, but there was no indication that Fladan heard or was even in the garden at all now.

So there was no way to send a message to his uncle. Lute sank to the floor, sitting on the thick rug, his fist against his mouth to keep from crying.

Why did they want him? The long tale of the Kings of Damaria, imprinted upon his mind since his birth, began to unroll. He and Riddle, alone of the Damarian branch of the Ancient Race, still lived here in the north of this continent. Blade and his family were kin, however, and Blade was the brother of Armor, Lute's great-uncle.

If Lute were dead, Riddle would be king. But if Riddle went beyond the ocean, that would leave only Blade in the direct line of descent. Was Blade a part of this plot?

Lute was dreadfully confused, for he knew his uncle trusted Blade. And their country, back to the south and east, was no longer open to those of their race, for the rebels had seized power there, killing all who were not of the New People.

They had slain Turnig for their fur, the Ancient Race because of their wisdom, and the furry men because they looked like men but were covered with fur.

Damaria was closed to those of the Ancient Race, perhaps forever. Why should Tulip plot to gain its throne?

Or, Lute wondered, burying his face in his arms to keep from bursting into tears, did she simply hate those who had come into this city because Riddle had not liked her? He had no way to know her reasons.

He only knew that he was here, locked in a room in a strange house, imprisoned by someone who struck him as being both very powerful and terribly unwise. A shiver went over him, bringing his skin up into goose pimples.

Would she go so far as to kill him? Others died, as he had seen with his own eyes on their journey.

Why should not Lute, King of Damaria, die too?

CHAPTER THIRTY-NINE

"...ill dreams can warn of danger...."
—Riddle

The ship was taking shape there in the dockside workplace, keeping Oakbeam and his sons, Riddle and Killeli, and even Lute close to the bustle of activity. Moonbeam missed their company, though Gorghoz had taken her welfare as his duty and kept close beside her all day, even as she exercised to regain her lost strength. At night small Chark slept in a trundle bed, near at hand in case the Dreamer needed assistance in the dark hours.

Though she was mending now, the process was slow. Very slow. Sometimes Moonlight all but lost hope that she would ever be strong and whole again, though the Goremin assured her that even the terrible price she had paid for their safety in the eastern lands could dwindle at last, leaving her strong in body, if not the Dreamer she had been.

She dreamed now, the nightmares that plagued other folk, dark adventures that left her shaking, wet with sweat, in the hours before dawn. And this night was one of the worst. She saw Lute, standing in a narrow passage in darkness, his small face tense with worry.

Again and again she dreamed, always waking with a jerk and a gasp to bring Chark to her side, concerned. When the sky beyond the window held light at last, the Dreamer sent her small attendant after Riddle. This was more than nightmare. This was a warning.

Riddle came, already dressed and ready to go to the docks to join Oakbeam. She beckoned him, and he came to sit on the edge of her couch, bending to hear her frightened whisper.

"I dreamed of Lute. In danger. Confined and frightened and alone. Riddle, I dreamed this many times in the night. Leave the boy here with me today. Gorghoz and I will tell him stories and teach him his lessons and keep him close. I am afraid, Poet. Today I fear for your nephew." She heard her voice shake, and she knew he thought her still in the grip of the sickness that had been a part of her life since their journey from Damaria.

He took her hand and held it in his warm grasp. "My dear friend," he said, "I know how frightening such dreams can be. I have had more than my share, since we came here two years ago, and often I am tempted to give in to their compulsion. But Lute is in no danger—who, here, would care or dare to harm him?

"He is under our eyes all the day, and he would be sorely disappointed to miss seeing the ship grow. No, Moonlight, you are overwrought. Sit in the garden and listen to the songbirds and the wind among the roses. All will be well." His kiss was gentle on her forehead, and then he went away, leaving her to shiver beneath the coverings that should not be needed in weather so warm.

The day passed slowly, and she did, indeed, sit in the garden with the Goremin, saying little but thinking hard. There had been an edge to those dreams that told her they were no wanderings of her own mind. Some danger hung like a dark cloud over this day.

The sun slid over the brow of the cape and the sky burned with the last light. But no weary Riddle and no train of hungry Turnig came trooping into the house by the wall, ready for baths and food. No one came at all, and the sky darkened, the stars sprang out in all their glittering numbers, and Moonlight sat in her room, her thought turned upon Lute.

She could not Dream, forming a vision in her own imagination until it became reality for another. That she had surrendered, with her youth and her innocence, in the battle with the Mover and Dinorm, there in the hills east of the City in the Mist.

But the odd talents that the Ancient Race had nurtured in her kind by careful teaching and breeding for useful traits held more than one capacity. As night deepened and no one came, and even Gorghoz grew tense and fearful, she found she could feel the fear of the child, though there was neither direction nor location. Her own fears she quelled mercilessly, leaving her mind open to the emotions of Lute.

He was in a small room, she thought, sitting on the floor with his chin in his hands, holding himself in check by exercise of that will peculiar to his race. She damped her own feelings to less than nothing as she focused upon that slender link with the child, trying to read his thoughts.

But that was impossible. Instead, she felt the cool floor beneath his bare legs, the hardness of the wall behind him, the pressure of chin on hand. And she heard a sound. The click of a latch being loosed.

Through Lute's eyes she saw the slit of light from the space beyond the door grow wider as the panel opened. A shadow, elongated in that beam, grew along the floor. And then a lamp kindled, and the soft glow lighted the room—a study, it seemed—into which the newcomer stepped.

"Lute?"

With a lurch, Moonlight felt her concentration break. Tulip! That presence had come to her with such intensity and ill-will she could not be mistaken, no matter where she encountered Riddle's cousin. Whether she had meant it to be so or not, Tulip had forged a bond between herself and this Dreamer she had intended making her victim.

Moonlight hissed into the dimness of her room. "Ssss!"

Chark was there at once. "Dreamer? You want?"

"Find Gorghoz, Chark. Has Riddle returned yet?" She knew he had not, for he would have come to her at once. It was not his way to let anyone worry needlessly.

"I find Gor'min. Back soon." The furry shape pattered away into the corridor, and Moonlight lay back, breathing rapidly, feeling her heart galloping as it dealt with the shock of her discovery.

Could those of the Ancient Race mean harm to their small kinsman? Moonlight could hardly credit that, for she had known only kindliness in all her dealings with the rulers of Damaria. Only here in this city so near the distortions of Dinorm in the north had she discovered one who seemed to be contaminated by the will of that destructive power.

As her breathing eased, the Dreamer heard the steps of the Goremin shuffling softly down the hallway to her door. When he stood in the opening, she called to him quietly.

"I have felt Lute. He is a prisoner in the house of Riddle's kinsmen. I saw only one, through his eyes. Tulip." She paused, holding herself still and calm, keeping her heart from skipping and pounding as it was wont to do now.

"There is a link between us, Gorghoz. She came to me more than once, until you shielded my mind from her. If you dropped that shield now, I might slip inside her. I might learn her purposes in taking Lute. I fear they are evil ones, my friend."

"I will send one of the Turnig after Riddle and those who help him in his search," the Goremin replied. "Only then, sitting beside you, holding your hands in my own, will I risk loosing that barrier that I have placed about you. But you are right—we must know what she intends. If you can learn, in this way, it will save much time and perhaps that may save the child."

She took the time while he was gone to dress warmly, as if she were going on a physical rather than a mental journey. Chark built up the fire in her grate, setting the driftwood logs in place until the flames burned blue and green and purple.

When the Goremin returned, they drew chairs close to the blaze and laid hand to hand, the grip of those furred fingers strong and comforting. Moonlight lay back in her deep cushions, letting her mind stray free of her skull, moving along that linkage that Tulip had, all unwittingly, formed between them.

She felt a misty unbeing for a moment. Then she was looking through the eyes of another—into a mirror. Tulip, seen for the first time with clarity, stared back into her own eyes. A secret smile touched her lips, as she brushed her dark hair with long, smooth strokes. Those eyes were filled with glimmers of purpose, bright slivers of thought sliding through their dark depths.

Moonlight, held for a moment by her own revulsion, relaxed her own will and slid deep inside that devious mind. Used to the order and clarity of a Dreamer's thoughts, she found herself awash with emotion, with cross purposes, and with an overwhelming sense of self. But she persisted, searching those tumultuous thoughts for a hint of the thing she sought.

And there was a glimpse of a tall, gray figure, one of the Lir-folk, out on the grassy hills. Beside him was a small shape, dark hair tumbled, golden tan face wary and filled with apprehension. She held on tightly for a long moment, and then she had it. With a sigh, she opened her eyes and found herself inside her own room, her hands safe in the clasp of the Goremin.

She shuddered, feeling her skin goose pimple, and sat straight, her hands still caught in his. "I know now," she said. "Call Riddle as soon as he comes, Gorghoz. I know what she intends."

The Goremin stroked her hands, warming them, for they had chilled even in his furry grasp. "What does she intend, Moonlight?" he whispered, his small eyes flickering blue-green in the light of the driftwood fire.

"She will send him south with the Lirfolk, back into the hands of Lorbek in Damaria. She would never manage killing him, for her people know nothing of her plotting, but once he is out of her hands she knows he will die. Lorbek could not allow him to live."

She stared into those wise old eyes, and she saw there the fury and the pain she felt within herself. What sort of mad folly would lead one of the Ancient Race to commit so terrible a crime? And against a child!

CHAPTER FORTY

"What sadder task than punishing one's child?"

—Riddle

When the Turnig sent by Gorghoz panted up, his fur bristling with excitement, Riddle felt certain his nephew had been found. Nothing else, he thought, would have caused those in his home to send for him with such urgency.

But Chal knew only that the Goremin had urged him to speed in locating the Poet, and no amount of questioning could elicit anything more, as the two trudged up the street in the dawnlight. When the house loomed ahead, Riddle hastened his steps even more, making for the stair as soon as he was inside.

He found Gorghoz waiting in the Dreamer's chamber. The two of them were sitting in chairs facing each other before the hearth, and in their stillness, their control, he read a message that he would rather not have learned.

"Lute?" Riddle asked, his voice choked. He dropped onto a stool at the Goremin's feet and looked up into those ancient eyes.

"Let the Dreamer tell you. It was she who found the boy."

"Found? But where...," and then he saw that he must listen if he would learn what had happened to Lute.

"He is with Tulip," said Moonlight. She leaned forward and put her hand on his shoulder, patting him comfortingly. "As yet, he is not harmed, only frightened. She shut him in a small room. I think on the second floor of Blade's house, but I could not be certain of that."

Riddle drew a long breath, calming himself, gathering his wits. Then he asked, his voice controlled, "She took him? Tulip? How do you know?"

So Moonlight told him of her dream, once more, her growing unease through the day before, and her nightmare that took her near the frightened child. "I saw through his eyes for the moment, and she opened the door and came into the room. It was Tulip, I know.

"That showed me the way. We are linked, as you may have guessed, because she tried to approach me until you set Gorghoz on guard. So we lowered that barrier and I went along the link, into Tulip herself."

The Dreamer's haggard face was even more drawn and weary than it had been when last the Poet saw it, and he ached for her as she continued. "She was alone in her chamber, brushing out her hair and thinking of her plan. She holds Lute, but she cannot harm him, for her father does not know he is there. The servants would not help her, and if Blade learned of her action he would punish her severely. So she intends to turn the child over to the Lirfolk to take away south to Lorbek."

Riddle jolted upright, his head pounding with sudden pressure. "When? And how?" he asked, his voice a gasp of sound.

"Soon," said Moonlight. "I read that much in her smugness. But I cannot tell you how. I suspect she may have a henchman who visits her father's house, and surely that is the one who will take the child away. You could learn more about it than I, for she was so sure of herself she did not worry over the details of her plan."

"Today," said Gorghoz. "It will not be safe for her to hold him for more than a few hours, and already he must have been in her hands since last evening. Go, Riddle, to your uncle. Put this into his hands."

"But is Blade to be trusted?" Riddle felt his confidence in his northern kindred waning to nothing, as he thought of his cousin's betrayal.

"Yes." That was Moonlight, now drooping in her chair, her face colorless except for the play of the firelight. "She dreaded his learning of what she is doing. Her only fear is that her father will find her out. Go, Riddle, and go secretly."

Her eyes widened. "I had forgotten that Wonder is here with us! He stays quiet and busy in his attic room, painting and painting, but he knows Blade and his house as none of us can. Ask Wonder, Poet, how to approach your uncle without letting Tulip know. If she sees you come, she may do something...fatal."

Her eyes closed, and Gorghoz lifted her limp form and carried her to the bed, covering her closely with a warm shawl. "She is done for now," he said. "She has little strength and may require years to attain more than just enough to survive. I will watch here. Good speed to you, Poet!"

Riddle touched the pale cheek on the pillow, looked up into the Goremin's eyes, and turned away. He must find Wonder at once.

The artist knew, of course, everything about the house where he had lived for centuries. Once Tulip had become the bane of his life, he had found ways of coming and going that she could not know, and he was delighted to take his cousin through the narrow ways on the other side of Blade's house, along the tunnels that served the wall, and through the passage he had cut with his own hands into the garden of his old home.

Riddle found himself, more quickly than he had thought, peering through the screening growth of a rosebush, now fragrant with a foam of golden blossom, at a little door set into the back wall of the house. Blade's study, with its wide windows, was around a curving stone bastion. It required only a quick moment to get them both inside unobserved.

"This way," Wonder whispered. He pushed at a tapestry panel, which swung inward to let him into a service corridor leading from the kitchens to the front of the house. "Blade has his own quarters, and Tulip seldom goes there without invitation. Once we find the service door—ah. Here it is."

He slid aside another panel, and Riddle remembered his visit and the sudden appearance of the servant with refreshment. A short hall led directly into the study, and Blade was sitting at his worktable, bent over a great leather-covered book. His pen was busy, and Riddle heard its scritching journey over the page, even before he emerged into the room.

"Uncle," he said softly. "Blade!"

The man looked up, his eyes refocusing with effort, as if his mind were far away from this chamber and this house. "What? Who? Wonder?"

Then he saw the pair as they came fully into view beyond his book-case. "Both of you." He laid his pen down carefully, as if he knew this was a visit of great importance.

Riddle moved to sit where he had sat before, and Wonder leaned against the wall, out of sight of anyone in the garden beyond the windows. Blade was staring at them, one to the other, as if dreading to learn what had brought them here so secretly.

"Uncle, we have brought a terrible problem to place in your hands," Riddle began. He saw Blade brace himself, waiting for the blow to come. The Ancient Race had the ability to know when danger threatened.

"My nephew Lute disappeared from the dock site yesterday, and when evening came he was nowhere to be found. We searched all night, but in first light a message came from those in my house. The Dreamer knew where he was." He looked into those brown eyes, now filled with pain, and he knew Blade's quick mind was running ahead of his words.

"She saw him in a room, dark and small. She saw a door open and Tulip come through to look down at the child. She believes Tulip intends to smuggle my nephew the King out of your house into the hands of the Lirfolk, sending him south to the one who now sits upon the throne of Damaria."

Wonder spoke from his hidden spot. "Today the messenger comes from the traders in the Merchants' Quarter to take our order for incoming goods. He knows nothing of our affairs here, and it would be easy for one of Tulip's skill to persuade him to take the child from this house into the city. Perhaps to turn him over to Arken, who has, I have often thought, more connection with the Lirfolk than Girnig would like, if he knew."

Blade's finely drawn face had gone parchment-pale, the bones standing out to make him suddenly show the centuries that had passed since he was young. His fingers gripped the pen so tightly his skin went white.

Then, releasing the polished bone of the instrument, he sat quite still, relaxing his body. Riddle could see the tension go out of his muscles; his face lost that old and rigid look, becoming again the familiar face of Blade, his uncle.

"We will go to find her," he said, his tone perfectly normal. "Come with me, both of you. I will need witnesses, for this is a thing that none of our family has been forced to do for thousands of years."

Riddle nodded, swallowing, feeling his heart turn cold and fill with dread. What was the penalty for such treachery among his kind? He had never been taught that, for there had not, in the three thousand years of his family in the north, been any need.

They moved into the main corridor that led from the front of the house to the back. Fladan came when Blade touched the silver chime at the door to the sitting-room.

"Is Silk in her rooms?" he asked. "And Tulip—where is she, now?"

The servant nodded. "Your cousin be, indeed, in her chamber, taken wi' a sudden chill in the night. She wasna able to rise for her morning meal, and we took her broth and milk. But your daughter be about the place, I canna say where. I will look, if that please you?"

Blade nodded sharply and led the two men up the stair. "Tell her that we will wait in the little study upstairs," he called back.

"Aye," came the reply as the old man hurried out of sight along the corridor.

The door of the small study was tightly closed, and when Blade lifted the latch it did not yield. "Locked," he murmured, fumbling along the door for the catch that secured it.

The thing clicked sharply, and the door moved when Blade touched it. They stepped inside, to find the room filled with light reflected from the wall facing the garden window. Lute sat on the narrow couch, regarding them with interest mingled with relief.

"I thought you might not know when to come, Uncle," he said to Riddle. "But here you are at last."

"You may thank Moonlight for that," said Riddle, catching the boy, well-grown as he was, up into his arms and hugging him tightly. "Things might have gone badly if she had not dreamed of you. I would never have thought to look here, of all places, for my lost one."

He let the boy slip down, and there Lute stood, staring up at Blade. "You are my great-uncle Blade?" he asked. "I think she was afraid you might find me. She told Fladan she had sent me home, back after dark when he asked if he should take me himself."

Blade bent and took the small hand that the King of Damaria offered him. Smudged and dusty thought it was, he kissed it gently, reverently. "Your Majesty," he said, "I am profoundly relieved to find you unharmed and still in my house. Do you want to see the punishment of your cousin Tulip?"

Lute looked up into those eyes, now bent closely above him. Something he saw there made him shiver and turn pale. "Thank you, Uncle, but no. I do not like her, but I would hate to see her hurt. Must you be severe with her?"

Blade straightened, his back like steel, his eyes hard and bright. "She is contaminated, Lute, by the Mover from the North. By Dinorm. By, it may be, some inborn weakness or wickedness that we could not see until the time came. Yes, she must be hurt."

Wonder caught his breath, his delicate face like paper in the soft light. "We will go to my rooms, high in the tower, Lute. There I will show you the paintings that were too large to move. I hid them away, so Tulip could not find them. You will like them, I think."

The boy took his hand, glad of this familiar member of his uncle's household in this strange house. He looked back at Riddle from the door, his gaze filled with understanding and pain.

He was, after all, the King of Damaria, with all the inherent intelligence of his kind. Lute knew this punishment would be one that would give more pain to him who administered it than to the one who must suffer it. Then he was gone, leaving the two men avoiding each other's eyes as they waited for Tulip to come to them.

CHAPTER FORTY-ONE

"The gift of life is also that of death."
                                        —Riddle

Blade waited for his daughter's step upon the stair. In the growing light of morning, there in the small study, he stared blindly into the garden, seeing the brilliance of the roses that clambered up the wall beyond, the glitter of dew on the vines draping the outside of the window.

His cousin said nothing, for which he was profoundly grateful. Riddle's presence might have caused this last and most terrible fall from grace into which Tulip had plunged, but her innate weakness and vanity could not be laid at his door. Tulip, daughter of Blade and his lost and almost forgotten Rose, had become evil. That was the bitter truth of it, and it was her father's duty to prevent more mischief to the innocent.

Fladan peered into the half-open door. "Your daughter comes," he said, his old voice almost a croak. "And the young masters be gone up into the tower to look at the pictures. Will y'need me longer, Master?"

"Go about your duties, Fladan," Blade said. "I will ring a bell if I need you." He did not look as the door closed softly and his cousin coughed and sat heavily on the couch where the boy had slept.

Blade had lived for a thousand years without feeling such pain. His wife's death had been sad, but they had not been close. She had been chosen and sent to him by her family in the south, and on her arrival they had found that though they did not dislike each other, they had no great liking either. No interest did they have in common, and they lived for many years, once they had achieved a child, as polite strangers in the house Blade's father had built.

Riddle rose and came to stand behind him. The younger man's hand touched his shoulder, and he turned to see a warning in his eyes. "She is coming," the Poet whispered. Blade felt a surge of sickness rise through him, almost making him retch. Now the tap of her shoe-heels was plain on the tiled stair, the rustle of her silken skirts whispering up the stairwell. He caught the light scent of her perfume as she stepped into the room and stopped, her apricot-warm cheeks paling as she saw him there.

When she turned her gaze and recognized Riddle, she swayed and almost went to her knees, but her cousin caught her and helped her to the couch. Once sitting, she looked up at her father, and in her eyes Blade saw the realization of her failure and her fate.

She was so very lovely. The golden silks of her gown echoed the tint of her skin. The lustrous darkness of her hair was repeated in her eyes. She was so like her cousin Silk, when she was young, that it wrenched at her father's heart.

"You know." Her gaze met his and did not falter.

He was proud of the fact that her voice did not waver, and she did not weep or plead. Whatever her faults, she was no coward, this wayward daughter of his.

He could not reply, but Riddle did it for him. "Yes, Tulip, we know. Lute is safe now, and whatever your purpose in taking him might be, that is over. But I must know why. Why did one of my own kind, bred for millennia to help and to heal and to mend, come to this?"

She raised her chin, her dark eyes flashing fire. "To help? Whom did you help, may I ask? Animals that walk like men! Monkeys and monsters, indeed, not true humankind of the Ancient Race. You are too weak to seize power and to hold it. Even the fool who governs here in the City in the Mist has the wit to take what he can and to grasp it unfalteringly.

"But you and the King and your brother and his people, all of them died because you were too weak-willed to forge armies, to train guards to keep you safe, to spy out those who meant you harm and to squash them without mercy. I am not so weak." Indeed, she looked like a queen, sitting there in her silks, her cheeks flushed and her eyes bright with passion.

"If you were gone west, and the child were dead, the throne of Damaria would be held by one of the New People, short-lived and weak of wit. Once he died, I could go there and take his place, for I have been negotiating for years with emissaries who move between this city and the Lirfolk in the hills. I would return our family to greatness, using an army that would lack the imagination to turn against me."

"An army," said Riddle, his tone soft and bitter. "Never in all the history of our kind in the north has there been the necessity for that. And if there should be, it is time we were gone and the country left to those better fit to rule it. In time Lorbek will fall, and others will come, and soon or late a good ruler will again sit upon the throne in Damaria. You would not have been that, cousin. No better than Lorbek's would be the government you imposed." He looked away, and Blade felt his hurt and his anger.

"Exactly," said Blade. "I regret that our family came north and kept you here all your life. You were too near to those who have troubled the land since the beginning. The flaws in your character were there, ready for their uses, and they corrupted you." He wiped his tears away on the back of one hand, unashamed of his grief.

"And now you must die. Your mother said, as she lay drawing her last breath, that she regretted your birth. She warned me that you were not a sound member of our race, and I should have watched you more closely. But she was sorely injured, near death, and I discounted her words. My fault! Oh, my fault!"

He stopped and calmed himself, drawing himself up to his full height and staring down at her, keeping his expression cold and unmoved, though inside his heart was chilled and filled with dread. "But that is in the past. Now you have proven her correct, and it is in my hands to halt you and the danger that you will ever sully the blood of our kind again."

He moved to the door and gestured for her to follow. "Come. We must go down to my own study. There we will end this terrible game."

She came to her feet without the help of Riddle's extended hand. Now she seemed subdued, her gaze guarded, and Blade knew that his daughter was plotting, still, trying like an animal in a trap to find a way of escape. He ached for her, but things had gone too far. He must end her mischief.

He had, somehow, expected that his study would be changed, simply because in the short span of time since he left it his own life had taken such a drastic turn. But no. The sun now streamed into the garden beyond the wide windows, and the golden roses clustered on the wall, dropping their heavy-petaled heads to peer into the room. He did not wait for his companions to enter but went directly to the tall chest, carven of black wood, that had traveled with his kind from their old home south of Damaria, over the roadless mountains and the long miles of forest and hill country. He had not opened it in hundreds of years, and when he touched the spring the panels were reluctant to move.

At last they gave, with a sigh and a creak, and he looked into the space where the poison lay. The vial was of wavery green glass, and the liquid inside gurgled as he lifted it out, turning blue-purple in the light.

"This is the easy way to die, Daughter," he said, turning to face her. "I would not have you suffer. We do not punish you so much as deter you from doing evil to others. And you would, you know quite well. I see it in your eyes."

Taking his courage in both hands, Blade poured the liquid into a delicate cup—a tulip, he noted with agony and irony—and handed it to her, looking at last fully into her face.

She dashed the cup onto the floor, shattering the fragile curves into glittering fragments. "I do not need a kind death, Father," she said in a steely tone. "If I die, you must kill me with your own hands. If you haven't the courage to stab me or to cut my throat, you do not have the right to order me to die by my own hand. I will not, do you hear? I will not!"

Blade stared at her, feeling the justice of her words. Then he glanced aside at Riddle. "She is right, you know. Will you stand beside me as I slay my child?"

The Poet took his cousin by the arm. "Outside," he said. "Among the roses. We will, otherwise, leave a mess for poor Fladan to clean."

Blade had never expected such cold practicality of his nephew. The words were like a dash of ice in his face, bringing him out of the stew of emotion that threatened to engulf him. He went again to the chest and took out a blade that had lain there so long the velvet of its scabbard had become a felt of dust.

"In the garden," he agreed. "Now." How long could he bear this? he wondered. Time seemed to stretch out before him, with no end of this agonizing scene in sight.

He moved into the garden, painfully sweet with the odor of roses, where the summer sunlight caught the light in the pool and reflected its ripples on the walls and the drawn faces of those who stood in the grass plot. Tulip's golden silks glimmered, her hair shone, her eyes were black puddles, withdrawn and lifeless now.

The sword caught the light, which quivered along the keen blade as he held it, facing his daughter. She held her head high, her throat revealed as an ivory column, ready for the cut.

He moved slowly, deliberately. He could not bear to make her suffer. She must die instantly, without pain, or he would be haunted for the rest of his bitterly long life with the memory of torturing her.

Then the blade moved, as if of its own will. Scarlet splashed down the golden gown, making random blossoms of brightness as it streamed, and Tulip went to her knees, huddling down and down until she sank into the billows of her skirt.

So sharp was the ancient sword that little blood adhered to its edge. Riddle took it from Blade's shaking hand and wiped away the pinkish trace with his own kerchief. Then he caught his kinsman about the shoulders and helped him to the stone bench beneath the drooping roses.

"Fladan!" Blade heard the raw pain in the younger man's voice, and he felt it echoed in his own throat, silent though he remained. "Ellever!" He turned to his uncle for more names of servants, but Blade shook his head, knowing that those two, old and faithful, would care for his dead daughter as if she were their own.

Then there came a sound at the door leading into the central corridor from the garden. Silk, frail almost to transparency, stood there, leaning on an ivory stick, her face blank with surprise.

She could not sustain such a shock, Blade was certain, and he rose and hurried to her side, turning her away from the bloody scene among the roses. But she looked up at him, her eyes knowing and wise, as they went into the hallway.

"So she is dead, Cousin. I could not say to you that your child was tainted, but I wanted for a long while to warn you. I do not want to know what she has done. If you have killed her, it means that her crime was wicked. I am relieved." She tottered, and he put his arm about her fragile shoulders.

Fladan came hurrying toward them. Blade gestured toward the garden, still holding Silk on her feet. "I will take my cousin to her chamber, Fladan. Help Ellever with...Tulip." His voice wavered, and he caught himself, again calming, stilling, controlling his grief.

"She is dead by my hand, as was my right and duty. See to the arrangements, my old friend. And comfort Riddle. He is out there, feeling guilty for her death, though she took his nephew and intended to see him dead."

The old man's eyes widened. But in an instant he had comprehended this strange turn of events and was again hurrying to the relief of his chosen masters.

Blade, concentrating upon the care of his cousin, moved to the stair and up, half carrying the slight figure beside him. Silk was relieved. Wonder would be delighted, he knew, though the artist had never complained of his cousin.

Only he, of all the family left in the north, would look with longing to see her bright shape at his door or in the garden. Only he would miss that lovely, evil daughter with all the passion of his lonely soul.

CHAPTER FORTY-TWO

"The creak of wood on wood, the rush of waves...."
—Riddle

The abduction of Lute shook Riddle's household from top to bottom. Moonlight and Gorghoz seemed unwilling to take their eyes off the child, and the Turnig set watches, telling off four of their number to guard the small King of Damaria in shifts.

Riddle was almost afraid to visit the shipyards, but he knew that the faster the ship progressed, the sooner he could take his mixed group of refugees away from the City in the Mist. He felt certain Arken had been involved with Tulip in the plot, and he could only assume Girnig was behind the entire project, although he could find no reason why the Sealord should try to slow the departure of those he evidently feared and hated so greatly.

The household of Oakbeam and Nilda was hardly less affected by the kidnapping. The builder was furious that such a thing could happen in his city, and his wife went about so puffed with indignation that she seemed to be about to float away with the heat of her own wrath.

Under the whip of Oakbeam's anger, those workers who had been reluctant to labor in his shipyard found the whispers of Arken and his henchmen less intimidating than the immediate threat of the builder's permanent embargo on their services. Again the yards swarmed with skilled laborers, finishing the many details of making a ship seaworthy, while the Turnig were freed to ready themselves and their families for departure.

Riddle was in the midst of everything, checking supplies as they were loaded into the massive holds, helping the Turnig decide which of their newly created art works were best taken with them and which made the finest gifts for those who had helped the refugees since their arrival in the City in the Mist. Yet he found the time to sit in his garden with Moonlight, trying to alter her decision.

"You will not be safe here," he said, holding her thin hand in his. "Girnig hates us all, though I have never found any reason, except the insecurity of his own mind, why that should be true. He may take steps against you, once we are gone."

"Oakbeam's son has promised to give me shelter and protection," said the Dreamer. She looked less frail since Tulip's assaults upon her mind were finished, though her face was still lined and drawn. Her chin was firmly set, and he saw no lessening of the resolve in her expression.

"I cannot leave this land, Riddle. There is reason for me to stay, although I cannot put it into words. Some instinct left from my days of Dreaming tells me that I may best serve us all by remaining behind. Do not urge me, for I long to go with you and all our friends to see those magical islands in the west, even as dimly as my eyes would now discern them. Your insistence only makes my task harder."

Riddle sighed and stood, brushing the lowest branch of the tree that shaded the spot and making a bright confetti of petals spill over his shoulders. He flicked them away absently as he regarded his friend. She was so brave and so helpless, now that her gift had been taken from her. Unable to Dream reality to confuse her enemies, how could she survive on this continent that had grown inimical to her kind?

"I will not speak of it again, Moonlight," he said at last. He reached to touch the streak of gray hair that sprang from her brow, remembering the terrible battle of wills she had fought on his behalf.

"But I will think of it always, and even as we sail toward the west I shall believe that you should be with us, going to a place of peace and safety." He turned toward the garden gate and the shortcut toward the docks. "We are almost ready. Oakbeam has pushed his men and his sons and himself almost to breaking, for he fears another attempt against one of us before we can sail."

"I am happy he is going with you," the Dreamer said. "He is old and needs some peace in his life. And those sons who go with them will find much of interest, there in the islands or farther west in those distant lands that send their silks and their spices to trade for our timber and minerals. They will be well out of this, I think."

She gazed across the garden at Chark, who was harvesting everything from her garden that could possibly be considered mature enough to dig or pick or cut. "I am glad the Turnig and Furry Men decided to accompany you. Even those who have lived here for many generations are beginning to feel pressure from the Sealord to leave his walls. I will be with you in thought, my friend."

He murmured a farewell and moved away toward the day's work at the ship. The time needed for completing the preparations for sailing had dwindled to a handful of days, and he felt even that was too much.

When the sun was down behind the cape, he turned his steps toward the house of his uncle, instead of toward his own home. Blade, always a lonely man, was now grim and sad as well. Though Wonder returned home at once, when his cousin was no longer there to torment him, and though Silk roused her weary heart to try cheering him, the master of their house remained depressed and silent.

Riddle knew he must say goodbye. He intended to try taking the entire household of the Ancient Race in the city with him on his quest for the Western Islands, feeling that such a change would be very good for them all, but he knew it would be hard to persuade Blade to leave the narrow grave beside his wall, beneath the golden roses.

Returning homeward beneath the stars of summer, he sighed, for he had failed. Silk was too old, too tired, too weakened by the lingering illness of many years to travel, and Blade would not leave her. Wonder, now that he could work in peace, withdrew from the voyage as well, and Riddle knew he stayed to comfort his uncle, though in his dark eyes the Poet saw a longing to see and paint distant places and kinds.

He had done his best, and now he must see to his own motley group of travelers.

* * * * * * *

With the first breath of the easterlies that came when summer turned, the ship was loaded and ready to depart. Riddle felt as if he had been laboring for years, building it with his own hands instead of the hundreds of other hands doing the work, for keeping the project moving had been harder than Oakbeam had thought possible.

Now, standing on the afterdeck of the *Refuge*, as he called his ship, and watching the line of Turnig move up the ramp to their midship quarters, he felt relief mixed with anticipation. Soon they would be out of this grimly decaying city, leaving behind the hostility of Girnig and Arken. Whatever their motives, those two, he was sure, had hampered each step, and he was glad to be rid of them.

He heard a bustle in the street leading down to his docking place and turned to stare at the group moving toward the pilings edging the platform. Blade! Wonder...and Silk, being carried in a sedan chair.

He hurried down his forward ramp and held out his hands. "Have you changed your minds? Are you coming with us?" he called.

Blade smiled and shook his head. "I could not allow my nephew to leave without a farewell from his own family," he said. "Wonder agreed, and Silk, to my amazement, insisted upon coming too. We wish you well, Nephew. We will miss you and your odd group of people. The old City will be lessened when you sail out of the harbor."

Moonlight, who had come with Oakbeam's married son and his family to bid the travelers goodbye, came toward them, and Riddle took her hand and presented her to Blade.

"This is our friend, of whom I told you. She will be staying with Egon, the son of Oakbeam, and his family. If you will, I would like for you to watch over her. She is very dear to us all."

"I will, indeed," said his uncle. "She might stay with us, if she chose, for we are lonely now we have no young woman to liven us up." For the first time the lines on his face eased, and he seemed to gain a bit of color.

"I will consider that," said the Dreamer. "If you truly want me. Egon has a merry brood of children to keep him cheerful, and I must admit they sometimes wear upon my nerves, though I love them dearly. I will, indeed, think of coming to you, if you are of the same mind in a week."

Garlock, the captain of the *Refuge*, hailed Riddle from the aft deck. "The tide is turning, Lord. It is time."

Riddle took Silk's fragile hand and bent to kiss her crepe-like cheek. "My love, Cousin." He turned to Wonder and clapped his shoulder. "Keep painting, my friend. You are indeed a wonder when you have your fingers upon a brush."

Then he turned from Blade's embrace and raced up the ramp to the deck beside the captain. The crew, a mix of professional seamen and specially trained Turnig, swarmed up the ratlines and loosed the middle one of the great sails from one set of ties, allowing the triangle of canvas to billow a third of its span in the growing breeze from the east.

Gorghoz waited, leaning on the rail beside Killeli, watching the city, the faces of those below, and the distant shape of Girnig, who was upon the balcony of his house, making certain these unwanted guests were leaving at last.

Riddle leaned beside the Goremin; now he turned his face toward the sea, as the ship moved slowly away from the dock and heeled slightly in the grip of the wind, taking aim for the slot that led out of the anchorage. The easterlies brought upon their gusty backs a hint of old scents, rousing memories of dangers and evils still walking the continent of his birth.

Now, surely, he and his nephew, who sat astride Gorghoz's broad shoulders, would be safe from the workings of Dinorm and his minion. These people who trusted him would find a haven at last.

And yet, turning for a last look at the dwindling shapes of his kindred and the Dreamer, he wondered. Was anyone ever safe, as long as he walked in flesh?

CHAPTER FORTY-THREE

"No voyage is safe until it has an end."
                                        —Riddle

They rounded the Cape and there the tide took them into the grip of the summer current, which carried the *Refuge* north and west. The triangular sails billowed and snapped, as the easterlies caught them.

"Out of our direct route," admitted Garlock, "but it will take us speedily out of the summer storms along the coast. Then we will loose the full expanse of sail and turn west, with the wind astern filling our canvas."

Riddle had come to know the captain quickly. He was Oakbeam's choice of all those master seamen available in the city, and he had worked for a year with the shipbuilder, lending his years of experience at ship-handling in creating this huge vessel. Now his weather-darkened face was wrinkled into thoughtful lines as he swept his glance from sea to sky, from wheel to mainmast, from watch-nest to the distant horizon.

"We have a fair start," he admitted at last. "But the sea is a dangerous road, Lord, and one never can take her moods lightly."

There seemed no need for concern, however, for the wind held and the current was swift. When they turned west, the easterlies did not fail them. They slept the nights through, except for those on watch, rocked by the gentle rolling of the ship. They spent their days on deck, watching the young Turnig and simian-descended children to keep them from tumbling overboard, or below, resting or doing the thousand and one small chores required to clothe and feed this large group.

Lute was in his element, Riddle knew, busy with other small ones, asking innumerable questions, even climbing the ratlines to sit astride the collar of the masts holding the pulleys that controlled raising and lowering one or the other of the three sails. From that perilous perch his uncle took him by the scruff of his neck, reminding him that a king never does anything to alarm his people.

That, more than any threats or warnings, seemed to tame the child a bit, and he took to sitting on the foredeck, watching the rush of water under the keel. That was why he was the one to spy the smoke billowing from a port low on the forward keel of the vessel.

"Fire!" came his shrill cry, and Riddle started awake from his doze as he lay on one of the hatch-covers.

At almost the same instant, there was a stir behind him and Gorghoz's deep voice cried, "Boat away aft!"

Riddle bounced to his feet and stared back to windward, where the escaping craft was dwindling rapidly as the ship plowed forward. Garlock ordered men and Turnig to the winches to close-haul the sails and aloft to tie them fast. The ship lost way and idled along in the water, while more smoke rose from the hatches forward and teams of men and Turnig ran to form bucket chains and to find the location of the blaze.

"We have a deserter," the captain said. He stood beside Riddle now, gazing at the speck that was no longer dwindling. He sounded both shocked and grieved.

"Never in all my career have I had a man desert a ship I command. And a fire! This is a thing I cannot explain, Lord."

Riddle moved to the aft hatch and raised its cover. "I suspect I can, when there is time, Captain. But for now I go below to see to the fire. Call if you need me."

He dropped down the ladder to land softly in the passage below, knowing that those beneath the forward hatch would be crowded with those seeking the fire. No smoke had gathered here, as yet, and he moved up the companionway that ran lengthwise of the vessel, banging on the doors of the different holds where his people rested or worked.

"Up! On deck! Quickly!" he shouted as he went. Halfway along, he began to smell smoke, and the lamps lighting the way were ringed with a yellow-gray haze. Riddle raised his head, focusing his acute senses upon the source of the fire, and he knew with sudden certainty where it had been set. The most flammable part of the ship! He motioned to the nearest Turnig and turned toward the sail locker.

"Girnig!" he said between gritted teeth. "And Arken, I'll be bound. A last greeting from the Sealord!"

He lifted a barrel of water, hooped against the wall of the passage against the chance of just such a catastrophe, and charged toward the sailmaker's shop near the bow. There the canvas was stored, with glue and line and fittings of all kinds. If all that mass of combustibles caught, the ship was doomed.

As he burst open the door, feet pounded behind him, and his cask of water, poured on the dancing flames about the edge of the canvas store, was joined by three more, before the endless chain of buckets of water began to arrive. Oakbeam and his two sons had joined in the effort. The fire sizzled and spat, while agile feet stamped and pranced as the four moved about the place, extinguishing any surviving sparks.

When they had all visible signs of the fire quenched, they gave way to a crew of sailors, who took the rolls of canvas, the coils of rope, the kegs of glue, up the ladders and onto the deck. There each was examined, bit by bit, for any remnant of smoldering material that might reignite.

As they watched the process, Riddle and Gorghoz, Oakbeam and Garlock murmured one name. "Arken, on behalf of Girnig. Perhaps on account of Tulip?"

Riddle knew his cousin, even dead, could manage such mischief. It had been laid bare, when Blade investigated after her death, that she had plotted with the Sealord's seneschal to send her small cousin southward with those of the Lirfolk with whom he held secret liaison.

The role Arken had played in slowing the construction of the ship became obvious when Riddle considered his cousin's intention of inveigling the guardian of the King of Damaria into marrying her. Slowing the ship gave her more time to gain her ends, but she had failed, as had her henchmen.

The failure must rankle with the Sealord and Arken, and this was its result, too late to accomplish any of their goals, he suspected. The suffering of innocent beings was no concern of any of the conspirators, the poet knew, if only they could feel they had taken revenge upon him and his people. The thought filled him with fury, but he held it controlled, as his people were taught to do from earliest childhood.

Once the damage was assessed and put right, as well as could be done at sea with no fresh supplies upon which to call, Riddle did not settle again into the dreamlike state that had held him. Instead, he kept a close watch upon the people in the holds, the sailors and the ship, even Gorghoz and Oakbeam and Killeli.

For as time passed and the ship bore westward, the close quarters and the boredom wore on everyone's nerves. Quarrels broke out among the Turnig, normally the most equable of people. Gorghoz grew morose and spent much of his time sitting near the bowsprit, gazing toward the horizon and ignoring the babble of talk and children behind him.

Killeli shadowed Riddle's footsteps, his skinny body tense, but he said nothing. Riddle read in his eyes an intuition of trouble to come, and he knew a similar foreboding, but he could find nothing that gave him clear warning. Only when the wind changed did he realize that he had been feeling the distant thought of Dinorm, fixed upon this escaping group, and now that thought was taking physical shape.

It had been years since Moonlight had quelled the Shaper and his minion in their own northern land. Even though she had soiled her spirit and ruined her youth in that encounter, she had known it would not be a permanent halt to the destructive plans of the two. Riddle had known it, as well, though he refused to talk of it with her.

Now, as cloud gathered to the north, piling up in pewter and gray and plum-blue mountains of wind and mist, he understood that the Shaper had revived, had grown strong again, and had turned his anger toward those who were going beyond his reach. If he could not possess them, he would destroy them, if it could be done.

Garlock furled the sails and had the sailors bind them fast to the masts. He readied masses of canvas for sea-anchors, in case such might be needed for riding out the storm that bore down swiftly, lit by the remnant of sun that peered beneath the western cloud-mass, turning it a sullen and sulfurous hue.

He sent everyone below at last and battened down the hatches, standing at the wheel as the ship scurried southward under bare poles, fleeing from the storm. He had lashings ready for binding the wheel, if the waves became too powerful to allow a man to hold course against them.

Riddle remained beside the captain, though Lute begged him to go below, and the Goremin grumbled at the risk as he bore the boy away. He turned his face into the wind, bracing his hands on the binnacle to hold himself steady. For now the swells had grown tall, and the buffeting of the gusts made the ship yaw like a startled steed beneath his feet.

The yellow light faded to a sickly gray as the cloud mass overtook the straining ship and a curtain of rain-squalls wrapped about it. Now Riddle stepped up beside the captain and laid his hands on the great wheel, for it was bucking against the seaman's hands as the wind beat first from north, then from west, carrying away every piece of gear that had not been secured well. Now the roar of the wind in his ears and the slash of rain about his face confused the poet, but he clung, following Garlock's motions, helping to control the wheel as the ship rose and plunged, rose and plunged through the steep seas. Sheets of water—rain or ocean, he could not determine which—dashed over the decks and swirled about his boots, and lightning cracked and lanced about the embattled vessel.

When it seemed that nothing could be worse than the present situation, the wind suddenly changed direction, catching them from the east and laying the length of the *Refuge* over in the boiling waters. But Oakbeam's deep keel and solid ballast held them, and the ship began rolling upright, only to be caught by a tremendous sea that battered down upon the masts as they came up again.

The longest mast cracked with a sound like that of the lightning. As the *Refuge* rolled upright again, the broken timber trailed offside like a broken wing, dragging in the water and making the wheel impossible to hold. The deck was canted at a dangerous angle by the weight of it.

Riddle helped to lash the spokes fast, and then he followed the captain as Garlock caught up an axe from its clamp and handed another to the poet. Together, they crossed the listing deck, amid the roar of wind and the shattering walls of water, to reach the broken mast.

Alternating their strokes, they chopped frantically at the tangle of canvas and lines, of wood and spar, freeing bits that they cast overboard until they came to the main body of the mast itself. Then they worked indeed, until the thing creaked shrilly, flew up, freed suddenly from its hold on its stump, and went overboard in a rush.

"Sea Anchor!" shouted Garlock, and Riddle staggered after him over the listing, bucking deck and helped to struggle with the rolled canvas, freeing it from its cupboard on the aft deck and letting it flow over the railing to settle onto the heaving sea.

Secured through metal eyes to metal anchor points with metal pins, the thing slowed the flight of the ship, controlled its motion through the waves, and kept it from yawing in the changing gusts. Now the wheel was steadier, held by the lashings, and the captain motioned for Riddle to follow him below.

Once they had shut the door of the captain's ladder behind them, Garlock turned to Riddle. "It will ride or it will not, and nothing a man can do will alter that now," he said. "With the sea anchor holding well, we should make it through the storm, but we are much off our course, carried south faster than we could have traveled if we had bent on all canvas and tried our best to make such time."

"And south was not our destination," the poet sighed. "Do you know an island where we might replace our mast and the lost canvas?"

"The islands in the southern seas are not inhabited, for the storms common to that area sweep them frequently. This that we have here is only a summer breeze compared to those terrible winds and tidal waves. And the continent beyond the ocean is many months away, far more than our jury-rigged ship could make it."

"Those islands," Riddle said, staring at the gimbaled lamp that swung back and forth on the wall, its flame upright, no matter what contortions its sealed oil container went through. "Is there timber?"

Garlock smiled. "There is timber and there is water. Stores are soaked below, or I miss my guess, and we will need to replace food-stuffs. There is an archipelago somewhere south and west of us, if we are anywhere near the area I guess as our position. I will have to take my star-glass and make readings, if the weather clears and the night is fine. We will find our location, and then I will know which islands to make for."

The poet nodded. Dinorm had managed, after all, to work his will upon them, even at such a distance and over water. That was an ill omen, he thought. But he was too weary now, too wet and bruised by the battering of wind and flying objects to worry about that now.

If they survived, he knew with sudden certainty, and reached the Western Islands, that would not be the end of it. His business with the Mover in the North and Dinorm was not done. This day had, if nothing else, convinced him of that.

CHAPTER FORTY-FOUR

"No haven is as safe as it may seem."
—Riddle

Oakbeam's house, even with Egon and his wife and their six children in residence, seemed strangely empty to one who had known it a-bustle with the builder and his wife, two more sons, and a gaggle of refugees. One wing was closed off until needed, for Oakbeam had added to the home of his father, expecting generations of his descendants to live there. But even then the rest seemed unduly vacant. Riddle's house, with its pleasant garden, was again empty, for no buyers could be found in the City in the Mist. Indeed, Moonlight could feel the city dying, day by day, as merchants and their families took ship for the distant homelands of the Sealords.

The heart had gone out of the place with the going of the King. Once Oakbeam was borne away on the *Refuge*, there was no builder left to repair and refurbish what fell apart or was damaged by storm.

Egon, sturdy and cheerful, was a builder of ships only, and he did not interest himself in building or repairing houses. The stones that fell into the streets from balconies and corbels did not trouble him, so long as he had a hull in his slip, taking shape beneath his eyes.

Girnig kept to his house as the summer became stormy and wet, sending the stones streaming water and the small river flooding roads and gardens along its length. Moonlight kept an ear tuned to the Sealord, for she had been kept abreast of Blade's investigations, and felt that her own safety might depend upon being warned of his movements. She engaged a small boy who hawked fish from door to door to keep her informed as to the Lord's activities, but he brought little news.

There was a strange mood abroad in the City in the Mist. Though many of the seagoing race had resented the presence of their refugee Turnig and Furred Men, even before the coming of Riddle and his people, once the other peoples were absent, they left many gaps where their busy hands had worked. Stone-carving was now rougher and less polished. Needlework was less artistic, holding fast without ornamenting the garments it held together. Wood was not worked with the same love and care as it had been by the hands of the simian people.

The gardens of the city languished, without little gardeners busy among flowers and vegetables. Egon commented upon that, wondering that he had never noticed the many things the Turnig did.

Moonlight only smiled, for she had traveled a long and terrible road among that kind, and she knew their stout hearts and many skills. Damaria was the poorer, she knew, for driving them out or skinning them for their fur. She suspected her native city also suffered for lack of their quick intelligence and their deft fingers.

But let Lorbek squirm. She had no sympathy for him, whatever happened.

As the weather cooled, wet though it was, she began to feel better than she had since coming from the east. Although Egon and Blade insisted that she must not go into the city streets alone, she found one or another of the shipbuilder's children willing to accompany her, and she began walking from the docks to the eastern wall, from the cliff backing into the cape to the shore fronting the harbor, feeling her strength increase, now, with every day.

As she went, she spoke with the people in the streets and the shops, gauging their mood. All seemed listless or depressed, and some even admitted the city was not what it had been.

The exercise helped her, and she grew stronger still. Her eyesight began to return, slowly and dimly, yet enough to allow her to see a bit more clearly. Yet the strength she gained was the strength of age, not of youth, and she knew, looking into her glass, that her blurred face was still withered and worn, her hair streaked with white. But again energy rose in her veins and muscles, and she felt like helping Egon's plump Talia with her household work and her constant mending, or when visiting Blade she helped Fladan in the garden.

She was again able to dream. Not the Dream of her kind, but night-dreams such as others had, reliving old times or experiencing skewed reflections of day-to-day affairs engaged her nights. As the days passed, she dreamed often of the ship and of Riddle and his people. She saw a terrible storm overtake the ship, and she watched as the crippled vessel limped away and out of her sight.

Waking, she worried, but there was no way of knowing if she had dreamed truly.

When in late summer the scent of the distant forests of her homeland drifted across the bay and tingled in her nostrils, she felt an irresistible desire to walk again. Talia urged her to go, and young Oakbeam, who was ten, was glad to leave his tasks and go with her.

She visited Blade and Silk and Wonder, in their solidly built home beside the wall. They talked of many matters, of their concern for the travelers, even of the strangeness that had seized Girnig and turned him into a sort of hermit, avoiding the eyes of his people.

They said nothing of Tulip, and Moonlight was glad of it. The pain of his loss sealed Blade's tongue, and those about him did not mention his daughter.

The shops did not hold her interest, for Moonlight had never craved the gaudy items they held, brought from distant lands beyond the sea. It was the harbor, with the fishing vessels bobbing at anchor or putting out to sea, that brought her back again and again. She longed to be on that westward-bound vessel, whatever its fate, knowing Riddle still lived.

But as she could not follow, she contented herself with watching the children of the fishermen as they mended nets or wove cord or built traps for the shellfish that thronged the shallows off the cape. She became so familiar there that the fisher folk seemed her friends, and young Oakbeam dared to scavenge along the beach or to play at toss-rocks with the other boys.

It seemed her life would be a long sameness now, secure among Egon's people, safe in the city. Yet, as she sat in the warm sand one afternoon, half dozing and half watching the quick feet of the children as they dashed about at play, she suddenly felt the grip of hard hands upon her arms.

Someone behind her said, "Catch her mouth, or she may cry out!"

A rough palm was crammed over her lips, and she felt herself lifted and carried swiftly off between the boats that were being scraped and painted, upside down on their supports. She smelled dead fish, a strong tang of brine and acid, the stink of unwashed flesh.

Then something went over her head, her hands were bound, and she smelled the mustiness of a fiber bag as she was borne along. The alleys along which they went smelled different from the well-trodden streets where sunlight came every day. The chill of the un-warmed stone, the echoes of the feet of her abductors, told her that she was not in the ways she knew.

Then a door creaked open and groaned shut, and she was dumped roughly onto a flagged floor, still damp and smelling of soap from a recent mopping. Whispers rustled about her, but they were at some distance, and she could not make out the words.

Again a hand seized her, pulling her upright and holding painfully to keep her from falling again. The bag was snatched away, and her bound wrists were freed, while she peered about her at what seemed a very ordinary rear passage leading to a kitchen.

And then she realized the one thing that made this a most unusual kitchen passage. Arken stood in an arched doorway, staring at her with narrowed eyes, his head cocked as if assessing her worth. His smile held no warmth as he finished his survey and nodded.

"Take her to the Lord," he said. "He'll make the judgment, but I doubt not that he'll think her not worth the killing. A hag only, of no value to anyone, even for sport."

With sudden thankfulness, Moonlight blessed her appearance of age. It would save her, she suspected, from indignities that she would as soon not suffer.

CHAPTER FORTY-FIVE

"We were delivered from the teeth of wind."
—Riddle

Gorghoz lay in his over-sized hammock, which swung madly as the ship plunged and rose in the gale. Beyond him, he could hear Killeli moaning in his own hammock, sick to his soul with the noise and the movement. From time to time the furred man dropped to the pitching deck and crawled to a bucket, set securely in loops against the bulkhead for his convenience. The stench of his sickness filled the small cabin.

Gorghoz was not seasick, which he considered interesting. He had never known a Goremin who went to sea, and so he had no measure of the resistance of his kind to motion sickness. But he was sick to his spirit because of the treachery that had accompanied the *Refuge* on its voyage.

They now knew the culprit who had set the fire and decamped with one of the lifeboats. Digon was a sailor chosen from among many by Garlock and Oakbeam. Skilled as he was at making sail and climbing ratlines, he had evidently held some grudge, or else Arken had found the asking price for his honor.

Digon, however, was no longer a matter of interest to anyone. He had certainly been caught when the storm bore down from the north, and the cockleshell boat in which he had thought to find land again must have been swamped and sunk in the first blast of the gale. Digon, whatever his motive, had now paid for his crime.

But the *Refuge* was flying before the wind, the sea anchor holding her fairly well, although it had begun to tatter the morning after the night of storm. Still the wind blasted from north and east, alternately, and rain pelted down fit to clear the decks of even the hardiest seaman.

The wheel was still lashed, and Riddle forbade even the captain to risk himself at the helm.

From time to time, hail as large as a man's fist came rattling down from the black-purple sky, and anyone standing uncovered would have had his brains dashed out, if he should be struck. They could only hope to ride out the storm. If the *Refuge*, designed and built with Oakbeam's best skill, could not survive, then Gorghoz thought there might not be a craft afloat that could. Now, hearing the timbers creak and groan, the joints snap, the seams of the great ship strain with the stresses it bore, he hoped with great intensity that the vessel could hold on.

No storm, even one sent by the Shaper, could last forever, and the farther the winds pushed them from the eastern continent, the weaker the power of that dark mind became. The warm southern seas set up their own weather patterns, and the chill north could not prevail there, he felt, although none of his kind had done more than read about those distant climates.

When, on the third day, the pitching eased, the decks lay something like level for more than an instant, and the noise died to a pitch that seemed almost silent, contrasted with what had gone before, he rose from his hammock and shook the miserable Killeli.

"Come, my small friend," he said. "We may be able to go on deck, and the fresh air in your face will make you feel much better." He caught the light body in his arms and lifted the furry man easily. He felt entirely too wasted and frail, and Gorghoz determined to trouble Chark for some of her rich broth, when the time came that his friend was able to eat.

As he emerged into the passageway, he found Riddle and Garlock there before him, waiting for Oakbeam and his sons to come from their cramped quarters to join them. Together, the group moved up into the dying wind, to find the cloud cover breaking up, its fragments blown away north again by a fresh breeze.

Setting Killeli on his wobbly feet, Gorghoz held him so he could feel the clean sea air and see the horizon, a serene line of blue in the distance. Now the ship had settled into a slow roll, and as Garlock freed the wheel and steered them westward, that line steadied, which helped to settle the furry one's disrupted belly.

The Turnig and the seamen were aloft in no time, untangling the lines, freeing the remnants of sail from the remaining masts. When fresh canvas was bent on, the breeze sent them scudding forward as energetically as a colt in a meadow. The loss of the central mast had not made the vessel unseaworthy at all, though it considerably reduced speed and maneuverability.

Everyone came on deck, once the sails were mended and the debris cleaned away. Turnig manned the tar-pots, sealing sprung seams in the hull with a mix of hot tar and tow, or washed and aired their bedding and clothing, musty from the long confinement below. Riddle and his nephew sat in the bow, watching the horizon as if willing land to come into view, and Gorghoz lent his will to theirs.

Everyone needed solid land beneath his feet, the smell of growing plants and sweet soil in his nostrils. They had been only three weeks on their voyage, but already, because of the storm and the confinement it had caused, tempers were growing short and more quarrels were arising among the motley group.

When Lute's piping voice rose shrilly from the bow, Gorghoz thought the boy was giving way, at last, to weariness and close quarters. But it was no complaint that he sent into the brilliant day.

"Land ho!" he shouted, and his uncle rose and lifted him high to see. Now Gorghoz could make out a line of darker blue against that horizon, only a dash of plum amid the sun-struck azures and sapphires of the southern sea, wearing a scarf of pale cloud. Then it was plain to see: a mountain stood against the sky, a collection of lower hills on either side, silhouetted against the billow of cloud above the bit of land.

They sped forward as if the *Refuge* itself craved a refuge of its own. Within the hour Gorghoz, now with his friends beside the foremast, could make out a curl of silver sand lining the arc of the lagoon. The brilliant glints of breakers foamed against the reefs flanking the channel that led into the protected anchorage.

Garlock was grinning, he found when he looked back, as if this were the grandest thing his eyes had ever beheld, and the Goremin was of a mind with him. To one used to the high places above the City of Damaria, where he had lived for so many generations of men, the confinement of a ship was hard to bear. He wanted the spring of turf beneath his feet, the steadiness of solid dirt and rock to hold him up.

Riddle turned to him, his eyes alight with gladness. "I see forests beyond the lagoon, climbing up the sides of the mountain. But is that steam floating from the top of the peak?"

Gorghoz had read among the writings of his kind of mountains that burned within, but he had never thought to see one. He peered upward, straining even his keen eyes to make out the details of that stony eminence.

He did see something like steam or smoke issuing from the mountain's top, but it was very light, almost invisible against the cloud. "I believe you are right, but it should not concern us. We will be here only a few days, and I have read that such burning mountains spew only at very long intervals, allowing generations to live and die without ever seeing such a thing."

He took Lute from his uncle and held him higher still, while the child crowed with delight at the coins of silver light dancing upon the waves of the lagoon, which they were on the verge of entering. As they came behind the point of land, the breeze was shut away, the sails went limp, and they could hear from the shore the sounds of many different birds or animals, calling in alien voices.

Even as they watched, a heavy-winged shape flew up from a tall tree beyond the beach and flapped over them, the sound of its laboring wings plain in the stillness. "Breeawww!" it squawked as it went, and Lute laughed.

A flock of white birds rose in a flutter of wings and a melody of fluting cries to follow its dismal lead. They circled the masts as Garlock ordered the anchor dropped and the boats lowered. Instead of flying away, they settled onto the water between the *Refuge* and the channel, as if guarding the harbor.

Gorghoz gazed toward the clean strip of sand, longing to set his splayed feet there, but he knew the small people, young and impatient as they were, needed to go ashore far worse than he did.

Riddle reached to touch his gray-furred shoulder. "I will remain aboard with the captain and some seamen. You go with the others, my friend. If there is danger there, the sight of you will frighten any enemy and make cautious any beast." The dark eyes were filled with light, as if the warmth inside the poet were finding its way up from the deep wells of compassion that lived in his kind.

Gorghoz was touched. Then, realizing how great was his need for privacy and the touch of soil, he knew Riddle had read him rightly. "I will," he said, setting Lute on his vast shoulders. "And if anyone threatens, I shall smile at him sweetly."

He grinned, stretching his wide mouth to its squarest dimensions, knowing the many layers of his teeth glinted fiercely in the sunlight. Few were those who could gaze unmoved upon the smile of a Goremin.

The boats were filling, as he took his small charge down and settled into the largest. Half the Turnig must wait, for in addition to those who had come with Riddle to the City in the Mist, there were a hundred more who had left their homes there to accompany their kindred westward.

The hundred who were to go fitted neatly into the five boats, for they were small and compact. A dozen of the seamen joined Gorghoz and Lute in the largest of the craft, and then they rowed for shore, amid a distant chirping and cheeping of many birds.

The sand was almost silver in the sunlight, as the Goremin

stepped ashore. There was a sudden stillness, as the presence of these strangers quieted the unseen voices in the nearby forest. Only the riffle of wind in the long, tattered leaves of the slender trees edging the water interrupted the silence.

Then the Turnig were ashore, and it immediately became a place of family games, washing and swimming, dashing and darting and shouting with mirth, as the tiny young ones exploded onto dry land.

Lute joined them, giggling as his legs, used to the heaving of the deck, wobbled beneath him.

Gorghoz, finding his own behaving oddly, came after the boy, glancing from the gamboling people on the shore to the bulk of the mountain that towered behind the woodland.

The scents of unknown blossoms rode the breeze, and he suspected that fruits of fine flavor might grow among the trees. They must send exploration parties inland, up the mountain even, in order to assess what they could use of the island's resources to replace the stores that had been ruined or damaged by sea water during the storm.

This was, indeed, a magical place, peaceful and untroubled. He could see no hint of the workings of hands anywhere about the lagoon. No print of any foot except those of his own party marred the evenly wind-combed sand.

From the grip of the storm, they had been delivered into a small Paradise. For that the Goremin found himself grateful, for he was becoming too old to bear too much hardship without some time to recover.

He waved toward the ship, semaphoring his great arms in a sign that all was well. In the distance there was a hail of acknowledgement. All was in order both ashore and afloat. It only remained to bring the rest ashore and to make out a duty roster for those who would take turns at watching aboard the *Refuge*. No competent seaman would leave his vessel unattended in strange waters, no matter how peaceful things might seem there.

Lifting Lute again, as the boy danced about his feet, Gorghoz drew a great lungful of the sweet air. As he exhaled, he paused, sniffed, sniffed again. Did he detect the scent of sulfur? Just the slightest indication, less than a normal sense of smell might notice at all? But a Goremin nose was a delicate instrument, and it told him there was indeed a taint of that element hanging over the island.

The volcano, of course. But it seemed to dream against the sky, its slopes shining gold in the sun and purple in the shadow, exhaling only the faintest plume of steam. Surely it posed no threat to these temporary visitors.

Again Gorghoz turned to stare at the ship. It seemed to list slightly to port, and he felt the faintest stirring of unease. Those strained seams must still be leaking; if the *Refuge* was to proceed on its journey, its people might do well to haul her close to shore and attend to its wounds.

That would take days. But surely there was no danger here, he assured himself, breathing the softly scented air and feeling the warmth of the fine sand between his toes.

CHAPTER FORTY-SIX

"Honor, once lost, seems infinitely precious."
                                    —Riddle

Girnig had thought his mind would rest when the King of Damaria and his rag-tag crew were gone from his city, leaving no rival ruler there to trouble his mind. In the beginning, he had talked long with Arken and those of the Council who were in agreement with his aims, trying to see the devious design beneath the seemingly straightforward conduct of Riddle and his people. Many guesses had been offered, but not one seemed apt.

When Arken suggested slowing work on the ship so as to give more time for learning what danger this expedition to the west might pose for the City in the Mist, the Sealord agreed, allowing the seneschal to weave his webs as he would. When Tulip, who had never deigned to notice his existence, visited his house at last, disguised, on a gray day in autumn, he had listened to her words, wanting them to be true.

She promised much, did the daughter of Blade, once she became a power in Damaria. For a time Girnig believed her, not because her plan was feasible, but because he so wanted it to be. Ridding himself forever of both Lute and Riddle, sending the Turnig and the Fur Men away from his walls and his harbor, those things would ease his heart and leave him secure in his rule of the city.

Yet once the word came to him of Tulip's death at the hands of her own father, Girnig felt something inside him shrivel with dread. The hope and ambition nourished by Tulip's plots withered to ashes, and he knew they had never been more than that. She had used him for her own ends, with Arken's help, and now those ends lay in ruins, and his own honor was stained past redemption.

The Council, without the solid intelligence and sensible advice of Oakbeam, was now a wishy-washy group, without power and useless even for sound counseling. As the first winter after the sailing of the *Refuge* set in, Girnig went into his chambers and closed the door against petitioners.

When Arken came with pleas from those needing the judgment of their Lord, he sent him away, feeling sick at the sight of that narrow face and those bright, knowing eyes. Why had he loosed his hold upon his own power, leaving it to the seneschal? He felt he had been enspelled, used by Tulip and this ancient and then cast adrift, helpless and alone.

His wife, frightened at the change in her lordly husband, said nothing and crept about their house like a shadow, afraid even to whisper to a servant or to scold her silent, wary children. When she moved from their bedroom, Girnig found himself glad she had gone. His nightmares woke her often, and the sound of her tense breathing disturbed him as much as the evil dreams that haunted his nights.

He had given away his birthright. That was borne in upon his mind more and more as time passed, winter turning toward spring and then to summer. The harbor was idle, for few ships now anchored there.

With Damaria lost to civilized trade, the City in the Mist did not offer a large enough market for merchantmen to risk the long eastward passage. Ships now went southward, to the subcontinent where the Ancient Race lived, without often beating up the coastline toward his city.

He spent hours gazing from his high window across the city at the shining waters and the channel leading out to sea. He longed for those days when he had been a seagoing Lord, commanding his own ship, his spirit haunted by no ill memories. But there was no returning for him, he knew. The thing that had influenced him, held his thoughts in thrall, guided his judgment to its own ruin, had not died with Tulip. She had entered his mind, and even in death the print of her presence still lived there.

At last he returned to the semblance of his former life, opening his doors once more to those needing justice, listening to Arken plead for the petitioners, though his ears shrank from the sound of the old man's voice. When the seneschal came to him, one evening in his chambers with another plan, Girnig knew at once that it was wrong, dangerous, and dishonorable.

"They left behind the hag they brought from Damaria," the ancient said, his head bent close to that of his master, his breath musty in Girnig's nostrils. "She is a witch, a danger, an evil thing to have in our city. We must rid ourselves of her, for it is because of her Tulip died and our plans were left in ruins."

The Sealord opened his mouth to protest, for even secluded as he had been, he knew the truth of Tulip's death. The abduction of a child, even in a city that was losing its sense of values, was still a crime calling for the death of the one who committed it.

But he found he could not speak. The remnant of that old compulsion forced him to nod, instead, as the husky voice went on.

"Egon is needed, for no other can build ships, and our stout keels are the only thing still bringing merchants to our shores. We cannot afford to anger him, for he might leave to follow his father.

"Yet we must rid ourselves of this Dreamer, for it is her influence that has diminished our city and brought its trade to a standstill. If we take her when she is walking about the streets, then there will be nothing to show who has carried her away. Egon may suspect, but if he cannot prove us guilty, he will have no excuse to leave us without a ship-builder."

The wrinkles crawled in the lamplight, as the seneschal bobbed his head, the straggles of white hair falling about his face. "A good plan, without any danger to anyone, eh?"

Again Girnig strained to protest, to utter scathing words of contempt for such a silly and useless plot, but he could not. The mark Tulip had made in his mind still lingered, forcing him to her will or that of her henchman. He felt like some helpless fly, caught in the sticky web wrought by a spider, and bile rose in his throat as he struggled to free himself. Yet he could not, and he nodded at last, without lending his voice to the plot. If he must damn himself, time after time, he refused to say the words.

* * * * * * *

Three days later, when the summer hung heavy over the city, and the streets hummed with small boys and vendors' carts and fitful breezes from the harbor, Arken came to his door. "We have her, Lord," he smirked. "Right and ready, if you will see her now."

Sighing, the Sealord rose from his chair beside the window of his study and turned to see who came. Two men held the slim shape of a woman, dragging her faster than her feet could follow, and thrust her into the room. She fell to her knees, for he saw that her hands were bound behind her and she was unable to keep her balance.

Girnig felt a surge of anger as he bent to lift her to her feet and helped her to a chair. "Loose her hands!" he said. The anger seemed to free him, somewhat, from his interior bondage.

Arken took the dagger from the sconce on the wall and sliced the ropes, though he kept looking sidewise at the Lord, as if wondering why he was able to assert himself in this way. As the bonds fell from her wrists, the woman straightened and rubbed her hands and forearms, as if they were painful after being tied so tightly.

"This is the Dreamer?" asked Girnig, finding that something of his old authority was returning to his heart. "The one you claim is a danger to our city?"

"Indeed. And she must be put to death, Lord, else we will have rebellion on our hands. The people are uneasy and want her punished."

Girnig knew that most of that was a lie, and yet there must be something of truth, too. He had heard, even in his seclusion, the echoes of dissatisfaction rising from the streets.

If he loosed this woman, sent her back to Egon's house, she would be killed. He saw that in the eyes of the seneschal, as well as those of the guardsmen standing on either side of the door, as if this frail creature might attack him and escape. But a sudden unwillingness to put her to death seized him, and he knew he would not consent to it.

"She will not be executed," he said. "I will not consent to that. Instead, you will supply her with food and clothing and a weapon, and you will put her ashore beyond the inlet, on the shores of Damaria. There she can do no harm, yet she will be able to survive, perhaps, on her own. This is my command."

The woman stared into his eyes, and deep in her fogged gaze he saw a distant, fleeting flicker of hope. She knew his heart, he saw with sudden clarity, and she understood his intentions. He offered her life, instead of death, if she had the capacity to use it.

She did not smile—that would have betrayed his purpose to Arken. But he saw a deepening of the wrinkles about her temples, and those cat-pupilled eyes warmed as they stared into his.

That seemed to melt something of the compulsion frozen into his mind. He relaxed a bit as he sat again in his chair and stared up into the astonished face of the seneschal.

"You will do this, Arken. See to it that he does," he said, turning to the guard Imond. "I shall want a report before nightfall that she is on the shore of Damaria, amid the forest, unbound and provided with what is needful for survival."

"But she will die anyway," said Arken. "Why not kill her now, neatly and quietly, and bury her beneath the wall? No one will know, and we will have no problems ever again with her."

"I will know," said Girnig. "I do not will it so. Obey my command, Arken, or surrender your staff and your keys to my house."

The old man all but reeled with the shock of those words. His eyes narrowed still more, and his mouth thinned to a slit as he bowed low, concealing that betraying expression, and turned from the room. Behind him went the men, now holding the Dreamer gently by either elbow and fitting their strides to hers.

Girnig stared down at the table before him. The papers there were old ones, neglected for days. His usefulness was at an end, he felt with sudden finality. He was no longer the Lord of the City in the Mist, but a puppet, a figurehead controlled by an ancient seneschal and a dead woman of the Ancient Race.

But he would have his will, one last time. He called for a servant and ordered her to watch until the Dreamer was taken from the house. When she reported to him that this had been done, he turned to the window, and before long he saw his own skiff pull out from the dock and set out across the bight of the bay, rounding the point into the channel leading to the open sea.

Only when it was beyond sight did he turn from his watching and move heavily toward his bedchamber, where he fell upon the couch and closed his eyes. He had fought battles, in his old seafaring days, that had not depleted his strength to such an extent. Fighting the dead will of Tulip had drained him of energy.

He heard a faint footfall and opened his eyes to see his wife looking down at him, her forehead furrowed with concern. "Are you well, Lord?" she asked.

"I am not ill," he said, moved by her presence. "Come and lie beside me, as we used to do, and talk with me of our children. I have not seen them for so long. Is young Girnig growing fast? Does he show skills that would interest me?"

She settled beside him and he felt her hand move to touch his. It had been a long, long while since they had been so close, and he felt comforted as she began to tell him of their children. His son, he realized with astonishment, was twelve winters of age, now, almost a man. It seemed strange.

At last his eyes closed, and he drifted into sleep.

Her struggle and sigh woke him, and he started up, only to fall back before the point of his own keen blade. He felt a warm stickiness on the hand his wife had held, and he knew that she was dead beside him, slain by this demonic seneschal, who even now was forcing him down and down to avoid that perilous point.

"I have worked with your son," said Arken in a breathless whisper. "He is my tool, Girnig Sealord. If you are not apt to my hand, I will have another, for the woman of the Ancient Race set her seal upon you both, without your understanding that. You may think that you rebelled and won, but that is an error.

"I have won, again and again, and I shall win this last, best battle. Die, Girnig, that your son may become Lord in your place.

"My tool, Lord. My puppet, as you have been for years now."

The blade came down, and Girnig felt himself drowning in his own blood as his hand sought that of his wife and clamped her fingers in his as he struggled and died.

* * * * * * *

Arken wiped the blade on the coverlets before wrapping both bodies in those and the hangings of the bed. He crept to the small door leading into the Lord's private passage and called softly into the darkness of the way.

Then, accompanied by four burdened men carrying a pair of hampers, two by two, he tiptoed down this secret corridor toward the alley leading to the shore. No one would know what had happened to the Lord and his Lady, but their children, left behind and bereft, would be safely in the care of Arken, seneschal of the City.

CHAPTER FORTY-SEVEN

"An island spiced with scents of lovely things...."
—Riddle

Riddle came ashore gladly, once Garlock decided the ship must be careened and repaired. The tide rose minimally in the lagoon, but they worked it close to the shelving shoreline. When the water receded they hauled the vessel as far as they could and built a rough slip with logs from the forest and rocks from the outcrops that made natural jetties along the beach line.

Even with so many hands and backs to lend to the enterprise, the travelers could not manage to drag the great ship out of the water entirely. However, they did slip it up into their makeshift cradle, leaving her sufficiently high and dry to allow them to work on her caulking. This was the work of weeks, not days, and they would take turns working on the hull.

Then, their vessel secured and shifts of hands busy with repairs, the rest of the group dispersed about the island, although Riddle found himself wondering about their safety. The Turnig were stout folk, and they went where they would, but he made certain that Lute went always with Gorghoz or Killeli or himself, for the safety of the small King was his primary concern.

He kept a close watch on the progress of caulking and sail making, as days turned into weeks, though Garlock supervised his crewmen at that demanding work. When it became clear his presence was a hindrance rather than a help to the workers, the poet took his nephew and roamed the beach, examining exotic seashells on the sand, naming the birds, searching out hidden caches of stones.

The rocky outcrops interrupting the beach puzzled him, for they were not coral, as he had expected, or lava, as the smoking mountain hinted. They were granite, solid and gray-white as that forming the bones of Damaria's own mountains. Although he had not studied geology deeply, he felt this to be subtly wrong.

Gorghoz agreed and pointed out, in addition, anomalies among the plants and trees of the island. Yet the blossoms were so vividly colored and so delicately scented that they intoxicated the poet's senses, and the fruits found on some of the bushes and trees tantalized the taste. He found it hard to think any real danger could lurk here, amid so much loveliness.

The Turnig agreed, and the small people ranged the island's shore and up the slopes behind, bringing out all sorts of edible things to fill in the gaps in their supplies. The stores were replenished, day after day, for Chark found roots that substituted for the flour that had been ruined by seawater, as well as fruits she insisted must be dried in the sun.

The bins and crates began filling again. Water casks were washed out with vinegar and re-filled from one of the freshwater brooks that tumbled down the slopes to spill into the lagoon.

When he had observed the entire area edging the beach, the poet decided it would be safe enough to take Lute up into the hills leading to the slopes of the mountain. Gorghoz and Killeli went as well, for they were curious as to what sorts of animals might live there, making the night sonorous with their cries.

The curved branches of the trees closed over his head as he carried Lute high on his shoulders into the forest. Motion above made them both look up, and behind them Killeli made a small sound of disbelief. A tiny animal, very like him in shape but obviously still only a beast, was staring down at them from a treetop, its eyes round and dark in its small white-furred face.

It seemed unafraid as it descended, dropping from hand to hand, catching convenient boughs or fronds as it came, to a point from which it could examine them more closely. Other creatures, especially birds, remained in place, staring down at the intruders with shiny, curious eyes. It was plain that no predatory two-legged people had walked here before.

As he climbed a ridge leading up onto the mountainside, Riddle paused and looked down the slope, which here was clear enough to allow them to see the harbor and their ship, careened and surrounded by busy crewmen. The ridge was almost snake-like, originating near the water and curving up and up until it disappeared into a crevice high above their present position. He handed Lute to Gorghoz to free himself as he examined that unusual formation.

It seemed almost artificial, and Riddle shivered. Since meeting Dinorm in its lair beneath the northern hills, he had felt a cold aversion to anything reptilian. Even as he entertained the thought, he fancied he felt the soil move beneath his feet, the long ridge rippling for an instant before his bemused gaze.

He shook himself and turned to make a joking comment to the Goremin, but when he looked up into those bright eyes he felt a chill go down his back. Gorghoz had fancied the same thing, he saw at a glance. And Lute, riding high on the shoulders of his large friend, was laughing.

"The ground danced, Uncle!" he said, pointing down the crooked way. "Make it do it again!"

Riddle tried to smile. "That was none of my doing, nephew," he said. But he was exchanging questions with the Goremin and Killeli, though no word was spoken among them. They needed to know what this island contained, and there could be no better spot from which to observe it in all directions than the flat spot just below the cone from which the smoke rose. If there was danger, it was better to learn what it might be now, considering how to deal with it sooner rather than later.

The other pairs of eyes held the same message. We shall go up, whatever the situation, and then we shall see. Riddle turned again to his climb, and behind him he heard the solid thud of the Goremin's great feet, the erratic patter of Killeli's hand-like ones, and the chime of Lute's laughter as birds flitted close overhead.

The air was cool, once they left the last fringe of trees, and hot though the sun might feel, the breezes off the ocean were refreshing. There was the scent of sulfur, and yet even so high the fragrant breath of the blossoming trees and shrubs found its way to Riddle's nostrils.

Below stretched an irregular quarter-moon shape, curved about the harbor into which they had sailed. The arms were thick, with heavy forest between the wide beaches along the lagoon and the narrower ones on the outward arc. Behind the mountain was an oval valley in the middle of which was a small lake, very blue in the midst of all the greenery.

The place looked like a small paradise, and the poet found a momentary wish they might remain there, safe and unburdened, for a longer time than looked possible. And then he turned again to stare down the slopes along the spine of that odd ridge.

He went cold from scalp to heels, and his hands clenched to control their tendency to shake. It was a great serpent, that shape, coiling up from the water to the crevice into which it went at the upper end. The rocks of which it was formed had weathered into the very semblance of scales, and though the shape was different from that of Dinorm, he had the same feeling of revulsion he had felt when he faced that destructive entity beneath the hills.

Behind him, he heard Gorghoz draw a deep, controlled breath. "So there are others," he said softly. "The Litati did not confine their creations to our own continent. They must have traveled widely, those ancient beings, to come so far and to leave a spawn of Dinorm's kind even here."

Again there came a ripple in the ground underfoot, and a belch of smoke rose from the cone behind them, as if the volcano itself agreed. Beneath the level of hearing, and yet quite perceptible to Riddle's body, there came the grinding of stones and the motions of something sliding deep beneath the island.

"That is his run," he said, half under his breath. "But I suspect he coils beneath the island itself. You said that kind shuns the water. I wonder if this one also is given pause when it reaches the endless ocean surrounding him?"

The Goremin shivered, causing the boy to look down at him inquiringly. "I would not say. Who knows if the Litati experimented with many kinds, back in the dawn of time before our kinds came into being? I would not venture to guess about this one. But it moves the ground when it squirms, there in its deep lair. I hope it remains quiet until we can finish the ship and leave this place. We are nearly done with our labors now."

As if his words were a signal, the ground moved more strongly. Riddle dropped flat beside Gorghoz and Killeli, all three holding fast to the rock and to the young King, whose initial pleasure at the unusual motion became alarm as the mountain seemed to sway beneath them.

There was a roar that shook the rock under Riddle's face, and a rush of gas and debris was flung high into the thin cloud hovering over the island. Pebbles and specks of molten rock pelted down upon the poet, who crawled forward to take refuge behind a cluster of boulders, evidently belched forth during an earlier and stronger eruption.

Holding fast to Lute and a knob of stone, he managed still to look down the long vista to the harbor. The ship quivered in its cradle; those who had worked about her were tiny specks, leaping away and flattening themselves on the sand so that the great bulk would not crash down upon them, if it should shake free.

What dismal fate had sent him to this place? the poet wondered. This group of people had been battered by hardship after hardship: war in a place that had never known war and cruelty in a country that had been only kind had set them to fleeing. Danger, battle, and death had dogged their terrible journey northward, and even at the walls of the City in the Mist they had found enemies waiting.

Surely they had earned rest and peace and refuge! But the storm that had sent them here had been no natural one. Riddle knew that, even while the ship pitched and the wind threatened to send his vessel to the bottom. It was no accident that the first land they found was this island, tenanted by one who was at least the distant kin of their old enemy.

Even as he celebrated the escape of his people from the eastern continent, Riddle wondered if he had been moved by the will of those who had destroyed his family, his country, and the dominance of the Ancient Race in Damaria.

CHAPTER FORTY-EIGHT

"Alone upon a dark, forgotten shore...."
                                                    —Riddle

As the rowers pulled, their backs heaving rhythmically, Moonlight sat in the bow of the small boat, facing back toward the seawall and the City in the Mist. Although it was dark, the lights along the wharves glinted their reflections into the polished waters. Beyond the line of docks, occasional lamps marked the lines of the streets raying outward from the port area until cut off by a dark line of sky topping the ridge, which divided the cape from the harbor area of the city.

She was cold despite the cloak her abductors had wrapped about her shoulders. At her feet lay a pack of supplies, which reassured her somewhat. If they intended to kill her, there would be no need to go to such lengths to deceive her first.

She had seen Arken from a distance, while living in the City, and now she had seen Girnig Windlord. There was no possible doubt that the ancient seneschal had assumed control of the port city; she had an intuition that the Sealord might even now be lying dead, while his erstwhile servant prepared to close his fist about the centers of power there.

They cleared the Cape, and the wind freshened from the northwest, blowing cool off the waves. She wondered if the ship bearing her friends westward had reached its goal. There had been almost enough time, for the sailors told her a few months would take a sound vessel to the Westward Islands. Riddle had been gone for a long while, and surely by now his mixed group of refugees had found the haven they sought.

While she...but she shook away the thought. When she faced the Shaper and the Mover in the hills east of the City, she had known what she risked. Her choice had been made freely, and when she knew she had won and the price was her gift, along with her youth, she had not begrudged it. The young King must live, she knew, and this was her contribution to his long life.

Now she shivered, but she concealed it beneath the dark cloak. These minions were nothing to her, neither villains nor heroes, and her business was none of theirs. They had been given their orders by Girnig himself, and if Arken had, indeed, seized the city for himself, they would not know until they returned from this errand.

The dark wind out of the northwest set favorably for the Damarian coast, off to the southeast. A rower rose and stepped the short mast, hoisting a triangular sail that formed a black blot against the stars of the spring sky. The craft surged forward, and Moonlight watched the dark bulk of the Cape sink slowly as she was borne away.

She twisted on the hard, flat seat, trying to see the line of darkness against the sky that would tell her they neared their goal. It was, as yet, lost at the edge of the sea and sky, where a mist seemed to be rising, blurring that line.

She felt her heart pick up its pace. If she were set ashore in a fog, that was a good omen, for she felt certain another party would be sent, very soon, to find and to finish her, if her guess about Arken's aims was a good one. She was descended from a feline race, with many of the enviable physical abilities of that kind. Even damaged as they were, her eyes, with their slitted pupils, could see where solely man-descended folk could not.

She didn't smile, for someone might be watching her, even in the darkness. But she clasped her hands tightly in her lap and waited for whatever might come next, as the boat slipped into the outer fringes of the mist. The moisture was clammy against her face, cold and unfriendly. The slap of the wavelets against the hull told her they were nearing something—probably the place where the shoreline shelved rapidly into the deeps.

There was now a deeper sound, a rushing and whispering caused by the waters against the shoreline. The rowers, dim blurs now in the fog, were no longer using their oars. Moonlight could dimly see their heads cocked, and she knew their ears were straining for the sound of water swashing about a rock that might smash their fragile vessel. Then the steersman grunted an order, and she heard the clatter of oars being shipped.

The boat bumped and grated, and someone hopped over the side to guide it up onto the invisible beach. Moonlight braced herself as the thing heeled and steadied, and then hard hands caught and lifted her. She staggered as they dropped her onto the shingle beach, which was uneven and slick beneath her shoes.

The cloak flapped about her as she moved away from the sound of the waves. Slipping through the mist, she ducked to avoid seeking arms, grateful for the sound of the waves, which hid the scrape of her steps on the shingle.

"Where is she?" came the question from the steersman, who had taken the orders concerning her. "I can't see anything in this forsaken fog!"

"Did we drop her in the water?" asked another voice. There was a bit of splashing, as if they searched there, and then it stopped.

"Wherever she be, we've done our task. Throw the supplies up on the beach and let's be gone. I mislike this place. It's filled with strange beasts that think they're men, since Damaria was taken."

Three thumps told Moonlight her supplies had been duly flung ashore for her, be she alive or dead. That told her much about Girnig's grip on his men, and she wondered if it would give Arken problems in the future. The stuff in the packs, be the contents food or whatever, could be sold in the City for gold and silver, and most guardsmen, she suspected, might have taken the opportunity to make a profit on this ungrateful task.

She waited in her tracks, afraid to move for fear of bringing their attention to herself, until the sounds of swearing and then the creak of oarlocks told her they were on their way. She waited still, for having been set free, she did not intend to be caught again. When there was no sound beyond the swash of waves and the drip of fog from the trees beyond the beach, only then did Moonlight feel her way over the small beach, seeking the supplies left for her use.

There was a large parcel wrapped in blankets, and she took that to be clothing and cooking pots. Two smaller ones might well be food and perhaps even medicine, against injury or illness.

The three would have been too much for her, a few months ago, but she had now recovered her strength. She managed to tie the small ones together and drape them over a shoulder, while dragging the larger behind her. That would, she knew, leave a readily discernible track, but once she reached the wood, which now showed dark crowns rising above the fog, she would divide the contents into what she could carry and find useful, and what she could not justify as a burden.

Her feet knew at once when she reached the edge of the wood. Springy mulch, squelching with damp, gave beneath her thin-soled shoes and made the passage of the dragging parcel more difficult than had the slippery shingle. The undergrowth became thick very soon, bushes and vines entangling her, impeding her burden, but she pushed ahead, panting now with exertion. The sound of the waves receded, and that of breeze rustling in branches took its place. Moonlight found a small clear spot, floored with packed dirt instead of dead leaves and branches, and she paused there to spread out her packs and examine their contents.

The smallest pack she opened first. Her seeking fingers found a small lightglass on the top of the contents, and with a sigh of relief she scritched the steel rasp against the flint. A spark jumped and caught the oil-soaked wick that she had rolled up from its sealed container.

The glimmer of light was not great, yet after the darkness of the past hours it seemed brilliant. She thrust the mounting spike in the bottom of the glass into the soil, and the glow steadied, showing her the contours of the other parcels.

Deeper in the first pack there was an oiled paper container of dried fruits, two loaves of nut-bread, which would last for a long while without spoiling, and thin strips of dried meat. A twist of salt, one of coriseed seasoning, and one of dried mint, suitable for making tea, completed the tally. Someone who knew about travel-rations and cared to see another person well found had prepared the foodstuff, she could see.

The second small parcel held tough trousers of wool, two durable shirts, a pair of boots that fitted her narrow feet comfortably, smallclothes enough to last for some time, and stockings both heavy and light, for varying sorts of weather. Sandals were rolled in a closely woven cape that could repel all but the worst rain.

The big package contained a set of heavy blankets, a ground cloth and overhead flap, a cook pot, a kettle, metal cup, plate, and long-handled spoon. Those were packed into a pail made of metal, and hidden in the handle of the spoon, Moonlight found a note written in the ornate script of the Sealords.

"Good fortune attend you. From a Friend." The note warmed her frozen heart. She had thought herself quite alone, surrounded by enemies, while she was being held in Girnig's house. Yet someone had known who she was. Someone had watched, had taken upon him or herself the opportunity to pack the supplies intended for the deportee.

If someone among the servants did know who was being sent away from the shores of the City, perhaps she might get word to Egon and his people...but that was unlikely. It might simply be one who disliked the ways of Arken and his master and wanted to ease the lot of any enemy of theirs.

Remaining near the coastline in order to wait for help might well bring more enemies in time. Moonlight regarded the mixture of equipment with close attention. She would need it all, for there was not one item that could be spared, if she had to live on this unsettled edge of Damaria for very long. She had no doubt of her ability to make what she needed, but that expended energy she no longer possessed. She must manage, in some way, to carry all this with her as she retreated into the depths of the forest of western Damaria.

Taking the groundsheet as a container, she repacked everything, putting the small into the large, rolling clothing and footwear into the blankets. Everything rolled bulkily into that providential groundsheet, the pack turning out to be as large around as her body, when she was done.

That completed, Moonlight leaned against the trunk of a tree and closed her eyes. Whatever came, she knew she must rest, for tomorrow she had to carry the weighty burden away into the forest. That was going to require strength, and she was exhausted. Fear and exertion had drained her, and even if some beast came while she slept and killed her, she could not remain awake another moment.

Strangely, as she sank into slumber there was not even the hint of a dream, good or evil, to trouble her rest.

* * * * * *

The island quivered, stones rolling away down the slope into the hills below. Riddle clung to his nephew and to the boulders, holding both of them in their shelter. For now a burning-hot rain of molten stone was pelting down, and he could smell the scorched fur of Gorghoz and the furry man, even over the stink of sulfur.

Lute, who had laughed at first to feel the earth tremble, now was crying silently. Only by the damp of tears against his blouse could his uncle know it. This was unendurable! Riddle would not have his small nephew terrified in this way by anyone, even an elemental created by the Litati. Crouched over the shivering body of the child, he groped through his mind for formulae that he had learned two hundred years before from the King of Damaria. There were matters that must be controlled, and the Ancient Race, living for millennia, had studied them and learned.

His eyes tightly closed, the poet focused his thought upon the mountain beneath his body. Down and down he traveled, visualizing the dark deeps, the layered rock, the upthrust lava, the burning heart of the thing. Lower he went, into the black bowels of stone below, where the creation of the Litati must dwell, roused now by the incursion of thinking beings into its domain.

It would be something like Dinorm, he was certain. Even a people as powerful and talented as those creators of the Worms had patterns of thinking to which they must adhere. So he saw, within himself, a shape, black on black, curled into a crypt far below the level of the ocean's floor, stirring its sluggish coils as it prepared to crawl up its runnel into the light of day.

Then he felt it, sensed it through all his frame. It knew he was there with it, under the thousand thousand tons of rock and soil between them. It moved, and the mountain shook to its roots, the lagoon below slopping about as if stirred from beneath.

Riddle forced his will into a narrow span, aiming it toward that squirming serpent. He recalled all the pain he had suffered at the will of its distant kin, there on the Eastern Continent. He remembered the sacrifice Moonlight had made, and her agony at being bereft of her ability to Dream.

All the pain, the deaths, the terrible, laboring effort of the journey his people had made he formed into a tenuous arrow, which he aimed toward the creature beneath the island. When it was charged with everything he could dredge from his own and others' suffering, he loosed it toward its goal, and the effort left him limp, protecting his nephew's body with his own while his weapon traveled upon its way.

The island went mad, shivering, the trees flapping their long leaves like hysterical hands, the rock dancing and the water rising in great dollops that fell straight back down again. The boulders began rolling away from his grasp, and Riddle tried vainly to hold his position by bracing his hands on the hot, gritty flank of the mountain itself.

Curved about Lute's small shape, he was struggling to keep from rolling after the boulders when great hands caught him and he was swept against the Goremin's furry breast. Mountains were the natural domain of his people, and Gorghoz stood steady on the bucking slope, Killeli clinging to his back, the poet and the child clasped to his heart with both powerful arms.

Without hesitation, he strode down the heaving mountainside as if it were a level walkway in the city, his long toes gripping every cranny when they came down, his long legs leaping great distances at every step. Riddle felt his huge body launch itself into the thick air, fly downward, land with muscle-cushioned softness, then take off again.

What a wondrous thing was a Goremin! he thought, riding down the mountain. Lord of mountains!

Then the motion of those soaring leaps began to make itself felt, and he almost gagged. In his arms, flattened against Gorghoz's fur,

Lute was whimpering with nausea, but better that by far than being shaken from the slope like vermin from the pelt of a beast.

When it became obvious that no more leaps would come, the poet opened his eyes. The Goremin set him carefully upon his feet and anchored him with one great arm.

"It is still shaking, but less," he said. "Whatever it was you did, and I felt something strange and powerful, it has stunned the thing, I believe."

Riddle turned in the circle of the shaggy arm and stared up at the cone above them. Though dark smoke and debris still puffed up at intervals, making it hard to see, there was no lava flowing forth. Indeed, the island was settling again into rest; the trees had almost stilled, though the disturbed water of the lagoon still swashed uneasily back and forth in its basin.

The poet drew a shuddering breath. Beside him, even the Goremin breathed heavily, and Killeli was gasping. The child peeped out of his uncle's arms. His tears dried almost at once, and he struggled to get down.

"Look! Look!" he cried, stooping and staring at something between his chubby feet. "Little worms, Uncle! Look!"

Riddle, a terrible dread gripping his belly, stooped beside the child, then went to his knees to examine the tiny creatures that seemed to be bursting from the soil in incredible numbers. Not worms. Serpents!

Gorghoz knew. He understood that as soon as he looked up and up into the huge being's eyes. The island was infested—a giant hatchery of unborn Dinorms, which were now freed by the disturbance caused by their parent beneath the rock.

Paradise...Riddle almost sobbed before he turned toward the shore. Running together, the four explorers dashed to the water and shouted to the still confused workers, "Launch her! Oh, launch her at once, ready or not! We must go now!"

Garlock came from behind the cradle, where he had been checking for damage to the hull.

"Leave? Because of this little quake? I've ridden out big ones without any trouble...."—but his voice died when he saw the faces of the three who now drew near, leaving Lute among the Turnig.

"It sleeps beneath the island, a worm something like that one we fled. Our presence woke it, and we have felt its stirrings below. The soil beyond the beach is infested with its young, hatched before their time because of the shaking of the ground." Riddle took the captain by the shoulders, shaking him with the force of his words.

"We will all die here, if we do not leave at once."

Garlock turned pale, but he was a stout captain for all that. "The hull is mended below the waterline," he said. "The cracks above can be done at sea from platforms slung alongside. Get the people ready, Sir, and I shall have the ship down the ramp and floating free before you have finished with that."

* * * * * * *

Before mid-afternoon the loaded vessel stood beyond the reef, and Riddle watched the island grow smaller as they tacked north and west. Something troubled him still, and only when Gorghoz joined him did he realize what it was.

"We can't leave things as they are, Gorghoz," he said, still looking toward the green peace of the land. "It is, indeed, a hatchery. In time, when the world changes, other hatchings may occur, flooding the continents with those destructive creatures. We should destroy the entire place."

A furry hand came down on his shoulder, as the Goremin shook his head. "There is no way to destroy an island," he rumbled. "Even if there were time, we could do nothing."

"I managed to prick the worm below," said Riddle. "And that was under stress, on a mountainside down which I felt I must fall almost at once. There are techniques my uncle taught to me long generations of men in the past. I think I might do it, if you agree it should be done."

Killeli had joined them, and Riddle told him what he proposed to do. The hairy man turned toward the bright cone, the fringe of trees, the soft curves of hills. Again a scarf of cloud floated from the peak.

"There were beasts there, and birds. Creatures without fault who will die. But I agree. It must be done, though I have no skills for doing it," he said.

"Then stand beside me while I try my strength against the bones of the earth," said the poet. "I was not made for such work, and it may destroy me, but I cannot leave such a danger in my world."

Again he closed his eyes, envisioning that deep lair, the squirming tangle that was the worm below the island. Once more he shaped an arrow, this one formed of Will garnered from centuries of life and training, ages of family lore, millennia of study on the part of his ancestors.

He could feel warm fur on his right, wiry strength on his left, bolstering his energies as he created a tool for breaking apart that now-distant island. Sweat ran from his skin, puddling in his sandals.

His muscles locked into cramps, and his belly rolled gently, but he ignored the physical pain of his creation.

For an hour he strained there in the stern of the *Refuge*. And then he cast free that bolt of energy he had engendered, sending it toward the roots of the island, the lair of the worm.

Gorghoz's hand clasped his arm and shook it gently. "Look, Poet! Oh look!" he gasped. Riddle looked. The island was now so distant that only the bright halo of cloud shone clearly in the sunlight.

Bright and brighter it glowed, as if great fires raged below it on the land. Then a dark gust of ash and smoke shot up into the pure blue of the sky, and a wave of hot gases and displaced water rolled toward the ship from the south and east.

"Hang on!" shouted Killeli to those on deck. "Hang on!"

They rushed for lifelines and wrapped themselves securely as the great rolling surge rushed toward them, towering above even the masts as it neared the vessel. With a shock it overtook the *Refuge*, but the stout ship rolled and righted herself, as the blind waters sped onward to dissipate in the ocean.

The sky to the southeast grew dark with debris, and even at such a distance Riddle heard chunks of rock and soil dropping into the waters about their hull. He turned to find Garlock staring at him with awe and fear in his eyes.

"I never thought you could destroy an island," the captain said, his tone that of shock and dismay.

Suddenly the poet was too weary to stand. Supported by Gorghoz's stout arm, he said, "I did not destroy the island. The worm did that. Confined as it was, blind to what goes on in the world, it was not one like Dinorm, old and wise in the ways of thinking beings.

"When I sent that bolt of energy into it, it panicked, as I hoped it might do. The power that destroyed its island was its own. It was the murderer of its own young, spawning in the soil of that little land. I was only the tool...." His legs gave way beneath him, and the Goremin swept him up in his arms.

"If he could do such things, do you think we would have fled from Damaria instead of remaining to uproot the cruel man who rules there?" asked Gorghoz. "No, this was a little war, and he forced the enemy to kill itself. But that was no small deed, captain, and songs should be sung by those who are able to sing them."

Riddle barely heard his words. He was sinking into a well of sleep, and there even the harsh memories of his life since leaving Damaria could not manage to intrude.

CHAPTER FORTY-NINE

"The forest bowed before the roaring wind...."
—Riddle

Moonlight did not halt her inland flight until the boom of the ocean against the stony outcrops bracketing the beaches could no longer be heard. She had no faith in the good will of anyone in power in the City now, and she did not intend to be recaptured, no matter how they might search for her.

The first morning was clear, after the mist of the night before, and the sun soon dried the damp from the air. Drips from the great crowns of the trees diminished and disappeared as she dragged her heavy burden through the forest. The trail she left behind was plain, but she felt it would be some time before any further problem might arise from those beyond the bay.

The forest was old, shaggy with moss and knotted together with vines of many sorts. The sky appeared from time to time, seeming distant and impossibly blue, but that allowed her to keep her bearings with brief glimpses of the sun. When she came at last to a shelf of rock at the foot of a cliff, she paused and examined the place with care.

Her badly needed supplies would be safe there, she thought, while she returned along her trail, obliterating its traces. But first she must rest and eat, for though her strength had returned in her years in the City, she had never regained her old vigor.

She laid a part of the pack cover tidily over the rock and set out a bit of nut-bread and a piece of dried fruit. Sitting in the cool shade of the cliff, she ate before leaning back to rest her weary limbs.

She sat in a small nook eaten by time and weather into the face of the rotted stone. The arm curving away to the south was layered rock, the courses as even as if laid by an expert mason, but between those rocky plates the soil had weathered away, leaving narrow crevices. As she gazed up the wall, she realized that many eyes observed her from the shelter of those slits.

She closed her own eyes for a moment, and when they opened again she could see small furry creatures of many kinds lurking in the crannies. A fennik lay flat, panting in the heat of midday, and above him were two round-eyed creatures, the like of which Moonlight had never seen before. Their small mouths were pursed as if to whistle, and they never glanced away for a moment from their intent watch on this intruder into their homeplace.

She closed her eyes again and slipped into a light doze, though some part of her remained alert. She no longer had the protection of her Gift; instead she must rely on her senses and her wits.

The soft rustle of scales on stone woke her. Some sense told her a serpent coiled within reach, and she opened her eyes slowly, slanting her gaze to right and left without turning her head. In the crack extending the length of the shelf, just to her left, there was a dark body, which was still moving out of its doorway toward her knee and the hand lying upon it.

The mottled shape was blue-black, stippled with a sickly gray-green, and she recognized the markings of the karet, eater of eggs and young, poisoner of larger prey when it took the fancy. Its fangs held death, and she remained frozen in place, her gaze fixed on its lazily rippling length.

The arrow-shaped head moved toward her knee, touched the tough fabric of her breeches, moved down her leg to her ankle, the forked tongue quivering rapidly as it examined this unexpected obstacle. Sweating, the Dreamer watched as the reptile raised its head, tongue tasting the air for danger, and slid over her boot and away down into the mulch of the forest floor.

A great sigh burst from her, and she realized she had held her breath all that time. Now, shaking with reaction, she breathed deeply, bringing her muscles and nerves under control. She must go back and erase her trail. No matter what happened, it must be done!

But it was hard—very hard!—to step off the rock into the rough footing of the forest. Any dead branch or pile of drifted leaves left from other years might hide a karet or something worse. She set her foot solidly onto the crunchy soil and moved away from her pack.

* * * * * *

It took the rest of the day to brush away the traces of her passing. Moonlight used the dead, leaf-laden top of a fallen branch, swishing it so the breeze of its passing blew leaves and dust and other debris over the swath left by her dragging pack. When she was done, it would have taken a better forester than those who lived by the sea to follow her.

When she came again to the cliff, the sun was setting, but she did not consider camping there. The karet would come again, and she did not intend to be there when he did. She rigged a line to a treetop high above the cliff top, throwing a weighted end until it caught in the branches. Then, using the doubled rope, she hauled her equipment up and managed to make it swing until she could dump it on solid ground. After that it was easy to use the line to help her climb the layered rock.

By the time she was beside her belongings, it was fully dark, and she blessed, once again, the thoughtful soul who had provided the lightglass. Even though the oil inside would soon be used up, it had served her well.

The night was so warm she considered sleeping on the ground cloth, but her months of travel the winter before had warned her not to trust the weather. Shaking with exhaustion, she found a suitable spot and tied down her protective flap to four young fir trees, laying her ground cloth and her blankets beneath it.

She had no strength left for cooking, and she again ate the bread and fruit, though she knew she must provide herself with meat, if she was to have the energy to survive here. At the bottom of the packs were small items of great value to one alone in the wilderness. Strips of leather, thongs and strings, metal loops and lengths of wire—all of those would serve to make traps, when the time came.

But now she must rest. She slipped off her boots and crawled under the shelter, listening to the rising note of wind in the tops of the trees. There was no way to see the sky, but she had the feeling that a storm was brewing, out to sea, and she was glad she had come so far inland. Even at such a distance, she could hear the boom of waves against the groins of rock that thrust out from shore, and she shivered to think of the wind and rain to come. She was too tired to deal with more stress, she thought, as her eyes closed.

Moonlight woke to a crack of thunder that brought her sitting upright under the flap. The trees holding it in place were bent under the wind, and lightning flashed so continuously she could see the forest in black and silver flashes. Her packs were under the trees and she crawled out and dragged them beneath the canvas, securing them under the groundsheet and sitting on top of everything to hold it down.

The wind, which had been moving through the treetops before, now was whipping everything violently, and she lay flat again, holding to the ground with fingers that dug frantically into the soil. One of the fir trees broke with a crash, but her rope held; the stub flipped madly at its end while the canvas cracked and snapped overhead.

Even the ground seemed to vibrate with the force of wind and thunder and rain, which now began pounding down in slanting sheets. It drove under the flap and drenched her to the skin.

She lay with her cheek in a runnel, her hands clenched in the soil, her toes locked on the other side of her pile of possessions. Never in all her life had Moonlight felt so lonely, so helpless, so much at the mercy of the uncontrolled elements. Even when she walked in the North, risking the wrath of Dinorm and the Mover, she had felt more able to deal with the world about her.

The storm raged, and the night seemed endless. Instead of slacking, the wind increased. Now she began hearing crashing roars as one or another of the ancient trees gave way at last, its roots loosening from the soil it had gripped for centuries. She knew if one fell here she was lost, and she hoped devoutly that those trees bending over her sleeping place would hold firm.

The sky grew almost imperceptibly lighter, and she could see, when she risked opening an eye, a pewter sky when treetops whipped aside. She lay now in gritty mud, her groundsheet soaked, her flap useless for protection, although the stout canvas and the new ropes still held, and the fir stub still flapped on its line.

When the wind died at last, she could hardly stand, but she forced herself up by rising on hands and knees and then catching one of the young trees to finish the task. All about her the forest looked beaten and tattered. A wide expanse of sky to eastward showed where one of the forest giants had fallen in the night, opening the ground beneath to air and sun.

A dead bird lay at the foot of the nearest large tree, dashed to its death by the wind. Fragments of wood and leaf were strewn everywhere, and she found bits even between her teeth, though she had thought to keep her mouth tightly shut during the worst of the storm.

Moonlight looked up into the heavy tree-crown above her head. Glints of sunlight shone in its uppermost layers, glittering brightly in coins of light on the new-washed leaves. She was alive. Her equipment, though wet, was intact. She had food, although she knew she must soon find a permanent place to set up a shelter and a trap line.

It took most of the morning to unpack and string out to dry her clothing and other necessities. Dipping her kettle into a pool held by the curving roots of a great oak, she washed her gritty hair and her clothing, waiting naked as both dried in the freshly minted sunshine.

By late afternoon most of her things had dried, and she was able to find enough tinder beneath the bark on the undersides of old deadfall to kindle a fire. She boiled a kettle of mint tea, and the fragrant steam made her feel a bit more human, though she knew that tomorrow she must move one last time.

There was one consolation for that storm, she decided, staring into the coals of her fire as she lay on her groundsheet, her back propped against her blanket rolls. It must have washed away any trace of her passing that she had left in the forest. No searcher from the City could possibly find her now.

Even a Turnig, wise tracker and forest expert though it might be, could not find her, she felt certain. As the thought touched her mind, she glanced up and went still.

Again, eyes were watching her from cover. Bright, dark eyes set in round furred faces. A pair of Turnig stared at her from beyond her blaze, their expressions wary and alert, and in their hands she saw well crafted lances with metal tips.

Even as she wondered, she realized that their trials in Damaria must have sent many clans of the small people fleeing to the west, out of range of the New People who had seized power in their old homeland. Their skilled hands, instead of creating gardens in small clearings in the forest and sculptures and paintings in deep burrows, had been turned to making weapons with which to defend themselves from harm.

They were a wise people. She smiled wearily, holding up a hand in a sign that long ago had meant peace.

If they understood, there was no indication of it. Without a sound, the pair vanished before her eyes, as if melting into the dimness of the twilight.

Moonlight lay flat and stared upward into the trees above. At least they had not killed her. That was something.

She knew that tomorrow she must go about her business as usual, packing everything handily, dragging the heavy burdens deeper into the forest. She would find a place and make a home there.

If the Turnig returned, she would make them welcome, for she had come to love the small people dearly, in that long trek that took her away from Damaria. But if they did not come, she would not allow it to trouble her mind.

She had endured, Moonlight knew, almost as much as she could. Anything more, once she allowed herself to relax from this new trial, would shatter her into tiny bits that would blow away on the wind.

CHAPTER FIFTY

"...for there are forces greater than are we...."
—Riddle

The storm that had taken the *Refuge* out of its original course had flung it far south of its intended route. It would require months, possibly, to find the islands for which they had set out. Garlock, a master navigator, took bearings, did esoteric calculations, and derived from those a position and a course, and Gorghoz could only marvel at his ingenuity. The Goremin did not do such mathematical wonders.

Instead, they studied the world about them, the tales of travelers, the records of their most ancient people. He had been a scholar among scholars, and his store of knowledge was great, even for his kind. The motions of stars and planets were recorded in his memory, the fluctuations of the crust of this world. The brief histories of men and the Ancient Race and the beings evolved from animals by selective breeding and the force of the Sealed Flame were only a footnote to his encyclopedic information.

Now, standing on the deck and staring into the horizon of swells and shadows, Gorghoz was thinking of the things he had seen on that island, now left far behind, even allowing for their constant tacking against the wind. That worm had been the kindred of Orm and Dinorm. Its physical power had been tremendous, but it had shown none of the subtle influence on the minds of lesser beings that its counterparts had displayed in the east.

He felt a touch on his elbow and turned to find the poet standing beside him, holding lightly to the rail to steady against the bucking of the deck. Riddle looked thoughtful, and the Goremin now knew him well enough to guess what passed in his mind.

"So what was that thing beneath the island? How did it survive, surrounded by water, which we know its kind dislikes? Why did it not warp our minds, as its cousin did those of the New People in

Damaria? I have been thinking hard about that. I believe I have formed an hypothesis."

"I thought you might," said Riddle. "Come and sit in the bow beside Lute and Chark and tell us what you think."

They made their way forward, the sails slapping above them as the ship came about to the northeast tack. Taking his place on the scrubbed deck, Gorghoz lifted Lute onto his furry lap, and stroked the child's dark curls as he began his tale.

"My people have recorded things concerning the world about them for longer than you children can imagine. The very mountains above Damaria came into being in the mid-life of my race. The oceans lay in different beds and in different configurations in the lifetimes of scholars who wrote of them in the oldest books of my kind.

"So I know the island behind us—or the island that used to lie there—may once have been a part of a land-mass much like the one we left. The worm may well have been forced back and back, until it was trapped beneath the ocean, coiled about that one bit of dry earth thrust up into the air and the sunlight."

"But that must have been so long ago, it is unthinkable," Riddle said. "And we know the Litati lived in Damaria within the lifetimes of your own ancestors. Surely such a movement of lands and waters must be too distant in time to involve any creation of those strange people."

"Who is to say how long the Litati lived upon this world? And who is to say that somewhere they may still not live, working their strange wills upon living matter, recording their activities upon those crystalline plates we found in their city?"

Chark shivered and leaned against the poet. "Small people fear such. Cannot understand, cannot see," she whispered.

"Bigger people than you cannot understand it," the poet said, patting her furry shoulder.

"No one understands. We can only guess," Gorghoz said. He settled Lute more comfortably against his great chest, and looked down into the boy's brown eyes, now wide with interest.

"Perhaps Damaria was only the latest of the places where the Litati have lived and worked. If they began their lives in the west, distant in both time and space from our lands, working eastward slowly, slowly, as the aeons rolled past, that would explain much.

"They may, even now, be settled into one of the countries east of the mountains that are my home, doing their inscrutable work among those savage warriors who used to come against the City in the Mist. Certainly those have not troubled the Sealords for a very long time, and this might explain that quiet among the easterners."

Lute squirmed to get down, and he released the boy, who dashed across the deck to hurl himself into a huddle of small Turnig. Riddle smiled, turning to face Gorghoz, and released Chark's small hand.

"I go watch," she said. "Small ones, they play, they forget hungry ocean down there."

Once they were alone, Riddle nodded, his expression thoughtful. "It may be you are correct, my friend. That thing back there may well be a lingering child of those elder folk, and somewhere they may be creating more. "Could it be..."—he sat straighter and his eyes brightened—"...that this, being an older version, did not possess the skills that Orm and Dinorm have? This would explain much. And what if somewhere to the east there is another version of the Worms, more powerful, more skilled yet?" He shuddered and stood to catch the rail and stare eastward as if dreading what he might see.

But Gorghoz, leaning against a bale, shook his head. Something told him, down where the instinctive wisdom of his people lived, that the Litati were wiser than this.

"No, I think Orm and Dinorm were mistakes. It may be they were the reason for the flight of their creators, for we found no other sign of disaster or disease. The Litati simply left the lands where they had lived for ages, leaving behind the worm that has plagued us since.

"Would they, pushed out of their homes by Dinorm, have made that same mistake again? I think not. Enigmatic they may be. Unguessable their motives undoubtedly are, but none has ever called them stupid."

* * * * * * *

Riddle thought often about that conversation as the ship struggled northward against a persistent headwind. The power of the Shaper and his master, distant though they might be, was the cause of the contrary winds, he felt certain, as they had been the cause of the storm that sent the *Refuge* into the realm of that remote cousin of the Worm.

The logic of Gorghoz was impeccable. It was somehow comforting to believe that another scourge was not being invented and nurtured in lands beyond his reach. There were enough problems in the here and now.

The sprung seams, mended as well as possible while the ship

was careened on the island, were now being strained again by the constant buffeting of wind and waves. They changed the set of sails, tacked to gain against the wind, league after league, moving ahead one league, perhaps, for every ten traveled back and forth across the wind-driven waters.

The Turnig were seasick, many of them, huddled in their cramped quarters in miserable balls of fur. The bilges were awash, and constant pumping was necessary to keep the vessel from growing too sluggish to handle. As the days passed, everyone able took turns at pumping or at tending the sick, and even Riddle grew doubtful that his charges would ever reach the western islands.

The calm, when it came, was a relief for a time. The ship rocked, becalmed, on a pewter sea whose ripples moved past in oily-smooth sequence, reflecting the spars and lipping against the hull. Again Riddle sat in the bow beside the Goremin and Garlock, whose work, for the time, was at a standstill.

"Better this than the wind," sighed the poet.

But the seaman shook his head. "Even with the wind, we moved toward our goal," he said. His fingers, ever busy, whittled a bit of wood into a fanciful figure for Lute. "While we sit here resting, we drift slowly on the current, which bears us to the south and west, rather than to the north and west as we wish to go. We are losing distance, even as we speak, yet there is nothing that can be done."

"Towing...," Riddle began, but Garlock shook his head.

"The men are exhausted, and the little people are sick. Look at their fur, Master. They are beginning to look dull and patchy, and that is a sign of sickness in furred creatures. Their eyes are glazed, and many cough.

"No, there are none of us, even you and I, who are able to pull at the oars of the longboats for hours at a watch, towing this heavy hull northward and west. And if we could, we would barely overcome the drift, and would more than likely remain in place."

"Then we must do something else," said Riddle, feeling inside himself a surge of impatience and a hint of a notion. Even as he began to speak, a plan was forming in his mind.

"We have no great powers, such as our enemies possess. We cannot even create illusion, as the Dreamer once could do. But we are strong and intelligent people, and our wills lack nothing, though our bodies have been overtaxed. Let us join our wills against the ocean and the winds. Let us envision gusts from the south, puffing out the canvas of our sails. Let us force this craft toward its goal, however it can be done. Are you willing to try?"

Garlock, practical man that he was, looked dubious, but

Gorghoz smiled, his toothy square of mouth looking even more forbidding than usual. Killeli, somewhat recovered, nodded briskly and rose to stand at the rail. Chark, beyond him, gave a chittering cry, and those Turnig who had come on deck began to gather about the group in the bow.

"Bring up all those below. It is better to be out in the fresh air than below in the stink of sickness. We will join our wills together, however long it takes, and force the winds to obey us." Riddle felt better than he had in many days, as he waited for the group to gather.

Surely so many wills, focused toward a common goal, could work some sort of magic upon the world. It was, after all, solely by will that the Worms did their work. What one being might use, another might learn to use.

When the entire complement sat on the deck, crowded together and waiting quietly for whatever might come next, he explained again what he intended to try. There was a rustle of interest. Dull eyes brightened. Small mutterings of talk stilled as he went on.

"Now think, my friends. Think of the sails up there billowing as a south breeze freshens. Think of the *Refuge* moving again, north and west, toward our goal. Together, all of us, we can do this. Close your eyes and think!"

He dropped to sit between Gorghoz and Killeli, closing his own eyes, forcing his mind to picture those sails filled with wind, the hull sliding smoothly through the waves. For hours they sat together, and Riddle found sweat puddling beneath him on the polished deck. His head ached with effort, and he felt as if he had, indeed, been pulling at those oars all day, towing the ship that had not moved except to drift.

Darkness fell, but no one stirred, and even the youngsters did not call for food. Everyone still focused upon their goal. About them the vessel creaked and groaned, and only the sound of the bilge pumps, manned by sequences of teams, interrupted the silence of the night.

Head bursting with pressure, eyes burning behind closed lids, Riddle strained still to force the winds to his will. Nothing happened, except the changes of shifts at the pumps. Lute lay asleep in the Goremin's lap, and Turnig were tumbled this way and that as they had succumbed to weariness. But many still held fast, hoping and wishing and willing with everything they possessed.

Sometime before midnight, a breeze touched Riddle's damp cheek. A line flapped, and a pulley groaned as the sails began to swell with wind.

Riddle, feeling limp and drained, looked up to see the sails bellying black against the black sky. Beneath him the ship began to move, slowly at first, and then with greater speed, until the *Refuge* was surging ahead toward their goal.

CHAPTER FIFTY-ONE

"The forest is a house of many rooms...."
—Riddle

The morning after the storm dawned glitteringly bright. Moonlight woke and stared off into the treetops across the space where the tree had fallen. The leaves were not yet withering on the downed giant, but she knew that before noon the relentless sun would begin its work. She wondered how many other great trees had gone down in the wind, as well as how much they would impede her progress deeper into the forest.

However, she must go, whatever the difficulty, for she was determined to settle herself into some sort of order before autumn passed and winter bore down upon the countryside again. If she intended to survive, she must have a shelter and she must augment the supplies she had been given.

She had a distaste for killing game, but her body demanded food, and roots and herbs would not provide all the sustenance she needed. She would go until she found something that could be formed into a hut, and then she would hunt out the area for places in which to set her traps.

Sighing, she rose and packed her gear carefully, reducing the size of her burdens as much as possible. As she checked out her route eastward, away from the coast, she realized the downed tree might offer help, and she broke off a spreading limb with its fan of leaves. Tying her packs onto the raying branches, she found she could drag the entire thing, leaving only a disturbance in the mulch and the bushes that did not hint at human passage at all.

She padded the cord saved out of one pack with some of the extra clothing, in order to save her shoulders from injury, and started away, angling north of east. The going was rough, for the soil beneath the ages of deadfall was spongy with wet, and vines and brush caught her ankles and her trailing cargo. Before noon she was hot and weary.

The day was a nightmare of effort and sweat, and she stopped for the night, and did not even try to build a fire to prepare hot food. She nibbled again at bread and fruit and a strip of dried meat, before falling into exhausted slumber.

When she woke again, she found herself wondering if someone had visited her camp in the night. Her things were disturbed—not obviously, but as if careful hands had sorted through her equipment and replaced it almost exactly as they found it.

This both disturbed and reassured her. If the searcher had meant her harm, she would be dead. As it was, she knew, whatever the motive, that midnight visitor did not intend to kill or injure her.

* * * * * * *

Before mid-afternoon, Moonlight found her new home. Another bastion of stone rose in the forest, this one solid and smooth. Granite, she thought, though she was no expert at identifying rocks. Against it, a gigantic beech had fallen to form a sort of lean-to, the branches on the down-side dug deeply into the ground to form a skeletal framework.

This was no new-fallen tree, for it was quite dead, the wood hardened with weather. The trunk's diameter was twice her height, forming a solid roof, and she knew she could weave limber branches and vines between the downward limbs, once she had removed those beneath that cluttered the area, and coat the entire "wall" with mud.

Behind her would be a sheer cliff some ten man-heights tall, down which only a foolhardy enemy would come. In the front of the stone face was a fluted cleft rising to the top of the cliff. She could build her fireplace there, safely walled with rocks on its outer edge.

For the first time in a long while, Moonlight smiled. She had always longed, in one part of her heart, to live alone in the woods, away from the demands of those who came to the doors of Dreamers for help and comfort. Now, strangely, painfully, through turmoil and terror, she had found her wish fulfilled.

Her feeling for Riddle she had put out of her mind, for there was no gain in regrets for possibilities lost. Her worry over the group who sailed west was fruitless. They would live or die on their own, and her worry would not aid them.

No, she would live as a creature of the forest, every day with its own problem or solution, every dawn a fresh beginning. She would forget the old days of Dreams. She would wall away in a secret place that terrible journey she had made with the refugees from

Damaria.

Moonlight would become an animal, thoughtless and without apprehension, living to and for herself. But even as she thought it, she felt saddened. It was not the way her people were trained. That was not the nature of her kind.

At the very bottom of the largest pack, Moonlight had found a small hatchet, put there by some knowing and sympathetic hand. Now she blessed her unknown benefactor still again, as she slipped between ribbed branches to stand beneath that fallen beech. Hacking away, she cleared space to work, but she found she must make a door through which to drag out the downed limbs. Once that was done, she kept her working area clean, and the grinding chore of chopping out the unwanted wood crutching between the tree-bole and the ground could go forward.

She camped against the granite but outside her proposed shelter, for it would require days of toil to clear an area sufficient for her needs. Anxious though she was to make her home tight and habitable, she knew she must not neglect her other needs. Her traps must be built and her snares set for hares and other small animals. Her store of firewood must begin to grow, even before the fireplace in which she would burn it was built. The discarded branches formed the beginning of her fuel supply.

There were predators, she knew, in the forest. The Groundbear, although infrequently found, was a real danger if one went too near his burrow. The red-furred cat craved flesh, and it did not care what sort it might be. Reptiles abounded, some poisonous, some not, though the bite of any of them could cause infection and death.

With these things in mind, she saved the biggest and straightest of the branches she cut away and laid them together, piling them as a barrier about her camp, with the cliff forming a solid wall behind. She built a fire pit in a crack of the stone and arranged her possessions so they would be protected from damp, far enough from her blaze to prevent random sparks from igniting anything.

This took a day and an evening, and though her thoughts kept turning toward house-building, she kept her attention sternly on her necessary duties. In the night, lying in a darkness lit only fitfully by glimpses of stars above the restless treetops, she found herself listening, listening, for any secretive footfall, any cautious approach by a predator.

Leaves rustled in the breeze overhead. The dead leaves underfoot crackled as some small burrower plowed along in search of grubs or insects. Distantly, a night bird called its silvery cry, and another answered almost directly above her.

There was nothing menacing in the night. She felt outward cautiously, all her wounded Dreamer's nerves shrinking from the attempt, but there was nothing there to answer her demand. All was lost, with her youth and her innocence, in that terrible battle with Dinorm and his lackey.

She breathed deeply, relaxing toes, legs, hips, torso, shoulders, arms, face. That was the way. Yes. She might sleep now.

Drifting, she heard with the edge of her consciousness the soft chittering talk in the undergrowth about her camp. Ah. The Turnig were there, watching her.

They had not harmed her before. Now their presence might well protect her from others not so well disposed toward intruders into the forest. Reassured, Moonlight turned on her side and slept.

* * * * * * *

In a handful of days of hard labor, she found herself well along in her preparations for life in the forest. The underside of the beech was now cleared of stubs, and the best of the material cut out of it was laid aside for other uses. Already she had her walls formed of interwoven vines and limber branches cut from trees downed in the recent storm. Her fireplace was built, and she slept, now, before her own hearth.

Sometimes she woke in the night, listening, and heard the soft sounds of Turnig moving about her house. It had been their hands, careful and curious, that had examined her possessions before, she was almost certain. She had no objection, for she thought they might have searched for weapons possibly to be used against them.

People who had been hunted for their fur had good reason to be cautious. She had suffered enough at the hands of the New People and their master Lorbek to feel sympathy for their fears.

Waking in the morning, she felt renewed purpose. Once she was settled, everything in order, perhaps those elusive little people would approach her. She missed Chark and her kindred, and she knew having Turnig as neighbors was far better than having any of the New Men nearby.

Once her snares were set along the faint runs of the small beasts, she began supplementing her diet with fresh meat. As there was no way of preserving such light flesh, she took only what she needed, freeing the other captives to go about their business. Her other traps, formed of cord and metal from her supplies, as well as limber withes cut from willows along the nearby stream, were set in the water.

Fish were plentiful, and she climbed the cliff and set up a drying rack on top of the rock, full in the sun and over a smoky fire, where her catch was dried for the winter. She must, she knew, hunt for heavier meat, and once her walls were daubed heavily with mud, she set out to supply that need.

A bow could be made easily from a downed ash. Arrows were easily formed, but sharpening them with the hatchet and the aid of a rough stone was not easy. Fletching them accurately with bird feathers she found in the forest was difficult as well.

She practiced with her weapons until she had developed fair skill, but she knew the horned beasts would be too large for her primitive weapons to bring down. With metal arrow points it could be done, but with wood that was not likely.

She hunted, instead, for the wild goats that roamed the forest, and as she wandered the trails, now roofed by tree-crowns of amber and gold and russet, she also located other game. There was a round, gruff-voiced creature she had never seen before. A third the size of a Groundbear, it looked something like that beast, although its fur was a different color.

Those were unwary and very stupid, and she found their flesh dried readily over her smoldering drying fire. Burdened with such a kill, she moved through the forest late one afternoon, and found herself face to face with a furry man.

She had not known any of the kind survived in Damaria, and she dropped her prey and held out both hands in a sign of welcome. She had learned something of the private language of that sort from Killeli, and she ventured to greet him.

"*K'aki letiko viga,*" she said, watching his face closely.

Although he had been tensed to run, the furred person paused, staring at her in astonishment. She wondered if he might be one of those wild ones whose stock had been the basis for the breeding program resulting in Killeli and his kind. Yet he looked too much like Killeli to be anything other than a true product of the work of the Ancient Ones.

He set down the bundle of sticks he carried, and approached her cautiously, studying her face, her clothing, and her weapons with wary interest. At last he nodded.

"You are Dreamer," he said in the odd, light voice of his kind. "From Damaria? I thought all were killed there, of your kind."

For the first time, Moonlight admitted to herself how she had missed the sound of another voice, the contact with another mind. Having found this fellow refugee, she determined not to lose him, if possible.

"Yes, a Dreamer, though injured so I can no longer Dream. Would you come with me to my house? I have more meat here than I can use tonight. We might eat and talk, for I am lonely in the forest." She hoped he would be tempted, for fresh company if nothing else, to accept her offer.

The spidery body relaxed, and the face grimaced into a smile. He, too, she thought, had been lonely.

She stooped to lift her game. When she stood straight again, he had resumed his burden of dry wood and stood ready to accompany her.

A great weight seemed lifted from her heart as she moved beside the furred person toward her new home. They would talk the night away, she knew, and when he left she would know a friend lived in the forest. Perhaps, after a time, the Turnig would learn that they also could trust this newcomer to their wood, and she would have other friends as well.

CHAPTER FIFTY-TWO

"After long wanderings we come home to rest."
—Riddle

The south wind, once roused by the wills of the travelers, seemed willing to continue without flagging. The *Refuge* forged ahead, its bow dipping into the rolling waters, lacy foam frilling along its sides. For many weeks it sped on its way, each day bringing it nearer its goal. And at last the scent of land told its passengers they were drawing very near indeed.

Riddle stood in his usual spot in the bow, staring ahead as the sails snapped and the pulleys creaked above his head. There in the northwest should lie the ancient refuge of his kind, those Western Islands that had received his kin for so many millennia.

The clean salt wind fluttered his hair from behind, and he breathed deeply, to scent the land that must lie beyond the silver-blue line of the horizon. A seabird swooped above the foremast, its thin cry sounding lonely and forlorn, and he looked up as the pale gray shape wheeled upward and away. That was a species that remained near land. The islands must be just over the horizon.

Chark, at his elbow, touched his side and pointed toward the edge of the sky. Pale ripples of wave rolled toward them from what seemed to be a bank of mist, and Riddle stared hard at the cloudy patch.

"Smell land!" said the Turnig. "Hear bird; listen!"

Then he, too, heard the shrilling of many seabirds as they wheeled around the clouded island that now became a pinpoint on the horizon. Turning aft, he cried, even as the lookout began to shout, "Land ahead!"

Garlock came to stand beside him, peering into the mists as they forged toward the fog bank. "This is always a very bewildering passage," he said. "You cannot see ahead or on either hand, and there are tall rocks thrusting up from the ocean that loom unexpectedly and make your heart stop with fright."

"I had no idea the approach was so dangerous," Riddle said. "My people avoid endangering Visitors, usually. We even hate hurting enemies."

Garlock laughed as he turned back to the steersman. Riddle, following, touched his arm. "Why do you laugh? It seems less than amusing to me."

"No legitimate visitor ever comes to harm here," Garlock said. "Some force controlled by your people on the islands guides unerringly any vessel allowed to enter the fog bank and the maze of rocks. I have heard that a pirate vessel from the far southwest once tried to force a passage. Only a single survivor was found, days later, clinging to a stone, whimpering strange words of phantoms and fear. Without guidance, no one passes here."

That seemed like his people, Riddle thought. He stood behind the steersman now, watching curls of mist explore the deck, finger the sails, damp the hair and fur of those above decks. On the foredeck, the auburn curls of Oakbeam's beard, Nilda's hair, and their sons' flaming locks caught the moisture and the fitful light.

The first monolith appeared like a wraith, draped in fog and black with threat. It frightened even Riddle, though the prow slid past smoothly, well clear of the ragged claws of broken stone. The Poet felt his heart cramp and ease as the obstacle came and went.

There was a light touch at his elbow. "Is place, yes?" asked Chark's small voice. He reached to pat her fur, which was beaded with damp. "This is, indeed, the place. If family tales are true, there lies one of the islands where a few of my kind live. It is grown up with great trees and many plants. I believe it may be much like the Forest Damariste."

Lute, beyond the Turnig, chortled softly in his throat, and Riddle reached to tousle his hair. It had been a long and terrible journey. Those left behind were a constant source of worry, but surely these new arrivals in the west were safe now, sheltered against any harm from the eastern continent.

His small nephew would live for thousands of years. In time, when he was grown, would he and others return to Damaria to take control there, where the new People had done inestimable damage to the developing species? Riddle sighed and gazed ahead eagerly.

The *Refuge* was nosing through a tangle of stony outcroppings, long natural jetties that ran like the spines of lizards above the level of the water, constantly lapped by waves. The oily wash of water about the hull and the slapping of waves against the rock created the only sounds in a world suddenly gone silent. The seabirds that had wheeled about the ship had not followed it into the mist. Those aboard did not speak, for there was a feeling of tension among them. Riddle knew, for it held his own breath taut in his throat.

An hour passed, two, three, and still they plowed through the rock-studded maze, blinded by fog, held by the fear and wonder of that journey. The steersman seemed moved by the wheel, rather than controlling it, and Lute climbed into Riddle's arms and nestled against his shoulder as they watched. Chark huddled into the tail of his cloak, her furry shape solid and warm against the poet's hip.

Something seemingly as large as the stones approached. In the eerie light, Gorghoz was a terrifying sight, featureless and huge against the background of foggy sky and misty sea. "We are almost there," he said, his voice soft, almost a sigh to match the moving waters. "It seemed, for a time, that we would not arrive at all, Poet. And we left behind....," but he didn't finish the sentence.

Riddle shivered. He, too, thought of Moonlight, left behind in the City in the Mist. Safe as she must be with Egon and Blade watching over her, it was a pain in his heart that she did not stand here with them, watching for some break in the dimness.

However long he lived, Riddle would always feel drawn toward the east, wondering how she fared and if she still lived. He felt as if he watched for her, as well as himself, staring ahead. Then he saw a glimmer of gold shimmering in the distance. He reached to take Gorghoz's hand, feeling Lute rouse and sit up in the crook of his other arm. Chark tugged at his cloak.

"We're coming out of it," said Garlock to the steersman. "Come to port. Easy now. Head for the point."

They emerged into a blinding blaze of sunlight, leaving the gray reaches behind them. Ahead sparkled a long beach frilled with lacy waves that rolled in and retreated rhythmically. A point of land thrust from the mainland, and the *Refuge* headed for that, driven by a light breeze that seemed to exist only within the ring of mist around the islands.

Riddle lifted Lute high, as they rounded the point and saw the harbor, with the city rising up the long slopes beyond it. The place was busy with small vessels, fishermen's craft, mainly, with a single great sailing ship that seemed to be offloading cargo alongside the largest dock. As he watched, a small boat, manned by eight oarsmen, shot off from the shore, headed for their ship.

"The inspector," said Garlock. "He always checks our cargo, our manifests, and any passengers intending to disembark. He is going to be surprised, this time. Watch—there he comes."

With neatness and speed, the cockleshell raced to the ship, came about precisely, and one of the sailors caught the ladder dropped over the side. A slight fellow with gingery braids wrapped about his ears popped over the railing. Riddle's heart came into his throat. This was one of the Dreamer kind, or he had lost his wits.

The cat-slitted eyes noted everyone on deck in one comprehensive glance. "Captain Garlock," he said, "not your usual vessel, Sir, nor your ordinary complement." Then he looked again at Riddle and his nephew, who were standing quietly behind the Captain, waiting to be recognized.

The fellow gasped, caught himself, and came with feline grace to stand before the poet. "It is always good to see another of your kind come west," he said. He glanced down at the tally-sheet held in the crook of his arm. "Your name, for the records? And your companions' names, if you will."

Riddle smiled. "Riddle, Poet of Damaria." he said, "and his nephew Lute. We are the last of the line of Kings of Damaria, save only our Uncle Blade and our cousins Silk and Wonder, who live in the City in the Mist. Bear to my kind in the city this word: we are refugees, homeless, driven from the lands we know. We beg their patience, as we seek a place here, for we are many and include Turnig, a furred man, one of the Goremin, and Sealords who desire sanctuary from those who now plague the eastern continent."

Oakbeam and his sons, trailed by Nilda, came aft and the shipbuilder greeted the inspector. "Mellet," he cried, taking the Dreamer's hands. "Little did I think, when you went west from the City, that I would meet you again so soon."

The young Dreamer smiled, his lips flattening into their characteristic catlike curve. "If you arrive with Oakbeam and Nilda, you are welcome indeed," he said to the poet. "We lack skilled builders now, since those who emigrated earlier have grown old. We have never had a Poet, they tell me. I will carry glad news back to my masters."

He saluted Garlock blithely. "Dock at the Butterfly Docks, Garlock, and I will have someone there to guide your complement to quarters in the city. " He slid over the side to land with a thump in the craft below. Soon it was skimming back across the harbor, as the *Refuge* made its way toward the dock he had indicated.

Amid the bustle of preparation for anchoring, the securing of sail, the anxious working into position, Riddle kept silent. It was good to find a Dreamer here. He hoped, when he came to shore, that he would also find kinsmen who might counsel him. Surely they would take the education of Lute in hand and make of him the king he should become, whether or not he ever returned to his homeland.

He caught the child up and, with Chark still clinging to his cloak and Gorghoz stalking grandly ahead, the Poet of Damaria set his feet at last upon the land toward which he had strained every effort for so long.

Before he could look about for guidance, someone came through the crowd of sailors and dockhands, onlookers and newly arrived Turnig, and caught him in a close embrace. "My blessing upon you, Poet," said a thin voice. He pushed away to look at the fragile old man, his face marked with the bony structure of the Ancient Race.

Riddle felt a surge of excitement and disbelief. Could this possibly be Granite, the father of his father?

"Grandfather?" he asked, knowing the reply. "How wonderful to meet you at last! King Armor and my Uncle Blade spoke of you, longing to know how you fared, once you set out for the west so many long years ago. The King of Damaria complained that your letters had grown so infrequent that he feared for your continued health. But now I know you have fared very well indeed."

Again the ancient hugged him, wrapping long thin arms about both Riddle and Lute. When he released them at last, he beckoned. "Come with me," he said. "My house is large. Most of your companions may shelter there until we find more permanent quarters for them.

"There are many kinds in the city who will be happy to host the Turnig. Never did I think to see one of those small people, for they became wise only after I departed from the east. Only through letters from my sons did I learn of them, over the centuries of their development."

Granite moved ahead, pushing his way through the busy throng with ease. When they stood at last on the steps leading up the steep street toward a rank of tall stone houses on the crest of the ridge, Riddle turned to look back. The harbor bustled with business. The sea sparkled under the westering sun. The barrier of fog blurred the horizon to a gray haze.

Riddle raised a hand, half in salute, half in farewell. If Riddle the Poet set sail once more, it would be toward the east, to set in order his lost homeland. But that lay far in the future, when the young King was an adult and when his people had learned all they could of the powers they might face.

Now he could rest, for his people had, at last, come to their new home.

* * * * * * *

The forest dripped with winter. Inside her snug house, before a crackling blaze, Moonlight sat carding the sheddings of Turnig, given her by her small neighbors. A felted cloak made of that material turned water and weather with equal ease. She had learned from Grik, who lived nearest her home, how to form the felt. Now she knew her way into the burrow that small person's family had dug for themselves in this country to which they had fled. Already the burrow was being decorated with new carvings and painted stones.

Moonlight's heart was almost at ease, although all her own kind were lost, along with their old homeland. Though she lived alone, she was not friendless. There were in these forests along the coast many refugees from the slaughter of the Turnig, the furry men, and even the Pazmi. A community of various peoples was forming, and this winter found them in fair condition, cooperating, sharing the things needful for survival.

Most comforting of all was her belief, arrived at suddenly and with total conviction, that her former companions had found refuge at last. One morning she woke with the sure intuition that Riddle had found the harbor he sought. With that worry eased, her transition into this new life was made easier.

There had been searches for her along the coast, of course, as she had expected. She smiled now, fingers busy, as she thought of that. Hidden high in a massive tree, with one of the hairy men, she had watched sailors and guardsmen stumble about, looking into shadows and through thickets, without knowing exactly what they sought or even what they were seeing. The storm had cleared away all trace of her passing, and the other people, warned that there might be a search, had kept well away from that part of the forest along the shoreline.

Arken had accompanied the last seekers, his skinny frame draped in a dun cloak, his face scarlet with rage. Shouting to his men, scrambling about among the rocks or scooting like some ungainly turtle through undergrowth, he had worn himself and his men to rags before giving up at last.

It seemed never to occur to him that she might have hidden deep inside the forest and was surviving there. He was looking for evidence of her death, it was plain from the places he rummaged out in his investigation. Just as well, she thought, laying aside a batch of carded fur and taking up another. He must think her safely dead, for no party had searched in late summer or in the fall.

Now she was secure in her strange little house, surrounded by those who shared her perils and her concerns. In time, she would learn to heal them with hands and herbs, for many were the hurts they sustained in this new country.

Moonlight's gaze turned inward. Riddle was safe, though she had no proof of it. That feeling did not die away but grew stronger by the day. Those she loved and cared for were beyond the reach of Dinorm or Verrainig or Lorbek, and she could set aside her worry.

There came a scratching at her door. She called softly, "Enter."

Grik pushed aside the felt draped over the opening and moved into the warm light, shaking the damp chill from her fur. "Bad day," she grumbled, crouching beside the fire. "Cold weather come now, very quick. You well?"

The former Dreamer smiled, her fingers moving amid the fur in her lap. "I am very well," she said, and nothing within her heart contradicted her words.

EPILOGUE

FAREWELL TO GLEAM

"Death moves behind us, nearer all the while,
and yet he seems a friend more than a foe."
                                        —Riddle the Poet

Lute, youngest heir of the Ancient Race, approached his home slowly, his shoulders slumped, his face a mask of worry. For more than four centuries he had lived on this island to which his uncle Riddle had brought him as a child. They had found friends, kinsfolk, work, and contentment here. Twice Lute had wed, each wife dear to his heart. And each time his kind's longevity had dictated that he must outlive his spouse. Now Gleam, the second, was very ill, and he dreaded what he would find when he entered the great house of Gorghoz, the Goremin, where he lived, along with his uncle and one of his married children.

Yet when he came into her chamber, Gleam managed a smile, her face revealing her pleasure that he had returned. Sitting in their dim bed-chamber, Lute heard his uncle's footsteps climb the stair and a heavier thumping marking the progress of the Goremin into his rooms. Lute leaned forward in his chair and touched Gleam's cheek. She closed her eyes and sighed.

In contrast to her husband, who still appeared to be little more than a stripling, Gleam had aged greatly during the forty years of their marriage. Her downy skin was crumpled like old silk, and her auburn hair was streaked with white. The cat-like pupils of her green-gold eyes focused with some difficulty as Lute lifted her and held a cup of water to her lips.

She sighed heavily as he laid her back on her high-piled pillows. "Will the children come today?" she asked him, her voice thin, as much with sickness as age. "I would like to see our grandchildren. I think...I think it will not be much longer now."

Lute nodded, knowing that she was correct. Never had he known such pain, for when his parents were slain he had been too young to understand. Now he was old enough, mature enough to comprehend just what this loss would mean to him—what such loss had meant to him in the past, as well as to generations of his kindred.

Even now he seemed far younger than his youngest son. With the loss of Gleam, he would become more like his children's sibling—or even their child—than their parent. His grandchildren considered him a young uncle already.

Yet he had lived for most of four hundred years, and his life had not been easy. The things he had learned could have been helpful to his descendants, but he knew that the older they grew, the less they would listen to him. One lesson he had learned was that the short-lived species discounted the words of those who seemed younger than they, whatever their true age or their wisdom.

He watched as Gleam dropped into a deep sleep, her heavy breaths barely raising her chest or fluttering her throat. His own chest grew heavy, and he dropped his face into his hands. The Turnig child who sat on a footstool beside him turned and patted his knee, and he felt vaguely comforted. The small furred people, who had begun their history as animals, had been altered by his kind over millennia to become wise and useful beings.

Lute looked down at him and said, "Chirek, will you go to my son Willem at his house? Tell him that his mother needs to see him. Then call Gerel and Salinda and all the grandchildren. They...they need to hurry, I think."

The little Turnig nodded, his small black eyes, bright in his furred face, turning toward the silent shape on the bed. "I go get," he said. "They come soon."

Willem alone, of all Lute's family, lived separately in one wing of the home of his wife's parents. Flicker was a Dreamer like his mother, and her people loved to live in family groups. Luckily, that house was not far from the home of Gorghoz, and Chirek ran as fast as his short legs would move, as Lute knew he would.

Waiting for his offspring to come, Lute dozed lightly while Gleam was resting. The sounds of small feet on the polished stone floor of the corridor woke him, and by the time Willem's group arrived all the siblings were assembled outside their parents' door.

As Lute joined them, Riddle came down the stair, attracted by the bustle below. Looking into his worried brown eyes, Lute nodded toward the door. His uncle understood, and his expression changed, settling into lines of sorrow. With sudden comprehension, Lute knew how very agonizing had been the loss of their people to his uncle, all those centuries ago. Riddle had tried to become father and mother to his nephew, and he had succeeded better than most could have done.

When the family entered Gleam's sleeping room, even the smallest were quiet and subdued. Going to his wife's side, Lute touched her hand, then her cheek. "Wake, my dearest. The children are here," he murmured into her ear. "Wake, my little Gleam!"

She gave a small moan and opened her eyes. "I dreamed," she said. "I dreamed of my own mother, and she beckoned to me. I am going to her soon, Lute."

Her husband took her hand. "No lovelier companion could you find, beyond the Shadow," he told her. "But now you must rouse yourself and speak with our children. The grandchildren are here, as well, and they are afraid, I think. Only you can reassure them, Gleam."

She aroused her dwindling energies by a deliberate effort of will. She breathed deeply for a moment, and a hint of her normal golden color came into her face. The cat-like eyes brightened with determination as she accepted his help to sit straighter against her pillows.

Then she gestured for their offspring to come to her, and they did, one at a time in the order of their ages. Tall Willem, brown-haired like his father but cat-eyed like his mother, bent over her and kissed her on the forehead.

Flicker followed her husband, and for a moment she gazed into the older Dreamer's eyes. She paused there as something deep but unspoken moved between their Dreamers' minds. Then they clasped their hands together strongly, and Flicker moved aside for Gerel and his wife. Gerel was more like the Ancient Race than his siblings. As he bent over his mother, Lute could see in his son a strong resemblance to Riddle. Salinda, behind him, was very like their mother.

While his young said goodbye to Gleam, Lute slipped from the room, unable to bear the emotions that burdened them all. In the corridor his uncle was waiting for him. Riddle laid a consoling hand on his shoulder. "I know about loss, my boy," he said. "If I could spare you this, I would. If I could have, I would have wed Moonlight, the Dreamer, all those years ago, and would have endured her loss, which would have come all too soon, as you must endure yours. That is the price of being one of the Ancient Race."

Lute nodded, knowing his words were true, but finding no

comfort in them. "It's the children," he said softly. "They are filled with such grief, and I cannot ease it for them. Even if I could, I think they would resent it, for they have begun to consider me a sort of child myself."

To that there was nothing to say. All of their kind had learned to deal with the grim realities of being who and what they were. In the end, it was likely the tension between their kind and its half-blood offspring that had led to the rebellion that brought an end to the Kingdom of Damaria and forced them into their long exile.

"I wonder," Lute mused, half to himself, "what happened to Lorbek, our uncle's half-blood son, after he took control of our homeland. Without the stability you have described, with Turnig, Dreamers, and simian people bearing their parts in creating a skilled work force and a balanced society, he must have found himself relying solely on his own kind."

Riddle shook his head. "Lorbek, in the short time I knew him, seemed to think that because his father was King, he himself must be exempt from any useful work, and was automatically competent to rule. Little did he know of the intricate pattern of skills that made our country exist in peace and plenty."

Lute raised his head. A sound beyond the door brought him around, and Riddle followed him into the outer chamber as he went into his wife's room. Willem, Gerel, and Salinda knelt beside their mother's bed, their hands linked, their heads bowed.

Willem rose as his father came and made room for him to approach the dying Dreamer. "She wants to Dream," he whispered, as Lute sat on the edge of the bed and took his wife's hands.

"My dearest, the effort is too much," he protested. "You will exhaust yourself."

"My time has run away like water, and what little is left must be made to serve my family and my own need," she murmured. "Gather close by my bed. Bring your uncle and our dear Gorghoz and make yourselves comfortable."

She shifted her shoulders. "Raise me higher, and prop me with pillows," she asked him. "I must be able to see...." Her voice trailed away.

Lute arranged her to her satisfaction. Then he made certain that comfortable chairs were placed in an arc, so all the family was near without being crowded. When all was ready, he turned back to Gleam. "It is done, my dear," he said. "For better or for worse, we are ready."

She smiled, her cat-pupiled eyes brightening for a moment with their old fire. "Seldom have I Dreamed in recent years, for Dream is motivated by the needs of people. Here we have been safe, and our needs have been only the small ones of daily life. But now I am going into the farthest land of all, and I must show you that this is nothing to fear but a thing of joyful anticipation."

She drew a deep breath, wearied by such long talk. Then she closed her Dreamer's eyes and her face relaxed.

Lute felt reality shift. He had never really become used to the tangible reality of the Dreamer's art, even though that power had saved his life, when he was small. Now he knew this to be the last gift he could offer to his wife, and he leaned back and waited to see what would form about him.

* * * * * * *

A cool breeze touched his cheek, and he realized that he now sat on a smooth stone overlooking a deep vale that ran down to a misty arm of the sea. The sun was evidently hidden behind the mist, which glowed with brilliant silver light, splashing with brightness the leaves of the low trees and the curves of the rocks about him.

He felt compelled to rise and follow the slight path leading down the slope. At the bottom, he found a narrow stream that rippled over colored stones, and he moved along the path beside it. There flowering trees bent over the water, dropping lavender petals to swirl on the current as jade and emerald frogs leaped away from his steps with bell-like shrieks of alarm.

There was an air of great peace there, and the scents of many blossoms perfumed the breeze. As he drew nearer the sea, the tang of salt tickled his nostrils, and the sound of an incoming tide began to growl on a pebbly beach.

Lute loved the sea, and that had always been the best thing about the islands. Yet this was no beach he had seen in his ramblings. There was a strangeness to the stone, the wind, the plants, and the smell of the air. This was a place beyond the world he knew, where strange things might happen before his wondering eyes.

Silvered by the mist, there were shapes on that beach that looked familiar. A tall one might have been his murdered great-uncle Armor, though the features were masked with droplets that shone in the strange light. Another brought a childhood memory, sharp and sweet, of his mother and father bending down from their great heights to lift him in loving arms. For an instant he smelled the flower scent that his mother had always worn.

The breeze grew stronger, and the mist swirled and eddied,

revealing other figures and then hiding them again. Beyond the beach he could now see vague outlines of dark ships at rest, waiting for the turn of the tide. He knew that one of the ships waited for Gleam. Where would it take her, once she came to join its complement? Were her mother and father aboard, ready to accompany her on her last journey?

He seemed to drift, without walking, toward the water, amid the cries of seabirds echoing from the cliffs. Like a ghost himself, he moved unseen among the tenuous figures on the beach, sometimes shivering as he passed entirely through one of them. He moved onto the water, his feet just above the tops of the waves, to approach the first ship. A banner whipped from its mast, streaming intermittent glimpses of crimson as it blew. The sails were furled against the booms, the lines a web-work of blackness against the pale mist, and the deck was shining with wet.

He felt the approach of a familiar presence, and he turned back toward the vale, where another came in his tracks. Gleam was approaching her end, nearing the ship that would carry her away from him. But as she came the mist cleared away and the changing light turned the sea and the ship and the waiting friends and kindred to gold.

Tears of joy filled Lute's eyes when he saw his wife taken into the arms of her mother and her father as they helped her onto the ship. The sails unfurled, drawn upward into gilded triangles filled with wind that now turned to blow seaward and bore the vessel slowly out to sea.

Lute saw Gleam look up at him as he rose higher and drifted over the deck. He held out his arms as if to seize her, but she was now otherwhere, and they could only smile and move apart.

* * * * * * *

When Lute returned to himself he was still sitting in his chair with his kindred about him. Gleam lay upon the bed, her face quiet and her breath stilled forever.

Willem rose and turned. "We saw. We all were there when the ship sailed, and we saw our mother taken to the lands beyond. She took us with her to say goodbye, and now, though we will miss her sorely, we can never grieve. We will all see her again. Come, Father, and let the Turnig prepare her body for its long rest."

He rose to join his children, and the grandchildren clustered about his knees. "Grandsir, did you see the birds? They were not like our gulls and terns and albatrosses. They were made of gold, with great wide wings that made the air sing as it passed over their feathers. What were they, Grandsir?"

That was Hellie, Salinda's youngest and almost his favorite. He lifted her and carried her along with the group. "Those were magical birds, I think, and we have no names for them. But we may give them a name, if we like. What would you like to call them?"

"The golden Gleam-birds," she said, her small voice carrying across the room. "Our Gran's birds that came to take her home."

A wave of smiles moved from face to face, as children and adults alike responded to her words. Gorghoz spread his hairy arms and said, "Well said, young Hellie. May we all be greeted by golden Gleam-birds when the time comes for us to set sail upon that final sea."

Feeling the solid warmth of the child in his arms and the presence of the others all about him, Lute released his pain and allowed simple grief to take its place. This was only the first of many losses, he knew, and he must not allow it to lessen him or to make him unable to attend to his chosen tasks.

Riddle, at his elbow, must have felt his easing. He spoke quietly into Lute's ear as they went forth from the house to sit on the wide lawn, and look up into the vast branches of the trees that shaded it. Lute sat in one of the white chairs and put Hellie down to run about the grass with her siblings and her cousins. He felt disoriented by the changes that seemed to have come upon him with terrible suddenness, despite Gleam's long illness.

"I am alone," he said to his uncle. "I must recover from that, and I must settle my heart. Who will comfort them while I mend my grief?"

"Do you forget our kindred here? Leaf and Rose and Silver and Flute live here on this island, within easy reach of your young ones. They have lived longer than you and I combined, and the store of wisdom they can consult is almost endless." Riddle paused, then continued, "A time comes when a parent must loose the grasp he holds upon his young. I have not had children of my own, but I learned much from our kindred."

Lute stared up into the rippling green of spring. The breeze, carrying a faint scent of the sea, seemed to lighten his spirit as it caressed his cheek. He leaned back in his chair and sighed, and the outgoing breath seemed to cleanse him of the darkness that had haunted him through his wife's illness. Then they sat quietly, listening to the children at play. After a time, Willem came and sat beside his father. His green-gold eyes were troubled, and he seemed hesitant to speak. At last he drew a deep breath and said, "Father...."

Lute looked into his face, reading his doubt as clearly as if he had spoken. "You want to know if the Dream was actual. That we saw what was real rather than an illusion your mother created to give us ease. Is that true?"

Willem nodded. "I thought at first that it must be completely real. But as I draw farther from the experience I have the feeling that our mother created that Dream just for us, to reassure us. Do you understand how it truly was?"

Lute turned to Riddle. "You understand the Dreamers better than anyone. You have walked inside their Dreams and lived within their visions. Will you explain this to my son?"

Riddle looked about, but all the others were busy with their own conversations and the children were resting in the grass. No one was near them. "I believe, although no one can ever be quite certain of what a Dreamer creates, that Gleam created that vision for herself and allowed us to join her there. It was, if I am correct, the way she wanted to go, and she allowed us to share her final Dream. Whether it was the way things will be for us or even actually for her, I cannot say. It was the thing she wanted you to remember when you think of her, and that should be enough."

Lute sighed. "That was what I thought as well, but I wanted to hear your views. So, Willem, remember your mother's final gift and take heart. Whatever lies beyond, she now knows, and in time we all will learn."

Yet Lute felt, not for the first time, what a burden a life counted in millennia could be to the one who must endure it.

ABOUT THE AUTHOR

The author of seventy books, more than forty of them published commercially, **ARDATH MAYHAR** began her career in the early eighties with science fiction novels from Doubleday and TSR. Atheneum published several of her young adult and children's novels. Changing focus, she wrote westerns (as **Frank Cannon**) and mountain man novels (as **John Killdeer**), four prehistoric Indian books under her own name, and historical western *High Mountain Winter* under the byline **Frances Hurst**.

Recently she has been working with on-line publishers. *A Road of Stars* was her first original novel to appear in print-on-demand format. Many of her out-of-print titles are now available from e-publishers fictionwise.com and renebooks.com; many other novels are being published by the Borgo Press Imprint of Wildside Press and Amazon.com.

Now in her seventies, Mayhar was widowed in 1999, after forty-one years of marriage, and has four grown sons. She now works at home, writing short fiction and nonfiction, and doing book doctoring professionally. Her web pages can be found at:

w2.netdot.com/ardathm/

and

http://ofearna.us/books/mayhar.html

www.ingramcontent.com/pod-product-compliance
Lightning Source LLC
Chambersburg PA
CBHW022220010726
47493CB00002B/533